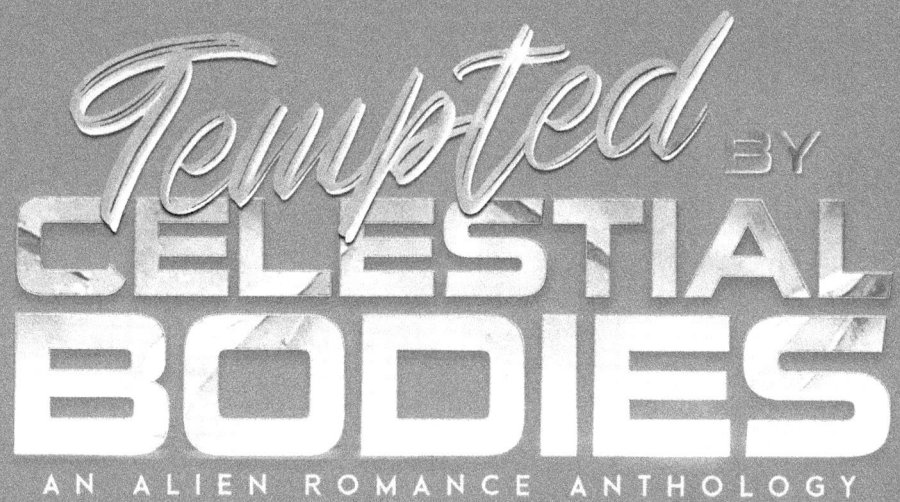

Tempted BY CELESTIAL BODIES

AN ALIEN ROMANCE ANTHOLOGY

EDITED BY LISA EDMONDS

tempted by celestial bodies

An Alien Romance Anthology

aurelie bell   charissa weaks

elisse hay   erin fulmer   j. e. mcdonald

jem zero   kristin jacques   lily riley

lisa edmonds   lita grey

megan van dyke   mindi briar

s. c. grayson   s. l. choi   winter elliott

STORYBOOK
House

authors' note

All stories and art within this volume (including the cover, chapter headers, and full-page character art) are original human creations.

The authors and artists associated with this volume stand with human creatives and against the use of derivative artificially generated text and images produced and marketed as human art.

content notes

This collection includes sexual content, some violence, and other material that may be triggering or disturbing to some readers. Reader discretion is advised.

A complete list of content notes for each story is available on our website.

CONTENT NOTES

To Flavia and Bojana—
For making our aliens sexy (and real) enough to abduct our hearts;

And to our beloved readers—
Thank you all.

praise dilf! a casino caper

Aurelie Bell

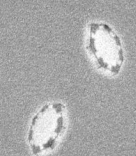

chapter one

zyndor

WHY WOULDN'T MY DILFDAMN LOINCLOTH STAY IN PLACE? IN THE ROOM of Preparation, I looked over my shoulder in the mirror to see if my ass was covered.

Blurodf rushed past me toward the stage, his costume aligned perfectly over his blue skin. "I can still see your dicks, Zyn."

"Thank you, Blurodf. Very helpful!" I shouted after him. "Dilfdamn idiot," I muttered to myself. That was the entire problem I was trying to solve. These strappy costumes weren't made for a Llurren's body, and if I couldn't look perfect, I didn't want to go out at all.

As if I had a choice.

I readjusted the thin golden chains that held the skinny loincloth over my privates. As a double-hung being, I had a harder time staying covered than dancers from different planetary races, especially when I was dancing. Sure, the crowd went wild whenever my loincloth flew out of place. But since that never happened to the other dancers, it shouldn't happen to me.

With my loincloth fixed, I checked the high braids on my head—not a blond hair out of place. Back on my home planet of Llurr, I'd cracked the secret to limitless energy. But thanks to a kidnapping and a subsequent botched rescue attempt that killed my rescuers and stranded me

3

on this planet, I was a former Surlep-Prizewinning energy scientist forced to dance like a sex object in the cabaret and casino of Daddy Skirkild the Unrighteous, Crime Lord of Jurdu.

Eyes closed, I visualized the steps to the dance I was about to perform. Without a laboratory and any real scientific work, I'd taken to obsessing over my dancing and appearance. Daddy Skirkild maintained tight control of his prisoners. After five early attempts to fabricate an escape by hacking the security system, the electrical system, and the water systems—and receiving harsh punishment in return—I had to focus on what I could control. For my own sanity.

Maybe worst of all, I missed PrettyScoundrel22. Dancers weren't allowed onto the galactic internet, so the last she'd heard from me was nearly six months ago. I needed her gentle encouragement, her wry sense of humor. By now she'd certainly found someone else on the LonelyStars chat site to flirt and talk with.

I stretched my back, exhaling jealousy from my body. Foolish to miss someone I'd only ever communicated with through a keyboard, but we'd had a real connection, one that had eluded me in my secluded assignment on Llurr.

No matter. Dancing, apparently, was my fate. I reapplied the gold lip paint required for all dancers which did nothing to differentiate my naturally gold lips from my naturally gold face except to conceal the darker swirls of my Llurren skin.

Did Skirkild even know what he had in me? I smacked my lips in the mirror and rubbed a stray smudge of lip paint away. He could've arranged a lucrative deal to hand me over to the Bahltoran President who'd ordered my kidnapping, or even my own Llurren Emperor, or—the lightbulb over my mirror flickered and went out—he could've had me update his entire facility with better lighting. I wouldn't charge him a single credit if he'd set me free.

Maybe Skirkild hadn't done those things because he didn't want the Bahltoran and Llurren armies on his doorstep. Then again, when his people found me in the wreckage of my rescuers' ship, he seemed to not know or care whether I might be worth anything beyond my body. "Grab that sssexy beassst," he'd said at the sight of me. Then his people scrubbed me clean, slapped a restraining collar on me, and handed me a dancing costume.

I took another look at myself in the mirror. Ridiculous—both the costume and the dancing.

Not that I wasn't rocking both. Because I was.

"Zyn," Vleneb called. "It's nearly time!"

I walked toward the other dancers backstage, trying to ignore the loud, sexual moaning coming from inside the Joining Rooms where patrons of the Casino were allowed to fuck any willing dancers, for a price. The dancers loved the gig—free food and board plus a cut of the credits, which they could save up to buy their freedom. But most simply chose to live in luxury with no plans to leave.

Blurodf eyed me. "Cheer up, Zyn. You always look so depressed. It could be worse—you could be Vleneb." He grinned, and the other dancers, including Vleneb, joined him in laughing.

Among the dancers, Vleneb had the least offers for joining, and I had the most. I shrugged. "What good does that do me?" Without the get-hard injections on Llurr, my dicks would only become erect if I encountered my biologically ideal partner, the likelihood of which was cosmically infinitesimal. Even Vleneb was rolling in money, but the only credits I had were the five pity credits Blurodf gave me when he first learned about Llurren mating biology.

Vleneb leaned a scaly claw on my shoulder. "You can perform plenty of sexual favors that aren't penetration, Zyn. Trust me." He snapped his claws together twice. "Only another Sciccorox wants this inside them, but my tongues are in *high* demand."

"True," I conceded, "but I can't bring myself to do anything without the desire."

My fellow dancers nodded their heads in pity, understanding of my dilemma even though they couldn't empathize with why I turned down every patron, even the beautiful ones. The irony wasn't lost on me that here, the crowd went wild at the sexualized dancing I'd perfected, and patrons threw themselves at me every night. But back home, the Llurren Emperor had isolated me in a cold northern laboratory so I wouldn't accidentally find a mate and leave my scientific research for the comforts of a home and family.

From behind the stage curtains, I peered at the hundreds of beings in the casino tonight. Back in my laboratory, I didn't have a Dilfdamn prayer of finding a mate. And although no Llurren woman would be caught dead on Jurdu, every night in the casino was technically another chance that a human female—really the only other species biologically compatible to mine—would light my body up with desire. Only five had passed through since I'd been here, none of them a match.

Every night brought an almost entirely new crowd of beings. Every night their arrival raised my hopes and dashed them all over again.

I leaned over and plucked one of Blurodf's fallen feathers from the floor. "I'd rather be Vleneb than have a feather fantail that erects so the whole casino can see when I'm aroused."

Amid laughing cries of *oooh*, Blurodf snatched his feather from my hand and stuck it in the strap of his costume, shaking his colorful tail feathers at me with a grin. "How else would I lure patrons to the Joining Rooms?"

The music began as he laughed, and he pranced onto the stage with the first troupe of dancers. The brass horns heralded the start of the next measure, and I fell in line to climb to the stage.

chapter two

roxy

"DON'T LET THEM SEE YOU, SHA," I WARNED.

My copilot shifted effortlessly from their Kelki form—all purple tentacles and beaks—into a human man as they flipped switches on our craft to land at the Aeon Trillium Cabaret & Casino.

"I swear to Dilf, Roxy, don't tell me how to shift my shape." Sha glanced at me and shifted their hair color closer to mine. "All humans look alike anyways."

I zipped my boots up under the long, red evening gown I'd chosen for this escapade. "You can't wing it, Sha. They don't look the same on visual record." I depressed the activation node on my infomatter. "Show me Count Borrdaff." I tossed it to Sha. "Here."

Sha spruced themself up with the new information, adjusting their face to a match for Borrdaff Kahcksuccerce, the Minor Crime Count of a nearby system. "I guess we'd better do a good job retrieving this Llurren for IFUCS. Maybe they'll throw us more business."

"I don't give a good fuck what IFUCS thinks," I said. "You know the Admiral of the Intergalactic Federation of United & Conjanct Starsystems wouldn't have hired us if they had better options. We're expendable to them, and don't forget it. We'll be lucky to make it out of here alive, much less successfully extract the Llurren scientist. But you're right about one thing—we can't afford to fumble this mission. We need the money."

"*Faaaa*," Sha balked, their voice modulating up and down along a lower register, trying to match the videos of Borrdaff they were now watching. "*You* can't afford to fumble this mission. I can't believe you're taking your half of the money to retire and leave me to my own devices."

I ignored that jab, placing the custom untraceable weapon-dampeners I'd fabricated onto my boots and leg straps, as well as a variety of other tricks and baubles. Sha only lashed out because they were going to miss me. We'd worked together a long time, traveling all over the galaxy as soldiers for hire. But this payout was all I needed to retire to the planet of my choice and continue inventing my anti-weapons. I'd even have enough to hack the LonelyStars database to find out what happened to the being I'd been messaging. Next week would mark six months since PowerPurr838 sent his last message: *Thank you, Pretty. I love talking to you.*

"I could retire on this haul if I wanted to," Sha said, breaking my thoughts from my lost...friend? Maybe future lover? Whatever me and Purr had been.

"Don't give me that shit, Sha. You don't have but a hundred credits saved. Do you know what I think?"

Sha's violet eyes rolled toward me as they flipped switches and our ship descended onto the casino's landing platform. "What?"

"Brown eyes, Sha. I think you love the adventure. I think you're addicted to being a mercenary."

Sha's eyes shifted brown as their human face grinned. "Been at it long before you were born, and I'll be at it long after you're gone, baby girl."

I stuck my tongue out playfully. "Why do you constantly have to rub my life expectancy in my face?"

Sha chuckled in Count Borrdaff's voice, and my eyes fell on the visual record of Planet Liminato I'd hung up in the cockpit, its green, rolling hills and blue skies calling me. I would've gone there long ago if I wasn't stuck, penniless, in this life. Purr was stuck, too, wherever in the galaxy he was. We both yearned for what we called "an afterlife while we're still alive," a peaceful life on a farm with someone we loved to balance out the strife we'd borne in our quarter-century of living.

I hoped he'd gotten unstuck, not gotten himself in trouble. I didn't know Purr's situation, but I'd been on the run since I ditched the orphanage on Hupfrair at sixteen to join a smugglers' guild. Thank Dilf that Sha found me at seventeen and took me away from those cutthroat criminals, teaching me almost everything I knew and letting me join their ship. They'd even indulged my tinkering, stealing endless amounts of equipment and supplies for it.

Smiling, I watched their hands shift between Kelki and human appendages at the controls as they prepped our ship for a quick getaway, just in case. I wrapped my little human arms around them, and they bore it with a smirk and a sigh.

"I love you, Sha." I would've added, *You're the closest thing I've ever had to a parent*, but that would just embarrass them.

"Sure, whatever." They accepted my human affection with feigned resignation but loved it all the same. I could tell by the way the shifted human skin on their hand involuntarily tinged green as they patted my arm.

They waited until I removed myself before adjusting their skin color back to a deep, tanned peach. "Didn't we get a visual record of the Llurren?"

I shook my head. "They didn't have one. He's been in a top-secret location and normally works alone."

Sha rubbed their whole human face with a purple tentacle before morphing it back into a human hand. "Llurrens. Remind me—tall and scaly? Or short and furry?"

I rolled my eyes and fixed my stare on them. "You know what a Llurren looks like. I've seen you impersonate at least ten of them in the time I've known you. Just imagine a tall human, maybe a range of six to eight feet. But with skin in colors like blue, green, and gold—our target's gold. Llurrens are really muscular—built like those ideal human joining droids. Pretty hairy."

"Are we talking full body hair?"

"Some do, but some have hair like humans—mostly on their head, chest, and limbs." I checked my weapons one last time. The docking crew approached our craft with a Gaming Ambassador, who, thanks to our impersonation of the Count and his daughter, would be our guide to the Casino and unwitting accomplice to our rescue of the Llurren.

I turned to Sha. "Ready?"

Sha ran a hand through their salt-and-pepper human hair. "I was hatched ready." They flipped the switch to open the craft door. "Wait," they stage-whispered. "What's my name again?"

"Oh sweet Dilf. You're Count Borrdaff Kahcksuccerce."

"*Cocksuckers*?"

"That's the name," I murmured, a haughty smile plastered to my face.

"Hello, gentleman," Sha boomed. A natural actor, they held their human arm out to me as if they'd done it a thousand times. "Thank you for your warm welcome. I'm Count Borrdaff Kahcksuccerce, and this is my daughter…"

Oh shit. Did they remember my name?

Sha turned to me with a wink. "Countina Sass Kahcksuccerce."

Whew. I curtseyed. "Delighted."

The Gaming Ambassador bowed both their waists low to the ground. "Welcome to the Aeon Trillium Cabaret and Casino, Count and Countina," one head said. The other inclined our way and spoke. "Daddy Skirkild the Unrighteous is pleased that you have chosen his humble palace for your gaming delights and nefarious trading."

Humble? The casino was built into Skirkild's fortress floating at the edge of a mountain range near the top of a trio of waterfalls. The palace was five square miles of luxury, and the casino alone was one-fifth of that. As we walked into the structure, I counted no less than twenty spires reaching high into the clouds, all ringed with balconies.

"Daddy Skirkild the Unrighteous is expecting me, of course," Sha said in Count Borrdaff's voice. "I've been working on some globular disintegrating blasters that the Unrighteous will find most useful *and* entertaining."

We passed through the long foyer of the casino and were spirited through the weapons check.

"Is this necessary?" Sha asked, lip curled beneath a silky mustache.

I held my breath as the guards powered the weapons finder. The screen lit up the dainty blaster tucked into my garter, but thank Dilf, none of my real weapons. I always liked to leave a little something small and dainty for them to find so they could feel like they were doing a good job.

A rather handsome Brachinme guard set his talons to his hips and his gaze on me. "Hand over the weapon, ma'am."

I turned on a full pout. "But you wouldn't take away a girl's only protection, would you?"

The Brachinme shrugged with a lascivious grin. "House rules."

I stepped my heeled foot up onto the weapons finder, the slit in my skirt running high up my leg attracting all the guards' attention. Most aliens considered humans attractive, so I played it up as often as I could.

I pulled the little pink blaster from my garter and handed it over with an eye flutter, tiptoeing my fingers up the Brachinme's chest. "Thank you for keeping us safe." I winked and smoothed my hands down my hips, flicking my finger across the muzzle of the untraceable sonic blast nullifier attached to my belt, hiding in plain sight.

Sha complained loudly to the Gaming Ambassador about the guards taking his weapons—also sacrificial for surrendering—then we were admitted into the elevator up to the casino.

Three steps in, I sized up the primary gaming room, which I'd only seen on visual record. A small, shallow balcony policed with guards encircled the top of the room, and the main floor was clogged with nearly a thousand beings collecting around gaming tables, several bars, and at least two stages. But I didn't see a single Llurren among them.

"Let me set my daughter up to play. Darling," Sha said to me, "here's eighty thousand credits to play with." Sha dropped a small fortune of the highest quality counterfeit credits on the exchange table.

The banker didn't blink one of her eight eyes at the gross display of wealth. She simply piled two slim trays of citrus-scented gaming chips before me, and I took them.

"Thank you, Pappa." I kissed Sha's cheek and let them lead me deeper into the room. Still no sign of a Llurren. This Dr. Tyos should've stuck out like a sore thumb—gold skin was pretty rare, even for a Llurren.

At least Sha and I had planned for a long game. It might take us days to locate him—if he was even on this planet—and even longer to extract him. I slid leisurely onto a stool at the castingo table, taking care to let my full leg show through the slit of my gown. A horned Ristoquarian raised his four eyebrows as his eyes scanned up my leg. I winked at him.

"Darling," Sha said, "will you be okay here while Pappa takes care of business?"

Code for *I'll pull off some of the heat, and you find out if anyone's seen the Llurren.*

"Yes of course, Pappa. I'll be fine."

Sha nodded to the Gaming Ambassador. "Bring me to Daddy Skirkild." A large contingent of guards followed Sha and the ambassador. I'd chosen the Count for this ruse for a reason—as a business partner, he notoriously offered both a high reward and a high risk. As predicted, Daddy Skirkild took the bait of illegal arms we dangled, but he knew well enough to keep the "count" guarded by his best men.

Dilf, this room was hot. I pulled my long hair back from my neck and shook it out, running my hand down my chest. Live music began from the direction of the stage, a pounding, sexual beat under the high notes of the brass and the low bass of the strings. The whooping and hollering of the crowd rose around the stage.

My next inhale caught a hint of the most intoxicating scent—spicy and fresh, almost like cinnamon and pine. A rush of aching pleasure infused my whole body, and my pussy stung from the rapid flow of blood. I grasped the table reflexively as a level of arousal I've never felt before overtook my senses. Sniffing the air like a cat on the hunt, I squirmed in my seat. Of the hundreds of smells in the room—the gambling chips, the body odor of at least three dozen alien species beneath snatches of perfumes and colognes—only one scent enthralled me, and its faintness was a tease.

There it was again. I shuddered, and with an effort, refrained from digging under my dress to pleasure myself in the middle of this room full of people. Had I been drugged? But no, I hadn't ingested anything.

The human at my table seemed unaffected, and Skirkild wouldn't be drugging the whole populace—that would shut his lucrative enterprise right down. By all accounts, Skirkild awarded death to anyone who endangered his patrons.

Another teasing whiff of the scent made my whole body shiver, and I suppressed a whimper. What in Dilf's name was this?

chapter three

zyndor

I STEPPED OUT WITH THE SECOND TROUPE ONTO THE STAGE AND TOOK MY place in the center. The thrumming of the synth percussion rumbled up through the soles of my feet, and I faced the crowd to dance. Arms above my head and legs planted in a stance so my loincloth hung free, I thrust my hips to the music in the way the patrons loved. I stomped my feet and roared with the other dancers, then executed a perfect turn to step aside so Blurodf could shake his erect feathered tail.

Vleneb and I exchanged amused glances. It didn't take much for Blurodf to be ready to join, and the crowd was always up for it.

On the side of the stage, I focused all my attention on completing the motions of the dance to perfection. *Three, four, stomp. Hips in a circle, then thrust, thrust.* The dance was sexuality in motion, and though I captured every nuance in my maneuvers, it was all for show. The dance never aroused me, the patrons never enchanted me. But perfection of movement—that, I could accomplish.

Blurodf's solo was nearly done, and I prepared to take my turn in the spotlight. As I whirled my hips across the stage, a fresh aroma of blooms and citrus in the spring slipped up my nose like a drug. My cocks twitched. Another breath in, and blood rushed to my groin, shivers shooting up and down my body. Holy Dilf—both of my dicks were hardening.

Extra-sensual prowess flowed into my movements on the stage. Where was the smell coming from? It was incalculably more effective than the get-hard injections at the Houses of Joining on Llurr where I learned how to fuck when I came of age. Lightheaded and aroused beyond all rational thought, my heart pounded with more than the exertion of the dance.

I was in the presence of my biologically ideal mate.

Nearly vibrating on the inside, I cast my gaze around the room. The most beautiful human I'd ever seen sat at the castingo table rubbing the bare, pale, peachy skin of her chest over a long red gown. My fingers ached to touch her, and all my senses centered on her as muscle memory overtook my dancing. The human woman ran her hand along her long, smooth bare leg then stood, slipping her hands down her hips as she walked with graceful ease. Her presence commanded the room, and her red dress hugged and bared the tops of her full breasts in a corset that cinched her small waist. I longed to dig my fingers into her full hips in passion. Her long hair was dark and curling like the bark of the stanian tree, and I wanted to twist it around my fingers.

What was a beautiful being like her doing in this Dilfawful place? She stepped away from the castingo table, and I threw myself harder into my dance, dancing only for her, finally feeling the sensuality others saw in my movements.

I'd prayed for this moment all my life, but now that it was here, doubt curled into my excitement. Why would the Almighty Dilf bring my mate into my life when I was a prisoner, unable to join with her or claim my life with her? Even if Daddy Skirkild had any mercy, throwing myself onto it wouldn't grant my freedom.

The literal clock to my life was counting down, and here I was thrusting into the air when I needed to be thrusting into *her*.

Because Llurrens who don't mate when the time comes, will die.

Survival kicked in. I needed her attention. I pushed to the front of the dancers, staring at my mate, bumping my hips to the beat, aware that my cocks were fully erect and being revealed as I danced, aware that my extra mouths were preparing to activate for the first time. The crowd's noise escalated into raucous shouting.

"Vleneb," Blurodf hissed from his position dancing beside me. "Zyn's erecting!"

"It's happening!" another dancer called.

I heard their growing, excited clamor, but I was locked into the orbit of the woman. I would do anything to bring her pleasure. I'd seen human women in the casino before, watched them joining with others and knew their bodies were similar to Llurren women, though usually smaller and more hairless. My mother'd been right, Dilf rest her soul. She said my future was with a human woman, and I hadn't believed her.

I threw every lust-teeming cell of my body into my dance. But if she didn't look my way soon, I'd have to leave my place onstage and risk everything.

chapter four

roxy

I NEEDED TO FUCK SOMETHING SOON, AND PREFERABLY THE ORIGIN OF THAT aroma. I followed it in a beeline toward the stage and stopped still as arousal-laced adrenaline shot through my body.

The Llurren.

What if it was the Llurren?

The unpartnered Emperor was adamant that we had to meet over a screen call because human pheromones were particularly compatible with those of Llurrens, and he didn't want to accidentally match with a *human*.

My heart pounded and my insides practically vibrated in anticipation. I should've taken more precautions. Because my body and brain were being hijacked by some horny Llurren—but no, it wasn't his fault. Llurren pheromones weren't just about biological compatibility. They were a highly advanced species, and their brain chemistry influenced the mixture of pheromones that were released and received, and Dilf in Their Infinite Wisdom judged this Llurren to be my ideal mate in mind and body.

Fuck that shit.

My heart raced, and I clutched my chips with white knuckles as if they were the only thing that kept my stomach from emptying its contents onto the ridiculously-patterned carpet. I made my own way. I made my own decisions. I had to find Purr. This was all without my consent and all out of order. What if I hated the Llurren? What if he was a horrible person? Was that possible? And would I actually die if I didn't fuck him, or did it just feel that way?

The biggest stage reeled me in as if an invisible, pulsing string was attached to my clit. A Feingraat with peacock-type feathers danced in the center, but when I looked to his right, my eyes met *his*, and my soul practically left my lust-filled body.

Sweet, heavenly Dilf, the golden Llurren was breathtaking. His dark brown eyes smoldered at me in a mischievous smirk between his thickly muscled, bent arms as he twirled on stage in the most seductive dance I'd ever seen. His bearded face was almost thoroughly human, and his heated gaze owned me. Over six feet tall, just as I'd thought. A thick head of dark golden hair was braided almost like depictions of ancient Earth Vikings, high on top of his head and along the sides, coming loose in wild waves and sticking to his sweaty neck and broad shoulders as he pumped his muscular arms in the sexual dance.

He pivoted and turned his muscular chest toward me, thrusting his hips as he danced closer. My gaze tracked down the sweaty hair on his muscled chest and stomach, down the trail leading into a loincloth slung low on his hips. Oh my Dilf—his gyrating hips revealed tantalizing glimpses of a double erection under his loincloth.

My swollen pussy clenched. How could I have forgotten that Llurren have two dicks, side by side like a brace of bananas? I walked toward him as if in a trance. I'd seen enough visual records of hot, naked Llurren men to know that what was bobbing under his loincloth were two meaty, human-like cocks. And I was definitely up for a good fuck or five.

He licked his lips, and my peaked nipples twinged nearly to the point of pain. A sheen of sweat laced his golden body as if he'd been dipped in metallic paint and was still wet. But not as wet as I was now. Swirls of darker markings covered his skin like tattoos, and I needed to trace each one with my tongue.

We neared each other. The closer our proximity, the stronger his scent, the more he filled me with overwhelming lust.

The things I would do to his body and let him do to mine.

The tempo of the dance changed, and an announcer barked over the speakers. "Dancers, choose your willing partners from the crowd!"

The dancers began pulling members of the audience onto the stage to dance, and Dr. Zyndor Tyos—because it could only be him— suddenly stepped in front of me. I was nearly five-foot-nine in heels, but I still had to tip my head back to meet his dark eyes as my body swayed toward his magnetic pull. I orgasmed the moment his big hands landed on my waist.

He held me upright as the waves of pleasure undulated deep in my body. I wanted to push him to the ground and straddle him in front of all these people. But he pulled me and lifted me onto the stage, never taking his eyes from mine. We began to dance, his hands on my waist. I ran my fingertips gently from the stretch of sensitive skin just above his loincloth, up his sweat-sheened chest, up to his broad shoulders. I leaned my breasts against his chest, and his hands slipped to my ass, pulling me tight against his erections as he thrust his hips against mine. I went up on my tiptoes, desperate to get both of his hard cocks closer to the wet, aching need between my legs.

And his eyes—dark brown, lit with amber. Fringed in dark lashes and maybe even kohl. The typical Llurren hairy forehead was absent in him—instead his thick eyebrows were just like a human's. He was a golden god, and his scorching gaze told me he wanted to fuck me into reverence.

He leaned his head down, his sweet breath tangling in mine. "Do you smell it, *gelsa*?"

Fuck me. His deep voice resonated down my body like a physical caress, its vibrations circling my clit. *Gelsa,* Llurren for *little red bird.*

I pressed closer. "Yes, Dr. Tyos."

His eyes widened when I said his name, and it broke the spell long enough for me to remember—I was here to break him out of this place.

Based on what we knew about the failed rescue attempt and Skirk-ild's palace, Sha and I made four different plans for the main types of prisoners he held: sanitation, chefs, ship and tech mechanics, and wait-staff. It never occurred to either of us that the scientist would be a dancer. It also never occurred to us that the scientist would be the hottest fuck in the galaxy and that a biological imperative would make me want to sit on his face until I died from rapture.

"Beautiful woman," he murmured in my ear, "we need to join soon, or I will die."

My face heated, and I tucked my hair behind my ear. "That's a little dramatic, isn't it?"

He shook his head in a frown. "It's a fact. I will literally perish if we don't."

"What?"

The Feingraat with the feathers poked his head into our little bubble. "It's true. I studied intergalactic mating rituals at university."

Come to think of it, the Emperor made a weird comment about Dr. Tyos's seclusion, something about not wanting to lose his best scientist because he wouldn't allow him to mate. I didn't get it at the time, but if I only *felt* like I might die if I didn't join with him…

"*Seriously?*" I hissed to Dr. Tyos.

He nodded, laying his forehead against mine and conveying his survival hunger for me with all ten fingertips pressed into the tender, naked skin of my lower back.

The hundreds of voices and pounding music around me was less distracting than the lust searing through my veins. And now Dr. Tyos was licking kisses down my neck and pulling my leg up against his side. This mission was already going wrong. My presence had put Dr. Tyos's life in danger, and the heated press of his body against mine was about to make all the decisions. I'd happily fuck the Llurren to save his life, but how could I get him alone?

"The Rooms of Joining are open!" The announcer boomed. "Just 500 credits will let you join with the dancer of your choice!"

"We're getting a room," I told him, grabbing his hand and pulling him toward the line. The other dancers patted his shoulder, congratu-lating him on his erections—weird, but at least they let us go to the front of the line.

Dr. Tyos wrapped his hands around my stomach, grinding his

cocks against my ass through my thin dress as one hand moved downward, cupping my pussy. His large middle finger pressed upward against me. I audibly whimpered. I needed him soon. If I prevented his death via fucking, it would buy us time to work on our plot to get him out of here.

I dropped my unspent stack of chips on the platter of the moneytaker. "Eighty thousand credits for our own room and as much time as we want," I said imperiously. "I'm going to wreck this Llurren. Repeatedly."

The moneytaker's green skin went pink as she looked from me to my chips. "Of course, Countina." She rushed into the hallway behind her and pulled open a closed door. "Everybody out!" she shouted.

Gasps and questioning yells emanated from the room, but an armed guard ducked inside, turned on the lights, and—

Dr. Tyos pushed me up against a wall as we waited, clamping his mouth on mine. His delicious, probing tongue claimed me even as his big hand grabbed my leg and pulled it up to his waist, my bare thigh against his skin. He ground his hard cocks against my center as he kissed me more passionately than I'd ever been kissed before.

The doctor's kisses dipped against the spill of my breasts over my corset top, and through my sex haze I saw dancers and their partners in varying stages of disrobing pouring from the room.

The moneytaker tapped gently on my shoulder. "The room is yours, Countina."

Dr. Tyos lifted me in his arms, my legs around his waist, and brought me into the room, slamming the door behind us.

"You think you're going to wreck me, hmmm, little Countina?" He swiped at a potted plant placed on a ledge as tall as me, sending it crashing to the floor in a pile of broken glass and dirt. Then he set me on the ledge.

"I'll do what I must to get paid, Dr. Tyos." My mouth spewed bravado, but my hands pulled my panties off and my legs popped open wide.

"How do you know my name?" he growled. His eyes fixed between my legs and his nostrils flared as he pulled my ass to the edge and huffed his warm breath across my sex.

I whimpered and dug my fingers into his braids. "I'm a soldier of fortune, not a countina. I'm Roxylira Starsprite—Roxy. And I'm here to get you out."

His gorgeous angular face lit up with a mischievous smile. "I'm Dr. Zyndor Tyos. And I'm here to get you off."

chapter five

zyndor

Roxy's nearly hairless, lust-engorged sex was possibly the most beautiful organ I'd ever seen, and it was mere inches from my face, exuding the highest concentration of the enrapturing scent I'd caught when she entered the casino. I inhaled deeply and met her gaze. She looked down at me with pure lust, her eyes glassy.

"We don't have time for this," she whimpered, spreading her legs wider and digging her hands into my braids, pulling my face closer to her body.

"I'd make time for this pussy any day." I placed my first lick, and her hips bucked so wildly that I had to hold them down as I attached my mouth to her sex. She tasted divine, sweeter than the sweetest yelvewine, her flesh soft and supple against my tongue, my lips. And as I suckled her in my mouth, devouring her scent straight from the source, her moans and desperate whimpers made my cocks hard and twitching. Soon she would activate their sonic vibrations, but not until both were inside the lush, hot haven of her body. But if I'd learned anything in the Houses of Joining on Llurren, I had to prepare her body for that.

She pulled a recording device from her belt, turned it on, and laid back, pulling me tighter with her leg around my neck. As if I wanted anything but her in my face. It made me feral to think she was recording our first encounter, and I redoubled my mouth's efforts, determined to make her pleasure perfect.

She cried out with every breath, and I knew I was building her closer to completion. I slipped my finger inside her, and she contracted against my mouth, around my digit. My cocks throbbed with the need to bury into her flesh.

"Oh, Dr. Tyos," she cried, tossing her long hair on the ledge, her big breasts heaving.

"Zyn," I said gruffly, running my hands up her body.

She sat up and pressed her mouth to mine, licking inside it and mingling her sex's taste with the honeyed taste of her mouth. "I need more," she panted, grasping my face while her kisses burned down my neck and the wet heat of her sex ground against my chest. "What do we need to do to keep you alive?"

"We have to join until I'm thoroughly spent."

"Fine by me." She slipped off the ledge and pushed me down onto a bed. Flipping up my loincloth, she freed my erections and loudly whimpered at the sight of me. Leaning down, she ran her wicked tongue up one of my shafts from base to tip. I shuddered, wild for her.

She double-fisted my cocks, pumping them and teasing the heads with her thumbs. My moan choked in my throat as she straddled me at an angle and enveloped one of them in the velvet of her sex. I cried out, her wet heat unraveling me. She ground herself against me hard and fast, her tight pussy choking one cock and her grasping hand on the other. My mate's breasts bounced, threatening to spill from her tight gown, so I freed them, sucking her luscious, peaked tip into my mouth.

Nothing had ever felt as divine as her sex enveloping mine, not even the joining droids on Llurren that were supposed to feel lifelike. I thrust my hips up against her over and over as she moaned and cried out. Even my yearning for Pretty faded to the back of my brain, though it left a searing shame. Shame for giving myself to another, and grief for her loss.

"Oh, my Dilf!" Roxy cried out, her dark hair swinging as she took me, as the tight heat of her body moving around mine drove all thoughts but her from my brain. "This is so…fucking *good*." Her vocalizations devolved into pants and short, guttural squeals, and then she threw her head back, her completion contracting around my cock.

My balls throbbed and my first completion with my mate throbbed deep inside her body and in her hand.

She looked down at my pulsating cock in her hand, confused. "There's no—didn't you come?"

"I'll have little emissions until later in the mating process." I sat up and slipped my hand around the back of her neck, digging my hands into her hair as I captured her delicious mouth with mine.

But she pulled back after a moment, her fluttering green eyes dazed. "So you're not…done yet?"

I shook my head no. A fresh rush of blood was engorging my cocks.

She raised her eyebrows with a smirk. "Good, because I want more." She stood and turned around, straddling me again, dropping her swollen sex to my mouth. I swirled my tongue around her bud as she ran hers around the tip of one of my cocks before plunging it deep into her hot, sucking mouth. I cried out in an agony of pleasure, and the vibrations of my crying made her writhe against my mouth. Her hand squeezed and pumped my free cock while I thrust up into her mouth.

My hands gripping her hips, I moaned against her ambrosial sex, suctioning my mouth to her as she ground my cock deep against the back of her throat. My tongue would never tire of its slide around her delicious clit, and as I slipped two of my thick fingers inside her tight pussy, my cock throbbed inside her mouth. Her orgasm clenched against my face, and her hot mouth closed over my other cock, quickly bringing me to orgasm again.

She launched herself into my arms, kissing me. "I think you… emitted a little that time. Why is it so delicious?" She moaned into the kiss.

I grinned. "It formulates based on my mate's tastes."

"Your…your *mate*?"

I nodded, licking up her neck and along her jaw. "Dilf has blessed me with the most beautiful mate."

She pushed against my chest and leveled her eyes at me. "Hold up,

Llurren. Just because I'm willing to fuck you dry doesn't mean I'm agreeing to be your mate."

"*Agreeing*?" I scoffed, tugging playfully at her hair. "There's nothing to agree to. We're either mates, or we're not. And we most certainly are mates. Dilf works in the most mysterious—"

"Where I come from, both people have to agree to being mates, and I'm only getting you off to get you out of here so I can get paid." She grabbed my face and sucked my kisses, as if she couldn't stop herself. "Surely you're good to go now." She pulled her dress up and stood, but I pulled her back into my lap, thrusting my already-hardening cocks up against her lovely bottom.

"No. The mating process can take weeks, and now that we've started—"

"Weeks?" she shrieked.

"Yes, and now that we've started, we can't stop."

"We can't stop what? Fucking? For weeks?" Her gaze dropped down. "My little human vagina can't handle those double barrels for weeks."

I popped her breasts back out again and licked my way across them both, squeezing them to the middle. "Trust me, Roxy." I ran my thumb around her clit. "You can take everything I have to give you."

"Dilfdamn," she lamented, "I need you again."

I slipped three fingers inside her and growled against her delicate ear. "When you make me cum, it'll heal any pain or discomfort, lengthen your climaxes, and drown your body in so much pleasure you can't say no to being my mate. And we need to leave soon to make this happen. Skirkild won't let me not dance for weeks while I bed you. And if I don't thoroughly bed you—"

"I'm not going to be your mate!" She almost shouted, writhing her sex against my hand and twining her hands into my hair, shoving her breast back into my mouth. "But your biological needs are wrecking my vagina *and* all my plans," she whimpered. "Sha and I just started reconnaissance—"

Jealousy roared in my chest, and I lightly nipped at her breast, redoubling my hand's efforts between her legs. "Who's this Sha?"

"My business…*ahhh*…partner. I need to tell them—" She cried out with her orgasm, her hands squeezing my shoulders. "Tell them we're leaving now."

She removed herself from me and pressed her finger to her ear as she stumbled toward the window. "Sha. Switch to Plan Sigma. The Llurren and I are—we have to leave. Now. Tell Skirkild you want a report on how I'm doing. They'll tell you I'm in a Joining Room with a dancer—it's Dr. Tyos. Do the 'Not my daughter!' play and go to the casino. I'll let you know when I'm in place, and if I've activated Plans Tau and Upsilon."

I stalked after her. The Rooms of Joining windows were sealed to prevent anyone from accidentally falling from their amorous activities into the raging depths of the sea below the waterfalls. She tapped along the window until she apparently heard a sound that made her smile, then she pulled a device from one of her boots and stuck it to the window.

"What are you doing, Roxy?" I uncovered my cocks and stroked them to fullness as I studied the thick lines of her bottom, imagining I was penetrating her again.

"We're swinging to the hotel across the way." She ripped the hem of her dress and part of the long skirt came apart in flat ropes. She looped them over her arm as the device she'd stuck to the window beeped, scoring a big circle around and around on the glass.

I wasn't sure where to look, her enticing legs or her devices. "Where did you get tech like that?"

She came to me with the ropes, affixing them in a harness around my chest and shoulders. "I made them."

My mate was intoxicating, beautiful, and brilliant too? I could only stare at her in wonder.

"We have to let everyone outside think we're still in here." She retrieved the recording device, and her clever thumbs raced across its controls. "And, you'll have to hold me while we jump." She set the device down, grasped two fistfuls of my braids, and pulled my mouth down to consume my kiss.

chapter six

roxy

Fuck me, but the Llurren made every sexual urge I'd ever had hit my body all at once. He kissed me like he owned me, and I was letting him do it. Encouraging it, even. Tonight, I was only supposed to *start finding out* where the Llurren was. Sha and I had several days' worth of plans to carefully lay with Skirkild to make an escape easier while not blowing our cover.

But fucking him—over and over again—consumed my thoughts. His pheromones might as well have been mind control. When I finally wore this golden god out, would his body lose its hold over me? I couldn't bind myself to a being I barely knew. Because Purr—Purr was out there, and he might be in trouble.

I broke from our long kiss with a smirk. "OH DILF, ZYN," I shouted. Then, I murmured in his ear, "We have to sound like we're having really loud sex. Don't forget my name's supposed to be Sass."

"SASS," Zyn bellowed. "OH SASS, MY MATE," he shouted, grinning at me mischievously. "TAKE MY COCKS. WRING ME DRY. MY BODY LIVES TO PLEASURE YOURS!" He ran his hands up my arms and murmured, "Why are we pretending when we could be doing?"

"FUCK ME, ZYN!" I shouted, "FUCK ME SO HARD I CAN'T WALK FOR WEEKS! Because we have to get out of here *now*."

"OH HEAVENLY DILF," he moaned with barely contained laughter, "FUCK ME WITH YOUR CONSTRICTIVE SEXUAL ORGAN! BOTH OF MY COCKS BELONG TO YOU!"

I snorted at our ridiculous dirty talk as I popped the grappling hook from my multitool and attached the ropes to his harness as he ran his fingers in circles around my clit.

As I moaned and cried, loud cheers erupted from the hallway outside the room.

"THAT'S RIGHT, SASS," his guttural voice in my ear heightened all my senses. "SCREAM FOR THEM. LET THEM KNOW WHOSE COCKS YOUR PUSSY BELONGS TO."

I moaned at his touch. "I need to be securely attached to you—"

Without warning, Zyn lifted me and thrust one cock balls-deep inside me, the other shaft shifting to rub against my clit. Dilfdamn, he was huge, a perfect, full fit. I wrapped my legs around him just as my glasscutter finished its revolutions. He banged one fist against the cut glass circle as he banged me. The cut window plummeted into the waterfalls, and their thundering still wasn't as loud as our lusty moaning.

Zyn laid me back over the open circle of glass, which was thick enough for me to backbend over while he fucked me. All I saw was the dark night sky as mist from the waterfalls settled cold on my bare chest around the hot torture of his mouth on my breast. I could barely speak. "Why...*ahhh*...are they cheering... *ohhhh, Zyn!*"

"They know...*unhhh*...I've found my mate...*ohhhhhh*. I've never participated in the Rooms of Joining before." He thrust harder and faster and his climax spurred mine. His orgasm inside me almost felt like a vibrator, and the sensation made me come again.

"Never?" I panted, my every breath freebasing his cosmically arousing scent straight to all my nerve endings while I pointedly ignored the word "mate" and devoured his skin with kisses. My whole body was ravenous for more of him. Thank Dilf the Llurren's singular cock fit at all.

What would it be like to take them both?

I was definitely taking them both before the night was over.

"You can't tell me no one's ever tried to buy you before—you're the most desirable being I've ever—Zyn, am I your first?"

"My first real being. I've joined only with droids before, to learn how. We have to be artificially aroused before we meet our mates." His cock inside me was already getting hard again, and I ground against it lustily, but he withdrew and replaced it with his other, even harder cock. The most depraved moan my body had ever made erupted from my mouth. "You are the only one who can make me hard, Roxy. Only you."

I devoured his mouth with mine. Something in my heart melted at the idea of Zyn being biologically unable to cheat on me—that'd be a first—but it still didn't mean I'd be his mate. He'd be able to move on from me. Right?

With a remote, I made the recording device stop and start playing back our lusty moaning and shouting, setting the device to mix our words around and vary our vocalizations so eavesdroppers wouldn't get suspicious.

I tucked my breasts away again and shot the grappling hook up to catch on an upper balcony of the second round tower of the casino's hotel, far across the dark abyss. I raised my eyebrows at him and wrapped my legs tighter as I writhed against his cock inside me. "Are you ready?"

He smiled and jumped through the window with his thick arms around me and his cock inside me. We swung through the darkness, slicing neatly between the neon purple and pink drone lights that illuminated the falling waters. His hands grasping my hips, he ground inside me all the way through the swing to the next balcony.

Zyn's long arm reached out at the height of our swing and grabbed the balcony railing of the hotel. He planted his feet on the balcony and his arms on the railing and thrust his hips up as I rode his hard body out in the open air. The cock that wasn't inside me rubbed between our bodies, applying the perfect amount of friction to my clit, tumbling me into ecstasy after ecstasy.

"Anyone could see us, Rox. Anyone could watch you fucking me."

"Let them be jealous," I cried.

Zyn's dark eyes watched my breasts bounce nearly out of my corset as he thrust up against me. Our every gasp, mewl, whimper, and grunt echoed back to us as our bodies built to climax and broke on each other's shores. Then Zyn leapt to the balcony with me in his arms and withdrew from my body, his already-hardening dicks bobbing. Hand in hand, we raced down the passageway, his double-tented loincloth fluttering through his legs.

We ran through an open balcony door into the hotel room of a surprised Ristoquarian and their partner, who both shrieked as we rushed past them and out their door. After jogging down the swirling spirals of the hallway to the base of the building, we tried to slip past the closed meeting rooms where Sha was supposed to be. But clomping feet approached from the exit we needed to take.

"Quick," I whispered to Zyn, pulling him behind the long flag of Jurdu hanging from the wall. Zyn lifted me backwards onto his shoulders behind the flag. My eyes peeked over the top of it just as Zyn's face buried into my sex. His hot mouth around my clit unraveled me, and I tried to hold in every whimper as the Gaming Ambassador from the dock knocked on the meeting room door.

It flung open. "There you are," Sha said. "How is my daughter? I do hope she's not taking the house for all it's worth. She tends to do that," they said in a proud fatherly voice.

"Count Kahcksuccerce," the Gaming Ambassador said, one of his voices trembling. "Your daughter…the Countina…"

"Out with it," a gravelly voice commanded. "Tell him about hisss daughter ssso we can get on with our negotiationsss."

That had to be the reptilian crime lord himself, Daddy Skirkild.

Oh Dilf, Zyn's mouth excelled at suction.

"Your Unrighteousness, she, um…" The Ambassador's voice broke. "She bought an entire Joining Room for herself and the Llurren."

"My sssexy beassst?" Daddy Skirkild's lament slithered into my ears just as Zyn's tongue slithered inside me, thrusting over and over.

Zyn's tongue was a god, and I would erect statues to it. His mouth clamped over my entire sex, gently sucking, and his tireless tongue swirling around my clit, slipping inside me, and back. Back and forth in a perfectly overwhelming dance. My hands twisting in his hair only seemed to make him go at me harder. His hands squeezed my bare ass, pulling me tighter against his mouth. I bit down hard on my lip to drown my cries of pleasure..

"What did you let my daughter do?" Sha hollered.

"Explain yoursssself and your daughter, Borrdaff," Daddy Skirkild said. "My Llurren never joinsss with anyone. He'sss my finessst dancsser!"

"Erm, the other dancers say…" One of the Ambassador's voices began, and the other finished. "They say he found his mate. They're in there right now…ehrm, mating."

"They're *what*?" A guttural give in the *what* nearly betrayed Sha's true voice, but they recovered. "Let me get this straight. My daughter is joining with a Llurren?" They sounded more confused than outraged. "Are we sure that's what's happening in that room?"

The Ambassador sighed heavily. "It sure sounds like it, Count."

A *thunk* against wood like someone's fist hitting a table. "That's preposterous. My daughter is an innocent virgin!" Sha bellowed. "She only has sex with other humans!"

I might've laughed at Sha's misunderstanding of the human construct of virginity, but behind the thin concealment of the flag, Zyn's mouth was thoroughly fucking me. Orgasm after orgasm cascaded through my body and one of his large hands expertly groped my breast.

"I'm gonna hold you responsible for this, Skirkild, and any babies that come from it." Sha rushed from the room with Daddy Skirkild close behind.

"Hold *me* resssponsssible?"

Whatever I'd expected the notorious Crime Lord of Jurdu to look like, the aged, skinny yellow-scaled reptile rushing from the room in a white-powdered wig was not it.

As Skirkild rushed down the hallway after Sha, bells tied to his tail with ribbons tinkled from below purple and gold embroidered robes. His shouting faded. "Your promissscuousss daughter can't have my Llurren! I found him fair and sssquare!"

The poor Ambassador followed, wringing his four hands.

The moment I judged them out of earshot, I released a string of expletives at Zyn's perfectly-timed release of a mind-numbing orgasm. He lifted me down, but I was unsteady on my feet. "Holy Dilf, Zyn."

He pulled me close against his chest, his strong arms encircling me, his heartbeat strong and steady under my ear. For the moment, I gave in to the quiet, the comfort. My face against the smooth, soft hair of his chest, his body exuding that irresistible scent while I tried to recover my shaking legs. This was no condition to be in for a job.

"You know, Roxy," he said, his deep voice soft and reverent in my ear. "I prayed to Dilf for a mate I would love—"

I pulled away and studied his soft brown eyes, my hands on his ridiculously muscled arms. Dilfdamnit he was beautiful. "Whoa. *Love?* Zyn, I'm not your mate. I'm being paid to rescue you from Jurdu and bring you to IFUCS, and—"

"But you *are* my mate. You're not only the ideal biochemical match for me, and—" He gave a small shrug and looked down as if bashful. "For producing Llurrlings, if we want, but—"

"Zyn, look. You're a great guy. Really. And yeah, right now with your mating…stuff kicking off, we're having a lot of fun. But I have important plans that this rescue is paying for, and—"

His shoulders sagged, his face pained. "What do you have to do that's more important than your mate?"

I sighed and pushed out from under the flag, and he followed me into an empty chamber. "Someone important to me is—" I hated to tell him I was emotionally involved with someone else, but he had to hear it sooner than later. "Someone I love is in trouble, I think. So I'm going to find him."

Zyn folded his arms, his thick eyebrows pulled into a foreboding frown. "*Him?*"

"And when I find him, we're going to go somewhere far from all of this—" I gestured around us. "This bullshit. Of arms dealers and mercenary jobs and rescues that almost never go right—" I put my hand on his arm reassuringly. "Oh but this one will, I promise! I've been doing this a long time, and I deserve a peaceful life, finally. The money from delivering you is going to buy me a retirement on a beautiful planet—"

"But we—"

"No." I put my hand on his chest. I needed his body again, but I didn't want to break his heart. He was making everything harder, especially my clit. "I'm taking this for myself, Zyn. What I want is an afterlife—"

He gasped. *"While you're still alive?"* His jaw dropped, those deep brown eyes staring intently into mine.

My heart kicked against my throat. "What did you say?"

The most beautiful smile bloomed on his face as he pressed his forehead against mine. "That's what you want. Isn't it, Pretty-Scoundrel22?"

I gasped. Only one person in the universe knew that handle. Knew that phrase. I grabbed either side of his face. "Purr?"

"PowerPurr838, in the flesh," he rumbled, softly skimming his lips against mine.

I kissed him. I held onto his face like I thought he'd disappear if I didn't, and I kissed him like I needed his mouth to stay alive. His arms snaked around me, and he lifted me, stepping to sit me on a table, grinding his cocks against my aching center.

This was my friend, the being whose kindness, humor, and gentleness got me through so many lonely nights, the shameless flirt who made me wonder who the stranger was behind the softhearted man I knew only through words on a screen.

His kisses trailed down my neck and one of his cocks drove inside my swollen sex, taking my breath away with deep, grinding thrusts that threatened to break the table. My Purr, the being I dreamed of and missed with all my heart. My…mate? My brain said no, but my heart shouted yes down every capillary. Why shouldn't I claim what's mine?

"I've missed you so much," he growled. "I have so many things to share with you."

"But how, Purr? How is it possible that we—"

He kissed my lips. "Shhh, my Pretty. Why question the will of Dilf when They bring us so many blessings?" He took his time building me until his climax shuddered inside me, infusing me with warmth and drawing long waves of pleasure from my body.

"We're getting off this planet tonight," I murmured. "We have to get to the landing platform."

Hand in hand with my mate, I ran down the hallway toward the exit on the ground floor.

chapter seven

zyndor

THE LANDING LEVEL OF THE COMPLEX WAS A LONG, OPEN-AIR DECK WITH lighting from the low ceiling directing pilots to park. I hadn't seen it since they first brought me in from the wreckage in the mountains to the north, but Roxy seemed to know exactly where we were going.

A troupe of guards passed, and I pulled my beautiful mate into concealment behind a ship. Her little bottom was delectable in that gown. I pressed my cocks against it and pulled her deeper into the shadows. She lifted her gown and ground her bare bottom against my cocks.

"Zyn, I want you, but we don't have time for—"

I spread her legs and thrust one cock deep into her body. "But I need to be inside you."

"Maybe we have a little time," she whimpered, grinding back against me.

My fingers dug into the flesh of her hips as I pulled her tight against me. She wrapped her hand around my other cock, pumping me against her clit and moaning as I worked her from behind.

I bent over and whimpered in her ear. "Roxy, my mate—"

"*Motherfucker*," she wailed softly, "you're so Dilfdamn good at fucking me—*oh!*" She gasped as one of her biggest completions yet squeezed around my cock. My emissions were starting to come through, taking away any pain she may feel and strengthening her climaxes. Soon, my mouths would activate.

My knees weakened as mine followed hers, but I withdrew, spun her around, and thrust my other cock inside her. "Dilf created me to make love to you, Roxy."

The roaring waterfalls drowned out our cries of lovemaking—almost.

Footsteps approached us—armed guards had us surrounded.

Roxy wrapped her legs tighter around my waist. "Lift me!" she commanded. I did what she asked, lifting her in my arms with my cock still buried deep inside her.

She pressed a button on her belt, and the hem of her dress unraveled higher in ribbons that shot up and around us, wrapping her tightly against me. Pulling weapons out from Dilf knew where, Roxy handed two to me and started shooting behind me. I planted my feet in a wide stance, thrusting into my mate as I shot at the guards running up toward us, nullifying their sonic blaster beams and sublimating them into fog. Then, driving myself inside her with every step, I ran through the fog, both of us shooting her brilliant anti-weapons until neither us nor the guards could see what was happening.

I dashed around a corner and pressed my mate against the wall to bring us to completion. Roxy uncoupled us and grabbed my hand, running with me to a ship that had just landed not far away. As soon as the occupants left, we snuck up the open landing steps and inside.

Roxy immediately began a domineering ownership of that little cockpit that made my balls ache. Flipping switches, setting controls, and pulling another cloaked device from her belt, she was breathtakingly beautiful and so clever. An intellect I could aspire to, and a body I could not stop pleasuring.

She twisted the ball-like device in her hands, and a light scanned down our bodies. "Let's hope this works."

"What is it?"

"Plan Tau. It mimics our life signatures so they'll think we stole this ship and left." She affixed it to the dash and pressed her finger against her ear again. "Sha? Time to go. Tell them I've sent you a goodbye message, and that I'm running away with the dancer. Plans Upsilon and Phi are a go." She listened for a second, smiled, and nodded to me. "They're on their way. Now we just have to get to our ship on the other side of the complex. Near the entrance."

I peered through the ship's windshield, squinting to see that far across the platform, even with my Llurren eyes. It was over a kilometer in diameter. "All the way across the platform?"

"Yep. I'll enact Plan Phi as we go. Come on."

Every so often as we ran, Roxy threw up devices that affixed to the low ceiling.

Just as I was about to ask what they were, all the vessels around us began to shift in appearance. Cruisers and short-rangers, large and small vessels of all shades of grays and blacks and silvers shifted into the appearance of a hot pink lightship cruiser covered in gold lightning bolts and emblazoned with the name "Count Borrdaff Kahcksuccerce." Below the name was an oversized portrait of an older human man surrounded by beautiful, half-naked beings from all over the galaxy.

"Who is this Count Borrdaff?"

Roxy chuckled. "Don't worry about it. There's my ship."

How did she know which was hers when they all looked like the Count's? I pulled at the metal ring around my neck. "Do you have a trinket up your skirts to remove this? If I try to leave the Jurdu atmosphere, it'll activate and kill me."

She turned to me, all concern on her beautiful face as she studied the collar. "I have something on the ship that'll take it off."

I pulled at her red dress. "I can't wait to take this off."

"Guards! Guards!"

A human man ran out onto the platform several vessels down and stopped short. It was the Count from the ships' portrait, and Daddy Skirkild was hurrying behind him.

"Who is this Count?" I asked. "Why is he here?"

"It's Sha," Roxy explained. "They're Kelki."

Several guards ran toward the shapeshifted Sha and Skirkild.

"Guards!" Sha shouted, holding up a communicator. "My daughter sent a message that she's running away with the dancer! And where is my ship? Why do all of these vessels look like my ship? I want to know who's responsible!"

With a grin, Roxy pressed a remote, and one of the Count Borrdaff vessels rose up and whooshed past. Everyone assembled shouted.

"Wasss that them?" Skirkild demanded. "Why do all of thessse ssshipsss look like your ssship?"

"You tell me, Skirkild," Sha said dangerously. "Did you have your dancer kidnap my daughter and cloak all the ships to look like mine?"

"Kidnap?" Skirkild bellowed.

One of the guards held up a scanner at the ship disappearing in the distance, and he went pale. "Two life forms. A human and..." he gulped, turning to Daddy Skirkild. "And a Llurren."

Roxy giggled softly beside me as Daddy Skirkild started shouting. "To your shipsss! Chassse them down!"

"You'd better bring my daughter back, Skirkild, or I swear to Dilf—"

Whatever Sha was shouting got lost in the shuffle as dozens of guards rushed in all directions trying to find their ships among all the duplicates.

Roxy cackled at the confusion. I lost sight of Sha altogether as one of the guards, who seemed particularly confused, directed his comrades in several different directions at once, then ran toward one of the Borrdaff ships.

"That's Sha," Roxy explained, grabbing my hand. "Get ready to make a run for it."

A great flock of Borrdaff ships rose into the air, heading after the decoy, but Daddy Skirkild remained on the platform between us and the ship Sha had gone into, shouting for the Count, yelling at all the Borrdaff ships taking off.

"Damnit, Skirkild," Roxy murmured. "You weren't supposed to be here." She pressed her finger to her ear. "Plan Chi, Sha. Ready for jump extraction."

My head snapped toward her as my stomach pre-fell. "Wait—jump extraction?"

Sha's ship lifted into the air with the others.

"That's right, lover." Roxy kissed me quick then pulled us into a loping run for the side of the platform.

The leaden fear in my legs slowed my pace to match Roxy's shorter one. Behind the metal railing ahead, the waterfalls and their two-thousand-meter drop looked like a death sentence. Jumping with a rope and harnesses to the balcony was one thing, but jumping with nothing to hold onto? That was madness.

"Ssstop! Sssomebody ssstop them!" Daddy Skirkild's voice and the cymbal-clangs of his platform shoes stomping the pavement rose above the cacophony. I glanced back to see him in a full-out sprint after us, one hand holding his robes up over his skinny reptilian legs as he closed in on us, a stun-phaser in the other hand.

Three red blasts shot past us. Just one hit would doom us, but I would take the perilous jump extraction that would lead me to a life with Roxy over this casino prison any day.

Roxy may've been brilliant and beautiful, but she was a slow runner on her heel-booted little legs. She pulled a blaster from the folds of her dress, and I picked her up from behind, increasing our speed as she shot at the metal railing ahead of us. It melted in a shower of sparks.

She gestured at the still-orange-hot hole with the blaster. "Jump!"

At the end of the platform, I jumped, sailing off the edge with Roxy in my arms into the vast empty air above the waterfall. My stomach leapt into my throat as we free-fell.

"Nooooo!" Skirkild's voice echoed down as we plummeted. "My sssexy beassst!"

Daddy Skirkild's scaly face faded into the distance almost instantly. I gripped my mate tight, my heart beating out of my chest as I buried my face against her warm neck. She laughed and whooped as the air rushed past, ruffling her hair and dress. She grabbed my face and kissed me, and at that moment, our freefall paused. The bright violet light of a tractor beam reeled us in.

Within minutes, we were sucked into the cargo hold of a ship. Roxy pulled me into a run toward the cockpit where a Kelki with purple tentacles and half of Count Bordaff's face was at the pilot's seat. They directed a tentacle toward me, and I shook it.

"Heya, you must be Dr. Tyos. Pleasure to make your acquaintance. I'm Sha. Sha Herdayn. Heya, Rox?"

"Don't leave the atmosphere, Sha. I have to get this restraining collar off of him." She rummaged through a tool chest, opening and shutting drawers, grabbing and discarding various pieces of equipment.

I peered through the windshield. Dozens of copycat ships swarmed in irregular flight patterns, winking in and out of cloaking, spinning and wheeling to avoid hitting each other as if they had barely any control over their steering panels. Sha's impressive evasive maneuvers would keep us alive for a bit, but we needed a more permanent solution.

"Yeah, well, we got another problem. Your little chameleon trick out there disoriented everybody else *and* was such a drain on our power that we can't shift into faster-than-light."

"Not enough power?" I eyed the gauge of the revolving nuclear core, which was dipping into critical. "I can fix that. Where are your spare fuel cells?"

I followed Sha's jutted tentacle toward a magnetic cabinet with dozens of outdated parts and empty plasma crunchers. Roxy followed, pointing a device at my collar. She tried and failed, recalibrated and tried again, over and over to get the collar to disengage.

"Got any chroniton cleaner?" I pulled two empty plasma crunchers, a fuel cell, and a lubricant injector from the cabinet.

"In here." Roxy kicked a metal trunk open with her booted heel, continuing her tinkering.

I cracked open the closed plasma cruncher with brute force and eyed the chroniton cleaner level in the canister. It was dangerous to mix these kinds of quantum materials outside the lab, but—

"We're not gonna make it," Sha said. "I'm shutting off the chameleon."

"No!" Roxy shouted, trying and failing another option to disengage my collar. "Their confusion is our only chance of escape."

Sha whooped at another near hit. "It's tanking anyway, Rox."

I shoved an eye protection shield over my mate's beautiful green eyes and poured what I hoped was a skillfully estimated amount of chroniton cleanser into the plasma cruncher. I dumped the whole thing into the fuel cell, igniting green flames from the cruncher shell. I leaned my head away as I brought the concoction toward Sha's panel.

"Faa!" they shouted. "Are you trying to blow us up?"

"Not today," I muttered, working around Roxy's continued efforts on my collar to disengage the superfluous fuel line. Blowing off the flames, I syringed the infusion up into the injector and shot it straight into the primary fuel line just as Roxy shut down my collar. As I shut the panel, my collar broke in half with a shrieking chirp and fell to the floor, no longer a threat.

And the ship rocketed into a stable yet meteoric acceleration.

"Go! Go!" Roxy shouted.

Sha jumped us into faster-than-light speed, and in seconds, we were surrounded not by Borrdaff ships but by the cocoon of a speed-induced wormhole.

Our cheering filled the cockpit, and Roxy jumped up into my arms, her legs around my waist.

Sha wiped their wide forehead with a tentacle. "So what in the ever-loving fuck was that all about?"

But my mouth was already clamped down over Roxy's as I stepped to push her against the wall. It would be weeks before our first mating frenzy was over, but I could feel my extra mouths activating, and I needed to get skin to skin with my mate as soon as possible.

"Zyn's my mate," Roxy explained as soon as my kisses slipped to her neck. "And we're going to need a few weeks to—" she moaned when I began grinding my cocks against her center. "Llurren mating—"

"Yeah yeah, wow, I know." Sha turned bright pink around their eyes and faced the windshield. "No one wants to watch that. You crazy kids go to Roxy's quarters and do what you need to. I got a friend on Verdalla, and we can lay low there for as long as you need. And when you come up for air and food—" they patted their suit pocket. "I got a surprise."

Roxy smiled wickedly. "Come on, then."

chapter eight

roxy

Zyn closed the door to my quarters. He nearly filled my room with his broad golden shoulders and tall stature, and my insides twisted at his wickedly sexy smile. He ripped my red gown to shreds as I unloaded all my hidden weapons. He unzipped my boots as I took a blade to the straps of his costume and the fine chains holding on his loincloth.

Finally, my golden dilf stood naked before me, both cocks erect, his scorching gaze traveling the length of my bare body. "Roxy, you are stunning." He ran his fingers lightly down my shoulders and cupped my breasts with his big hands, teasing my nipples with his thumbs. "Your breasts are the perfect fit for my hands…" One hand slipped lower, dipping thick fingers inside me. "Your pussy is ready to take all of me."

I ran my hands up his muscled arms and tangled my hands in the wavy hair that hung loose from his braids. "I'm ready for you, my mate. Take me—I'm all yours."

Zyn laid me down and plunged his face between my legs, the wet heat of his mouth untangling any traces of stress that remained from our escape, bringing me to the height of pleasure and letting me unwind against his tongue.

"Your beautiful body is prepared, Roxy, and mine is too." Zyn widened his stance on the ground and lifted me up into his arms where he stood. I wrapped my legs around his waist as I'd done so many times before. But this time, Zyn carefully pushed both his cocks inside me.

And oh Dilf, the immensity of them filled me like nothing else could have, and I squeezed my legs tighter around his waist, pulling him deeper.

"Oh, Roxy," Zyn cried, his deep voice almost desperate with heightened pleasure. "It's happening! My mouths are activating!"

"Your what are *what*?" And then I felt them. Hot sucking mouths opened from Zyn's body, clasping onto one of my breasts, then the other, tongues flicking across my nipples. "Oh Dilf, Zyn—" but then I had no words, only moaning to express the ultimate pleasure attainable by a being. Because a final mouth gently suctioned around my clit, its tongue swirling perfect ecstasy in gentle, heated drags that almost took my breath away. I was immobile with pleasure until his cocks inside me began to vibrate. Then I moaned and writhed desperately against his body, shouting, as orgasm after orgasm cascaded through me.

Zyn captured my moans with his kiss. "Shh, my mate," he murmured, his low voice almost caressing my body as his cocks hardened and he went at me again. "This is how I'll fuck you, Roxy, over and over. I'll dissolve you into a mind-numbing state of orgasmic ecstasy, the sonic vibrations of my cocks will cause me to partially emit, and only when your orgasms last for full minutes will I fully cum inside you. And when we're both spent, we'll rest before beginning again, over and over, for weeks, until our mating bond is solid."

He ground his vibrating cocks slowly inside me, and the heightened sensations of my body reached a fever pitch until my initial shock melted into a blessed euphoria. My orgasms built up longer and higher and released out more slowly. I didn't think the human body was capable of such bliss, but maybe it was his cum that I felt spurting inside me that caused it, as he said it would. Because I felt no pain, only the rapture of my mate's mouths sucking and licking me, his full luxurious thrusting, and a languid orgasm that undulated in great, rhapsodic waves through my body and into infinity.

zyndor

CARRYING IN A BASKET OVERFLOWING WITH SWEET YELVES FOR OUR cupboard, I breathed out a contented sigh at the hills covered with wildflowers. Verdalla was our promised land, mine and Roxy's.

I pushed the door open to her shop. "Roxy, look at this bounty!" I set the basket onto a worktable and a couple of ripe yelves bounced out. My chest puffed with pride to provide such a harvest for my mate.

Roxy's beautiful smile lit my heart. She set down her tools and jumped up from her workbench to sit on the table beside the basket. I picked up a yelve and started peeling it, picking off a supple piece of the fruit and offering it to my lover's mouth.

She giggled as she took a bite, the purple juice slipping down her chin. Her long, dark hair was pulled back in a high horsetail of braids, similar to mine, and a smudge of grease darkened her smiling brow. "Mmmm, Zyn, I swear. You're going to spoil me rotten," she said around her chewing. "This crop is even more delicious than last year's."

She tipped her face up to me and I kissed her, slipping my tongue into her mouth to share the juice of the yelve. My mate's arms stole around my neck, and her spread legs welcomed me against her core.

I'd not known such bliss existed in the universe as these two years with Roxy. Sha and their crafty tentacles had indeed snagged a surprise for us, one of Daddy Skirkild's prized diamonds, which they sold for five hundred thousand credits. It was enough to buy us this farm, build our dream residence, and even build a factory for Roxy's anti-weapons designs on Hupfrair, for which Sha was the face and primary salesperson.

"What have you been working on, my love?" I asked her.

Her face lit up and she pulled a gadget from her workbench. "I call it the harmony-synching serotonin flooder—HARSSAF for short." She waved her hand. "I'll work on the name. It emits a barrage of tones that floods the systems of most beings with serotonin. It de-escalates most situations, and fosters empathy between combatants, hopefully inspiring them to lay down their arms."

I took it gently from her and studied the little valves and gears. "That's so cool, Rox. I love the peaceful things your beautiful brain creates."

"It's no recipe for limitless energy," she said with a smile, "but it's a pretty good contribution."

"It's more than pretty good," I gently chastised, carefully replacing her device on the workbench. "I only created one thing to share with the universe, but you keep creating new things." With my blessing, Sha had blasted my formulas for limitless energy first to all the poorest planets, those on the verge of extinction and in need of clean water, food, and shelter. And finally to the richer planets, but only so they wouldn't use force to take it from others.

Roxy nudged her core against my erections. "But your energy is powering the factory, so really, my little devices wouldn't leave my workshop, if it wasn't for you."

"I think what you mean to say is that if wasn't for Sha's sticky tentacles, nothing in our paradise would be possible."

Roxy laughed. "That's probably true. But no matter what, you'd still be my love and my mate." She pressed her mouth to mine and kissed me, her hands slipping across the surface of my skin and pulling at the fastenings of my shirt and pants. "I'm glad there's no one else around for miles." She grinned. "Because I plan to wreck this Llurren—repeatedly."

"Whatever my mate wants." I dropped my clothing to the floor to stand naked before her. Another mating frenzy was upon us. My erections began to vibrate, and my mouths awaited only the bliss of her skin to activate.

"But first," she said, leaning back on her hands on the workbench with a mischievous smile, "I want you to dance for me."

I threw my head back and laughed. "Dance for you?"

"That's right," she said, slipping her clothes off and spreading her legs to give me the most blessed view. "Rock out with your cocks out, and *then* I'll take them both inside."

So I danced for my mate, only for her. I stomped and thrust my hips in the dance, her eyes never stopping their roving over me, my gaze tracing the curves of her beloved body and watching her hand slip between her legs to pleasure herself as she watched me. And when neither of us could stand the teasing any longer, I joined with my mate here in our promised land, and brought her to heightening pleasures again, and again, and again.

about aurelie bell

Aurelie Bell writes erotic, magical romances with witches, retold fairy tales, and lots of spice from Southeast Louisiana.

When she's not writing, you can find her buying crystals, consulting her tarot cards, and daydreaming about her next book.

She is the author of *Sin and Sapphire*, (A Fairy Tales of Ravellore Novella), available now.

To learn more, aureliebellbooks.my.canva.site/aurelie

bound to the primal prince

Charissa Weaks

chapter one

"I CAN DO THIS."

I stare up at my guest chambers' gilded ceilings, a sick feeling swirling in my stomach. With each passing minute, a duty I can't avoid draws closer.

I swallow my dread and turn around.

The holographic woman staring back at me looks every bit the princess bride she is, resplendent in a gold ponsilk gown with a poofy skirt and swaths of matching ethrille trailing from the sleeves. If that woman wasn't me, I'd say she looks ready to wed.

But she *is* me, and I'd make a break for it if I could.

I run my palms down the hand-beaded bodice. I'm not sure if I'm being masochistic or just mentally preparing myself—or both—as I recite the three words that will unite my future with that of an Otharan prince:

"I. Choose. You."

From behind me, my best friend, Korrah, meets my stare in the hologram. With her old-fashioned measuring ribbon hanging around her neck, she studies me, her opalescent face bright in the light. She takes in every inch of my dress—her beautiful creation.

"You're absolutely breathtaking, Adeira. I truly adore the new you! You look like home. Like a Krythian seaside sunset."

A Krythian seaside sunset. I think Korrah is just trying to ease my nerves.

I've lived on planet Othara for three months. The first month was a period of planetary acclimation spent in a med bay in Segen's Sector General, something Korrah didn't require since there isn't a drop of human blood in her veins. During that time, my hosts downloaded the Otharan language and various dialects via a port implanted in my brain. After that, I was assigned an attendant named Groyo from Segen Palace who helped me get settled and took me on a tour of the bustling city.

Both Groyo and I were confused when the increasing exposure to a new atmosphere changed my appearance. The medics at Sector General deemed me fit and well, though my long and once-vibrant orange hair is now bright pink, with a few strands fading to soft coral.

And my skin…

I've always been the image of my half-human mother, though my skin matched my Krythian father's sparkly magenta tone. Now my skin is more human in appearance, a golden tan that hardly glitters anymore—the Otharan suns taking their toll. The look is fine, I suppose, but I worry what will happen with time.

"I'm so glad your father let me come along." Korrah squeezes me gently. "I wouldn't have missed these last weeks with you for anything. And you *can* do this, Adeira. Trust your instincts, and just be your magnificent self."

I force a sly smirk and raise the narrow, pin-tucked sleeves of my wedding dress to cover my bare shoulders. "*This* woman?"

Korrah laughs but arches a white eyebrow and yanks the sleeves back down. "No hiding," she insists, and I can't help but grimace, to which she rolls her eyes. "What are you so scared of? That your new husband might actually find his bride irresistible?"

Annoyed, I give her my frostiest look. "That's *exactly* what scares me. I don't *want* an Otharan to find me irresistible. If I must be trapped on this planet, I prefer to become the unwanted wife who's free to relax in a lush palace or go wherever she wants, so long as it's nowhere near her husband."

"So what you're saying is you want a marriage like your mother's," Korrah says flatly. "Love is not a consideration."

I ponder the notion of love with an Otharan. Like me, my late mother had to marry someone from another world. Father liked their arrangement. Physically, they were compatible, which is the main reason the dying human race sought refuge in our galaxy in the first place. But my parents had many differences, and my parents were not in love.

"Should it be?" I ask. "How can two people—two *enemies*—who are forced together possibly find passion and adoration as well?" I glance back at the bride in gold. "Mother was happy enough. I just need to choose my prince wisely. All will be fine if I make the right choice."

Korrah strips the measuring ribbon from her neck and comes to stand in front of me. "You said you were leaning toward Prince Mehro. Now you're telling me you still don't know which prince to pick?"

My heart sinks. "Not in the least."

Korrah's eyes go round. "You *did* read the dossiers of all six princes, yes?"

I slip my fingers into my hair and feel the port's metal ring at the base of my skull. "I did! To the best of my ability, anyway."

The dossiers were delivered the same day Korrah and my father arrived from Krythia. I'd been so happy to see my best friend that the last thing I wanted to talk about was my future husband.

Her eyes narrow. "To the best of your ability? What exactly does that mean?"

"It means I skimmed for the information I needed and ignored the rest. I know there's one prince whose people live in cold caves in the north, and another whose kingdom is mostly farmland. At least he lives by the sea, though it said he lives in a *hut*. I couldn't read any more. My choices are exceptionally limited."

Korrah's brow raises. "Adeira."

"What? Don't scold me. Those files were longer than our university texts. I'll give you one guess why."

"Politics," she says without missing a beat.

"Exactly. And I don't care to read hundreds of pages about inter-planetary politics ever again."

"You're the daughter of a viceroy," she reminds me. "Krythia's hope at real peace with Othara. The path to proper trade for our lands. Politics comes with the territory, my friend."

The sick feeling returns. The truth in Korrah's words is nothing I haven't accepted, but knowing your fate and facing it are two different things.

Before I can respond, someone says, "Lady Adeira?"

I turn to find Groyo standing in the doorway wearing a fine red and silver suit, his thick, black coif sitting atop his head like a frozen oceanic wave.

"Yes, Groyo?"

His crimson face softens as he enters the room and presents the most gorgeous and aromatic bouquet of pink and coral emetta blossoms from behind his back.

"It's time," he says.

Even with the distance between me and the Great Hall, I hear the growing chatter of the ceremony's attendees. My throat constricts and my stomach lurches, but I accept the flowers and force another smile.

Unable to avoid my fate any longer, I allow Groyo and Korrah to escort me to the Great Hall. At the entryway, two sentinels flank a pair of golden doors. Between them stands my father, dressed in a white suit with Krythia's gold and silver flag stripes stitched down his jacket sleeves. The white is so lovely against his magenta skin, and with his Krythian insignia embroidered on his chest and the roped aiguillettes dangling across his shoulders, he looks truly regal.

The wide ridges flared across his forehead grow more pronounced as he raises his eyebrows and looks me over, from golden crown to silken slipper. He seems pleased, if sad.

"You are the bravest Krythian I know, Adeira." Tenderly, he grips my shoulders and kisses my temples. "Your people will never forget this day, my darling. How greatly you honor them."

I don't feel brave, but I don't tell *him* that. Instead, I say, "Thank you, Father. I hope to make our homeland proud."

He holds out his arm. I take it, and we move toward the doors. I stand silent, clutching my bouquet, wishing someone would vaporize me so I don't have to do this.

The sentinels slide lidless eyes toward Groyo, who looks at me. "Are you ready, your ladyship?" he asks.

I most certainly am not, but I offer a simple *yes,* and the doors to my future swing wide.

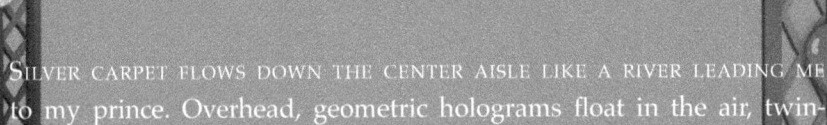

chapter two

SILVER CARPET FLOWS DOWN THE CENTER AISLE LIKE A RIVER LEADING ME to my prince. Overhead, geometric holograms float in the air, twinkling like stars, even in the ambient light illuminating the hall.

Beyond those holograms, metallic gold fabric and fluffy pink and coral emetta garlands hang draped from the domed skylight at the center of the lofty ceiling and waterfall down the white marble sidewalls. More blossoms line the aisle too.

I swallow hard and lower my gaze to the dais at the end of the room. Four white stone columns with gilded finishes have been crowned with wreaths of flowers. Standing in front of those columns are six Otharan rulers, dressed in their country's ceremonial garb. With them is the High Chancellor of Segen.

Each prince faces me, hands, claws, and tentacles behind their backs.

Trembling, I lift my foot to move toward them.

With every step, I push through the tension drifting back and forth across the aisle as enemies face one another for the promise of a truce. Feeling every inch a political sacrifice, I concentrate on my bouquet and breathing, and soon enough, Father kisses my cheek and offers my hand to the High Chancellor, who leads me to the center of the dais.

While I'm trying not to pass out, the High Chancellor begins his speech. I hear the first several words—*My fellow Otharans and Krythi-*

ans, we have gathered this night for The Selection, a ceremony that will bind—

Everything else becomes a clamor in my ears, until the High Chancellor touches my back and says, "Lady Adeira, did you hear me?"

Startled, I look up into his single gray eye before leaning closer, embarrassed. "I'm sorry. Can you repeat that? My mind was elsewhere."

Several people in the crowd laugh, and my face heats. I forgot the chancellor's voice is amplified by a special device on his lapel, and I just spoke into it. Where else could my mind possibly be but on the ceremony?

Wonderful first impression, Adeira.

"I asked if you were ready to begin The Selection," he replies.

"Of course," I answer.

Ready as I'll ever be.

A young girl rushes across the dais and takes my bouquet as the chancellor gestures for the first prince to approach. Prince Vanor. With long, hard-booted strides, he steps forward, and the chancellor backs away, allowing us privacy.

I call up a basic summary Korrah helped me create from the dossier. *Lord of Belroth. Northern territory. Ash-colored hair and skin. Red eyes. Fangs. Can shift into a silver Atyr, a massive beast similar to what my mother's ancestors would've called a bear. Has THREE penises, one of which can form a knot that traps his lover, ensuring breeding.*

Nothing I'm quite ready for.

I extend my hand. With two long-nailed fingers, Vanor accepts, touching me like I'm made of poison.

Carefully, he pecks a quick and wary kiss on my knuckles, then clears his throat, smiles. "Lady Adeira. You are a vision. This night, when we consummate our marriage, I will pump my seed inside your fragile quim, Lady until your soft belly becomes distended with my spawn, filled with an heir who will see my lands secured in a future where Otharans and Krythians must coexist."

Oh, seven moons. I'll pass.

Though difficult, I unclench my teeth and school my features while mentally erasing Vanor, his deadly maw, and all three cocks from the list of possibilities. We bow to one another, then the second prince takes Vanor's place.

I look up. *And up.*

Prince Trevian. *Lord of Sorcia, the arid southeastern islands. Yellow hair and emerald skin. Razor-sharp horns. Golden eyes with vertical, black slits. A massive prehensile tail that can pleasure or kill. Can shift into an enormous lizard. No information on his penis/penises, only that Sorcians pleasure one another with their tails.*

I glance at Trevian's gargantuan tail, which is the size of my calf and inwardly cringe. There's just something about the idea of his tail accidentally splitting me open during the consummation that makes it easier to strike him from my options.

The next three princes are just as easy to decline.

Prince Dorian. *The four-armed, clawed fool.*

Prince Xindax. *The tentacled, arrogant bastard.*

And Prince Mehro. Sadly, *the handsome coward.*

Anxious, I wait to meet the last prince. At first, I can't even look at him. My resolve from earlier is fading, and my stomach churns again.

He takes his time but eventually approaches, keeping a greater distance between us than the other princes. Still, his scent reaches me, all salty sea winds and warm suns.

Prince Thane. Lord of Cenia. Southwestern provinces. Deep purple hair. Amethyst-indigo skin that develops iridescent scales when he shifts into a water breather. Coral irises that glow in the dark. Spinal and shoulder spikes he can summon at will as a defense mechanism. One penis. Elongating tongue. Also, primal warrior.

Primal warrior. I should probably be more concerned about the fact that this is the prince who lives in a *hut,* but…

I try to call up more information on what *primal warrior* means, but the download skips across static that tickles my ears in a not-so-pleasant way, making me flinch. If that isn't enough, what's left of my brain completely short-circuits when Prince Thane, unlike the other princes, calls me by my formal title.

"Hello, Lady Hale."

When I lift my head, one eye pinched, he's staring back at me with an expression that couldn't be less impressed. As the static in my ears dims and I relax, he inhales deeply, as if breathing me in.

At least there's no ogling. And he isn't scary at all. He's just a pretty purple prince with a pair of lovely dusk-and-sunset eyes that are so steady they'd feel like a strong embrace—*if* they didn't also reflect their owner's irritation.

A bit breathless, I lift my hand. "Prince Thane."

He takes a single step closer and accepts my offering, never looking away. Not even when he presses his perfect lips to my skin.

Though he's unexpectedly warm—I'd imagined cold skin for a water-breather—a rogue chill chases through me. The panic that consumed me moments before shifts, my pulse throbbing for an entirely different reason. Suddenly, no matter how provincial his kingdom might be, all thoughts of being forced to live a life like my mother's vanish, replaced with the unthinkable.

Possibility.

Thane possesses the kind of beauty I could stare at for days. The kind I didn't expect thanks to his image in the dossier, a casual capture taken in a field, blurred by sunlight. It didn't do him justice, which perhaps was his intent.

At a glance, he could pass for a human/Krythian hybrid in shape and design, but with a closer look, his luminous eyes, sleek skin, dark nails, and the slight webbing between his fingers, paint a different tale. Still, our differences don't seem extreme.

Though he's no giant, he's taller than me by several inches. He's lean but broad through the shoulders, clearly hiding a muscular physique beneath his black suit, the stiff fabric ornamented with cosmic pink and polished brass accents. His dark purple hair falls in loose waves, brushing the golden epaulets at his shoulders.

I spot the collar around his throat, lined with the emerald, fuchsia, and gold of the Cenian flag. I also note an embroidered silver planet and its many rings and moons on his chest. He was—or is—a captain in Othara's space navy.

Where the other princes each held their own interesting attributes, Thane exudes something surprising: *Power. Goodness. A pure heart.* I can *see* it in him. It's as if he floats within his own dominion among the other princes. Even his touch is different. The others either barely made contact, gripped me too possessively, or trembled as if a wife is something to fear.

Thane's big, calloused hand is as steady as his eyes and just as sure, hiding the promise of brute force as well as brutal pleasure.

And that jawline…

Those full lips…

That deep, silken voice…

Oblivious to our audience, I find myself trapped by his enchanting stare. I slide my feet closer, thoughts wandering to what it might be like to kiss him, even to consummate this marriage with him tonight. He might be Otharan, but I doubt it would be unpleasant, and entertaining that idea at all, much less with actual desire, is more than I ever hoped for.

Pulse thundering in my ears, I nearly swoon when Thane takes my chin between his thumb and forefinger. But then he looks me dead in the eyes and whispers, "Lady Hale. *I am not the one.*"

Rattled back to reality, I blink up at him. "Wh-*what*?"

His lavender eyes, with their bright irises and non-existent pupils, narrow to sharp slits, filled with judgment. "You didn't read my dossier."

"Of course, I did." My face burns, and I hate how defensive I feel. "What kind of fool do you take me for?"

Now he just looks angry.

"I never called you a fool." His voice lowers even further. "But I'm beginning to wonder, because you're lying to a very important Otharan right now."

"I am *not* lying," I whisper-shout as I indeed lie again and train my face for our attentive crowd.

"You *are*. I smell your dishonesty. Your fear of becoming a bride." He holds up a finger. "Which leads me to my point. Your fear and worry are valid. My kingdom is not like your homeland in Krythia or even like Segen. There will be no city to explore when you're bored, and you *will* be bored. You will find no fine accommodations or host of servants like here or at your father's estate." With an arched brow, he looks me up and down. "No fancy dresses or crowns, either. We work the land and fish the seas."

Fine. So much for life at a lush palace. Bucolic countryside and a hut by the sea actually sounds nice now. I'd prefer it over Vanor's cold caves, Xindax's isolated islands, or Mehro's castle where his overbearing mother reigns.

I offer Prince Thane a forced smile. "Perhaps you didn't study *my* dossier either. If you had, you'd know how much I adore my father's staff, and that I prefer pants and trousers any day over dresses and gowns. I never minded a little work, either."

He reaches for my hand. I let him take it, and he studies my neatly manicured nails.

Then he laughs. *In my face.*

"These hands have never held a shovel. And I'm certain you own more clothing than wedding dresses and ball gowns, but you *do* have servants and friends to keep you company. At my home, you will be *alone*."

He lets go of me. Though I'm still processing that he can *smell* my lies, I recall my chat with Korrah yesterday. This is what I wanted: to perform my marriage duty and be left to my own devices. Perhaps not *completely* alone, especially not if I'm married to Thane. Physical allure is not enough to carry a marriage, but it seems torturous to face a lifetime with a prince like him and never discover the pleasure of that body.

Though I could already do without his ability to speak.

Thane taps the symbol on his chest. "My life is solitary and dangerous. I used to sail the galaxy, often fighting your people. Now I sail Othara's Dead Seas. Have you any idea what that means?"

I shake my head, wishing I could lie again, but I want to know the answer.

"It means there is no place for you at my side, Lady Hale."

My spine turns to graphene. "Prince Thane, you will call me by the name my late mother gave me. *Adeira*. And there's something *you* need to understand as well: where I belong is for *me* to decide."

"Apologies for your mother," he says. "And it most certainly is your choice. It would serve you well to choose wisely. That means you should select anyone else on this dais to be your husband." With those brilliant coral eyes penetrating to my core, he leans down, so close I can feel his breath across my lips. "Anyone but *me*."

He releases my chin, steps back, and bows, ending our meeting, whether I want it to be over or not. Though shaking from the encounter, I bow and try to decide what in the seven moons I'm going to do.

I'm still undecided when the High Chancellor hands me the golden ribbon that will bind my hand to my future husband's. All I have to do is choose the lucky groom, place the ribbon around his neck, and seal my selection with a kiss.

Vanor seems smug, chin held far too high. Trevian looks completely disinterested. Xindax wears a cocky grin, Dorian watches the holograms above with childlike wonder, and Mehro gnaws on his lip, terrified. Then there's Thane, the only prince who seems truly self-aware and secure. He just also happens to come with a smart mouth and enough red flags to fill a cargo ship.

But the truth is that I'm not scared of Thane or a life in Cenia. Any danger he exudes is only a call to adventure for this Krythian female, certainly after realizing he was in the space navy and now sails the *Dead Seas*. Whatever those are.

Finally, I make my choice. It's easier than I ever dreamed, because only one prince truly intrigues me. Only one ignited a spark of desire and determination at the same time.

And so I walk toward him, Prince Thane of Cenia, even as his jaw muscles ripple from clenching his teeth. I see and feel the *NO* he's shouting with his eyes and posture, the way his spine stiffens as if he wishes to recoil. Yet I don't balk as I say the three words that seemed so dreadful yesterday:

"I choose you."

More gasps race through the crowd as I rise on my toes and place the golden ribbon around Thane's neck. His lips press into a tight line as I take his smooth, handsome face in my hands, but those eyes reveal a glint of weakness.

"You're being impossible," he snaps. "This is a mistake—"

I shut him up by kissing him, the official sign of a selection made, warnings be damned. At first, Thane doesn't respond, but with the soft coaxing of my tongue, he eventually sighs and opens his mouth, letting me inside. His warm lips soften, his tongue learning the newness of me as I learn the newness of him. I can't believe how much I'm enjoying this, especially when Thane grips my waist and tugs me closer.

A thrill chases through me as the hard lines of his body meet the soft curves of mine. I half think he's trying to scare me—if so, he's failing. But another part thinks he's just as intrigued by this kiss as I am.

Enraptured, I melt in his firm grasp and thread my fingers into his thick hair. A groan rumbles loose from his chest when I drag his bottom lip between my teeth.

"Fuck," he murmurs, hungrily nipping me back, igniting a fire inside me. Suddenly, I feel like the victor of some great battle, one that was far easier to win than I imagined.

The attendees break into applause.

Thane jerks away and stares at me, eyes wide. He looks so confused, brow furrowing as he touches his glistening lips, as if he cannot believe he kissed a Krythian and liked it.

The High Chancellor calms the crowd, and a disoriented Thane and I are positioned face to face. As my heart races, a Segen priest approaches with a silver knife perched on a red pillow. The priest takes the blade and cuts a small diagonal line on my left hand and another on Thane's right.

With blood pooling in our palms, the High Chancellor chants a string of words in an old Otharan language, then instructs us to hold hands. As we do, he wraps the golden ribbon around and around, binding us together, a symbol of our inseparable union.

Proudly, the chancellor presents us to the standing crowd. "People of Ranuth! I give you Prince Thane and Princess Adeira of Cenia! May their joining unite Othara and Krythia forever!"

Trying to mask how unnerved he is, Thane paints on a fake, close-lipped smile and lifts our hands between us. Horns sound, and the holograms overhead shatter into a million flecks of glittering light. I can't help but smile when I spot Korrah's grinning face in the crowd. Bouncing, she gives me a thumbs up.

My smile is real. Thane may be guarded, and he may not want this marriage any more than I did half an hour ago, but I've *never* shared a kiss like that with anyone. I listened to my instinct, and it told me to choose him. I couldn't have chosen wrong.

But when we turn to leave the Great Hall, fear and doubt creep in, because as we head off to be prepared for our wedding night and marriage bed, Thane looks at me with the most disappointed stare and says, "Don't say I didn't warn you, princess. You're going to wish you'd listened."

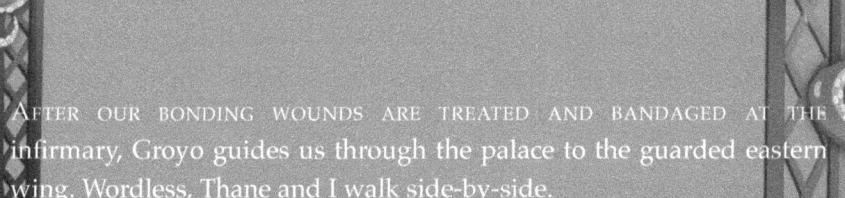

AFTER OUR BONDING WOUNDS ARE TREATED AND BANDAGED AT THE infirmary, Groyo guides us through the palace to the guarded eastern wing. Wordless, Thane and I walk side-by-side.

Toward our room.

Still dressed in our wedding attire, we follow Groyo until he stops in front of a shielded entryway. "Your hand, Prince Thane?" Groyo gestures to a recog panel shining red against the door's wall of white, humming light. "Or yours, Your Highness," he adds, glancing at me with a soft smile.

Your Highness. How strange hearing those words.

Thane is closer, so he scans his uninjured palm. A graphene panel materializes and slides open to allow us inside.

Thane sweeps his arm toward the room. "Much as I can't believe I'm doing this, the bride should go first." When I frown at his tone, he rolls his eyes. "What, you don't trust me, *wife*?"

That word hits me like a plasma bolt. Not Lady Hale. Certainly not Adeira. Not even princess.

Wife.

I cross my arms over my middle and search for a snarky comeback to match Thane's snarky tone, but I can't think clearly with him staring at me like that.

He sighs. "It's a Cenian tradition for the bride to go first. For marital good luck."

I scoff. "Moons know we're going to need loads of that."

He arches a brow and gestures again. "Then stop talking and get moving."

Annoyed, I flash a quick smile at Groyo, then I slice my gaze toward Thane. Once I'm a matter of inches from his face, I find my comeback. "I think I'm already beginning to hate your grumpiness and that wicked tongue."

The cocky smirk that forms on his lips shouldn't be as attractive as it is. "Too bad. You wouldn't listen, so you're stuck with me forever now."

Irritated, I force myself to turn away and cross the glowing threshold. The first thing that draws my attention is a gold filigree bed in the center of the room. A domed canopy covered in multicolored gems sparkles under the blue light emitted from intricate stained-glass lamps hanging from the ceiling. More emetta bouquets decorate the space, with several blossoms scattered across the floor and bed.

Behind me, the door slides closed. Thane steps past, raking his fingers through his hair, sending a waft of his aroma into my personal space. It's annoyingly divine.

Pretending to study our accommodations, I watch from my periphery as he removes his jacket and vest and tosses them on a nearby chair. He then discards his captain's collar and unbuttons his crisp, white shirt at the throat.

Moons know I try to ignore the smooth, amethyst-indigo skin now exposed down the middle of his unbelievable chest, or how his shoulders, biceps, and wide, tapered back test the limits of the shirt's thin fabric. Not to mention the effort I exert to tear my eyes from the absolutely obscene things his ass and powerful thighs are doing to those pants.

But it's impossible. He's gorgeous, and he really is built very similar to my people. At least I know what I'm dealing with when it comes to sex. *I think.* Much could be hiding beneath those clothes.

I do recall the mention of spikes. I see none, though I remember the summary said he could summon them at will. I can't help but wonder how they work and when he'll actually reveal them.

Thankfully, Thane doesn't notice my lingering attention. Instead, he heads straight for the liquor bar where he unstops a crystal decanter and pours a glass of whiskey. "One of the best invention humans ever gave us," he says. "Though wine isn't far behind. Want some?"

"I think I'll pass." I can't endure Thane's presence while inebriated. That would be a disaster.

Far more relaxed than me, he turns around and leans his perfect ass against the bar, crossing his feet at the ankles, drink held in an easy grasp. He slides his other hand into his trouser pocket and glances at my fidgeting fingers.

"If you're worried about what this night holds, there's no reason. I know I can be a prick, but understand that the danger you face being part of my life will never come at my hand, or anyone else's if I have anything to say about it. You're my wife now, and I'm your protector," he says matter-of-factly, though the words are followed by a soft sigh of resignation. "I have a feeling you might test my patience from time to time, but I swear you're safe with me."

The anxiety tightening my chest eases. "You didn't seem the kind of Otharan who would harm your wife."

He stares at me like I'm a complex book he's trying to decipher. "And you believe that's a norm with Otharans? Being cruel to our wives? Is that what your government teaches you about us?"

I shrug. "We aren't taught to trust you, that's for sure. But Prince Vanor didn't give me faith in my safety. Nor Prince Xindax. Nor any of them, really."

"But *I* did? You didn't read my dossier. How could you have possibly known I'm harmless when it comes to you?"

I stand straighter. Lift my chin. "I read *some* of your dossier. I had what I believed were the important details at my disposal. The rest was instinct."

A half-smile tugs his lips to one side. "Instinct."

I'm too distracted to care about his mocking tone, however slight, because for the first time, I see the white teeth that all but bit me—in a good way—during the ceremony. They aren't straight cut like human teeth, but not a ragged mess of daggers like Prince Vanor's either.

Thane has a mouth full of perfect canines.

"That's why you chose me, then," he says. "Because your *instincts* convinced you I was the lesser evil."

"I did the best I could. This hasn't been easy, nor has it been fun. I'm on another planet, forced to select a life-mate from a group of enemy princes, and now my new husband is questioning why I chose him. You by far seemed the best option. It's as simple and as complicated as that."

A heartbeat passes, and Thane tilts his head toward the waiting bed. "So what you're so nervous about isn't your safety. You're worried about mating with me."

I narrow a look at him. "I venture to think most anyone would have reservations about sleeping with the enemy."

And concern for how badly they want *that enemy.* My skin is on fire, damn him.

"Oh, I agree," he says wholeheartedly. "I half expect you to put a blade to my throat once I close my eyes in ecstasy. But after that kiss you leveled me with in front of six hundred people, I didn't think you were *most anyone*. You seemed… so bold. So brave. Defiant, even. And certainly not reserved. I figured you'd handle the consummation in much the same manner, if you didn't kill me first."

That word—*consummation*—causes dread and desire to tangle inside me at the same time. Nervously, I glance down and rub the bandage around my hand. "It seems such courage is more difficult in reality than in theory. My feelings are understandably twisted, but I've accepted my duty, and I'm ready to meet it."

Thane crosses the short distance between us, his nearness unnerving, especially when he widens his stance, lowering himself to my level. "Look at me, wife."

I stare at his fingers, loosely clasping his glass as it dangles at his side. Slowly, I lift my head.

"I've accepted my duty too," he says. "To my people and to you. We don't have to know one another well to mate. Strangers do it all the time, for far less noble reasons than ours. But for things to go that far between us, I require honesty and your complete consent. You chose me without understanding what mating and life with me means, so there are matters we need to discuss before I carry you to that bed."

Again, my face heats. "Fine. Explain whatever it is you need to say."

He takes a deep breath. "It's true that I don't know you, and you don't know me. But what I do know is that you're already physically affected by me, whether you really desire me or not, and that's problematic for me." He leans his head down, closing the last few inches of height separating us, his hair falling forward like a curtain. "Do you not smell that?"

I stare at his luscious lips. How easily my nipples harden to points of pleasure-pain, imagining that mouth roaming my body.

"Smell what?" I ask, my voice breathy.

"*Me.*"

I *do* smell him. That scent of salty waves and golden suns, which is somehow more potent than the flowers filling the room. He smells like sex under summer moons. On a sandy beach. Near crashing waves.

At the thought of him naked, I grow wet between my legs, aching to be touched. I close my eyes, trying to tamp down the inexplicable need setting my every nerve ending alight. When I open them, Thane's nostrils flare, just like when he approached me on the dais.

"That lust you're feeling isn't real," he says, and I blink in confusion. "Truthfully, without time to clear your head, you will never know your true feelings for me, because my DNA will always get in the way."

I can't stop the frown that takes over my face. "What are you saying?"

He tucks my hair behind my ear and leans down, pressing his mouth there. "I smell your sweet, wet heat, wife." His tongue darts out, sneaking the barest taste of my skin, making my heart race, even as I gasp for breath and hold it. "I bet your pretty thighs are slick with your desire, and all I had to do was get close to you to make that happen." He nuzzles his nose in my hair and inhales. "Now you want me inside you, don't you? Deep as you can get me."

A quiver rocks me to my core, his words leaving me yearning and panting because I want *exactly* that. Just the thought makes my body involuntarily clench, longing to be filled.

"The reason for this war inside you," he says, "is *me*. My pheromones. A billion pesky chemicals that tell you to ache for me." When he pulls back and drags his nose across my cheek, his lush mouth so close I taste the whiskey on his breath, panic strikes.

"Pheromones?" The breath I'd been holding *whooshes* out of me. "*That's* what this is?"

He straightens, brows darting up. "I'm a primal prince. What did you expect?"

There's that word again.

"If you'd read my dossier, you'd know that Cenians are a very old species," he adds. "My people possessed powerful pheromones that allowed them to overcome adversaries on the sea by poisoning their minds. The only time those pheromones are a problem is when a primal becomes bound to another being. The moment the sensory nerves in my cut palm detected your blood, my pheromones became attuned to my life-mate. So now, when you're around, they're all for you. To make you crave me, even if you despise me." He tosses back a swig of liquor. "So see? I wasn't lying when I said you'd wish you'd listened."

Everything inside me sinks. We're bound for life, and in all that time, no matter how long that might be, will I ever be able to discern between lust and love with Thane? If love is even possible?

I stamp my foot like a child. "Why didn't you tell me this at the ceremony?"

He cocks a brow. "I'm honor-bound to tell no one outside of my people. No one speaks of it. Even your attendant would've committed a punishable crime by telling you. All anyone could say was that I'm a primal warrior. I had to hope you were a curious enough woman to research what that meant."

I drag the heels of my hands across my eyes, suddenly weary and so worried.

"There's nothing to be done for it now," Thane says. "You made your choice."

I lower my hands, feeling helpless, because he's right. "We just need to get this night over with, then. Consummate the union. Then we can deal with the complications later."

He looks at me as if a tentacle sprouted from my forehead. "We *cannot* mate tonight. You don't even really want me. What you feel is just *chemical.*" He points at the bed. "If we mate, the moment I leave your side tomorrow and take my pheromones with me, a clear head will find you, and there you'll be, loathing me for taking something you didn't want to give."

I think back to the first moment I looked into his eyes. Heard his voice. Felt his touch. Tasted his kiss. It was instant attraction, but it's difficult to believe none of it was real. I felt something spark between us *before* the blood binding, especially when we kissed.

Something… *electric.*

"I wanted that kiss we shared," I boldly admit. "And when you kissed me back, I didn't fear the thought of you claiming me tonight. I was excited for it, until you seemed to want anything *but* that. And there was no blood bond between us at that point, just true physical attraction. At least for me."

His gaze roves over my face, and I have to wonder if he finds this Krythian beautiful or terrifyingly ugly.

As if reading my mind, he says, "You are a very desirable woman, make no mistake. I would happily bed you right now had if I had no honor. But if we join tonight, it won't be because you're in love with me or even because you really want me. Do you understand that? Your mind and body are not your own anymore."

"Please don't tell me what I feel and want. I would've slept with you before all of this."

He laughs, eyes widening with disbelief. "I bet you say that to all the princes."

Though I see his instant regret at his choice of words, I arch a brow and sharpen my voice. "I take that as an insult, and from my husband no less. If you must know, I chose you for several reasons, one of which was because I knew I would've been miserable if I had to spend my wedding night with any of the other princes on that dais. I

73

wouldn't have been in love with any of them either, but based on the spark I felt between you and I, not to mention the kiss, we could've, at the very least, navigated our way toward bliss tonight."

"*This* could've led to bliss?" He shoots a glance at my hands, balled into fists at my side. "You look like you could throttle me. Beyond that, you don't even understand how my body works, nor do I understand yours. I can't imagine euphoric orgasms from a woman who might not even be able to fit me inside her."

That should probably inspire worry. Instead, I just grow hotter and wetter and needier. Thane clearly notices, because he groans a muffled *fuck* as he scrubs his hand down his face.

"We will have to learn one another as any husband and wife," I say. "Surely you understood that was part of this assignment, regardless of who I married."

"Oh, I understood, but *you* didn't. You're the wife of a primal prince now."

I place my hands on my hips, ready to fuck or fight—I'm not sure which. "So you keep reminding me!"

He draws his shoulders back, and my gaze drifts down that sleek sliver of bare chest, muscles still straining his shirt buttons. I could mount him right now.

"I'm reminding you for good reason." His stern voice splinters my thoughts. "I'm not the same as other males of my kind, or any other Otharan, for that matter. Once I take you, and the taking is a brutal wonder, my name will be written on your soul and yours on mine. Mating with a primal is a holy act, a union far greater than a simple blood bond and leagues beyond fucking. *You will become my treasure.* I will pleasure you to the point of mindlessness every time I scent your need. I will scour the galaxy for anything you desire and slaughter anyone who dishonors your name. There will be no deed too great and no command too small, because to possess the devotion of a primal prince is to be seen as divinity in their eyes. You will be worshiped daily on the altar of my bed. My heart and endless endurance will serve as my sacrifice, your orgasms and favor my every reward. My world will turn *only* for you."

I stand frozen, my tongue thoroughly and utterly silenced, my body more ready than ever.

It takes much effort, but I find my words. "You don't want that, do you? To be so devoted to another?"

He exhales an exasperated breath. "I don't know. I've asked myself that question since I first saw you."

His coral gaze dips to the swell of my breasts, heaving hard against my low-cut bodice. For a long moment, the tension between us draws so tight I wait for it to snap, for my husband to lose control the way I so wish he would.

Clearly aroused and yet frustrated as well, he licks his lips and hands me his drink. "Take it. You look like you need it."

This time, I readily accept and drain the glass. Thane slips both hands in his pockets, as if he needs the restraint, and glances at the bed again, his jaw muscle rippling like mad, like he can't decide what to do.

"The consummation can wait," he finally says. "No one can know we didn't join, however, except for us. It's a secret I do not wish to carry, as it creates a dereliction of duty that could be devastating to both our home worlds." He turns back to me. "I will give you time tonight to clear your head of me, and if you still want me when I return, we can talk then. But I won't bed a woman who can't truly choose me, no matter how beautiful she is or how fucking delicious she smells."

My mind stutters at that. All of it. "Wait. What does that mean? I smell *delicious*?"

Does he scent my paltry human pheromone levels the way I smell his?

He takes one small step closer. "It means that when I said you'd test my patience, I meant it. Just being in this room with you makes my mouth water. *We're bonded.* The aroma between your legs is torture for me, and once we mate the need I feel will only grow more intense. Even now, I could bury myself inside you and never leave."

Feeling like I could shatter if he touched me, I whisper his name, aching for him.

He swallows hard and lifts a hand, tracing the line of my face with the backs of his fingers. "It also means I have to leave, right now, before I do something we'll both regret." He turns and snatches his jacket from the chair, then heads toward the door. "I'll be back before dawn."

Struggling to catch my breath, I spin around. "But someone will see you!"

Or maybe they won't, because he's already gone.

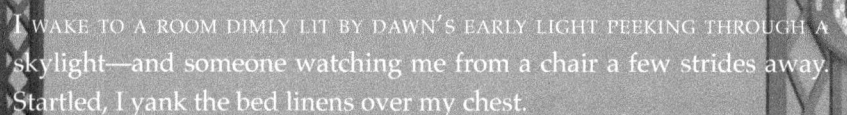

chapter four

I WAKE TO A ROOM DIMLY LIT BY DAWN'S EARLY LIGHT PEEKING THROUGH A skylight—and someone watching me from a chair a few strides away. Startled, I yank the bed linens over my chest.

"It's just me," a deep, familiar voice says.

I rub my eyes, and my sleep-blurred vision clears. Two coral orbs shine in the darkness.

Thane.

It takes mere seconds for a new wave of desire to rush across the short distance between us and crash into me. Trying to ignore the jolt of need coiling in my belly, I sit up and tap the lamp beside the bed once for the lowest setting, so as not to hurt our eyes.

My breath catches at the sight of my new husband, the way his big, beautiful body sprawls in the chair, his elbows at rest on the curved arms, knees spread wide. Though he's cast in shadow, I can see that he's shirtless. His muscular silhouette and that unblinking, luminous stare set my already pounding pulse into a frenzy.

"I didn't mean to wake you," he says.

I focus on my pulse, doing my damnedest to steady my heartbeat. "It's all right. We have a busy day anyway. Did anyone see you?"

"Not a soul. I'm quite skilled at not being seen." Before I can ask for an explanation, he changes the subject. "I thought you'd have skin like your father's. Your file said your skin was magenta. Not that I mind the gold. It's lovely. I've been sitting here for an hour, admiring the view."

I glance down, realizing how much of my skin is exposed. Not only my arms and shoulders, but my leg is bare to the curve of my hip. The covers and my rucked-up sleeping gown only shield my torso and breasts.

"You can see in the dark?"

He nods. "Night has little power over me."

How interesting. And oddly alluring.

I circle back to his other question. "Something about the Otharan atmosphere changed my skin and hair. The medics say I'm fine. I'm still trying to get used to it and hoping it doesn't get worse."

"Still beautiful," he says, his voice deep and smooth.

Heat rushes through me as several moments of silence pass. Then...

"How did you feel after I left you?"

There's an easiness to this conversation that didn't exist last night. A calmness to Thane that radiates from his every word and tempers the hurt, bitterness, and worry I think we both felt acutely after the ceremony.

"Lonely," I answer honestly. "I never thought I'd spend my wedding night on a foreign planet by myself."

A regretful sigh whispers from across the room. "I'm sorry. Forgive me. But we both needed to think with a clear head, and I needed you to sit with the truth of your feelings, without my presence clouding your judgment."

I pick at a loose thread dangling from the blanket. "I know. I understood what you were doing, but I still preferred you here with me."

He tilts his head. "Even after your desire faded?"

I don't know how to tell him that I needed him so badly I had to pleasure myself twice, or that when the longing finally passed, I still wished he were here so that we might talk about his life and my new home in Cenia. I wanted him to hold me like a husband holds a wife and tell me stories from his childhood until I fell asleep in his arms.

So I simply say, "Yes. I wanted you here. With me. In this bed. *Espe-*

cially after the desire faded. I want this marriage to be a happy one. I want to desire my husband and be desired in return." I pause, watching him in the dim light. "What did *you* feel?"

"Torn. Worried I might not be able to give you the life you want. Struggling to stay away because your fierceness and fire make me want this to work too. And because even once I could breathe without smelling you, I still wanted you."

Relief eases the tension in my muscles, but then Thane stands, and I curl my fingers in the sheets. He walks toward me, until he's standing beside the bed, half-naked and hair damp, dressed in gray sleeping trousers. Beneath his pheromones hides the lingering scent of juniper soap on his skin. I never heard him in the lavatory, but he's clearly been there.

He gestures toward the edge of the bed. "May I?"

I nod and he sits, facing me.

It's impossible to keep my eyes from swallowing every inch of his body. His rounded shoulders. Those thick arms corded with muscle and veins that match his skin. That perfectly sculpted chest with purple, erect nipples. And his abdomen... rows of chiseled lines that vanish behind the gathered waistband of his pants. The only thing I still don't see are the spikes. Somehow, I imagine they'll only make me want him more, when and if they ever make an appearance.

"Are you *trying* to be cruel?" I clutch the blanket to my chest. I can barely think around my desire, his scent overpowering all efforts to appear unaffected. He has to know what his nakedness and nearness are doing to me.

"Never." He plants one hand on my other side, caging me in. "But if you truly wanted me after I left, and if I have your true consent, I only wish to ease your longing, and to ease mine as well."

My breathing deepens, need and excitement rushing through my veins. "I might actually die if you don't."

Now he smiles, though it's there and gone so fast I could've just as easily missed it.

"I only have one condition," he says.

He reaches for the blanket trapped in my grasp. As I let go, he pulls it away, revealing my bridal sleeping gown. One satin strap lies fallen from my shoulder, and my nipples are visible, peeking through sheer, white lace.

The light in Thane's eyes brightens until his irises glow. "The condition is that you let me learn your body first. Let me claim you the way I need to. We have two hours before my guards retrieve us for the ride home, and that's not enough time for a primal mating." He trails a long look down my body and back up. "That can happen once we reach Cenia. We can take our time then, and I can show you what true pleasure really is."

This mating grows more appealing by the second, and though I don't want to wait, I also know I must make the first compromise of our marriage.

"Learn me, then." Slowly and deliberately, I slip the unfallen strap from my shoulder and slide my arms free so he can see my naked breasts.

"May I touch them?" he asks, so gentlemanly.

I arch my back. "I'm all but begging you to."

He cups one breast in his warm hand, the contact sending goosebumps across my skin. A long, shaky breath escapes me. *Finally.*

"Cenian women don't have heavy breasts like this. They only have nipples for feeding younglings." His grip flexes as he tests the weight in his hand. "Your breasts are for more than children, yes?"

I can't help but smile. "You've never been with a part-human/part-Krythian woman before?"

He cocks a brow. "You've never been with a primal Cenian man?"

"Fair enough. And the answer is yes. They are for much more than children. The right touch, kiss, and grasp can make other, more important parts of my body come alive with sensation and need."

"Do they come?" he asks so seriously, and I giggle.

"No, sadly. But other parts do. Fondling my breasts just helps that happen."

He stares at my body with newfound hunger, then leans down until his mouth is a breath from mine. "Would you have me taste your nipples, wife? Suck them? Torture them with my teeth and tongue?"

He teases a hardened tip between his fingers, plucking and pinching, sending a tingle straight to my sex.

I dig my fingers into his strong forearm. "Yes. Please, yes. All of it."

His nostrils flare, no doubt scenting how badly I want him, but that calm I noticed before abides. He has such *control.* Like he fully understands the importance of enjoying every exquisite moment rather than rushing past them.

Thane slants his mouth over mine, and I open for him, my lips parting on a gasp as he squeezes my breast. His tongue slides in deep, tangling with mine, until he captures it and sucks.

When he descends to my nipples, I watch as his kisses turn ruthless. His lavender tongue, quite flexible at the tip, feels so powerful as it circles my taut flesh and flicks the aching buds over and over.

I bury my fingers in Thane's damp hair and watch as he tastes me, moving from one breast to the other, clutching them both now, pressing them together. When he looks up and meets my stare, drawing both nipples deep into his mouth, a moan tears from my chest.

He releases me with a wet, audible *pop,* just as he drags his unbandaged hand down my hip and kneads my ass. That hand soon moves lower, trailing the curve of my outer thigh to my knee, then back up the inside.

"Tell me what you'd have me call this." He traces a line along the center of my drenched underwear. "I want *your* words."

He lowers his mouth to my breasts again, sucking and nibbling and licking, even as he stokes a fire between my legs. The word I want to hear him say rolls off my tongue with far more ease than I expect.

"Pussy," I tell him as his finger rolls over another very important part of my anatomy. "And that... that's my clit."

These are human terms, but humans place much more sexuality on certain words than Krythians. Over my years as an adult woman, I've learned to enjoy the heightened arousal such language can elicit, and right now, I can't think of anything I'd like better than hearing Prince Thane of Cenia utter every filthy word I can possibly imagine.

His fingers work harder, teasing me through the fabric as he kisses a scorching path up my neck, dragging those canines along my sensitive flesh. "Will your little clit spurt cum for me like a Krythian? Or is it more human?"

I dig my nails into his shoulders, feeling like I might combust as he licks the shell of my ear, but I'm so glad he knows at least *one* thing about my hybrid state.

"It will come for you. It will come so hard."

A soft moan tickles my ear. "Good. I can't wait to drink every precious drop."

Seven moons

Thane crawls atop me, using his knees to settle his heavy body between my spread thighs. I help him drag my gown over my head, then he tosses it to the floor. Arching my breasts against his warm chest, I roll my hips upward, seeking his cock as I trail my palms over his wide shoulders and down his long back. He stiffens at my roaming touch, and I go still as a statue.

"What are these?" I ask, feeling firm knots forming under his skin. There are several on each shoulder, and more rising from the divots of his spine.

An almost wicked half-smile curves his lips. "Those are my spikes."

Ah. The elusive spikes.

"They weren't there before."

"No." He kisses me, torturously sucking on my bottom lip. "Because my cock wasn't hard. Now it's so stiff it hurts."

I shake my head, confused. "I thought they were for defense. Your cock must be hard in order to defend yourself?"

He lowers his forehead to mine and laughs. It's such a genuine, heartwarming sound.

"Also no, but I'm happy to hear that you did, in fact, read a little about me." Sweetly, he kisses the tip of my nose. "I can summon them for defense, but to use them for sex, I have to be thoroughly aroused." Another kiss. Slower this time. "And wife, *I am thoroughly aroused*."

Needing to feel him, and more than a little curious, I wrap my legs around his waist and curl my hips. This time, he pushes up, supporting his weight on his hands, and slides his cock back and forth between my legs.

When I look down between us, every thought in my head spirals to one thing: his impossibly thick and rock-hard length, rubbing me, jutting from the waist of his sleeping trousers. Several ridges wrap the girth, rippling up and down his length in gentle waves, leading to a swollen, dark purple tip, replete with a shimmering pearl of coral-colored cum just waiting to fall.

"Oh my," are the only words I can manage. Mind filled with questions, I meet his stare, but again, my thoughts swirl, because the knots across Thane's shoulders grow before my eyes, lengthening and hardening to points, like they're erect. "You're just one big surprise. I...I really thought those were only for defense."

Wearing an amused smile, Thane leans down on an elbow, shielding me from his weight. He kisses the line of my collarbone before tenderly biting my breast, making me gasp and writhe against his cock, now firmly pressed between us.

"They *are* for defense." His voice falls a shade deeper. "But they're also for seizing prey, and for making certain my wife never leaves my bed without feeling thoroughly had." He lifts his eyes, and his spikes soften and lengthen into tendrils, trailing from his shoulders and spine until they're slithering across the bed, much like prehensile tentacles, only more slender than any I've ever seen.

My pulse kicks up a few notches, and my legs tighten around him as I try not to recoil. Prince Thane of Cenia is beginning to feel like a lot to handle.

Thane shakes his head and *tsks* like I've been naughty. In response, two of his spikes wrap around my wrists before dragging my hands above my head and gently pinning them to the upholstered headboard. I feel vulnerable in the most erotic way, all while a trickle of fear drips into my veins. These appendages are smooth and warm, but I sense their withheld strength. Knowing what Thane is capable of only makes me want him to squeeze me tighter.

"I feel your pulse pounding," he says. "Please know that I will never hurt you. Remember that." He bends down and nips at my throat. "But I *will* play a game of chase if that's what you wish." Another nip. "Or I can play the captor. Become your sweet punisher."

All fear fades, and I shudder and ache, probably enjoying being trapped in Thane's hold far more than I should. But I want everything he just said, and I know I can have it.

"I can let you go," he continues, and the spikes' grip lessens before tightening the way I wished for. "Or I can hold you down and make you take everything I want to give." He presses his hot cock against me. "Your choice, wife."

"Hold me down," I plead, barely recognizing my voice or the dark desire saturating every word. I can't explain this feeling, even to myself, especially given that I hardly know Thane. But being at his sexual mercy is more arousing than anything else my mind can conjure right now, and I've never felt safer.

Two more spikes tickle my ankles and vine up my calves before wrapping around my thighs. Gently, they peel my legs from Thane's waist and spread my knees wide on the bed.

With a violent jerk, Thane's spikes rip away my underwear, making me cry out with need. The others press my wrists and knees firmly to the mattress as my husband begins the slowest, most tormenting descent down my body.

He takes his time, painting a map of kisses across my skin with his tongue, sampling and sucking my flesh, his hands tracing every curve. By the time he nudges his broad shoulders between my legs, and his spikes drag my knees even higher, opening me fully, I am nothing but a wanton mess, my clit throbbing and pleading for relief.

Thane's coral eyes flick up. "You have two beautiful holes."

"Krythian," is the only word I can speak. The sight of him between my legs, lips already swollen and glistening, eyes bright with hunger, is just too much.

He looks pleased by my answer, and I gather he understands what that means. Unlike a human, my body uses food in its entirety for energy. There's nothing left over. Like a Krythian, those parts are meant for sex and pleasure alone, thank the stars.

"You're so deliciously pink." He sucks hard on my preening clit. "And you are so, so wet for me, wife."

"Please, Thane." Every muscle in my body quivers with want. "I need you. I can't wait another second."

That wicked grin teases his mouth, then he dips his head and plunges his tongue inside me. I cry out, and a tremor of pleasure rolls through me.

Barely able to gather a breath, I stare down at him, his eyes still fixed on my face as his tongue does miraculous things to my body. For one, it feels huge and very much like a cock, except for that dexterous tip teasing the place deep within that makes my muscles clench, already threatening release.

Using his fingers, he plays with my clit as two more spikes roam up the bed and curl around my breasts, undulating like the steady massage of soft, warm hands, the ends flicking back and forth across my turgid nipples, mimicking what his fingers are doing elsewhere.

More spikes drift over me, caressing and stroking, and I'm certain the pleasure coursing through me can't get better.

But then there's a gentle prodding at the entrance of my second hole, like the soft knock at a door, asking to come in. I gasp, feeling a different sensation. This spike is slick, as ready as I am for penetration.

Incapable of doing anything more than nodding my head, I murmur one word: *please.*

Just like that, I'm being fucked with Thane's tongue and spike, deep and hard, every erogenous part of my body fully tended to. I rock against both intrusions, feeling stretched and filled, struggling to believe this isn't a dream as the tense need in my core tightens and coils.

"Thane. Stars and moons. I think I'm… *Thane.*"

I thrash against his grip, but his spikes hold me pinned, my orgasm rising fast. As if he senses the end approaching, he withdraws that lavender tongue and refills the emptiness with his talented fingers.

Eyelids heavy with lust, he licks swirls along my inner thigh. "I'm going to eat your sweet pussy every day for as long as we live. Do you understand me?"

I nod, and barely a second passes before he dips his head once more.

Thane utterly devours my clit, fingers and spike pumping inside me, his mouth hungry and possessive as he sucks and flicks and moans, grinding his hips hard into the mattress. I become lost in him. In his scent filling the air. In his body filling mine. In every part of his being carrying me to a precipice from which I will happily career.

He holds my gaze all the while, eyes filled with starving desire and fragile restraint. But it's his voice that finally breaks me. The moment when he begs against my flesh and finally speaks my name.

"Come for me, beautiful Adeira. Let me taste you."

Mindless, I arch off the bed, swept away in the euphoria crashing through me, my body clenching his, each rippling pulse of ecstasy as powerful as a resounding clap of thunder. Thane doesn't let me go. Just as he said, he keeps his mouth fastened to my clit, drinking every drop of spurting release.

I don't stop falling for what feels like eternity, but when I finally drift back to my husband, he's lying atop me, hands buried in my hair as he sprinkles tender kisses across my face, my lips, my racing pulse.

"That was... mind-blowing," I admit. "Absolutely, unfathomably incredible."

He smiles against my throat. "Still hate my wicked tongue, wife?"

"Not in the least. Do you still hate me?"

He lifts his dark head, his thumb rubbing small circles at my temple. "I never hated you. Krythian or not, human or not, stranger or not, when you walked down that aisle, I thought you were the most stunning creature I'd ever seen. The longer I watched you on that dais, the more I was struck by how desperately I wished I felt like I was good enough for you. I wanted you to choose me, but I couldn't imagine you'd want me given my pheromone situation, and I hated that I had to try to convince you to select someone else."

With the most unexpected happiness in my heart, I draw him down into a slow, sweet kiss. We haven't had time to fall in love, but I can't say this is a bad start.

When we finally part, Thane shifts, and suddenly his cock is lying between us again, still so hard and huge and heavy.

"It's your turn," I whisper, my voice ragged with want. I slide my hands down his spikeless back and under his sleeping trousers, feeling the curve of his ass. "Surely there's time for me to get to know my husband better."

Chills rise on his skin as he grazes his warm lips across mine. "Swear you won't kill me?"

I bite back a smile. "Only if you die from pleasure."

"Then I would love nothing more."

I work up the nerve to fold my hand around him. With a soft moan, he jerks in my grasp, and those interesting ridges begin rippling and undulating as I stroke. Though I have many questions, I'm excited to explore him, to tease him, to watch him lose all control.

But I'm not given the chance.

Because someone buzzes our door.

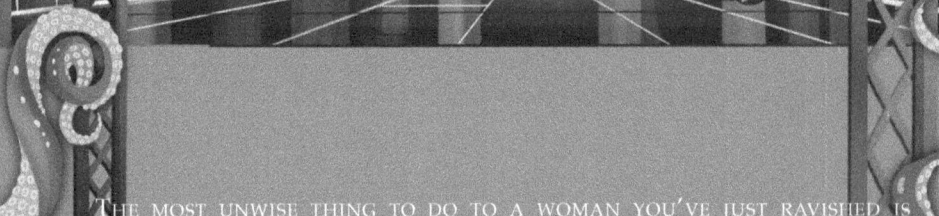

chapter five

THE MOST UNWISE THING TO DO TO A WOMAN YOU'VE JUST RAVISHED IS leave her.

"I don't understand why I can't go with you," I say.

Thane stands on the opposite side of the bed, dressed in nothing but a pair of rugged green cargo pants and shiny black boots, stuffing last night's uniform into his duffle without a care.

"And I don't have time to explain any more than I already have." He snatches a folded green shirt from his pack and shrugs it on. The fitted material all but melts over his physique. "Can you even swim?"

Hands on my hips, I stare at him with disbelief, as if it will matter. "Yes, I can swim. Stop trying to change the subject. You should've told me who you really are last night."

He gives me a sidelong look, though that coral gaze slides down my body. I'm wearing nothing but his white shirt, unbuttoned.

Slowly, he drags his eyes back to mine. "I've never lied about who I am. Everything you needed to know about me was in my dossier. I told you at the ceremony that my life is dangerous and that I sail the Dead Seas. Last night, there was too much other information to cover. I thought I had time to explain the finer details of my *job*."

"You're a prince! That should be your job! But no! You're a *monster hunter*. A *princely* monster hunter. I would've appreciated knowing that before you were called to the high seas, leaving me to travel to Cenia with a troop of guards I don't even know."

"You met Fedder," he says, speaking of his right-hand guard who interrupted us earlier. "And Groyo is welcome to travel with you as well, if that makes you more comfortable." He zips his bag and sighs, then slings the duffle across his shoulder and rounds the bed. He stands over me, gentle hand caressing my face. "You'll be safe in Cenia. My people may not like you, but they know better than to do anything but guard you until I'm there to do it myself."

I clutch his shirt, honing in on his worry. "I'm safer with *you*."

"Normally, yes. But not where I'm going."

He's a wall I'm not going to tear down, no matter what I do. I've tried ever since Fedder delivered the urgent message that Thane's services were needed at sea.

"Just don't make me a widow on what should be my honeymoon," I say. "I'd rather not rule your kingdom alone."

"Have no fear. There are many dangerous creatures in the Dead Seas. And yes, it's *my* job to protect the coastlines that suffer their wrath, namely my own, which is why I must go. But there's one thing more deadly than any beast lurking below those deceptive turquoise waters." When I give him a questioning look, he answers, "*Me.*"

Trying to find comfort in that, I walk him to the door, my arms folded around my middle. Thane stops and faces me, dropping his bag at our feet. He clasps my face in both hands, and after staring into my eyes, kisses me so deeply that by the time it's over, my tense body is languid in his arms.

"My ship sails fast," he says. "And I've killed many gordrusks before. You'll be in the comfort of my hut within a few days, and I won't be far behind. Fedder will take the best care of you until my return."

"Just promise you *will* return."

He smiles. "I promise. You won't get rid of me that easily."

Moments later, I watch Thane walk down the hall, shake Fedder's hand, and vanish around the corner. I return to our room alone, truly believing his promise is enough to sustain me, and that I can let him go and be the dutiful Princess Adeira of Cenia who obeys her new husband and goes to her new home without protest.

Unfortunately, I still feel like Lady Adeira of Krythia, and she never really much liked being told what to do.

chapter six

Escaping Segen Palace requires three things.

One, convincing Korrah to don my veil and clothes, skip the ship ride to Krythia, and pretend to be me, which isn't hard to do after she's seen Fedder. Two, stealing a staff jumpsuit from a cleaning closet and stuffing my hair under a hat Groyo bought me weeks ago. And three, flirting with the guard at the exit since I don't have an identification badge.

Before I go, the guard winks and hands me a pair of eye shields and face mask being offered to those heading outside.

"Sandstorm passed through last night," he says. "Still windy out."

I slip on the mask and eye shields and step into the dust-filled air. Visibility is low, and though I roamed the city with Groyo and walked past the docks as well, I don't know my way around. With every turn down every sandy street, I worry I'm moving in the wrong direction.

I listen for any sound that might signal I'm getting closer—the torgulls squawking over the ships, the vessels' humming engines, the low waves lapping the hulls. But with the hover lanes roaring above and the wind, I can't make out anything distinct.

Finally, though, I turn a corner and spot the various sails of hundreds of gleaming waterships floating in the harbor. I don't know much about Otharan sailing vessels, only what Groyo explained. They fly above the water's surface but can hover and sail the seas as well. I suppose, given that this planet's oceans hide monsters, being able to quickly escape via the sky makes sense. At the very least, it gives me comfort for the journey ahead.

Now to locate Thane's vessel.

As I walk down the docks, one watership stands out above the rest: the one with *Predator* painted in Otharan across the side. It has a sleek, blue graphene alloy hull that reminds me of the underside of a fannawhale's mouth, down to the ventral pleats. The ship's decks are vast and covered in dark, shining wood, its pale green sails stretching higher than any other ship in the harbor. They remind me more of folded wings than the typical wind sails back home.

Dozens of people rush on and off the deck, hurriedly loading supplies, while others inspect the vessel itself. And there, at the helm, stands a tall, purple figure dressed in dark green, a captain directing his crew.

Like everyone else, Thane wears a mask. I dislike the sand—it's getting everywhere, even inside my clothes—but I'm glad I can hide my face, and that a salty, earthy scent saturates the air. Thankfully, I can smell little save for sand, the sea, and my own breath. I shouldn't notice Thane's pheromones for a while, nor he mine, at least until we're clear of these winds.

There's only one way onto the vessel, so I slip into a cluster of people and grab a crate of squirming squidlets—bait for the gordrusk Thane's hunting, I suppose—and make my way on board. Before I can make it up the ramp, I'm stopped by a woman—clearly the quarter-master—who holds her hand over her squinting eyes to block the suns.

"I'm Varley." She looks me up and down. "Who are you?"

I try not to panic, but my nerves get the better of me. I answer with the first response that flashes through my brain. "Name's Korrah. Fedder sent me."

"Fedder, eh? Where is that big jerk, anyway?"

Simple enough question, but I detect the woman's effort to catch me in a lie. I may not know Thane as well as her, but I highly doubt he failed to tell his main crew members where his bride is.

"He's seeing Princess Adeira home. He wanted to make sure the crew had enough hands. Fucking gordrusks."

Varley studies my eye shields and mask for a moment, then she huffs a tight laugh. "Fucking gordrusks, indeed." She jerks her head. "Get those squidlets to the stern then come collect another load."

Much to my surprise, that's the extent of our encounter, possibly because the urgency to leave is palpable. When we do set sail, I stand at the railing, back aching from carrying a dozen crates, heart pounding at my impending adventure, bandaged hand pressing down on my hat lest the wind blow away my disguise. I would've never imagined such a rush of excitement as the watership drifts into the harbor, then slowly rises into the air and begins a steady hover toward open seas.

But my stomach flips, and the widest grin imaginable spreads across my face.

I spin around, gaze landing on my beautiful new husband, the sun reflecting on his amethyst-indigo skin, the wind tangling in his dark locks. A strange-looking weapon—almost like a curved sword— hangs from his hip.

One powerful hand grips the helm, steering us southward, while the other pulls a lever that releases the massive wings at the vessel's sides. They flap in long arcs, carrying us at least thirty feet above the water's surface, then rowing the vessel forward at a speed quick enough I have to strap myself into a seat on the deck like the rest of the crew.

Wide-eyed, I watch as Segen's shining skyline, hidden behind a sandy veil, vanishes in the distance. But I'm drawn back to Thane. When I finally make myself known, the Prince of Cenia may show me an entirely different side of himself and scold me for such defiance with a lesson in rage.

But the truth is, right now, I don't care.

Because there's nowhere else I'd rather be.

* * *

THE FACT that I remain hidden from Thane's view for three days is nothing short of a small miracle.

Each morning, I help in the kitchens to stay out of sight, though I do venture above every few hours—with my hat, mask, and eye shields firmly in place. No one seems to think it's odd. The suns are brutal on everyone's vision, and a cough here and there goes a long way with ensuring I'm avoided.

At night, I camp in a corner bunk in the crew's berthing compartment. Once Varley comes below, I know Thane has settled in his cabin, so I stroll to the main deck to feel the wind on my face and watch the universe sparkle overhead.

This morning, the deck is fairly quiet. Dawn will arrive in a couple of hours, and then we face the hunt. Most everyone's still resting, save for a few early-morning risers lingering near the stern, the men tasked with watching the sails, and of course the fore-top master, sitting high above us all, spying the Dead Seas.

And me. Too excited to keep sleeping, I lean onto the rail at the prow, listening to the sails cutting the wind as the glittering, inky sea drifts below. With a soft mist kissing my exposed skin, I stare into the lavender and sapphire expanse ahead, imagining my new home of Cenia, a land mass that's out there just waiting. Somewhere.

"Beautiful, isn't it?"

The moment that deep voice reaches my ears, icy panic seizes me. I stiffen but remain still, swallowing the knot in my throat. I feel like a cornered animal, especially without my eye shields.

In my periphery, Thane settles his sinewy forearms on the rail beside me, hands clasped. His bandage from our wedding is gone, as is mine, thankfully.

Like me, he aims his gaze at the ocean of bruised darkness stretching wide before us. "You know, I've sailed the seas for a long time. A captain knows when something is off on his vessel. Whether something's gone wrong with the ship itself, or maybe the weather ten miles out is turning for the worst, and he feels it in his bones." An awkward moment of silence passes, then he looks at me, and I swear I feel those coral irises burning a hole into the side of my face. "Or maybe, just maybe, there's a new member of the crew who doesn't feel as though they quite belong."

My stomach sinks, and my cheeks burn. Pulse racing, I tug my hat down over my eyes, as if that's an adequate way to hide right now. It's a nervous reaction that elicits an amused laugh from my groom.

"My quartermaster questioned me shortly after we set sail, about the new crew hand Fedder sent. I was too busy to think much of it, but then I spotted someone last night. A woman dressed in an oversized jumpsuit and a rather expensive hat, still wearing a mask though we're clear of the sands. I couldn't help but watch as she crossed the deck and vanished downstairs for the evening." He leans close. "The getup was a good idea, but you forget I've held that plump ass in my hand, moments before I devoured your pussy," he says brazenly, sending chills in a mad rush over my skin. "I've worshiped those magnificent breasts and memorized those long, stunning legs. If you don't think I know your walk and the way you hold your head high as you sway those lovely hips, regardless of what you're wearing, then you clearly didn't notice the way I absorbed your every move at our wedding ceremony."

He reaches for my hat, and I can do nothing but let him remove it. When my hair tumbles around my shoulders, I finally slide my mask off and look up at him, guilt seeping from my every pore as I wait for the sharp bite of reprimand.

It never comes.

Thane just shakes his head. "Is this level of disobedience what I can expect for the rest of our lives?"

"Not if you let me come on adventures with my husband." I shrug innocently. "At least you can't blame pheromones. I haven't smelled you for days, and yet I'm still so happy to be here."

An exasperated sigh escapes him, and he scrubs his hand down his handsome face before settling his palm on the hilt of the weapon he wears without fail now. "This is not an adventure, Adeira. This is a monster hunt. It's dangerous. We're nearing infested waters."

"And if you think I care about danger, then you're ignoring the fact that I'm here right now. I know this is dangerous. That's half the allure."

He narrows his eyes and moves closer. "What's the other half?"

I grip his shirt, fingertips grazing his hard nipples. *Now* I smell him. Just the slightest whiff of pheromones, carried away on the briny wind.

It's still enough to steer me toward desire, though I would've ended up there with or without the help, I'm certain.

"*You* are the other half. And not because of your chemicals, but because I think I just like being near you."

Thane slips his hand into my hair and closes his hand around my neck, his thumb stroking a line up and down my throat. With a look edged in hunger, he tugs me flush against him. With the promise of rapture in his eyes, he descends slowly and kisses me, so achingly slow. He tastes like sun and sex and salty sea mist.

Just like that, I'm swept up in the moment—in the pleasure of his addicting, talented mouth, the warmth of his strong arms as they fold around me in the most wonderful embrace, the comforting shield of his powerful body. I don't know how I stayed away for three days, because even though this relationship is still so new, I've missed this.

Missed *him*.

Thane slows our kiss and reluctantly pulls his lips from mine. "It's a good thing I didn't know you were here before now. You are my greatest temptation. We would've faced quite the struggle staying apart these last few days."

"I'm struggling right now," I admit. "The things I could do to you…"

He groans. "Adeira. As badly as I want to, I cannot mate with you on this ship. I may have to discipline you, though." He drags his teeth over my throat. "My naughty wife."

A thrill dances down my spine. "Will you be my sweet punisher?"

The most decadent, deep sound rumbles in his chest. "Mmm, is there any other kind?"

"Then by all means, teach me a lesson, Captain."

More than ready, I slide my arms around his neck. One corner of his mouth quirks up, though the expression quickly fades.

"Just understand something," he says. "I know you want to be here, and a part of me is truly glad you'll get to see what I face when I go to sea. But you must promise to listen to me, Adeira. No disobedience when I'm hunting tomorrow. This is *my* territory. If you're this determined to learn about what I do, I will teach you. But my first job is to keep you safe."

Quite happy with the second official compromise of our marriage, I reply with, "I promise. I'll do whatever you command."

He arches a brow. "Then we're going to my cabin. We don't have long before sunrise, but this tongue can work fast."

Thane drapes his arm across my shoulders, and I wrap my arm around his waist. Together, we stroll across the deck, grinning like the newlyweds we are.

"Just one question," he says before we turn for the stairs. "What did you do with Fedder?"

Smiling, I open my mouth to tell him about Korrah, but a horn blows, and someone shouts. The fore-top master. "Gordrusks, Captain! Port side! Four of them!"

No sooner does his voice reach our ears, than an ear-piercing shriek cuts the air.

A moment later, something strikes the watership, jarring the entire vessel, toppling crates of squidlets, their slimy forms wriggling across the deck.

Thane yanks me into his arms as a dozen screams fill the early morning. I have to blink at what I'm seeing when a pink tentacle, thicker than a mast and covered with hundreds of rooting suckers, reaches up from the darkness below, water sluicing from its length as it latches onto the port side sail and demolishes it in one horrific swipe.

"Fucking bastard!" Thane covers my head as seawater, splintered wood, and shredded canvas rain down, and the watership's left side begins to tilt.

And tilt.

High into the air it goes, even as more tentacles wrap around the railing, lifting, as if the beast means to heave us over. The last thing I see as my husband and I lose our footing, stumble then careen toward the helm as seawater pours down the deck, is those giant tentacles, slinking under the ship. Pushing.

As we slide, Thane turns us so that his big body shields mine from the final impact. He flinches when we crash, the wheel's wooden handles jabbing into his ribs, but he grabs on, keeping us from falling further.

Coral eyes bright, Thane scans the destroyed sail. He then shoots a look over his shoulder at the sail flying starboard, damaged from falling debris. The crewman responsible for tending the wing clings to the rail.

In a split-second decision, Thane grabs nearby rigging hanging from a hook. With deft hands, he jerks me to my knees, making me straddle him as he quickly wraps the rope around our waists, securing us to the helm before pulling the line tight. He ties off a complex knot so smoothly it's clear he's done it a thousand and one times before.

"Wrap your legs around me and hold on! Don't let go!" He grips one of the helm handles again and presses me against him, just as the vessel's port side drops and the entire watership free falls.

Arms and legs fastened around my husband, I bury my head in the crook of his shoulder. My body floods with adrenaline as wind and mist rush over us, the sudden descent *whooshing* in my ears and stealing my breath.

When the ship slams against the water below, finally righted, we're jarred so hard my teeth clack as we bounce. The following several minutes are a blur. People rush everywhere—some hurrying above deck while others run below. Thane unbinds us, and the next thing I know, he's kissing me like he may never get to kiss me again.

He lets me go too quickly, and before I can ask him what to do, I'm handed to Varley, who gives me a vest that will inflate should I find myself tossed overboard.

"Strip off some of that garb, Your Highness," she orders. "You must be able to move freely if you're forced to swim."

I'm too rattled to care that she knows I lied my way onto this ship. Instead, I shed my too-big jumpsuit, thankful I wore leggings and a blouse underneath today.

Varley helps me fasten the vest, then grips my shoulders and looks me in the eyes. "I want you to—"

The watership lurches and smacks against the water again, as if a gordrusk nudged it, sending us stumbling.

"Lights!" I hear Thane shout. "And for fuck's sake, shoot those motherfuckers!"

Brightness blooms from underneath the ship, floodlights illuminating the waters below. I don't get a chance to see much more before

Varley leads me to a small cranny near the stairs, tucking me safely between a sidewall and the stairwell.

"Stay here," she orders. "If things go wrong, Prince Thane or I will get you to a skiff. Now cover your ears."

Just as I do, the ship rocks with the force of plasma cannons expelling their bolts into the sea. Blue light crackles like miniature lightning fracturing the darkened dawn.

Please kill them, please kill them, please kill them.

I wait for what feels like forever, long enough that the suns begin to rise, lighting the sky with plum light.

The guns go off at least a dozen times as Thane steers the wounded *Predator* toward his home, to waters he knows well, sailing so fast the wind whistles into my nook. I only know we're aiming for the Cenian coast because Thane shouted it to his crew. He wants to run the gordrusks aground, make them mad enough to chase us, and trap them where they're easier to kill.

I can't believe there are four of them. Dark pink, blue, green, and yellow, according to Thane. Surely hunting this many at once isn't normal.

A hard *thunk* strikes the bottom of the boat. My pulse ratchets higher, but my curiosity is peaked. I need to see these things.

Though I know it isn't wise, I creep from my hole and crawl over one too many squidlets toward the railing. When I peer over the edge, I expect to see foamy water, or maybe one of the creatures swimming past. I'm truly not prepared to meet the stare of two gargantuan black eyes bulging from an enormous, bulbous head rising from the depths, nor face the sight of a horrendous, bleeding maw filled with rings upon rings of jagged teeth.

With a yelp, I shove off the rail as the gordrusk dives forward and snaps. Hissing a terrible screech, it clamps down on the rail between us, destroying the barrier before vanishing under the water line, away from the light beneath the ship.

Before I can shake off my stunned stupor, someone grabs me from behind and spins me around. "Adeira! Don't you dare go near that railing again, do you hear me?"

I look up into Thane's face. Sheer panic carves every line.

I can't help but note that he's shirtless, his shoulders and spine lined with stiff spikes.

"I-I'm sorry. I just—"

"Wanted to see the gordrusks," he finishes for me, nostrils flaring. "I'm well aware. We're going to have to work on your self-control, *if* we survive this."

The guns pulse again. Three rippling rounds boom from below. Thane pulls me close, the ship rocking from the gunmen's efforts. I notice his wounds then. Big, round welts across his bare chest and shoulders, as if he got into a fight with a...a...

Suckered tentacle.

With hopeful expectation in his eyes, he stares across the sea, a captain waiting for the sign that his enemies have finally met their end. That hope is quickly dashed as his gaze latches onto something behind me and widen with dread.

An eerie sensation climbs up my back a second before a fountain of water jets into the sky overhead. Thane and I raise our arms at the same time, shielding our faces as a pink tentacle slams down on the deck beside us, shattering the wood as though the thick planks are made of glass.

"Oh, fuck," is all Thane gets the chance to say before that tentacle closes around us, and a giant, monstrous fist drags the Prince and Princess of Cenia from the ship.

chapter seven

I TAKE ONE DEEP BREATH BEFORE THE GORDRUSK BURIES US UNDER THE Dead Seas.

In the pale light reaching from our ship through the watery abyss, I spot my safety vest floating away, torn from my body as easily as wet paper.

I look into Thane's eyes—and then look lower and lower. Everything about him is different. His skin has turned to scales, iridescent even in the murky water, and two wide, silver flaps ruffle on the sides of his head. His eyes even seem further apart, and two long slits have opened on either side of his throat.

Water-breather. I never even saw the shift.

He jerks his head to the side, as if trying to get me to see something. And do I ever. Thane's bare feet, now webbed and wider than normal. But beyond that, I glimpse the monster below us. It's all mouth and teeth and tentacles, beady eyes dancing from side to side as it drags us deeper.

I won't make it long like this. I require air and plenty of it.

Thane fights against the beast's hold, as do I. Some of his spikes remain stiff and sharp while others lengthen, working to loosen the gordrusk's grip. But even in the midst of all of this, Thane seems focused on something within the creature's grasp other than us.

Suddenly, a mighty pulse ripples through the sea just as a beam of light scans past, the crew likely searching for us from above. That light glints off glowing metal before all illumination from the ship goes dark.

The weapon that had been at Thane's side. That's what I saw shining. It's now clasped in his webbed hand.

With a mighty flex of muscle, he arches his back, ramming his spikes into the gordrusk's tentacle. The monster shrieks as thin ribbons of blood drift through the water, and its hold loosens in a momentary reprieve.

Thane jerks his arm free and, with a powerful downward stroke, slices the curved blade straight through the tentacle wrapped around us. Another shriek sounds, echoing mournfully under the water, and the appendage falls toward the sea floor, leaving a blooming trail of bright red blood in its wake.

Holding onto me, Thane sheathes his weapon and swims with the long stroke of one arm, kicking his feet, leading us from danger and toward freedom. He soon lets me go and urges me ahead, nodding for me to swim on my own.

I drag my arms through the water, desperate to breathe as I propel myself upward, sure that my husband is right behind me. But when I break the surface, gasping for air, he's not there.

In the day's lavender light, I turn and turn, paddling to stay afloat, searching. Thane is nowhere to be seen. Neither are the gordrusks. Or the ship. All I see is the sprawl of land to the north, a wide stretch of beach becoming more visible as the suns begin their rise. I could probably swim there. Maybe. But I can't leave this water without Thane.

And where in the seven moons is the ship? It was just here.

More shrieks resonate from the sea. Driven by worry and panic, I inhale a deep breath and dive back under. I don't have to swim too far before I spot the light of Thane's sword and the shimmer of his scales.

And three gordrusks. Pink, blue, and yellow. Surrounding him.

He moves like a purple serpent, his body elongated in a manner it wasn't before. I'm taken aback by his speed, and the way he dips and dives so smoothly, slicing his weapon through tentacle after tentacle, stabbing the creatures' open maws and startled eyes. Blood clouds the water, but the spectacle below me is still visible, like a dance in shadow.

A primal prince, slaying the beasts terrorizing his sea.

As the gordrusks' dying bodies fall away, Thane turns, ready to swim to the surface when he spots me. I never would've dreamed I'd see him like this today, or that, after all this horror, he'd be smiling. But he is, and so with a kick of my feet, I head back to the surface for air and wait with a thrumming pulse for my prince to join me.

When he does, he's still in his water-breather form. Mindful of his spikes, I slip my arms around his neck and hold on tight, highly aware of how much bigger and longer he is against me.

"Your ship's gone," I tell him, my lungs burning for air.

He turns us around and scans the brightening sky and sea. "Not good. We need to get to shore and send out a search party." He touches my face with a webbed hand and kisses me softly. "Tell me you're all right."

As water drips into my eyes, mingling with tears, I shake my head. "I'm not. At all. But I'm not hurt, if that's what you mean."

"Good enough." Another kiss, this time on my forehead. "I can get us close to the shore quickly, but we'll have to swim separately the last few hundred feet. I'll need to shift back before I step on land, and it weakens me."

I climb on his back as he instructs me, his spikes now smooth knots down his shoulders and spine. Making certain the ship is still nowhere to be found, I glance back, only to spot the green gordrusk shooting out of the water behind us because. That gaping, toothy maw opens wide, closing in fast. Before I even grasp what I'm doing, I've ripped Thane's glowing sword free from its sheath.

With all my strength, I swing the weapon in a wide arc, slitting the gordrusk's throat before it can devour us whole. Thane's blade slices through the beast's slick skin with far more ease than should be normal.

The monster flails, jerking away from me, even as its blood spills, staining the water red.

Thane spins and shoves me behind him before he realizes what I've done. The green gordrusk's eyes lose their light, then the last of this hunt's beasts collapses into the seafoam, its massive body vanishing into the deep.

Thane faces me, eyes wild. "Adeira. You just killed a gordrusk."

I nod and hand him his weapon, shaking so badly I can hardly hold it. "This is a special sword, isn't it?"

I could feel its power inside me. I couldn't have done anything if not for that.

He nods and takes it from me. "Very special, but not as special as you. That sword allows no one to wield it but me. And you now, too, it seems."

I'm glad his sword approves of me, but…

"Will you take me home?" My voice trembles as the adrenaline that fueled me before flees my blood, replaced with cold shock.

His face softens with such sweet tenderness. "Of course I will, my brave little monster hunter."

Protectively, Thane helps me ride out a powerful wave, then he slips me onto his back. I fold my arms around his neck, thankful he's here and that I'm with him, though longing for the moment when we reach Cenia's shores. When this is over, I might still want the adventurous life of hunting and killing sea beasts with my husband.

But right now, I just want to be a princess.

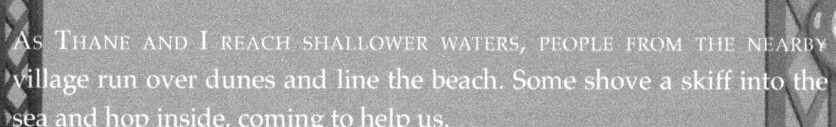

chapter eight

As Thane and I reach shallower waters, people from the nearby village run over dunes and line the beach. Some shove a skiff into the sea and hop inside, coming to help us.

I know no one in Cenia, but even from this distance, and even with the morning's waves crashing wild around us, I see a young woman, opalescent arms waving: Korrah. Seeing her helps me fight as Thane and I struggle against the water and exhaustion.

Now back in his Cenian form, Thane clings to my hand as we move side by side, our feet winning the battle with the shifting sand—until a wave slams into us, separating us, knocking me to my knees.

Thane powers toward me, the look in his eyes rattling my soul. It's an expression of devotion and respect and a thing I cannot name because no one has ever looked at me that way before.

He clasps my face and kisses me, his lips salty and warm, his scent an aroma that will forever find me.

"I am in awe of you, Adeira. Now come. I'm carrying you home."

Thane reaches under the water. Though I know his body is weary and wounded, he scoops me into his arms anyway and carries me to the shore, battling the pounding waves alone. Even once we're safe in the skiff, he keeps me in his grasp, nestled in his lap, my head against his naked chest as I listen to his raging heart.

One of the boatmen hands Thane a device that he slips into his ear.

A radio. The *Predator* and its crew are safe, the vessel having washed ashore down the beach after being launched across the ocean by that angry green gordrusk.

Once we're finally on land, we're loaded into an open-air hover vehicle with Fedder and Korrah in the front seats. Thane still doesn't let me go, his strong hands checking for injuries he won't find, soothing me as my trembling wanes.

Korrah's face is a mask of worry. She reaches back and takes my hand. Thane notices and gives me a perceptive look, as if he understands exactly what we did to fool Fedder so I could hitch a ride on that watership.

"Do you need medics?" Fedder asks.

"I think we're fine," Thane replies. "Just take us to my hut for now."

I look at Korrah and manage a weak smile.

"His *hut*," she whispers, and we both laugh under our breath.

And perhaps it *is* a hut. To Prince Thane, anyway. To me, it looks like the most perfect home by the sea. It has two levels with white mud-brick walls and a thick grass roof. Large windows cover the ocean-facing side, their blue shutters open wide for the day, letting in the breeze. Sheer pale pink curtains blow in the wind.

"Should you need anything at all..." Fedder says, his words trailing.

Thane inclines his head. "I know where to find you. But I think I just need to be alone with my wife for a few days."

Korrah's eyes go wide, and I bite my lip, relieved and suddenly anxious.

Thane insists on carrying me inside. Once we cross the threshold, I'm surprised there's no talk of what we just experienced. Nothing but a need for closeness.

We shower together in the shade of a lush, open garden off Thane's bedroom, taking turns scrubbing one another's body and hair, ridding ourselves of any last bits of gordrusk and sand. I study each of Thane's wounds, black bruises he insists are painless thanks to Cenian medicine.

Our hands most certainly roam as we bathe. We taste the temptation of naked flesh and hungry kisses, not to mention the arousal of seeing and teasing and touching one another in such bold light.

With water softly raining down upon us, Thane presses me against the shower wall and slips a finger inside me, moving in and out as I ride his hand and stroke his rigid length. We kiss with unmatched desire, our needy mouths never once parting. Not until we climax, anyway, in one another's hand.

When we step back into the bedroom, I think our mating will *finally* happen, but the moment we sink into Thane's plush bed, we're done for. We sleep like the dead, deep into the next afternoon.

But oh, when we wake…

Thane lies curled behind me, the warm press of his body melded with mine. His heavy arm is slung over my middle, his hand cradling my breast.

As desire replaces my need for sleep, I close my eyes once more, relishing the moment. It's almost impossible not to roll my hips along that thick, hot erection nestled against the curve of my ass. What a wonderful thing to wake up to.

For a while, I just lie there, aroused yet quiet and still, absorbing Thane's scent as his steady breaths tickle my neck. Then I turn over and face him, only to find him already staring at me.

Slow smiles form on both our mouths as I slide my hand into his hair, instantly inhaling a waft of pheromones and all the power they hold over me. Power in which I willingly lose myself.

"Can we finally mate now?" I ask.

His pretty lips quirk up higher on one side. "I've been lying here for the last three hours hard as a meteorite, trying not to wake you, wanting exactly that."

"Wanting exactly what?" I tease.

He kisses me, licking his tongue into my waiting mouth. "To be buried inside you. To feel you grow wetter and wetter as I pleasure you in ways you have never been pleasured before."

I tap his nose. "So confident."

"Perhaps I have a reason to be."

That just makes my desire worse.

I'm beyond eager, my nerve endings wide awake and wanting. But there's one thing I need before we officially unite.

I press my hands against Thane's chest, urging him back onto the pillows, though he doesn't budge. "I never got the chance to explore you the way you did me," I complain. "Seems only fair."

He arches a dangerous brow, but that's all it takes for my husband to submit with ease. "I suppose I must endure the agony of discovery, then," he sighs.

Smiling, I straddle him, mindful of his bruises. My pulse begins a steady thrumming as I trail kisses down his beautiful body, pausing to tease his hard nipples.

His spine arches a little, and he gasps, strong fingers fisting in my hair, holding me close. If *this* has such an effect, I can't imagine how he'll respond when I do the same thing to his cock.

It isn't long before I find out. I settle between his legs, mesmerized by the intense aroma of pheromones and Thane's beautiful, throbbing cock. There's so much to see now that I'm closer, observing him with the late afternoon light spilling through the house.

I drag a fingertip up the underside, following a thick, pulsing vein to his swollen tip. Unable to resist, I take his wide head into my mouth and roll my tongue over and over him, flicking back and forth through that center slit, tasting his already-rising arousal when I suck.

Thane moans my name, and his hands tighten in my hair, urging me into a steady rhythm, his gently grinding hips all but begging me to take him deeper.

I take all I can, until the first ridge is inside my mouth, and Thane's control slips. He begins a shallow thrusting, clearly longing to see me swallow more of him, but we're closing in on a place I don't want to go yet. So I release him, noting the deep rise and fall of his chest, and how his eyes have already glazed over with the shimmer of lust and desire and near orgasm.

"Tell me what I need to know," I say, lapping hungrily at his tip.

His eyes roll back in his head, and that hand in my hair…

But he comes back to himself, breathing hard, shaking his head at me with a tight stare. "You make it incredibly difficult to think."

"Yes, well, you and your pheromones make it incredibly difficult to be patient, but I need to know what I'm in for."

He stuffs another pillow behind his head. "You once said I'm full of surprises." He rubs his thumb across my bottom lip. "Do you want to see how many?"

The delight that courses through me is probably abnormal, but I feel like I'm receiving a gift, so I nod. With vigor.

Thane closes his hand around the base of his cock. "I'm similar to human and Krythian males in that I enjoy being touched like this." He strokes and strokes, then his other hand arrives, fondling his balls. "These are sensitive too. Squeezing and tugging them heightens my pleasure."

Unable to resist, I suck one into my mouth before dragging my tongue up their center, feeling his smooth skin tighten. But I can't just stop there. I drag a taste all the way up the length of his delicious cock, claiming a sweet drop of coral cum waiting for me at the tip.

Thane shudders, heavy-lidded eyes intent on mine. "If you keep doing that, my surprises are going to be just that. *Surprises.* Because I'm either going to come or I'm going to flip you over and mount you like the desperate primal I am."

Much as I ache for that scenario, I force myself toward restraint. "All right. I'll be good…for now. Please continue."

"These ridges"—he strokes his cock again—"undulate for both of us. For me, when I'm ready to release, it's like a second stroke. For you, the motion supposedly feels wonderful, the ridges stretching you wide as they swell with cum, throbbing and pulsating until I explode."

I clench the sheets to keep from touching him. "That sounds… exciting."

He winks. "It will be. But now for the real surprises." He touches a small dark purple line between the base of his cock and balls. "See this?"

I frown. "Is it a scar?"

"No scar. An opening."

Before I can ask what it's for, a second cock head appears through the slit. I gasp aloud, watching in utter amazement as a fully erect penis introduces itself. It's shaped exactly like the other one, only a bit smaller.

"For your second hole," he says, fisting it. "Cenian women have three holes. We males are built to please."

Seven moons. I cannot even fathom my luck at this moment. The things I'm going to do to this poor prince.

But…

"Your dossier said you only had one penis."

Thane barks a laugh. "Is that all you cared to know? What was between our legs?"

I make a face. "It matters! And Korrah thought it was certainly information I needed to consider before taking a life mate."

"Korrah seems like the kind of friend who truly looks out for you. And, technically, it *is* just one penis. The other bits come from the main root, so…"

I narrow my eyes. "You purposely left this information out of your dossier."

He smiles. "Perhaps."

"And what do you mean by surpris*es* and *bits*? I only see *one* surprise and one extra bit."

A devious gleam shines in his eyes as he presses his first cock down with the palm of his hand, his long fingers not even reaching the head. At the top of its base, there's another slit.

My mind starts tumbling over unbidden images. Things are getting crowded for this part-human/part-Krythian girl. Cenian women might be able to take three cocks, but I'm not sure what I'll do with a third one.

What appears from that second slit, however, is not another penis.

"This is my spur." Thane flicks his finger back and forth over the new appendage that looks very much like a short, forked tongue. "It vibrates and works in a licking motion. It can elongate, too, much like the rest of me." His eyes meet mine, bright as two summer suns. "But for us," he says, his voice deepening, "I think my spur is perfect for making your little clit cum for me."

Any restraint from before vanishes, replaced with unbridled craving. I crawl up Thane's body and crash into him, my mouth and chest colliding with his.

He grabs my waist as I reach for his main cock, angling it just so, and then I sink onto him, gasping and shaking and yearning to be filled.

Thane crushes my mouth to his and thrusts his hips, burying his massive cock inside me. A cry escapes me, my fingers tangling and tightening in his hair as a shiver rockets up my spine. I gasp for breath, but he swallows both my cry and my air, rolling his hips, pressing so deep I'm not sure where I begin and he ends.

Panting, Thane rips his mouth from mine. "I feel like I've been waiting ages for this. To feel you wrapped around my cock. To see you sitting atop me like the princess you are. You're so fucking beautiful, Adeira. I could live and die right here in this bed."

"It's been four days," I remind him, and he laughs. The sexy, rough sound does delightful things to my heart and my pussy.

Thane kisses my temple. "Does it feel good? Having me inside you like this?"

"You know it does." Barely able to think about anything else, I drag a tender bite up his throat. "And I want more."

He slides his hand down my back and over my ass. "Take all you need. I am nothing if not a slave for your desires."

My thighs quake at that, my core clenching as I reach back and position his second cock. It takes a little maneuvering, but soon he's double-seated inside me, and I'm trying to remember my own name when we haven't even truly started yet.

But then we begin, and the dance of our joined bodies is far sweeter than anything I could've ever dreamed. As I rock slowly against Thane, learning him, his hands trace maps of memory over my skin, his mouth hot and needy as he sucks and nips and moans against my dangling breasts. He touches me wherever he can, reaching between us and behind me to feel where we meet, even as we smother one another's desperate moans with fevered kisses.

I lean down, my forearms beside his head, my breasts pressed against his warm chest, and revel in ecstasy as he thrusts into me, his spur licking and vibrating against my clit, edging me so quickly toward release. It's a test of restraint, because I take my time, making love to him until the late afternoon sun turns to soft shadows across the room.

This game of back and forth is a subtle destruction, one that nearly destroys me, but I'm determined not to give in. Slowing, I push myself up until I'm sitting upright on Thane's cocks.

I cannot believe I get to have this for the rest of my life. I am the luckiest princess in the galaxy.

I drop my head back, losing myself in the euphoria of being so gloriously filled. Patient and admiring, Thane caresses my body, from my shoulders to my breasts, to the soft curve of my belly, and finally my clit.

When I lift my head and meet his eyes, I see the maddening hunger there, the ache and longing he's barely controlling.

"I need to claim you," he says, his voice ragged. "To bend you over and come inside you until my seed runs down your lovely thighs."

I can't begin to deny him. The air is saturated with his pheromones and us and raw, wonderful sex.

There's nothing like the moment when I give myself over to him. Every dark need that has ever lived inside me suddenly feels satiated once I'm on my knees with the primal Prince of Cenia kneeling behind me, gripping my waist in his powerful hands, thrusting deep with both cocks throbbing, their ridges moving with the most tender undulation.

I don't get the benefit of Thane's spur like this, but my husband is thorough. An elongated spike slips between my legs and begins a tender torture all its own, sending me tumbling toward that sweet cliff of release, only to relent just long enough to prevent me from falling, all before returning to take me on the journey once again.

I groan and rock, back arching, anything to take Thane deeper, riding him with a hint of violence burning in my blood, a need far greater than anything I've known before this moment.

As if sensing that dark hunger, he seizes a fistful of my hair and wrenches my head back. Like the warrior he is, he leans down and devastates my mouth so thoroughly a sob leaves me the moment we separate.

"My stunning wife," he whispers, lips still close to mine. "My Adeira. My treasure. Forever."

I crumble under his words and hands. There's nothing in the world then, save for the pounding of our bodies, the rippling pleasure pulsating like a threat between my legs, and a strange oneness pouring through me like the universe itself lives within my blood.

A true binding—a uniting of souls I sense in my very essence.

Instinctively, Thane knows when I'm hanging from the cliff of my orgasm, and with artful ministrations, times my climax with his own. Suddenly, he's chanting my name, his grip on me tightening as the throbbing pulse of his swelling cocks turns so powerful I can feel his seed rising, each stroke of my body and his undulating ridges priming him toward release.

When we erupt, I swear our climaxes radiate through every part of me, scattering like shattered starlight. I feel open and vulnerable, but there's no fear in this. Just joy and bliss and a tender security the girl from Krythia has never known. It's as if I've given something precious away yet received something just as great in return.

The devoted heart of a primal prince. That's what I've gained.

When the height of our rapture passes, we sink into Thane's bed, ruined and ravaged victims of the fire still burning between us. Our bodies are slick with sweat and pleasure, but that doesn't stop my husband from kissing me from the tip of my nose to that tender place on the inside of my ankle.

After, we lie in a peaceful tangle, racing heartbeats slowing as we caress one another, until the day's last light fades.

Thane finally rises on his elbow, head at rest in his hand as he looks down upon me. "Fate or no fate, monster-hunting or no monster-hunting, duty or no duty, I want you to know that I'm so very glad you chose me."

With the sweetest sincerity in his eyes, he kisses me again, and we both smile, tasting the curve of one another's lips, the happiness lighting us from within, bright as the suns that hang high over Othara.

I touch his face, fully aware of how much I still have to learn about this new life and the many things I've yet to discover about my handsome, fierce, primal prince.

But I utter the truest words I have ever said: "I'm so very glad I chose you too."

about charissa weaks

Charissa Weaks is an award-winning Amazon Top 100 author of romantic and historical fantasy. She crafts stories with time travel, magick, myth, history, a dash of spice, and the occasional apocalyptic quest.

Her debut novel *The Witch Collector*—the first of five books planned in the Witch Walker series—earned a Best of BookTok flag and is published in several languages.

Charissa resides just south of Nashville with her family and two wrinkly English Bulldogs. When she's not writing, you can find her lost in a good book or digging through four-hundred-year-old texts for research.

To learn more, visit direct.me/charissaweaksauthor

crocheter's guide to alien conservation

Elisse Hay

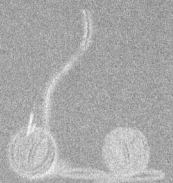

chapter one

eve

I'D HOPED NEXT TIME I OPENED MY EYES THAT HEAVY SENSE OF hopelessness would be gone. I'd hoped, but I hadn't really expected it. So as I watched the guy in front of me coming into focus and that elephant was still on my chest, I wasn't really *disappointed* so much as resigned.

I *was* disappointed by the accommodations. I lay on some sort of smooth table, there was *sky* above me, and why did I feel like I'd been hit by a bus? If I'd swapped the hopelessness of the daily grind for broken ribs, I probably could've lived with it, but this was just the worst of both worlds.

The guy glanced over and I closed my eyes. *It's a side-effect from the medically induced nap for the journey*, I told myself. *Your eyesight is fine. He isn't purple.*

Or…I was talking to an *alien*. Aliens *ate* us.

"I wish you a pleasant waking," he said, his voice a deep, vibrating timbre that made it almost impossible to keep my eyes scrunched closed. "Is your body comfortable?"

Was my *body* comfortable? I looked up at where he towered over me, his dark green hair falling to frame his exaggeratedly square jaw and strong, beak-like nose. Whatever I was going to say dried up.

He wasn't purple. He was *lilac.*

I was utterly fucked. I wasn't supposed to be anywhere beyond humanity's reach. My destination was only two planets over from Original Earth. No aliens, no way. I was going to be the saltiest snack this guy had had in awhile because *fuck. this.*

"Do you recall how you came to be here?" he asked me, but the movement of his lips didn't match the words.

I closed my eyes again. Five years ago, I'd married my dream guy, I'd just landed my dream job, and I'd been organising to move into my dream home. Except they hadn't really been that; they were only dreams if they came from the *Dream* region in France. They'd just been sparkling toxicity. And now I had dreams of being able to afford more yarn for my knitting.

"Oh yeah," I told him, grimly. "Yeah, I do."

"Have you anyone remaining?" he asked me, the question so gentle I kind of wanted to throat-punch him.

I'd signed up for *new* and *different* and, sure, the program had obviously been predatory. They didn't invite plebs like me to assist in populating a relatively new planet without adding some catches, and I hadn't felt the need to ask a lot of questions. I could have an adventure with predators. At least I'd known what I was getting into. *Go away, leave everything behind, have a fresh start, sell my soul to a different megacorporation and eat cereal for dinner on a different planet.*

I hadn't signed up for *therapy.* I'd signed up for *get the fuck out of here.*

"Nope." I tried to sit up and pain radiated through my whole body, taking my breath away. My eyes popped open, but he wasn't about to try to hold me down or whatever. He was just standing there, like a big, weird, lilac lump.

Maybe this was some sort of mindfuck orchestrated by the program to ensure my compliance? I watched him, giving myself at least four chins with the unflattering angle of my face and in way too much pain to care. He watched me back. Behind him, the indigo sky seemed so close I could almost reach out and touch it. It had a different texture to what I was used to. Velvety. The stars glowed in unfamiliar patterns behind him and I wished I could try to figure them out, but I *hurt.*

"What's the deal?" I asked, and the question came out somewhat pleading, because the bench I was on made all the other hurts into bigger, shittier hurts.

"You have a need to be comfortable," he said, and I sure as hell didn't disagree. But it was a weird way to say it, and again the movement of his lips still didn't match the sounds he was making.

In the background, I could hear waves, and for some reason that normalcy alongside this alien's strange speech made me want to puke.

"I am not informed of your body's requirements," he added. "I do not recognize how to aid."

That's what they all say. I cleared my throat and glanced around, but couldn't see anyone. Someone had built rough-hewn stone walls arranged aesthetically around us to make it a semi-sheltered outdoor area. I saw some baskets that probably would've cost a fortune at the local farmer's market and a lot of sand. Everything was a strange colour palette, though. Was this a side-effect of the medically induced sleep? That would probably make sense, if their drugs had fucked my vision.

Unease overcame hopelessness and pain. I struggled up despite the bolts of pain that shot from my chest and up one leg, though my head swam and my stomach rebelled. I looked down at my body and was utterly unsurprised by the rudimentary splint on my left leg. I was scraped, bruised, and one of my favourite shoes was missing. If I tossed my cookies on this guy, well, he wouldn't be the first to suffer that fate.

There had been hundreds of us. We'd smiled and sat and run our phones down waiting for our turn to be put into long-term sleep and sent to the mystery land where we'd start over.

I couldn't see anyone, though. Only rocks, plants I didn't recognise, and a choppy, uninviting sea crouching over the horizon in various purples and oranges with the odd splash of pink for that sweet accent shade. "Where's everyone else?" I demanded.

He shook his head. Black hair that shone with green highlights swung hypnotically around his strong neck and settled on his shoulders. "No others lived. I express regret and sadness appropriate."

My head spun. "What happened?"

He frowned, a little. "You said you are knowing?"

For fuck's sake. Tears rose in a wave and I struggled not to drown. "Where am I?"

"We are by the Centre of All," he said, the words kind. "You have been Called."

Great. Just fucking great. I wiped away tears. "You better explain that, too, buddy."

He glanced at one of the moons hanging over my shoulder. I followed his gaze and stared at where the second one sat, low and fat, in the velvety purple sky, the source of the light that let me see with relative clarity. "A Bio-resonant Signal Not Yet Identified In Your Language alerted you to your importance by the Centre of All," he said, slowly, as if this might help me understand. "This is not phenomena your people are knowing?"

I couldn't begin to list every phenomenon my people weren't knowing. I struggled to wrap my head around the fact that I'd somehow crash-landed on an alien planet and the locals were using culty justification to make it all okay.

"What's your name?" I asked him, survival instincts kicking in.

"It will be not correct to your ears," he said, passing me what looked like a crutch, made of polished driftwood with pretty, sea aesthetic shit carved into it. It would've been fit for a water wizard in a high budget movie on Original. "The meaning maker will shift the words. But it is Dreamdiver."

Dreamdiver. What the fuck. I scooted to the edge of the table, my whole body aching. "Okay, Dreamdiver." I could play along. "Where are we going?"

He looked at me with so much patience I damn near swung the crutch at his belly. "You should travel to cot." He waved a hand toward the side of stone where I could make out some sort of path between the tumble of rocks and purple-tinged plant life. At least the rocks were greenish, to break up all the purple.

I was more interested in his hand, though. And the way his fingers sort of...*flowed.* I blinked, trying to focus, but he'd dropped his hand to his side.

Regardless of the danger of aliens, if he'd planned to eat me, I'd already have been nommed. My leg was *actually* broken and my every-thing hurt. If I was about to be alien chow, then I'd cross that bridge later.

The crutch was ungainly but the moment I touched my foot even gingerly to the ground, agony made my head spin.

He stood silently, watching me try to balance without puking or crying from the pain. I gritted my teeth and it wasn't enough. Tears itched on my cheeks.

"Can you help?" I demanded, but it sounded more like a sad mewl and I *hated* that.

He made something adjacent to a grunt that came from deep in his chest, and a moment later the whole world, such as it was, tilted. His arms were barely softer than the table I'd been on, and he smelt like the sea.

Like *Original* sea, not some weird alien sea, and for some reason that made me relax as he carried me along.

I closed my eyes and let myself enjoy the ride.

Next time I opened them, everything hurt a whole lot more, but I was inside, at least, and he was setting me down on a huge chair made out of driftwood, except with some pretty washes to add color. I leant my upper body against the table and watched him move about the big, airy, boho beach-chic hut decorated with driftwood, strange purple plants, and the odd off-white or dark silver cylinder, stand, or rectangle that I suspected were his tech. He arranged a blanket-adja-cent creation in what looked like a sized-up cat bed. I didn't hate it.

"This is not a superior cot," he said, and with his back turned I realised the pattern I could see wasn't a quirky shirt but the texture on his lilac skin. "It has been many rotations since I last met someone similar to your body. I have not the ideal furnishings for your comfort."

Hypnotised, I watched his hands. Well, his tentacles. Halfway down what would've been a forearm on a human, darker purple, tentacle-like digits split out from his arm. Webbing flared between them as he extended one away from the bunch and I watched as they flowed over the covers, suckers the size of the pad of my pinky clutching to some pieces and releasing others as he adjusted it.

I couldn't remember feeling them on me when he'd carried me. My head spun as I watched this evidence that I was utterly, hopelessly lost.

He straightened and offered me the crutch in mass of *tentacles*. "Is it best for your comfort if I haul you?"

Haul. I scowled at his word choice. "Fuck you, buddy."

His chest and neck flushed a deeper purple. "That is a kind offer, but it would be inappropriate for us, as you are in my care."

I barely heard the words, watching the dark, blotchy purple flush. "Wait." I held up a hand, wishing my head wasn't so full of cotton wool. "Wait." There was no point asking him if he was trustworthy. He'd tell me yes either way.

I was stuck with an alien guy on an alien planet, everyone I'd been transported with was dead, and I was stranded.

No time like the present to remember your survival skills, Eve.

"I'm sorry," I said, slowly. "I didn't mean to be rude." Yeah, better not piss off the locals.

He tilted up his particularly square jaw and waved at his temple, where a series of circles were tattooed in blue. "The universal speaker affordance is not deprived of drawbacks. You were not asking me to fornicate?"

It sucked that he looked kind of relieved. "Nope," I said, taking the crutch he was offering and grimly forcing myself to my feet. "I was upset by the word you used for helping me move." I paused, though, and ran a finger over my own temple. A shiver of unease went up my spine as I felt hard, circular ridges beneath my fingertips.

"You did not have the universal speaker," he said, tentatively. "I am not knowing how you moved through locations without it, and I am not feeling you are less important because of it. Forgiveness is desirable." And he looked at me with big, soft green eyes that could've been used to sell anything from pet food to adult toys back on Original.

I really did need that nap. "Do I sound as weird as you?"

He looked puzzled. "I am not knowing how you mean." And he was blushing again, his throat and chest going a deep purple as his eyes dipped down to my throat.

Had I just accidentally hit on an alien?

This whole thing was too bizarre. "You know what?" I put the crutch down. "I hurt and I'm tired. Please haul me to the bed."

He hesitated a moment, but scooped me up again. This time I paid attention, but still couldn't feel his hands—tentacles—on me, and he held me much lower, almost at hip height. There was some sort of scar running from the centre of his lip down his throat and it was comfortingly silver. I don't know why the colour of his scar made me feel better, but it did, just like the smell of salt that clung to him.

It was about three steps, but in those three steps I'd realised he didn't have body hair, that his skin was a little rough, and that he didn't have nipples.

That kinda seemed like a shame?

"Are you a mammal?" I asked, then wished I could snatch the word back.

He set me down in the giant cat bed like I was a snake. "I am a Sea People Not Yet Identified In Your Language."

"I'm sorry." I grabbed the blanket, struggling between fury at the situation and absolute shame that I was making such a mess of it. "Look, I'm going to try not to be a dick, but it comes naturally to me. I'll have to work on it."

His eyes ran over me as his colour deepened. "I do not think the universal speaker is working for this," he said. "I am not knowing how to help you be comfortable, but please use words if you have concepts to share."

I'd just called myself a dick and he'd taken it literally.

Wordlessly, I nodded, curled up like a cat, and pulled the blanket over my head. If I was eaten, that probably would only be a good thing, at this point.

I ASSUMED IT WAS NIGHT, because when he returned, he turned on a glowing lamp thing that crouched in a driftwood cage and emitted a pale pink glow. I watched, fuzzy-headed from sleep and pain, as he moved around in a kitchen area. He glanced over at one point and I tried not to think about our communication breakdowns. "Hi," I said. "I'm Eve."

He rolled his hand at me in a weird way, then touched it to his chest. "I am eager to have seen you, Before. How is your body comfort?"

Before? A moment of confusion was all it took before I realised my name had a literal translation and he probably just got it. I was "Before."

Jesus Christ. I didn't have the brain juice for this. "My body isn't comfortable." I didn't know what painkillers would translate to, but surely that statement and my best puppy eyes would do it.

He nodded. "I can help reduce your body being uncomfortable, if you will allow me to haul you through water."

There he went with the hauling again. It was lucky my possibly-vegetarian alien looked like he could deadlift a truck. "Sure." *Don't be a dick, Eve.* "If you're okay to do that. Thank you, Dreamdiver."

He nodded again, turning his back quickly and bringing whatever passed for food to his mouth. Pain pounded me as I waited. Moving was hard, but I got to my feet to make his job a bit easier. My throat was dry as a desert. Before I could figure out how to express that, he was in front of me, holding out his arms.

I wanted coffee, some paracetamol, and a couple ibuprofen with a tequila chaser. That was a beachy mix, right?

When he picked me up and started walking, I settled back as much as my aching body would allow. Outside, the sky was dark. The obligatory two moons hung in the sky. They showed similar amounts of shadow. Shouldn't they be different?

He carried me in silence away from the hut. I wanted to be able to enjoy the landscape, but I *hurt*. And also, for some reason this guy *didn't have nipples*. He was straight up and down, no abs, no pecs. Just rough, streamlined purple flesh.

"We will enter water soon," he said to me. "You are not a Sea People or Name of Aquatic Beings Not Yet Identified In Your Language, so you will need to hold onto me."

I heard splashing before that could process. Aquatic beings I didn't know about? The image of merfolk swam through my head. I surprised myself by wondering if Dreamdiver could answer the age-old question of how they reproduced.

"I will put you in the water to shift how my hold is on your body," he said.

The universal word thing was unhinged. "Cool." I glanced over the water, uneasy, as he lowered me. Flashes of deep burgundy with frothy pink waves were all I could process. The water was warm, but the pain was phenomenal.

I struggled to breathe and he held me gently, leaning over me with that kind expression on his face and too many moons behind him. And his tentacles wrapped around me with the sweetness of a thousand forehead kisses.

"Draw in air," he said, kindly.

As if I'd ever stopped? The water's movement against my splinted leg was agonising, and something brushed against my back. Alarm spurted through me. I jackknifed, and spots swam over my vision.

The sense of being submerged, of water rushing and his body moving beside mine, made the panic flutter. I clutched at him. Darkness, cool water, stinging bubbles. Above me the moons appeared distorted, but the light travelled through the water in a way that didn't make sense, exposing endless purple depths and silhouetting underwater forests far away. My heart was hitting my ribs like my ex smashing the *ring for service* bell.

"We have a little distance to travel now," he said. "Remain not panicking."

I could hear him talking underwater. Somewhere, in the back of my brain, I realised how deeply fucked up that was. But the majority of my mind was taken up by the fact that we were *underwater* and going deeper at a rate that I suspected wasn't good for my poor, up-fucked body.

We turned a corner and the moon was suddenly gone, but a soft green glow came from somewhere that I couldn't see. He was still swimming. He didn't know I couldn't breathe water. I was going to drown. Alien man was going to drown me.

I tried to kick my good leg and felt his attention on me. But if we could go *faster*, maybe I'd live. Maybe. A bubble escaped my mouth and I watched it vanish into the dark water above me.

And then we ran into the faintest barrier, and the water was left behind.

I sucked in air, grabbing hold of the stone lip of the cave entrance. Green lights, steel, shelves full of wicker baskets that were neatly labelled in a curving, fluid-looking writing I couldn't read. A big, messy net puddled to the side. Beakers and glass science-y stuff sat along one wall. Tanks of some sort of fish were stacked, the creatures staring at me in their individual glass houses. I didn't know enough about caves to know if it was natural, but it was *big*. Not like, stage-a-concert big. As in, could fit a family of five and still have pets sort of big.

With his tentacles still wrapped gently around me, he climbed out of the water. "It is with much courage that you swam," he said, smiling at me. "Allow me to provide you with A Medication That Is Similar To Opiates Not Yet Identified In Your Language."

I couldn't speak. I didn't have the air, or the backbone, or something. He rolled me onto a steel platform and the green glow above me increased. A dark green metallic disc thing floated above me.

"There will be no pain from my medical treatment," he said, and he put on glasses.

Glasses.

I lay back and let the darkness take me.

chapter two

irosabsuul

HER OXYGEN LEVELS WERE GOOD, AND HER INJURIES EXTENSIVE BUT NOT medically significant. Satisfied it was the pain that had resulted in her loss of consciousness, I checked her weight, metabolism, and species information against the Blue Tipped Keldra serum to make sure I hadn't miscalculated.

I was *qualified* to do this, but not *practiced*. If she'd been awake, it would have been much more comfortable. I could have provided her with the serum and she could've taken it, or not. And even knowing that her species didn't use their oral opening for recreation and repro-duction the way mine did, it still felt unethical to put my digits on her jaw and ease her lips apart.

Drawing in a deep breath, I took the dropper, administered the dose, and was glad when my mind didn't sexualise her.

While the pain medication did its work, I assessed the damage again on the scanner. She'd been sent for a reason. Everyone was. She'd move on to the city. She'd do something that would help sustain the Centre. This was a small notation on the tertiary level of my job. Sometimes, a being would be in need who was not within my usual role. I wasn't going to turn them away.

Her damaged limb was stiff, with brittle bones. Her feet showed harm done by improper foot positioning, and my quick study showed little pieces of cartilage growing where they shouldn't be. What had she done to her poor feet before landing here? Furthermore, her hormones were out of balance, and there were nonlethal but troublesome cysts on her ovaries that would cause her significant discomfort monthly.

That needed to be dealt with sooner rather than later. But she'd come to me because of her leg and sore chest, so I focused on those concerns. There wasn't much I could do about her bruised ribs except marvel at the way her species had evolved such a flawed spine. But her leg I wrapped in bright, fresh Volett leaf, then tied and set beneath a light cast. It would take her a few weeks to heal, but that would hold it still, and the Volett would protect the muscles while she held the limb immobile and encourage blood flow. And if the Refugee Support Services arrived before then, they'd equip her with the higher tech version of what I'd just done.

I spent some time looking at her toes, each one like a little, only barely functional limb. I wondered what her home planet was like. To have existed without the universal translator, either she was incredibly wealthy...or unbelievably impoverished.

Her eyes fluttered open and I braced myself for her fear as her eyes ran over the contents of my lab. She probably hadn't been able to think very clearly before.

"Good sunup," she said, then scrubbed her hand over her face with those strangely firm fingers that I didn't stare at. "My body is a large amount less painful. I am happy."

She didn't look happy, but I was familiar with the translator's quirks, and knew many of our languages included reassuring phrases that didn't necessarily translate well. "Your leg has been treated. It will heal over the coming weeks. For now, try to let it rest."

She nodded, scooting over to the edge of the bed. "I must be rocked as intercourse," she said. "Because my pain is greatly reduced. The fish look low temperature."

Why she spoke of intercourse so often I was unsure, but I gathered it was another, albeit unusual, turn of phrase. I offered her my arm to lean on and brought her over to the bio-recovery area. She hobbled along beside me, her gaze everywhere, her words coming fast and making only limited sense. I stopped listening to the exact terms she used, but instead watched her round, pink face flushed with increase blood flow as she laboured to get around.

Her happy noises were pleasant.

She crouched down before the bio-recovery unit of a fingerling who'd been brought to me with a damaged tail and some bite-marks. "A leaf is adhered to it," she said, looking at me accusingly.

"It's medical," I told her.

She shook her head. "No, look. It's a leaf."

I nodded, then indicated toward her leg. "Volett," I said, slowly. "It is good for increasing blood-flow, and will stay on even when you're in the water."

She looked at me, then her leg, then the fish. "Are you a medical responder for unaware beings?"

"I help sea life," I agreed, hoping that would prevent misunderstandings.

"And me," she said, her eyes huge as she stared at me, her lips so full and flushed, parted ever so slightly. As I watched, her tongue flicked out tentatively, the briefest flicker of pink. Heat rushed through me and I tore my eyes away. It wasn't appropriate for a patient to stir such feelings, even if we were biologically compatible.

"You needed help. I helped." I cleared my aching throat. I had no right to lust after her. If she came back, later… I cleared my throat again. "This one should be ready to release soon."

She turned her gaze back to the fingerling, slowing her pace to watch the fish. Her shifting attention allowing me to observe her unusual roundness, the soft pillows of her body that felt so lovely against me. The clothing she wore was not protective. The darkness of it was made more pronounced by the water it appeared to hold onto. The cloth clung to her fragile skin like the Volett leaf. I could see every dip and ripple of her short, but generous body.

My mouth watered.

My eyes traced the dip of her spine, the curve of her behind, the dimples in her thighs and the valley behind her knees. The backs of her legs rippled like the sandbars after a storm. I swallowed and tore my eyes away, but the peaks and troughs of her were seared into my lids.

She was injured, and in my care. It had been years since I'd had romantic company, but those years had been fulfilling, even joyous, and I hadn't felt the lack of partner.

This poor woman had just had her life torn apart. Who knew who she'd lost, what she had left. The Call was rarely without cost. The nagging irritation in the lead-up, the navigation as you needed to iden- tify what, exactly, your Calling was. One day, we'd learn more about the Heartbeat that stabilised the galaxy and fuelled this planet as well as providing the source of its biobeacons that ensured ongoing, high level care of the entire system. One day, we'd decode the biobeacon so it could be read like a holotext, rather than interpreted like a nagging worry. For today... I was simply here to ensure she survived and continued along her way.

As if she was the Heartbeat, though, my gaze drew inexorably back. My throat felt too tight as my eyes drew upward, this time, over the roundness of her belly and the peaks of her breast tissue, to her beautiful neck where tendrils of fine, dark hair curled against her strangely pale skin.

Creases in her skin begged to be traced. Her bones formed a beau- tiful vee at the base of her throat that I couldn't see from this angle, but I knew was there.

You shouldn't look at injured beings.

She had control of her faculties now, though, and for the next few hours. I couldn't help but notice her bone structure and flesh created pleasing forms.

Her jaw was painfully delicate. It was one of the first things I'd noticed when I'd thrown the torn pieces of steel off her. The wreck was huge, and the fires had been high, but one outflung arm had caught my eye. And there she'd been. Pale, dirty, and half-covered by rubble, needing my assistance every bit as much as the fingerling she was staring at now. Unlike the fingerling, she'd have external help soon enough. The thought was unsettling. I followed, with my eyes, the line of her jaw and the curve of her cheek. Her lips were curved up, now, in amusement.

Horror struck me as I saw she was watching me watch her in the reflection of the tank. I swallowed again, trying to regain some semblance of control.

"I should identify how to leave," she said, and while the translator smoothed the jumble of sounds that came from her mouth, it kept the tone. Amusement, but also, the first trace of concern.

I was glad she was coming back to herself, and glad that she had the usual survival reflexes, even if hers seemed to have been buried beneath the pain.

"Whenever you want, I can take you to the city," I told her, keeping my worry to myself at that idea. "Or I can summon the Refugee Support Services."

I only had a week or so before the Heartfins migrated, and preparation would take every moment of my time. Their numbers had been reduced in a storm, and were crucial to maintain for the Heartbeat's health. No other fish was as efficient at eating the Unngild forests that could choke the Heartlines and congest our ability to sustainably harvest the biofuels.

"Population centre?" she repeated, frowning. "There's a city?"

"There is." I considered picking up the net now, but I was exhausted, and threading the fine, stretchy fibres into the correct shape made my digits ache just to think about. "Did you want to see it?"

She opened her mouth, but no sound came out. I was treated to a view of her tongue and a single row of teeth that curved with her delicate jaw, an unbroken pattern of them. She closed her mouth, and I drew in a deep, patient breath. She didn't know what that meant, I could only assume. She didn't know how she was affecting me and I needed to keep it that way.

"I have no currency."

I considered the ship she'd crashed on. Likely there was something they'd be able to repair so she could access her financials. The Heartland was well placed to support her even if that failed. "You've been registered with the support service," I assured her. "They know of your injuries and the location of your landing. They'll help you find your purpose."

When I'd first found her, I hadn't hesitated to provide first aid.

Once I was confident she was stable, I'd followed standard protocol to report it all. They knew she was physically well and in my care.

But I hadn't *wanted* to tell anyone. And the thought of them arriving, of taking her away for scans, questionnaires, and instructional holo-vids made my belly feel tight. It didn't make sense, so I ignored it.

"What will they do?"

Despite my exhaustion, I felt for her. "Give you the basics, and support to identify your Call, or at least your Temporary Call. We don't rush the process. But they won't come for a few days, as they know I've provided you with medical care." I ought to contact them again, tell her she needed their help sooner rather than later.

She wasn't my first refugee. She wouldn't be my last. They knew that, while caring for injured beings wasn't my Calling, supporting others to access their Call was everyone's priority. She needed to heal, and she would, here. They wouldn't hurry.

It all seemed simultaneously too far away…and not far enough.

chapter three

eve

THE RETURNING ACHE CHASED ME BACK TO CONSCIOUSNESS. I LAY STILL, feeling my heart beating heavily, barely aware of the warmth of the air or the comfortable covers. He had painkillers. I needed them. He wasn't giving them to me. Where was he?

As if summoned by my thoughts, his sleek purple form passed by a window.

His steps were quick and his movements hurried when he appeared before me, kneeling low and offering me a dropper full of a bright blue liquid. "For your pain," he said.

I opened my mouth and took the drops gratefully. The taste was something like blueberries, and also like nori. I'd had worse things. I collapsed back in the bed, the pain a bone-deep ache that set my teeth on edge and rattled my brain in my skull.

"It'll take a few moments to work," he told me.

I didn't try to respond. He got up and moved around and I just drifted, waiting for his alien juice to work.

Relief came like the pull of the tide, slowly and surely. I struggled up and ate the soup-like substance he'd put beside me. Salty and a little spicy, it was filling, and by the time I'd finished it I felt much more human.

Meanwhile, he'd seated himself at a table, his legs folded together to one side, a screen of some sort in front of him. His feet were some sort of variation of flippers, arranged to look graceful as hell. His tentacle fingers wiggled through the air deftly, rearranging images and streaks that looked like a bunch of tiny barcodes among icons.

With some difficulty, I manoeuvred myself up, curious. But he glanced up as if he'd forgotten I was there, blinking at me. He wasn't wearing his glasses. "I regret my distraction," he said, with a flick of a bunch of tentacles that made it all vanish. "Is your body comfortable?"

"My body is comfortable," I told him, which wasn't too much of a lie now the painkillers had kicked in and my belly was full. "What were you doing?"

"Current type exodus pattern interpretation Aquatic Species Native To This Planet," he said, in answer. "Distraction will happen for some days, I am socially sad, reminder it is central to the unending achievement of existence."

I tried to sift through that, but all I got was that he had a problem. "What's happening?" I asked, thinking about global warming and plastic pollution and the state of our oceans on Earth. I hadn't seen any litter here, but I wouldn't necessarily see it at home, either.

It surprised me to feel a twist of regret at this strangely calm little patch of purple ocean being under threat. I wasn't a monster, but I was accustomed to living under the mantle of constant dread of the future.

"The state is complex," he said, hesitantly, not in a patronizing way but with a concerned glance that made me wonder how many people had ignored his interests in the past. "It is not my wish to tire you with additional information not required."

"I get tired fastest from doing nothing," I pointed out. I doubted he'd like me when I was bored. "And I'm interested, anyway." Imagine my luck to accidentally find myself freed from a doubtless predatory situation, only to crash-land in the middle of a trash-fire of a planet. That sounded like exactly my style.

He hesitated, looking up at me from his seat at the table. "I could explain it to you, but I need to travel below the surface to my laboratory."

I remembered the deep-dive and those cute-ass fish he had all over the place. And how I'd seen him staring at me in the reflection of the glass.

Trash-fire planet with hot alien was probably still an upgrade from where I'd been.

"Can I come?" I asked him, and when he just nodded I assumed the accidental double entendre hadn't worked with the universal translator. That probably was a good thing, really. I had no idea how his anatomy worked, whether he was single or if he'd eat me afterwards.

His lips were unsmiling as he turned his face toward me. I didn't stare at their shape, mostly because navigating the sandy surface on crutches was a pain in the ass. If he was impatient at how slowly I moved toward the water, he didn't indicate it. I kind of liked the slow, relaxed way he strolled alongside me, his shoulder-length black-green hair ruffling in the wind and his expression thoughtful, bordering on sexily brooding.

Maybe the soup was full of aphrodisiacs. Maybe I'm high. I didn't hate the idea.

"If you remain calm, you will find the descent simpler," he advised me, seriously, as we approached the water. "I will need to remove your mobility devices to wait above the high tide mark. It is safest if you sit."

I let him take the crutches without complaint, glad to see the back of them. My poor clothing was still ever so slightly damp from the last trip down, however many hours ago. It was lucky it wasn't cold.

I followed his advice and sat, wondering if I could get a fresh change of underwear and a new bra at some point, or if I'd need to hope they had size 18E coconuts. And if I didn't get out of these jeans, I was going to need medical treatment for thrush, as well as the killer chafing I was doubtless going to feel once I sobered up.

"Do those painkillers make you, uh, think differently?" I asked him, as he hurried back to me, his large feet steady on the sand. He basically had snowshoes, except for sand. Their splayed shape tightened as he entered the water, so he didn't even have the downside of flippers. I had anatomy envy.

"The medication should not impact your thoughts," he said, frowning. "Are you experiencing side-effects?"

Hell, if it was from the soup, I wasn't complaining. "I feel somewhat inebriated," I admitted. "Not badly. My thoughts are just more weird than usual."

He paused, looking down at me, puzzled. "I will complete an analysis of your body. It may be the food I provided was not ideal."

"It felt pretty ideal," I disagreed, grinning. "So, you were telling me about how your planet is also about to go up in flames? Do you have orcas, by any chance? I hear they do good work."

His frown deepened and he reached down. Without thinking, I held up my hands, and felt those tentacles wrap firmly around me. They caught hold of my arms, each little cup sucking lightly on my skin. Delight rippled up my spine. "We have many marine creatures who are apex predators and hunt in packs, yes, and they are important to maintaining the balance within the ecosystem." I stood on my unbroken leg, keeping my butt out of the thick, gritty sand, knowing I didn't look half as sexy as I felt. The cold water lapped around me as he pulled me a little deeper, until I was floating entirely in his arms.

I held onto him, wondering why this entire situation wasn't freaking me out more. The soup *must've* been good shit. "On my planet, orcas sink the boats of billionaires," I explained, generalising for the sake of speed. "It's kind of a joke."

He paused, treading water with me, frowning. "Why were marine mammals damaging property, and why is that good?"

It was all very far away. He was warm under my hands, his skin bumpy and comfortingly resilient. His eyes were a dark green and I felt like I was falling into them. At least if I was tripping, it wasn't a bad one. "There are no good billionaires."

His mouth moved slowly, his brow furrowed. "Why do you have money hoarders?"

I blinked. "Don't you have billionaires?"

He shook his head, lips unmoving.

I looked around, realising suddenly how far out we were. Last time I'd been in too much pain to notice much of anything. His little shack on the shore seemed an impossible distance, though I could swim, if I wasn't too off my face to stay on task. The pain wasn't a barrier. At all. "Weird world," I mused aloud.

"We come from different places," he agreed, the words polite. "We were both Called, though, because this is where we belong."

My hackles rose. I'd never liked being told what I ought to do. I'd learned to accept it occasionally as an adult, but only due to trial and error—emphasis on *error*. And I didn't believe in fate and magic and shit.

"You dislike that," he said, frowning a little. "But I am concerned for your mental state and sobriety, so we must prioritise getting you to the bioscanner. Fill your lungs to receive my gratitude."

The waves carried us through a dip and swell, but never came near my mouth. My hair was going to be *ruined* by all the salt, but I wondered if I looked like some sort of cute, fat mermaid with it fanning out in the water. I liked the idea.

I barely had time to suck in air before he was taking us under.

"You do not have air for conversation underwater," he told me, as he swam. "I advise questions be asked after we arrive. But if you look to your right you will see one Power Source As Yet Unnamed In Your Language glowing."

I kicked along with him and followed his outstretched arm. My eyes caught on the tentacles and a shiver of delight rippled through me as I remembered feeling them tugging delightfully against my skin.

He'd be the *best* hugger.

Beyond his arm, though, or whatever the fuck those limbs were called, there was a bright pink glow that made something deep inside me twist and ache, like when I listened to one of those songs that was a gut-punch, or a good, misty sunrise spent blissfully alone.

"Do not expel your air," he said, and the alarm in his tone made my attention snap back to his worried expression. The green of his hair danced around his face and his eyes turned forward. They held so much awe as he took in his future that it made my heart hurt to see. "It calls to us. The Vibration of Energy Particles In a Method Not Yet Identified In Your Language makes our bodies hunger to find our place, keeping us unsettled until we are in our role."

And here was me thinking I just had undiagnosed ADHD.

Why not both?

"The Small Fish Not Yet Identified In Your Language interact with

The Vibration of Energy Particles In a Method Not Yet Identified In Your Language every twomoon." His lips were still moving. I didn't see any gills, though? And how did that work under water, anyway? I just stared at him, drinking it all in. "There was a storm last twomoon, and we lost many Small Fish Not Yet Identified In Your Language."

That was it? That didn't sound like the worst trash-fire. I wanted to ask if there was only like fifty of them left in the wild, but my lungs were burning and I just kept on kicking as he guided me around the big rock and toward where his lab glowed in welcome.

"Population would recover in a few years if they were left," he added. "However, any small proceedings can commence a chain of events that can have catastrophic impacts."

A stitch in time saves nine. I recalled words from a hazily remembered educator at my before school care program when I was little. I couldn't remember the woman's name, but she'd smelled of lanolin, and she'd been patient. I'd wondered if I'd acquired her love of crocheting simply because she'd existed alongside me at the right time in my life. What would've happened if I'd hung out with someone who liked hedge funds?

We surfaced in the peaceful pocket of his lab and I looked around again, little details jumping out at me that I hadn't taken in last time. The soft shape of the glowing lights, the clinical but not cold tanks that had clean sand and colourful vegetation, the bits of driftwood hung up like decorations or hooks against the smooth stone walls.

I probably wouldn't be here if I'd got good at hedge funds instead of wool. He waited, watching me with worry, while I processed whether that would be a good thing.

"You don't have billionaires?" I asked, looking around. "But you do have people, right? And money?"

"We do not have wealth hoarders," he confirmed. "We work for the Heart, here." And I remembered that pink glow that made something deep inside me tighten. "And we all benefit from the bounty."

Maybe I was stoned, but it *did* make sense that billionaires would tell us anything to continue to exploit us—including that aliens would eat us. And I'd *known* the program was predatory. I'd basically signed up to move to a colony alongside a bunch of other non-billionaire folks to fuel the corporations that made Original Earth less liveable by the day.

Maybe working for this Heart wasn't so bad, when I thought about it.

I boosted myself up, wishing I knew smart questions to ask to figure out if this was a legit alien utopia or just a good trip.

"We have many people who have access to currency used to trade for goods and services." He pulled himself out of the water beside me, and my mouth went dry to see how graceful he was. That seemed unfair. How come he was so coordinated underwater *and* above it? I couldn't even manage *one* of those two. "The Heartland Refugee Support Services."

Was that the second time he'd said that? I accepted his help to stand and leant on him as I hobbled over to the examination table where I was pretty sure I'd got my first dose of whatever these drugs were.

"What does that mean for me?" I asked him, worry sparking as a myriad of situations ran through my head, each worse than the last.

"You will be provided with a building to shelter you, and food to nourish you, and aid to repair you." He laid me down and fiddled with some technical looking, glowy stuff, but I was stuck on this idea of all the free assistance. "They will provide you opportunity to find what Calls you."

I watched the gadget hover over my body, those images scrolling above it. Most of his attention seemed to be on the information it was projecting.

They were going to feed me, house me, fix me up, and find me a job that made me happy, huh?

"What's the catch?" I asked, feeling sick.

He was interacting with the information with his tentacles. "I do not know what you will be snagged on," he said, absently. "Whatever obstacles cause you delay, the Reps will assist you to overcome. It is their Calling, and they are accomplished at their roles." He was frowning at the information. "It appears a combination of four foods and Trace Mineral Not Yet Identified In Your Language has a unimportantly exciting effect on your form."

I didn't think excitement was unimportant, but what the hell. "What's the side effects, doc?"

His head cocked a little to one side. "The short-term variations seem to be restricted to influence on your meditation. Modification of decision-making capacity, coordination, or physical health in any way is a low chance. Additional opportunity is required to construe long term impacts, but no momentous warnings are attention attaching." He peered down at me. "Do these results sit beside your interpretation of your comfort?"

He stood, his hand still buried in that small, colourful projection of data as if it was his keyboard. Maybe it was. And, as if any of that had made sense, he reached over and lazily snagged glasses, settling them on his nose with a practiced flick before peering at me again.

It *did* make him look more trustworthy.

"You're a vet?" I asked, slowly. "Or...a marine biologist?"

His brow furrowed. "These terms are close to my role. Your people have a similar ecosystem to protect?"

"Probably," I said with a sigh. "But we fucked it up."

Colour rose up his throat. "I do not think the universal translator works for this phrase."

His neck was thickly corded, compared to his other wiry limbs. Why hadn't I ever noticed that? And it darkened so much when I swore.

"My planet," I explained. "My people didn't care for it." That was a fair summary, and saved me misrepresenting science I didn't really understand to someone who probably would've. He looked at me over his glasses and my legs went soft. *Hot alien nerd.* Jesus. "Is there a way we can communicate better than the translators allow?" Flirting was going to be hard with the synonyms getting all messed up all the time.

He hesitated, then turned his head and showed me the vague blue outline at his temple and raised a single tentacle. "The device has the ability to be turned off for language learning purposes. I require my attention on other tasks, my regret." And, to underscore the disappointment in his tone, his eyes lingered for just a moment on my lips.

I sighed, surprised that it was my regret, too.

chapter four

irosabsuul

She sat at the table, mincing up the food for the fingerlings, while I did my rounds. "What will the Refugee Support Services do to me?" she asked, without looking up.

That the idea of support brought her distress didn't make sense to me, but then, I hadn't paid much attention to stories of systems without the Responders, who would help people meet their basic needs and identify their Call. Maybe I should've. "As I told you, they'll look after you. They won't ask for anything except that you answer the Call, which you'll want to do, anyway."

She expelled air from her nose in a manner that spoke of amusement, but not joy. "Is this true?"

Her intelligence wasn't any lower than mine, so I knew she understood my statement and guessed this was an expression of disbelief. "Is your planet unsafe?" I asked, remembering how she'd asked about wealth accumulators multiple times.

"The answer is dependant on your comparison data," she said, but beneath the translated words I could hear unhappiness in her voice.

I didn't like that she'd come from a cruel place, but it might make it easier for her to settle here. "You can go back, if you want," I told her.

"We will provide you everything you need for the journey and return you safely."

"Why in the intercourse would I go back?" she asked, as I'd suspected she might. "My existence vacuum sealed."

If she'd been kept in a vacuum, she shouldn't have such damage to her feet. *Another turn of phrase.* I noted it. "I thought it might help you feel better if you knew that you were free."

"Your statement is consistent, but reality may not match it," she said, shaking her head aggressively. "How long will employment be required of me? What category of employment? What are the circumstances, and the time? Do you permit unions?"

My heart ached at the grim tone of her words. Her hands held tightly to the tool in her hand. "I'm sorry I don't know the customs of your culture," I said, hoping the translator would carry my meaning clearly. "I would like to comfort you, and reassure you that no harm will come and nothing will be asked of you, but I do not know how."

She went still, looking up at me. Her hair hung in dark streamers around her face and framed her neck. My mouth watered, but I wasn't so young and foolish as to glance at that soft, exposed flesh.

"That is the sweetest concept anyone has ever vocalised to me," she said. And then she gave another laugh that was without joy. "I am unsure how to formulate a response."

I nodded, going over to the net. "No response is needed." It seemed as if telling her was enough. Given her disbelief that she would be safe, it made my heart sit a little lighter that she could, at least, believe that I wanted to help.

I moved to where some net was stored, pulling it out heavily. As jobs went, it was my least favourite, but one of the most important to reduce the larger Trefinns which would compete with the Heartfins for food at their breeding ground.

"Tell me the tale of your existence," she said, stretching out her inefficient, but delightfully curved, spine.

I didn't let my eyes dip down to the pink line of her neck, forcing my gaze back to the thick green cord I was untangling. The nets hadn't been used in decades. Many lengths were still as sturdy as when they'd been painstakingly woven together. But parts of it had disintegrated with age, and a net was only as good as its weakest point.

"I was Called young," I told her, surprised to find I was happy to discuss myself. Maybe I'd been alone too long. "My sister and I trained under the Dreyth'khar researcher who tended these waters before us. She works further out, in the depths. If you're still here in a tenday, you'll meet her." I doubted she would be, but stranger things had happened. "I've been here since."

She was frowning at me. I didn't mind. The food she was preparing would keep for a long time at room temperature, and any help she gave me was gratefully received. I found one end of the net and sat down on the ground, tugging it into my lap.

"You remain alone?" she asked. "How many cycles of the sun have you lived?"

"Eight-and-thirty," I told her. "You should be wary who you ask that question of. Inferring people are too infantile can be distressing for some travellers." I glanced up, hoping she hadn't taken offence.

"Regrets," she said, her big, unusually brown eyes full of guilt. "My cycles of the sun are similar. Thirty and six. What other duties should I identify?"

I shook my head. "You will be fully trained by the Responders. If I try, I might teach you the wrong, or overly simple, information. Responding is not my Calling."

She made a noise that didn't have a direct translation but sounded like a worried noise. "What are you undertaking?"

I held up a segment of the net. "Repairing."

She accepted this in silence, but had spun around on the seat so she sat twisted at a strange angle, one foot beneath her curved behind. Her anatomy was curiously designed, superficially similar to my own, but softer, more delicate. She'd be vulnerable to temperature fluctuations and would need specialty equipment if she was to stay, moving between sea, shore and the underwater setup I called Sanctuary. I could vividly remember how her body had felt against mine, but I didn't have words to describe the way our bodies met, and how it felt both entirely strange and like the most normal sensation.

I shook myself. She'd be gone soon, and while the trip to and from the surface to the sanctuary might not be comfortable for her, it was only for a little longer.

"I have not viewed any other beings," she said, and I gladly accepted the new topic. "Does anyone else attend this location?"

"Every tenday or so I will receive supplies," I told her. "And my sister will visit when it is beneficial for us." That wouldn't happen until after the twomoon. I hoped we'd be able to bask at the tidepools and compare stories with joy and only a few worries. I could imagine it now, the cze'lekk skewers she'd bring and the flasks of fermented esterbyrry I'd been saving to share, and the slow descent of the sun over the waves.

In my mind, the-woman-known-as-Before was there too, smiling up at the sky as she lay across my lap, her strange, beautiful hands moving as she spoke with animation about her first Heartfin migration.

"What of your other family or intimate companions?" she asked me.

I shook my head, giving the heavy weight of the net a flick and continuing to feed it through my hands as I checked it carefully. "I thought I had found a lifepartner, but they were a periodpartner." I couldn't resist the desire to look up and see her expression and found her watching me closely. Energy tingled down my limbs. "They remained with me for a period of my life," I explained, hoping the translators might receive an update soon. "We enriched each other's experiences for a set time, rather than our entire lifespan."

She blinked at me again. "That is the most surprisingly benevolent method of description about a previous intimate partner."

I suspected her sceptical nature had developed, probably unconsciously, to protect her from her challenging surroundings. The thought made me ache. My eyes went to one of the injured Heartfins, only visible away from the plants in its tank because we weren't nearby. I knew what the Heartfin had suffered, in the storm-whipped seas. I didn't know what she'd suffered, and it surprised me that I wanted to.

As I worked, I considered what I'd learned of her, and whether it was worth pushing through the barrier of the universal translator to try to gather more information.

"Do you have a lifepartner?" I asked her. The thought had barely even condensed in my mind before it had slipped from my traitorous lips, and I felt heat climb up my suddenly aching neck. She'd said she had no one, but did that mean they had passed on? Was she grieving, and that was why she was so withdrawn?

"No," she said. Just one word. The tone was firm, and the statement final. Her shoulders were hunched over, like she had digestive issues, and her movements were aggressive as she finished up with the patients' food.

She must have had a period-partner who treated her poorly. The rush of anger that swept through me took me off guard but I used it to fuel my work on the net, sorting and searching faster. The rope ran through my hand, a little stiff now it was dry. A frayed part caught my attention, but it wasn't in the section I was searching. If I was doing this, I may as well do it properly.

From her place by the bench, she let out a noise of relief and stretched her spine. The movement made the damp fabric stretch tight over the soft folds of her body and I felt all the suckers on my digits contract in response. The net tangled up against me, piles of it falling awkwardly. She glanced over at the noise and, humiliated, I tried to extract myself.

The leg she'd been sitting on unfurled from beneath her like the graceful leaves of a freynza, reaching out toward the moons at night. "Are you adequate?" she asked me.

Adequate to what? I couldn't grasp all of her at once. There was so much softness that it would overflow my hold. I hadn't really *tried*, before. Not to hold her against me, to swim together, tangled up and tender. I'd held her like an injured party, yes. Not like a potential-partner. But I could adequately cradle her, I was sure of it. Our anatomy would work. I knew it would.

"Dreamdiver?" she asked, and hearing the words on her tongue made me jolt. That was my name, as she heard it. "Are you adequate?"

"I don't know what you mean," I said, and finally my suckers released and the tangled mess fell at my feet. I ruffled the fins on my legs, trying to settle. "To assist you?" She was crossing to me, an awkward hopping shuffle that made my protective instincts compete with the desire to watch her body jiggle appealingly. "You will injure your limb further if you continue to move like this. The medicine stops it from hurting, but does not knit together bone."

She let out a quick noise that sounded frustrated and reached out, steadying herself against me. The digits on her hand were both strangely firm and simultaneously limited. "I'm moderate quality," she told me, and I managed, somehow, not to object. "Are you?"

"Am I moderate quality?" She was so close I could see the strangely beautiful pinkish brown tone of her skin and the deeper brownish orange flecks in the blue in her eyes.

Translator, I reminded myself. "Is your pain manageable?" I asked her, the words struggling to free themselves from my aching throat.

A smile split her face and my suckers flexed again against nothing, helplessly. "My health is moderate quality. What occurred with the net?"

There were words in my head but I wasn't getting them out. I just reached over, trying not to fumble and hoping I wasn't visibly shaking, offering her the offending tangle.

She frowned, her brow creasing in a way that made her round cheeks sit lower against her facial structure. I wondered what that roundness would feel like beneath my suckers. I wondered what it might feel like…beneath my lips.

"You require repairing of this item?" she asked me. "Can I assist?"

I nodded, mute.

Her firm-but-limited fingers grasped the threads with more confidence than I'd expected. "Where does the weave reside?" she asked. I stood and, wordlessly, retrieved the rope that I'd brought to do the repairs. Her broken limb stretched out along the floor and her small, bony digits grasped the rope firmly. "I do this for recreational activities frequently," she said, and the words were cheerful. Then she paused and looked up at me. "Do I have permission?"

There was no chance of a word escaping through my throat. She looked unnatural, sprawled on the ground like that. But her eyes were huge and her throat bare, her hair curling softly to provide a beautiful frame for it.

Her lips rolled inward and the bottom flesh was caught between sweet little teeth. She worried at the surface as if it was irritating her. I tore my eyes away and removed myself physically, my body throbbing.

I'd seen the scans of her body. I knew exactly how we could fit together. But she was injured, and in my care.

Behind me I heard her working steadily on the net, the slip and slide of the twisted fibres slipping against the rock. I stored the food she'd prepared and busied myself until I had myself in hand. It took far longer than it should've. Long enough that I'd begun to be concerned for her energy levels. Which was hypocritical of me, considering what I'd wanted to do to her earlier.

My sanctuary in order, I found she'd made surprisingly quick progress with the net. With a clearer head, I was able to enjoy the sight of her digits deftly dancing over the twisted threads. The places she'd repaired would've been imperceptible if not for the way the colour had leeched from the old net.

"That looks wonderful," I said, pleasantly surprised.

She smiled up at me, and it felt like the first touch of the water on my feet in the morning. "As I communicated, I do this frequently for recreation. Not *this*." She flopped the net. "But similar, at home."

I shook my head, hope blooming in my chest. I struggled to contain it. "Are you willing to return tomorrow to help?"

"Without question," she agreed, and held up her hands to me. "Can you assist?"

Bracing myself, I wrapped my digits around her arms and helped lift her to her one working limb. "We'll get some dinner," I told her, my mind returning to the issue of the stew I'd prepared and its impact on her. It shouldn't be strong enough to keep her awake, but I wasn't sure. "I will ready you a different meal. It may take some time." Tiredness dragged at me, but she kept a hand on me as she hopped along awkwardly, and I was grateful for the slower pace as we crossed the sanctuary.

"I don't brain," she said.

I glanced over, but she didn't look confused, so I let it go and slipped into the water with some relief. The soft tug of the current said *it's time to rest* and my cells accepted the message.

She sat on the edge and scooted forward, her stiff limbs, the broken and the whole, dipping into the water. "My hair is going to be injured by this liquid," she said, but she didn't sound sad, so I didn't try to make sense of the words. My digits coiled around her arms, my suckers clinging to the softness of her flesh and my throat aching.

Her mouth parted as she drew in a breath. My head swam. *Stop.* I clenched my jaws as I hadn't needed to in over a decade, and guided her into the deep.

chapter five

eve

THERE WAS NO ALIEN BONER ON DISPLAY, BUT I WAS PRETTY SURE I HADN'T misread all those long looks and clinging tentacles. He didn't talk as we swam through the dark water that probably should've been terrifying. It wasn't, though. Not with him propelling us. A few fish swam past, glowing soft pinks and oranges, and I wished I could hang out and have a look. Maybe one day I'd get a diving tank or something and he could take me on a tour of his backyard...hopefully before the random aliens came to take me away.

We broke the surface of the water. Two moons hung above us, not quite ripe. Their glow was a deep orange that called to me in the same way the pink glow underwater had, making my belly tighten and my skin prickle.

I didn't believe in fate, but I'd always felt peaceful when swimming, and crocheting was a go-to soothing activity. Maybe it was a coincidence...or maybe it was science.

He tipped onto his back, holding me with just one arm as he moved us along. On the surface, his pace seemed a lot slower. Was he not rushing because I could breathe? Or did he feel it, too?

Was science calling me to this man I could barely even speak to?

Come to think of it, I'd had less meaningful conversations with plenty of losers I'd fucked.

He stood and I followed suit, seeing his hut up the beach aways, perched in the welcoming peach light like something out of a beach getaway acid trip.

I was impulsive. It had caused plenty of issues in my life. But I didn't think it would cause issues this time when I planted my foot in the sand beneath us and tugged him back to me.

He turned, his eyes zeroing in on my mouth, and heat flooded my veins. *For science,* I told myself, holding onto him with both hands so I was flush against him. I breathed deep in a way that had already become second-nature and, buoyed by the water, pressed my lips to his.

A groan of pleasure came from somewhere in the vicinity of his chest and I understood it even without the translator. The last lingering splinters of doubt removed, I felt the hungry ache start, low in my belly.

In my arms, he felt warm and oddly unyielding, his lips firm and his hold on me even more so. When I opened my mouth and swept my tongue against his lips that groan came again, making his whole body vibrate. He held me so close to him no water could get between us. Through my sodden jeans I felt one branch of his tentacle suckers latch onto my thighs, the other on my upper back, and my head spun as I thought of all the places he could use those suckers.

His mouth opened for me. His tongue, short and smooth, met mine without hesitation. I tugged it into my mouth and he groaned again. Between my fingers, his hair felt like clumps of good satin ribbon and I sucked in air deeply, desperate to figure out the next step and also entirely willing to rub myself against him until my brain would work. Would those tentacles fit under my jeans? He clutched me closer and the wet cloth was suffocating, infuriating.

He pulled back to look around and started towing us toward land, his expression settling into one of determination. Joy rippled through me. I could count the amount of actually good guys I'd seduced on one finger. Nice guys, sure—but not *good* guys.

Mentally high-fiving myself, I grinned as he scooped me up and

from the water. I could feel the drum of his heart behind
...med he'd have ribs, though his torso felt different to mine.
...ing to explore every single difference.

Eventually.

The suckers on his tentacles clung to me and I ran my hand up his
chest. His mouth popped open and he looked down at me, eyes
searching, as if shocked.

He'd reacted pretty strongly to the word *fuck*. But what kind of
beach alien was a puritan?

Worry began to creep in as we went and his expression didn't
change from that grim determination. He wasn't striding like a man
who was about to get his dick wet.

By the time he put me down gently in the giant cat-bed, I was
gearing up to be totally ready for the ground to open and swallow me
whole.

"Sorry," I said, hollowly, as he stepped back hastily.

He shook his head, the movement aggressive.

Well, he obviously *was*. "No hard feelings," I said, trying to play it
cool while in actuality I was wondering how fast I could get out of
there. "I should've asked, really. So yeah, that's on me."

His eyes closed. "Patient of mine," he said, the words thick.

The shame still curled, dark and sticky, but I forcibly reined in my
thoughts. He'd wanted me, there was no way he hadn't.

"First, do no harm," I reminded him. "Sex is definitely going to
help me feel better."

He shook his head again, turning away. I didn't know if he got the
joke or not, but apparently, I wasn't getting the D.

My mind ran over every single stupid decision I'd made and my
body throbbed despite the shame. He bustled around, presumably
preparing food, and I wondered what he'd do if I started sadly mastur-
bating. *Jesus, Eve.*

I was confident he'd wanted me, but I wasn't quite confident
enough to go there solo. So I curled up and tried to be sensible. And I
fell asleep.

chapter six

irosabsuul

I WASN'T SURPRISED WHEN THE HEARTLAND REFUGEE SERVICE representatives arrived before dawn the next day. I'd never had reason to prompt their attendance before, but I couldn't trust myself around her. What else could I do, except call for their assistance?

She'd looked…closed off. The way she had when she'd first opened her eyes, her distrust palpable, her resignation worn like battletech.

Still, she'd trusted *me* swiftly. All they needed to do was give her somewhere dry to sleep and a bit of food, and she'd realise the Reps were no more likely to hurt her than I was. We all thrived working together, and we were safest as part of a strong community.

"I can walk," she told the rep who offered to assist her out the door to the hoversled.

Last night she'd smiled up at me as *I'd* carried her. She'd wrapped herself around me like I was her rock.

"You can visit any time you wish," I told her, in case she thought she wasn't welcome. "You know how to get to the sanctuary, or summon me, and I'll come and get you."

The look she sent me was swift and unreadable. The smile that curved her mouth wasn't the same one I'd seen last night, full of joy.

"Gratitude, Dreamdiver," she told me, and the literal translation of my name made me ache strangely. "Don't tangle up my net."

My digits stuck to the underside of the bench. The Reps farewelled me. I listened to them helping her onto the hoversled, then the soft whir as it left.

I might not ever see her again. She might find her Calling and work in a rewarding, challenging field I never even knew about.

Or she might be back tomorrow. The thought nagged at me throughout the day. They'd be giving her more official medical care. She'd view the introduction holos, settle into her temporary apartment, tour the city, get to practice some of the new customs. She'd have the opportunity to contact anyone who might be concerned for her.

The thought drove me to the water and I swam deep. She'd told me there was no one, and I believed her.

She'd come back. I felt the familiar tug of the current against my fins and closed my eyes, breathing deeply and feeling the water cling to me.

Her lips had been so soft. So hungry.

The changing temperature prompted me to open my eyes, and I swam into the sanctuary, but the tasks I needed to do felt hollow and the net stared at me from where we'd left it. Her work was wonderful. She hadn't done terribly with making the food, either.

The anxious Heartfin in the tank heavy with vegetation darted out of my sight with just a flash of purple, and the incomplete net mocked me.

Surely, she'd recognize the Call.

Back to me. Back to Sanctuary.

I rubbed my neck, knowing I couldn't rush her, that she'd choose to answer or not and either way, I'd do well to continue my work.

It would've been easy to put it down to how unsettling her visit had been, or how worried I was about the incomplete preparations before the twomoon, but it was purely because I missed her that the days went slowly. I forced myself to work on the net and imagined her exploring the infohub, enjoying the Heartspring, and tasting food. I wondered if she'd find someone to take her on as an apprentice weaver, or if she'd go into tailoring, or spinning, or whether there were other professions I hadn't even considered that might allow her to answer her Calling. I wondered what she'd look like after one rotation, and six, and twenty, whether I'd recognise her still and whether she'd realise before our lifespans ebbed.

I wished I knew her so I could guess.

I wished I hadn't called the Reps.

In bed at night I fell asleep thinking about her returning right as the twomoons rose over the sea and the Heartfins swam. I imagined the way she'd smile and it would make all of her soften with joy, her hard-won wariness put aside. She'd stroke my neckslit and suck my tongue and I'd spread her out in the shallows, with the migration behind us, and match scientific with practical knowledge.

It was an excellent fantasy, and I clung to it as the days ticked down even knowing I'd probably see this migration out as I often did, finding joy by myself watching the ebb and flow of the bioresonant sensitive marine life.

I was in Sanctuary when the alert popped up on the holoalarm to the side of the cave, only a day and a half until the twomoon rise.

The image showed she was climbing out of the hoversled by my home, proper mobility aids clasped in her firm digits and wrapped around her forearms. She manoeuvred them as if they were new. I couldn't make out the detail of her expression, but she lifted one hand in a strange motion, then touched her chest in farewell to whoever had driven the hoversled.

She was back. On my beach. In my domain.

The tags I'd been checking teetered in my digits, my suckers forgetting to hold them, as the holoalarm switched off. The quiet reverberation of the sea suddenly felt agonisingly crushing without her. Tags forgotten, I turned and made my way to the water's entrance.

I'd never been a speed swimmer, better built for endurance than moving swiftly. But today…

I'd felt the Call. I hadn't known it, but I'd felt it anyway, the kick of my pulse, the agitation, the urge to *do*, the peace once the path was begun. It had been so many years since I'd felt that gnawing uncertainty I hadn't even recognised it.

The beach felt like such a long way away, but when I broke the surface of the sea she was there. She'd shed the dark, heavy clothes she'd landed in for the pale, form-fitting, robust garb preferred by soft-skinned beings. Her brown hair was piled atop her head and clasped in an unusual fashion. There was colour in her cheeks, and happiness in her eyes.

"I perceive you have a net to restoration," she said.

I slowed, though my heart kept racing toward her. She'd heard part of the Call. That was enough, for now. "I do." Some bags sat by my home and I forced myself to settle. "I'll find you somewhere for your things."

She glanced back where I indicated. "Oh, that's to haul down to the science room with us. It's for the nets. Some is entire, if you want to start hanging it where you've gaps."

My mouth went dry. I'd been set to have it more or less complete by the twomoon rise, but it wouldn't have been done as effectively as I would've liked.

"I cannot swim well as yet," she said, and waved a hand at where a standardised dark purple wrap encased her leg in a thin layer of what was essentially Volett. It made folks feel good, to think medicine had advanced so far. I missed the big leaves against the dramatic curve of her legs, but now I could see the ripples in her thighs, like the marks the tide left on the sand. My suckers latched onto my own thighs for lack of anything else to hold.

"Irosabsuul?" And her lips moved in perfect time with the sounds that fell from her lips.

My name—my *real* name—on her tongue made my fins flare and the water tangled around my feet like I was an overexcited fingerling. She'd learned my name. She'd disconnected the translator, and learned how to make the sounds in my language. She'd gone to all that effort *to learn my name.* "Yes?" I managed, somehow.

"I enquired if you can take me and the equipment submerged at the same period, or if I should delay."

The sun tossed its reflection back at me and the waves tugged at our feet, trying to draw us in.

She'd learned how to say my name.

"I can take you and the bags," I said, hoarsely. I could've taken the entire city, in that moment. "I'm happy you came back."

Maybe the translator did something strange to my words, or maybe she felt as lightheaded as I did, because she laughed. The sound was like the rushing of Heartfins through the great Volett underwater forests and my heart sat brightly within me.

Questions poured through my mind, and they made no sense. I knew what she'd seen and experienced. I knew she'd come back to answer the Call. What I didn't know was how she felt about it, how it had looked from behind her eyes. She collapsed the mobility aids and hooked their clasps to the standard issue belt she wore around her hips. I hurried to get the bags.

"How drives the preparation?" she asked me.

"Well." Joy shimmered in me as she continued to look at me expectantly. "Most of the injured Heartfins are ready to be released come migration," I said, because she was genuinely interested. "The weather has been perfect. I was low on tags for the new fish this twomoon, but the drop came earlier today."

"Why do we label them?" she asked, as I secured both bags over one shoulder and reached for her. "You identify where they travel, don't you? You trail their bioresonance?"

My suckers were flexing before she was even within reach and I drew a slow breath. She was here for the nets. *We.* The word leapt out at me. She slipped into my hold as if she'd never left. "I'm tagging family groups to ensure a healthy diversity. We don't trace individuals' paths. That wouldn't be efficient."

She softened, letting me take her weight and breathing air deeply into her surface-loving lungs, the picture of comfort in my hold.

eve

THE CHANCES OF THE COUNCIL WHO RAN THIS BELT OF PLANETS BEING truly benevolent had seemed pretty slim to me, but they'd looked after me. I had my own apartment, free food and medical care, basic clothing, and training in anything I could want to learn. I couldn't see the cost to anyone or anything...and I'd looked.

The weight of Irosabsuul's eyes on me made me smile. I wasn't buying the whole fate schtick, but if I was in a fish cult, at least it seemed to be based on helping people find their joy.

"How did you locate the Refugee Service?" he asked me, under the soft glow of the mosses that covered the roof of the underwater cavern.

Locate? Find. "They didn't have much sense of humour, but they were okay." The whole universal translator killed wordplay. And then sometimes raised it from the dead. I gave the rope an absent flick to unspool some more, feeding it into the net I was weaving with the new, softer, silvery rope. It was a gazillion times better than whatever trashy shit he'd had on hand. Watching all their informational projection video things had been a lot less annoying once I realised they wouldn't be upset if I wove while I watched.

It hadn't been my fault that I'd naturally just made a net-shaped creation. It was the last thing I'd worked on, after all. My brain was tired. Two weeks ago, I didn't know aliens were friendly, after all. They were lucky they didn't all get cute crocheted dicks. *Here, fishy, this is a Jacob's ladder.*

He'd been shocked by how much I'd made already. Obviously *he'd* never sat through the onboarding protocol. I'd forgotten ninety-five percent of it and the remaining information was mostly useless factoids entirely removed from any beneficial context, but by hell I'd made a badass net.

And at some point, I'd figured out where I was supposed to be, too.

While he was swimming out to secure it over the ocean trench thing, or whatever it was called on this planet, I stayed in the peace of the underwater lab, listening to the quiet sounds of the fish in the tanks and a few of the potions dripping through beakers and vials as he distilled something that probably was really important for the fish's scale strength or some shit.

I did wonder what it *really* was for.

When my ass went to sleep, I explored, and the cool retractable crutches made snooping around much more satisfying. I wished I could read the glyphs he'd stored in the little holographic notepad things, or decipher the reasoning behind the seemingly healthy fish in some of the tanks. It would come with time.

I could get used to the musical sound of falling water. I turned, following the noise, and found him boosting himself into the lab, seawater running from his beautiful lilac skin.

Whatever their bullshit "Calling" science said, he didn't make me less agitated and I didn't believe for a second their bioresonance crap had anything to do with my ADHD, but he *was* hot. And I did really like chilling out with him.

He looked at me as if relieved to find me still present, and I felt a small, answering twinge in the vicinity of my heart.

"We should return," he said. "You require a meal."

I made my way over to him. The sea behind him was dark, but something large and pale swam past. A chill went up my spine, but he looked over to me as if inviting me to admire something particularly special.

"That won't eat us?" I asked him.

His eyes crinkled but he didn't smile. "No. They won't eat us."

Cool. So, a whale-like creature, then. I paused beside him to collapse the crutches and tuck them away. One day, I wouldn't need them. Meanwhile, at least their painkillers were amazing.

"The net you made was high standard," he said, his expression earnest.

I wondered if maybe *he'd* like a crocheted little dick. Or a beanie done to look like a boob, with a nipple on top. "It was pretty good," I agreed. "Was it the right size?"

"It fit precisely," he said. "Just like you do."

I knew instantly he wasn't talking about me sitting around in his lab, and it surprised me that the sentiment made my belly twist pleasantly. He was right: I kind of *did* fit. I didn't need to talk to anyone except him, here, didn't need to do much except swim and weave and look at fish. I'd never thought it was possible, so I'd never dreamed it. Now I was here…

I couldn't imagine wanting anything else.

"Science, right?" I asked, unsure if I was amused or irritated.

He offered me one bundle of tentacles at the end of his arm, and I put my hand into the mass without hesitation. The sensation of being firmly held was comforting.

"You have currency?" he asked me. "And autonomy?"

Something low in my belly twisted. "Isn't that all standard-issue?" He'd told me it was, before.

"You are choosing to be present," he said, and I felt the suckers tugging pleasantly on my skin, like a million tiny kisses. I hadn't known I'd wanted that, especially not on my forearm. The sensation was so distracting I barely mustered up a nod for him, lowering myself to sit on the stony edge of the water. He still held my hand. Given how dark and huge the sea was beyond us, I didn't mind that.

He lowered himself with me, slipping in ahead of me as he always did. But he was too close for me to climb into the water alongside him, gazing up at me with a hungry expression that didn't require a shared language to be clearly understood.

Heat unfurled slowly in my limbs as he settled his torso between my knees, gazing up at me. "I do not know your social norms to ascertain your wishes," he said. "I would enjoy intimate contact with you."

A wash of nerves went through me, unexpectedly disorienting. Agreement was on the tip of my tongue. *You sure would, buddy.* My body hummed, and I remembered how I'd kissed him, how he'd wrapped himself in me and carried me like the most precious thing he'd ever touched.

"Same," I said, holding onto the shit-stirring for later, when I knew more of his language, or he knew more of mine, and we could spar on even footing. Because there would be a later. "How do we do this?"

His tentacles unwrapped from my hand and went to the centre of my chest. I let him lay me back across the cold stone, my broken leg floating beside him, painless and safely wrapped. The other he settled over his shoulder.

Surprise, and amusement, ran through me, lightning fast. I resisted the urge to prop up on my elbow and ask if we could kiss or something first. When I felt his cheek rub against my inner thigh and the touch of his suckers across my belly I was glad I had. The new, made-to-purpose clothing I wore was peeled off slowly. The air was cool where it was removed, his touch warm. I closed my eyes and felt him exploring the curve of my belly, the dip in my waist and the sides of my breasts. The world could've vanished, right then, and I wouldn't have known it. There must have been a million points of contact—each tentacle had dozens of suckers, and each sucker was warm and firm against my skin, the sensations all clamouring for my attention.

The silvery sound of water running from his body as he lifted himself a little higher met my ears. I felt it trickle over my leg and shuddered. Heat pooled as one set of his tentacles explored the curve of my breast. I felt them slipping beneath, wrapping around, flattening over. My breath caught as his other arm draped up my body to wrap around my throat, a tender caress. Something brushed the corner of my lip and I opened my eyes as the warmth slipped into my mouth a short distance and latched onto the end of my tongue, holding gently. Every point of contact was a siren's song in my head, a symphony that overwhelmed all thought.

Between my legs I heard him groan and a shiver ran up my spine in answer to his call. Those points of contact became more intense, like the dial had been turned up on the suckers all at once, then relaxed.

I turned my head a little, better to take what I could of a tentacle into my mouth, and was rewarded with another groan and a flex of pressure on my neck in the most delicious fashion.

On my thigh I felt his lips press, hard, into my skin. Careful to not jostle him I found his head and twisted my fingers into those ribbons of hair, cradling his skull.

As if he'd been waiting for permission he turned and latched onto my clit, and bright lights exploded in my vision. My legs jerked and he gentled, his tongue sweeping rhythmically. On my breast, his touch found my nipples and I gasped, my body arching involuntarily. Thoughts of what I wanted next were simultaneously crystal clear and utterly impossible for me to grasp as I struggled to process the myriad of sensations. His tongue swept over me and the fantasies ebbed and flowed as hunger coiled. Inside my mouth, he stroked my tongue and it was all I could do not to pant. I was held entirely exposed and felt like the most fragile, precious thing in existence.

I was climbing toward my peak when his touch slipped away from my breast. A mewl of disappointment slipped from me, my body throbbing with hunger. I tried to move, to look and see what was happening, but his arm along my body pressed me back with a gentle pressure and his licking tongue was joined by a light suction that made the muscles deep inside of me flex and shudder.

His touch moved down my thigh and I parted my legs further, the thought of feeling him inside of me bringing me to the edge. But he held my leg tightly. In his hair my hand flexed, wordlessly begging him for more.

The moan he let out stole my air. Something hot and hard nudged at my cunt a moment later and I arched again, out of sheer reflex, pressing close to that rigid promise.

I couldn't make sense of it and it didn't matter, because a moment later he was deep inside of me, aggressively lapping at my clit and thrusting into me at the same time, and all I could do was close my lips around the warm appendage in my mouth and let the sensations sweep over me. The white lights dancing in my vision joined together and the echoes of my own gasping breaths were all I could hear. My hips moved helplessly as the muscles inside of me flexed, contracted, and locked down, hungrily holding him close.

His groan was deeper and joined my own desperate breaths perfectly, the sweetest fucking song. My legs clamped around his head but his movements never once faltered, not until I'd come apart and his moan chased mine. A moment later I felt his orgasm pulse through his body, the rhythmic throbs of it making him bob in the water and dragging us a little deeper, muscles in his shoulders spasming beneath my calves.

My balance unsettled, I threw out an arm and caught myself against the lab floor where I was perched with my ass in the water and my back against the stone, then realised a moment later it was an unnecessary precaution. He'd rightened us both, boosting me further up and away from the water, his breaths as quick as mine.

I glanced down in time to see a softened, but decidedly phallic, organ slip out of me. The hand that had been on my thigh quickly tossed some water over his chin and the slit in his throat and chest as he did a quick clean-up of his softening cock. The grip he'd had on my own throat stroked the same spot on me that his slit was, tenderly, as his organ slipped away. It retreated behind the slit in his neck and chest. Now I knew what it was, I could see the faint, almost invisible silvery line tracing down his throat, and recalled noticing it when I'd first seen him.

I wonder if "sex-starved" is a thing for his people. I flopped back, confident that wouldn't be a problem for him while I was around, and definitely too happy to give a fuck about the mechanics of it. He nuzzled again at my thigh and a shiver went up my back. My clit throbbed in contentment, responding to him still.

"Is your body comfortable?" he asked me, the words low and rumbly.

Something deep inside of me squirmed in pleasure at the timbre change of his voice. I'd done that to him. "It is."

"Can I make you more comfortable?" he asked me, and there was definitely suggestion in that question.

If I was any more comfortable, I might die. "Nup."

He nuzzled again. "We should return home," he said, and sighed in regret.

I blew out a long breath. I *did* need to go home. That was why I'd organised a flying car back here, to him. "I don't think *either* of my legs work now."

He was quiet for a minute. When I caught his eye, he was looking at me thoughtfully. "In the future, I will endeavour to stop your arms from working, too."

Amusement swept through me. Apparently, we were figuring out this translator stuff. "Is that your calling? To fuck me out of my mind?"

He rested his cheek against my thigh, that mischievous twinkle in his eye. "It has eased my agitation. It must be true."

With a gentle, confident touch, he pulled me fully into his arms. I breathed deeply, then let him take us into the deep. As theories went, it was pretty solid.

about elisse hay

Elisse lives on the unceded land of the Kulin Nation in Australia. She loves hanging out with her three awesome kids, plays a variety of the nerdiest games she can find with her partner in crime, and considers a week incomplete if she hasn't eaten pesto. You'll most likely find her somewhere comfy with a coffee, a cat or dog and space to share with good humans.

She is the author of the Something Wicked series, available now.

To learn more, visit elissehay.com

resonant drives

Erin Fulmer

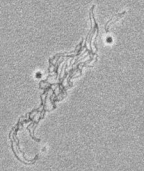

resonant drives

In the vast and lightless interstellar void, time ceased to hold real meaning for the traveler eons ago.

He does not fear death, because death cannot touch him. He does not fear age, because he is ageless. He does not fear pain, because he's already survived the worst pain he can imagine.

But he survived. He's still here. He has eternity to wait. And he fears eternity most of all.

He could wait forever, and what he waits for—craves—*requires*—might never come again.

He may never find *her*. Never feel her. Never free himself from this empty, echoing expanse, an endless shrine to everything he lost. He may never fully live again.

He's alone in the dark, the way his kind was never meant to be alone. Without a pilot, without his mate, he's lost and will stay lost.

In the deep void, he waits, still, silent, searching. He stretches his senses and his will across vast distances, to every far-off star within his reach, but finds only a hundred, a thousand, a million barren planets.

One in a million times, hope flares, quickly extinguished when he scans rock after rock seeded with simple life, single cells, nothing to sate him. Again and again, the life he finds strives only to fade away. The failures stay with him like they're his own. Maybe they are. If only he hadn't let her go, if she had stayed, they could have tended this little corner of the galaxy until it overflowed with life.

Then, against all odds, something changes. How did this small blue jewel bound to a yellow star escape his notice? How did he miss its flowering, closer than he'd ever guessed, almost in his own orbit?

No matter. Because he couldn't have missed the call that draws him now.

Find me. Take me. Claim me. Fill me.

The tether snaps into place, a sudden, tangible gravity that shivers across his iridescent shell, exposed as always to the relentless, enveloping cold of the void. It cracks him open and unfolds him, lighting up long-dormant pathways in his neural net, echoing in abandoned corridors of the vessel which contains his multitudes.

She's mortal. Unfamiliar. Human. And yet...

Come for me.

It's her. He knows her. Needs her. Has to have her.

His by fate, by right, she's the one he's been waiting for. She'll give him everything. Take him everywhere. And in return, she'll have all the pleasure he can wring from her, forever.

He has his heading, and there's no power in the universe that can stop him from claiming her.

His core ignites. He shudders. Rumbles. Roars.

I'm coming.

KAT HAYWORTH SHOULDN'T BE awake at 2 a.m. But she can't put her book down *now*. She's just getting to the good part.

Her long workdays at the lab don't leave much room for letting off steam. Not safely, at least. Experimental fusion drives aren't quite rocket science, but they *could* be, someday. Kat wants to be around to see that day.

For now, she's a first-year postdoc fellow in a large cohort, the lowest rung on a mercilessly competitive ladder. The real rocket scientists get paid for genius, not kindness. The other postdocs are no more than frenemies on a good day.

That's where smutty literature comes in clutch. When the cruelly hot antihero corners the protagonist on the page, she can trust they'll eventually have their happy ending, or at least a lot of lovingly described orgasms.

Her male colleagues might be able to find exoplanets or split the atom, but the mechanics of the clit still escape them. By contrast, the love interest in her latest book has aphrodisiac venom, a vibrating cock, an inhuman devotion to feminine pleasure, *and* is wildly, obsessively in love with his ordinary human mate.

And now he has her at his mercy, bound and begging for release.

Kat props her e-book reader against the pillow and lies back. She *will* have a crick in her neck tomorrow morning. Her free hand wanders down to tweak a nipple tenting the thin fabric of her t-shirt. Biting her lip, she turns the page and slips her fingers under the waistband of her panties. Scanning the page with frenzied eyes, mouth dry, she chases her own release.

Her fingers aren't enough. She needs more. With a low moan of frustration, she throws back the covers, book forgotten as she yanks her favorite vibrator from the drawer and plugs it in. Finally, she falls back into the bed and switches the wand on at its highest setting.

God, she needs to come so bad. She'll do anything. She imagines a shadowy form above her, pushing inside her with brutal force, calling her *mine.* Taking her, claiming her, filling her until her brain whites out and she falls apart around him.

Her back arches, poised at the edge of a sudden, shattering orgasm when all the lights go out and the vibrator stills in her hand.

"*Fuck!*" she screams, the waves of pleasure ebbing as fast as they rolled over her. "Not again. The wiring in this place, I swear to God…"

It's not the first time she's thrown a fuse. Once the entire apartment complex had gone dark and didn't come back on for hours. One neighbor, wondering aloud who'd used enough joules to blow the fuse box, had mentioned they'd heard someone using a power tool, which was…not incorrect.

Flushed, panting, she lies in the dark, her heartbeat thumping in her ears, almost lightheaded. Even cut short, her toy packs a hell of a punch. She can still almost feel its hum in the air, in her body, shaking the windows—

That's not the vibrator at all. It comes from outside, a deep rumble that seems to reach all the way to the marrow of her bones.

She tries to roll over, sit up in bed, but her body won't respond. She can't even turn her head.

Harsh light flashes over her, bright enough to bring tears to her eyes. It paralyzes her. She can't speak or scream.

The mind-numbing vibration draws closer, right outside her window now, shaking her apart, squeezing the breath from her lungs. It's loud enough to wake the dead, let alone her nosy neighbors.

But no one comes to save her, and amid the overwhelming thrum of *whatever* is outside, she realizes: she's not in bed anymore.

She's floating on air, body rigid, drenched in light that pulls her inexorably—*elsewhere.*

Abruptly, the light fades away. In Kat's last conscious moments, the darkness comes as a relief, until—

Hello, sweetling.

Held helpless in the dark, she shudders. The voice caresses her, velvety and deep as night unending.

Now you belong to me.

* * *

TAKING HER IS EASY.

Her desire flares across the empty reaches, a beacon drawing him into her orbit. This small blue world and its riotous gravity of life isn't all *her*, of course, but his mind balks at the concept.

He exists as a collective, a network of individual neural nodes and bodies with separate functions, but all *his*, all *himself*. He *is* the vessel floating in the void, and its protective shell, and all it contains within. Each experiences its life as linked inextricably with the whole, forming an integral part of a singular entity.

His scans tell him that she is one among billions, like and unlike her, each life autonomous, without the cohesion perfected by his kind. Not just millions of individuals but millions of *species*, an overwhelming variety, a wild proliferation of biomass. He can hardly picture such a wealth of difference.

It's everything that he has waited and watched for, this world. But it requires a brand new frame of reference.

How lonely it must be, how strange, how small and separate she must feel, even among billions. That profound difference intoxicates him. It holds an irresistible, terrifying promise. In her truest essence, she's unknowable, and at the same time, she must be unknowing too: *incapable* both of fully knowing him or being known by him.

An encounter with such a unique entity could create something entirely new, unpredictable, unstable, *dangerous*…and powerful.

Similar alchemy once created this world in its dizzying variety. It's not entirely unfamiliar to him, and what he does know of it revives something new and old within him: a restless dissonance, a *loss* of wholeness.

He knew what that was like, once. So long ago, now, that he's forgotten how it works—worked—must work again, if he's to live as he once did. Worse, he's forgotten why it *didn't* work, in the end, why it left him echoing and hollow.

Did he try to forget, or did he lose that knowledge, one small part of everything that ending took from him?

The question grips him at his core. It spills from the empty places inside him as he drops into synchronous orbit with her position on the landmass. He *aches* with it, as if the line between him above and her below has pinned him at the balance point.

Already parts of him reach out to her, long arms unfolding from where he hangs suspended at her zenith. Now, hidden in her world's shadow, he hesitates.

In that pause, the space of one of her short breaths, her pleasure hits its peak. Even at this distance, it electrifies him. A slender thread of exotic energy—*her* energy—sparks from the ground upwards, racing along his length toward his center.

With that brief pulse of her essence against his, he's well and truly lost. All sense of caution, all sense of himself *as* himself, fails in an instant. Only for an instant—but it's enough.

He won't have another chance, not like this, locked onto her and shrouded on the dark side of her world, in a night that's all too short. If he lets go, velocity will slingshot him out of orbit, faster than her gravity can hold him still.

It's now or never. He reaches for her, curling fingers of force and shadow around her. She trembles, going rigid at his touch.

She fears him. The realization shakes him. Her terror flows out like a black wave. Her call fades into silence.

No. No, no, no. Panic flaring, he folds her closer, his body shielding her from gravity, acceleration, heat as he places her in emergency stasis. It's too cold for her in his hold, even at his core.

Now that he *has* her, the singular hunger that drew him temporarily sated, he can spare attention for logistics, long-term plans. A thousand processes launch at once. His sensors back online and working overtime, he samples her home environment, running comparisons.

Even the atmosphere in his hold is wrong. She needs oxygen most, but tempered with nitrogen, argon, trace amounts of carbon dioxide, neon, helium, and methane, with enough water vapor to keep her body supple and skin hydrated, all at a very specific mercurial pressure.

Void take him for a fool, she'll need so many things. Air, warmth, water, sustenance. Human biosignatures mark them as omnivores, but what *this* human prefers will be individual, unique, unknown. Her den yields few clues, but he gleans enough to make a start.

What brought her to the peak of ecstasy that called to him across the light-years? From her small surface den, he collects a handheld data pad and a stimulator tool of some sort, a starting point for study and iteration. But to master her species' expectations for mating rituals, he must satisfy her in *every* way, not merely fulfill physical necessities.

He must delight her mind and tantalize her senses. He needs her to *feel* for him. His nanoprobes range more widely, gathering samples from local food sources, tapping into a million data streams to gather cultural context, physiological diagrams, electronic libraries, human attempts to parse the mystery of their own sexual diversity.

He keeps her in stasis while he prepares to host her. He must get this right. That brief burst of energy she gave him, all unknowing, told him everything he hoped and feared was true.

She's perfect. She's everything he craved in those long epochs of waiting, his end and his beginning.

His fate. His fuel. His freedom.

With the power she holds, she can save him…or destroy his last chance to fulfill his purpose. But no matter how his gambit ends, he knows one thing.

He's not alone anymore. It's more than he thought possible. And for a moment, with her wrapped safe and sound within his hold, it's enough to drive him forward.

* ..... ,,,, °

HE STALKS CLOSER *with a smirk playing across his beautiful face. His eyes glow red as a predator's, one native to the shadows gathered close around her. They hold her rooted in place, helpless before his slow advance.*

"How you tremble for me, little one." His voice rumbles low and deep, poised between a purr and a growl. It seems to stroke her very skin, raising chills along her spine. "How your heart races. You can't hide that from me. Not your fear, and not how much you want this."

"I don't," she whispers. Lying. Every word, every step toward her stokes the ache in her core, even as she shrinks from him. Heat throbs between her legs as tendrils of shadow tighten at her calves, her wrists, and gently, inexorably, around her throat.

"Your body betrays you." He really growls this time, eyes flashing. His shadows twine around her thighs, an inexorable caress that spreads her open. They pull her down to her knees, and she tips her head back, rewarded by the faint curve of his mouth.

The proximity overwhelms her. She could beg him to stop, to leave her alone, and yet. She cannot bear it. "Please…"

He nudges himself against her lips—silky, hot, hard as steel. When she flicks her tongue over his tip, eagerly tasting the precum glistening there, his groan shakes them both. Gripping the back of her head, hands fisted in her hair, he pushes in deeper, fucking her mouth with abandon.

His shadows are more solid now. They slither between her legs, strum-

ming her clit. She cries out around his cock as one thick, heavy tendril pushes into her pussy, while a second presses warm and insistent below it, gently working her open.

Then they pull back, and she moans with a sense of utter loss. She was lost the second she dreamed of belonging to him.

"Please," she whimpers, lips numb, jaw aching. "I want you everywhere. I want—"

Before she can finish, he's there. Everywhere. Deep in her pussy, spearing her ass, invading her airway, growling in her ear.

"You...are...already...MINE."

And she comes apart, lost in a sharp and shattering pleasure, a surrender so complete she could fall into it forever.

Kat wakes with a start, her own wordless cry still echoing in her ears.

The dream dissolves, already no more than shreds and flashes of half-remembered depravity, but heat still pulses through her body, and her panties cling damply to her skin. She reaches down to relieve the heavy desire suffusing her limbs—

She can't move. Her limbs are bound by something supple, strong, and oddly, warm. She's lying on her back, the surface below her soft but not yielding. It too carries a strange current of warmth, like she's held and supported by something living.

It takes a moment of trying to open her eyes before she realizes they already are, wide and staring into darkness so complete, she wonders if she's gone blind.

"Where on earth am I?" The words rasp from a dry mouth and aching throat. A flash of her dream returns—something thick and hard stretching her lips wide and pushing deep into her esophagus.

Was it only a thirsty dream?

She licks cracked lips. Thirsty indeed. "Hello?"

Her voice cracks. That's embarrassing, assuming there is anyone here to listen. But someone must have brought her here, bound her here, left her in this lightless place.

The air here smells fresh, faintly sweet, almost heady. It's not cold— it's almost perfectly matched to her body temperature—but there's no draft or movement across her exposed skin. None of that is much comfort, though.

The last hazy dregs of arousal drain away. Fear builds in its wake. Her heart hammers in her ears. She's in the dark, bound hand and foot, with no idea where she is.

Before her dream of dark and endless pleasure, before the voice that thrilled and threatened her, she'd been at home, alone, with a filthy book and her favorite toy. The lights had all gone out, and then—

She doesn't believe in out-of-body experiences. The bright spotlight falling over her, how she floated up into it, limbs frozen and mind awake, the hum in the air—it's all too much like something from that old show her mom has obsessed over for twenty years. *The X-Files*, or whatever.

That's silly. Of course she hasn't been *abducted by aliens*.

Maybe that was all part of the dream. Maybe whoever kidnapped her drugged her first. That makes more sense. She would have screamed her head off and fought back, otherwise. But she couldn't kick anyone in the balls if they shot her full of sedatives and hallucinogens.

More likely, it has to do with the fusion lab. They don't have a working reactor yet, but they might someday, if Kat's wildest theories on quantum energy fields prove correct. If she can get her dissertation through the committee. If she can get her faculty mentor on board. She'd pitched the most hinged part of it at office hours the other day, while he stared at her as if she were speaking another language.

Focus, Kaitlyn. Now's not the time to engage in postgraduate angst. Her universal resonance theorem can wait until she gets out of this fix. Whatever it is.

Who knows? Maybe her unknown kidnappers will accept her untested equations in exchange for getting back to her boring little lab rat life. It's probably the best chance for her ideas to see the light of day, if she's honest with herself.

She opens her mouth, then pauses at a soft sound in the dark, a furtive footstep. The faintest breeze brushes her skin. Her heart thumps unevenly.

"Who's there?" she calls, as loudly as her wrecked vocal cords will allow.

"You're awake. Good." The voice that answers her is deep, velvet, resonant, and impossibly familiar. It makes her belly flip, but a chill creeps upward from the base of her spine and settles at the back of her neck.

"Do I know you?"

"Not yet. All in good time, my dear." A pause, as if thinking better of this. "I've waited for you for so long, you see. You must forgive my familiarity."

"The hell I do," she spits, struggling against the bonds to no avail. "What is this place? Who are you? *What do you want from me?* Show yourself!"

"Of course, you have a lot of questions." A faint light flares in the darkness—no, *two* lights. Twin stars, glinting red, trained on her with a predator's intensity. "We should talk, before—"

Kat *shrieks.* "I'm not going to talk to you until you *let me go,* you FREAK!"

The two red lights in the distance switch off abruptly, leaving her in total darkness once more. When she lifts her head, something tugs at her hair and scalp—multiple points of contact with a sticky, tacky sensation that makes her shudder. *Blood? Or worse?*

"Please." The voice sounds taken aback.

"What the fuck did you *do* to me?"

"You must lie still. You'll injure yourself."

With that, real light creeps back in around the edges of her vision, a warm yellow glow that comes up slowly as if on a dimmer switch. Kat squints, eyes watering.

The light sources blooming in midair look for all the world like *chandeliers.* They hang from an unseen ceiling, but the space beyond the small circle of light remains lost in deep shadow. She's lying on a table—an exam bed, maybe. The black, flexible restraints on her wrists and legs look like thick PVC tubing or rubber cords, but they reflect the soft lamplight with a faint oily sheen that seems to shift and flow when she doesn't look at it directly.

There's no sign of whoever had spoken. Maybe she scared him

away. That deep voice was certainly a *him,* whatever else he might prove to be.

She blinks until her eyes adjust, hauling herself up on her elbows as far as the bonds will allow. Whatever had tugged at her scalp releases its hold abruptly, though the sticky sensation still makes her scalp crawl.

A thicker tube hangs from a hook at the side of the table near her head. It looks like the same material as the restraints, with what looks like an oddly shaped oxygen mask at the end. Its small attachments remind her of earbuds in their size and shape. It doesn't look like any medical device she's familiar with, but between her sore throat and the location of the tube, she can make an educated guess about its purpose.

Hell. They intubated me. She checks herself over as best as she can, but despite the unseen person's warning, she doesn't have any visible injuries. Rather than a hospital gown, she has on the same clothes she wore in her last waking memory, soft sleeping shorts and an old T-shirt several sizes too large. Her feet are bare.

It still doesn't make sense, yet in the absence of any immediate danger, her heart rate slows. The air smells subtly different now: sweeter, softer, almost…*comforting.*

"That's better," the voice says unexpectedly, from somewhere behind her head. She doesn't even jump. Her heart keeps up its steady rhythm as she breathes in the strange, sweet air. It reminds her of cookies baking, of cinnamon and vanilla, laundry fresh from the dryer, the warmth of home.

Soft footsteps draw closer, still out of view, but she's not afraid. She's not angry anymore. She's not numb. She simply *is,* while whoever or whatever captured her draws closer on stealthy feet.

"Don't come any closer." She hears herself speak with impossible calm. "I know what you're doing. Drugging me won't get you what you want."

His voice is soft and low, now, unthreatening. "I only want to keep you safe. Your biometrics spiked far past their recommended range."

He must be monitoring her vitals somehow. Maybe the restraints have more function than simply holding her still. "Yeah, waking up in a strange place bound hand and foot tends to do that to a girl. You *could* just release me."

"If I did so while your body was primed to flee, you might fall from the table in your haste to escape, or trip over something when you run into the dark. There are many ways you could come to harm before I could intervene. You'd likely fight me if I tried."

"If you think I won't fight back when I'm stone-cold calm, you have another think coming."

"It seems likely," he admits with surprising readiness. "If you must fight me, however, I would prefer you do so with a clear head. But I can give you back your fear, if you wish."

"I can't help but notice you still haven't released me. Or shown your face."

A pause lengthens. Has he just...left her there? *Alone in the dark or alone with my captor...which is worse?* With the "clear head" he's granted her, she decides *both* are objectively terrible options.

Then he says, in an oddly tentative tone, "Would you like to see me, Kaitlyn?"

"I'd like you to stop lurking behind me, yes."

He knows my name. Under the artificial calm, her panic beats against the bars of its chemical cage, desperate to kick off another round of adrenaline.

The worst part is that he's *right*: all other factors remaining equal, she would rather face whatever this is, whoever he turns out to be, with dispassionate logic instead of raw instinct. If he bottled whatever he's pumping into the air, he could make a killing marketing it to the military industrial complex. Her petty pack of infighting colleagues could use some cooler heads too.

A shadow falls over her, a quiet footfall her only warning as he circles into her field of view.

Even though her pulse holds rock-steady, she draws in a long breath. Words unexpectedly elude her, because the man standing before her is *beautiful*. Objectively. Aesthetically. Undeniably a physical specimen of a quality only reached by professional athletes or leading men with a team of nutritionists and trainers at their beck and call. Or the subjects of romance novel covers, but that was just a fantasy. This man is flesh and blood, standing close enough to touch if her hands were free.

He's bare-chested, slender, abs taut and defined, his pants well-fitted enough to leave little to the imagination. Calm or not, heat rises in her cheeks and belly.

When she belatedly catches herself staring at the outline of the bulge between his legs, she tears her gaze up to his face with its strong jaw, high cheekbones, and full lips. Shadowed by a dark wave of hair falling over his forehead, his intense, hooded eyes meet hers. They're a striking color, a deep hazel that almost looks red-gold in this light.

"Well?" he says in that rich, low voice of his. "You've seen me, now."

"Uh. Wow. Hi." *Smart. I went to MIT, but I can't talk to a hot guy like a normal person. Classic Kat.*

"Hello." A trace of a smile flits over his gorgeous features. "If I loosen your restraints, will you run from me now?"

"I'm not making any promises. Would you chase me if I did?" The words slip out before she can stop them, and her stomach flips again. For a moment she pictures this gorgeous man pursuing her, catching her, tackling her to the ground—

What is wrong with me? He kidnapped me! Whatever chemical cocktail she's breathing in doesn't seem to have dialed down her libido.

He cocks his head, a long, assessing look. "Do you want me to?"

"*No.*" Her denial rings out too loud, too fast. "That's not what I said. Don't put words in my mouth."

"I was only asking," he says mildly. "I would prefer it if you don't run. Personally."

"Are you going to let me go, or what?"

She's hardly finished saying it when the bindings on her ankles loosen and slip away, brushing over her skin with a silky, light touch that brings goosebumps up on her bare arms. She bends her knees, feet flat on the table, sighing with relief.

Her stiff joints and shaky muscles protest the movement. *How long did I lie here, unconscious, at his mercy?* The restraints on her wrists uncoil as she pushes herself to a seated position.

What *are* those restraints made of? They move with a sinuous grace that makes them look organic, *alive* for a split second before they go limp, hanging from the table's edges like so much rubber tubing. They were *warm*…She shivers again, rubbing the goosebumps from her arms.

"Are you cold? I can make this space warmer if you like. Or perhaps—" A moment later, he's at her side, tucking a plush covering around her shoulders. "That's better. You were not, hm, *wearing* much when we—when I found you."

She pulls the exquisitely soft blanket over her bare arms and legs, feeling exposed but unable to find her way back to fear. At least she has her t-shirt on. It's some small comfort. Besides, his balls are *right there*. She could easily reach out and—

Taking refuge in the strange, unrelenting calm, she swings her legs over the edge of the table, deliberately putting her back to him. Her feet dangle a few inches off the floor as she takes stock of her surroundings again now that she has a wider field of view.

Nothing here looks unfamiliar, exactly. The shapes seem right, but she can't identify any of the materials. The floor, which has the same subtle iridescence as the equipment. It's not metal, wood, or stone, but a dark, almost springy texture with a rippling quality, as if some current moves beneath its surface. The intricate molding of the chandelier-like lamps branches into lighted tips with a subtle, organic asymmetry. They sway gently, glowing hypnotically, in an otherwise undetectable breeze.

"I think you better tell me what is going on," she says, with dream-like serenity.

Her captor—or rescuer—clears his throat. "You're not running, it seems."

"Not yet," she agrees. "So don't give me a reason. Tell me where we are and how you found me. Tell me *why*."

"These are not easy questions to answer." His tone sounds almost apologetic, but he says nothing further.

Wearing the furry blanket like a cape, she lets her bare soles meet the smooth, unidentifiable surface of the floor. It has the slightest bit of springy give and exudes a gentle warmth.

"I don't care how hard it is for you." Her legs hold her, and her knees prove only a little watery as she turns to face him across the table. "You're the one who's left me in the dark so far. *Try.*"

"And if you don't like the answers?" His throat jumps. Is he *nervous*? Does the air not grant him the same calm it does her?

She folds her arms, brows raised, waiting. "I promise you I won't like them less than *not* knowing them."

"Very well," he says, and sighs. "This is not—but no matter. You asked where we are, and what I've done to you. The simplest explanation is that you...*We* are very far away from home. We had limited resources and very little time, so I admit we took some—liberties."

"*Liberties* is one way of putting it." She really should be panicking. Her continued fearlessness doesn't feel like a gift anymore. Suddenly, she misses the ability to understand in her body, as well as her mind, why all of this should alarm her. No way she'll fess up to that now, though. "That doesn't tell me much of anything, except that you're admitting to kidnapping me. And who's 'we'?"

"I didn't kidnap you." His brow knits, and he casts a glance toward the invisible, cavernous ceiling, as if seeking help from some unseen observer. "Not exactly. I'm here to help you. Care for you. All you must do is ask, and I can provide it. *Anything.*"

Even without fear, a cold determination straightens her spine, slips into her voice. "I'm asking you for answers—real ones. Starting with where on Earth, *specifically*, you or whoever you're working for has taken me."

She's circling toward him now. He steps hastily the other way, keeping the table between them. "I can't."

"You don't know either. Is that it?"

He *laughs*, a little huff out of his perfect, Grecian nose. "No. Your request can't be granted. Not the way you asked it."

"I don't see why that's funny. Stop playing games with me."

"I promise you, I'm not." The spark of amusement drains away as he faces her, eyes wide and pleading. "I believe the most culturally appropriate phrase is...Hm. *We're not in Kansas anymore.*"

"I live in *California*," she says. "But fine, I'll play along. Just how far away from *Kansas* are we?"

"Approximately five thousand of your astronomical units." He stands at the edge of the circle of light now, their combined path tracing an elliptical orbit from its center.

Blank, she stares at him. "I'm sorry." Nothing about this makes sense. *I liked the last dream better.* "I thought you said…"

He inclines his head, his gaze oddly melancholy. "Would you prefer I provide the conversion in a different unit of distance? It is a very great number of miles, but I could—"

If her memory served, that would mean somewhere on the inner edge of the Oort Cloud. Past the current reach of any Earth missions, even past the Voyager probes with their half-century head start. Farther than any woman has ever gone before.

"I know what astronomical units are," she says, numb-lipped and frozen. *No kidding. The temperature at that distance would be 50 Kelvin. Negative 360 Fahrenheit. This* must *be a dream.*

"Then you did hear me."

"That means we're in space. *Interstellar* space."

"True, in a sense, though you could not survive in space."

She glances around her, disbelieving, recontextualizing, rejecting the conclusions that follow. *Impossible.* Objectively. "So, this place is—"

"I believe you would call it a starship."

Play along. Maybe he's a spy. Some foreign power wants our rocket science, and this is all a ruse to get the intel. That sounds more believable than a fucking *starship.* "What do *you* call it?"

"I call it home," he says softly. "And I hope that someday, so will you."

● ﹨﹨﹨﹨   ⁄⁄⁄⁄ ●

FROM ALL THE data he collected while she lay in stasis, he expected fear would feed her passion, but instead she gets *angry.* She awakens strong, spirited, full of unexpected defiance, forcing him to recalibrate swiftly.

He assigns an aspect more compatible with her chemistry, with promising results. Her pheromone levels tick up. She stops yelling at him and waits to find out more.

But as the small truths she asked for take hold, she staggers where she stands. A flush painted her cheeks when she looked at the form he chose, but the color drains away now, leaving her skin pale. Even her lips lose their color.

She sinks like he's cut her legs out from under her. On her knees, head bowed, she braces herself against his surface with hands icy as the void outside. He registers a precipitous drop in her electrodermal activity.

The human-bodied individual rushes to her side. Specialized in both form and function, this one performs a particular role in service to the colony's reproductive imperative: a gonozooid, defined by his adaptive ability to protect his mate, comfort her, provide for her, and please her. Meanwhile, the collective's core neural network races through the human medical databases acquired in orbit around her world.

Her home, the one by her side murmurs. *We took her from her home.*

Lowered skin conductivity can indicate an onset of negative mood states, reduced capacity for pleasure, even loss of personality coherence. The data doesn't offer any certainty—*how do humans live with such imprecise understanding of their own biology?* —but it doesn't allay their collective concern, either.

His chosen mate cannot fear him in this moment, but she can still experience *despair.*

You told her too much, too fast.

She asked. The individual gonozooid's response has a strangely frantic edge of emotion, as though human feeling somehow follows human form. *She left me no room to prevaricate. It would have made her angrier.*

The warning throws the colony into an unfamiliar state of conflict. Yet every part of him knows that this moment, this meeting, is essential. It must go well, or they—*he* will lose his last chance to fulfill his mission.

He could offer her euphoria, but she already accused him of drugging her. He's studied the language enough to understand the connotations, and he will not steal her autonomy.

All his focus turns to her chambers, to the two individuals at the edge of the small circle of light. The gonozooid kneels before her, reaching out with tentative tentillae—*fingers*—to move aside the matted tangle of keratinous filaments—*her hair*—that's fallen across her face. He needs to see her.

She looks up with dull eyes, uncomprehending, but she doesn't shy away. She lets him brush her hair back with a gentle hand.

We've already broken her.

I'm not so sure. The one at her side offers a surprisingly vehement counter. *She's already proven more resilient than expected.*

"You're an alien," she whispers.

He sits back, considering this. "I suppose I am, to you."

"This isn't a dream. Or a lie. Or a trick."

"No, Kaitlyn," he says softly. "You asked me for the truth."

"I..." She clears her throat, wiping a wrist across her face. "I don't even know your name."

He hardly knows how to answer her. *I am many. I am one. I am eternal. An exile. Alone and yet legion.* But he was not always alone. When he had a pilot, a mate, a companion, she had called him by many different names. *Dear. Darling. Love. My everything.* But there were others, too, the ones that came later. *Parasite. Wretch. Bore. Destroyer. Brute. Life-ruiner. Tyrant.*

Monster.

If this is what we've become, his love said, leaving him, *if you refuse to change your ways, you will always be alone.*

I never had a choice, he'd cried out, but she was too far gone by then to hear him. *This is what I am. I can't be anything else.*

"You must have a name," Kaitlyn says now, his tearstained mate, his only hope, his fate, his likely doom. "Even aliens need names."

Of course, humans love names. They require them, a precursor to any intimacy. He should have thought of that.

He casts his seeking mind through databases, encyclopedias, still tasting her salt-sweet tang in the back of his avatar's throat like a promise. Finds something that seems fitting, or close enough.

"You may call me Cassiel," he says, choosing a name from a human mythos that resonates, a watchful entity of solitude and grief. *Archangel.* A curious sort of creature, one he can find no biological reference for, other than beings of their wide salt seas: angel fish, angel shark, sea angels, anglerfish…It seems oddly appropriate. Their oceans contain creatures not entirely unlike him. Besides, she wouldn't find *polymorphic colony* as comforting.

"Cassiel." She draws the sounds out on her tongue, hard and sibilant becoming almost musical at the end. Something shifts inside him, settles into place. Her head comes up, her eyes glazed and shining. "You haven't told me *why*. If you are…what you say you are—why abduct me?"

"We—*I* needed you. If I could have done it differently—but I had no choice."

"You needed me. For what? Am I…a research subject, or a hostage?" Fluid leaks from her glittering eyes, dampening the epidermal membrane beneath her. "Or am I *prey*?"

The vessel's membrane drinks up the droplet of her immediately. It's a small gift and he's hungry for whatever she offers him, anything to help him know her better, map a way forward.

For such a tiny sample, the lachrymal secretion offers a complex, distracting wealth of new information: saline, enzymes, limbic hormones, trace minerals, electrolytes, opioid peptides…*Tears*. The rich flavor races through his distributed awareness with intoxicating intensity, near-erotic in its force. For a moment he loses himself in it, chasing a dream or half-forgotten genetic memory of his species' ancient prehistory, before they left the oceans of their Mother World and evolved to live among the stars.

She tastes like a home he's never known, and he wants more of her. He wants to sample all of her, in every mood.

"No! Not like that." His avatar stammers, off-balance in the tide of his desire. She *isn't* prey, but there are more pleasurable ways to taste her, for them both. "I have no wish to harm you. Quite the opposite."

"I don't understand."

How can she? It would break her even more.

"Please don't cry," he says, still kneeling before her. "Are you hungry? Thirsty? You must remain hydrated, and this—" He waves a hand at her face, glistening from the moisture running from her eyes and now her nose. "It can't be helping."

"Yes," she hiccups. "No! Please just—leave me *alone*." With that, her strength resurfaces. Relieved, he stands and backs away.

"I'll leave you now," he says, and walks away, faster than is strictly necessary. She makes no move to follow him.

He will always remember the taste of her tears, no matter what happens afterward.

● ⟍⟍⟍⟍   ⟋⟋⟋⟋ ●

SHE CRIES herself out on that strange warm floor, wrapped in the blanket he gave her. When she finally pulls herself together—scoured, empty, and as he predicted, terribly thirsty—more lights have appeared.

The hanging candelabras come up in a line, like an invitation, still *not quite right*, organic, *alien*. They lead to a perfect, ordinary, normal wooden door.

Distrustful, she lays a palm flat against it, then snatches her hand back with a sharp, in-drawn breath as it swings open under her touch. Beyond it waits a lushly furnished suite with a wide canopy bed, an oversized chair, and a standing wardrobe. The blue-black walls curve gently, concave between floor and ceiling, shimmering in the soft light with a faint iridescence.

"You had all this right here," she mutters, "and you still woke me up on a lab table like some half-baked alien autopsy video? Here I thought E.T. would be *smart*."

Shrugging off the inexplicable impression of unseen attention keenly focused on her, she steps cautiously inside. A crystal carafe waits on a bedside table, with a delicate, subtly asymmetrical glass beside it filled to the brim of blessedly cold water. She gulps down a glassful, then pours another from the jug, starting to feel a little more… human. Further exploration reveals another door, and behind it recognizable bathroom facilities with a huge, sunken tub set in the center of its floor, already full and steaming.

"Ok," she mutters. "I could get used to this."

She still doesn't want to think about whatever unidentified gunk is drying stiff and tacky on her scalp. Now she can wash it off and hope-fully never think of it again.

When she's finally clean and pleasurably boneless, she emerges from the tub and wraps herself in a huge, plush towel, then stops short. She heard no one come in, noticed no movement, yet her discarded clothes somehow vanished from the floor.

"What the hell?"

The door opens before she can shove at it. She almost stumbles into the larger room, dripping water onto the floor, ready to scream at whatever beautiful, unearthly man or monster waits for her. But no one's there, just that same watchful feeling—and an envelope lying on the bedside table.

She snatches it up. The paper has a unique aesthetic, thin, flexible, but crackling with a finely ribbed texture, and single sheet inside bears a message in flowing script.

My dear Kaitlyn,

You've come a very long way in a very short time. I fear I've proven myself a poor host who has failed to adequately consider the needs of your mind or body.

If you allow me, I'll endeavor to remedy these failures to your satisfaction. Please join me for a meal when you're ready.

Cassiel.

A quiet creak startles her as the wardrobe door swings open. It doesn't look big enough to contain everything inside: silky, slinky gowns, billowing princess skirts, shimmery cocktail dresses, a confec-tion of black lace and chenille with a bodice to match.

Running her hand over the soft fabric, she lands on a flowy, leaf-green satin jumpsuit with long sleeves and a plunged neckline. She's not about to pick something she can't run in. Nothing here resembles a bra or panties, so she goes without. The sensation of the satin between her thighs, sliding across her bare nipples, sends a shiver up her spine.

She's trillions of miles from home, in a starship of unknown origin, captive of a man with unknown intent, and yet every new detail she encounters seem to offer a frisson of pleasure, as though charged with latent eroticism. If she ruins this satin romper because he didn't leave her any underwear and his mothership is unreasonably sexy, that's *his* fault, not hers.

For all the room's luxury, it lacks a mirror. She settles for finger-combing her hair as it dries, twisting the bulk of it into a knot at her neck. Strands fall around her face in messy tendrils, but it will have to do.

Outside, the lights now curve around and somehow *up*, an unwinding spiral inviting her to an unseen higher level. When she looks down, only thick shadows lie beneath. She doesn't look down again.

Where the slope levels out, a bone-pale, intricately carved archway rises high above her head, laced with unintelligible patterns. Beyond it, more shadows await. The sense of unseen watchfulness redoubles. Meanwhile, the lights that led her safely to this threshold wink out, all but the last one.

No going back now. She holds her head high and steps through the archway.

"Hello? Is anyone there?"

A breeze from nowhere swirls around her, stirring the loose hair around her face and setting off a flurry of echoes. They build into a storm of far-off whispers, almost musical, then dissonant, like wind in pine boughs or the ghost of an orchestra tuning. The air carries a rich, sweet scent with it, and her mouth waters despite itself.

"Cassiel?"

"I'm here." He must be closer than she would have guessed, yet that mysterious calm settles over her again. A flood of golden light illuminates him all at once, standing above her on a dais. Behind him waits a long table, laden with a feast.

He, too, dressed for this occasion, in a sweeping, dark red coat embroidered with curls of silver, slim black trousers, a scalloped frill of white shirt escaping from his lapels. For a split second, she catches an odd expression on his handsome face, gone before she can interpret it. His lips curve when his gaze meets hers, like her stunned reaction pleases him.

He's a stranger. An alien kidnapper. A dangerous unknown.

He's *magnificent*, and she's in so much trouble.

HER SHARP GASP cuts through him—has he miscalculated, frightened her further? Then his higher processing kicks in. Data gleaned during his brief orbit of her world and the pheromone spike in her salt-sweet biochemistry provide context for her parted lips, her wide, startled eyes, the slide of her long, graceful throat.

She's hungry in more ways than one, drinking the sight of him like he's a wellspring on a dust-dry moon.

He didn't expect her to choose the garment she did. It suits her, a splash of green in his empty halls. It belongs to the world he stole her from, the color of photosynthesis, life that builds kingdoms out of air and light.

"This is…" she says. "You're…"

He waits for additional morphemes that will make sense of her speech. With none apparently forthcoming, he chooses an appropriate response at random. "I wasn't certain you would come."

This seems to jolt her out of her daze. Her posture closes, brow creasing and mouth pressed into a thin line. "Did I really have a choice?"

"Of course. I would have sent sustenance to your chamber, had you asked it of me."

"Right," she says. "Like a prisoner."

"Like a guest," he corrects her, as the hope her initial response sparked in him sputters and fades.

"An unwilling guest, yes. So very different from a prisoner."

It takes him a long interval to parse her tone, a mere fraction of one of her seconds. "You don't mean that."

"You don't have sarcasm where you come from, do you?"

Such feints and games of meaning make little sense from the colony's perspective. He's almost forgotten what it's like, interacting as an individual with another discrete organism, her inner processes unknowable to him. "I am, you might say, long out of practice."

The fluidity in her emotional affect has him straining to adapt. Her expression changes again, and she steps toward him, stopping at the bottom of the wide, shallow steps. She's hungry, still, but hiding it, examining him as if running her own analysis. "Where *do* you come from, anyway? Are you alone in this place? Or are there..." She swallows. "Others, here. Like you."

How to answer such questions? "Come," he says, instead. "Sit. Eat. And then if you like...perhaps I can show you."

He *can* show her where he came from, even if it's not what she meant. He is alone, but not, and there are others, like him and not. He can embody any preference, give her almost anything she wants, except an explanation that will make sense to a member of a species with binary definitions of *alone* and *together*.

There are so many of him. There is only one *him*.

And now, her. Singular. Alone, with me. Together...

He extends a hand, inviting her to move closer, to join. For another long moment, she stares at his hand, then at him. Some Earthly threat assessment runs in the background of her gaze before she finally seems to come to a decision.

Her movements deliberate, almost challenging, she takes his hand and lets him lead her to the table, but frowns again when she takes in the foodstuffs spread there. "That can't be—mac and cheese? If we're so far from Earth, then where...Did you *make* all this?"

"I wasn't sure what you liked," he says. "You seemed partial to a prepackaged form, but I prepared a variety of other dishes popular in your home region."

She's already plunked herself down in a chair. For a moment he stands still and closes his eyes, feeling what it's like to hold her, the warm weight of her thighs pressing into this other part of him. In the cleft between her legs, her heat pulses like a beacon, satin fabric clinging to the slick folds at her core.

With a shudder, he drags his awareness back from the whole to focus on this interaction. Oblivious to his lapse, she heaps food on her plate: the ground-wheat paste, shaped and boiled, that she calls *macaroni*, hot and dripping with molten, creamy cheese and topped with tidbits of cured meat; starchy tubers cut into straws, fried to a light crisp and salted well; greens and protein in a spiced sauce over soft, steamed whole grains.

She tries a bite of each, tentative at first with wide eyes, then with a soft sound in her throat that calls his every cell to attention. Her pleasure, his prerogative, a pull as steady as a magnet.

"This is *amazing*," she says, and then opens her eyes to frown at him. "I suppose I should thank you for not eating me instead."

"I told you," he says, stung. "That's not why I brought you here." Then he swallows, hard, as the still, breathless part of him now cupping the curves of her seated body whispers, *not to eat, no. But to taste…*

"Right. That's the part you haven't explained." She pops another forkful of food into her mouth, savoring it this time, and he tries not to fixate on the way her lips wrap around the implement and pull it into the hot, wet depths of her mouth. "Why *did* you bring me here, Cassiel? Seems like a lot of trouble to go through, just to ask a girl to a fancy dinner date."

He almost laughs because of how *not wrong* she is, but he knows he must take special care with this. He doesn't want to make her cry again. The next time he tastes her, he wants to know her joy, not her despair.

"You called out," he says, cautiously. "We came. And then— perhaps we, or I, acted too quickly. You were so beautiful, you see."

Her fork pauses halfway to her lips. "What are you talking about?"

"Perhaps you didn't mean to, but I heard you. All the way across the system, out here in the black—it had been a long time since…We had little choice. I had to follow it. I had to know whose call it was."

"I don't know what *call* you're talking about."

There's no way around it. He must tell her, sooner or later. "It sang to me like a…symphony," he tells her, soft with the memory of it. "Or perhaps your myths would liken it to a siren's spell."

"You're saying I *enchanted* you." She sounds skeptical, suspicious even, but her eyes are locked on his, as if some part of her can already read between the lines. "How?"

"Your pleasure. Your desire. You must understand," he hastens, at her deepening frown. "I didn't know, exactly…To our kind, such a call, ecstasy spooled out across the stars, we hear it in a different way—"

Her fork clatters to the table. "This call. Please tell me it's not—"

"I can't." He circles toward her around the table in case she tries to run again. "It woke me from a long sleep and pulled me toward you. I didn't know you, but I knew what you were. *My mate.*"

"A mating call." She leaps to her feet. "*Fuck me.*"

Surprised, he freezes behind her, a little to her right. "Are you sure?"

"*That's not what I meant.*" She wheels on him. Her skin is flushed, deep pink and deeply becoming. Heat rolls off her in a wave. "While I was innocently, uh, enjoying myself, *you* were listening in. Getting off on some free earth girl porn."

"I didn't intend to! I couldn't help it. I don't make a habit of listening in on, hm, *earth girls.* Just you."

"Just me," she repeats, uncertainly.

"The call is a rare thing for my species."

She folds her arms over her chest, jaw set. "How rare?"

"We…I was locked," he says, "in distant orbit in this system, quiescent, for five hundred million of your planet's years."

A heavy silence falls. They face each other on the dais he made for her, the fate of his world hanging in the balance between them.

"You were out here, alone, all that time."

"Yes."

"That means you're older than humanity. Older than *sharks.*"

"…Sharks?"

"Never mind." She waves the question away, impatient now. "It's not possible. No species can survive that long without…reproducing."

"No *Earth* species. We…my people are travelers. Explorers. Builders, when the time is right. But we're spacefarers first, and space takes a very long time to cross. Longer still, to find what we're looking for."

"What does that mean?"

It means I need you. "Your pleasure awakened me. It brought me to you. It made all this—for you." *It made me what I am.* While the greater organism he serves is as old as he said, this body made in the image of her desire has only known an ambulatory existence for a few rotations of her world.

"You still haven't told me *why*."

"This vessel's power source, its light, its warmth…it's you."

"Come again?"

"*Union* fuels my people's journeys between stars. If you let me in, let me taste you…" He swallows, his mouth watering. "It would mean everything. It would mean we could go anywhere. We could know home, again."

He emerged from the greater whole for one purpose. That purpose now stands before him, ready to scream, or run, or maybe hit him, or all three at once. He can't read the complicated emotions storming across her face without far more data and time to study.

We don't have all the time in the worlds. Not anymore.

But she doesn't do any of those things. "*Union*," she repeats, thoughtfully. "You're saying you abducted me because you want me for sex. For *mating*."

"That's not—"

"And then you'd take me home? Back to Earth?"

She's *brave*, his mate. Brave, unexpected, and oh, so beautiful. In the distant stretches of the colony's awareness, the individual who now calls himself Cassiel feels a sea change, a sensation of something essential, breaking. She's shaken him. He can feel the utter ebb of grief, the way it will inevitably come crashing down on him. Like the sea after a tremor, echoes of yet another primordial dream.

In this moment, he doesn't care about that. He's lost sight of the mission. All he can see now is her.

"My heart," he says, naming the wild beat inside him. His adopted physiology seems to be developing a mind of its own. Wanting inexplicable things. *Individuating.* "It's the only way I *can*."

● 〜〜〜〜   〜〜〜〜 ●

"YOU'LL REALLY TAKE ME HOME?" Kat asks the alien. "Promise?"

He reaches for her, as if to stroke her cheek or pull her close. Then he pauses, his hand suspended in mid-air. "Are you sure this is what you want?"

It's not an easy question when posed by a beautiful man, one who keeps talking about her pleasure like it's all-powerful, holy, necessary to his very being. He *did* kidnap her, though. Maybe she shouldn't be so ready to let that slide. "I'm still not sure I have much of a choice."

"Of course you have a choice. You could pleasure *yourself*...it will still power the journey. I collected your stimulator wand when I came for you."

"You stole my *vibrator*?" She suppresses a snicker. "You really are a freak."

"It seemed important to you. I've been studying it," he added, almost defensive, "and I think I could improve on a few functions, so if you'd like..."

"And that would work for you?"

"You could have anything, anyone you wish. It doesn't have to be me. I could show you—"

"*No*," she says, and he stops, looking both worried and absurdly hopeful. "If we're doing this, we're *doing* it. I want it to be you."

It's the opportunity of a lifetime, isn't it? She gets to have it all: fuck a gorgeous self-proclaimed alien in real life *and* go home again. Her favorite book heroines would kill for a chance like this.

"All right," he says, without moving toward her.

If it was him, in her dream—he certainly spoke with a voice that sounded the same—she almost misses the claiming, the overwhelming force he'd shown then. Her cheeks flare all over again. *He can't read my mind, can he?* But he doesn't stir, so...probably not.

"How does this work? Should I just kiss you now, or...?"

This seems to penetrate whatever daze he's fallen under. He laughs softly, and then, all at once, he descends upon her, sweeping her up in his arms to pull her flush against him.

We're explorers, he told her, and his kiss starts as an exploration—tasting, testing, probing—and then, abruptly, a conquering assault. His tongue feels human when it sweeps across hers, even if the teeth capturing her lip seem sharper than she's used to.

He feels human elsewhere, too, though the hard ridge growing against her belly does seem, well, *larger than life*. When she grinds up against it, an experimental investigation of exactly what she's gotten herself into, he makes a very human sound into her mouth, half growl, half moan. His hands—which, she notes, have five fingers, nails nicely clipped, with smooth, warm, human skin—slip down around her ass to the backs of her thighs. He lifts her off the ground as if to slot her onto him, if only they were both naked.

Pulling back just enough, his lips brush hers as he murmurs, "I hope you're done eating, my beauty."

"Why," she asks, breathless, "were you hungry, too?"

"In a manner of speaking." He licks into her mouth again. It *is* a hungry kiss, thirsty even, like a man finding an oasis in the desert. "It's my turn to have my fill, I think."

As he turns them around, her legs still wrapped around his middle, she realizes dimly that the table has disappeared entirely. In its place waits a bed much like the one in her chambers—no, identical to it. Hands busy with the back of her jumpsuit as she clings to him, he takes a few strides forward and spreads her on the bed. Kneeling over her with his eyes bright and wild, he tears the green satin from her body easily as ripping tissue paper, laying her bare.

"I knew you were going to eat me," she gasps. "Just…not like this."

"I *could*, you know." He bares his teeth, suddenly sharper than before. "Eat you, like that. Just a little. If that's what you want."

"Um." Her laugh quavers, high and nervous. "I'll pass."

"If you're sure." Leaning over her, he presses parted lips to her neck, over her collarbone, across the swell of her breasts. "I aim to please, remember?"

"How did you do that? You sound human. You *feel* human. But you can change?"

"Some things, I can." He doesn't bite down, but his tongue swirls around her nipple in lazy circles, tasting her before fastening on and suckling.

Pleasure ripples outward and she arches, crying his name. "Cassiel!"

"What do you want, little mate?"

Mate. The word settles hot in her belly. She tugs at his pants, looking for a button. "I want to see you, too."

"Then you shall," he says. "But there are other things I can show you. I can give you so much more. Heighten your pleasure just as I eased your fear."

"Yes," she whispers. "I want more."

With a sinuous, slithering noise, oil-black restraints whip out from somewhere beneath her—from somewhere, it seems, *inside* the bed itself. They wrap around her wrists, pulling her hands back from his body and pinning them against the mattress. Tight but not painful, inexorable but with that strange, warm give, almost like living flesh. She's helpless beneath him, a knowledge that builds the heat at her core. When he presses his hips forward so the ridge of his cock scrapes over her naked sex, she bucks into him and moans.

"You like to fight me, don't you?" He does it again. "Especially when you can't win."

"Those are yours," she says. "They're *you.*" Then she gasps again as another glistening black tendril twines around her leg, coiling upward along her sensitive inner thigh toward her core. A wave of euphoria spills over her, pleasure layering upon pleasure: her helplessness, his eyes on her, his mouth on her other nipple now, drawing another moan from her throat.

"Oh, sweet little love." He draws back, a wrenching loss of his touch. "Haven't you noticed? *Everything* here is."

Little love... "It was you, in my dream." The tendril climbs higher. *Exploring*, delicate as a single finger dancing a slow path between her legs, insinuating itself among her folds, spreading her slick around her opening and making her tremble. "*Ah.* Did that...happen?"

"It was still a dream, mostly. Merely a test. I had a lot of material to analyze, and much of it was contradictory. Nonsensical." A wry grin flashes over his face and he drops his head to kiss his way up along the opposite leg from the tendril now ever-so-slowly coiling around her aching clit. "And alarming, at times. Do human women really prefer a *shadow daddy?*"

"Shadow—*what material?*" A terrible thought assembles itself from the wreckage of her higher brain functions. He took her vibrator when he picked her up, like an X-rated Barbie accessory, so what if he… "Cassiel! Have you been reading my Kindle library? Those books aren't educational! They're fiction. No fucking *wonder*."

He raises his head, blinking at her. "It seemed like rather a lot of fucking, to me. And very educational."

"Oh, so now you're sassy too? What gives you the *right*?"

"I hoped I could persuade you to forgive me." His tongue flicks over her, then away, making her twitch and whine. "I had an imperative to fulfill, and I didn't have much left in me. If I couldn't keep you warm, fed, breathing…space is very cold and very dark, you see."

"You could have *told me*!"

"Would you have believed me?"

"No," she sighs, as he settles between her thighs. "But it's not… ah…what I like reading is a *fantasy*. When it comes to reality, I prefer…"

"What?"

"*Honesty*."

He looks up at her, eyes darker than she remembers. "Then," he says, "*honestly*, all I want right now is to make you come."

* \\\\\   //// •

SHE TASTES like the rich salt of ancestral seas, like the tang of an alien spring, like rich air he's never breathed.

She tastes like *home*.

Her ecstasy washes over him, a rising tide. She keens and moans, music marked by breathy little gasps, variations of the song that called him across the empty darkness to her small, bright world.

He laps hungrily at her, finding his new center of gravity in the small bundle of nerves at the top of her slit, where her pleasure builds, wave upon wave. Her body trembles beneath him, her legs shaking around him. She opens like a flower, frilled lips slick with her arousal.

Exploring her, he runs his tongue lower, drawn to her entrance by her heady, coaxing scent. *Here* is where he wants to sink himself deep inside her, give her all he has. Instead, he works her gently open with a tendril, the slender, deft appendage finding the most sensitive spot within her. Rhythmic pressure draws a desperate, wanton noise from her throat, and then, in broken syllables, the name he gave her to call him by.

"Cassiel…"

The sound is too sweet. He wants to hear it again. With gently increasing pressure, he plunges deeper inside, redoubles his attention at her clitoral bud, and spreads her open with his fingers, seeking more access, more sensation, more breathless noises as his own intoxication grows. Drunk on her juices, achingly hard, he can barely maintain control over the surging instinct that demands he follow through on his imperative. He could take her, rut her, breed her here and now.

He shudders at the thought of filling her, spilling his seed within her until her belly swells with the promise of new life, new worlds, *potential energy*.

But he made her a promise.

Instead, he brings her to her peak again and again, thrusting his fingers inside as he explores further. The press of another tendril against her lower hole raises the pitch of her frenzied cries to gratifying new heights. She instantly yields to his invasion there, her muscles fluttering as they clutch and spasm around him. *"God,"* she whimpers, "yes, please fill me. I want you inside me. *Everywhere."*

He pushes deeper into her tight warmth, fingers working her cunt in rhythm as he suckles her swollen clit. Her words dissolve into inarticulate screams, her limbs shaking as she comes apart, and he loses himself in her climax. Every part of him shudders now, not just the one atop her. The colony trembles as the power of her pleasure flows through it, moves it, drives it toward its inevitable end.

She pulls him back to himself, fingers clawing at his shoulders in a bid to draw him upward, to cover her further. It takes a few of her seconds for him to process her breathless, panting words.

"I want your cock," she says. "Let me see you. Feel you."

In a moment of weakness, he lets her guide his position over her, his member straining against the fabric of the tight-fitting clothing he wore for her. Her heat sears through him as she wraps her legs around him. Belatedly, he realizes he has released the restraints at her ankles.

"Fuck me, Cassiel. I mean it this time."

It would be so easy to drive himself into her, lock their bodies together, claim her and seal their fates. It takes every ounce of free will to hold himself back.

"What is it?" A strange look crosses her face. The small hands that grasped his shoulders now stroke over his skin, come up to cup his face with a tenderness that almost breaks him. "If your equipment is… you know, different…I don't care. I swear. I told you, if we're going to do this, we should *do* it. I don't want to go home without knowing what it's like to fuck…" She stops, biting her lip.

"What?" he grates out, from the edge of his control. "An alien? A monster? *Say it.*"

"*You.*"

He can't help it. He drops his head into the curve of her shoulder, breathing in the wild scent of her, his life's elixir, the overwhelming cocktail of pheromones screaming at him that she's ready, willing, and wanting. That she literally *asked for it.*

But she doesn't know what she's asking for. She's not asking for eternity, to be taken away from everything she's ever known, to become his goddess, his purpose, his world. She only wants to try this body out before she leaves him in the dark forever.

"I can't," he whispers. "*We* can't. Please, don't ask it of me."

"Why not? You said you wanted to mate." Her legs tighten around his waist, and the heat at her center scalds him and soaks through to the cock she's begging for.

"*No.*" The effort in that single word almost breaks him. Dimly, he can hear the uproar of the colony mind. The rest of him doesn't understand what he's waiting for. "Trust me on this. You don't want this. You just think you do. *Don't* ask me again."

He's out of synchrony, at cross-purposes with himself. As an individual, this body was made with a singular purpose: to love her, to protect her with his very life. He knows what this life will hold for her. Even if letting her go means the colony's end, or another few millennia floating senseless in the dark, he can't claim her like that.

But he won't have the will to hold back any longer if she *begs* him for it.

"I don't understand."

He pulls away from her. His chest aches, and the lungs designed to breathe her atmosphere seem determined to malfunction. This body isn't *him*, not really. If she saw the rest of him, she wouldn't look so bereft and so eager all at once.

"There would be no going back," he says. "You'd be *mine*, if I entered you like that. Neither of us would have a choice, then." *Not a meaningful one, at least.* His lost love had chosen certain death over eternity with him. She'd taken a part of him with her into the void when she went.

"You don't want me." Her voice comes out small, and pain tightens in her face.

"Kat. *No.* Every part of me wants to make you mine. But it would… change you. Change both of us. It would bind us, permanently."

"Oh." She goes still, silent, wide eyes searching his. "Then…"

"I will *not* do this," he says softly. "I promised to take you home. But I am more than happy to have you in other ways. I'll give you as many orgasms as your body can take, until we're back within your planet's orbit, safe and sound."

Her expression shifts. She nods, but mischief sparks in her eyes, and her mouth curves slightly as she says, "I said I wanted you everywhere. It seems like you have more than enough ways to be inside me. I didn't say *what* had to go where."

"What…?"

"Come here," she says, and then when he still doesn't move, she scoots down lower on the bed. She tugs at his waistband, pulling it down his hips until his cock springs free, hard and throbbing, pre-ejaculate beading at its head. "How much of that dream of mine did you see, Cassiel? What do you remember?"

His voice almost doesn't come, and when it does, it's a rough rasp, nearly a growl. "All of it," he says. "Kaitlyn, I remember *everything*."

It wasn't *him*, in the dream she means, not exactly. Hormones and electrical stimulation stimulated her brain to create a fantasy that justified her unconscious arousal. But the information he gleaned from it gave him plenty to work with. He never thought that she would remember it, much less like this, her pupils wide and dark with unbridled lust as she drinks in the sight of him bare before her.

"Fuck my mouth like that," she says. "Let me taste you. Please? That wouldn't be the same as you..." Her breath catches and her small pink tongue sweeps across her lips. She swallows hard. "*Mating* with me, in the way you said before."

She's perfect. She's everything he could want, even if he can't have her, not like that. But she's giving him *this*.

A groan rises in his chest as he looks down at her, spread out on the mattress for him. Eyes heavy-lidded, she opens her mouth and tips her head back, tongue curling up with anticipatory eagerness.

He can't resist the invitation. When he drives his cock between her lips, her choked moan makes his hips jerk forward. Carefully, he thrusts deeper into the wet warmth. His girth stretches her little mouth open farther than he imagined possible, and he pulls back before he pushes her gag reflex too far.

"Please," she says, when he withdraws, her lips still brushing him. "I can take it. Let me try, at least."

"I can...make adjustments, if you'd like me to suppress that reflex." It's an easy enough biochemical fix, at least temporarily.

Eyes wide, she nods again, and he pushes deep once more, experimenting with minute hormonal changes in the fluids she's so greedily suckling from him. Returning his tendrils to her pussy, he makes another involuntary, guttural sound when he finds her soaking with even more moisture than before. He works into her everywhere, just like she asked for, strumming her clit, invading her holes, and she cries out around his cock, helpless and impaled on him.

Three ways he *can* have her, and she surrenders all of them to him.

Her climax cuts through him with a sharp sweetness close to agony. He roars, spending himself in her, coating the back of her throat with his seed. Her throat squeezes him, vise-tight, as she swallows, and he almost comes a second time, his cock over-sensitized and throbbing, buried in her.

He wants more. He wants everything. But this will have to be enough.

He takes her again, rides her mercilessly from peak to gasping peak, and with everything she gives him, he carries her home.

A DIM, pale blue glow seeps into the room, cold and diffuse as dawn. Roused by a new chill in the air, Kat opens her eyes to find herself alone.

She stirs, her muscles sore, but deliciously so, each ache an exquisite memory of the pleasure Cassiel wrung from her. Nothing binds her here anymore. Her green satin jumpsuit lies crumpled beneath her, torn and shed like a skin. She pulls a sheet from the bed and wraps it around her instead.

"Hello?" she calls softly. "Cassiel? Where did you go?"

No answer. Her bare feet meet a chilly, quiescent surface, no longer humming with electric warmth. Shivering, she tilts her head up, trying to gauge the dimensions of the ship's hull.

A fathomless dark expanse stretches above her, its dizzying depths pierced here and there by a faint point of light. *Stars.*

She stands beneath a translucent dome, a shell of sorts, its curvature visible only in the refraction of light. Seeking the source of that faint illumination, she turns in place, then stops with a soft gasp.

For a moment she doesn't understand what she's looking at, as a sliver at the meridian grows to a wide, shallow crescent of white light. Then it expands into a curving slice marbled with blue and speckled white, here and there broken by greenish-brown—

Earth.

"Holy shit," she breathes, and the bright half-circle blurs, her eyes wet with sudden tears.

"Your world is beautiful."

She jumps at the voice. The transparent dome brightens with the bluish glow of Earthrise, but Cassiel is nowhere in sight. And this voice isn't quite the same: more resonant, less *human.* It echoes from everywhere and nowhere, leaving whispers trailing through the air behind it.

"Where are you?" she says. "Where did you go?"

"If you mean the one who brought you here," the voice says calmly, "he is gone. He served his purpose. Not well, in the end, but he did the best he could."

smaller space to amplify it. "This place was not made for you. It's not safe."

"Oh, shut up," she snaps, but when she rounds the next corner, the corridor opens up, and her own voice fails her.

Bodies. They line this long, tiered chamber, tens of them, hundreds of them. Each hangs suspended in a glowing blue-green pod, not so different from the one she ran from. Some are human, or at least humanoid with bestial or monstrous features: curled horns, folded leathery wings, scales or fur, tusks or tentacles…but all naked, and all *unmistakably* male.

Kat stares, half in horror, half in fascination at the wide array of phallic diversity. Then she shudders. None of these people are *awake.* It feels wrong to stare at them, hanging there like slabs of meat, no matter how impressive a display of the meat in question.

"We didn't mean for you to see them. Not like this." The voice sounds almost worried. Apologetic, even.

She doesn't know where to look. "Like what? *Flaccid*? I'm sure it happens to all the…" *Say it.* She didn't want to hurt him, when he said that before. Now… "Monsters. No offense."

For the first time, amusement tinges the disembodied voice. "Of course it must look alarming. We weren't certain what you liked, so we may have over-prepared."

"Wait. You're saying—these are all *you.*"

"Yes," he—it—they say. "You could have had any of these, more than one. All of them. You only had to ask."

Made to order from her very own why-choose catalogue. *Intriguing. Horrifying. Checks out.* "And they're all…alive?"

"In a sense. They are only segments, undifferentiated from the whole."

"But when they differentiate, they're still you. They're all the same."

"Genetically identical. Our zooids exist in synchrony but act independently. These are specialists."

She doesn't have to ask what specialty. "This is where Cassiel came from. Made for one purpose." She picks up her pace. "You used him. He was just *bait.*"

Bait, who had defied his collective's will to send her home.

"No!" The voice seems shaken, for once. "For a much higher purpose. Some might say the *most* essential."

"You mean fucking."

"*Mating*," the voice rumbles, and despite herself, her stomach flips.

"And here I thought aliens would be enlightened." She rolls her eyes, walking faster, deeper into that rogue's gallery of masculine fantasies. "Apparently male single-mindedness is universal. Why him?"

Her unseen companion takes a moment to answer, as if nonplussed. "What?"

"Out of all these," she sweeps an arm wide, encompassing a thousand variations on a theme of cock, "he was the chosen one. I want to know why."

"We didn't choose him," the voice says, after another long pause. "He was the one *you* chose."

"Oh, fuck *off*. When did I get to choose?" She peers into each translucent pod as she passes. Not at their…attributes, now, but at their faces. "I was asleep. And then I was afraid. And he made me feel…not afraid at all. But that was a trick. He didn't even deny it."

"Biochemical compatibility. Not a trick. You knew him in your body." Then, dropping lower, "Didn't you?"

"Stop it," she grates out. "Trick or no trick, *you* don't get to play me. Whoever and *whatever* you are. Tell me where he is."

"Why?" It's the second time he's questioned her, instead of the other way around, and she can't deny how good it feels to throw him off-balance.

She's tired of asking. "Cassiel must be here somewhere. I want to see him."

"That's not possible."

"You keep saying that." Her fists clench at her sides. "If you've hurt him, punished him because he wouldn't impregnate me or fulfill whatever weird hellish plan you had for us, I'll *destroy* you."

A heavy silence falls.

"Oh, now you've got nothing to say? Come on, you coward! You could at least show me your true face. You owe me that, at least. Look me in the eye when you tell me what you've done to my—"

She snaps her mouth shut around the word, but it seems to hang there anyway in the quiet corridor, at home among the rest of the attractive horrors.

My mate.

"I don't understand." It's a murmur, one she has to strain her ears to hear. "You didn't want that. Didn't want to stay."

"Yeah, well. Humans are *complicated.*" She casts a glance around at the gallery of rogues and monsters. For a moment, it's like she's trapped in a hall of mirrors, every reflection a facet of...*her.* Her own lust, in all the shapes it's taken. "There's so many of you, but we can hold a whole host of conflicting desires in one individual psyche. I can want ten impossible things before breakfast. Maybe that's *our* specialty."

The voice doesn't respond.

"Hello?" She strides forward again. The entire vessel can't be devoted to the production of sex objects. "Are you even listening? I can want to go home, and also want the stars. I can miss the earth, and also miss the guy who made me come until I'm pretty sure I actually passed out, but more importantly, was *kind* to me. He *cared.* I can love you for letting me have him, and be willing to wreck you for taking him away."

She catches a sobbing breath and finds herself at the end of the assembly line, staring at what could be a door. Or a wall to break herself on. *"That's* what humans are like. That's what *I'm* like. Is that why you won't let me stay?"

Raising her hand, she places it flat against the smooth, cool shell in front of her. Exhaustion overtakes her, suddenly, and she leans her forehead against it.

When it shifts, irises outward in a spiral motion, she almost falls forward on her face.

"*Asshole.* You could have warned me!"

The corridor that's opened up to her doesn't light up the way the upper level did. It absorbs light, an absence so intense it hurts her eyes.

"Are you sure you want to know?" The words come low and pained out of the darkness, without echoes, as from a single throat.

"I want to see you." But she doesn't have to. She already knows him, even in the dark.

There's no answer, just a long, ragged hiss like an in-drawn breath.

She takes a step forward into the darkness, lets it swallow her. "I told you I wanted honesty. Give me that, at least."

In the absence of light, a strange, sweet scent, *his* scent, suddenly fills her senses. Her trepidation drains away.

With her next step, her foot meets nothing but empty air, and she falls.

This is it, she thinks, still without a trace of fear. *It's clearly a trap. A classic honey pot. Now I'm* definitely *going to get eaten.*

And then, something supple and rippling as corded muscle whips soundlessly out of the dark to wrap around her waist, stopping her fall.

It lowers her gently until her feet touch down on something solid. As it releases her, the darkness ebbs, and she can see *him.*

Cassiel's eyes meet hers, wide and wild, his pupils blown. His beautiful face twists with something close to agony. He's seated on a chair of sorts—*a throne?* Thick cords bind his wrists and ankles, holding him in place, the same kind that bound her when she first awakened on this ship.

He's also naked, fully erect, his cock jutting between his parted legs and swelling further under her gaze. "You shouldn't have come," he grates out, teeth bared. "It's not safe."

The chamber doesn't *look* safe. More of the iridescent dark cords line the walls and snake across the floor. They move in waves and coils, with a strange, sinuous synchrony.

"I'm not afraid."

His chin falls forward onto his bare chest, as if he can't hold it high any longer. "You should be."

"I can't be. Not around you." She steps carefully forward. The tentacle-like cords seem to make way for her, clearing themselves courteously to the sides. "What did they do to you?"

The chair he's bound to has a curving, organic shape, but it's part of something larger. The bindings pulse where they touch his skin, and bruise-purple veins stand out rigid and dark on his forearms.

There's technology here, of a sort, and a tangible crackle of energy, an ultraviolet phosphorescence. She can see it if she doesn't try to look right at it, like an alien magic eye puzzle.

"I told myself you couldn't destroy me." He doesn't raise his head, his voice quiet enough she strains to hear him over the deep electric hum in the air, at the very edge of audible frequencies.

"I didn't mean that," she says, flushing. "I didn't mean *you*."

"It doesn't matter. You already have."

"What? *Why?*"

"Your pleasure," he says, voice tight. "Our power. We're almost finished now."

"Power…" She stares around her. "This is an *engine* room, isn't it?" A half-formed idea teases her mind. *Unity. Resonance. Fusion.*

Connection lies at the core of this alien technology, potential energy released by the merging of wildly different elements. It answers a question she didn't know to ask until she came here, saw this, knew *him*. It blows her pet theorems out of the water, upends them in an instant. It changes everything.

Experimental physics comes with inherent risks. A good scientist must cultivate the will to understand the incomprehensible, to unmake the knowns of the universe to account for new data.

"I said I'd bring you home." Cassiel writhes in the chair—*a pilot's chair?*—as if he's trying to escape his bonds, and he bites his lip like he's in pain. "I made you a promise. Why won't you let me keep it?"

You already did. "They plugged you in like a battery. They're *using* you, Cassiel."

"This is what I *am*," he grates between bared teeth. "I told you. You should…leave. *She* did."

That gives her pause. "*She* who?"

"It doesn't matter." The tentacles whip out from the throne, from the walls. They push her backward. "It was…a long time ago."

Apparently even aliens have ex-girlfriend trauma. "I'm not *her*, ok?" Digging in, she slaps the whipping tendrils back. "I'm not going anywhere. *My* choice."

"We're out of time, love." He pants, his body flexing against the restraints. "I don't know how much longer I can hold on."

"Hold on how?" Why *is* he holding back? He seems to have some sway over the cord-like tentacles in this room, but if so, that means he could have made them release him.

"I'm weak, Kaitlyn. Don't you understand?" His back arches, his cock rigid and swelling larger still, dark, ropy veins standing out along his length. "I'm weak for you. I could lose control, and then…"

"Then you'd take me," she says calmly. "You'd make me your mate."

"*Don't.* Tempt me."

"Try and stop me," she counters, pushing at the resistance of the tendrils. All at once, they make way for her. She strides unimpeded toward his throne.

Finally, he raises his head as she stands looking down on him. "Kaitlyn. *Please.* I warned you not to—"

"Shh." She reaches out, places a finger over his mouth. "I don't care."

His lips part under her touch, his expression dazed. She poises herself over him, bare under her t-shirt, and a feral sound rises in his throat as the tip of his cock nudges against her entrance. The contact jolts through her, electric pleasure with the force of a live wire. It heats her from the inside out, and she's instantly slick with overwhelming need that coats him and trickles agonizingly down the insides of her thighs.

"You can't…" His voice breaks, torment and desire mingling in his eyes. "This will change everything. You won't be able to go home."

He thinks he's saving me. But she doesn't want to be saved. Somewhere between the promise he made her and all the ways they found to have each other, in the long dark journey back from the edge of the solar system, the change he threatened must have taken hold. She can't imagine leaving him, not like this, not now.

He warned her of an unbreakable, permanent bond. He didn't mention it would come with an all-consuming need to have him in her, over her, around her, as close and in as many ways as possible. She would crawl inside his skin, as if it weren't enough that the ship that carries her is just another part of him.

Is it really my choice?

The answer resonates in every cell of her being. She can't go back to her life before this, not without having him, not after he laid the universe at her feet.

"Cassiel." She leans her forehead against his. "I *am* home."

She lowers herself onto him, inch by inch, her body straining to contain him. His head drops back against the coiling shell of the seat, and he bucks his hips up, pushing deep inside her. Driving himself home. Stretching her as the base of his cock swells to fill her even more. When she tries to rise again, she can't go far.

His eyes meet hers, fathomless, dark, and heated with an infrared glow more felt than seen, a relentless, inexorable gravity drawing her into him, molten at her core. "I warned you. No…going back."

"Bound together. I want that. God, I can *feel* it." A fractional lift of her hips, and then she slides back down, the curve of him hitting every secret place inside her with exquisite friction. "Fuck, Cassiel…It's so good, it's too much, *I can't…*"

His hands close around her hips, gripping them hard enough to bruise, but she's beyond caring. He moves her on him, slamming deeper inside her with each thrust. Then, with a growl and a fluid movement, he surges forward, bearing her down to the floor. She moans at the pressure and sensation as the knot at his base takes more of her weight, dragging her along with him. He's locked inside her, and she couldn't stop this if she wanted to, not anymore. Maybe she never could.

She doesn't want to, doesn't want anything but this pleasure, forever and always.

The thought almost frightens her before it dissolves in a dizzying, abrupt peak, her cries echoing wildly in her ears. He bears down on her with slow, agonizingly short thrusts. "You take me so well, little mate," he groans into her neck. "Want to breed you. Make you mine."

"*God, yes.*" She wants him spilling inside her, wants to take his seed over and over until her body overflows with him. "I need it. Need you. Please—"

Her plea dissolves into a helpless scream of pleasure as he rises to his knees and spins her away from him, still sheathed as deep as he can go, her hands scrabbling for purchase as he pounds into her. His rhythm turns ragged, and suddenly he's not holding back anymore. Each thrust shakes her body, rattling her bones and sending sparks of ecstasy up her spine. He grips her thighs for purchase, pulling her half off the ground as he ruts into her with ragged panting gasps that roll hot and sweet over her neck.

Then, with a roar, he closes his teeth over her nape. With one last shuddering thrust, his release floods into her. Exquisitely sensitized, she cries out with every pump of his seed, each pulling another white-hot wave of orgasmic pleasure from her.

"Cassiel?" Dimly, she realizes he's fucking her through her climax, picking up speed again.

"Yes, love?"

She can hardly manage words, but this seems important. "What-ever...happens. You need...to know. I...*aaahhh*. I chose this. I chose you. My mate."

"*Mine*," he says, driving hard and deep inside her, and she has no more words to give him. Keening, incoherent, she's barely human anymore, an entity of pure energy, pure sensation, and utterly, entirely *his*.

This time, when he spends himself inside her and they come together, she sees stars.

● ＼＼＼＼   ／／／／ ◗

"Cassiel," his mate says, a long time later. "What comes next?"

They're lying together on the floor of the ship's core, still joined. The frantic force of the first mating frenzy has loosened its hold, at least enough that they have breath to speak with.

Breath. It fascinates him, how quickly he's acclimated to this shape, her shape, this body that fits her so well. And with it, how his will has strengthened, until he holds sway over the colony. It doesn't rule him anymore. He rules it.

Some functions have accepted that easily. The ship-form responds to his every thought now without resistance, but other parts need more time to adjust. He has much to learn about what it means to choose for himself in this new form.

"You come next." He rolls his hips lazily, drawing a gratifying noise from the human woman beneath him. He's still buried deep within her, her body fluttering with orgasmic contractions around him. Her inner muscles grip him like she doesn't want to let him go. "And then, maybe me again."

"I'm serious," she gasps, when they can speak once more. "I want to know what happens now."

"That depends on you." He says it into the soft skin at her neck, just to feel her shiver. "I meant every word, when I said we could go anywhere."

"We can go anywhere, but I can never leave. Is that right?"

He stretches his awareness toward his greater whole, receiving a grudging answer. The colony doesn't want her setting foot outside its reach, not after what happened last time. It wants control. But that belongs to him, now.

"I cannot be apart from you." He says it with some uncertainty at first, but in speaking it, he can feel the truth in it. "But I won't keep you here against your will." He doesn't like that much either, but she chose him once. Maybe she will again.

"I don't want to leave *you*." She strokes his back, his hair, with gentle fingers as if sensing his distress. "What if...would you come with me? Could you survive outside the ship?"

He rolls onto his back, pulling her with him and over him. The mating tendrils released their hold hours ago, satisfied by how well he'd filled her, as his seed spilled down her thighs in softly phosphorescent rivulets. He had gone on rutting her on this floor because she begged him to, because he wanted to, because it felt so good. Not biological imperative, but his choice and hers, together.

How far does his new freedom extend?

"I don't know. We could try." The colony likes this even less, flooding his mind with warnings about contamination, hostile environments, and violent planet-dwellers, but he ignores them. "It has never been done before, but we never mated with a human, either."

"All right." She grins up at him, a challenge and an invitation. "My place or yours?"

"If you want to visit Earth, we're already in orbit."

"We can start there." Then she laughs. "At the very least, I should take you home to meet my mother."

"Your…mother?" Honestly, that sounds terrifying. An alien planet, with alien customs, in an environment wholly out of his influence, on the home turf of his mate's progenitor, and yet…

She's been so brave for him. It seems right that he should do the same for her.

"I'd like that," he says, and his courage begins with her kiss.

about erin fulmer

Erin Fulmer (she/her) is a legal aid attorney by day, author of urban fantasy and science fiction by night. A 2020 Pitch Wars alumna, she lives in sunny Northern California with her husband and two spoiled cats. When she's not writing or working, she enjoys soaking in nature, taking pictures of the sky, playing board games with friends, and napping like it's an Olympic sport.

Her urban fantasy trilogy, the Cambion series, is now available in brand new indie editions!

To learn more, visit erinfulmer.com

.

dream broker

J. E. McDonald

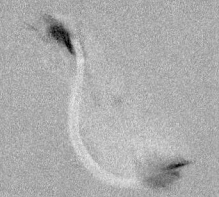

chapter one

THE DUST STORMS OF ROJAB ONE, NOTORIOUS FOR KILLING TOURISTS, HAD almost claimed me as a victim.

"It's an event of a century, they said," I muttered, shoving my hands deeper into the pockets of my cargo pants while I walked, shoulders hunched. Tourists of all shapes and sizes, all colors and species, including humans, packed the winding cobble-lined sidewalk, taking advantage of Carlow City's entertainment district.

"You won't want to miss it, they said." Gritting my teeth, I tried to appreciate my surroundings since I'd only been here for a few days and never this far down Prime Street.

Food carts sizzled with confections while individuals waited in long lines for tubers on a stick; fried scents washed over everything. Orange lamps graced the street in regular intervals, creating orbs of light at my feet. Darkness shrouded the city almost constantly except for part of the year, when the planet tilted and the horizon glowed to signal "day." For a woman used to four seasons and a twenty-four-hour clock, the constant night had done a number on my head. Colorful illumination adorned every structure, highlighting windows, doorways, and architectural marvels. In some ways, the aesthetic reminded me of the Christmas village my grandmother used to set up in her living room every winter back on Earth.

"It'll be *fun*, they said." The safari had been about as fun as getting sandblasted by a herd of dust sharks on the hottest day of the year.

Oh, wait. That was exactly what had happened.

And it was all Jordan's fault. *The fucker.*

My stomach squeezed uncomfortably like every time I thought of him. "Forget about him, Monroe," I told myself, a sentence I'd spoken aloud more than once. Hard to do when he'd put me in this mess.

Ignoring the nausea conjured by thoughts of him, I pressed my hand to my overly exfoliated cheek, then ran a chafed palm over my hair. Grit and dust particles stuck to my skin despite having showered three times already. It was a wonder I had any flesh left after the damn sandstorm. I didn't have time to go shower again at the hostel, not if I planned on catching a transport in the morning. I needed money, and I needed it yesterday.

Up ahead, a neon blue sign flashed above the sidewalk, an arrow pointing left with the words Glow Road beneath it. The audio translators we'd been given when we started this tour didn't work for signs, but Rojab One catered to tourists. Their technology translated signs too. I had no idea how it worked, but it was seriously cool.

A gust of hot wind lifted the ends of my hair but did nothing to remove the sweat on my nape. For the millionth time I considered shaving my head, but knew I'd miss my long, brown waves once returning home. Another gust pressed against me and I flapped the front of my tank top in an attempt to dry the perspiration collecting under my ample boobs. Hot climates and I never seemed to get along.

I slowed my pace, then stopped under the sign, staring down the narrow street. It wasn't as well-lit as the main tourist drags, the shadows deepening. Trash gathered in the places wind couldn't sweep it away. The road cleaners must not turn down this side lane. Instead of cobblestones, black pavement curved away from me, then disappeared out of sight between buildings as the street twisted and narrowed further. Non-humans walked in and out of shops, but only a fraction of the crowd as strolled behind me.

Heinrick's words from last night echoed through my head. The old human backpacker had seen and done everything, but claimed the Rojab System always enticed him to return for one reason or another.

My first stroke of luck since arriving in this system came when we discovered we hailed from the same continent on Earth and he remarked I reminded him of someone he used to know. I'd shared my sob story over two pints of this world's cheapest lager.

"You'll get your money from Khor Drath," Heinrick said with a nod. "You give him one night and you'll have enough cash to take ten interstellar tours."

I almost spit my beer across the bar top. "You're delusional if you think I'm going to sleep with someone for money."

Heinrick cackled, slapping the counter. "Not sleep with him, Monroe. Sleep for him. He doesn't even touch you, girl." He glanced over his shoulder, scanning the room, then leaned into me, voice lowered. "He's a dream broker and will siphon your dreams."

A shiver of unease cascaded down my spine. "Siphon?"

"It's not what you would call common knowledge," he said, his volume only above a whisper—disconcerting because he'd been a boisterous soul ever since I'd arrived on Rojab One. "Most tourists don't ever learn of the thing Rojabians really want from us." He shrugged and took another swig, wiping his mouth with the back of his hand. "Fuck, I'd go sell my sweet dreams to Khor Drath right now if the big bastard wasn't sick of me and my fantasies." He scratched his stubbly chin. "Tell him I sent you and maybe he'll give me a cut. That would be nice."

The rest of the conversation was fuzzy, but I did remember one last thing Heinrick said: *He might be scary as fuck, but he wouldn't lay a hand on you. The epitome of a businessman, eh?*

With the blue sign flashing over my head, I glanced over my shoulder to squint at the brightness of Prime Street. It appeared unnatural after staring down the subtle shadows of Glow Road for so long. Families and couples from across a dozen systems enjoyed the open hospitality of Rojarians with laughter and chatter. My chest ached.

Because I was alone.

And abandoned.

I took a deep breath and stepped onto black pavement. I'd officially entered the blue light district.

chapter two

Tʜᴇ ꜱᴜʙᴅᴜᴇᴅ ʟɪɢʜᴛꜱ ᴏꜰ Gʟᴏᴡ Rᴏᴀᴅ'ꜱ ᴍᴀɴʏ ꜱʜᴏᴘꜱ ᴅɪꜱᴀᴘᴘᴇᴀʀᴇᴅ ɪɴᴛᴏ the pavement beneath my feet. I kept my pace brisk, but casual, hoping I blended in. The scents of street food gave way to stray wafts of perfume, then shifted to the stench of old garbage. The farther I traveled down the twisty road, the more I garnered interested stares from the aliens hanging out in front of the shops.

This planet was a study in contrasts. Rojab One orbited as close to a sun as you could get without becoming barbecue. The sun-facing side remained unlivable to most species except those born here. I'd only met one Sun Rojabian. Some might find their textured, rock-like skin or their towering stature unnerving, but their three eyelids over two sets of eyeballs, one on the back of their head and one on the front, was what sent shivers across my skin.

Then came the Night Rojabians. Their darker skin and glowing eyes distinguished them from their sun-loving counterparts. They ruled Carlow City and all the tourist destinations along The Span, the boundary where the darkness met the light. Aliens from all over came here to trade, or work, thanks to the flourishing mining and entertainment industries.

"Hey lovely, are you here for a ride of a lifetime?"

The satiny smooth voice pulled me out of my thoughts and I spun on my heel. A two-headed alien with a body similar to a horse swayed in front of me. I'd seen this species before, but didn't know what planet they came from. The building behind them towered over the ones flanking it, at least six stories tall. The sign glowing softly on its facade read "Dream Land."

I returned my attention to the alien's heads.

"My eyes are down here."

The irritated voice snapped my attention to the middle of the being's chest, where two cartoonishly cute eyes glared at me. I grimaced.

So, not two-headed after all. Two-breasted? This wasn't the first time I'd made an alien *faux pas* and it wouldn't be the last.

"Sorry, not interested," I murmured and scurried farther down the street, praying the being wouldn't come after me for the slight.

Heinrick provided specific instructions on how to reach the dream broker's lab. I needed to walk down Glow Road until it split in two directions, then take the right fork to the dead end. Sounded simple, but the further I walked, the fewer people I encountered, and the more I checked over my shoulder, paranoid. Shadows cloaked doorways instead of the array of fixtures I'd come to accept as the Rojabian norm. My shoulders inched toward my ears, my stomach swirling with nerves.

I would turn back right now if I could, but I didn't have any other options thanks to Jordan and transport incident. *Dickhead ex-boyfriend. Dickhead dust storm.*

Rojab One didn't use biometric credits like most of the planets in this system. They used credit sticks. I'd downloaded a good chunk from my Earth account at the exchange terminals when I'd arrived, and ignorantly didn't check off the "added insurance" box when I signed up for this little jaunt back on Rojab Six.

"Don't live with regrets, they said." My mutter turned into a whisper. The dark buildings on either side of the road narrowed so much a transport wouldn't fit through. I stole another glance over my shoulder, and kept walking.

I had more regrets than sense at this point. The tour transport carried my group to the other side of the mountains beyond The Span. With the planet's natural tilt, the sunrise effect with the chemicals in the upper atmosphere occurred only once every hundred years. I'd heard the experience was supposed to be life-changing. At least, that was what the travel agent on Rojab Six had promised.

I tried not to cry in defeat at the irony.

A dust storm developed halfway to our intended destination. The planet had ample warning systems in place, and we would have made it back in time if it hadn't been for the dust sharks. I resisted the urge to rub my raw cheeks again. The sharks took some of the tourists as a late-night snack, and the rest of us huddled in the transport's wreck until rescue arrived. I'd been grateful for my life, but being stranded wasn't the worst part.

I'd lost my credit stick to the desert. After the rescue, I'd tried to access my off-world funds and my accounts were empty. That piece of shit Jordan had stolen from me. We'd joined our accounts when we'd moved in together. What a mistake. Had he planned it all along? Seemed stupid to invest two years of his life for one measly bank account. He'd probably done it to impress his new green girlfriend. As soon as I returned to Earth, I was going to nail the fucker to the wall.

But that legal action waited for another day.

If it weren't for Heinrick lending me a few credits and sharing the other bunk in his room at the hostel, I would've been sleeping on the street.

The passageway divided, the shadows lengthening even more. My feet slowed while nerves renewed their dance in my belly. I took another peek over my shoulder. All the artificial light from Prime Street had disappeared, leaving the dim of Glow Road in its place. I squinted ahead. None of the façades were lit along this strip. Illumination came from the occasional light orb on the ground and the slice of stars between the top of the buildings.

I shoved my hands in my pockets and tried to think of another way out of this mess, but came up empty. I couldn't afford *not* to do this. Inhaling a fortifying breath through my nose, I aimed myself at the right side of the fork and forged ahead.

Heinrick told me the deeper a broker traveled into the Night side, the higher the price they'd pay for my dreams. With zero credits to my name, that made Khor Drath my only option. For such a ubiquitous entertainment staple on this planet, I couldn't decide if it were ironic or appropriate that dream brokers lived in the shadows of Carlow City.

The walkway stopped abruptly. The darkened walls of the buildings seemed to curve inward they stretched so high, blocking out the stars. My eyes adjusted enough to see the indentations between the organic-shaped black brick which constructed most of the buildings on this world, but it took me a minute to make out the door inset into the dark surface.

My heart pounding with apprehension, I reached my hand forward, searching for the key pad Heinrick said would be in the center of the door. The rough stone felt surprising cool compared to the heat of the planet. I brushed my fingers back and forth until I connected with smooth metal.

A screen activated, the glare almost blinding in the dim of the dead end. I blinked, then pressed the circular button to announce my arrival.

"What do you want?" came a brusque voice a moment later.

"Uh…" I licked my lips and swallowed. "I'm here for the dream broker." It would be just my luck if I'd arrived at the wrong location and wound up applying for a job as a Mannramm milker by accident.

The door clicked, a sliver of light spilling between the gap. I lifted my hand to push it open when it swung inward. More light washed over me and I squinted. A form blocked the doorway, and I looked up, and up, past a bare chest and wide shoulders before I reached his face.

Silver-white eyes shone down on me, glowing like the brightest of stars. My breath left me in a whoosh. Awareness tingled over my body like a living thing.

Heinrick hadn't told me what species Khor Drath was. I'd assumed a Night Rojabian, but I'd assumed wrong. Khor Drath was a Sawarstian, the warrior race who notoriously kept to themselves when not fighting someone else's war. I'd heard it said we were all made of stars, but not Sawarstian. No, they were made of nebulae.

I'd never seen someone so breathtaking in my life.

Swirls of color, both subtle and bright, over a backdrop of dark, composed the skin of his chest, his face, his arms. *Everywhere.* Navy blue, teal, and deep purple dust-like movement moved like a living, breathing entity. It was all an effect, like how a chameleon changed its skin when camouflaged, but it mesmerized. I couldn't tear my eyes away. I'd seen a lot of aliens since beginning this fiasco of an interstellar tour, but I'd only heard whispers about Sawarstians, and had never seen one in the flesh.

He didn't have hair, but thick cords of flesh that extended from his scalp, then tapered to delicate points to rest on broad shoulders. They swirled with color like the rest of him. His skin appeared as smooth as a dolphin's and he had to be over seven feet tall, his rigid posture adding to his height. He braced one of his hands against the door frame and the other curled around the top of the door, five thick fingers on each in proportion to the rest of him.

My gaze dropped below his waist, noting the bulge beneath his black pants, the only clothing he wore. *Definitely in proportion.* My chafed cheeks burned and my eyes snapped back to his. Mortification constricted my chest, but he didn't react to me noticing the size of his package.

Because he stared at me in the most disconcerting way, like he could see right through me, *inside* me, and knew my true nature. Or like he peeled my skin layer by layer like an onion, leaving me exposed to his gaze. The longer he stared, the more my body flushed with heat.

Since I'd begun the tour, aliens hadn't done it for me *at all.* Until now. I mean, I could see the appeal of the green girl Jordan dumped me for, but other than her, no one had turned my head in a sexual way.

But this guy? *Holy hell.* He was something else. Standing this close to him prickled my body with humming interest. Thick jaw, high cheekbones, fierce scowl—his face alone could probably launch a thousand spaceships.

And he kept staring at me.

I stared back.

Tension crackled between us.

His fingers tightened on the door frame, making it creak.

Did his species have some sort of welcoming ritual? The old backpacker hadn't said a word about it. Was this even Khor Drath?

"Heinrick sent me." The words left my lips in an embarrassing squeak.

He shook himself and straightened away from the door. His eyes scanned me again, this time taking in my features, clocking the scraped skin of my cheeks and forehead, then downward over my wind-torn clothes.

When he opened his mouth to speak, I held my breath in anticipation

"Dust sharks?" he asked.

chapter three

His voice rumbled through me, deep. *So deep.* It vibrated through my belly and down between my legs. Every other thought I'd had up until this point escaped out my ears in a puff of smoke. I went stupid, forgetting why I was here.

He peered down at me in charged, silent expectation, like he waited for an answer.

I didn't remember the question, but he kept staring, and the blood rushed to my head in a volcanic surge, and if I didn't say something soon I was probably going to scream, or he'd shut the door in my face and I'd continue to be broke and stranded.

"MynameisMonroeandIamhereforthedreamthing." The words tumbled out so quickly, I gulped a breath to compensate. The sound bounced loudly off the brick caging me in.

Khor Drath's eyes narrowed, intensifying their white glow. "Monroe?" His deep voice penetrated my stomach then lower, a whole new sensation enveloping me. Could a voice curl into your underpants? I'd heard of Sawarstian allure before, but this was ridiculous.

I nodded, maybe a little too frantically, because he tilted his head, forehead furrowing. "That's me. Yeppers. Totally me." Now it sounded like I was lying, and from the way Khor Drath crossed his arms over his chest, he thought so too.

But the chest-crossing thing? It was a problem. A big, sinewy one because the muscles of his forearms shifted with nebulous colors of turquoise, purple, and orange.

I cleared my throat. "So, yeah. Heinrick sent me, said you might need some fresh dreams. He asked for a cut because of the referral."

The corner of Khor Drath's mouth twitched and curled up. My heart fluttered. Why did humor on this big, color-changing dude look so hot? Why did *everything* about him seem to steam up the air? Maybe I needed revenge sex and this was the first being to twinge my lady parts since Jordan. Wait, why was I thinking about sex? Yesterday, I was adamant about *not* having sex with a random alien. I came here for the dream thing, nothing more, no matter how hot the dream broker turned out to be. *Heinrick should have warned me, the bastard.*

"*Are* you Khor Drath?" Probably should have cleared that up first thing.

He tilted his head slightly in acknowledgment, then stepped back. "Follow me." Leaving the door open, he led the way deeper into the building.

God, his voice. *So deep.* It made me want to roll over and call him Daddy. *Space Daddy.*

I stepped fully inside and scanned the space. Warm-toned light cast everything in a soothing glow. I blinked repeatedly as my eyes adjusted from the contrast to the dark outside. The walls were curved, stretching into a dome-shaped ceiling that appeared almost cave-like. This entryway served as a waiting room of sorts, but no one sat upon the comfortable sofas—if you could call the bulbous shapes that—or the matching poofs in green, gray, and blue big enough to fit a Sawars- tian or two. Three corridors led off the main space, and the darkness of the narrow passages reminded me a lot of the streets I'd just walked.

Khor Drath disappeared down the middle corridor and I jogged to catch up, leaving the inviting entry room behind. Already, the sweat on my body dried in the cooler air. I pulled my tank top away from my skin to speed up the process, then gave my armpit a surreptitious sniff to make sure I didn't stink too much.

We were only in the narrow hallway a moment before it opened up into a domed kitchen. Shelves upon shelves lined one curved wall, full of jars and supplies. I squinted at the row in the middle dedicated to pickles from worlds beyond this one—the edible ones, not the self-pleasuring kind. Maroon, mustard, teal, and lime green...pickles of every color were jarred and wrapped in labels from other systems. This guy appeared to be a true alien pickle aficionado.

"So, what do I call you?" I asked, jogging to catch up where he'd crossed into another curved tunnel. "Khor? Mr. Drath? KD?"

He stopped suddenly and glanced over his shoulder. I sucked in a sharp breath at the way his eyes shone like beacons in the dim light, then nearly ran into him because my feet kept moving.

"My name is Khor Drath."

Right. Okay. Not one for informality, then.

This close, I craned my neck to meet his gaze. The body heat he exuded warmed my already flushed skin. Even in this darkened space, his nebulous skin pulsed with color. The moment stretched, affecting my body like I floated weightless in space while staring into the depths of a binary star system surrounded by the beauty of nebulae. The walls, the floor, the ceiling, all melted away.

He turned and strode toward the opposite end of the corridor, the abrupt movement jarring after I'd felt so adrift.

I put some pep in my step to catch up, pulled deeper into another narrow and dark corridor. "Can you tell me more about this process?" I asked when there were only a few feet between us, my voice echoing off the curved walls.

"First we'll give you a scan, make sure you're healthy." His words traveled back to me. "I'll show you the contract, see if you have any questions, then go from there."

Khor Drath led me into a domed-shaped lab and my nerves reawakened in my stomach. The room smelled sterile, like he cleaned it on the regular with antiseptic-type soap. Curved work surfaces extended from the doorway in opposite directions. Monitors, terminals, and all sorts of technical equipment I'd never seen before filled the rear wall and a desk-like workstation. Wires, so many wires it looked like they exploded from them, reached toward the ceiling then cascaded down into the middle of the room.

One chair, covered in plush ekku leather, took up the center of the room as if on a stage. Though wider and taller than a dentist's chair, the way it eased back at an angle reminded me of one, or the gaming lounger we bought for our apartment on Earth.

Our apartment.

Fuck, Jordan. I'd successfully not thought about him for a few minutes while wrapped in the amazingness that was Khor Drath, and it soured my mood to think of him now. Not like I'd been in a stellar mood right before the thought—more of a half terrified, half horny state which I was trying to mentally accept and move on from, but still. Definitely didn't want the cheating, backstabbing bastard on my mind. Not when I had Space Daddy getting comfortable on a stool behind one of the biggest monitors.

I'd frozen by the door to take in the room, but hopped forward when he gestured to the stool near him at the end of the curved table. A swallow lodged itself in my throat as I passed a multitude of instruments: a scanner, a prober, and an old-style tool that resembled calipers. And another jar of pickles, half full and bright pink, hailing from the Anitih sector from the writing on its label.

The man likes his snacks.

I settled on the stool and examined everything from Khor Drath's angle. Three of his monitors revealed views of the room, recording the chair at different angles. Alien code scrolled along the others, or at least what looked like code. Three of the screens were blank.

"How does this work, exactly?" I asked, eying the hanging wires in the center of the room with a healthy dose of distrust.

Instead of answering, he picked up a medical wand from beside one of his monitors and aimed it at my head.

"Hey!" I swatted it away.

He frowned at me before bringing the scanner back between us. "Need to make sure you're healthy enough for the process." He waggled the rod. "Are you afraid of a little scan?"

I swallowed at the question. No, I wasn't afraid of a medical scan, but it didn't stop the nerves in my stomach from surging into my chest. "I'm only sleeping, right? Why would that matter? It's not like my dreams are dangerous on any other regular night."

He shrugged his wide, purple-blue shoulders and turned on the scanner. "I strive to anticipate every potential situation." His voice rumbled through me, making me squirm. "Haven't lost a client yet."

The rod hummed over my head and around my shoulders and I had the urge to swat at it again to see what he would do. "Why would you say that? Why would it even be a possibility?" This stupid idea was getting stupider by the second. I didn't have "Death by dream machine" on my bingo card for this year.

Fuck that. I didn't have "get dumped by my boyfriend for a hotter alien" on my bingo card either.

"A precaution only." He finished his scan and set the rod on the counter beside me. "I keep some of your awareness synapses conscious. The experience is closer to a lucid dream, meaning you can control what you experience if you like."

I pressed my thighs together in an attempt to ward off the way his words stroked me.

"Certain kinds of dreams sell better than others, so you can guide yourself through scenarios if you want one more than another."

I hated to ask... "What sells?" If I was going to do this, I might as well get top dollar. What had Heinrick said? Enough for ten interstellar tours?

Khor Drath's brow ridge quirked. "Top two sellers are sex and fear."

My heart rate kicked up again. Heinrick had said as much. I'd never been into horror movies. They scared me too much, felt too real. Nightmares weren't my entertainment, even if they gave Rojabians their kicks, and I couldn't see guiding myself into one just because.

I swallowed around the growing lump of nerves in my throat and eyed the big guy with the shifting skin.

Sex it is.

K<small>HOR</small> D<small>RATH</small> <small>PICKED UP A TABLET FROM HIS DESK AND PASSED IT TO ME.</small>
"Here's the contract." The metal felt cool against my skin, but light.
"Take your time. Once you've signed, your dreams belong to me."

His words sounded like a promise, one I didn't know if I wanted,
but it sent a shiver down my spine. The text on the screen blurred for a
moment, then solidified in English like the signs on the street. The first
page was all "the client this" and "the client that," then turned into
"the broker this" and "the broker that" along with a bunch of legalese
definitions which created a pulsing ache in my temple.

I swiped to the next page. My stomach plummeted when the
bottom of the screen read two of one hundred twenty-two. *Shit.* I only
had tonight to do this if I wanted to catch the transport back to Earth in
the morning. Reading through everything would take up all my time. I
jerked my eyes down the page, trying to get the gist of it all before
swiping to the next. By page twenty I was skimming hard-core.

Swipe. Swipe. Swipe. Swipe. All the words blended together. Exhaling
with frustration, I dropped the tablet in my lap and peered up at the
big, swirling nebulous guy. "How do I know I'm going to be safe here
while I'm sleeping?"

"You didn't read page seventy-seven, did you?" His eyes crinkled
with humor and I kind of hated him for it.

"Just tell me."

"The only thing to touch you are the synapse nodes. It's why the whole thing is recorded. You'll be sent a copy of the external recording at the digital address you provide upon completing the contract."

My fingers flexed on the edge of the tablet. "And the ones buying my dreams, they won't know it's me? It remains anonymous, right?" When he gestured to the contract and looked like he was going to tell me to read it, I held up my hand. "Give me the gist of it."

One of his brow ridges—teal now from the way the color on his body shifted—rose in what appeared to be both disbelief and superiority, but he replied, "They experience the dream through your eyes, so no. Not unless you're standing in front of a bunch of mirrors, and I can scrub reflections in post."

It sounded like he'd been doing this thing for a long time. "What's a Sawarstian like you doing in a place like this?" The question blurted out of my mouth before I could think better of it. "Stealing people's dreams? Aren't you supposed to be fighting other planets' wars for them or something?"

His expression shuttered and I immediately regretted the brash statement. He didn't know me and didn't owe me answers.

Tapping on the terminal in front of him, he turned away. "Any other questions about the contract?" He didn't look at me when he spoke.

I shook my head, though I knew I should be asking a million more —if I had any other options.

He gestured at the contract. "Name, date, DNA signature, and digital address on the last page."

I kept swiping until I landed on page one hundred twenty-two, filled out my information, then passed the tablet into his waiting hand.

"Pick a unique phrase," he said tossing it to the side of his desk without looking at it. "I'll program the dream machine to wake you when you speak it. Fail-safe."

I swallowed against the nerves renewing their path up my throat. "Pineapple pizza." Where in the world had that thought come from? I didn't even like pineapple.

"Pineapple pizza," he repeated, his brow ridge, now burgundy, inching its way up into his hairline.

"I said what I said," I muttered, too embarrassed to change it now.

He tapped on his terminal, then gestured to the chair in the middle of the room. "Make yourself comfortable."

My focus narrowed on the black padded seat. I approached it and the tangle of wires like a nest of vipers. Acid swirled in my stomach with each hesitant step.

The ekku leather squeaked beneath me as I sat on the edge and felt soft and cool under my palms. Every shift of my body increased the sound until I settled my weight fully, my neck supported by the pillow-like top and my legs stretched long. The scuffs and dirt on my black boots glared at me, sand from outside trickling from the bottoms to the pristine seat. I grimaced, snapping my head in Khor Drath's direction to see if he noticed I'd dirtied his chair, but his focus was on the screens in front of him, not me.

Fidgeting, I lay back and stared at the ceiling. The wires above seemed even more tangled, a chaotic swirl of black, red, white, and blue. Not quite as mesmerizing as Khor Drath's nebulous skin, but hypnotic nonetheless.

His face loomed above me and I startled, not having heard him move. The nebula on his skin had shifted to reds and oranges. Did his mood affect the change? I was about to ask, when he reached into the mess of wires, pulling a bundled strand of blue and white with a suction cup node on the end.

I tensed, bracing my hands against the arm rests of the chair, then stayed still as he guided the node toward my temple. His fingers were warm, electric, against the cooling sweat on my forehead. I shivered, though the touch remained brief and professional. Another strand of wires came at me, this bunch red and black, and he secured it to the other side of my head with the same efficiency. For a second, I leaned into the touch, then forced my body to keep still.

The chair lurched as he braced his hand above my head and stretched further within the tangled wires. Rose-colored abdominal muscles rippled inches away from my face. Moisture filled my mouth like it would when presented with a decadent dessert. I swallowed, then looked away from his flawless example of physical fitness, forcing my gaze upward again. The wires swayed and jiggled while he searched. My eyes kept straying to his abs. He yanked hard and out popped another node, this one with a wide, clear hat-like cap.

I sank into the chair as far as I could go, fingernails digging into the armrests. Khor Drath tilted his head at me, eyes laughing like he wanted to call me a sissy or something. Scowling, I jerked my chin in challenge, egging him on even though my heart pounded in my throat.

The lines in the corners of his eyes deepened as he sat the curved cap on my head. Something pinched. I hissed through my teeth, frowning up at him.

"Page fifty-four." His voice rumbled through me.

I blinked, not following. "Huh?"

"On page fifty-four of the contract it states the main synapse node may cause mild discomfort."

"Right, yeah. Of course." The fucker knew I hadn't read the contract. *Jerk*. Big, beautiful, jerk.

After one last adjustment, he stepped away from the chair, giving me the once over. "As soon as you close your eyes, we'll begin."

I wondered if I looked like Medusa with all this shit attached to me. Guess I'd find out in the replay recordings. Khor Drath strode across the room. My eyes took in every flex and shift of his back muscles before he settled behind his desk. He tapped on his terminal, and the lights around the perimeter of the room darkened, circling me in a ring of light.

Fortifying myself, I took a deep breath and closed my eyes.

chapter five

AT FIRST, NOTHING HAPPENED. OF COURSE IT DIDN'T. I WAS DISPLAYED LIKE a lab specimen in an experiment, spotlight included. With my eyes closed, I became aware of the low hum of the recording equipment in the room, the flow of air from an atmosphere purifier, and the way my shaky breaths sounded in my head.

I tried to calm myself, taking a deep breath in through my nose, then exhaling through my mouth. It didn't really help. My fingers shifted on the chair arms, the leather squeaking. I inhaled again, forcing my shoulders down into the chair, embracing the fact I needed to chill out if I actually wanted to fall asleep.

What should I dream about?

As soon as I had the thought, the dark behind my eyelids deepened. The subtle noises around me faded away. A strange sensation tugged at my nape and fingertips. The chair beneath me disappeared in a swooping motion. I opened my eyes.

My surroundings passed by me in a blur, like I was in a worm hole, or blasting through space in a pod with an invisible hull. Colors and stars swirled. I caught snippets of images—people, settings, objects— and when I concentrated, those images became clearer.

I rode a rainbow unicorn through a field of blue sunflowers.

I stood atop a mountain, clouds twirling around my feet.

I waited at the starting line of a space race in my very own cruiser.

I shot beyond Earth's solar system in the interstellar tour space transport.

Jordan and I floated in bright green water along with the rest of the tour group. That had been our first stop, the one with the porpoise-like creatures who tickled our toes.

My chest panged painfully at how content and happy I'd felt right then. I moved on.

Jordan eating breakfast at the dining table.

I almost passed the moment to the next one, when I forced myself to back up and keep hold. This wasn't a dream, it was a memory.

My feet settled onto hard ground. I was home. On Earth. Six months in the past.

I'd never remembered my dreams looking or feeling so real before, but this apartment appeared almost exactly as we'd left it a month ago to take our interstellar journey, complete with dirty dishes stacked beside the sink, the half-folded laundry from a basket spread across the sofa, and Jordan drinking coffee while reading the morning media reports off his tablet at our little eat-in table.

Someone burst through our front door, making me jump backward. My spine hit a hard object that shouldn't be there, and I spun around. Khor Drath stood behind me, his skin tones colorful, matching the load of clothes strewn across the surface of the sofa in yellows, greens, and bright blue. My heart jumped into my throat.

"What are you doing here?" I panted, shocked by his close proximity in my memory.

Loud excitement on the other side of the room smothered the question. I spun back to the scene. The person who had burst through the door was me. The old me. And I held the interstellar tours poster in my hand, the one I'd ripped off the train station wall. I shook it in Jordan's face.

"We need to do this! It'll be amazing!" I'd thought the trip would give us a change in focus, take us away from the day-to-day drudgery that had become our lives.

Jordan looked up from his tablet slowly, measured, like I'd inconvenienced him with my presence.

I didn't need to listen to this conversation, I'd lived it, but watching the scene from this angle, I saw the grimace cross his face. *He hadn't wanted to go.* He barely paid attention while I told him all the reasons we should do it. How come I'd never noticed this before? That he didn't care about what I cared about? That no excitement remained between us?

I fisted my hands, angry at myself and him. I'd blindly remained in a relationship which only survived on a thread of the status quo.

"You don't need to be here." Khor Drath's voice had the same effect on my body as it did in real life, the deep of it resonating low in my stomach to spread downwards between my legs.

His statement pushed me onward, past my memories and to things I no longer recognized, worlds I would never have been able to dream up on my own. Yellow skies. Purple water. Blue fire erupting from the ground to turn into mist. A fleet of ships. Laser fire. A battle where one faction resembled Khor Drath.

I stopped and held onto the vision.

Bright sunlight from dual suns stabbed towards me. I squinted against the glare, shielding my eyes with my hand. I stood in a field, in some plant like clover, but the foliage blazed neon pink against navy blue undergrowth.

This felt like a memory too. But not *my* memory.

Hundreds of aircraft blotted the sky. No, not aircraft, warships. They descended through the atmosphere, hulls bright red where they broke through the stratosphere. The ones closer to the surface glinted a deep purple color, almost black.

The closer they came, the more shadows cloaked everything. The hum of the engines mutated into a deafening rumble. I covered my ears. Some of the ships landed in the distance, in front of a yellow and white forest. Others flew overhead continuing toward a massive opposing army. More hovered right above me.

Boom. Something exploded. I turned in time to see a pulse shot from one of the ships to the army below. Shielding shimmered over the group and they remained unharmed.

Tethers dropped from the hovering ships above. My breath caught as I watched warriors spin down those tethers with unfathomable ease. They hit the ground. *Thunk. Thunk. Thunk. Thunk.* Their skin twisted with colors of pink, dark blue, and black. All sorts of gleaming weapons covered the bare skin of their bodies.

I kicked myself for not asking more questions when Sawarstians came up in past conversations, but rifled through what I'd heard.

It was said their mere presence won the war.

That they shared some sort of telepathic hive mind when in close proximity.

That they chose their battles based on ethics, not by the amount of money promised.

That they lived hundreds, if not thousands, of years.

And when not at war, they searched for their fated mates.

One of the Sawarstians landed right in front of me, then strode forward. I gasped as he walked right through me.

Oh, right. I was dreaming. I'd forgotten because everything felt so real.

Then I spotted Khor Drath. Except it wasn't the Khor Drath I'd met at his lab. This Khor Drath wore the same dark burgundy pants as his fellow warriors, numerous deadly weapons strapped to his body, blades and blasters alike. I swallowed the sudden moisture in my mouth. He shouted to the heavens amid the warriors, then surged ahead.

Dear. Fucking. God.

I couldn't move, though somehow kept sight of him as he cut a path through his enemy. One hand held a blade that slashed and stabbed, the other a pulse gun that leveled those who dared step in his way. Blood sprayed everywhere.

All saliva dried in my mouth as I stood frozen in both horror and awe. Why was I dreaming this? *How* was I watching this? Was it real? In my wildest dreams I didn't think I could have come up with something like this. My dreams last night had consisted of me trying to push Jordan and his new girlfriend out a malfunctioning airlock.

"Battle dreams are a dime a dozen."

I jumped at the nearness of Khor Drath's voice behind me, so close his breath grazed against my ear. The heat of his body warmed my spine.

"What are you doing here?" I knew with my whole being the Khor

Drath at my back wasn't the same as the Khor Drath caught in the scene.

"This is your dream." His voice rumbled through my spine as surly as the weapons fire made me flinch. "Ask yourself that question."

The battle thundered too loudly for me to think.

"Better to take yourself somewhere familiar. You can go wherever you want to." His eyes burned bright, centered entirely on me when I peered at him over my shoulder. "The possibilities are endless."

I closed my eyes and focused on what I loved most in the world. For long moments, the blood and gore played behind my eyelids in a kaleidoscope of pink, blue, yellow, and red.

Then the battle cries around me faded.

chapter six

WHEN I OPENED MY EYES, THE SOUND OF RUSHING WATER FILLED MY HEAD. Blinking against subdued sunlight and blue sky, it took a moment to orient myself. Cool air brushed my skin for the first time in what felt like forever after visiting so many warm planets. I was surrounded by forest: tall pines, and birch, and poplars. The familiar sight of Earth's trees relaxed my shoulders a fraction. A creek gurgled in front of me, only a few meters wide, steam rising from its surface. Up the embankment, a waterfall gushed off a squat ledge, pummeling into the pool below. If I stood beneath it, I knew it would be warm, and filled with enough power to knock me over.

I gasped as recognition flooded me. *I know this place.* It was a remote waterfall in British Columbia, one I'd trekked to over the course of three days with two other nineteen-year-olds I'd met while backpacking. This was before I'd met Jordan, before I'd settled in the city for good. *Before my life got boring.*

And one of my fondest memories.

A figure floated, naked, in the center of the deep pool. From the tips of his toes to the thick cords of his hair, skin swirled with the greens of the trees, yellows of the moss, and blues of the sky. His cock lay against his thigh, thick like my arm, and pulsed with the same colors as the rest of him.

I swallowed against the sudden dryness in my throat. "There are still two of you?" Without looking, I knew another Khor Drath stood behind me, though I didn't know why I knew that. Maybe the heat of him warming my spine, or the way the air moved around both of us, his body protective.

"It appears so."

I turned at his tone. He rubbed the bridge of his nose, forehead furrowed the same as when I'd first met him at his door, like he processed a thought as deep as his voice. "This is a place you've been before?"

I nodded and took in the landscape in front of me. "This is my home world, in a remote, secret hot spring not many are privileged enough to see." My eyes returned to the naked figure in front of me. "Why are you here? Why are there two of you?"

"This is your dreamscape."

His voice whispered against me ear, but when I tilted my head to look into his silver-white eyes, he was gone, the wind brushing my spine in his absence.

I spun around, panicked he'd disappeared. No matter where I searched, I couldn't find the second Khor Drath, the one who'd felt as real as me.

My eyes landed on the version of him floating in the pond. This was my fantasy, and my way off Rojab One. I swallowed, then grabbed the hem of my tank top.

Khor Drath moved suddenly, waves sloshing around his body as he straightened. Water dripped from the cords atop his head, splashing to the surface.

Pausing with my shirt half-way up my torso, my gaze remained captured by his form as he swam toward me. I stayed frozen when his feet hit the bottom of the pond and he stood to his full height. Gaze locked on mine, he walked toward me. Water sluiced down his muscled chest, his hips, his cock, and legs.

Dear lord, why had I imagined his cock so big? He was going to split me in half.

This is only a dream.

Right. My dream pussy could take it.

Pushing my nerves aside, I yanked my shirt over my head. My nipples hardened in the cool air.

Where had my bra gone?

This is a dream. Only a dream.

Why did I keep forgetting that?

Probably because you're dreaming.

Fantasy Khor Drath stood in front of me, only inches away. Water dripped from his cords and down his arms. I kept my eyes averted from his cock, though the temptation to stare below his waist was a big one.

You can do whatever you want! It's your dream!

Yeah, but that meant the real Khor Drath would see this! The big guy probably sat at his desk right now and laughed at the size I imagined him. And I was about to take advantage of this dream form. Embarrassment made my heart race all over again.

Dear lord.

Before I could let mortification completely take over, fantasy Khor Drath reached and grabbed my hand. Wet, but warm, skin slid across mine as he tugged me toward the edge of the water.

"Hold on. Hold on." I pulled away from him. "Don't want to soak my clothes." I reached for the button of my cargo pants.

He smirked. In a flash, my pants disappeared. Cool air swirled between my thighs. I glanced down at my naked body. My hiking boots were gone too, the soles of my feet pressing into uneven, damp, stones.

My head whipped up to meet his amused stare. "Did I do that or did you do that?"

And if he did that, why would he have control of *my* dream?

Instead of answering, he pulled me forward with a gentle tug. The warmth of the water spread across my feet and tickled my ankles. The rocks turned to silty sand, puffs of gray blooming below the surface as I kicked up the soft substance. Warm water lapped at my calves, then knees. All the while, Khor Drath's eyes swept over my curvy body in appreciation, heating me more than the hot spring ever could.

I chanced a look downward, and the tree trunk between his legs grew larger. My fingers flexed in his, my free hand twitching at my side.

"This is your dream," he said pulling me closer. "You're in charge."

I'm in charge.

With my next step, the water lapped around my thighs. I pressed my hand against his chest, like I'd wanted to do since I first saw him filling his doorway, and stroked over his smooth pectoral muscles. He sucked in a breath as I passed over his forest green nipple.

His reaction filled me with courage. I wanted to make this large, spectacular man feel good, even if it was in a dream. I wanted to watch him come undone.

I pulled my other hand free and caressed over his shoulders. His silver-bright eyes lit up. The strangest sensation swept through me, that this wasn't the dream Khor Drath I'd seen when first arriving to this scene, that he was the Khor Drath who'd been standing behind me since the beginning of the dream session.

But that wouldn't make sense. Would it?

I shook the thought from my head and decided that no matter what happened in this dream, I was going to enjoy myself.

Because a better dream means a bigger sale, right?

The money didn't seem to matter anymore as I petted the big guy in front of me, his skin shifting colors beneath my hands. His body temperature ran hotter than the water and I couldn't get enough. I skimmed my palms along his ribs, over his abdominals, then up towards his throat.

He stepped further into the pond, and I followed, not wanting to stop touching him. I gasped. The water swirled between my thighs, caressing the edges of my lips in warm laps. He noted my reaction, his eyes narrowing on my face, the intense focus lighting my skin.

"What do you need?" His voice deepened, making my already sensitive pussy quiver.

"I need you to touch me." The words came out husky and raw.

A low growl rumbled from his chest, vibrating through my fingers to race down my arms. His palms skimmed my hips, pulling me closer. He towered over me despite the way the bottom of the pond sloped gently downward. Our bodies collided and we groaned. Naked Khor Drath felt amazing. Muscles, and heat, and damp skin, and everything I needed in my life. He stroked my arms, my back, then grasped both my ass cheeks in his big palms and pulled me hard against him.

His baseball bat cock swelled, pressing against my curls. I shifted upward a little, letting it slide between my thighs. He groaned. I sighed. God, that felt good. It pressed against me with such insistence. When I widened my stance, a small tilt of my hips rubbed my clit against him at just the right spot.

Back and forth I moved, my eyes glued to his as he let me get myself off.

"I want to kiss you," he murmured, a plea in his tone.

Dream Khor Drath was so polite. And I was extremely grateful dream Khor Drath knew what kissing was. Not every alien did.

"I want that too."

His bright eyes beaming down on me, he bent his head.

I met him halfway, impatient, gripping his neck to keep my balance. Our lips smashed together, inelegant for a dream, but hot. *So hot.* Pleasure coursed through me, making me lightheaded. His lips tasted sweet, like candies from the corner store. The scent of him, a comforting spice I didn't recognize, surrounded my body. His tongue must be longer than a human's because it explored the entirety of my mouth like it had a mind of its own. My fingers dug into the flesh of his neck, holding on tight as he plundered. My head swam with sensation. I wouldn't have thought a tongue could be electric, but sparks shot off between us, increasing the pleasure.

Dear lord, how would this tongue feel between my legs?

Like he heard my thought, he lifted his head and smirked down at me.

Then he took over, my feet no longer touching bottom as he pulled me up against him. My legs automatically wrapped around his hips and I pushed up. This was a better angle now, our mouths and tongues gliding over each other's at equal height.

My open pussy pressed against his abdominals. I tilted my hips up and down, creating more friction, wet on washboard. His cock kicked up against my ass and all I could think about was how much I wanted it inside me—no matter how big it was. My desperate fingers grabbed hold of the thick cords of his head. Khor Drath hissed against my lips, sounding partly in pleasure and partly in pain.

"Harder," he demanded, right before kissing me again.

I tugged. He groaned. I kept gripping him tight as our kiss increased in temperature, loving the way his tongue took possession of my mouth.

His hand skimmed up from my ass, across my ribs, to my breast, leaving goosebumps in its wake. While his tongue plundered, his fingers kneaded the flesh of my breast, then toyed with my nipple. Electricity zipped through my body, amping up my desire.

A pulse of pleasure rocked my clit. I couldn't stop jerking my hips. The heat within me grew until there was nothing left except the need to explode. Faster and faster I thrust against him until he stopped playing with my breast, thrust his hand between us, and speared me with two of his thick fingers, his thumb pressing and swirling against my clit.

I detonated with a scream against his lips, the sharp sound echoing off the trees. He swallowed the sounds with his mouth and tongue, licking into me while his fingers and thumb pulled every drop of pleasure from between my legs. I twitched and thrust, movements slowing as I returned to Earth.

A murmur of discontent escaped me when he pulled his fingers from my core. With his one hand gripping my ass tight and holding me against him, his other came between us, wet with my juices. I watched, transfixed, as he licked his digits clean, his amazing tongue not missing a single drop. My pussy clenched on nothing. My heart had started to slow, but sped up again while I stared at the heated look in his silver-white eyes, like I was the most delicious thing he'd ever tasted.

Dropping his hand, he kissed me again, holding me tight against him. I flexed my thighs and pulled on his cords, wanting to give him as much pleasure as he'd given me.

"I want to take you somewhere," he said, breaking the kiss to grin down on me.

I swallowed. "I'm pretty sure I'd allow you to take me any time, any place."

His grin grew, then the forest faded away, and I was nestled in space, in the arms of a nebula.

chapter seven

MY BREATH CAUGHT IN MY THROAT AT THE BEAUTY OF IT. PURPLE, magenta, navy, and teal dust particles and gases swirled around us and beyond as far as I could see, all co-existing on a backdrop of pitch black dotted by pinprick stars. Snaps of electricity lit up sections in waves. This was more beautiful than anything I could have ever imagined on my own.

We floated together, weightless. My grip tightened around Khor Drath's neck, holding him close to squish my cheek against his shoulder as I took it all in. Silence pressed in from all directions. Back at the hot spring, it had been quiet because we were the only people around, but the soothing wind and gurgling water, the rustle of leaves and the buzz of insects, had all composed the ambient soundtrack.

Here, in the black of space, there was nothing, the silence haunting and absolute. Not even the pulsing electricity made a sound.

I should be freezing. Space was a killer—colder than ice with no air. But here, warmth surrounded me, my breaths able to flow freely, my skin as comfortable as it had been in the steam of the hot spring. I lifted my head and looked up at Khor Drath, wanting to know why we were here.

This is where my people are birthed, he said in my mind, pushing all other thoughts from my head, his voice as deep and transformative as it was in his lab. *Somewhere humans can never go.*

I straightened a little, trying to process what he said. Birthed? "You can breathe in space?" My question was silent, the sound disappearing as air passed my lips.

How was it possible to be birthed in space? I scanned my surroundings with care, trying to figure out if I was in a nebula, or something completely different.

If my kind don't encounter their mate within the nebulae, we quest across the stars until we find them.

Movement caught my eye, the colors rippling a fair distance away. I squinted. *What is that?* Two undulating forms materialized the longer I stared, people, *aliens* like Khor Drath. They were trapped in a sensuous embrace, rocking together in erotic motion. My lungs tightened. The silver-white of their eyes blended in with the background beyond, their coloring making it almost impossible to see their forms.

Khor Drath moved around me in a fluid way I couldn't comprehend, fingers skimming my skin, creating shivers.

I will make you forget every unworthy partner who has come before me.

His large hand took possession of my left breast, while the other slid between my legs.

I will protect and cherish you as only one of my people can. Provide for you in any way you can conceive.

The heat of his body pulsed through my spine from shoulder to ass as he dipped his fingers back inside me. A moan wanted to escape me but was smothered by the void. I widened my legs and he delved deeper, stroking, pleasing, drawing whimpers that made no sound.

Not only do I want to take you here in your pleasure center, but in your mind as well. I need to entwine our souls and learn your secrets, your desires, your needs.

Sensuous tendrils of sentience caressed my mind, alerting me to his presence deeper than what his voice touched. For a second, I tensed, but then relaxed into the sensation, giving him permission to explore me fully.

That's it. His voice inside my head took possession of me as wholly as his fingers. I thrust my hips, gyrating. *Take it all.* His digits scissored inside of me, intensifying the stretch, while his cock pressed insistently between my upper thighs. *So good for me.*

The force of his mind in mine wasn't an invasion, but another way to make love to a part of me, eliciting a silent gasp from my lips as he discovered the inner secrets of my soul and shared every facet of his. How he'd acquired a fortune over several lifetimes waiting for me. How he longed to give me the world, the universe. How once he took a mate, his lifespan would align and he would no longer be an eternal creature with no purpose. How he'd prayed to all the gods and goddesses who would listen that each new day would be the one when he found the person meant for him.

Then his mind wrapped around my past, seeing the goals I'd envisioned then abandoned, how I'd never wanted to stop traveling, but my money ran out, forcing me to make a life for myself in the city. How I'd met Jordan through friends, and for a time how things had seemed perfect.

Khor Drath's mind stroked each of these thoughts, comforting, soothing, and my blooming bitterness gave way to contentment. The sensation felt tangible, even though I knew it couldn't be. We existed in a dream. I couldn't really be here in this nebula surviving in only my skin, but my mind didn't want to accept that.

And the more he touched me, the more needy noises wanted to escape my lips, but were snatched away before I could make them. My eyes remained fixed on the other couple as they twisted and churned around one another, their erotic display adding to the heat building inside me.

The longer I stared, the more couples manifested, trios and larger groups too, all of them ensnared in sensual embraces, taking and receiving pleasure. *Space orgy*. They were much like humans, but oh, so different. My eyes skimmed over breasts, and cocks, and cords, and pussies, and fingers.

Every touch from Khor Drath stoked my fire. I didn't know where to look, and couldn't contain my fevered emotions. A flick of his finger over my nipple shot charged heat directly to my clit. I gasped, then pulled his fingers from my breast to suck on them. The taste of his electric skin coated my tongue.

Need you. Need you. Need you. I chanted the words inside my head in time with pulls of my mouth, hoping beyond hope he understood what I wanted.

He spread me wider, his cock nudging my entrance. *Yes. Yes. Yes.* I needed him inside me so bad—to the point if it didn't happen, I'd die of unfulfillment.

Can't have that. Lust and humor tinged his tone. His cock probed, then pulled away. He did it again, and had me panting, his fingers circling my clit over and over.

Don't tease. I bit down on his fingers then soothed the area with my tongue. *Want you inside me.*

Finally, he thrust upward. Stars went supernova behind my eyelids. The first two inches of him was the best thing I'd ever experienced. Floating like this, I had nothing to brace against, but did my best to push back and take him. Our movements propelled us in a different direction, the nebula's colors spinning. Each new inch of him made me moan and sweat, eager to take more, though it felt like I'd already been stretched to the max. His hand moved from my mouth to my stomach and he held me close, bracing our masses together.

That's it. Take me. So tight. So perfect for me, my mate.

The endearment pinged around in my head, refusing to settle, but meaning everything. Reaching behind me, I gripped one of his cords, my other hand digging into the meat of his thigh. A soundless groan vibrated through his body as he bottomed out, the stretch unreal.

Fuck, yeah. I knew he would split me apart. And it hurt *so good.* I'd never been stuffed so full in my life.

He began to move, small thrusts at first, then became insistent with powerful jerks of his hips in and out. *Yeeesss.* I loved it. Couldn't get enough. Wanted more. Never experienced anything like it. The fingers of his one hand moved to my clit, while the other pinched my nipple. We created as carnal a display as any of the pairings and groups around us.

Our tempo increased and so did my breaths. With each slide of his cock inside me, my pleasure climbed higher, his thickness hitting just the right spot over and over again. His lips, then teeth, skimmed my neck, my shoulder, and I turned my head to capture his mouth.

The silver-white of his eyes shone down on me as our tongues tangled and stroked. My emotions swelled, a poignant, pinching sensation growing within my breast. This felt so right. So perfect.

His movements turned frantic, feral, undisciplined. His hunger fed my own passion. The two of us were trapped in a cyclone without escape, the intensity increasing. I didn't want to escape the chaos, not at all, and dug my fingernails into the skin of his cord and thigh.

Another soundless groan vibrated through my spine. His hot cum exploded inside of me, setting off my own orgasm. I left my body then, my cells turning into specks of dust in the nebula, soaked in pleasure, the inside of my head buzzing. I floated away in a million little fragments.

Thick arms wrapped around me tight, holding me close as I returned to myself. I opened my eyes to see a different view of the nebula. Pink, mauve, and red beings undulated to a silent beat, mesmerizing in a fundamental way. *Every time I see a nebula from this day forward, I will wonder if beings are having orgies in them.*

Khor Drath moved behind me, and I gripped his thigh tighter to keep him still. I didn't want to separate from him, didn't want to lose this weightless joy we'd attained with one another. His lips pressed against my hair, my neck, my shoulder. I turned my head and he kissed me, the touch filled with emotion and longing. We drifted, fused together, for what seemed like hours.

I jolted from our peaceful state when he began to pull out. The slow slide of his cock out of my channel sent aftershocks of pleasure through my nerve endings. My gasp disappeared before it passed my lips. He turned me in his arms, and I wrapped my body around his to hold him tight. I buried my face in his throat, inhaling the electric spice of his skin.

A sadness overtook my mind. I could never visit this place, be with this man like this, in real life. *I wish we could stay here forever.* Why did it have to be a dream?

The thought woke me, and I gasped, my eyes flying open, to find myself lying on a black leather chair in the middle of the lab.

chapter eight

I BLINKED AS I RETURNED TO MYSELF, MY BREATHS COMING FAST AND HARD like I'd just run a marathon. My fingers fluttered down my body, taking inventory. I wore the same tank top and cargoes I'd had on when I'd arrived. Scuffed boots stared at me from the end of the footrest. My nipples were as hard as rock, and my pussy soaked, but not sore like it should have been if what I'd dreamed actually happened.

My head whipped to the left. Khor Drath was where I'd left him, on the other side of his desk behind his numerous monitors. His silver-white eyes met mine. *Fucking hell.* Heat scorched my cheeks. He must have seen everything I'd dreamed about him. That was the point of all this, wasn't it? To record my dreams?

"What was that?" I pressed my hands to my hot cheeks, wishing the chair would eat me like a real ekku would so I didn't have to face my mortification. "It felt so real, like you were there with me."

He stood from his seat, his gaze fixed on mine over the screens. Was it unhinged to think those eyes held heat? That he'd liked my dream? An echoing warmth spread through my belly and I clutched at the arms of the chair to hide the reaction.

With measured movements, he walked around his desk, then toward me. My heart raced with each step closer.

"My people have the ability to dream walk," he said, his growly voice rumbling through the room. "But only with a select few…significant people who are…important to them."

"What do you mean?" I whispered, my breaths coming faster and faster as he drew near. "You were really there with me?"

He stopped beside the chair, his thighs almost touching the arm where my fingernails had left indentations in the leather, and nodded once.

My heart stopped. It wasn't only that he had seen what I'd fantasized, but he'd lived it? As an active, willing participant? If the bulge in his tight pants was an indication, then he really had. Would he be the same size in real life?

My gaze flew back up to his when the other thing he said hit me. *Important people to them.* "You called me your mate," I blurted, my fingernails digging into the chair to keep me still, to not dive for him like my body was telling me to do. "It's said your kind search for your mates an entire lifetime."

He nodded again, a small movement. "An oracle on Deeha Prime told me I'd meet my mate on Rojab One." His hand lifted, then stretched toward my temple where he tucked a stray piece of hair behind my ear. "When I saw you at my door, I knew my wait was over."

The air in my lungs froze. I was his *mate?* Truly? The idea was too far-fetched, too fantastical to entertain. But the fluttering of my stomach, the blood pumping thick in my veins, wanted it to be true.

"How long have you lived here?" I was both scared of and *needed* the answer.

His fingers skimmed across my cheek to cup my jaw, creating tingles in their wake. "Almost two hundred years."

He'd waited that long for me? My head, my whole body, went weightless in realization. In the next breath, I launched myself at him. I kissed his cheeks, his nose, his forehead and pulled on his cords of his hair. He captured my lips with a groan, squeezing me tight to his bare chest. And suddenly, there was too much clothing between us.

He seemed to be thinking the same thing, because his hands fumbled with the top of my cargoes.

I broke the kiss to pant, "What was the talking in my head thing?"

Like this? And there he was, filling my mind. Exactly where he was supposed to be. He unzipped my pants. *Need your flavor on my tongue.*

"Yes." It was exactly what I needed. Especially with how long and thick I'd managed to make that appendage in my dream. What had been him and what had been my imagination?

The nebula definitely had to have been his creation. I couldn't have thought it up on my own.

He laid me back on the seat, then slid my pants and underwear down my legs. The cool air of the lab swirled between my thighs. I was as wet as I had been in the dream. He tossed my clothing over his shoulder and hunkered down in front of me, hooking his arms around my thighs to pull me closer to the end of the chair.

This. He pressed my knees up and wide, exposing my center to his hot gaze. *This is how I need to taste my mate.*

The position made me feel vulnerable, but also powerful beyond words. That I could bring this spectacular being to his knees. That his need to pleasure me was so great. I gripped the edge of the chair and held on for dear life.

"Oh, God." The first swipe of his tongue from my ass to clit sent electricity through my body like I'd stuck wet fingers into a live power junction.

So good. His voice in my head was as intimate as his tongue against my body. *So perfect for me.*

His tongue delved deep, as thick as some human cocks, but more satisfying with the way it stroked my G-Spot with unerring accuracy.

I want your scent on my skin.

Him being able to stuff his face and speak to me at the same time was a whole new level of erotic. He licked and sucked, then focused all of his attention on my clit, swirling his tongue around and around.

I love the way your petals feel against my tongue. The scent of your arousal on my chin. The silk of your thighs against my cheeks. I want to bathe in your fragrance.

He thrust two fingers inside me, stretching my needy pussy. It pinched then gave way to pleasure and I wanted more.

You feel amazing, like this pussy was made to be pounded by my cock again and again.

I bucked against him, unable to stop the thrusting motions of my hips, searching for the peak of my pleasure.

You like that? When I tell you my deepest fantasies, all my lustful thoughts?

"Yes!"

You want me to tell you everything I've wished for in a mate and now that you're in front of me, you're even better, more perfect than anything I could have imagined?

Yes!

Never in a million years could I have imagined anyone as pleasing as you.

The heat inside of me climbed, entwined with the presence of his mind. I felt split open, not only my thighs and how he played between my legs, but in my psyche. Any misgivings I still held disappeared. His mind licked at me, coiled with mine as tangibly as his fingers curling inside of me and how his tongue circled my clit.

His mind stroked the outside of my body too, like a hundred hands on my skin, my breasts, my nipples, igniting my desire past any point of comprehension.

I exploded again, fireworks and stars behind my eyes, my whole body lurching forward. I bowed over Khor Drath's head, the warmth of his cords pressing through the thin material of my shirt. I held him tight against my breasts. My legs shook as pleasure rippled through me. I clutched at him, afraid to let go. Never *wanting* to let go.

My breaths slowed as I dissolved back into myself. I released my hold and melted into the chair, blinking the stars from my eyes. Khor Drath stood in all his nebulous glory. His arms released my legs in a silky glide, creating shivers everywhere. Pleasure and satisfaction covered his face as surely as my glistening juices.

His fingers twitched at his sides, like he wanted to grab me but held himself back. His hungry eyes took in my form. My legs remained spread, open to his gaze, and another wave of heat swept over my skin.

I licked my lips, loving the look of him, then swallowed. He'd given me amazing orgasms; he'd called me his mate. *Where do we go from here?* I asked the question in my mind, hoping he'd hear.

He didn't answer, and I leaned back in a huff, my gaze fixed on the ceiling as I grappled with a mix of emotions. A sense of unreality swept over me the longer I stared at the smooth ceiling above.

Something wasn't right.

My stomach plummeted into my toes, panic squirreling around me in the wake of the free fall. The tangle of wires was missing, no longer hanging above. I touched my head. I'd had no nodes attached to me when I woke.

I lifted my head a bit, meeting Khor Drath's eyes. *What the hell is going on? Where am I?* He didn't move, didn't twitch. The nebula on his skin no longer swirled.

Dread rising inside me, I opened my mouth and said, "Pineapple pizza."

chapter nine

I JOLTED INTO MYSELF AND SQUINTED AGAINST THE GLARE OF THE BRIGHT lights from above. My hand lifted, blocking most of it as the tangled wires came into focus above me. Black, white, red, and blue—they hung heavy like a serpent in the way they had when I'd arrived. The sharp scent of antiseptic cleaner filled my head. My clothing stuck to me in odd ways from the sweat that had dried to my body.

This was real life.

The stuff that had come before…none of it had been real.

The sense of loss following the realization was painful. *Too much.*

I scrambled from my reposed position, yanking at the wires attached to my head and rolling to my feet. My chest rose and fell in fast breaths, overwhelmed, and I met Khor Drath's gaze across the room.

He wasn't sitting at his desk like I'd imagined, but standing at the counter beside it, rigid, his grip digging so hard into its surface it creaked.

I couldn't catch my breath, like I was having some sort of panic attack. My fists clenched and relaxed over and over again, my thoughts disjointed because the world spun chaotically around me. Nothing made any sense.

"What is this?" My voice came out hoarse, like I'd been screaming for hours. I stared at the chair in front of me, at the little crescents my nails had made in the leather. Perhaps I had been. "What happened?"

I knew my questions didn't make sense. Everything was becoming clearer the longer I stood here. *It was all a dream.* My reality solidified around me. I'd come here because I'd lost everything in that fucking sandstorm. Jordan had betrayed me, abandoned me, then took everything. Heinrick had told me to come.

Erotic dreams sold the best.

But those dreams had changed me—deconstructed, then rebuilt me. And they probably meant *nothing* to Khor Drath except that he'd been the star of the show. Just some stupid human's wishful, *sad*, pathetic fantasies. I couldn't meet his eyes and stared at the chair instead.

I swallowed, my chest burning in shame and loss. "Are you going to sell them when you're in them all?" It probably wasn't good for business.

"No." Surprised by the harshness of his answer, I lifted my chin to gauge his expression. It was strange to hear his voice aloud after him being in my mind for so long. "Your dreams belong to me, *mate.*"

I sucked in a sharp breath. Was this true? Had what happened in my dreams have anything to do with the real world? "I don't understand."

He pushed off the counter and the whole surface groaned. "Like I told you, my species can dream walk with our mates. You pulled me in as soon as you fell asleep." He stalked between the counter and the desk, then headed straight to me, eyes burning bright white.

I took an involuntary step back and shook my head. "What are you even saying?" None of what had happened in the dream could be true, could it?

When he stopped, the only thing separating us was the chair. *I knew the moment I saw you that you were my mate.*

The sound of him in my head was like slipping into a soothing, warm bath. My exhale came out shaky, and I realized I'd pressed my hands to my heart. "And you've been here for two hundred years?"

He nodded once, his cords falling over his shoulders.

Relief spread through me. None of it had been fake. But could I trust that?

"Pineapple pizza." I'd never been more terrified to say two words in my entire life.

Nothing happened except a smile bloomed on his face. *I can assure you this is quite real.* He braced his hands on the chair and leaned forward. My body bent toward him of its own volition. *From what I showed you to everything I said.*

"You're my mate?" My voice sounded ragged.

He nodded again.

"And you've been waiting for me?"

Another nod.

"And you want to be with me, and protect me, and live the rest of your life with me?"

With every fiber of my being.

My skin broke out into a cold sweat at how much I wanted that too. "Even when my lifespan is as short as heartbeat when compared to yours?"

I've lived too many lifetimes without you to give up one by your side in exchange for more loneliness.

My chest tightened in a painful way. I could hear, could *feel,* the sincerity in those words when he spoke in my mind.

This was everything I'd ever wanted, to share my life with someone worthy, to be in a partnership which meant something. And from his mind probe earlier, he knew it too.

I wanted this, wanted *him,* more than I'd wanted anything in my life.

"So why are you way over there and not touching me?"

His fingers dug into the leather of the chair. "You signed a contract. I've vowed not to touch you."

My eyes scanned to his desk where he'd tossed the tablet, then deep into his glowing eyes. "That's the only thing holding you back?"

One more nod.

"I verbally break the contract!" I shouted, the sound way too loud in this small space, but I wanted it on record. "You are no longer held by its terms!"

He leaped over the chair like something out of superhero movie, landing in front of me. *Thunk.* I launched myself at him, my legs wrapping around his waist. One of his strong arms tucked under my ass to hold my weight and the other cupped the back of my skull. Even with all my clothes on, the reality of him holding me was so much better than the dream had been. And that had been mind-blowing. I braced my hands on his shoulders, loving the feel of his smooth skin beneath my palms, mesmerized by the swirls of color.

I could stare at him all day, every day, and it floored me I'd get the chance to do just that.

His head lowered to mine and I met him halfway. We both groaned into the kiss. His lips were incredible, soft, and firm. *And delicious.* Better than the dream because I knew he cared. I knew this was real. I knew there would be more—as amazing as that truth was.

The kiss went on and on, both of us content to enjoy this moment and not take it any further. We would have a lifetime for everything else. I could feel him in my mind too, stroking, investigating, the sensation more right than intrusive.

You'll be able to stroke my mind with practice as well.

I wanted that. I wanted to know him on every level like he was getting to know me, to explore the glimpses I'd seen during the first part of my dream.

That and more.

It was his promise, and I would hold him to it.

We broke the kiss, and I stared into his star-bright eyes. My arms flexed around his neck, keeping him close. "So how long is your tongue, really?"

A warm, baritone of a laugh rumbled from his chest into mine. "I will take you to our bedroom, my mate, and you will soon find out."

I returned his grin. "Stellar plan, KD. Just stellar."

about j. e. mcdonald

J.E. McDonald was born and raised in Saskatchewan, Canada, the Land of the Living Skies. As a child, she was either searching the clouds for identifiable shapes, or star-gazing way past her bedtime. She's an anti-morning person who wakes up at 5am to write. Needless to say, coffee is a morning requirement.

She cut her teeth watching Star Trek, James Bond movies, and reading the Harlequin novels her mother left in the bathroom—which resulted in an extremely skewed sense of sex education by age eleven. All of these factors contribute to her love of writing paranormal romance with humor, mystery, and lots of spice.

J.E. resides in Saskatchewan with her husband and three daughters. She is the author of the Wickwood Chronicles, Goldenlach Shifters, and Blueshift series, all available now.

To learn more, visit www.jemcdonald.net

an indelicate negotiation

jem zero

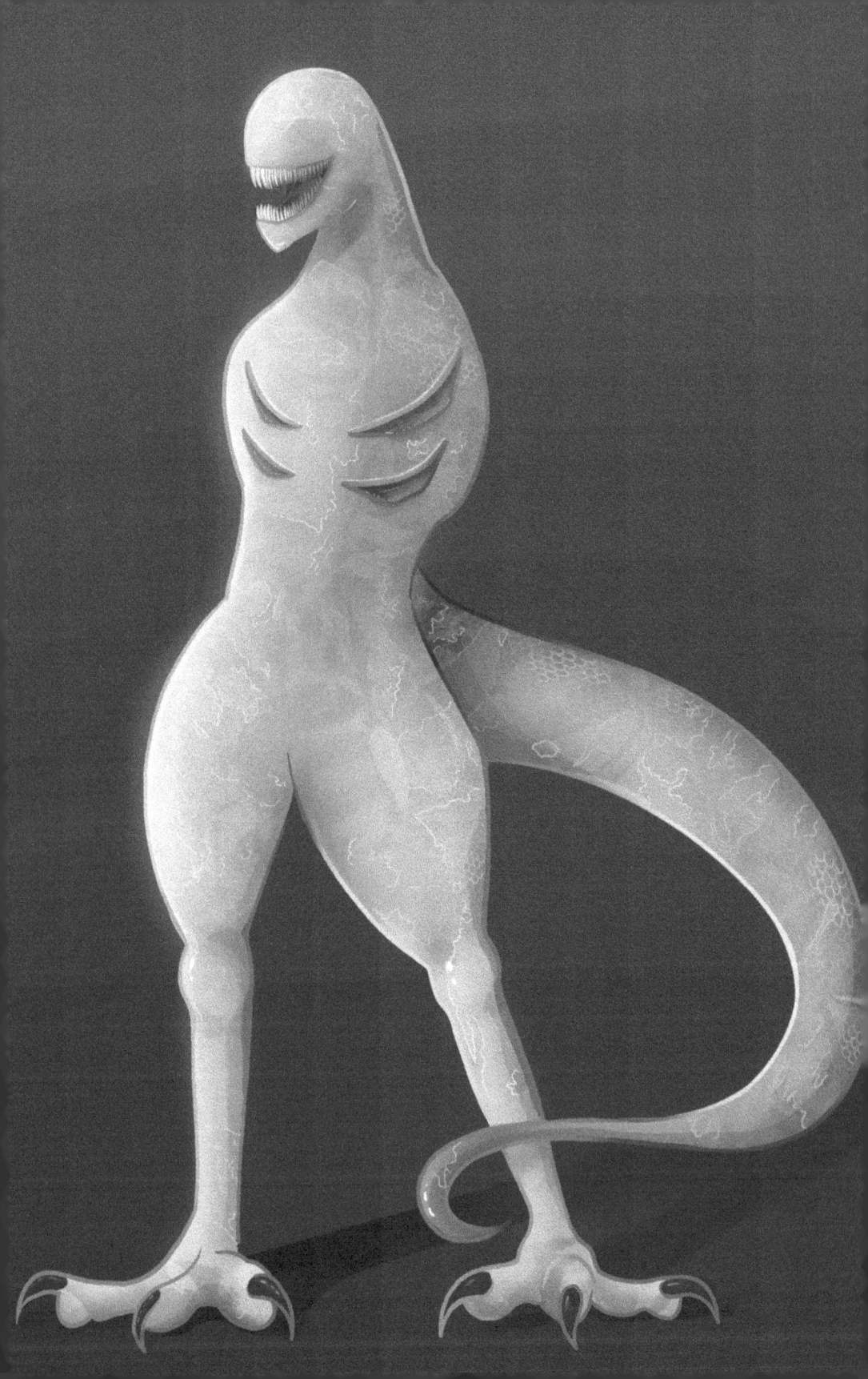

an indelicate negotiation

THE THIRD TIME I'M PASSED OVER FOR A PROMOTION TO PEACEKEEPER, I strongly consider throwing myself out the airlock. It wouldn't accomplish much, considering the *Mainstay* is currently grounded on Oïe, but the melodrama might make me feel better.

This time I was certain I'd make it. I started writing *Peacekeeper Chance Landfall* in my notebooks like a middle schooler with a crush, except the crush was on the position of intergalactic negotiator. My current job is a government position I don't hate. I reach out on behalf of various Earth companies seeking to license trade agreements. The past three weeks, I have worked as a liaison for a hydroponics company looking to acquire harvests of aquatic grasses from brackish Oïe waters.

It's not a bad position. Of my six-person team, I'm the one most consistently pulling in high ratings for successful deals. I'm confident I'll be able to get this company their seaweed in a timely manner.

I take my role in intergalactic trade very seriously. However, my skills are wasted on negotiating issues such as the exchange of CO_2-rich fertilizer for a company that wants to make luxury rugs using wool from a species of alien fauna. Not when I could be leading campaigns to halt potential conflicts and initiate first contact with the inhabitants of other planets.

When each new planet or species takes months to prepare for intro-

271

ductions alone, professionalism is integral. Eight years of encounters and I've never experienced a total loss, unlike several of my coworkers. Researching customs and social etiquette makes a good impression, and I enjoy learning. If I were a Peacekeeper, the fruits of that labor would go *so much further*.

And yet! Not this time. Maybe not ever.

With my office lights dialed down to minimum brightness, the professional space sinks into a hazy, low-vibration liminality, its atmosphere demanding stillness. No one ought to disturb the humming, empty halls of *Mainstay's* business wing, and yet I'm here, feeling terribly out-of-body. It's late, and I should be in my pinhead-sized bed quarters. Asleep.

Except the stress of yet another rejection has snapped my self-control like a brittle twig.

After switching off the automatic opener for my office door, I manually slide it aside just enough to slip into the dark hall. I stay close to the entryway so as to not trigger the motion sensor lighting panels built into the walls.

It's an unnecessary precaution, because a figure turns the corner a moment after I emerge, their armless silhouette a void within the shadows for a scant second before the first light flickers on. As each subsequent panel clicks to life, their progression seems akin to the descending of a celestial being. I can tell when they've spotted me, because the forward march of their powerful raptor legs evolves into an upbeat trot.

A thrill races down my spine.

By the time the Öiet spokesperson, Nuj, stops in front of me, the hall has become fully illuminated, and I feel as if I'm being stared down by a marble statue come to life. Öiet can present a variety of colors, opalescent like polished gemstones, while a closer look reveals a landscape of tiny scales. Nuj's scales are pink shot through with white streaks, and as they shift in the artificial light, bright green highlights erupt across their form.

"Greetings, Mr. Landfall," Nuj says, their voice fractured by static. The translator implanted in their long, sloping neck hasn't yet been properly adjusted to the Öiet voice box. The engineers are working on it, but for now, Nuj's speech assumes a surreal quality, as if they're speaking to me through distant radio waves even though I could reach out and touch.

As the representatives of our respective species, Nuj and I have spent most of the past three weeks in each other's company, but we're not usually *alone* together. Tonight is the first time we've agreed to meet outside of professional hours, and I'm full of wild, nervous energy.

Clearing my throat, I say, "We're not in negotiations, Nuj. Don't you think you can call me Chance?"

"That would be improper," Nuj responds, and gives me a light, playful shove using their radia—an orb of kinesthetic mental currents Ȯiet use to manipulate their surroundings.

The sensation is like being hit by a wave of strong, warm water, reaching deeper than my skin, applying pressure I can feel around my bones. Being invisible, the radia allows Nuj to jostle and nudge me during our meetings without anyone else knowing, leaving me to blame my flustered blush and shortness of breath on my asthma, if questioned by other coworkers.

I've sat with aliens possessing an endless array of unique traits and features. My training ensures I treat every species with the respect they deserve, but the Ȯiet can be unnerving. Most stand slightly shorter than average human height, bearing a resemblance to Velociraptors from the Earth's Cretaceous epoch. Below angular jawlines Ȯiet have no arms, just a torso descending into muscular hips and thighs, raptor legs, and a massive reptilian tail. Thus the radia, because as Nuj has explained, orthotic manipulation is annoying, as their clawed toes frequently fumble and puncture items they'd rather not ruin. None of that even begins to address the alarming fact that they don't have *eyes*.

They are generally a curious, peaceful species, but as ignorant as it may be, the Ȯiet's appearance screams '*Predator!*' to the average human.

Still, I don't fear for my safety around the Ȯiet; if I did, I wouldn't be meeting Nuj alone. No, the reason I'm here is because the predatory way they regard me, the way they smile while drawing inappropriately near, fills me with the most delicious terror I've ever felt.

And I'm painfully into it.

Nuj leans in so close I can see the shallow hills and valleys of skin above their wide rictus smile, thin lips peeled back to reveal hundreds of short, needle-thin teeth. Visually, Öiet faces are nearly impossible to differentiate. They identify one another using a combination of their radia and a type of echolocation to trace the contours of their facial folds; to a sighted species, discerning one from another might as well be palm reading. Öiet don't wear clothes other than the occasional neck wrap with names and credentials. To make things even worse, their pronoun designators are untranslatable—or, at least, the Intergalactic Standard Trade language to which the translators are programmed isn't yet broad enough to grasp the cultural complexity.

All-in-all, a political relations nightmare.

Fortunately, Nuj always makes sure I know who they are, having established unique ways of invading my space. Can't guarantee I wouldn't lose sight of them in a crowd, but I've become deeply attuned to their presence.

I pause to consider them properly—their wholeness, not just their appearance and whether it does or does not intimidate me, and for which reasons. This is a do-or-die moment. Finally, I open my mouth, murmuring, "Well, Spokesperson Nuj. Maybe we can forego propriety if we find some way to be alone."

A laugh crackles in Nuj's throat. "Quick thinking, Landfall. I might be able to arrange that." Then they hip-check the door to my office the rest of the way open and saunter inside, tail swishing behind them.

Tonight is merely a blip in my usual standard for maintaining professional distance. I'll go back to being a perfectly respectable coworker tomorrow.

Drawing one last bracing inhale, I follow Nuj back inside. I engage the lock just in case of attempted intrusion, then turn to see Nuj considering the chess table I set up in preparation of our, uhm, *lesson*. While we were in the office yesterday, Nuj had loudly inquired about the grid-based Earth game; in response, I very innocently offered to show them. No one else would have been privy to their radia slowly drawing pressure down my spine, dipping dangerously low before I shivered and shook them off.

Not here. Not now.

Well, it is presently both *here* and *now*, and as Nuj makes their presence known in my space, the reality of the situation has my palms beginning to sweat.

There are two olfactory organs positioned bilaterally on either side of an Öiet's ribcage: long, angled vents with thin interlocking bars buried about a centimeter deep inside the gaping mouth of each orifice. These are what Öiet use for breathing, smelling, and spatial awareness. Thus, instead of turning their head to examine the game, Nuj shifts their weight and adjusts the angle of their torso.

It reminds me of a chicken holding its head still while its body adjusts to maintain balance. Imagining Nuj as a giant domesticated fowl forces me to choke down a somewhat hysterical laugh, drawing their attention from the chessboard. They smirk with their sharp gash of a mouth, and a shudder raises hairs on the back of my neck.

"Do I want to know what you're chuckling over, Chance?" they ask sweetly.

"Probably not," I admit.

Nuj tilts their head, switching their intense consideration to… me. I suddenly regret distracting them from the game table, because even without eyes, Nuj's gaze is so hot it burns. And their attention lasts and lasts, agonizing because it's impossible to approximate a sightline, and thus I have no idea what they're looking at.

Just before I combust, Nuj purses their lips, then takes a small step toward me. They go still with one foot in the air, the knob of their ankle twitching as they make a silent decision. Then they snap into a blur of movement, scales dark mauve and emerald in the low light. The wide arc of their tail knocks over the game table, scattering chess pieces across the office floor. Nuj doesn't seem to care, and I have more important things on which to focus my attention—such as the fact that they're now in my face, steering me backward. I'm a few centimeters taller, but the size difference hardly tips the scale in my favor, not with them crowding me into the notch between the wall and a bookshelf.

Nuj rumbles, their chest vibrating where it's pressed against mine. "How should we do this?"

Words catch in my throat. I'm not sure how to answer, because what I'm thinking is '*any way we can, with whatever parts are compatible, and however we can wiggle them to get each other off.*'

At my soft choked noise, Nuj laughs like a creaking hinge. "Worry not. We'll figure it out as we go."

Then they kiss me, because at the very least, oral foreplay seems fairly universal.

The entire time we've been working together, I haven't touched Nuj —not once. Without hands to shake or clasp, I learned how to express politeness via body language, shifting weight and nodding my head at different angles and degrees. Observing the other Öiet gave me an excuse to stare at Nuj, taking note of their figure from their dainty shoulders to the pristine obsidian of their wickedly curved claws. Half the time my heart rate would surge in fear of getting caught, knowing Nuj wouldn't let me live it down. Other times I found myself hoping they *would* notice—obviously they did. They've learned much faster than me.

I open my mouth, allowing passage to a cool, sinuous tongue. Nuj is careful with their teeth, not pricking me as they wriggle that tongue farther down until it's fucking into my throat. Pressure from their radia guides my hands forward until I feel the smooth texture of their scales under my sweating palms. I squeeze to test the firmness of their waist. It's more resistant than a human stomach, but still pliant, and the faint texture of their scales makes it satisfying to massage.

Nuj moves one thick-boned leg to settle between my feet so they can press against my front, putting their thigh squarely against my crotch. When they roll their weight, I choke on their tongue.

Nuj pulls away, inspecting me with what seems like concern, until understanding dawns. "*Oh!*" Visibly pleased, they adjust to consider where our lower bodies meet.

It isn't even a lot of contact, just undulating pressure, but the adrenaline has me twice as sensitive, so when I manage words it's only a strained, "Fuck, Nuj…"

They laugh. "Yes, I suppose so."

I rock forward on their thigh as I kiss them again. Their lips are firm and sleek, teeth still politely omitted from the negotiation. I get a wild impulse to ask them to bite me—gently. I've never objected to a blunt-toothed partner getting mouthy before, but this is different. There's an inherent terror of trusting someone who could divorce my larynx from the rest of my anatomy to merely give enough to be pleasurable. It makes my stomach clench in unbearable anticipation.

Nuj touches me with their radia, starting at my neck and moving down. It's a wildly strange sensation—a solid wave similar to the mechanisms in a massage chair, but smoother. The pressure seems to originate from *inside* me before radiating outward. When Nuj reaches my hips they pin me firmly against the wall, running the tip of their tongue along the inside of my teeth, experimental and searching. I'm still too afraid to return the favor lest they accidentally nip it off, but take the opportunity to suck lewdly on their tongue instead.

The noise that rattles free of them startles me, until I realize it was a moan. Nuj repeats the grating sound, then plunges their tongue farther down my throat. I suck harder, eliciting a full body jerk. Nuj rubs against me more insistently, and I join them with a moan of my own. Then they withdraw their tongue, moving to press their mouth to my neck, hissing through their teeth as they nuzzle my throat. I feel their lips peel back, the flats of those teeth running along the length of my jaw with a predatory precision.

Curious and motivated by their budding exploration, I drag my hands lower along the contours of their body, to the tops of their thighs. I don't find anything reminiscent of genitals, not even a slit. I flatten my palm between their legs and press, just in case, but Nuj doesn't react until I reach farther down, running over their scaled skin until I reach the underside of their tail. There's a fold there, but Nuj twitches, flicking their tail to dislodge me, so I reroute, switching to the small of their back. I let my fingers trace the base of their spine, and this time they shudder, mouth opening to release a series of clicks while their teeth-points coming *dangerously* close to my skin. Instead of biting, Nuj latches on and sucks.

My hair is in my eyes, blonde streaks blurring my vision. Groaning, I close my eyes against the distraction. I usually keep my hair styled back, away from my forehead, but the nervous sweat has worked against the product I use. I lift a shaking hand to push it aside, but Nuj catches me by the wrist, trapping it against the wall beside my head.

Their radia continues to roll *against-into* me as their lips move down. They use their tongue to explore, touching my clavicle with intense curiosity before deeming it safe to greet with the rest of their mouth. Desperate to give them more space I try to free my left hand, but they refuse to release it, so I fumble the tiny button at my stiff, high collar with my right hand alone. I succeed, barely, but that's as far as I get, because Nuj follows my example and in one swift gesture pops all my buttons—actually rips one off entirely, sending it plinking onto the floor amongst the game figures. This leaves my shirt hanging open, exposing my bare chest and the thick scars beneath my pectorals where unwanted breasts used to be.

Nuj prods them curiously. "What are these?"

"Scar tissue," I explain. "I had parts of my chest removed."

"Oh." Tongue flicking out, Nuj traces one of them. "What was on your chest? Why would you remove it? Were they parasitic?"

Briefly embarrassed for failing to consider our biological differences, I pause to wrack my brain for terms that will translate to a reptilian alien. Öiet are a unisex species without gender designators, so I need to choose my words carefully. "Mammalian species feed offspring with swollen chest glands." I've no idea how to search their expression for understanding, but they don't interject, so I continue. "Juvenile female humans grow mammary glands on their chests, but some individuals… don't want them."

"But you are a human male," Nuj says as if it's a fact. Behind them, their tail lashes, which I recognize as a signal of curiosity.

Explaining transgenderism to a person wholly unfamiliar with gender as a concept is not the sexiest way to spend our time together, so I rush through the rest. "I was born female, but I was uncomfortable with how that felt. So I changed some things, and now I feel better."

After another moment of contemplation, Nuj says, "There are plenty of species who change sex." Then they fold, dropping to their knees.

Tucking their thick toes in the space between my ankles, Nuj wraps their tail around themself, the tip slithering up the bottom of my pant leg. Their upper body twists, breastbone arching in a manner that would be impossible for an earth herptile, neck bending out of the way so they can see-smell my response. My face reddens both when I'm flustered and when I'm turned on, and right now I'm both, so I must look like a damned spectacle. Hopefully my approach—less smooth sailing and more floundering shipwreck—still manages to inspire arousal.

I consider Nuj with stunned wonderment and a bit of unavoidable discomfort at the unsettling anatomical positioning. The foreign visual further increases my excitement. Palms hot, pressed flat against the cool surface of the metal wall, I try to shake my hair out of my face so I can see better. Nuj smiles, shifting until their head looks dislocated on their neck—and pushes my bangs back for me.

I lose interest in musing on how I look when they lean in, allowing the tiniest edge of their teeth to intimidate the hollow beside my hipbone. The area is unbearably sensitive; I buck in terror so sharp it's nearly painful, arousal surging to ripe agony.

"I liked that," Nuj says, like we're having a normal conversation, and repeats it with more insistence.

Screaming in pleasure might still trigger the distress sensors, so I cover my mouth and bite into the meat of my palm. Nuj continues working their mouth around that soft, vulnerable skin, right above the waistband of my uniform pants, and that's when I feel their radia pat around between my legs. They know I have something erogenous in that area, but haven't yet found where stimulation will reduce me to dust.

Anticipatory, I yank the zipper of my pants, forgetting that there's an inner latch so that when I try to tug my fly open and fail, I let out an embarrassingly distressed sound.

Nuj must know how pants work, because they calmly bat my hands away, gentle like a warm ocean current, and perfunctorily unfasten the clasp. I want to shove the pants to my ankles, but I also want to see what they'll do, so I make what might be a risky move and set my hands on the top of their head, stroking chipped-gemstone scales. Doing so seems to be the right move, when Nuj rubs their temple into my palm and makes a chittering sound that registers as their own pleasure.

I shudder when they lave their tongue up the inside of my wrist.

"You're so fun to play with, Chance," Nuj informs me. Then they peel away the front panels of my pants, pushing them down to my knees, exposing my undergarments. Their radia prods the squishy material of my packer, held in place by my tight boxer briefs.

Another thing I forgot.

"This is human male anatomy?" The confusion in their voice has me realizing they've probably never seen a penis before—at least not a human one.

"An imitation of one, yeah. But let's not talk about it any further, alright?"

Nuj huffs a quiet laugh. "Acknowledged." Regaining control of the situation, they guide the stretchy material down my thighs, then arch to inspect the offerings of my crotch.

I keep my body hair trimmed, so the view of my testosterone-thickened clit is unobstructed, though I prefer to call it a cock nowadays. I'm near-embarrassingly wet, enough to feel slick between my thighs when I shift. Uncomfortable with my restrictive, disheveled clothing, I awkwardly toe off my shoes, then squirm out of my lower garments, leaving me in just my unbuttoned shirt when I straighten. I stand there, cunt fully exposed, and wait for Nuj's next move.

In a way, we're playing a game after all, except unlike chess it lacks defined rules. Flying blind—quite literally, in Nuj's case.

After drawing in a deep breath—fuck, are they *smelling* me?—Nuj smiles. "Very interesting, Chance Landfall. May I touch?"

A giddy laugh bursts from me. "Please. *Please.*"

I'm so turned on I might combust. I have no idea what to expect, but when their tongue slides up my inner thigh to wiggle up inside me, I just about die.

I try to be gentle as I cup my fingers against the back of Nuj's head, dragging them closer while cautious of nicking myself on their teeth. Nuj seems unperturbed: their tongue moves within me like no toy nor dick ever has, and I've had fairly satisfying variants of both. They spread my thighs, then apparently decide there still isn't enough room, because they lift my left leg from under me and settle it over their shoulder. I tense, but Nuj keeps me steady with their radia, increasing pressure on my hips until I stop my panicked squirming. Once I relax,

I'm overwhelmed by the powerfully new sensation of their writhing tongue, only half-wondering how strong Nuj is to be supporting my weight as if it's nothing.

I do my best to muffle the sounds that force their way out of me, and pray the distress sensors know the difference between being stabbed and being fucked.

Nuj's tongue slithers so deep their teeth end up pressed against my pubis. By now I trust them enough to get off on the danger aspect without the unsexy sort of fear. After a few different attempts to stimulate my cock, Nuj figures out how to apply suction with their radia, pumping me like a full-sized dick. No longer able to control my harsh, desperate noises, I buck down, fucking myself on the powerful muscle.

Sex is enjoyable most of the time, but it's not uncommon for me to approach partners with some level of self-consciousness. I can't relax until I'm sure they won't be put off by my body. In contrast, the whole point of this encounter is to *not* relax, and furthermore the person fucking me is so phenomenally, bone-chillingly alien that it's impossible to waste brainspace on judging my potential anatomical shortcomings. None of the usual nerves are there when I seize up, orgasm ripping through me like a plasma ray.

Apparently, the sensors *can* tell the difference between an orgasmic wail and shouts of genuine distress.

"Fucking… tits on a plane," I gasp when I can form words again. That was *fast*, lightspeed compared to the effort previous partners have had to exert to force me toward climax. At some point Nuj returned my leg to the ground, but my muscles are so weakened Nuj has remained supporting me. Quite considerate of them.

"What are tits?" Nuj asks as they adjust, gently lowering my body to their level, settling me with my knees spread on either side of their knobby ankles. My cunt is still sensitive, and the movement alone makes me twitch.

"It's what these used to be." I touch my top scars, which healed more thickly than I'd have preferred, puffy and dark pink. When Nuj adds to the pressure of my fingertips with a brush of their radia, I shudder, even though the area's sensitivity was reduced to nearly

nothing after the surgical procedure. Endeared by their gentle exploration, I ask, "Now, how do I make you feel that good?"

Nuj whistles out a pleased chuckle, then pats my sternum. "Put
your hand here, on me."

I blink. "Where?" All I see are the four slits of their olfactory
organs. Unless—

When I don't move on my own, Nuj leads my hand to the lower set
of openings on their chest.

Oh. My stars.

My fingertips brush the ridges where their scales dip into one of the
slashes, stopping when they bump into the vertical barring sealing it
off. "How do—?" My question cuts off when the barrier begins to shift,
parting into thin protrusions, and I realize with fascination and
outright horror that they are *more teeth.* "What in the endless celestial
fuck, Nuj. Holy shit."

"Don't worry, Chance," Nuj purrs, apparently satisfied with my
reaction rather than offended. "I won't hurt you."

But they *could.*

I proceed slowly, despite being obscenely excited to explore their
unknown. The teeth recede, sucked into the surrounding flesh and
leaving a bluish opening, a dark spot in the otherwise iridescent
swirling pink of their skin. Pushing forth, I'm surprised by Nuj's
internal temperature; their scaled skin isn't cold externally, but within
feels like lying underwater. Undulating pressure, cool and surreal.
Thick wetness seeps from pulsing walls, squeezing my fingers then
letting go.

It dawns upon me that I am hand-fucking another species' organs.

The thrill is so powerful I catch Nuj's mouth with my own,
plunging my tongue between their lips, even though I can't fuck them
like they did me. Obliging, they wrap the tip of their tongue around
mine, squeezing like they're sucking. I moan against the lingering taste
of my own come. As we kiss, I ease my fingers farther into their chest.
A high, wheedling sound, unlike any I've heard Nuj make before,
reaches my ears like music. My hand slides in up to the last row of
knuckles, and Nuj's head hits my shoulder.

"Should I—" I demonstrate, pushing my fingers in and out. "Or…"

I don't know what other motions to use as an example, too worried of messing up with my hand halfway inside their thoracic cavity.

Nuj grunts and rolls their spine so my fingers slip farther inside, saying something in the Öiet language that doesn't translate. After a scorching pause, they grit out, "Just move them," voice even more gravelly than usual.

Okay.

I cautiously roll my fingertips in a wave against the bottom wall of their opening and shiver when they clench around me, like a pussy but flat and cold and nothing like a pussy at all, actually.

Emboldened by the positive response, I leverage the pads of my fingers to press upward, fucking in deep, and clasp the back of Nuj's head when they jerk and moan. I continue to try different things, most of them mindless, twisting and stroking and, most importantly, never slowing the steady stream of movement. They seem to prefer depth, so I try not to pull out while getting creative with gestures.

It doesn't take long for me to conclude that I can do better than this.

I unclasp my fingers from Nuj's swanlike neck, dragging my palm down their chest before plunging my left hand inside their other opening to match the right. Blue fluid squishes out between my fingers, dripping down my wrist, staining the white fabric of my uniform shirt. I can't push the sleeves up, so I ignore it.

Kissing them again, I work both my hands, sometimes in unison and sometimes individually, riveted on the challenge of deciphering their vocal responses. Most of what they vocalize isn't translated, which is fine. This is more primal, me fucking their chest until my elbows are wet while mouthing at their smooth scales, licking the sharp blade of their jaw. They mewl when I bite down on the long column of their neck, and their ribcage heaves when I keep descending.

The cold blue slick tastes like water, slightly tangy. It isn't bad in the least, so when Nuj arches their back with a desperate groan, I lean in with more purpose, tonguing the upper length of their slit. I shift the fingers of my right hand just far enough to the side to allow me to get my mouth onto them properly, sucking along their opening. I can feel faint rows of bumps where their protective teeth hide, capable of snapping closed at any moment should someone prove themself a threat.

But not me. All I want is to move my left hand in and out, rounding the shape to provide a better stretch, while the right fingers flex and rub, leaving space for indigo slick to coat my lips and chin. Nuj's tongue passes through breathless lips, the tip tracing the shell of my ear so I gasp against them, choking on a mouthful of thick fluid. My arms tremble, not helped by Nuj's ministrations, but as I switch my mouth to pleasure the left opening, my right hand creates a waving undulation; palm down, pressure firm and direct and unyielding and—

Nuj muffles a screech against my throat, their devolving control finally allowing their teeth to nick my skin, but I'm unbothered by the pinpricks of pain. I push down as hard as I can, rubbing steadily as they ride out their orgasm, insides tightening around me so snugly that all I can do is push back. Eventually Nuj's thoracic muscles relax, and they nuzzle my temple before slowly drawing away, leaving a string of thick mucous connecting my hands to their swollen, throbbing openings.

I watch the teeth close, and shiver.

We end up slumped side-by-side on the floor, both shaking and wracked by the occasional twitch. Our mutual affliction presents an interesting counterpoint to our physical differences, the way Nuj has to angle themself to avoid crushing their tail against the wall, their chest moving in heaving gasps despite their lips being closed.

Eventually Nuj shifts, humming. "I drew blood," they inform me, not sounding pleased about it. My wet fingers drift to the tiny punctures I barely feel, only for Nuj to smack them away. "Wash first," they scold, only to shamelessly lick the beads of blood drying with the sweat on my neck.

"I've got wipes in my desk," I mumble, not inclined to struggle or argue.

Nuj rises with a groan, taking a moment to ensure their feet are steady before drifting to my desk. The floor is made of a low-impact material, rubbery with a grip to prevent slips, and I can hear the quiet scrape of claws over the ridges.

Raising my voice, I tell them, "Second drawer on the right," but still hear multiple drawers being opened. A small, delirious smile tugs at my wet lips as I listen to Nuj snooping through my personal items. After they allowed me to manually fuck their internal organs, it hardly feels like an invasion of privacy.

Eventually Nuj returns with the wipes, a guileless smile on their face. They clean me up with surprising tenderness, wiping my body all over from my oversensitive cunt to the spaces between my blue-tinged fingers. Hopefully the pigment fades with a much-needed shower, otherwise I'll have some extremely awkward explaining to do.

"Well," Nuj says finally, nudging me to my feet—which I allow, though reluctantly. "I'm impressed, Chance Landfall."

I sway, but they don't let me fall. "What's impressed you?" I can't help a bit of fishing for praise. The denied promotion is all the sting my pride can handle for one-day cycle.

A sawing laugh explodes from Nuj's chest, suggesting they know exactly what I'm doing, but they oblige anyway: "In addition to your exceptional negotiation skills, that was the best I've ever been fucked by another species. Commendable professionalism, Mr. Landfall."

"You consider that *professionalism?*"

Nuj only sighs in contentment.

I shake my head, then slide my ruined, no-longer-white shirt off my shoulders, leaving me completely naked—and I can tell Nuj notices by the abrupt tilt of their head.

"Like what you see?" I tease, before the faux pas hits me. "Oh, fuck. You don't have—"

Throwing their head back, Nuj cackles. "Now *that* was not professional. I'll dock your points for cultural insensitivity."

"Shit."

"And that's another penalty for foul language." Nuj tuts. "I'm afraid one more infraction merits a failing grade."

My lips part, but I can't think of an appropriate repartee.

Nuj saves me with a bump of their shoulder, grinning like a hanged skeleton in possession of forbidden knowledge. "It's all right. If you're that concerned about your grade, I'll allow you to re-take the exam."

I arch an eyebrow. "You'll *allow* me, hm?"

"Generously," they clarify.

"Extremely so," I agree, crossing my arms over my bare chest. "Would you mind handing me my blazer?"

"And if I do mind?"

"Then I'll accept my near-failing grade and report the mission failure to my program director."

Without further protest Nuj grabs the clothing item from the back of my desk chair, then plucks my pants and undergarments from the floor as well. I don't miss their curious squish of the silicone penis prosthetic before they hand everything over, and their smile informs me they couldn't care less that I noticed.

Once I'm dressed—doing my best to ignore the weight of Nuj's unwavering attention—I take a moment to prop my ass against my desk. I consider Nuj, who is now standing across the room, on the other side of the scattered chess pieces.

My heart begins to pound as I take a reckless shot. "Did…" I swallow hard. "Do you think my performance tonight merits a repeat, Spokesperson?"

"Haven't the foggiest idea what you mean, Mr. Landfall."

Ah, fuck.

"My mistake," I say with an unavoidable twinge of disappoint-ment. "Of course I don't expect a prolonged arrangement. That would be presumptuous and possibly compromise our professional deci-sions." I hazard a weak smile. "Wouldn't want you to get soft on me during negotiations, after all."

I didn't fuck Nuj for professional gain, and am loath for it to appear as if that was my goal in pursuing an affair. In the interest of not revealing my foolishly hurt feelings, I turn the toppled game table upright and resolve to pick up all the pieces tomorrow, then navigate through them to the control panel. I reset the automatic sensor on the office door and set the lights to turn off in ninety seconds. Just enough time to make a dignified retreat.

Except when I try to leave, Nuj doesn't move. Their smaller figure allows me to see the only exit with pained longing, but I don't dare push past them. If they didn't grab me with their radia, its full strength still unbeknownst to me, a mere flick of that powerful tail would send me flying.

One long stride brings Nuj achingly close. They brush damp hair out of my eyes, then lean in until our lips graze, just shy of kissing. "Discard your fears, Mr. Landfall," they purr. "I plan to inform our superiors about how impressed I am by your *exceptional* proficiency at business negotiations. We'll proceed with a fresh mutual understanding. And…"

Nut stretches to murmur in my ear. My breath catches when their chest rubs against the bare skin exposed by my partially unbuttoned blazer.

"In the meanwhile, I've found the rules of chess are much more complex than I had expected. Therefore, another lesson is in order. And perhaps a few more after that, if we find our gameplay enjoyable."

I try desperately not to grin, but fail. "That's more than all right on my end. Now, if you'll excuse me, I have to figure out how to bleach my uniform shirt before tomorrow's meeting without raising any suspicions."

Nuj flicks the tip of their tongue over the spot on my neck where their teeth nicked, then withdraws from my space. They swish their tail behind them so the office door slides open with a whisper, then step into the hallway. Just as the door is closing behind them, I hear: "Good luck with that, Chance."

I linger, unmoving, until the timer runs out and the light flicks off, leaving me standing rumpled and alone in the dark.

about jem zero

jem zero (they/them) is an autistic and disabled transmasc who lives with their family in a house built by their great-grandfather. They primarily write queer SFF with strong themes of love and social justice. They have nonfiction personal essays, short fiction, and poetry published by the Thinx Blog, Between the Lines newspaper, The New Smut Project, and Gertrude Press, among others.

More of their work can be found on their website, including their full-length romance novels and award-winning sci-fi erotic short, A STUDY IN CIRCUITS AND CHARCOAL.

To learn more, visit jemzero.com

ratchet and clanked

Kristin Jacques

chapter one

kori

ONE FINAL TWIST TO TIGHTEN A RUSTED-OUT BOLT ON THIS METEOR-RIDDEN undercarriage and Kori would be done for the night. A fine tremor had settled into her arm muscles, aching after wrestling with the damned personal craft for hours. Sweat plastered her grease-stained tunic to her back, the heat in the shop stifling after so many hours of gritty labor despite the filtered air blasting through the vents. Flecks of oxidized metal coated her gloves as she coaxed the worn threads on the ancient junker to cinch completely shut. The rust was a problem. She'd have to talk to the reluctant owner about properly sealing the outer hull before it ruptured on them and made the small craft into a crumpled metal coffin. But that was a problem for future Kori.

The stubborn bolt squealed with the sound of metal on metal that made her back teeth grind. It was as tight as she could make it. Kori draped her quivering arms over the top of the craft, the metal a fraction cooler than the repair bay air and a welcome relief. Her sonic wrench would have shaved hours off this job if the hull paneling wasn't held together with rust and a prayer. Damn Vox—he knew that and still dumped it in her bay before he and the entire crew fucked off for shore leave.

Groaning, she hooked her fingers over the craft's stabilizing fins and straightened up. Through the starboard viewing panel, she caught a glimpse of the massive cerulean planet surrounded by swirls of glittering gold dust that moved through the outer atmosphere like a shifting veil. Vega Surong, the premier vacation destination for the discerning galactic tourist, and an ideal shore leave planet for any overworked waystation mechanic. Which is exactly what her entire crew did, drawing lots over who would stay behind to man the emergency bay while their waystation set up temporary orbit in the planet's outer atmosphere.

Kori sighed, stripping off her gloves. Right now, she could be lounging on one of Vega Surong's sapphire sand beaches, soaking up the sun. Maybe having her clit sucked by one of the natives, who were notoriously receptive to trysts with tourists. An underappreciated highlight of the planet in her opinion, if the rumor about their split tongues was true.

"Fucking short straw," she muttered.

After vacuuming down her work area, Kori stepped into the cleansing pod and let the steam lift the rust stains from her skin.

Freshly scrubbed, she pulled on a clean shirt and shorts before crawling onto the cot set up at the back of the emergency bay. Kori missed her private bunk, but as the lone mechanic on call for the next sixty-nine rotations, the accommodations were necessary. Exhaustion and the thorough cleanse left her limbs pleasantly sluggish, yet sleep hovered just out of reach. She glanced out the viewing panel, lulled by the undulating golden mists that surrounded the planet.

Her lazy fingers drifted down her stomach, slipping beneath the waistline of her shorts to carelessly play between her legs. Her half-hearted movements weren't enough to climax, but she let her mind float on the sensations, shedding the tension her muscles still carried. Her thoughts spiraled out, sinking into an unconscious blank slate, until the incessant chime of the intercom scratched through her groggy brain.

Kori sat up so fast her head spun, tipping sideways off the cot before her body registered the scant hours she'd slept. She tapped the intercom, mumbling a sleepy *Hello?* A disconnected click answered her. Squinting, she finally registered the source of the ongoing chime.

Not the intercom, but the proximity alert. Clumsily slapping at the controls, she shifted the viewing panel to the opposite wall, revealing the object that tripped the alarm.

She gaped. "What in Sagan's black hole is that?"

A sleek craft sped toward the waystation's upper decks in an uncontrolled tumble. Her mind registered the diminutive size of the ship as its trajectory curved, caught in the planet's gravitational pull. Not a craft, but an escape pod. And this close, she could see the faint buckling of the pod's hull against Vega Surong's outer atmosphere.

"Fuck!" Kori flung herself across the controls, holding her breath as the emergency retrieval bot burst out of the rear bay. Her gaze fastened to the pod, counting the vital seconds in her head as the bot drew near it. Retrieval nets burst forth in a silvery bloom that enveloped the ship.

Relief rolled through her when the bot slowly pulled back toward the station, the pod firmly snared in its nets. The moment both were safely within the confines of the rear repair bay, she took off. Her bare feet slapped across the patterned metal floor, but she ignored the discomfort as she reached the damaged pod. The bot had already extracted the craft from its netting, revealing the extent of the damage. Dread pooled in her belly. Chances were slim to none the occupant was still alive, but she had to be sure.

The brush with the planet's atmosphere had distorted the outer hull of the pod, trapping whoever or whatever occupied the craft. Snagging a laser cutter from the tool rack, Kori dropped to her knees, the corrugated metal flooring biting her exposed kneecaps. She paid no attention to the sharp sting of pain, her hands steady despite the fluttering panic in her chest as she carefully cut into the crumpled paneling until the pressurized interior released with a pop. The warped metal cracked, made brittle and fragile by the extreme heat. Kori winced, fearing the worst as she gently pried the panels away to reveal the pod's lone occupant.

She froze in mid thought, caught off guard by the most beautiful person she'd ever seen. Like the cursed royalty of old Earth fairy tales, they lay locked in stasis, pale hands clasped over a flat stomach. Their features were nearly Elverin in appearance, with all the sharp, smooth angles of androgynous beauty the race was famous for, except this person had a lush mouth and cleft tipped nose. Human features, both highlighted by simple golden piercings, caught her eye: a small septum hoop and lip stud that drew the eye to their full bottom lip. Metal caps tipped their ears, connected by delicate chains to a daith piercing. Tousled white-blond hair framed that stunning face, like threads of tangled silk that darkened to lavender at the ends and brushed up and over their bare shoulders. A black sleeveless tunic drew attention to the paleness of their skin, molding over a lean masculine-presenting chest. Her gaze caught on the golden rings that adorned their long, elegant fingers and manicured nails painted an iridescent pearl white.

She absorbed all these details in seconds, her rapt gaze drifting back to the stranger's still features to snag on the tell-tale metallic plating embedded in their right cheek, tracing their jawline. An altered being, a seamless creation of biological and mechanical; the integrated technology alone was enough to make her mouth water.

Kori sucked in a sharp breath. The outer hull panel slipped from her slack fingers, landing with a loud clang that made the passenger flinch, a single crease marring their smooth brow. Their eyelids fluttered open. Silver eyes peered up at her. Despite the lack of visible pupils or sclera, she could feel their gaze tracking over her face. Their brows drew together, a subtle tensing of muscles rolling through their frame that she noticed a moment too late. Their body moved far faster than her frazzled mind could follow, tackling her.

"Shit!" Kori barked. The laser cutter skittered across the floor as she slammed back hard on the unforgiving floor. She hissed in pain, her wrists caught in a crushing grip. Velvet clad thighs bracketed her waist, the soft fabric rubbing against her skin where her nightshirt had ridden up. The stranger loomed over her, ombre hair falling in a tangled curtain while their silver eyes gleamed down at her. No pupils or irises to break up the metallic gleam that seemed to exude malice.

"Whatever the Consortium is paying you, I assure you it's not worth your life." Their voice washed over her, far deeper than expected and laced with a hollow echo that hinted at the cybernetic enhancements hidden beneath their skin. Their thighs squeezed around her waist with a strength that made her wheeze. Kori made the unfortunate discovery her body enjoyed the sensation to a startling degree.

Heat washed over her, flushing through her cheeks and lips as her nipples pebbled, a reaction made blatantly obvious by her thin shirt. "I—I don't know who *they* are," she sputtered. Was she *panting*?

Those silver eyes roved her form before something shifted behind their imperious expression, flaring with calculated interest. Their thighs shifted lower, settling directly over her hips while they effortlessly shifted their hold to clasp her wrists in one hand, the other trailing lazy fingers down her side.

"Then tell me who you work for, pet. Perhaps I can make a better offer." The octaves of their voice modulated into a throaty purr that scrambled her thoughts. They grinned down at her, all perfect teeth and panty-melting charm. Who the hell was she dealing with here? Enhanced or not, they handled her with frightening strength, and the sudden flip from aggression to suggestion should have sent her screaming, but Kori felt the insane urge to shimmy her hips into better alignment with her captor.

She'd been on this station too damned long.

Her fingers spasmed, arm muscles straining against that relentless hold. Kori licked her lips and swallowed, keenly aware those silver eyes observed every reaction. "I work for Vox, and he doesn't work for anybody. Though, I guess, he kind of works for the Alliance like everyone else in the quadrant. Listen, we're above board and certified here—"

"What are you talking about?" The sultry expression faltered. A frown knotted their brow. "Who are you?"

"K-Kori," she stuttered. "The on-duty mechanic."

Their eyes widened. "Mechanic?" They glanced up, finally noticing the state of their pod and surrounding repair bay. "Shit."

The weight of their body vanished. Kori shivered, slowly righting herself to peer at the stranger. They caught her rubbing her wrists and looked away, a faint pink staining their pale face.

"I apologize. I fear I've made a terrible mistake," they murmured, tracing their ringed fingers along the crumpled outer paneling of their craft without looking at her. "Could you please tell me how I came to be here?"

Kori cleared her throat and shuffled closer to the damaged ship, eyeing the interior to see what clues it might offer. A charred control panel answered why it had been careening through space. "Your automated guidance system appears to have shorted out. I won't know more without examining the crash data, but your craft was about to be torn apart by Vega Surong's atmosphere."

Her gaze snagged on a more curious object tucked against the interior. Although the metal case itself wasn't noteworthy, the familiar symbol etched on its side was. The blooming ferienne, a suggestive petal and protruding stamen arrangement, was a well-known symbol for those who practiced a certain profession. Realization caressed her senses. Now she knew why the stranger was so very alluring. Courtesan houses were common throughout the galaxy, boasting many reputable establishments, but not all of them followed the set code of humane conduct. That she didn't recognize the Consortium was telling. She breathed in a delicate floral scent, aware the stranger drew closer, their heat radiating against her back.

"What would overload the system like that?" Their arm brushed against her as they reached out to pry open the blackened panel. The melted mess of wires and circuits made them both wince. "I don't suppose you have transport to the planet's surface from your station?"

Kori shook her head before they finished speaking. "We're operating on a bare bones crew right now for extended shore leave. Won't return for another sixty-nine rotations, give or take." She'd managed a scant amount of sleep before everything went sideways, and now that the rush of adrenaline was fading from her system, exhaustion dragged her hard.

"Stars, I still need to log all of this. We don't exactly have guest quarters in this part of the ship." She rubbed a hand over her face, trying to scrub the sleep from her eyes. "But you can stay in my bunk for now. Sheets are clean." She glanced up to find the stranger hovering far closer than expected, causing her to flinch.

Those intense silver orbs logged every micro movement in her features. "Log? Is that a report? Who would read this report?"

Kori cleared her throat. "A report would be sent to the station commander. She will probably send out a general transmission to make sure there are no ships in distress or other escape pods that need to be picked up." A standard procedure, though she had a suspicion that was not the case. There had been no other debris or signs of other pods. A lone ship, spiraling through space.

They pulled back a step. "There are no other pods." Their gaze shifted back to the open pod, where the metal case gleamed beneath the bay lights. "You said you were alone here. Perhaps, we could discuss the nature of your report first?" Suggestion wove through the delicate curve of their brow and Kori's mouth went dry.

"I don't even know your name," she murmured, shocked by the flush of heat that flooded her system. That indistinguishable floral scent intensified as the stranger reached for her, their thumb caressing her lower lip. Golden circuitry lit up under their skin, rippling up their arm as their face drew closer. Close enough to kiss. Why shouldn't she? They *were* alone.

That sobering thought made her jerk back. She huffed, flapping her hand in front of her face to disperse whatever pheromones were currently cloying her senses. Kori glared at the stranger. "I know what the symbol on that case means." She crossed her arms, ignoring the sensitive brush of her nipples against the inside of her shirt. Little she could do about that now. "Does this Consortium hold your contract? Is that why you tried to roofie me to keep me from reporting your escape pod?"

They blinked, a flash of calculation crossing their features before they bowed their head. "I apologize, Miss..."

Shit, she hadn't bothered to introduce herself either. Embarrassment pinkened her cheeks. "Kori."

"Kori." They licked their lips as if they savored the taste of her name in their mouth. Something dangerous and wild fluttered in her chest. The strength of her desire worried her, and she could tell by the gleam in their metallic gaze they saw it too.

chapter two

wrex

Wrex studied the biological metrics feeding through their sensors. Not that they truly needed them. A short-sighted skiskant could see the female's body was responsive, from the delectable peek of her nipples through her thin nightshirt to the way her skin flushed that alluring pink when they spoke her name. The pheromone glands implanted beneath their collar bones pulsed, sensing her arousal, eager to enhance her pleasure. They gave off a pleasant odor, but only an aroused individual could scent them.

"I assure you; I am not attempting to 'roofie' you," they said, lips turned up in a knowing smile.

This interaction required a more tactical approach, because Wrex could not abide it if her report somehow reached the Consortium. How much distance had they managed to travel from their station? The Consortium's reach was far, and fear twisted Wrex's morals into shades of gray. They would never go back to that living Hell, no matter what they had to do to ensure otherwise. Though they didn't *want* to hurt the female to do so. This woman, Kori, was far pleasanter fare compared to others they had been forced to service under the Consortium's brutal grip.

The sight of her biceps alone made their mouth water, a body toned and built for endurance. Kori nearly matched them in height. Banked desire glazed her bright blue eyes and plumped her full lips. Her sleep-tousled hair was as black as the space between stars, and rose in a messy crest, the sides shaved short.

A scent teased their sensors, and Wrex clenched their hands behind their back. Receptive, yes, and the right amount of suggestion could sway this delicious female to their perspective.

"My designation is Wrexler Trivane, but you may address me as Wrex." They properly bowed to her, hiding their grin when she nibbled on her soft bottom lip. A single touch would be enough to confirm how pleasant it would be to kiss those lips. They kept their proximity to the female, enjoying the little huffs and puffs she emitted in her vain attempts to maintain decorum. Wrex wondered what she would look like undone and what it would take to tip her over that edge.

"Wrex," she breathed. They liked the sound of her voice speaking their name. To their surprise, she closed the distance first, taking their hand in a firm hold, calloused fingertips massaging the smooth skin of their wrist. "Can you help me understand your situation? Tell me what happened?"

Her touch created sparks of desire beneath their skin. Wrex leaned in, skimming the tip of their nose along the curve of her ear. Kori froze.

"Will you report the pod if I don't?" Their breath fanned over her face, stirring the short black strands of hair at her temples.

"I—I, wait, this is—"

Wrex captured her mouth, swallowing her words and the groan that followed, drawn closer by soft lips and slick tongue that they wanted to suck and nip at leisure. They moved further into her space until their clothed chest brushed against her. By the glory, they could feel the peaked buds of her nipples straining through the layers of fabric between them. A problem Wrex planned to remedy momentarily as they reached for the hem of their shirt, breaking the kiss to whip the garment over their head.

The brief break in contact was a mistake. "Whoa, hang on there, stud," Kori wheezed, slapping her palm against their naked chest. "I need answers."

Wrex bit back a scowl, but their disappointment must have been evident in their expression. A burst of panic surged through their system. That small taste of her mouth was enough to keep them calm. Seduction was the key to their survival here, and Wrex was determined to never force anyone the way the Consortium did.

But that didn't mean they could trust this intriguing female to help them evade any retrieval crews sent after them. The Consortium held a contract in Wrex's name, and in this part of the galaxy, that would be legally binding.

"I'm afraid I can't provide all the answers, lovely one," they said, delighted by the deepening shades of red on her skin.

She frowned at them. "What *can* you tell me?"

Wrex pursed their lips. "That I won't be going back." They'd shove themselves out the nearest airlock to suffocate first. That would kill them as surely as any other living thing; their lungs were still flesh and blood.

Kori's fingers shifted over their pectoral muscles. They grinned. She hadn't removed her hand from their chest.

Kori didn't seem to notice where her hand traveled, still nibbling on her bottom lip. "Were you forced into a contract?"

The question made their shoulders go tight, tension spoiling the simmering lust they'd enjoyed until that moment. "My decisions were my own," said Wrex, dislodging her hand with a shrug. "The contract is all above board, if that is what you're asking." They stared, waiting for her to pass judgement.

Her chin lifted. "That doesn't mean it was a good one. Were you mistreated? I haven't personally heard of this Consortium, but most courtesan houses adhere to strict rules of conduct for their contracted and their clientele."

There were rules of conduct? Wrex kept their expression impassive, but the implications of her words wedged an unpleasant truth in their mind. The Consortium might have trapped them after they signed, but this level of ignorance was their fault and that left a hollow ache in their chest. Regardless, their new temporary companion picked up on the inner turmoil, gently gripping their hand.

"I've been on the clock too long. Let me show you to my bunk. The report can wait and maybe, after I get some actual sleep, we can work through this mess. Okay?" Her tone coaxed them forward, letting her lead them away from the wrecked escape pod to an offset hallway lined with sealed doors. Kori stopped at the third one, tapping the biometric lock to the unit.

A modest bunk greeted them, the welcome scent of freshly cleansed bedding lingering in the filtered air. The opposite wall featured a desk that spanned the length of the room, cluttered with deconstructed gadgets and tech in various states of repair. Other than that central bit of chaos, the space was tidy. Kori pulled back the fresh sheets for them to climb inside, taking care not to brush against them as she backed out of the room.

"I'll disengage the bio-lock for the night." She hovered in the doorway, her expressive face cycling through various emotions without settling on one.

Wrex raised a brow. No bio-lock meant they could roam the ship at their leisure. "That's an awful lot of trust for a stranger."

There she went, nibbling her lip again. Wrex wanted to catch her lips between their teeth and take over the teasing.

"I'm a fair judge of people," she said, letting the sentence hang, an unfinished possibility.

How could she be so sure of a stranger? Wrex sat on the bed, their weight sinking towards the center. "Thank you," they said. Perhaps cordiality was best for the moment, but they didn't miss her final lingering glance. A body, willing and receptive, was something they could work with.

chapter three

kori

Sleep was an evasive bitch. Kori glowered at her ceiling. She'd returned to the cot in the control room hours ago. Unfortunately, her mind refused to stop mulling over her guest. Exhaustion left her loose-limbed and foggy. Coupled with her annoyingly persistent, lingering arousal that left her restless and agitated, it was driving her crazy.

Sex work was a universal profession, one Kori respected as she did any other occupation. And just like any physical job, one that came with risks. The crew knew all the reputable courtesan houses in this quadrant of space and often visited them when shore leave allowed. Their current destination, Vega Surong, was a highly regarded pleasure planet, boasting the highest number of established houses in the galaxy. With no working knowledge of the Consortium or where they were located, she could only guess if and when they would come after Wrex. If Wrex's intended destination was Vega Surong and their contract holder enforced the terms, then the authority on the planet would turn them over in a heartbeat.

Thoughts of what she would do regarding her guest continued to churn through her mind until she finally drifted off into a fitful state of rest. A mouth-watering aroma teased her consciousness to the surface.

She floated, too tired to roll off the cot just yet as she enjoyed the warmth of her bedding.

Not just her bedding. Fingertips danced across her stomach, circling her navel before deliberately dipping southward. Awareness slammed through her. Kori opened her eyes and turned her head. Wrex knelt beside the cot, bracing their chin with their free hand while the other hovered expectantly, low over her belly.

"Good morning, lovely," they murmured, their husky voice making her shiver. Their presence should have irritated her, but her arousal flooded back in a rush. It didn't help to have their shockingly gorgeous face in such proximity.

"What are you doing here?" she rasped, keenly aware of all her titillated bits and that hovering hand. In truth, their presence didn't shock her in the least. The moment Wrex woke in the pod, she'd sensed a magnetic energy between them. Their precarious situation coupled with their seductive skillset explained why they kept coming on to her, though that didn't stifle her body's reaction to them.

"Would you believe that I crave your company?" Wrex revealed a devastating smile that made her toes curl at the end of the bed. Despite her body's visceral reaction, she couldn't stop her small snort at their tease.

"Please. Does that line work on your clients?" Kori eyed their hand, but it hadn't moved. Waiting for permission.

The smile twisted into something more self-depreciating. "My clients don't need much convincing." There it was, that flicker of emotion that had convinced her to break protocol and delay her report.

Kori sighed, wrapping her fingers around their wrist. "Wrex, I know you're hesitant to tell me why and how you were in that pod, but I'm not going to report this incident. You don't have to do this."

Their lips parted, those silver orbs flickering over her features. "No, I don't. But I'd like to." Wrex paused. Their elegant throat worked in a nervous swallow. "If you're interested."

She sucked in a breath. The slick rub of her thighs certainly confirmed her body was on board. To think this stunning being was remotely interested in her did all sorts of things to her ego...if they were telling the truth. It was her mind that hesitated. She studied them, nibbling on her bottom lip, trying to push through the haze of her lust to gauge the truth.

Wrex seemed to register her internal flailing. Their gaze fastened on her mouth. "I've thought about doing this since last night." They leaned forward, breath fanning her face before they gently seized her bottom lip between their teeth. They teased and nipped, soothing the sting of those gentle bites with swipes of their smooth tongue.

Kori shoved their hand into her shorts. Wrex chuckled against her lips, immediately burrowing between her legs to find her pussy slick and greedy for the plunge of those elegant fingers. Her hips jerked off the bed as single digit hooked inside her, padding that secret textured spot with pinpoint accuracy. Her mind struggled to process the sensations as pressure bore down on her clit, coupled with a delicate brush along her labia and a tentative prod against her sensitive ass in angles that didn't make sense.

Not that she could make much sense of anything. She reached up to tangle her fingers in Wrex's white-blond hair and massaged the base of their neck.

Wrex groaned into her mouth just as the fingertips inside her shorts began to vibrate.

"Fuck!" Kori yelped, her body jerking at the force of her orgasm. Her vision whited out for a second, and then Wrex's face slowly came back into focus.

They grinned at her. "Would you like to continue?"

"Continue?" Kori lifted herself up on her elbows, feeling slightly dazed. Wrex's grin turned wicked.

Their hand emerged from her shorts. She watched, barely able to breathe as Wrex lifted their glistening fingers to their mouth and sucked them clean.

"Stars," she uttered.

"Exquisite," said Wrex. "But not enough."

Kori gasped when they seized her hips, effortlessly maneuvering her body sideways until her legs draped over Wrex's shoulders.

"I hope you're not too attached to these shorts," they said. She shook her head, wide eyed. The fabric shredded to bits in Wrex's grip, fluttering around her waist to expose her damp sex. The influx of cool air made her twitch, but strong fingers gripped her thighs, holding her in place as Wrex's warm breath teased over her still-throbbing clit.

A stray thought darted through her lust-soaked brain, wondering with dark glee if Wrex's tongue vibrated like their fingers. Her musings stalled when their tongue extended and split. Kori squealed as they plunged that tongue inside her, tracing a deep intricate pattern that had her writhing and screaming in ten seconds flat. It was too much, more pleasure than she'd ever experienced with anyone, and she'd visited quite a few brothels in her time.

Wrex finally eased away from her. "Remember to breathe, lovely," they said, their expression concerned.

Kori sucked in air, her heart pounding against her ribs. She was certain she'd lost consciousness at some point. If this was Wrex's head game, what would the main event look like? Would she survive it? There were worse ways to go.

Somehow managing to shimmy into a sitting position, she cupped Wrex's chin, pulling them closer for a kiss, the taste of herself on their lips. "My turn. Why don't you join me up here on the cot?"

"Oh, I don't think that is a good idea," they said. They rose up on their knees, putting some of their weight on the bed until the hinges creaked.

"Oops," Kori giggled. "Then let's move to my bunk. It's got some stability." This close, she caught the flash of strain in their smile before they turned away, snagging the case she hadn't noticed resting on the floor. A flicker of unease rose through her satiated haze.

It didn't bother her that Wrex woke her up ready for seduction. They still let her lead, and she could have said no. But she couldn't shake the feeling she was missing something.

Wrex distracted her, offering her hand up. "Lead the way."

chapter four

wrex

APPREHENSION STIPPLED THROUGH THEIR NERVES. THE TASTE OF KORI lingered on their tongue, a lush profile they wanted to sample again as soon as she let them. Her throaty moans and mewling screams, the beautiful flex of her muscles as she held on for dear life…they wanted, no, *craved* more. There was no obligation, no contractual pressure, and that freedom was a heady experience.

Yet the idea of her reciprocation made Wrex inwardly cringe. They'd never wanted something so very badly while fearing it in equal measure.

Their fingers tightened on the handle of their travel case, the contents a welcome distraction. Kori set the control panel to alert her to any incoming signals and led them back to her bunk, her blanket wrapped around her waist, though they'd already seen her delectable bottom.

She smiled at them when she found her sheets tucked in, exactly how they were before she pulled them back for Wrex to sleep last night. Kori dropped the blanket with a blush and sat on the bed. Wrex sat down next to her and set the case between them, watching her wide-eyed expression when they clicked open the internal latches.

The case sprang open with a flourish, revealing two rows deep and two columns wide of specially crafted attachments shaped for their body. The Consortium had outfitted Wrex with a variety of manufactured genitalia to appease over two hundred and fifty different species of clientele along a varied gender spectrum. Instruments built for singular and dual penetration, others for insertion, and a few designed for both activities at once.

Wrex picked up a piece, a soft silicate that replicated the feel of flesh on contact. "This one has a micro interdimensional expansion inside which accommodates the length and girth of most species."

Kori blinked. "You have a pocket dimension pussy?"

They chuckled. "Yes, exactly. It is a popular attachment," they said. Wrex placed it back in the case in favor of another. "This one is also a client favorite."

Her lips parted at the sight of the engineered phallus, textured to provide the epitome of pleasure. "Does that one adjust in size, too?"

"Of course," said Wrex, puzzled why she would ask. "It wouldn't do much good if it didn't fit the client exactly."

Excitement lit up her face, and Wrex couldn't stop staring until she grasped their wrists. "Which one do you want to wear?"

They frowned, thrown by her question. "You...you want me to choose?" Their brow furrowed, unsure how to proceed. "Which do you prefer?"

Kori flapped a careless hand. "I enjoy both," she said. "I promise, no matter what you wear, I'll make sure you feel good too."

They swallowed hard, knowing it was a vow she couldn't keep. Their smile was tight as they held up the "pocket dimension pussy." "Want to explore this one?"

"Ooo, think I can fit my whole arm in there?" She wiggled her eyebrows at them, her infectious mirth turning their smile genuine.

"Are you always this serious in the bedroom?" They teased. Wrex slid off the bed and stood to divest themselves of the remainder of their clothes.

"If you can't be goofy with your clothes off, you're not doing it right," she said. Her brows drew up when their pants rolled down their waist, revealing the smooth paneled juncture between their legs. "You don't wear everyday genitalia?"

They shrugged, unwilling to clarify. "Give me but a moment," they said. The panels dislodged with a quiet click. Wrex braced their legs apart, inserting the piece into place where it blended in seamlessly with their flesh.

Kori licked her lips, drawing Wrex back down onto the bed. She kept moving them, until she laid them onto their back, crawling up between their legs in a position that mirrored their earlier activities.

"I don't know if I can make you pass out, but I can at least take you on a trip through the stars." She winked at them, lowering her head. Wrex watched her intently, waiting for the moment her mouth contacted the piece before they *reacted*.

They moaned and shifted, letting their knees fall open. The sight of her in motion was erotic. Her lashes were downcast, fluttering against her cheeks while her dark hair tickled their inner thighs. Wrex's legs rested on the woman's thick biceps, her hands splayed over their belly and around their ass, supporting their body in a way that they loved. An enthralling act that deserved a worthy reaction.

Wrex threw their head back to mimic the breathy gasps they'd heard from dozens of other clients. However, taking their eyes off Kori was a mistake.

"Wrex," she said, her voice quiet.

Dread pooled in their belly. They tipped their face to look at her, the familiar sense of shame and disgust crawling up their throat.

"You can't feel my touch," she whispered.

"No," they said. She hadn't posed it as a question, but Wrex needed to answer her. Somehow, this female noticed immediately what so many of their clients had not. Though, if Wrex was honest with themselves, most simply didn't care.

kori

FURY MADE HER HANDS SHAKE AS SHE DUG THROUGH HER DRAWERS FOR A fresh pair of shorts. Wrex still sat on her bed, their pants back on, looking miserable. Did they think she was angry with them?

Kori dropped to her knees, clasping their hands. "Who did this hack job to you?"

Wrex looked away, jaw muscles tight. The circuitry beneath their skin emitted a faint light that glowed gold through the surface epidermal tattoos on their arm. "It's a standard procedure in the Consortium. All contracted courtesans are cybernetically and biochemically enhanced to service a wide clientele base."

"How horrifically clinical," Kori sneered. There were plenty of courtesans who chose to upgrade their bodies with all sorts of enhancements. This Consortium appeared to take the choice out of the equation. And a House that could subject their courtesans to mandatory alterations was capable of any number of unsavory activities. How these bastards managed to maintain legality for such activities was questionable, but right now, she had to help Wrex. She squeezed their wrists. "Will you let me examine the internal circuitry?"

They frowned at her. "Why?"

Kori hesitated. She had a terrible suspicion that the bio mechanic who worked on Wrex left them in this physical limbo on purpose. "How do these implants work during sex if you can't physically feel them?"

Another shrug while Wrex refused to meet her eyes. "Mechanically, they perform in accordance with the actions of the client."

It was true that the pocket dimension pussy had reacted to her, twitching and contracting like living muscle, but she'd still noticed the disparity between her stimulation and Wrex's reaction. "Please let me look."

Indecision warred on Wrex's beautiful face. Kori waited them out. After several long, silent minutes, Wrex sighed and rolled over onto their stomach, hugging her pillow to their face. Kori snagged her precision toolkit from her desk and sat on the floor beside them. Her fingers traced down their spine, searching for the camouflaged seam in that smooth expanse of pale skin.

The shift in texture let her know she'd found it, tapping her fingers at the edges until it rippled open to reveal the delicate tangle of circuitry interwoven with living tissue and nerves. Kori bit the inside of her cheek to silence her visceral reaction. Those assholes had soldered Wrex's nerve endings, leaving them scarred and unanchored. A cruel, careless job, but a *fixable* one. Kori would stake her professional reputation on it.

"Wrex." She laid her hand on their shoulder, their silver eyes loaded with tension when they peered back at her. "I can fix this for you if you give me the time, but you must remain still. Do you trust me to work on you?"

They sucked in a sharp breath, worrying their lip stud with their tongue. Wrex swallowed once, twice, hands clenching and unclenching on the sides of her pillow before they gave one definitive nod.

Kori went to work.

chapter six

wrex

TIME SPOOLED AROUND THEM IN A LAZY SKEIN OF SENSATIONS. WREX breathed into Kori's pillow, the clean scent of soap mingling with the faint pleasant musk of the woman herself. Warmth bathed their skin from the head lamp Kori wore to illuminate her task, and pressed into their sides where she rested her forearms. Welcome sensations compared to the previous teeth-gritting agony they bore while Kori shaved away their deadened nerve endings.

No numbing agent under the stars could completely nullify that, though Kori did everything in her power to make the experience a quick one. Once that task was complete, she settled into the far more meticulous task of routing and repairing the connective circuitry the Consortium's surgeons had left a mess.

Kori hummed while she worked. Wrex hid their smile, ruminating over their current predicament. There hadn't been much of a plan in place for escaping the Consortium's reach. Vega Surong was a well-known destination known for frequent visitors, ones Wrex could barter with for passage to parts of the galaxy where their former employer and jailer held less legal sway.

They wondered if the commodity of their body would have been enough. Wrex had existed for years in this malfunctional state, using their wits and skill to survive the Consortium's hold. If Kori hadn't intercepted their pod, they would have kept using their body like a tool, never free from the ones that made them.

What would Wrex do once Kori "fixed" them? What possibilities did the stars hold? Their focus narrowed, where the possibility of what they could experience anew with this delectable woman eclipsed the uncertain future.

Anticipation scratched at the underside of their skin. They must keep still while Kori tinkered, but energy thrummed through their system, begging for release.

The song paused. "And got it," said Kori.

Electricity rolled through their nerves. Wrex sucked in a breath as the current shot down their spine, tracing their nerves straight to the vortex of sensation gathering at their core.

"Now, to test it," Kori murmured. The panel over their spine slid back into smooth seamless skin that she trailed her fingers across. Wrex shivered, bare skin pebbling beneath the tortuously gentle path of her touch. It'd been so long since they experienced pleasure in their sexual organs. The distant memory suddenly rekindled through Kori's careful ministrations.

At the first whisper-soft brush of her fingers over their mound, a jolt shot through their system, lightning tracing under their skin in a burn of pleasure that bordered on pain. Wrex crushed the pillow, shocked by the intensity of the sensation after so long without, but their companion wasn't done.

Their entire universe narrowed down to the juncture between their thighs, and the callused fingertips that worked Wrex's silicate flesh with expert care. Their legs shook as those fingers worked them open, before Kori's breath fanned their entrance. Her tongue swept over and inward, in long strokes that ended with a flick at the nub of artificial nerves now finally connected directly to Wrex's system.

A hoarse cry tore from their lips, overwhelmed by the influx of pleasure, true actual pleasure. Moisture clumped in their lashes, spilling down their cheeks. It was too much. It wasn't enough. Their mind blanked when Kori's fingers slid inside, and Wrex felt every twitch and flex. Her exploration brushed against something that sent their senses reeling. Warmth suffused their body, afloat in a sparkling wave of white, until Kori's giggle grounded them back to the moment.

"You really can fit your whole arm in here." She grinned up at them, elbow deep in the pocket dimension pussy.

"Don't lose any jewelry," Wrex wheezed. They flopped back on the bed, struggling to breathe through the aftershocks of the most intense orgasm of their life while Kori wiggled her fingers inside them.

Clear that Wrex was satisfied and satiated, she withdrew her arm and climbed onto the bed beside them. "Well, we know that attachment works."

Wrex went still, turning to look at her. "We should really test the others."

Kori nodded, nudging the case on the floor with her foot. "Need to make sure the integrity of that rewiring works with all your gadgets."

"All of them?" Wrex wasn't sure they'd survive it. Kori laughed, resting her head on their shoulder.

"Don't worry—we can take our time."

Time Wrex now had, finally complete and whole. For the first time since they fled in the pod, they felt free of the Consortium's shadow. That sort of revelation gave them a second wind.

"Did you know the phallus also vibrates?"

chapter seven

kori

There was something to be said about the benefits of cybernetic strength. Used to being the physically stronger individual in a relationship, Kori's current position pinned to the wall of her bunkroom by Wrex's thrusts was a novel experience.

Couldn't fault that cyborg stamina either.

Kori tightened the grip of her thighs around their hips, her body a taut line of winding tension as Wrex swiveled that perfectly manufactured cock inside her body like they were signing the secrets of the universe. Another mind-shattering orgasm bore down on her while Wrex's hands and tongue and cock created an ideal equation of ecstasy. They lavished attention on erogenous zones she hadn't known existed, giving equal homage to her kiss-bruised nipples as they did the simple indent above her collarbone.

The two of them were a panting sweaty mess and Kori no longer regretted drawing the short straw for the crew's shore leave. Luckily, there had been no further proximity alerts or patrons seeking repairs. The hours passed in physical bliss, though Kori knew their time together was running out.

The building crescendo stalled for a moment. Kori stared down at Wrex's beautiful face, caught in the throes of genuine pleasure. She touched their cheek, meeting their mesmerizing silver eyes as the enormity of the moment stole over her. Once the crew returned, would Wrex leave for Vega Surong? Would she ever see them again? She'd never had a partner so in tune with her body and needs, or one that she wanted to give pleasure to in equal measures and more. The knowledge that Wrex had gone so long without, used by this despicable Consortium, fostered a deep need to give them those experiences. To see the chords of their neck muscles tight, their expression lost to the sensations of their body, renewed and relearned.

In sixty-nine rotations of fucking and chatting, she'd grown to know Wrex better than partners she'd had for years. Their leaving would hurt, but Kori knew they needed the freedom to make that choice.

"What will you do once we've tested all these wonderful devices of yours?" She brushed a hand down the side of their face, the metal plate along their jaw the same temperature as their skin. A smile tugged at her lips. This amazing being chose to be with her, a fact that humbled her as much as it thrilled her. No matter what Wrex chose to do next, she would carry their time together for the rest of her life.

They paused in their ministrations, one hand squeezing her thigh while the other cupped her chin. Wrex studied her face, their expression somehow more intimate than the cock throbbing inside her. "What place would there be for me here?"

The question threw her, a lance of ice through her pleasant buzz. A sensible question, one she couldn't flippantly answer with something selfish and thoughtless like "in my bed." Wrex had spent years in a terrible contract, servicing countless patrons who didn't give a damn about them, their body, or their mind. She didn't want Wrex to feel indebted to her for fixing what those bastards took from them, nor did she want them to feel like the only place for them was in the bedroom. Kori didn't have a ready answer, but before she could mitigate the situation, her comms burst to life.

"Kori, why is there a wrecked pod in my bay?" Vox's gravelly voice thundered through her room via the intercom, a rumble that shook her back to the reality of the present.

"Ah, fuck," said Kori, frantically gesturing for Wrex to put her down. She whimpered as they withdrew, her final orgasm truly thwarted and her emotions a tangled mess. Scrambling into her clothes, she couldn't quite look at Wrex as she explained. "That's my boss. Which means the crew has returned from shore leave. You can stay here, if you want. I'll take care of this."

Wrex hesitated, slowly pulling on their trousers. "Could I come with you?"

She nodded, though she didn't relish a witness to the epic chew-out Vox was about to give her. "Vox is rough around the edges, but he's secretly a softie. Don't let his bluster fool you."

Kori shoved her feet into her regulation boots, barely taking the time to fasten them properly as she counted the seconds in her head. She barreled out of her room with Wrex on her heels approximately seventy-six seconds after Vox called for her, which meant he'd spent at least forty-six of those seconds getting good and steamed.

Hurtling out into the repair bay, Kori winced at the audience waiting for her, the entire crew milling about like the cluster of gossipy ninnies they were. Vox scowled at her entrance, but his expression turned to confusion when Wrex appeared. Despite that, the mighty glower returned in full force once she rocked to a stop in front of him.

He gestured to the pile of scrap metal Kori had inconveniently left in the middle of the floor. It had been a busy sixty-nine rotations. "What is this? And why is it here?" His gaze flickered to Wrex who stepped up beside her, ready to answer. Vox squinted at them.

"Report, Mechanic Ross!" Vox barked. Wrex jumped at the boom of his voice and Kori sighed up at the seven-foot gray-skinned Titanae.

"The pod tripped a proximity alarm, sir," she said. "The navigational drive burnt itself out and the planet's atmosphere was about to tear it apart. I brought it on board to assist any passengers."

Vox raised a thick brow, pointedly examining Wrex. "Your shirt's on backwards, Mechanic Ross."

Kori closed her eyes to the chorus of snickers behind them. It didn't matter; she knew where they slept.

Vox glared at the crew. "Don't you lot have duties to catch up with?" He addressed Wrex as the others scuttled out of the bay. "This is a Class S escape pod, but there aren't many permanent orbital stations in this quadrant."

They both flinched. Vox had years of knowledge and experience over her, and he likely had a firm idea from whom and where Wrex had fled.

Continuing the pattern of inconvenient timing, the proximity alarm shrilled through the bay. Vox rolled his eyes. "Mechanic Reeve, what is that nonsense about?"

Reeve hustled to the console, still wearing a thick smear of sunscreen down his nose. "Uh, some spiky-looking vessel, sir. Don't recognize the make of it, but they're hailing us."

Vox folded his arms, not taking his squint off her. "And what do they want, Mechanic Reeve?"

The beleaguered Reeve squinted at the screen, clearly wishing he was still enjoying the sun on Vega Surong. "An envoy from something called the Consortium. They demand the return of their contractual property."

Horrified, Kori shot Wrex a look, shaking her head. "I didn't, I swear I didn't—"

"Of course you didn't, Mechanic Ross," Vox snapped. He kicked the wrecked pod. "All Class S escape pods have an internal tracking device."

Kori wanted to shake herself at her own stupidity. Even if she'd delayed her report, she should have checked the craft for such devices. "I'm sorry," she whispered to Wrex.

"It's not your fault," they said, reaching for her hand. Vox caught the gesture, inhaling deep through his nose.

"Right," he said. "Reeve, get your unit and make that craft disappear."

"Sir?" Reeve glanced between the three of them.

"Down to the last scrap, Reeve. Was I not clear the first time?" Vox sneered.

Reeve went into action while the head mechanic turned and strolled to the wall at the far end of the bay. Kori didn't know what the hell he was doing, but knew without being told she was meant to follow. When they reached their destination, Vox slammed one meaty fist against the corner of a seemingly random panel, popping it free to reveal a sizeable space inside the walls.

"Hop in, you two," he ordered.

"Sir?" Kori shared an incredulous glance with Wrex. "Both of us?"

Vox gave her a look. "Mechanic Ross, I need to convince this Consortium idiot their contract has fled for parts unknown, and you look well and truly fucked. Get in the wall."

He caught her arm when she went to follow Wrex inside. "These assholes are bad news, Ross. No matter what position you friend was in," his eyebrows twitched, "we wouldn't give them up."

Kori nodded, relieved to have someone like Vox in their corner as she let her boss close them in the wall.

chapter eight

wrex

Unable to dwell on the fact that the gruff Titanean held their fate in his hands, Wrex decided to occupy themselves. There wasn't room to stand, but the two of them were comfortable if snug sitting side by side in the wall space. The distance simply wouldn't do. They pulled Kori into their lap, burying their face in her chest.

"I know you didn't bring them here," they said, their voice muffled by her lovely breasts. Despite their precarious situation, their cock stirred to life. Blame it on years of deprivation.

"Wrex, you know I am more than willing, but time and place, darling," whispered Kori.

Tension wound in a painful progression through their body. "Nope, can't wait," they stated. If the Titanean failed to convince the Consortium to leave empty handed, these could be their last moments together. Wrex wanted to be in her every second they could manage. Kori squealed when they lifted her, turning her around as they yanked her pants down far enough to give them access. They didn't give their own garments the same courtesy, ripping the seams to free their stiffened cock.

"What are you—" she gasped, swallowing her words when they slid into her welcoming heat, still slick from their marathon session.

They drew her down fully, groaning when their cock lengthened and thickened to accommodate their position.

Wrex wanted this, not just the sex, but this woman. They wanted her laughter and her talented hands and whatever burgeoning connection was forming between them. They wanted her wonderful mouth and calloused fingers buried inside them. They wanted her panting with their cock seated throbbing inside her, while their hands explored all the hard muscles and lush curves of her body. They wanted *her*.

"Wrex," Kori whispered, her tone frantic through her uneven breaths. "My boss is right outside, lying to the Consortium. I can't. I can't do this," she whined, wiggling against them. Wrex nipped the back of her neck, sending a gentle vibration through their cock that made her inner muscles lock around them.

"Then we must be very quiet," they said with a wink.

Kori's arm reached back, wrapping around their neck while she whimpered and shook with them through a slow-burning orgasm.

Wrex remained seated inside her once they finished, content in the feel of her around them. "I want to stay with you, even if I have no other skills to offer you than this."

Kori released him, her head drooping forward. "You are so much more, Wrex," she said. "You could become a mechanic or learn any other job on this ship. You could leave and see the galaxy. You could go anywhere. What do you want to do?"

Wrex squeezed her to them. "If I leave, would you come with me?"

She hesitated, clearly torn by the life she had on this station, and the unknown. "Maybe."

They kissed her shoulder. "Then I'll stay."

The two of them hovered in a state of cozy bliss until the sharp rap of Vox's knuckles intruded.

"They're gone, Mechanic Ross." Vox's voice boomed through the thick metal panel. Kori barely suppressed her giggle as she glanced at their rumpled and torn clothes. "I offered them the pod's core, explaining we retrieved it after the vessel disintegrated in the planet's atmosphere. No survivors. They weren't happy at the loss of their merchandise, but they can go suck a Tagor's nutsack."

Kori glanced back at Wrex, both of their expressions lit by hope.

"You hear me, Mechanic?" Vox tapped the outside, seeming to remind Kori of their entangled state.

"Y-yes sir, I understand," she gasped, her inner muscles squeezing a quiet groan out of Wrex. A pause followed her answer.

"You're hosing down the inside of that cubby, Ross."

Laughter burst out of her, while Wrex nipped at her shoulder. "Yes, sir," she wheezed.

"Please return to your quarters, Mechanic Ross," said Vox. "When you're decent."

Kori tried and failed to muffle her humor, Wrex content to feel the fine movements of her body. Finally, she managed to steady herself, turning to look at them. "What do we do now?"

Contentment suffused Wrex's circuits. No matter what happened now, their choices were their own, and Kori was their first choice. "Would you like to try the dual attachment?"

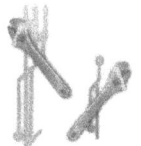

about kristin jacques

Kristin Jacques is an award-winning author of fantasy fiction for teens and adults. She currently lives in a small town in Connecticut with her partner, kiddos, and two trash goblins who think they are cats. When not writing, she's usually reading, gaming, or catching some excellent B-horror movies. She is currently working on projects full of magic, mystery, and delight.

Kristin is the author of many books, including *A Bargain of Blood and Gold*, *Ragnarök Unwound*, and *Poison & Poultice*, all available now.

To learn more, visit www.kristinjacques.com

blue moon

Lily Riley

chapter one

anya

There's a dead body outside my window. It's definitely not human.

I stare at it for a moment, keeping my panic tightly leashed thanks to extensive training and sheer force of will. *You can't panic in space. Observe first, then freak out.*

Five irregular limbs sprout from a bulbous, wolf-sized body—or possibly a head. Short, reddish-orange fur covers it completely and I can't make out any discernible facial characteristics. It reminds me of a five-legged ginger tarantula, except for its massive size. *What the hell is it?*

There's no way it came from Earth. The creature doesn't look like any of the known alien species I recognize from my training. I squint slightly, and I can see a light dusting of fine gray silt coating its fur where it touches the ground in a small impact crater. Yet, there are no footprints or tracks marring the powdery soil anywhere near it. Did it crash into the surface from some distant trajectory?

Or did something put it there?

I'm supposed to be alone on this shithole lunar station while the rest of my crew takes their well-earned leave. My restrained panic finally breaks its tether and I suck in deep, rasping breaths. Icy dread raises goosebumps on my skin and my heart hammers a tattoo of fear in my chest when I consider that perhaps I'm not as alone here as I thought.

Whatever the corpse is, it certainly wasn't there when I went to sleep last night at zero dark thirty. I glance down at my bio-cuff to check the time—well, *Earth Nova* ship time—0530. That means that at some point in the last five hours, a dead alien creature crash-landed right outside my room in the *Alpha Lunis* station. But there's no other disturbance I can see from my small round window, and the fact the body didn't vaporize on impact suggests...

No. It couldn't have been placed there. Surely, there'd be tracks. The station's scanners would've picked up a signal from another ship. I would have seen something, heard something, or sensed something. It can't be there. *How is it there?*

I squeeze my eyes shut and turn away from the window. *Maybe when I look again, it'll be gone.* There's a comforting hum from the station's artificial gravity generators and if I stand still enough, I can feel the distant vibrations of the massive football stadium-sized plasma heaters working around the clock to melt the ice embedded in the lunar poles. The off-gassing vents mile-high geysers of steam into the air, which slowly condenses into what will become the new atmosphere on the moon. Humanity's last resort and fledgling hope.

I take a sip of water from the aluminum flask tied to my bunk's bedpost and turn back to the window.

The body is still there—not a hallucination, then. My pulse races fast enough that my bio-cuff beeps in warning, asking if I'm having a medical emergency.

"Calm down, Anya," I tell myself. "First thing's first: figure out what you're dealing with and then send in a report. Someone will come. It's a fucking alien—they *have* to come."

My soft voice has a metallic echo in the spartan bedroom, but it gives me a strange sense of courage to hear my plan out loud. Heartened, I strip off my thin cotton pajamas and start layering my daily uniform: insulating layer first, followed by thick, utilitarian coveralls and my metal-soled boots. I twist my platinum blonde hair into a severe knot on top of my head, wash my face and brush my teeth in the tiny sink in my room. One of the best parts about living here alone is that I can listen to my choice of music without anyone giving me a hard time, so I crank Billie Holiday through the station's PA speakers. "Blue Moon" warbles throughout the dead space and soothes my frazzled nerves. I mentally prepare for my next task: searching the entirety of the *Alpha Lunis* station for an interloper.

If there's even the remotest possibility of an alien intruder, I should be smart and bring protection with me, but this outpost isn't a military installation and weapons are hard to come by. Plasma blasters are forbidden inside the station due to risk of depressurizing accidents, so the best I can do is grab an eighteen-inch monkey wrench and a small, handheld plasma torch from my toolbox.

My stomach rebels at the thought of breakfast, but I manage to choke down a bland green nutri-cube to power me through my search. With that, I steel my nerves, roll some of the tension from my shoulders, and open the heavy door leading into the main corridor of the station living quarters.

Blue-white LED lights flicker on as I make my way through the station, barely daring to breathe. I search rows of empty berths in the living quarters, all pristine and ready for the relief crew that will arrive in four months. I quickly clear the med bay, science labs, and the mess hall, all sealed and untouched in sanitary stasis. No signs of life.

The command pod in the center of the complex is my second-to-last stop. I consider taking the time to contact the base and let them know I'm not alone on this station. *How would they respond?* I wonder.

Looking out the main window of the command pod, I watch the distant formerly blue-green marble swirl in desolate streaks of brown and white. In the velvety blackness beyond, stars twinkle and shimmer —evidence the plasma heaters and lunar steam are starting to work and the beginnings of the new, proto-atmosphere are forming. In my opinion, there's something warped about altering the landscape of our ever-constant, gentle gray moon, but it makes for one hell of a view.

Too bad there's no one to share it with.

A soft throb of loneliness unfurls in my chest, but I shove it down.

My crew is a month out on their way to the *Earth Nova* colony ship and the next group won't arrive for some time. *Not that I'd sit and watch the stars with anyone on my crew.* A hysterical giggle bursts from my lips when I think of the dead alien in my front yard—perhaps they came for the view, too.

Not likely.

When humans first made contact with extraterrestrials ten years ago, it was all so anticlimactic. No abductions, no invasions, no two-way contact: just the confirmation that somewhere in the distance, other beings existed. More importantly, they existed and wanted nothing to do with us. Who could blame them? What sentient species would care about a decimated population on a dying world? We're a guttering candle too dim to bother extinguishing.

The remnants of humanity evacuated into hideous, unwieldy colony ships that still orbit the parched, choked, utterly cooked rock I can't bring myself to miss. My family was gone long before the colony ships were built, and besides, I've always been too in love with the endlessness of space and the promise of the stars to feel homesick for Earth.

As a kid, I dreamed of being an astronaut. I wanted to explore distant galaxies, befriend alien species, discover new worlds. Instead, I'm as good as a graveyard shift grease monkey trying to turn an old, abandoned deep space research station into a terraforming luxury resort. Apparently, I'm the only unattached solitary loser they could find to help lead the re-engineering mission on the old lunar station, tasked with getting it prepped and ready for the first wave of colonists wealthy enough to buy their way off the ships.

I rub at the hollow ache in my chest when I think about all the couples and families planning on a future here on *Alpha Lunis*. What I wouldn't give to have the hope of my childhood dreams again. My own future stretches out before me like space: vast, unknowable, embarrassingly isolated.

Assuming, of course, the dead alien outside isn't a sci-fi portent of doom. *Yeah, one thing at a time, Anya.* I have bigger problems than contemplating the lonesomeness of my pathetic existence or trying to figure out how to turn an outdated laboratory into luxury living accommodations.

Sighing, I turn on the main computer and key in my ID code. A symphony of grating beeps and clicks shatters the silence of the command pod, and I type out an urgent message to my team on the base. Just as I'm about to hit Send, I pause. I've seen *Alien*. What if they want me to bring the thing back for study or something? Or worse— what if they don't believe me in the first place? What if they think I've gone nuts from too much solitude and solar radiation?

Unease twists my stomach into knots and stutters my pulse. I should get some kind of proof, but what if the thing isn't really dead? What if it's hibernating? Or gestating? The last thing I want to do is go outside, especially when I still have no idea where it came from. If something put it there, that something could still be hanging around using the dead tarantula alien as bait, maybe.

It sounds crazy. I *feel* crazy. I feel like I'm going to look out my window again and there won't be anything there. It will have been a trick of the light, or a fever dream from eating an expired ration, or something. *Something.*

The anxiety I've been brutalizing deep down in my gut rears its head and I delete my message one heavy keystroke at a time.

I scroll back through yesterday's station data, but there's nothing out of the ordinary. A tide of worry laps at the fringes of my mind as I consider my next move. I don't think I can handle all this alone. At some point, I'll need to contact the ship and tell them, but I don't want to risk everything I've worked for. If they think I've lost it, they'll cart me back to *Earth Nova* and I'll lose my chance to lead the engineering team on the next space station, which is the closest I'll get to exploring the stars.

Earth Nova has to believe me. That leaves me with one nauseating option: finish searching the last remaining section—the garage and landing decks—then head outside and document the carcass.

Grabbing my wrench and plasma torch, I venture from the sterile sanctuary of the command pod and take the service elevator down six decks to the lowest level. This is the area I've been dreading—the biggest, most labyrinthine, and most likely to harbor some alien invader bent on terrorizing the station's hapless human meatsicle.

I start in the garage by inspecting the rows of lunar rovers. The maintenance lockers, storage bunkers, and machining shop are all as they should be, with nary a swipe of grease or dusty footprint to be seen. By the time I finish searching, my stomach is rumbling and my bio-cuff beeps, reminding me that I haven't eaten since my depressing breakfast eight hours ago. I'm exhausted, sweaty, famished, and my nerves feel as if they've been stretched into spun glass and shattered.

"Almost done," I remind myself. "Then it's a hot shower and a full ration for dinner."

With leaden limbs, I pull on my heavy spacesuit and wait for it to pressurize in the garage's outer chamber. When the preliminary tests indicate everything is copacetic, I smash my fist into the airlock release and step out onto the surface of the moon.

Without the assistance of the station's artificial gravity, it takes me ages to leap and plod and shuffle toward the dreadful heap of ginger limbs outside the window near my berth. The hairs on the back of my neck stand up and I feel as if I'm being watched, but I can't tell if it's my proximity to the alien carcass or the odd sensation of standing on the chalky lunar regolith staring out at the boundlessness of space.

I toe the corpse, but the lifeless body is frozen solid. I want some kind of proof to show the base that I'm *not* crazy and yes, there *are* aliens knocking on the door of our brand-new home. As I study the corpse, something catches my eye—in the silty soil, strange slithery tracks I didn't see earlier encircle the alien body. Like desert sand after the rain, there's no real pattern to them and no evidence they move off in any singular direction. Perhaps they're not tracks at all, and it's a natural phenomenon. We're growing an atmosphere; maybe this is where some water has condensed.

Grimacing, I bend down to grab one of the furry legs and tug it with me onto the lower loading bay that opens into the garage. In zero gravity, I can manage the weight, but as soon as I get inside, I'll need a hover cart to help me transport it to the cryo-freezers in the lab. I figure keeping it frozen and entombed in the lab is my safest bet until I can convince everyone on the *Earth Nova* ship, and then I'm going to fling this creepy bastard back out into space…or vaporize it with one of the plasma heaters. I'm not taking any chances.

The trek to the lab is uneventful—well, except for the fact that I'm lugging a dead alien through the hallways of a lunar station. But the moment I seal it inside the cryo-freezer, I exhale with a jittery kind of relief.

Despite the overall horror show of the day, I feel much better by the time I trudge back into my room. I take a twenty-minute volcanically hot shower, stuff a full dinner ration of rehydrated spaghetti into my face, and tenderly pull on my pajamas. My bio-cuff reads 2200 *Earth Nova* time, which is a little earlier than I normally turn in, but I'm glad for the extra rest.

Tomorrow morning, everything will go back to normal. I'll send in my report *with* evidence, get a security team here to help watch my back, and dive back into work. In another few months, I'll have earned my own fancy suite on *Alpha Lunis* and then be right in line to lead my team on the next galactic adventure. Maybe the dilapidated Mars outpost. Now *there* would be a fun challenge.

I snuggle into my covers, trying not to allow the emptiness of the station, my room, my life suffocate me. I refuse to let my mind wander to the mysterious dead thing stashed in the lab's freezer or the unnerving marks in the dirt outside that don't seem scientifically possible. I did my best today and tomorrow, everything will be fine.

I'll be fine.

＊ ＼＼＼＼　　　／／／／ ＊

JUST AFTER I manage to drift off, a nightmare sends adrenaline surging through my body and I leap out of bed, convinced there's someone—something—here with me. I reach for my wrench, tucked safely beneath my pillow. Sweat beads on my skin and my bio-cuff beeps at my elevated heart rate and respiratory distress.

But once again, I'm alone. *Always alone.* Even so, it takes several minutes for me to calm down, and as the stress finally starts to ebb from my muscles, I make the mistake of opening my eyes and peering out my window.

There is another dead body outside.

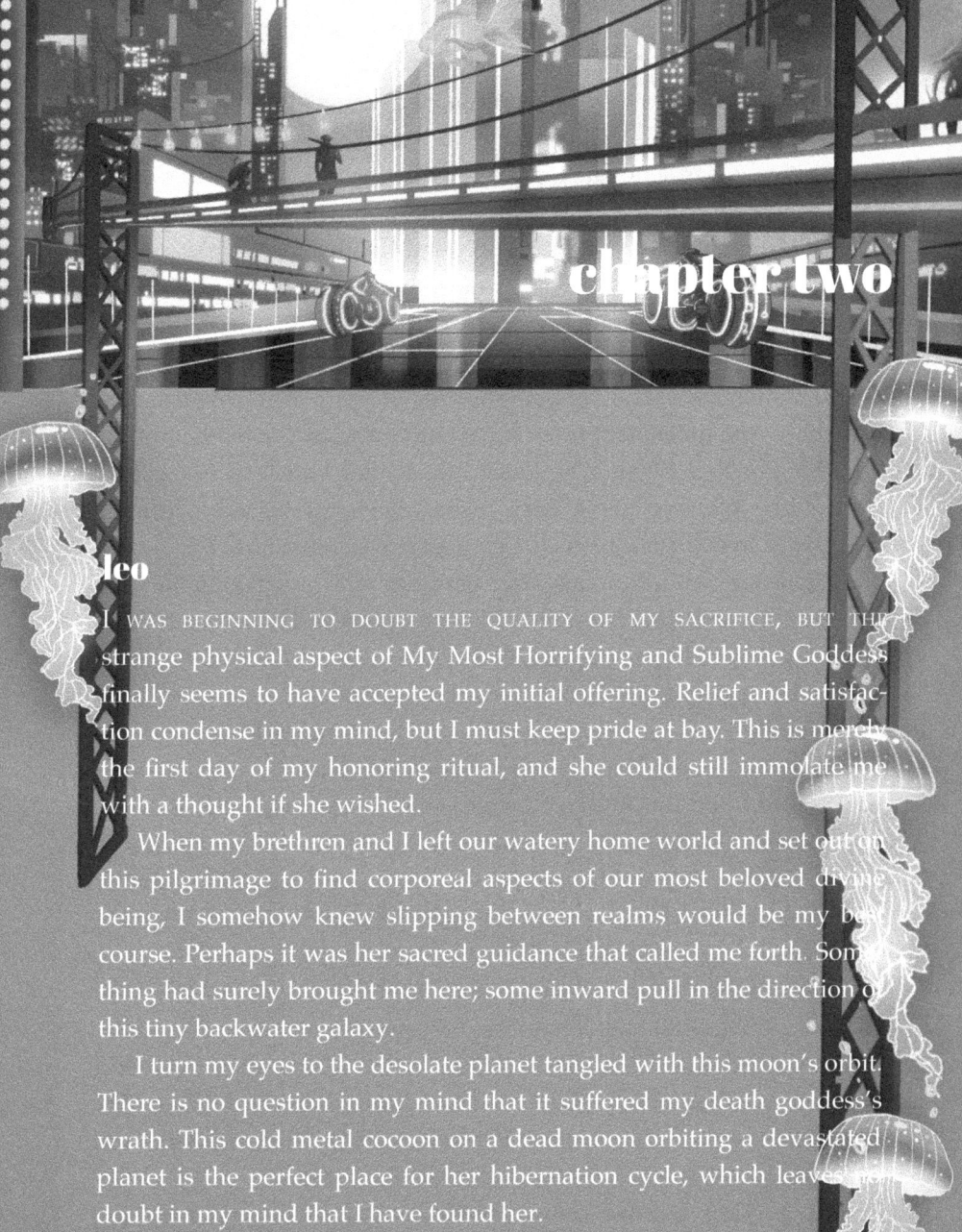

chapter two

leo

I WAS BEGINNING TO DOUBT THE QUALITY OF MY SACRIFICE, BUT THIS strange physical aspect of My Most Horrifying and Sublime Goddess finally seems to have accepted my initial offering. Relief and satisfaction condense in my mind, but I must keep pride at bay. This is merely the first day of my honoring ritual, and she could still immolate me with a thought if she wished.

When my brethren and I left our watery home world and set out on this pilgrimage to find corporeal aspects of our most beloved divine being, I somehow knew slipping between realms would be my best course. Perhaps it was her sacred guidance that called me forth. Something had surely brought me here; some inward pull in the direction of this tiny backwater galaxy.

I turn my eyes to the desolate planet tangled with this moon's orbit. There is no question in my mind that it suffered my death goddess's wrath. This cold metal cocoon on a dead moon orbiting a devastated planet is the perfect place for her hibernation cycle, which leaves no doubt in my mind that I have found her.

I would never question her judgment, but the location does make my honoring ritual challenging. Collecting living sacrifices on unworthy males would be much more manageable if there were shreds of life on the slowly rotating brown rock below.

Honorable Sindaria obviously means to test my mettle for the next thirteen turns. Finding dishonorable flesh for her consumption is my duty and privilege. I am taken aback slightly by her choice of corporeal body, as it seems small and weak in comparison with mine, along with the rest of our devoted priests. I don't find it altogether unpleasant to behold—this four-limbed aspect of meat and bone—but it does make me wonder: *Where does my divine lady hide her monstrous, world-rending tentacles?*

No matter. I question her not. The idea of being near her—*with* her—is almost too much happiness to bear after my long, solitary journey. The thought that I won't be alone any longer buoys me as I float through the Void Between Things. If she accepts my second sacrifice, I will gladly shift to match her shape, reveal myself to her, and complete the ritual and my pilgrimage. My brethren will be envious, indeed, that after searching for our immortal death goddess, I have found Fearsome Sindaria hidden away in this odd little galaxy with so little life to sustain her prodigious, incomprehensible desires.

I feel the small vibrations of her body and watch with all my eyes as she paces in the large metal cocoon. Her garb is different than earlier, and I find this much more pleasing. It's thinner, softer-looking, and brushes against her limbs when she moves. The rate of her vibrations increases, as if she's excited or in distress, and it's all I can do not to flail my tentacles with pride. She must be pleased with my second sacrifice.

It's difficult for me to wait camouflaged out here in the Void Between Things, but the pain of cold only adds to my feelings of devotion. When Glorious Sindaria exits her metal cocoon again to collect the body of the three-legged Cha'orth I brought her, I will take the opportunity to scan her form so I can replicate it. Then, my real work begins.

My goddess has disappeared from view, and I sense her making her way to the lower part of the cocoon. Anticipation sends ripples through my hood. This was how she emerged last time—I must be ready.

Disappointment flutters through me when she exits the cocoon wrapped in the same robes as before, the thick, ugly ones that obscure her body and encase her omnipotent brain in a round crystal. It will be difficult for me to scan her as such, but not impossible. It simply means I must get closer to her to do so.

This time, she brings a metal cart with her, and I shake with barely restrained joy when she hefts the Cha'orth on top of it. Slowly, I float down behind her and softly caress one of my sensory tentacles across the outer surface of her raiment. The touch is not enough for her to sense me, but it is enough for me to absorb the anatomical guidelines coded within this aspect's genes. She pauses for a moment, then whips around, searching for my phantom touch. This close, I can see more of her shape, and there is such alien beauty to it, I nearly collapse.

She only has two eyes that I can see inside her crystalline head covering, but they are as blue as the deep waters of my home. White-blonde hair covers the top of her head, reminding me of thin icicles that form in the northern seas. Her flesh is covered by skin that looks almost as soft as my hood, and pale pink lips the color of my favorite stellar nursery twist in a frown. I'm certain these lips disguise fearsome sharp teeth, because otherwise, my Delicious Sindaria has chosen an aspect with very little to offer besides obvious visual enjoyment.

Her coloring, however, leaves little room for doubt. Her sea blue eyes, ice-white hair, aurora pink lips...she is borne of the oceans of Oseuth. *She belongs to me.*

Beautiful Sindaria turns around again and tugs the cart with the dead Cha'orth into the bowels of the metal cocoon. Seeing her disappear from my view leaves me with a longing that borders on pain. *No time for that now.* I've gathered what I need to begin my transformation. I'm ready to become the perfect biological mate for my Fierce One.

I sift through her genes, taking what I require and discarding others. I weave my flesh into her form's echo, relying on my imagination and the inspiration of her divine guidance to finish knitting myself into a four-limbed body that I pray will please her. My final action is to pull my tentacles into my new form, absorbing the filaments of my sensory and stinging cells. I send those cells to the tips of this body's fingers.

When I'm satisfied that I've done my best, I follow Sindaria's foot-prints to the lower section of the metal cocoon. I'm dismayed for the merest of moments when I see the electronic box on the outer door but realize I can match the sonic signature of the box with my sonar. This must be the first test, which surely means we're proceeding with the ritual. The door opens with a hiss of air and as I step into the cocoon, heavy gravity presses in from all sides. I stagger forward, my body's new limbs adjusting to the musculoskeletal limitations and unfamiliar gravitational pressure. Pain radiates from my many new organs, and I suck in a startled breath.

Ah, so this is what her lungs breathe!

Kneeling on the cold floor, I take a few moments to accustom myself to new thoughts and sensations.

It is warm in here—not quite as warm as the tropical seas on Oseuth, but certainly more pleasant than the icy Void Between Things. It's strange to see with only two eyes, to smell with my air breather on my face, and hear sounds from the sides of my head. In my true form, I sense almost everything with my tentacles, and these new experiences cause a kind of sensory overload. I close my eyes to center myself—to pray for guidance and search for clues to this body within my divine lady's chosen DNA.

Some time passes, but I'm not sure how much. I move awkwardly at first, but mimic the confident gait of My Goddess and eventually make progress through the lower parts of the metal cocoon. I send out a few sonar clicks to better locate Stunning Sindaria since I'm not used to these sensory organs and follow her delightful vibrations down a strange tunnel. My two eyes take in such an odd world around me, all sharp edges and cold metal and electronic signatures. Lights flicker on above me, but I cannot see what manner of creature emits the glow.

A single heart beats in my chest and my pulse begins to race as I near the chamber where Sindaria prefers to slumber. In her goddess form, she does not need sleep, of course, but this lovely fleshy version of her seems to require it in staggering amounts. If that is what she desires, I will exhaust her with worship and pleasure and then see nothing disturbs her. I will massage her limbs and wreath her in my tentacles—or rather, I will wrap her in these limbs until her fearsome appetites are sated.

I hear soft noises from the other side of this wall, and I think perhaps it is Sindaria returning to bed. The thought of her in her thinner robes excites me in a carnal way, and I notice that my new body's reproductive appendage hardens in anticipation of my sexual worship. *Curious.* I wonder how these bodies will come together. Hopefully Sindaria will be satisfied enough with my honoring sacrifices, and she will show me how to please her. *What will it feel like?* Tentatively, I run a fingertip down the length of my engorged flesh and the pleasure of the touch zings through every nerve, filling me with a primal need to bury the organ in my goddess and rut until she overflows with my seed and holy benedictions spill from our lips.

Encouraged, I step forward and press my hand to the smooth, cool metal separating me from My Most Horrifying and Sublime Goddess. My mouth lifts in a joyful smile as the wall slides to the side with a soft *whoosh* and lo, there she lies—sleeping peacefully, resplendent upon a bed that faces a view of the Void Between Things and the devastated planet that somehow elicited her displeasure and deserved wrath.

She is singularly breathtaking, and I have only just learned to breathe. As her fathomless blue eyes open, I sink to my knees and bow before her. I do not know how these aspects communicate, so I stroke my consciousness against hers until she opens her mind to me, and I convey my thoughts with all manner of deference and respect. The ritual words, memorized thousands of times for a thousand years, are as natural to me as anything.

Fearsome Sindaria, I have come to you across universes separated by space and time, from the depths of the seas on Oseuth, all to journey in holy contemplation and devotion to your might. I have begun my honoring ritual and mean to worship you with gifts of sacrifice and pleasure for the next thirteen cycles. Accept me, Devastating One, and bless me with your presence.

When I dare to raise my head from the floor, Sindaria's vibrations are fast and erratic. I'm convinced it's a match for my lust and excitement, until she opens her mouth and lets out a piercing scream. Terrified she's about to wrench my cells apart in rage, I recoil and try to run from her chamber. In my haste, however, I have forgotten how these moving metal walls work, and run headlong into the surface. Pain explodes across my face before I collapse to the floor again, and darkness wraps me in a dreamless embrace.

anya

Fuck. Fuck. Fuck.

"What the fuck?" I hiss into the silence. This time, instead of my voice offering some kind of comfort, its echo exacerbates my hysteria.

It's an alien. There is a fucking *alien* in my room, and he did something *weird* to my mind, like some kind of telepathy but with images and feelings instead of words, and…holy shit.

He's completely naked. Naked and unconscious and weirdly humanoid—totally unlike what we've found evidence of on other worlds.

His body is roped in lean muscle, like a swimmer, and his skin moonstone pale—paler than mine—with a soft, velvety sheen to it. Long, powder blue hair falls just below his shoulders, or it would, if it wasn't currently obscuring his insensate face. I hold my breath and gently pull it back, taking in an angular jaw, brutally sharp cheekbones, full, lush lips and a long aquiline nose dusted with a spray of glowing, bioluminescent freckles.

He looks like blue starlight made human.

Suddenly, his brow furrows and he shifts slightly, and I yank my hand away as if I've been scalded. I twist back to my bed and grab my wrench, brandishing it in front of me, but the sleeping cerulean being does not wake.

Biting my lip, I devise a quick course of action. I'm reasonably certain he doesn't mean to kill me, given he had the opportunity to do so and ended up on his knees before me instead, but since I don't know what the hell he's doing here or why he's more nude than Venus on a clamshell, I need to be smart about this.

Glancing around, I pull my wheeled office chair out from my desk and yank a length of cable from the spare parts I keep on my workstation table.

"I'm going to tie you up," I say softly, though I hope he doesn't come to. It's possible, nay probable, I've completely lost it now and am experiencing fully tactile hallucinations, but I guess it doesn't hurt to be polite. "I'm sorry if that freaks you out."

I heft his body into the office chair, keeping my wrench in my line of sight the entire time. Still, he doesn't stir. A traitorous thrill buzzes through me when I touch his skin—the most contact I've had with anyone or anything in months. I catch myself inhaling at the crook of his neck. The scent of his skin is faintly saline, as if he just stepped out of the ocean. The buried, wild part of me has a suicidal urge to lick him, but I stumble back in horror when I realize how messed up that compulsion is.

After tying his wrists to the chair's arms, I bend to tie his feet to the legs and—wow. *Wow*. Ugh…is it weird that I'm scoping out this creature's dick? I'm only human, after all, and it's been such a long time, and none of my boyfriends have been quite *that* blessed.

"Congrats," I mumble, startling myself. "Sorry! I'm sorry, I didn't mean to get an eyeful of your dick. It's just…it is right there! And it's glowing blue! And…buddy, are you already semi-hard?"

The awkward, incredulous words tumble from my lips before I can quarantine them behind my sanity barrier. Shaking myself, I finish tying the alien to the chair and sit back to study him again. Uneasily, I toss a blanket across his lap to cover some of his nudity, despite acknowledging that his nudity is pretty pleasant to witness. There's a nasty cut on his forehead, arcing down across his left eyebrow and syrupy, glow stick-like blood drips down his cheek.

"That looks bad," I say with a wince. "I hope you don't have acid blood like in *Alien*."

I swipe a mostly clean rag across it and when the rag doesn't disintegrate, I'm mollified. Resigned, I decide to take him to the med bay to patch him up. Who knows how he'll react when he comes to? Maybe if I help him out a little, he won't want to abduct me for terrifying experiments, or whatever it is these aliens do.

As I wheel my unconscious intruder down the corridor, several thoughts occur to me simultaneously.

One, it's likely this alien is the reason for the other two dead aliens in my cryo-freezer, and two, it's probably a good thing I didn't contact *Earth Nova*, because I've obviously lost my ever-loving mind. Yesterday, my day was normal. *I* was normal. A little tired and a little lonely, sure, but otherwise normal. And today?

Today I've got two dead aliens in the freezer and a third one strapped to my desk chair, rolling with a comical squeak down an otherwise silent hallway in a soon-to-be terraformed resort on the goddamned moon.

Manic laughter stutters out from me as I reach the sealed doors to the med bay and swipe my badge. When the doors slide closed and the too-bright lights kick on, my mystery guest finally huffs a breath and rolls his head back. I tense, gripping my wrench tighter. Fear and agitation have me primed to clobber this thing faster than you can say *anal probe*.

The alien's head lolls on his chest before he lifts it blearily, blinking up at me with eyes the same bioluminescent blue as his freckles. A wide, sultry smile plays upon his lips and heat of unmistakable intent flickers in his gaze.

I aim my wrench at his chest.

"I'm going to ask you some questions," I say, as calmly as I can.

The alien blinks.

"Can you understand me?" I ask.

He tilts his head to the side, examining me with interest, then nods. *Yes.*

But he doesn't speak it—his lips remain closed in that almost-cocky grin. It's not really a word, so much as it's a feeling. The sensation of

Lily Riley

agreement takes shape in the back of my mind—a foreign presence that leaves me further untethered from reality.

"Can you speak?" I ask.

I do not know. I have never tried.

"Okay, this is really fucking weird," I mutter to myself. "Obviously, this is a new level of hallucination for me. Hey! You better not be rooting around in my head."

His grin falters, and he looks appalled by the thought.

I would never attempt such an invasion, Exalted One.

"Exalted One?" I echo. Must be a weird translation thing. "Right, well, good. Let's get down to it. Who are you and what the fuck are you doing here?"

The alien looks puzzled by my questions, which bodes ill for me. We haven't even gotten to the tough ones yet.

I am of the Oseuthans. But you know this, My Goddess. It is your divine guidance which has called me here. Do you show me favor with this gift of cloth?

His nods to the blanket in his lap and I stare at him, my eyebrows lifted in surprise.

"First of all, it's not a gift of cloth, it's a blanket. You showed up here totally naked and that's unnerving as far as introductions go. Second, I've never heard of Oh-soo-thans. Third, that's a real sweet term of endearment and all, but at no point have I ever offered anything that could be considered divine guidance. I can't even give sound advice, because I am clearly not of sound mind anymore."

He appears confused at first, then shakes his head.

This is no hallucination, Beloved One. No, you brought me here. I offered you my pledge, remember? I mean to worship you with gifts of sacrifice and pleasure.

"Your pledge? Sacrifice? Are you telling me you're not here to abduct me?"

The alien's eyes widen in fear and surprise.

Does My Goddess wish to be abducted?

I'm not considering it—of course I'm not. I've worked too hard to get to where I'm at, right? Who wouldn't want to stick around in a lonely tin can stuck on the moon when a hot, possibly radioactive alien

346

offers you a ticket to the stars? I swallow thickly and check to see if my bio-cuff indicates some kind of brain bleed.

"Abducted...no! And you've got it wrong there, pal. I'm no goddess; I'm just a human. A lone mechanical engineer whose job it is to get this station up and running," I explain, unnerved by this obvious case of mistaken identity.

Mechanical engineer? Is that the name of this divine aspect?

"What the fuck are you talking about?" I whisper, more to myself than to him. This is nuts. I am having some kind of mental breakdown and am going to need to be sedated. "No, engineer is a job. It's my profession."

The alien's shoulders sag with relief.

That is good. I do not wish to waste time now that the ritual has begun. I had hoped you would find this form I have chosen pleasing.

"Form? This isn't what you normally look like?" I ask, my curiosity getting the better of me. If this is insanity, maybe I should just go with it.

He nods again, and then an image condenses in my mind's eye.

I'm floating in a warm, fathomless sea. All around me, massive gelatinous blobs decked with glittering rainbow tentacles drift together as one. Sunlight filters in through waves above me and all around, bizarre fish and invertebrates dart through huge coral and rock pillars.

"Whoa," I breathe. "That's you? You're like, giant space jellyfish!"

He tilts his head again, and this time he reminds me of a bewildered puppy. It's oddly endearing. *What the hell am I saying?* I ask myself. I can't be thinking the figment of my psychotic mind is endearing. Or hot. Definitely not hot.

I do not know this jellyfish. I must say, Venerable Sindaria, your responses to my pledge have me...perplexed.

"You're not the only one," I say. "Right, let's start there. My name isn't Sindaria. It's Anya. I'm not a goddess. I'm a human, from Earth. See? That rocky brown planet just outside the window? That's where I'm from originally. Lately, we've all been hanging out on colony ships, though, because our home world can't support life anymore."

Realization seems to dawn, because the hot alien frowns up at me.

You...you did not devastate that world with your brutal wrath?

"Sorry, buddy. It took generations of humans to wreak that kind of havoc. I don't even like killing spiders. Well, I didn't, anyway, before they all died out."

That is not something the Goddess of Death and Carnal Pleasures would say.

My face twists in sympathy, but he continues.

...unless she were truly testing my devotion. Beautiful Sindaria, I will not fail you.

I blow out a resigned sigh.

"Do you have a name, jelly guy?" I ask.

A name? We are the Oseuthans.

"No, I mean you personally," I say. "Like, my name is Anya, not Sindaria. Anya."

I see. If you wish to be called Anya, I will do as you ask, My Terrifying One. Glorious Anya, we do not need names. The Oseuthans are linked in consciousness. We are all Brother to each other.

"I've got to have something to call you, unless you want me to keep calling you Jelly Guy," I gripe.

I would be honored to receive any name you would offer me.

"Sure. Fine," I say, wracking my brain. Long-forgotten memories of high school biology surface. "You know, the Latin name for moon jelly is *aurelia aurita*. How about Leo for short?"

Leo. Yes. This pleases me. Thank you, Divine Anya.

"It's just Anya, Leo. Anya the human."

Just Anya. You are more than "just" anything, My Goddess, but I will honor your wish. Anya.

He smiles again, his long hair falling forward and sticking in the blood on his face. A flinch of surprise and pain tugs at his features.

"Can I help clean that up? I don't know if you're susceptible to the same infections that humans get, but I wouldn't want it to fester," I say.

Leo's lower lip quivers in a sad little pout and his eyes flick to the ground. My heart lurches in my chest.

I have had this form for such a short period of time, and I have already damaged it. I do not deserve your care or your mercy, Div—Anya.

"Tell you what. I'll get you bandaged up and you can tell me more about why you're here, why you're naked, and what the hell this ritual is all about. Then I'll decide if I'm going to untie you or stick you in the cryo-freezer with your two dead buddies," I offer, waving my wrench menacingly before I put it down on the table behind me. Keeping one eye on him, I turn to pull a first aid kit from one of the drawers.

Leo's luminous blue eyes seem to get brighter as he sits up. He grins again, this time flashing teeth that are faintly pointed—halfway between shark teeth and blunt human teeth. I shiver, but don't know if it's from fear or interest.

I'm here for you, My Anya. Every fifty-two spans on Oseuth, my brethren and I set forth on a great pilgrimage to honor our gods and goddesses. I am one of the brothers who primarily honor you—Fearsome and Desirable Sindaria, Goddess of Death and Carnal Pleasure. We search universes across space and time until we find a corporeal aspect Sindaria inhabits, and we spend the next thirteen cycles performing our honoring ritual.

I swipe a cotton pad doused with antiseptic across the cut. I expect him to react, but the pain doesn't seem to register. Leo simply stares up at me with dreamlike wonder. It's utterly intoxicating. I've never been thought of as a catch before, let alone a goddess, and even if he's barking up the wrong tree, it strokes my ego in just the right way. Clearing my throat and stepping back, I pull out a small bandage.

"Well, um, the good news is the cut on your head doesn't look too bad," I say, embarrassed to be enjoying my descent into madness as much as I am. I press the bandage against his wound and absently stroke one fingertip against the impossibly soft skin of his cheek.

Leo tilts his head into my touch.

You have not mentioned my first two sacrifices. My gifts to you, so that you may feast upon the flesh of unworthy males. It is how the ritual begins.

"You mean the dead things out left outside? Yeah, that was really gross. I stuck them in the cryo-freezer. I'm *not* going to eat them," I grumble. "But, uh, thank you."

His too-beautiful face falls and as I watch, the cables tying him to the chair melt away, as if they're being corroded by acid. *Holy shit.* Before I can turn and run, Leo falls to the floor in front of me, bowing down so far, his forehead rests on the floor and his hair spills out around my feet. The blanket slides from his lap to the floor, forgotten. *Oh, wow.*

Forgive me, Venerable One. I should have found more worthy sacrifices for you. You deserve the finest of everything. I offer you my own body to use as you see fit. Punish me, if you will—let my pain sate your wonderfully cruel appetites.

Well, shit. I've made a huge misstep. I didn't mean to offend the poor guy, but I can't have him unearthing galactic horrors and showing up with them like some fucked up bouquet of flowers. But… it's probably not a great idea to antagonize an alien who can melt twelve-gauge cables from mere skin contact.

"I mean, um. Leo, your sacrifices were wonderful. You did great, champ, you really did. I just wanted to save them for later, okay? That's why they're in the freezer. You didn't displease me, but just…no more killing. Cool?"

He peeks up at me through the curtain of glittering blue hair.

"That was a neat little trick with the cords," I huff nervously. "How'd you do that?"

I still retain many of my abilities, even in this form. I may look human, but I am still Oseuthan.

"Abilities. Right. So, I was right to worry about the acid blood, I guess," I mutter.

You have nothing to fear from me, human goddess Anya.

He slowly lifts his head and sits back on his heels. In this position, it's hard not to notice the way his lean muscles flex beneath his velvety skin. His muscular thighs and sculpted abdomen appear more in line with a Grecian marble than what I pictured on an extraterrestrial humanoid.

"Tell me more about the ritual," I say in a rush, hoping he doesn't notice the blush stealing across my cheeks.

It is your ritual. He smiles coyly at me and something predatory enters his electric gaze again.

"Humor me," I all but shout, suddenly feeling very warm in my thin pajamas.

Six cycles of flesh and blood. Six cycles of pain and pleasure. One cycle of death.

The panic that has been strangely absent for this conversation rips through me again. I back away from him slowly, groping behind me for my wrench.

"So much for having nothing to fear from you! Blood? Pain? Death? You better start explaining yourself, or you're about to become a sexy alien cryo-popsicle," I snarl.

I do not understand many of these words, My Anya, or why you would have me explain your own ritual to you. If it is to test me and ensure I know my sacred texts, I am happy to oblige.

Leo rises slowly and steps forward, palms raised in a gesture of submission.

The six cycles of flesh and blood are meant to provide sustenance to your chosen form and sate the first of your divine appetites. Slake your thirst for the blood of cruel, unworthy males and feast on their traitorous flesh. We priests must bring these to you. We search galaxies for them.

I nod, lowering my wrench slightly. That's not great, but at least I'm not on the menu.

"Okay, so you bring me bad guys to eat. What next? Pain and pleasure? What's that all about?" I ask, surprised by my own breathlessness.

He takes another step in my direction, the slow movement like a graceful predator trying not to startle its prey. Desire burns in his luminous gaze, and the smile he gives me is sin itself.

Can you not guess, My Goddess?

The very last shred of rational thought is snuffed out like a spent match, leaving a trail of heated lust in its wake. He reaches up to run a finger across my lips and the gentle, exploratory touch paralyzes me with an onslaught of emotions: confusion, excitement, wariness, and above all, instinctive, brutal lust.

"And the cycle of death?" I hear myself whispering.

He's a breath from me now, sliding his fingers through my hair, scraping nails against my scalp. My hair comes loose and falls around my shoulders, and he makes an odd noise of approval in his throat—almost like a purr.

This body has sensory receptors everywhere. One might die from the pleasure of sensation alone.

His fingers tighten in my hair, pulling just enough to tip my mouth up to his and send bolts of desire arcing through my entire body. Heat pools between my legs and I swallow a whimper.

"D-d-die?" I stammer, dangerously close to his lips. "Does that mean you're going to kill me, after all?"

What is pleasure without a little death?

"I hope you're referring to orgasms," I breathe. Honestly, I don't know that I care at this point. Being fucked to death by a hot alien is probably better than a lifetime of loneliness on a lunar space station.

I sense you're amenable to the idea, my Anya. Do you wish to proceed with the ritual?

Leo's hand snakes down from my scalp to my neck, then traces my breasts through the thin fabric of my pajamas. My nipples harden instantly, and this time I can't stop the moan that gives sound to my need. Proceed with the ritual? What the hell am I getting myself into?

Cool, firm fingertips find their way beneath my shirt and stroke my abdomen, sliding low to the waistband of my pants.

Give me leave to worship you, My Goddess. My Anya. Show me how you want to be touched, tell me the words you wish to hear, let me fill your body with unbearable pleasure until you feel as if this flesh will come apart at the seams. Only then will I fuck you—only then will our bodies join. Only then will I paint this holy human body with my release.

With the onslaught of images and sensations he's broadcasting through my brain, I'm about to go out of my mind with sexual need. Some distant part of my brain keeps reminding me about the afore-mentioned death involved in this ritual, but would it be so bad to enjoy being worshipped in bed for a little while? Logic says yes, but my libido drowns it out with the drumbeat of fiery passion flowing to my erogenous zones.

Leo leans into me, sliding his hands down the curves of my ass. He pulls me against him, and I feel the firmness of his erection pressing against my stomach, igniting the primal part of my brain that can only focus on one thing. His wild smile takes on a feral edge and he dips his head to lick the sensitive skin beneath my ear.

Tell me yes, My Anya. Tell me yes, and then show me what this body can do.

chapter four

Leo

I HAVE EXPERIENCED SEX IN MANY DIFFERENT FORMS THROUGHOUT MY existence, but nothing has prepared me for the tidal wave of blinding want that My Goddess's firm, four-limbed body elicits. I am desperate for her.

Her interrogation leaves me with more questions than answers. Is it possible this beautiful creature is not, in fact, my Divine Sindarae? Faint warnings flit through me, but they're almost immediately silenced by my new body's lust for her. If she's not the embodiment of the Goddess of Carnal Desires, I don't know what she is. I have never hungered for another so much, so instantaneously.

"This is crazy," Anya murmurs, her lips a whisper away from mine. The throatiness of her voice is a rough scrape of desire in my ears, and I find myself dreaming of all the peculiar sounds she might make with that lush mouth.

My Anya, will you let me touch you? Taste you? Will you open your mind to me so I may learn how these bodies are best used?

I'm trying to be patient, but even the fabric of her clothing feels delicious against my skin and some strange new instinct has me pressing my body against hers.

"Open my mind to you? What do you mean?" she asks. Her hands are tentative on the skin of my abdomen—she seems particularly interested in the flat ridges of my stomach.

Show me in your mind how humans find pleasure with each other.

Her strange round pupils are blown wide, nearly swallowing the blue of her eyes. She sucks her bottom lip into her mouth and worries it with her small, blunt teeth, and finally nods in agreement. This time, when I stroke my consciousness against hers, she relaxes into me and a flood of images, words, sounds, and sensations cascades over my mind. I grasp onto fragments of her memories, desperate to understand how to make her feel good. One image returns again and again.

I weave my fingers through her silky hair again and pull her face to mine. Tilting my head slightly, I brush my lips against hers. A pleasant sensation, but I'm confused as to its meaning.

My face must show my dismay, because Anya chuckles.

"Kiss," she says. "It's a kiss. Of course you don't understand kissing—jellyfish don't have lips."

Her lips move gently against mine again and her small, pink tongue slips out to lick at the seam of my lips. Startled, I open my mouth, and she uses the opportunity to lean in, stroking my tongue with hers. The feeling is slick and wet and electrifies my nerves. Suddenly, I'm ravenous for this kiss. I return the movement, and Anya makes a soft mewl of pleasure, then wraps her hands around my neck. *Yes. I understand this now.*

I lift her small human body from the floor to keep our mouths together, because after learning the movements of lips and tongue and teeth, I find I would rather endure great pain than cease this kissing. Anya rocks against me, and my engorged "dick"—as she called it—rubs against her. The feeling lights a fire of sexual hunger that I know will not be slaked any time soon.

"God, your cock feels incredible against me," she mumbles against my lips. "How bad would it be for me to have sex with a hot alien I met an hour ago?"

I want to explore her body, so I let one of my hands slide back down beneath her clothes. The scent of her need perfumes her skin, a heady mixture of pheromones and her body priming itself for mine.

Not bad. Good. It would be very, very good, My Anya. Do you want this,

Sweet Goddess? Do you want me to plunge my hard cock into your wet heat? Or would you allow me to lick your dripping cunt until your body shudders with release first?

"For your first day in a human-like body, you've learned pretty quickly," she says with a grin.

You showed me all I need to know, My Anya. Your body will tell me the rest.

"You aren't trying to get me pregnant with a bunch of alien babies, are you? You're not going to lay eggs in my chest or anything, right?" she asks, suddenly concerned, but not concerned enough to cease rocking against my groin.

No, Devastating One. I chuckle. *Oseuthans do not lay eggs, and we do not make young during the ritual, unless you decide it should be so. I would be honored to sire your divine offspring, if you so choose, but that is not the point of this ritual.*

My reassurance relaxes her slightly, but I still sense there is something weighing on My Goddess's mind.

May I take you to a comfortable place while you decide what you want, My Anya?

She considers the question, and I'm delighted when her cheeks darken to a deep pink.

What does this signify? Can human bodies change colors?

I pulse my photophores in response and she brushes her fingertips across the glowing spots on my skin. My soft blue light dims to a deep, vivid purple and when she gasps in delight, my cock twitches at the noise. I wish to wring such a sound from her lips.

"Kind of," she says. "Actually, yeah, maybe I need to take a minute to think. I know somewhere we can go."

She takes my hand and leads me out to the main corridor. "Come with me. Tell me more about your planet—your brethren, as you call them."

Truly, Fierce One, there is not much to tell. We live simple, spare lives on Oseuth. We want for little, but we need little. We venture forth on holy pilgrimages every now and then, but those who never find a holy aspect return to the seas of Oseuth and must wait for another opportunity to seek their tribute.

Sadness blooms in me momentarily.

Though we're linked in mind, it's a solitary life. I've lost count of the pilgrimages I've made—lost track of my purpose more times that I can count, lost count of the worlds I've explored and the failures I've acquired. But that's behind me now, My Goddess, now that I've found you.

Anya winces slightly and casts a pitying look my way. "I'm not your goddess, Leo. I told you before—I'm just a human. I wish you'd believe me."

Again, this refusal. I am beginning to take her words as truth and not a test of faith from Sindaria. I do not understand the vehemence of my feelings for her—this lust which exists unparalleled in my intimate memories. If she is *not* Sindaria, then she must be a gift from the Goddess of Carnal Pleasures, for My Anya is most certainly divine in origin.

So you say. Well, if that is the case, I'd much rather hear about how you ended up in this desolate metal cocoon orbiting a planet you claim you did not destroy. Why are you here alone?

Anya sighs. "Promise you won't think I'm a pathetic excuse for a human?"

Shock pauses my footsteps through the claustrophobic metal corridor, and I turn to her in confusion.

I do not understand. You are the force that guides my existence. You are perfection and destruction given form. How could you be anything but divine?

She clears her throat and flicks her gaze to mine.

"I'm from the last generation born on that planet. I come from a long line of engineers: my mom, my grandfather, my great-grandfather. After my parents passed away, I left to join the Federation, thinking it would bring me to the stars. I've always felt this pull to the stars, but I suppose watching your home world shrivel and die will do that to anyone. You just long for something better because you know it's got to be out there, right?"

Her eyes begin to make water, which confuses me at first, but now that I can sense her emotions more clearly, I understand this to be a human expression of sadness. It's beautiful, really, that her lovely blue eyes produce the element that sustains life on my planet. The longing she speaks of plucks at my heart in kinship. I wish to tell her that I know this feeling, that my entire existence is predicated upon it. The endless search for a fearsome divinity who always seems to elude my tentacles; it has carved out a hollow in my insides. I do not feel this emptiness with my little human. Perhaps that is what led me to her moon in the first place. And perhaps that is why I cannot summon the familiar feelings of disappointment at the realization that Anya is *not*, in fact, Sindaria, but she might be the divine being I have scoured universes to find.

She wipes the moisture from her eyes and shakes her head, offering me a sad little smile that elicits a fluttering sensation in my organs. I am nearly overcome with the urge to fight something and present her with its corpse, but she has forbidden me from doing so. I will find other ways to honor her, then.

"Anyway, I spent a lot of my time working on the colony ships, and then this post opened. I came to lead the preliminary crew to start work on the station, to turn it into a luxury resort," Anya says, twisting her long ice-colored hair back into a knot on top of her head. Her vibrations are frenzied, but it's not from the surge of lust we shared earlier. It's as if she is anxious to say these things to me.

You answered a call to the stars. Why?

"Why did I come?" she repeats for clarification. Then, like the first rays of sunlight breaking through a sky of platinum clouds, she smiles. She's stopped walking now and we stand in front of a large chamber. "Here, I'll show you."

Pressing her hand to a panel, the wall slides open, and she pulls me inside the room. She gestures expansively and her pulse flutters with pride and happiness.

"The post gives me the chance to lead more crews on bigger, longer missions. Plus, the prelim crew gets their pick of the luxe cabins here," she says. "I chose this one. It's the furthest away from Earth, and you can only see it for a few hours in the day when I'm usually out working. I hate looking at it." She shudders. "Every time I do, it just reminds me how we all failed."

I admire the room that brings My Anya such satisfaction. The walls, ceiling, and floor appear to be made of a smooth, white stone, polished until it gleams. The window faces the Void Between Things and the infinite stars beyond. Along one wall lies a raised platform, decked in plush pillows and blankets. Anya presses something on the wall, and soft golden orange light filters in, giving the impression of a soothing summer sunset.

You have chosen well, my Anya. This is indeed a comfortable, luxurious place. How clever you are to have secured such a home for yourself.

"Thanks, Leo," she says, looking out the window. "It's nice to be able to brag about it a little. I've been a little sad not to be able to share it with someone."

As I come to stand next to her, the loneliness in her ocean eyes pierces my singular heart with another barb of empathy. All this time, I must wonder if it is Sindaria I've been searching for or if it's this odd little human. No one in all the universes feels as perfectly matched to me as this miraculous creature. I have lusted after others, but never have I wished to protect, to serve, to give up my brethren and priesthood…to stay. I want to take away her pain, her loneliness, her self doubt. She may not be Sindaria, but she is every inch a goddess I was made to worship.

I am honored you are sharing this with me. It is a gift I will treasure for the rest of my life.

Anya smiles again as we stare out into the Void Between Things, watching the stars. After a moment, her fingers interlace with mine—a curious, charming gesture.

"I'm sorry you crossed universes and didn't find Sindaria. I hate to think of your wasted effort, starting your ritual for a silly human on a space station. You should be off exploring other galaxies, where you can find your goddess," Anya says, sadness tainting her words.

Perhaps I have not found Sindaria, but I have found My Goddess.

I can bear her sadness no longer, and I pull her into my arms for another of her strange, wonderful kisses. She melts into my embrace like the last ice floes of spring and in less than a heartbeat, my desire surges with the force of a tidal wave.

Anya slides her hands around my neck and hops up to wrap her legs around my waist again, and I walk her back towards the cushioned platform along the wall.

"Yes, Leo, the bed—take me to the bed," she says against my lips.

Are you certain you truly want this to happen, Anya? I would die before I sparked your regret. But know that if you say yes, I will bring you such pleasure, you will be forever changed.

She's already tugging her garments up over her head as I drop her on the soft surface.

"Someone sounds a little full of himself," she chuckles, leaning back against the pillows.

I'm momentarily stunned by the sight of her breasts and soft, round abdomen. Nothing has ever been so beautiful to me.

The rest of your garments—may I remove them?

Anya nods and I kneel between her legs to gently pull them down her legs. When I discard them and focus back on her, I am in awe. Her flushed skin is smooth all over, except for a small triangle of light curls covering her sex. Her dusky pink nipples are peaked on the tips of her luscious, round breasts, and I am overcome with the need to taste her all over. As I crawl forward to her, I can't help but tremble in anticipation. I feel like a fledgling Oseuthan, unloved and untried. She will be my rebirth.

I brush tentative fingertips up her legs, and the feel of her skin is better than I imagined. I rub my cheek against the inside of her thigh, reveling in the warm, heady scent of her arousal. It's the most exquisite perfume and my mouth waters at the thought of how she will taste on my tongue.

Experimentally, I lick the skin of her glorious, rounded hip and my eyes almost roll back into my head. *Truly divine.*

Anya moans softly and runs her fingers through my hair as I nuzzle my way up her body. I alternate kisses, licks, and gentle, claiming nips from my teeth and catalog the way she squirms and whimpers and pants beneath my touch.

If I had another millennium of life, it would not be enough to memorize every expression, every twitch of muscle, every ferocious uptake of breath when My Goddess's pleasure begins to build. Returning to her mouth, I take her lips and tongue again in a greedy kiss. I want to devour her. Fierce possessiveness burns through my veins like venom, and I fight an onslaught of hunger that is so powerful, it makes my blue green photophores flicker crimson.

Anya notices and pauses.

"Leo? Is everything all right? What was that?" she rasps, her voice thick with passion.

I need to calm myself—to gather my thoughts. I inhale at the junction of her neck and shoulder, then trail kisses down her chest to score my teeth against the pebbled tip of her nipple. She gasps and bucks against me. I draw it into my mouth, lathing my tongue across it and sucking harder when Anya's moans take on a keening pitch.

Inspired, I knead her other breast with my palm and summon some of my dormant tentacles' stinging cells to my fingertips. As Anya writhes beneath me, I unleash a sharp sting upon her oversensitive nipple—not enough to damage her perfect breasts, but enough to send her a jolt of pleasure-goading pain. She arches up against me with a shriek.

"Holy fuck! What was that?" she cries. "God, Leo, that was amazing—do it again."

This time, I send some of the cells to the tip of my tongue where it swirls around her nipple. Again, the sharp shock of pain elicits a beautiful, shrill scream from her throat, and I scent a renewed flood of arousal between her legs.

Your body is so responsive to pleasure and pain. I've never seen anything like it. It's like you were made to be worshipped in this way by me. Is this good for you, My Goddess? Do you want me to continue?

"I'm halfway to coming and you haven't even touched my pussy yet," Anya says. "If you stop now, I will vaporize you in the plasma heaters."

I chuckle at her lascivious violence.

Perhaps there is something of the Goddess of Death and Carnal Pleasures in you, after all. Now, lie back and spread those legs for me, Fierce One, so that I may feast upon that divine cunt.

Anya mutters many coarse words to herself, but does as I ask. She spreads her legs too slowly to match the ferocity of my hunger, though, and I eagerly wrench her thighs apart. The sight of her human sex— soft, pink, and dripping with arousal for me—is too much to bear. My righteous priest's control snaps in an instant, and I dive forward to lay my unworthy mouth upon her.

With the first swipe of my tongue, all my thoughts stutter to a stop. She tastes of the sea. Warm, saline, faintly sweet…My Anya tastes so much like home, it's all I can do not to sink inside her and live there forever.

Her moan brings me back to myself, and I pull her down toward me so I can explore her slick folds more thoroughly. I eagerly lap at the wetness coating her flesh, then flick my tongue against the small bundle of nerves at the top of her sex. As soon as I do, Anya moans encouragement, then holds my head more firmly.

Ah, so this is where you want my attention…

"It's so good—feels so good, please keep going. Keep licking my clit," she groans. "More."

I take some time experimenting with my touch, swirling tight circles, alternating with wide sweeps, then almost losing myself entirely when I thrust my tongue up into her hot channel. Each action whips her into a frenzy, and I sense she's building toward her climax. Her pleasure has my nerves crackling and muscles tensing in my desperation to claim her.

"Leo," she chokes out on a whine. "I'm so close, please, I need more. I need…"

I know what you need, Anya. I know what your sweet cunt needs and I'm going to give it to you. Your pleasure is my greatest work—it is yours, and it is mine. Do you understand, Beloved One?

I slide one finger inside her and there is a faint roar of ocean waves in my ears. My mind is close to short circuiting from the utter perfection of her slippery sex. Anya tries to grind against my mouth and hand, and I press her back down on the bed.

No, My Goddess. This is mine for now. Yes?

"Yes," she says with a shudder.

With another chuckle, I slide a second finger inside her, pumping them in time with her pulse. She still writhes, clearly needing more, so I twist my fingers in her and curl them against a spongy spot on her inner walls where I sense the electricity sparking just beneath the surface. Again, she bows up off the bed and I must push her back down again.

Mine, I remind her.

She's close now, and my need to experience her release is all-consuming. Again, I summon the stinging cells to the tip of my tongue, and I time one final, punishing thrust of my fingers with the electric lick of pain against her clit, and she shatters beneath me. Her tight core clenches around my fingers and her panting breaths cease for a beat as I feel pleasure roll over her in successive waves. Finally, all the tension leaves My Goddess, and her limbs fall to her sides on a satisfied groan.

"Oh my god—that was the best oral sex I've ever had in my life," Anya says, languidly reaching for me. "Will you come up here and hold me for a bit?"

My own sexual need claws at me, but I turn away from it in the face of her sweet request.

It would be my honor, My Anya.

The barest trace of disappointment at not finding Sindaria evaporates with Anya's sweet sigh of satisfaction, and I know I will give up everything to stay with her always. I cannot feel sadness or despair over the realization. As I crawl up to wrap my new limbs around my little human goddess, I cannot feel anything but complete and utter contentment.

anya

LEO WRAPS ME IN HIS LIMBS AND PRESSES HIS FACE TO THE CROOK OF MY neck, as if I'm going to float away on the tide. I chuckle a bit, then remember he's never cuddled a human before, and a wave of tenderness overtakes me.

"Thank you," I say, trying to power through my awkwardness. "It's been a long time since anyone's done...*that*...for me and I wasn't kidding when I said you were the best I've ever had."

Leo grins and cracks one bright eye open at me.

I am glad you enjoyed it. Though I can't say I am pleased hearing about others who have failed to serve your pleasure.

"Don't tell me you're jealous," I laugh.

Not jealous. Just disappointed in the skill of your previous partners. An unsatisfied goddess is dangerous and irresponsible. Who knows what horrors she would unleash?

He runs a feather-light touch over my abdomen, and I chuckle when I realize he's teasing me. His hard cock presses against my hip, and I reach down to wrap my fingers around it. Immediately, he tenses.

"What about you, Leo? What pleasure do you get from your

al?" I ask. I stroke my hand up and down his hot length and every muscle in his body goes taut like a stretched rubber band.

My pleasure comes from yours, My Goddess. I do not need release.

"What if your goddess wants you to have one, anyway?" I press, swinging my leg over his and straddling his hips in one smooth movement.

I squeeze the base of his cock gently and his eyes widen in surprise.

I would never deny My Goddess anything.

"Good," I murmur as I bend down to run my tongue over the glowing precum beading at the tip.

Leo's hands fist in the sheets at his sides, then unclench and reach for my hair.

I...I have not known pleasure like this, Anya. I don't...I don't know what...

I slide my lips around him and take him fully in my mouth. When I swirl my tongue around his pleasantly salty skin, there's a faint ripping sound, and I open my eyes to see the sheets shredded beneath dagger-like claws that have erupted from his fingers.

It's too good. I don't...I can't...

Suddenly, he sits up and pulls me off him, and he slides out of my mouth with a wet pop. His movements are rough but restrained, and I can tell he's barely able to maintain control. It's a lit match on the tinderbox of my lust, and my rapidly kindling need is about to become an inferno.

"Can I show you what comes next?" I ask. "Do you want to keep going?"

His thoughts come through in fragments now, unlike the clear conversations we've had thus far. He's a dark well of voracious need—this is truly the priest of a goddess of sex and death. The glowing blue green of his eyes darkens to an electric violet, and he finally nods at me.

Gripping his cock again, I position him at my entrance, taking a moment to slide the tip through my slick folds. His hands claw at my hips—fingers digging into the soft flesh of my sides in a not-unpleasant way. Slowly, I sink down onto him until he's sheathed to the hilt. I'm stretched with the fullness of him, but it's good—so good I don't think I've ever felt like this before.

His gaze is riveted on the place where our bodies join, and when I start moving, rising above him and rhythmically lowering myself back onto his hard length, his eyes drift close in instinctive bliss.

My Anya. My Goddess. Yes, Goddess—you feel so incredible. My body hasn't known pleasure like this. My soul hasn't known joy like this. It feels like coming home. I am forever yours, My Anya.

His words send a thrill through me, as if my loneliness has found its answering call. My whole life I thought I longed for the stars, but maybe my need was for more than that. Maybe it was a sense of home, of belonging, of adventure, of joy—all things I'm feeling with Leo. Emotion forms a tight ball in my throat as I pick up speed, and Leo's desperate panting is coming in sharp gasps.

As if he's reading my mind—hell, maybe he is—he suddenly hooks one leg around mine and flips me beneath him. He lifts one of my thighs up to adjust his angle of penetration, and then he's pistoning into me with the exact amount of force I need to sight an oncoming orgasm on my horizon.

Do you wish for more, My Goddess?

His hand snakes low and one clever thumb begins to circle my clit.

"Yes," I rasp. "More, Leo—give me more."

Everything. I would give you my life force itself. But for now—I will give you what your perfect human body needs.

His pace slows ever-so-slightly and blue-violet eyes flicker momentarily, and suddenly there's a slight pressure around the tight pucker of my ass.

"Holy shit," I say, the sound breathless and shrill. "What is that?"

Leo leans down to scrape his sharp teeth down my neck and the building heat in my body threatens to burn us both to ashes.

A tentacle. I altered my shape slightly—I sense there are more pleasure receptors in this part of your body.

The mystery tentacle slips inside me from behind while Leo continues to thrust, and the dual appendages working me over have electrified every nerve until I'm practically coming out of my skin.

It's too much—it's not enough. It's too many layers of pleasure stacking on top of each other in a tower of sin that reaches the heavens.

Anya, you feel so good, I can't hold it back...

"Don't hold back!" I scream, just as I feel the most intense orgasm of my life start to break.

Come for me, My Goddess. Come with me.

With that blinding demand, my body shudders with my violent release and the stars outside my window blur in front of my eyes. Wave after wave of pleasure drags me down until I'm convinced I've devolved into a boneless, one-celled organism.

I feel Leo shudder and grunt—the only sound I've ever heard him make—and I feel his hot release inside of me.

On one final, languid thrust, Leo nearly collapses on top of me, but rolls over and drags me into his side. Before either of us can say anything, he wraps his limbs around me again, as if he's too afraid to let me go.

I have never experienced pleasure like that. I am convinced you are a gift from Glorious Sindaria—even if you are not her in physical form.

A thread of unease winds through me.

"You're not angry? Or disappointed?" I ask.

He lifts his head to look at me with the most gut-wrenching, heart-stopping expression of pure adoration, it nearly steals my breath.

My seed leaks from your divine cunt even now, My Goddess. Anger and disappointment are not even in the same universe as we are.

I breathe a sigh of relief.

"Well, now that you know I'm not Sindaria, what will you do? Will you go back to Oseuth? Will you..." I pause, suddenly overcome by dread and sadness so poignant, it aches. "Will you keep searching the universe for your goddess?"

I have searched many universes, Anya. And I have found My Goddess. I think, perhaps, Sindaria brought us together for some unknowable reason. If you will have me, I will stay with you. We can live in your metal cocoon, if you wish. Or we can take our chances and explore the galaxy. There are those who could help us with a ship, and many worlds you may wish to see.

The emotions clogging my throat finally overwhelm me and tears spring to my eyes. The chance to explore the stars, and to share it *with* someone, is within my grasp. Literally.

"You would do that? You would give it all up after one night with some random human?" I ask.

Leo tucks a strand of hair behind my ear and smiles.

If you're asking if I'd forfeit a lonely quest to find love and acceptance from one goddess when I have love and acceptance in my arms from another goddess, the question seems absurd. I would stay with you, My Anya. My devotion is a fearsome thing. Is that what you want?

Given everything that's happened over the last day, my answer is as natural as it is alien.

"Yes," I say. "I want you to stay. I want to explore the universe with you."

His smile is terrifying and breathtaking as he holds me close, trailing light touches down my arms. I sigh with contentment and press a few buttons on my bio-cuff. Music filters into the room as we watch the sun rise on the lunar surface. Billie's melodious voice gives sound to my thoughts in a too-perfect verse.

Blue moon
Now I'm no longer alone
Without a dream in my heart
Without a love of my own.

about lily riley

Lily Riley is a romance author writing sci-fi romance, paranormal romance, and fantasy romance books that feature a little bit of cheek and a lot of steam.

When Lily isn't writing about dreamy aliens and 18th-century French vampires, she enjoys sipping wine, eating cake, and dancing naked by the light of the full moon.

She is the author of the Vampires of Versailles series, available now.

To learn more, visit www.authorlilyriley.com

swept away in stardust

Lisa Edmonds

chapter one

gen

"Come on, baby," I coaxed. "You know I always treat you good. You've got one more in you, I just know it. Do it for me, okay?"

Unfortunately, I didn't think *Nebula* had one more in her—for me or anyone else.

With a sigh, I sat back on my heels, cleaned lubricant from my hands with a rag, and studied the engine's core. "Just one more job before you need drydock maintenance," I told my ship. "That's all I'm asking. I need one more job after this to afford downtime and then we can both take a break. I'll find an outpost where you can get some parts replaced and I can get laid. Then we'll both be happy. Well, as happy as either of us are likely to get."

My ship groaned and creaked. I couldn't tell if that was an agreement with my plan or a derisive sniff at my ambition to find someone at an outpost worth sharing a bunk with. Or just the strain of another deep-space run at hyperspeed with a fully loaded cargo bay. *Nebula* was a moody bitch when she wanted to be. I supposed I could relate.

I shut the access panel to the core and rose.

"You require sleep, Captain Drae." My maintenance robot rolled to my side from the open access panel where it had been repairing wires. The tall, many-appendaged 'bot had a male voice today with a

373

distinctly Raxian accent. It knew I disliked Raxians, but it kept that voice in its rotation—I suspected just to annoy me, like the reminders about needing rest.

"You know there's no rest for the wicked, Mechabot." I headed for the cockpit. "Work on this conduit instead, okay? Contact me immediately if you see anything else leaking or sparking."

"Affirmative, Captain." The 'bot turned its attention to the open access panel and the leaky tube that had given us trouble lately.

Unfortunately, it wasn't the only leak on my ship, and even more unfortunately, that conduit was part of *Nebula*'s life support system.

I suspected I was more concerned about the leak than Mechabot. The robot could function perfectly fine if life support failed. After I asphyxiated, it would even roll past my corpse to pilot my ship to Ymar II. It was the coldest of comforts, I reflected wryly, to know my untimely death wouldn't stop the food, weapons, and other supplies in my cargo hold from making it to one of the most dreaded prison colonies in the galaxy.

A paycheck is a paycheck, I reminded myself. The prison colony paid top rates for speedy delivery from reliable freight captains. I was lucky to be on their roster. Whatever I thought of the colony itself, these gigs paid for my fuel, ship maintenance, and my infrequent planetary or outpost stopovers.

Not that I got as much enjoyment from shore leave as someone who didn't have my past. I never stayed long in one place, and I never really relaxed, no matter how luxurious the accommodations. My instincts urged me to keep moving. Too many people wanted me dead. A target who stayed in motion was much more difficult to take out.

Right now, all I wanted was to deliver my cargo to Ymar II, get paid, and set course for Outpost 600. If I was lucky, my favorite freighter mechanic would still be living and working there, and both *Nebula* and I could get well-serviced during our stay.

Nebula was a mid-sized single pilot freighter with a cockpit, a captain's quarters, and two small cabins I used for storage since I had no crew but Mechabot. The ship also included an engine control room, a minimal medical bay, and its enormous cargo hold. I would be the first to admit she was fully utilitarian and would never win any beauty contests, but she was reliable, tough, and perfect for a former mercenary soldier who preferred the solitude of lengthy deep-space freight runs.

I'd only made it halfway to the cockpit from the engine room when an alarm sounded and warning lights flashed red all around me. "Stasis pod systems failure detected in the cargo hold," the ship's computer announced.

"What the hells?" I stopped in the middle of the corridor. "Computer, *what* stasis pod?"

"Unidentified stasis pod detected in the cargo hold." The computer's utterly unemotional voice contrasted sharply with my anger and confusion. "Life-threatening conditions observed. Do you wish to cancel this alert?"

"No, I do not wish to cancel the alert," I snapped. "But silence the alarm so I can *think*."

The noise shut off abruptly. The emergency lights along the corridor remained on. Not really necessary, since I was seeing red anyway.

What the hells stasis pod? I fumed.

The cargo manifest for this job had not included a stasis pod. If it had, I wouldn't have taken the gig. Every booking agent I worked with knew I did not transport people aboard my freighter for any price— not as passengers, not as crew, and most *definitely* not as cargo. So someone had snuck this pod aboard my ship, hidden among the supplies intended for the Ymar II colony.

I opened my weapons storage, stuck my pulse gun and a couple of my favorite blades into my thigh holsters, and ran for the closest entrance to the cargo bay.

At the entry, I pressed my palm to the scanner and unlocked the hold. The doors rattled and whined as they opened. I sighed. I really needed to get Mechabot to fix these doors once it repaired life support.

Nebula's cargo bay made up three quarters of the ship's total volume—typical of mid-sized deep space freighters. The supplies ordered by the Ymar II colony filled the bay completely. I'd supervised the load-in and not spotted the stasis pod, so it was hidden somewhere among the mountains of stacked containers.

"Computer, location of the malfunctioning stasis pod?" I called.

The computer chirped to signal that it was scanning. "Quadrant Delta," it replied. "Container listed on manifest as XKDP6335, food waste processing unit and related materials."

Luckily, Quadrant Delta was against the hull on the starboard side of the hold and easily accessible. Once I got close, urgent beeping led me straight to one container in particular. XKDP6335 turned out to be a large unit about four meters wide by five meters tall and twelve meters long. Two more identical units were stacked on top of it.

The shipping agent had locked the container. According to my contract, I had to leave that lock intact or risk a deduction from my payout for its compromised contents. Given the work I needed done on my ship, money had a strong claim to the top of my list of concerns. However, slightly above that was wanting to know who the hells was stashed in this container. Plus I still had six Earth-standard days of travel to get to Ymar II and I didn't want to spend them with a corpse in the cargo hold.

I had to consider that this could be a ploy to get me to open the container, where an assassin might lie in wait. Despite how carefully I had built my new identity since leaving the mercenary guild, a past enemy could have tracked me down or hired someone to find me. That was an argument for leaving the container locked, dropping it on Ymar II, and letting its contents be their problem.

On the other hand, if a potential assassin didn't have a way to open it from the inside, they would hardly have locked themselves in and gambled I'd voluntarily open it. So either I had to open it now or risk the person inside opening it later.

Meanwhile, the beeping had turned into a full-fledged alarm that indicated the stasis pod had reached critical failure. If there really *was* someone in the pod, I was about to have a corpse on my hands who wouldn't be able to answer any questions without the help of a medium.

"Shit," I muttered.

I typed my override code into the container door's keypad, got ready to shoot anything that moved, and yanked the door open.

chapter two

kerian

I AM DYING.

From the depths of an unconsciousness darker and more abyssal than I'd ever experienced before, I struggled to reach the surface and wake. My chest heaved as I gasped for air and my body ached down to the bones.

Instinct told me to move, to get away from whatever caused me pain and stifled my breathing. But when I reached out, my hands struck something solid about thirty centimeters from my face. I saw nothing but pitch black, though I felt sure my eyes were open.

What was right in front of me felt like a glass window. When I rapped on it with my knuckles, the sound confirmed it. Everything else around me smelled like metal. A metal cocoon. But with a window?

My wheezing breath brought in no air.

Thinking was difficult, but even in my foggy brain, the links of evidence formed a chain: I had woken in a stasis pod. A stasis pod that was about to become my coffin.

Fumbling, my fingers and toes numb from what I now recognized as the effects of long-term stasis, I searched the interior of the pod for an emergency release and found none.

I drew back my fists as much as the pod would allow and punched the glass with all my might. Now *that* pain I felt very clearly. I had no breath with which to curse. The window creaked but didn't break. The ringing in my ears grew louder. Unconsciousness was moments away and death right behind it.

I had not survived the horrors of genetic manipulation on my home planet and ten years of service as a spy in the Gandarian army to die in this gods-damned pod.

With darkness closing in, I hit the window one last time with my fists, my feet, everything I had. I felt the door give, but I thought it was probably lack of oxygen or wishful thinking—

—Until my shuddering breath drew in a lungful of stale air and I began to cough. The ringing in my ears cut off abruptly. An alarm of some kind? I couldn't think about that now. All that mattered was breathing.

To my sensitive nose and antennae, the air reeked of machine parts, industrial solvents, and recycled ventilation, but I had seldom smelled anything sweeter.

When I opened my eyes, I found myself staring at the business end of a pulse gun pointed directly at my face. Holding the weapon was a human woman in a captain's jumpsuit. She had long blonde hair in a braid, the physique of someone who worked hard every day of her life, and a smear of what appeared to be engine coolant on her forehead.

She also had the coldest eyes I had ever seen that weren't in the mirror looking back at my own.

"Who. The *fuck*. Are you?" she demanded. Each word promised death.

I recognized the tone, the look, the way she held her gun and the kinds of blades she wore in her thigh holsters. She might be a ship's captain now, but at some point in the very recent past, we'd been in roughly the same business.

With numbness in my extremities and my brain still muddled by long-term stasis, I couldn't move fast enough to disarm her—not when her finger was already on the trigger.

On the other hand, she had opened my pod before I asphyxiated and hadn't shot me on sight. That meant I had a chance to survive.

"I'm Kerian Nos, Captain." My voice sounded hoarse. I coughed. My throat and lungs hurt from gasping for air. "Permission to come aboard?"

Behind her, through the open door of this shipping container, I saw a large cargo hold full of identical units. I had no idea how I got here, or where *here* was, other than the amount of cargo, thrumming of engines, and smell of recycled air indicated a freighter traveling at hyperspeed.

I had no memory of where I'd been before this except hazy impressions of sitting in a bar on the planet Erzia and meeting a woman with red hair and a scar on her shoulder. After that…nothing. Not a gods-damned thing.

It occurred to me then, very belatedly, that I was naked.

The sight of my body tended to elicit one of two reactions: amazement or disgust. The captain's gaze never left my face, however, and I saw no reaction to my body at all—revulsion or otherwise. I might have been as human as her or as bizarre as a Hardanian lava squid or anything in between for all she cared. All she apparently saw was an enemy.

When my cramped and aching wings fluttered and changed colors and my antennae leaned toward the captain, her index finger moved on the trigger. I tucked my wings back into the pod at my sides.

She studied me, reading my eyes, face, and body language in the same way I looked at others: as a trained killer assessing a threat and deciding whether to ask questions and then shoot, or just shoot. "Give me one reason not to kill you now," she said.

"I'm polite?" I rasped.

She scoffed. "I've killed a lot of polite men."

"Fair enough." I wanted to massage my aching limbs but figured any movement would get me shot, so I stayed perfectly still. "Well, I didn't put myself in this pod. I think we'd both like to find out who did, so we can kill them."

"We are not a *we*." Her icy blue eyes narrowed. "If you have no information for me, I see no reason not to shoot you."

"I didn't say I have no information," I countered. "I just don't know *yet* who put me on your ship. It's got to be someone who wanted me gone. Without me, you'll have no chance to figure it out. I doubt I'm here because of something *you* did."

In the middle of that sentence, the shape of her eyes changed. That look activated my every cell and flooded my body with adrenaline.

My offhand comment about not being aboard her ship because of something she'd done had the opposite effect than I'd intended and made her think that was exactly why I was here. She must have already suspected I'd come to kill her.

A millisecond before she squeezed the trigger of her pulse gun, I launched myself out of the pod with a desperate leap. My legs and wings had recovered just enough to help me avoid the blast. The bolt of plasma sizzled under me and hit the stasis pod, leaving a smoking hole right where my chest had been.

I landed on an enormous food waste processing machine next to the pod, flipped off of it, and dropped on top of the captain. As we fell, I grabbed the gun to keep it pointed away from my body. She grunted and fired again when we hit the floor. That shot barely missed my torso. The plasma left a white-hot burn on my left side, singed my wing, and melted through one of the legs of the machine, causing it to wobble.

I smashed the captain's right hand twice against the container's floor to loosen her grip. The gun went skidding into a dark corner. She already had a blade in her other hand. With astonishing dexterity, she spun it and drove its point straight up at the center of my primary heart like a highly trained killer. She recognized my physiology and knew where to stab, though my kind were extremely rare. Who *was* this woman?

Before she could plunge the blade into my heart, I forced the knife's point away from my chest and toward her throat as I pinned her lower body with my legs and feet.

The captain's fiery gaze locked on my face as her chest heaved against mine. In this position, my bare cock pressed into the warmth between her thighs.

I couldn't tell how much of her fury resulted from being pinned down with a knife at her throat versus the unfortunate location of my dick. I wanted to apologize for the latter, but our position was an accident. And it wasn't like I'd asked to end up on this ship.

She smelled of grease and her ship and hard work and anger. Whether it was my years of army service, or my brief foray into life as a mercenary, or just my own peculiar tastes in women, I found myself breathing in her scent and enjoying it. I liked how she felt beneath me and wished I did not have a knife in my hand.

Unfortunately, judging by her glare, she understood that nothing prevented me from slicing her throat other than my decision not to. I'd bested her in three moves. Given the chance, she'd likely gut me like a Pallasian mettlefish and toss my corpse out the closest airlock.

"I don't want to kill you," I said, holding her knife above her jugular. "I just want to find out where I am and why I'm on this ship."

"Fuck you, Kerian Nos," she said coldly. "You'd better kill me now or you won't get another chance."

Alarms split the air. The cargo bay plunged into darkness except for red emergency lights.

An ominous rumble rolled through the ship. The deck shuddered and heaved violently, throwing us roughly against the base of the food waste processing machine damaged earlier by the pulse gun blast. I took a painful blow to my ribs and lost my grip on the captain. She rolled away from me toward the container door.

The enormous machine's other front leg buckled. It toppled over, nearly crushing my stasis pod. The pod held up just enough to keep the machine from killing me outright, but I ended up trapped between the machine and what remained of the pod.

From somewhere to my left, the captain cried out as all the small shipping crates stacked on top of and around the machine fell in a potentially deadly avalanche. Her scream cut off abruptly.

My stomach clenched. *Oh no.*

As the shaking stilled, more emergency lights activated in the bay, bathing my surroundings in hazy red. I belly-crawled from under the machine and spotted the captain pinned under a fallen crate. A rivulet of blood snaked its way across the floor from her body.

"Captain!" I shouted. "Captain, can you hear me?" She did not respond or move.

I got to my feet and staggered to the captain to assess her condition. One of the small supply crates had landed on her chest. The corner of another had apparently struck her in the head, knocked her unconscious, and left a bloody gash on her forehead.

To my relief, she was still breathing, but the sound was rough and labored. The blood on the container floor came from under the crate and not from her head. She likely had severe internal injuries.

My body ached from my time in stasis and hitting the machine, but I was no stranger to agony. I set the pain aside, picked up the crate with care, and dropped it a few feet away from the captain's unmoving body.

"Emergency alert," a computerized voice stated in Alliance standard, its voice echoing in the cargo bay. "Impact by debris has caused a hull breach and significant damage. Life support and other crucial systems are failing. Captain, please proceed immediately to your emergency refuge and seal the door. The ship will maintain course to its destination. Repeating. Impact by debris has caused a hull breach and significant damage. Life support and other crucial systems are failing. Captain, please proceed…"

I cursed and crouched to touch the captain's face. "Captain, can you hear me? Where is the emergency cabin?"

She did not stir.

I had to get her to shelter. Doing so risked compounding her injuries, but it was either move her or leave her here to die.

Would she save my life if the situation were reversed? I wondered. Probably not. She did just try to blow a hole through me. Now I had to keep her from dying or face surviving this calamity and the journey to our unknown destination alone.

And I didn't even know her name.

As gently as possible, I scooped the captain up in my arms. The scent of her blood filled my nose and made my antennae twitch. The air had already become thin. The hull breach sucked it from the ship much faster than the failing life support system could replace it.

"Computer," I called, hoping it would respond to my voice. "Where is the emergency refuge?"

"The captain's cabin is the designated emergency habitat," the computer said. "Ship's port side, aft section. Follow the lighted path. Emergency alert. Impact by debris—"

"I heard you, Computer." Careful not to jostle the captain too much, I ran from the cargo bay. In the corridor, the red emergency lights flashed in a pattern that directed me to my left. "Computer, what is the captain's name?" I called.

"The ship *Nebula Traveler* is under the command of Captain Gen Drae. Please proceed immediately to the emergency cabin and seal the door."

At a run, I followed the red lights down one corridor, turned right, and down another until they led me to an open doorway and what was unmistakably the captain's quarters.

The spartan interior matched the utilitarian appearance of the rest of the vessel. The main room contained a wide bunk, desk, chair, and food preparation station. Above the captain's bunk, a large window showed a view of stars passing at hyperspeed. To my left, an alcove led to the washroom and what appeared to be storage for clothing and other personal belongings.

Carefully, I settled her on the bunk, and then ran back the way I'd come to a door labeled *Medical Bay*. By the time I reached it, I struggled to get a breath.

I stuffed two emergency medical kits with everything I could get my hands on that I might need to treat the captain's injuries, plus a couple of large medic's coveralls I thought I could use as clothing.

My journey back to the captain's quarters seemed to take four times longer than the trip to the medical bay. I gasped for air and pulled myself along the wall a few steps at a time. Within a minute, I guessed there would be no more air to breathe on the ship other than in the emergency cabin.

Just before I reached the captain, a ship's maintenance robot with a half-dozen arms rolled past, presumably on its way to the cockpit to take control of the ship. If it recognized me as an intruder, it must not have been programmed to attack.

"Keep us on course and alive," I gasped.

The 'bot's head rotated one hundred and eighty degrees to face me as it continued without pausing. "Affirmative," it said, and disappeared around a corner.

I staggered inside the captain's cabin and fumbled for the door controls. They were labeled in Raxian—not surprising, since many freighters this size were built in Raxia's busy shipyards. I pushed the one labeled *Emergency Seal*, hit *Confirm*, and collapsed to the deck.

On the bunk, the captain wheezed, her face and lips tinged blue.

The door slid closed, locked, and sealed. Immediately after, I heard and felt a welcome *whoosh* of air as the cabin pressurized. A ship's designated emergency habitat typically had its own self-contained life support, climate system, stores of food and water, and power source. If the captain survived her injuries, those resources would keep us alive until we reached the ship's destination—assuming we suffered no more calamities in the meantime.

A few fortifying gulps of air gave me enough strength to drag the medical bags to the bed. The bunk was surprisingly oversized, apparently made to accommodate species larger than humans. For all her defiance and anger, the captain was about average height for a human female. She appeared small in comparison to the bed and almost fragile—a far cry from the warrior I'd met only minutes before.

In the short time it had taken for me to get to the medical bay and back, her blood had soaked through her uniform and bedding and puddled on the floor beside the bunk. When I ripped her jumpsuit open, I let out a hiss of dismay and anger at the sight of her badly lacerated torso. The crate had come so very close to killing her instantly. Another half-meter to the right, and I could have done nothing to save her. As it was, her survival was anything but certain.

I brushed loose hair back from her face. "Stay alive, Captain," I said.

Captain Gen Drae. Killer of polite men and stowaways and probably many others besides, who smelled like heaven and home to me.

I dumped the medical bags out on the bunk and went to work, fighting to save the life of the woman who'd just done her damnedest to end mine.

chapter three

gen

Great gods above and below, did I feel like shit.

I opened my eyes and blinked a few times to bring my surroundings into focus. The room was dark except for a few faint lights, but I recognized my own quarters. I lay on my side on my bunk as I always did, facing the door.

The first odd thing I noticed—other than how much my whole body hurt—were the scents around me. My bedding smelled freshly cleaned, as did my cabin, and the distinctive odor of medical equipment hung in the air. Strangely, I also smelled something that reminded me of a jungle, but that didn't make any sense.

I let out a groan and started to roll onto my back, only to find myself held in place by a strong hand on my hip.

"Stay still," a man said from behind me, his voice gentle.

Fury and fear, in equal amounts, sent an icy chill down my spine. Thanks to my muddled mind and aching body, I hadn't realized I was not alone.

"No sudden movements," the man behind me added. "You got knocked out and all your wounds are still healing. Don't rip anything open again."

I had no memory of being knocked out and no reason to take this man at his word, but my entire body did hurt, especially my head and my chest.

"Who are you?" I demanded. I sounded hoarse, as though I had been unconscious for a long time. "What the hells are you doing on my ship? *And in my bunk?*"

"My name is Kerian Nos," he murmured. Despite my anger, he kept his voice quiet and calm and deliberately nonthreatening.

It didn't escape my notice that he'd put himself between me and the wall, leaving me free to get away if I wanted while allowing himself to be in the more vulnerable position. He'd done everything he could to anticipate my anger and confusion and assuage my fear.

"You found me in your cargo hold, trapped in a malfunctioning stasis pod," he added, now with definite concern in his voice. "Then the ship was severely damaged. Do you not remember?"

The more I tried to recall details of who he was and what had happened, the fuzzier my memory became. I supposed that supported his claim of a head injury. I also had a dim recollection of trying to shoot him. Obviously I hadn't succeeded in killing him if we were in my cabin, and in my bunk.

And speaking of which…

Under my blanket, I wore sleepwear, and my skin smelled of cleanser. "Where is my uniform?" I demanded.

"I removed your clothes, but I took no liberties. I am a trained army medic." His gentle voice became clinical. "Once you were healed, I cleaned away the blood and changed your clothing."

Indeed, several new scars crisscrossed my torso. More evidence of how close I'd come to death, and of how much he'd had to do to save my life. My sluggish brain had a difficult time processing this information.

"How did I get injured?" I asked.

He explained about the damage to the ship and that we were still on course for Ymar II, piloted by Mechabot.

"I knew that robot would get into the cockpit someday," I muttered, then raised my voice. "Computer, what caused the damage to the ship?"

"Scans indicate a collision with a derelict vessel," the computer replied.

"Ship's status?"

"Hull breaches on the starboard side, aft section, and widespread system damage. Shipwide life support and interspace communications remain offline. You are advised to remain sequestered in your cabin until the ship reaches its destination."

My ship. My gut contracted.

For all her moodiness and leaky conduits and sparking wires, *Nebula* was mine—the only thing I'd ever had that truly belonged to me.

Floating debris posed a constant danger for deep space travelers, but usually they weren't large enough to cause anything more than minor damage. If we'd struck a derelict vessel at hyperspeed, we were lucky to be alive, and even luckier to be able to continue to Ymar II.

"Why save my life?" I asked. I wanted my voice to be steady, but it wasn't. I felt like my own pain reflected *Nebula*'s suffering too.

The bunk dipped behind me for a moment, as if he'd started to move toward me then thought better of it.

"I'd have to explain once we arrived why you were dead and I wasn't on any manifest," he said. "We had a disagreement about why I was aboard your ship, but you *did* open my stasis pod before I asphyxiated. And it's almost a standard week to Ymar II. A long time to be sealed in a cabin alone."

Well, that made sense.

I still felt like I'd been trampled by a horde of Hardanian war-pigs, but I wanted to look at this man's face because try as I might, I could not remember what he looked like.

"I'm turning over," I said. "Give me some room."

The entire bunk moved when he scooted away from me. I sensed he was much larger than me, and when I carefully rolled to my back, I found I was right.

Kerian Nos, my stowaway and apparent savior, sat with his back against the bulkhead, with one knee raised and the other leg folded. Even sitting, I could tell he dwarfed me by more than half a meter.

I immediately recognized him as a Fortusian, a race of humanoids who enhanced themselves through genetic engineering and manipulation, utilizing biological material from species across the known galaxy.

Like most Fortusians, Kerian's astonishingly beautiful body appeared almost entirely human, but his dark blue skin had green patterns that reminded me of leaves. Thick, dark hair with streaks of blue and green hung just below his ears. Lavender antennae, about twenty-five centimeters in length, sprouted from each side of the crown of his head. They twitched and swiveled, one toward me and the other in various directions, maybe scenting the air and listening for sounds aboard the ship.

He had folded his exquisite, brightly colored, moth-like wings behind his back. Their colors and patterns captivated me.

I must have taken quite a hit to the head to knock my memory of this man from my brain. The only impressions of him I'd had until this moment were suspicion and the desire to kill him for stowing away aboard my ship.

But then he'd gotten me to safety, saved my life, and watched over me until I woke. He hadn't had to do any of those things. It would have been easy enough to claim he couldn't save me. The damage to the ship, his stasis pod, and Mechabot's records would back up his story about the disaster. I couldn't help but wonder if he'd had some other reason to keep me alive. What it might be, I had no idea, given I'd really done my best to kill him.

He'd apparently improvised clothing for himself using a coverall he must have found in the medical bay. I felt a little disappointed by the fact he was clothed and then wondered what in the hells was wrong with me.

The jumpsuit was designed to adapt to a wide range of body types, but his size strained its fabric. He'd had to tear off the sleeves to accommodate his long, muscular arms, and cut open the back for his wings. I couldn't help but notice those details—along with the way the jumpsuit hugged the area of his groin in a way that implied what was under the fabric was proportionate to the rest of him.

Well, of course I'm curious about his body, I reasoned. *Nothing wrong with that.* I'd only met a few Fortusians and each was entirely unique.

Genetic engineering created infinite possibilities. I didn't know the source of the genes that created his wings and antennae and whatever other enhancements he had, but he was a magnificent male.

"I'm sorry for staring," I said, though I wasn't. And why I felt compelled to be polite to a strange stowaway was as much of a mystery as his presence on my ship.

"You are not sorry." His mouth turned up at the corners in a wry smile. "And no apology is necessary. I'm used to stares—though few are as admiring as yours. I usually evoke disgust."

"I wasn't admiring," I retorted, while wondering who in any galaxy would look at him with disgust. "I've just never seen someone with your particular modifications. It's scientific curiosity, nothing more."

He regarded me. "I suppose it's not in my best interest to tell you this, but I can smell lies and deception." He pointed to his antennae. "My senses are all very acute."

Well, shit. If he could smell a lie, he could probably also smell that the sight of his body had elicited a definite reaction in some very personal places.

I had been in space for a long time. I certainly had ways of providing my own pleasure, but no species, no matter how technologically advanced, had come up with a substitute as good as the real thing.

Now both of his antennae swiveled in my direction.

Damn it, damn it, damn it to all the hells, I thought.

I tried to think about cold water, Raxian basketmaking, and even the leaky plasma conduit that had probably ruptured during the accident and taken out the ship's life support system, but for every non-sexual thought I managed to have, two more thoughts and images of him invaded my brain. I knew I shouldn't have waited so long for my ship's drydock repairs. Now both *Nebula* and I were desperately in need of attention.

More to the point, the fact he didn't leave me to die in the cargo hold stirred something in my heart—something I'd never expected to feel. A kind of camaraderie, or kinship, at least, brought on by barely surviving one of the many calamities that lurked in space.

Add to that the way he smiled at me, as if he knew exactly what I had on my mind, and I could no longer think of anything but how warm and strong he looked and how much I wanted to see everything under that jumpsuit.

Stop it, I lectured myself. *You're just lonely and horny from being in space too long. You don't owe this man a damn thing.*

Except I *did* owe him something. Not sex, because that wasn't a commodity I traded, but I did owe him a debt. He'd saved my life. Maybe because he needed me alive when the ship arrived at the colony, and maybe because he didn't want to spend the next few days alone. Whatever his motivation, I owed him a ride to Ymar II. After that, he was on his own.

Only then did I realize how tired he appeared. I'd been so caught up in admiring him and thinking dirty thoughts that I hadn't spotted the slump of his shoulders or the dullness in his eyes. He'd barely woken from stasis when disaster struck, and he'd spent the hours since ensuring I didn't die.

As my adrenaline wore off, exhaustion swept over me too. Healing and blood loss had sapped my strength. I might not be bleeding everywhere anymore, but I'd still taken a beating.

Neither of us were in any shape to do anything about whatever this was stirring between us. Not right now, anyway. Later, once we'd slept off our exhaustion, I'd let myself think more about how it would feel to have Kerian on top of me—or under me. I was willing to bet it would feel pretty damn good.

"We should sleep." I rolled to my side to face him and tucked my bent arm under my pillow. "You look like you're about to pass out sitting up."

"I was made to not need rest very often."

"Maybe so, but you need to sleep now." I pointed to the pillow beside mine, the one nearer the bulkhead. "Lie down and face the window, please."

"I will sleep." He tilted his head. "But I must sleep facing the door."

I frowned. "The ship is uninhabitable. Nothing's coming through that door. Mechabot will contact me on the comms if it needs to tell me something."

He shrugged. I figured his instincts demanded he never put his back to a door, especially in an unfamiliar place. I always slept facing the door myself, so it was odd that I'd settled in facing him instead.

It doesn't mean anything, I told myself. *I just don't want to turn my back on him. I can't trust him.*

Except I did.

"Okay," I said. "Face the door, if that will help you sleep."

He must have been exhausted because he lay down immediately, his beautiful wings folded neatly behind his back and tucked close to his body. He mirrored my position, with one bent arm under his pillow.

We studied one another with weary eyes, neither willing to be the first to fall asleep. His rain forest scent seemed to fill the air. I longed to touch his wings and wondered if they felt as soft and silky as they looked.

To my surprise, my fatigue caught up to me before his did. I wasn't aware my eyelids had drifted closed until I heard Kerian murmur something from the soft darkness beyond them. It sounded like he said *I like how you smell.*

I like how you smell too, I thought.

A heartbeat later, I was sound asleep.

chapter four

kerian

I SLEPT FOR ALMOST SIX HOURS—TWICE AS LONG AS I NORMALLY SLEPT IN two standard days—and woke refreshed, with clear thoughts for the first time since regaining consciousness aboard *Nebula Traveler*. But try as I might, I still had no memory of how I'd ended up in the stasis pod or on this ship.

When I opened my eyes, I found myself staring at the back of Gen's head and her long blonde hair fanned out over her pillow. She did not strike me as a woman who gave her trust easily, but she'd fallen asleep quickly and then turned over in her sleep to face the door, putting her back to a stranger in her bed.

A stranger who, believing she had already fallen asleep, had confessed he liked her scent, only to have her murmur *I like how you smell too* in reply before she'd drifted off.

I had certainly caught the scent of her desire before she declared it was time for us to sleep. Maybe she'd somehow sensed my attraction too. I hoped so.

All my adult life, first as a soldier and then as a mercenary, I had relied on my instincts to keep me alive, to keep me one step ahead of my enemies and one step behind my targets. But in this moment, every fiber of my being sang of her and nothing else, to the point I couldn't trust my instincts at all. It left me feeling completely adrift. I needed an anchor—something I knew was real.

Gen slept deeply, with a light snore I found strangely endearing. I listened to the sound for several minutes before I wound her hair through my fingers, careful not to tug the strands and wake her. The smell of her drove every other thought from my mind except how much I wanted to feel her bare skin against mine. Her body looked like it would fit perfectly to my own.

The fact that made no sense did not stop me from thinking it.

Once we arrived at Ymar II, I would have to begin my search for answers to how and why someone had put me aboard this ship. I had so many questions. Why in stasis? Why *this* ship? I hoped the stasis pod wasn't too damaged to give me some clues about where to start.

My gaze returned to Gen as she let out a little sigh in her sleep. She'd kicked off her blanket while we'd slept and lay partially on her stomach with one knee bent. Her pose invited me to lie next to her with my chest against her back and my arm around her middle, but I did not dare. Not unless I knew she wished me to do so.

As I pictured leaving her behind, a strange thing happened. An unfamiliar vibration ran through my abdominal and back muscles and made my wings flutter restlessly. A few moments later, they spasmed again more powerfully. I had to hold back a groan as the discomfort became pain.

In thirty-two standard years of life, I had never experienced this sensation, and it was truly terrible.

The pain became an urge, but I didn't know what I needed to do to alleviate the agony. I sat up carefully, trying not to disturb Gen's sleep. Six hours of rest might be more than enough for me to recover, but not nearly sufficient for her needs. Not after how badly she'd been injured.

With one last wrenching spasm, my wings unfolded of their own accord, snapping open like a sail caught in a gale-force wind. My back bowed and my head hit the window behind me.

The cabin filled with sparkling dust in every color.

For a moment, I thought I had hit my head hard enough to see stars, but that was not the case.

My wings spasmed again, releasing another blizzard of sparkling dust. I slumped against the wall, my chest heaving with ragged breaths. The dust, stirred by the air vents and my fluttering wings, swirled around us before settling on every surface in a two-meter radius.

And it covered Gen from head to toe.

I froze, fearing she would wake coughing and sneezing and demanding to know what the hells I'd done. Instead, she made a contented sound and snuggled deeper into the bed. I had not thought it possible for her to look any more lovely to me, but covered with the strange, sparkling dust from my wings, she appeared closer to a goddess than a human woman.

I did not want to wake her, but I didn't know what effect my dust might have. "Captain," I murmured and touched her shoulder. "Captain Drae."

She opened her eyes and blinked at her shimmering, dusted arm. My heartbeats thundered in my ears.

Her brow furrowed, Gen raised her hand to study the dust more closely, turning it in the dim light provided by the comms panel above the bed and the starlight streaking by outside the window.

"Good morning, or whatever time of day it is," she said, flicking her gaze up to my face. "Is this from you? Did you have a good dream?"

I started to protest, but her tone was light. Her lips had turned up at their corners too. She was teasing me.

Utterly at a loss, I said, "I am sorry."

"No, you're not." She stretched with a groan, then rolled over to face me and prop her head on her hand. As she moved, the dust caught the light and shimmered like a galaxy of stars. "No more sorry than I was when I stared at you earlier, wondering how you look under that uniform." She gestured at the dust. "So, what is this?"

"I don't know," I admitted. "My wings...this has never happened before."

She marveled at her hand, turning it to see the dust shimmer. "This is so beautiful, and it smells like you—like a rain forest." Her gaze swept over my wings and entire body before returning to my face. "You've painted me to look like you. Did you want to do that?"

"No," I said, and then reconsidered. With her, I thought honesty would serve me better than evasiveness. "But I am very glad it happened."

"Why?"

I decided to risk speaking the words I'd been thinking since the moment I'd lain on top of her in the cargo hold with my cock between her thighs and her scent calling me home. "Before this, you were the most beautiful woman I've ever seen. Now you are the most beautiful woman in the galaxy."

Her smile grew. "That's a good line, Kerian Nos. But I'm immune to lines. Do better."

I dared to lean close and run my keen nose and one of my antennae along her shoulder and up the graceful curve of her neck. "It's only a line if it's not true," I murmured into her ear. She shivered. "I wish you could see yourself through my eyes, Captain Drae. Then you would know I'm speaking the truth."

She chuckled low in her throat. "Call me Gen, Kerian. I'm covered in your stardust. I think we're on a first-name basis now." She turned her head so her mouth was near mine. Even her lips shimmered. I longed to kiss them. "If you've never made this stardust before, what's going on here?" she asked.

"How can I tell you?" I caressed her shoulder and neck again, this time with both my antennae so I could drink in her taste, her scent, the silky smoothness of her skin. "I cannot explain it to myself."

"Then I'll explain it." She slipped her free hand around the back of my neck. My hearts raced at her cool touch. "We survived a disaster in space. Nearly dying has a way of making us want to enjoy the best things about being alive."

I did not imagine it; she wanted me. Her desire shone in her eyes. The smell of her arousal made my antennae twitch and my cock harden.

"Yes, it does," I said, my lips on her jaw. "What did you have in mind?"

"I think you know." She shivered again. "If you'd like me to spell it out for you, I will. I was disappointed when I saw you'd put clothes on."

Gods above, if I'd thought she would want to see my naked body in her bed, I would have left these uncomfortable coveralls in the medical bay.

"I want to know what you look like, from your antennae to your feet," she continued. She ran her fingertip along one of my antennae, her touch as light as a feather, and the scent and taste of her felt like a bolt of lightning down my spine. "You saw me naked," she said, her smile a playful pout. "But I don't remember how you looked in the stasis pod because of the damn concussion. It's not fair."

"I only saw you as a medic who treated a patient," I countered, but my voice shook because she'd begun stroking my scalp and running her fingers through my hair. Her flesh was at least ten or fifteen degrees cooler than mine, and the sensation of her touching me made it difficult to think clearly.

"Fair enough. But I'm no longer your patient. I'm healed and rested and feeling very good about being alive." She slid her hand from my head to my chest and rested her shimmering palm above my primary heart. "I'd like you to look at me in a very different way now."

What would she think if I admitted I had looked at her in the way she described when she'd tried to stab me in the very place her hand rested now? As strange as those words might sound to someone else, I thought she might understand.

But does she want my touch because I saved her life, or for some other, deeper reason? I wondered. Perhaps the answer should not matter to me, but it did.

Gen pressed her lips to my chest, then met my gaze. "I can guess what you're thinking because I'd be thinking the same thing. I'll tell you plainly so there's no misunderstanding. You saved my life even after I tried to kill you. In return, I'm letting you stay on my ship and share my limited emergency resources all the way to Ymar II." She rolled to her knees so she was closer to eye level with me. "What we do on this bed is not a reward for services rendered."

"I'm relieved to hear it," I said. "For the record, I would not have turned you down, but it makes a difference."

"Of course it does. We each have rules that we live by."

"What are your rules, Gen?"

Her smile turned brittle. "No passengers aboard my ship, ever. No one in my bunk when my alarm wakes me in the morning. No touches from anyone I think might want anything more than a few pleasurable hours. No one at my back. Those rules have kept me alive a lot longer than someone like me has any right to expect."

She curled her fingers so her nails dug into my skin through the jumpsuit. It hurt, but I liked this kind of pain. I wanted more of it.

"And yet here *you* are," she continued. "On *my* ship, in *my* bunk, at *my* back. You were here when I woke up covered with your stardust. I'm breaking all my rules for you."

"Why?" I genuinely wanted a truthful answer, and wondered if she'd give me one.

She twisted her fist in my jumpsuit and pulled me closer until our lips almost touched.

"Because I've always liked being cold," she said. "I like being in front, in the lead, taking charge and giving orders. I like making decisions, issuing commands, and keeping myself alive and my ship fueled and full of cargo. I have a good life, especially compared to the ones I've left behind. But now I want heat, and I want you to give it to me."

I didn't need my enhanced senses to discern that she had spoken the rawest kind of truth, in words she might never have even articulated to herself.

"How much heat do you want?" I asked.

"All you can give me." She flicked my lower lip with the tip of her tongue. The movement mesmerized me.

"Until we get to Ymar II?" My voice sounded strained with the effort of holding back as the scent of her arousal grew.

"Until then." She looked up at me, her eyes dark with desire and some other emotion I couldn't identify. "By the time we dock, we'll know whether we want to keep breaking our rules or go back to the people we were before." Her expression changed, became something almost feral. "I'm cold, Kerian. I'm so fucking cold. Give me heat."

If Gen wanted heat, by all the gods above and below, I would not stop until she blazed like a sun.

I pulled her body to mine and kissed her.

chapter five

gen

KERIAN'S KISS WAS UNLIKE ANY I HAD EVER FELT BEFORE.

He kissed me with hunger, possessiveness, and need, as if my lips, mouth, and tongue were his to claim and do with as he pleased. I had never felt so *wanted* by a man's mouth before.

His lush jungle scent grew until it filled my lungs and seemed to soak into my skin. It had undercurrents that reminded me of wines and spices I'd tasted on some other world years ago, long before I'd become the captain of the *Nebula* and left my old life behind.

His hot tongue slid over my lips and shimmered with stardust. I opened my mouth again, inviting him to share the taste of the dust with me. The moment our tongues touched, a jolt of pleasure ran straight through me like a bolt of plasma, causing my thighs to clench. I moaned.

"Please take off your nightclothes," Kerian rasped. His dark eyes glowed like starlight. "Before I ruin them."

I pulled the soft sleeveless tunic over my head. Rather than toss it aside, I rubbed the cloth over my breasts and stomach, transferring the shimmering stardust to my bare skin.

"Let me," he said, and took my top from me. He swept it over every inch of my back, from my shoulders to my waist, and then nudged me to lie flat so he could do the same to my chest. His finger-tips grazed my hard nipples. I cupped my breasts for his attentions and he took his time ensuring every quivering centimeter glimmered.

With my upper body now coated in dust, he slipped his fingers into the waistband of my pants and drew them slowly down my legs, dusting my skin with the shirt as he went.

The moment my pants were halfway to my knees, he leaned over to drag his tongue over my abdomen and then farther down. I moaned, my hands clutching at the bedding.

His tongue delved between my barely parted thighs. I cried out and tried to open my legs, but he held me still as he flicked his tongue on my most delicate and sensitive skin. This was torture.

"Take off my pants," I told him breathlessly. "Don't make me wait."

"You like giving orders." He gave me a smile that sent a shiver through my entire body. He slid my pants down my legs until they were off, and then dragged them between my thighs as he crawled back up my body to kiss me again.

"And?" I panted as the soft fabric ran over my inner thighs. The stardust tingled on my skin, heightening my sensitivity until I swore I could feel each individual particle of dust.

"And I like taking them," he murmured against my lips. "But please turn over so I can get your back as well."

I turned to my stomach so he could swirl the dust-covered pants over my ass and down the backs of my legs. He took his time. Every slow sweep of the soft fabric made me shake, shiver, and moan.

"Done," he said, and rolled me onto my back. I stared.

He'd somehow performed magic and removed his jumpsuit while I'd turned away, and now I saw all of his body for the first time. Well, the first time that I remembered, given my memories of our meeting in the cargo hold were nothing but blurry impressions.

The same dark blue skin and green leafy patterns covered his entire body, including a cock as beautiful as it was thick and inviting. It curved upward toward his abdomen. I licked my lips.

"Tell me what kind of heat you want," Kerian said. His hot finger-tips ran up my thigh and over my hip to my waist. An old scar ran almost halfway around my abdomen. He must have seen it, along with all the others, when he treated my injuries, but they didn't seem to bother him. And he didn't ask how I'd gotten them. He'd probably already guessed I'd made my living with guns and blades before becoming captain of the *Nebula*.

"This kind." I spread my legs for him, marveling at how my skin shimmered in every color. He'd even dusted my toes. "How do I look now?"

"Like a dream I never want to wake up from. Like the sweetest dessert in the galaxy." Kerian slid down the bed and kissed his way up my inner thighs. "I love to eat dessert first," he murmured, and raised my hips so he could slip his tongue between my legs for a series of long, sinuous licks.

Oh, gods. I twisted my fists into the bedding.

"No." He raised his head, his gaze dark with need. "If you want to grab something, hold on to me."

I let go of the comforter and slipped my fingers through his hair. He rewarded me with flicks of his tongue, and more when I clutched his hair and pulled.

No one had touched me like this in far too long, and Kerian's life-saving talents paled in comparison to the way he plucked and played every sensitive place like a stringed instrument. When his hot fingers slipped inside me, I came apart on his tongue, screaming and grinding against his face and hand.

I expected him to stop, but he didn't. He didn't even pause, as if my cries weren't as loud or desperate as he wanted them to be. And when his fingers curled inside me, stroking and searching, I came undone again, this time with a scream.

Kerian moved up my body, his fingers still stroking inside me so I writhed and panted. "Tell me what kind of heat you want now." He dipped his head to lick and suck my nipples, biting each time I raised my hips to grind against his hand. His hot cock rubbed against my thigh, collecting more stardust with each movement he made.

"More of this," I gasped, clutching his head so he would keep teasing my nipples with his tongue and teeth.

"Stroke my antennae," he ground out, his tongue laving my breast until I wanted to scream with how good it felt. "Be gentle."

I drew my fingertips from the base of one of his antennae to the top. He shuddered hard. "Again," he said. "Please, Gen."

His plea melted me all the way to my core. I repeated the movement, alternating between the antennae so I could keep one hand on the back of his neck. I had no idea what sensations this gave him, but he trembled against me as he drew more pleasure from me with his tongue, lips, and fingertips.

He lay half on his side, leaning over without putting his weight actually on me. His skin felt so much warmer than mine. I wanted—I *needed*—more heat.

"Put your body on mine," I told him, raising his chin so I could look into his beautiful glowing eyes. "I want all of it. I want all of you."

Bracing himself with one hand, he moved his knees between my thighs to keep his weight from crushing me into the bed. He ran his lips, tongue, nose, and antennae over me, tasting and smelling my skin, and even licked his fingers before slipping them back between my legs.

I wanted to taste him too, but I needed to feel his heat warming me from the inside. I wrapped my legs around his hips and urged him closer.

Instead of obeying, he resisted, looking down at me from above.

"What's wrong?" I asked, breathless. My fingertips traveled across his chest, following the lines of his muscles.

"I don't know how I ended up on this ship." He dipped his head into the crook of my neck and shoulder and inhaled deeply, as if he wanted to drink in every atom of my scent. "I intend to kill whoever did this to me. But I owe them a *thank you* before they die."

"You did say you are a polite man." I cupped his face with my palm. "Anything else on your mind?"

"Only you." He rested one hand on my shoulder to hold me in place and pressed his lips to my ear. "Only...*this*."

He thrust deep into me with his shimmering, stardust-covered cock in one powerful stroke.

We cried out at the same time. The entire bunk shook beneath me. I couldn't tell if I was writhing from head to toe or if he was, or both.

The burn and pleasure of his thrust turned into a series of

orgasms that rolled through my body, one after the other, with no pauses and no mercy. I screamed. I sobbed. I cried out Kerian's name, sometimes as only syllables and sometimes as the whole word. My vision tunneled into a kaleidoscope of the colors of his wings, as if we were tumbling through space and he'd wrapped them around me. I felt weightless, free, transformed…and yet perfectly safe.

I had only marginal awareness of my body—just enough to know I was thrashing uncontrollably in Kerian's arms.

The stardust, I thought, the words so hazy they barely registered. Beautiful as a galaxy and as combustible as a supernova.

A million little explosions later, I opened my eyes to find myself lying on Kerian's chest. "Gen," he said, squeezing me gently. "Gen, can you hear me?"

"Your wings," I gasped, my voice raspy. Had I screamed myself hoarse? "We're lying on your wings!"

"It does not hurt me." He pressed a kiss to the top of my head. "Are you all right?"

I tried to laugh, but I trembled so badly that apparently Kerian didn't realize what sound I'd tried to make. His entire body tensed, and his antennae bent toward me, quivering in what might have been worry. "Did I hurt you?"

"No." I moved my head so I could look into his eyes. "No, you didn't. I'm not hurt at all. I'm…" I couldn't find the right words for coming down off all-body orgasms that sent me into another universe altogether, so I rasped, "I feel very good. What about you?"

"I feel very good too." He relaxed, his arms loosening around me. "I am sorry. I had no idea that would happen."

"Please do not apologize for the best orgasm of my life—or *orgasms*," I amended. "I'm a fan of that dust from your wings."

He smiled. "Only my dust?"

I rubbed my nose against his chest. The multicolored dust covered both of us from head to toe now, and I liked the sight of our matching, glimmering skin even more than I'd imagined I would. "I am a fan of everything about you, Kerian Nos."

"I feel the same, Gen Drae."

We lay like that for a long time, with me listening to the beatings of his hearts and him languidly stroking my side and hip with his hand.

"Are you warmer now?" he asked, his hand coming to rest on the curve of my ass. "Too warm? Not warm enough?"

Did I detect a hint of hope in that last question?

"Not warm enough. Not yet." I slid down his body.

He seemed reluctant to let me move until I wrapped my hand around him and stroked gently a few times, and then not so gently.

He sucked in a breath. "Gen…"

I took him into my mouth, tentatively at first because I wasn't sure how he would react, and then more deeply when he groaned and let me do what I wanted. His stardust and rich jungle taste sent pleasure spiraling through my entire body. I couldn't help but slip my free hand between my thighs with a muffled moan.

"Come to me," Kerian said, his voice guttural.

I let him reposition me with my body on top of him and my knees on either side of his chest so he could return his talented tongue to the place I wanted it most.

Lost again in a haze of pleasure, I made him writhe and groan with my mouth and hands. In return, he held me firmly in place, refusing to let me move away or escape until he'd wrung two more orgasms from me.

When I collapsed on his chest, gasping for breath and unable to move on my own, he wrapped me in his arms almost lovingly and rolled us over so he could cover my body with his. This time he thrust much more slowly, moving what felt like a centimeter at a time. Our first coupling had been a supernova; the second, a perfect series of tidal waves or earthquakes that rolled over us both each time he moved.

Once he finally filled me to the hilt, I wrapped my trembling arms and legs around his back and hips, marveling at the way his muscles flexed under his skin and the delicious sensation of the edges of his wings brushing against my calves. The tingling stardust made even those gentle touches spark and blaze with pleasure, as if the feeling of his hot length stroking in and out of me wasn't breathtaking enough.

"Can I touch your wings?" I asked.

In wordless answer, he nuzzled my neck and draped them over us.

I ran my fingertips over his wings and gasped in wonder. They were as silky as I'd imagined, but each color had a slightly different texture. The edges had a fringe of tiny hairs. When I caressed those hairs, Kerian shuddered and his pace increased before he regained control and slowed again.

"Don't be gentle with me," I told him, cupping his jaw with my hand. "I'm not fragile."

"But I am very strong." He kissed my forehead. "I'm afraid I will hurt you."

"I'm not afraid of that happening." I smiled up at him and ran my thumb over his lips. "But if you're worried, let me take over."

He rolled us over in one smooth, almost acrobatic movement while keeping me filled and let his wings drape across the bunk beneath us.

In the soft starlight that streamed through the window, he watched me ride him, his hot hands on my thighs and my hips as if to guide me. I moved faster and he met me halfway, using the leverage of his feet on the bed to drive himself deeper and harder as I braced myself on his chest. Our cries echoed in my cabin.

He threw his head back, his fingers tightening on my hips until I knew I'd have bruises, and rasped, "Gen."

The sound of my name said like a prayer and the feeling of this beautiful man lost in pleasure beneath me sent me over the edge with a wail. I collapsed on his chest, lost in bliss. But he wasn't ready to let me rest. Instead, he changed our position once more, curling up behind me and hooking my leg over his arm so he could thrust gently.

"Watch," he said, his dark eyes meeting mine before he looked at where our bodies were joined. "Watch how well you take me, my beautiful Gen."

My beautiful Gen. I had never been anyone's Gen. Strange that I didn't mind when he'd called me his.

I watched as he'd asked me to until he found the angle that made my head fall back against his chest, and then I saw nothing but a haze of stars until I came once more, softly this time, wrapped his arms.

Kerian pressed his lips to my ear. "Are you warm enough now?"

"Almost." I ground against him a few times, enjoying how he

groaned each time I slid up and down his length, and then slipped free to lie on my back, my knees open in an invitation he immediately accepted.

The stars streaking by the window reflected in his dark eyes as he moved above me. Maybe it was that soft starlight that made me murmur, "Tell me what you want."

He kissed my forehead and drew back to look directly into my eyes. "I want to come inside you. It is safe for me to do so. I am without disease, and I am voluntarily sterile."

"I am too." I cupped his face with my hand and whimpered when he did something magical with his hips. "You may come inside me, but only when I say you may."

His smile told me he liked what I'd said. I'd suspected he would.

He bent to kiss my jaw and increased his pace once more. "Beautiful Gen," he murmured against my lips. "Captain of the *Nebula*. Tell me when I may come."

For a long time I made him thrust harder and faster, until he'd gone wild with need and almost feverish with the effort of holding back. He called my name again and again in a litany that was part plea and part exultation.

I came apart one final time with a soft cry, my fingernails digging into his shoulders as he watched from above. "Now," I gasped.

He threw his head back with a groan, his beautiful body wracked with shudders from his antennae to his feet as he finally allowed himself to come. The heat of his release filled me in waves, one after another, until he was spent.

He lowered himself to cover my body once more with his own, but with most of his weight on his elbows and knees.

"Pin me down," I whispered. "The way you did in the cargo hold."

His startled expression and sudden smile made me think my words resonated with him in a way I hadn't anticipated. Maybe he'd been drawn to me even then.

"Yes," he rasped, and put his body on mine with his face nestled into the pillow beside my head.

With his muscular torso pressed against mine, I felt his hearts pounding and the rise and fall of his chest as he breathed. Finally, I was wonderfully, wonderfully warm.

Beneath me, the familiar hum of *Nebula*'s engine comforted me through my bunk. For years, that thrumming had soothed me all the way to my bones.

Now the sensation was a reminder that my ship was now four days from docking at Ymar II, and then I'd have arrange for *Nebula* to be towed to the nearest drydock shipyard for repairs. Meanwhile, Kerian would depart on his search for how and why he'd ended up in my cargo hold.

I hoped repairs would be possible and I could find a way to finance them. With Kerian gone, I would have to face that hurdle on my own, coldly and efficiently, along with all the obstacles that would come after.

At least I was warm for now. That would have to do.

chapter six

kerian

FOR FOUR MORE DAYS, I KEPT GEN WARM.

When the cabin's climate system began malfunctioning two days from Ymar II, my body heat became a matter of not only comfort and pleasure for her, but also survival.

The power to the food preparation unit went offline the next day. More of the ship's systems failed one after another as *Nebula*'s condition deteriorated. Some of the light faded from Gen's eyes. The damage to the ship was clearly far worse than we'd originally thought. The odds of her being able to repair it for any amount of money were dwindling.

Whatever she thought about the ship and its future, she didn't share it with me. She simply asked for more warmth. At least beneath me and in my arms she seemed happy and content.

Twelve hours from our destination, we lost communication with the ship's maintenance robot in the cockpit. Not long after, three loud rumbles rolled through the ship. We didn't know what the silence from the cockpit or the shaking meant. In a way it didn't matter. They could not signify anything good. I suspected more of the ship had started to break apart under the strain.

With six hours to go, as our breathing made puffs in the air, Gen stopped looking at the screen above the bunk that gave our location and time to destination. I switched it off. We lay in near darkness now except for the starlight outside the cabin's window. The only lights still glowing were those by the door, a few on the control panel above the desk, and the ones by the vents that still feebly pumped air into the cabin.

On her bunk, under our pile of blankets, I drew Gen to my chest and tucked her head under my chin. "What can I do?" I asked.

I expected her to ask for warmth, as she'd done so many times. Instead, she said, "I need to ask you a question, and I want you to tell me the truth, no matter what it is."

It disturbed me that she didn't move so she could see my face. Gen always looked me in the eye. "I will never lie to you," I promised.

"If we get to Ymar II, what are you going to do?" Her tone was deliberately flat, as if she thought she knew what my answer would be and had already begun the process of pulling away.

My uneasiness increased when I realized she had said *If we get to Ymar II* instead of *when*. I had been so careful to never let on that I doubted we would survive this journey. Maybe it was she who had stayed hopeful up to now, for my sake.

I had long since decided what I would do if by some miracle we reached our destination. My focus then became Gen's pleasure, warmth, and well-being. And I had never wavered in my choice—not even for a moment.

"If we get to Ymar II," I said, "I want to go with you, wherever you go."

"What about finding out how you ended up on my ship?" Now she sounded incredulous. "If I'd woken up in a stasis pod with no memory of how I got there, I'd tear the universe apart to get the answer."

Of that, I had no doubt. "I *do* want to know those answers," I told her. "But now there's something more important."

"What could *possibly* be more important?"

"Keeping you warm, Gen Drae." I pressed my lips to her hair. "I never want you to feel cold again."

She raised her head. Her eyes had deep shadows and dehydration and hunger had taken their toll, but she was as beautiful to me as the moment I'd first seen her.

"That's a good line, Kerian Nos," she said with a ghost of a smile. "But I'm immune to lines. Do better."

"How about this, then." I kissed her forehead. "I am addicted to how you look covered in the dust from my wings and the sounds you make when you come for me. And it's an addiction I have no intention of recovering from."

She tried to laugh, but it came out as a kind of strangled half sob. "Well, that's definitely better."

Another rumble shook the ship. A light on the ceiling began flashing and the air vents sputtered. We were still hours from Ymar II. The colony might as well have been a galaxy away.

She snuggled closer with her face against my chest. "That was the emergency life support starting to fail." Her voice was muffled.

"Yes." I tucked the blankets more tightly around us. "I will keep you warm, Captain Drae."

"I know." She kissed my hot skin above my primary heart. "I'm glad I got to know what that feels like."

"Me too," I murmured.

I had been a soldier and fighter all my life. I would have battled any foe who tried to harm this woman. But a disintegrating freighter and the heartlessness of space itself were not enemies I could defeat.

Even so, I lay facing the cabin's doors, ever on watch, with Gen wrapped in my arms. My own body temperature began to drop as the cabin grew colder by the minute. I tried not to shiver, afraid that would alarm her, but after a while I could no longer keep still. She let me hold her so tightly that our body temperatures almost matched, and I lost track of where my body ended and hers began.

For a long time we drifted in and out of consciousness, murmuring words to each other that neither could really understand but that were still comforting.

Some hazy time later, I hallucinated that the ship jolted sharply and alarms sounded. The life support system seemed to power on with a blast of breathable air and the cabin grew noticeably warmer.

This is a good dream to have just before the end, I thought, and closed my eyes again.

Not long after, a series of urgent beeps roused me once more. The doors to the cabin groaned open, revealing a familiar robot with six arms. Behind it stood three uniformed Ymarians carrying medical kits.

"Captain Drae and unidentified passenger," the 'bot said, in the same tone I imagined it used for everything, including apparently to announce miracles. "We have reached Ymar II."

Was I alive? Was I dreaming? And most importantly, did Gen still live? I almost feared looking at her—but when I did, her red-rimmed eyes blinked blearily up at me. The slow beating of her heart and her raspy breathing were the sweetest sounds I'd ever heard.

I took her face in my hands and kissed her. What the Ymarians thought of me and the sparkling dust that had spread to every surface in the cabin, I had no idea, and I did not care.

"Captain Drae," the 'bot repeated. Was I imagining it, or did it sound impatient? "The commanding officer of the Ymarian rescue team requests a report."

"Mechabot." Gen's weak voice still carried the undercurrent of deadly danger that made my hearts race. "If you don't give us a damn minute to celebrate the fact we're alive, so help me I will sell you for scrap."

"Understood, Captain." The robot retreated hastily, along with the Ymarian medics. Even if they hadn't understood her words, her tone needed no translation.

Gen and I stared at each other.

"What you said—" she began.

"Nothing has changed," I told her. "I meant what I said. Wherever you go, I go, if you will have me. Maybe we can seek the answers together."

"Okay." She took a deep, shuddering breath. "My ship isn't salvageable, is she?"

"I don't think so." I rested my forehead on hers. "I'm sorry. But we are alive."

"One out of two ain't bad." Gen looked up at me with defiance and tears shining in her beautiful blue eyes. "I am going to get emotional about this for exactly forty-five seconds. And if you ever tell *anyone*, especially that damn robot, I will—"

"I know." I kissed her again and sucked gently at her lower lip, which trembled. "My bloody, twitching corpse goes straight out the nearest airlock."

"One hundred percent," she said.

Before the Ymarian medics and Mechabot returned, she'd already let me kiss her tears away.

about lisa edmonds

Lisa Edmonds was born and raised in Kansas. She studied English and forensic criminology at Wichita State University. After acquiring her Bachelor's degree, she considered a career in law enforcement as a behavioral analyst before earning a Master's in English from Wichita State and then a Ph.D. in English from Texas A&M University.

For ten years, she was an associate professor of English at a college in Texas, where she taught a variety of writing and literature courses. Now a full-time author, she shares a cute Victorian-style home called the Storybook House with her husband Bill and their cats, and enjoys writing, reading, traveling, spoiling her niece and nephew, and singing karaoke.

Lisa is the author of the Amazon Top 100 Alice Worth urban fantasy/paranormal mystery series, available now.

To learn more, visit www.lisaedmonds.com

cosmic cravings

Lita Grey

chapter one

ariel

HE'S GOING TO RUN. I JUST KNOW IT.

I wiped the counter for the third time and scrubbed at a stain that hadn't budged in three years. Out of the corner of my eye, I watched my solitary dine-in customer take another sip of coffee in an almost reverent way. That might have flattered me if I didn't know my coffee could double as an engine de-greaser and multi-purpose solvent.

Those deliberate sips—and the way he watched me when he didn't think I noticed—had tipped me off that he intended to skip out without paying, even before he'd lingered over his food for nearly an hour. And he'd savored every bite like I'd plopped a Bacorian feast in front of him rather than about three kilograms of standard outpost fare seasoned with whatever Kitbot felt like throwing in with the synthetic meat and vegetables today. I never asked exactly what ingredients that robot used as long as he didn't kill any customers. Bad for business.

Plus body disposal here on Outpost 406 was a real pain in the ass. I'd established the Last Chance Diner on Deck 4, about midway along the starboard docking platform where smaller ships came into port for maintenance. The crews liked to stretch their legs, so this was a perfect location for customers to find me, but I couldn't just throw a corpse out an airlock and risk it floating past the outpost's windows and nearby docked spaceships—not to mention outpost security would catch it all on camera. Too many awkward questions. The very last thing any business owner out here on the galactic frontier wanted was too many questions, or worst of all, a visit from the Licensing Baron.

I could drag Mr. Mysterious's corpse to the incinerator, but I'd have to do it in pieces because the guy was huge. Even then I'd risk one of the Pallasians who operated the incineration facility finding the guy's legs or something and then I'd have to pay them off to keep them quiet.

Now I was grumpy about having to get rid of his body and he hadn't even tried to make a run for it yet.

You're over-selling it, I wanted to tell Mr. Mysterious. *The key to sneaking out on a bill is to act like a regular customer. Not take an hour to eat while stalling for time, you gorgeous moron.*

And gorgeous he was, even by human standards, though I figured him for—at minimum—a thief. Well over two meters tall, with broad shoulders, crimson skin, and short horns that curled back from his hairline. He'd strung beads and what looked like pieces of bone throughout his long black hair, which hung loose down his back nearly to his knees.

Scars crisscrossed his hands and face, which were the only other parts of his body I could see since he hadn't taken off his long black coat. Another sign of a plan to run. Most customers removed their coats if they stayed to eat. I didn't keep my place cold. Many species of travelers who passed through this outpost came from hot planets. Takeout made up most of my business, but even so, my tips went up when the temp was up too. Nobody felt generous if their genitals shriveled from the cold.

When Mr. Mysterious reached for a napkin, his sleeve pulled back to reveal a significant scar on his forearm. So maybe not *just* a thief, then, I mused, as I tossed my rag on the counter and made a show of checking on my prize Bacorian-made coffeemaker. That kind of wound only came from combat. He had the physique of a gladiator, but no ring around his neck bearing the name of his owner.

My eyes narrowed. He was probably a mercenary. I'd checked the docking logs when he sat down and seen his ship and its registration.

It looked like it had a lot of light-years on it, so he was probably a deep-space raider—the kind who killed without mercy for money or stolen goods. I would definitely not let him walk out without paying. He owed me for his food, water, and air, and for dirtying my diner with his presence.

I tapped my foot three times to activate the sensor that bolted the airlock door. Then I made a trip to the kitchen, where Kitbot had docked himself in his charging station awaiting the next order. I checked the charge on my pulse gun, in case Mr. Mysterious decided to fight or beat the location of the door-lock switch out of me. He wouldn't be the first to try.

Lots of beings who passed through thought this part of the galaxy was lawless and they could do as they pleased. They were wrong. There might not be much *official* law enforcement out here, but that meant we were each tasked with upholding the law. That included preventing and punishing theft, especially in places where resources were tough to come by.

Come to think of it, putting Mr. Mysterious in a stasis pod on display out front might actually be a good deterrent against future attempts. A neat solution to my problem of what to do with him if he didn't hand over my money. No body to get rid of. No muss, no fuss.

From the dining area, a bellow rolled through the whole diner, rattling my plates and cups on their shelves. I'd never heard the man make a sound beyond a grunt of greeting and another of thanks when I brought his food, but I recognized his voice all the same.

I grinned.

I might not be the first diner owner he'd tried to skip out on without paying, but I was damn sure going to be the last.

thalan

SHE LOCKED ME IN!

I roared and pulled on the airlock's handle. No, no give at all. Bolted and sealed. Even with sharp vision and hearing, I had not seen her trigger the locking mechanism or heard it activate.

I pounded on the door, but it was as solid as the hull. I would have more luck pulling the tusks from a Hardanian war-pig than making a dent in either of them.

A peal of laughter made me spin around with a growl.

The diner's owner leaned against the doorway to the kitchen, her arms crossed as she laughed at my attempts to escape. She had slipped a pulse gun into her thigh holster. It looked fully charged and capable of blowing a hole through me. For all they lacked in size compared to my own kind, human women who lived in the frontier range could shoot and fight with surprising ferocity—enough to have long ago earned my grudging respect.

I had watched her so closely. Been so sure she did not have a clue what I had planned to do. But she had sniffed me out and locked me in.

Enraged as much by how she had outsmarted me as my captivity, I spread my arms, raised my chin, and roared, baring my teeth and flaring the ridges that ran down the sides of my neck. I had made more than one opponent shit themselves and run with that act alone.

But she did not run. And she did not unlock the gods-damned door.

Instead, she watched me, the corner of her mouth turned up in something between a smirk and a wry smile. And then, to my absolute consternation, she applauded.

"Very scary," she said, her tone mocking. "So very scary. Or it would be, if I hadn't just dealt with an infestation of Muravii fang beetles last week."

That was an insult of breathtaking proportions. Muravii fang beetles were five centimeters in length and their bites hurt less than a stubbed toe.

"Open. This. Door." I spoke each word clearly, deliberately, every syllable dripping with the promise of death and suffering.

Utterly unfazed, she pointed to the glowing number next to my empty plates. "Payment due," she said. "If you please. Local currency or outer rim credits."

"No one imprisons me." I took two slow steps forward. Not quickly enough for her to want to pull her weapon, but to close the distance between us and use my height to frighten her. "Least of all a lone human woman running a vermin-infested diner."

"No one steals from me." Her voice had changed to match my own in both coldness and anger. "*Least of all* a murdering raider who wears all black to hide the blood."

My cocks twitched at her tone.

She had flipped a switch from soft and almost playful to tough and threatening and I would be damned if it did not make me hard.

Usually human women did not interest me. My unexpected desire, however, made me take note of her beauty. She appeared strong and curvy rather than pale and wiry, as many human women in the outer rim of the galaxy tended to be. Life aboard an outpost station might be less desperate than on a colonized planet, but she worked hard, as evidenced by the toned muscles in her arms and legs. Her sleeveless shirt and skintight pants, both standard attire for the outpost, showed off her strength, as well as a very fine, round ass.

Her hands curled into fists at her sides, ready to fight for what I owed.

The problem was, I could not pay, even if I wanted to.

My now-former copilot had robbed me of every last credit. The only money I carried was Raxian and I doubted she would accept it, even if I did not need it to pay for fuel to make it to a system where my former squad could not find me. Because if they tracked me down, I would die slowly, in agony, over weeks or months. Or *years*. They did things to traitors that were beyond nightmares.

The longer I stayed locked in this diner, the more likely someone would spot my ship. I had forged its registration well enough to fool the outpost's bored docking officer, but it would not stand up to real scrutiny. Any member of my former squad would recognize my ship on sight.

I was strong enough to rip the head off a Gandarian mule ox—and had done so, on two occasions—but I could not get through the airlock. The appropriately named Last Chance Diner had no windows to the corridor outside that I could attempt to break, and this was the only exit. Its door, walls, floor, and ceiling were designed to withstand a breach of the outpost's outer hull, so I had no chance of getting through.

I could try to force the diner's owner to open the door. No doubt someone else in my position would have done exactly that, but I had lost my taste for violence. After my squad's raid on Genrus III, I had even signed my own death warrant by leaving in my ship while my comrades were distracted celebrating their ill-gotten gains among the colony's smoking ruins.

And most importantly, I would be gods-damned if I would tell this smirking, well-armed woman I had no money. Because I might own a secondhand ship *and* be running from my squad *and* be flat broke after my partner robbed me, but I still had my pride.

Perhaps this could go a different way. I had something else besides money to offer—something she might want.

A human woman living in a shithole outpost did not exactly have her choice of sources of pleasure, even if she was not all that particular. I *was* particular about my bedmates, as any longtime raider with a host of enemies would be. If we could come to an agreement, however, I doubted finding pleasure between this beauty's legs would prove difficult for me. Barely a hardship at all. I was hard already just thinking about bending her over a table or throwing her on the counter and spreading her legs as she screamed my name.

I lowered my neck ridges, opened my coat, and slid my hands into my pockets. Her gaze, still flinty and cold, scoured the prominent lines of my chest and abdominal muscles visible through my shirt and landed on the bulge below my belt. She licked her lips—a quick little dart of pink tongue that made my cocks throb.

Oh, yes. She was *hungry*. I could sate that hunger…and then some.

I let myself smile for the first time in a very long time.

"Surely we can barter," I said.

chapter three

ariel

BARTER? IS HE SERIOUS?

"Does this look like a swap meet?" I demanded, forcing myself to look away from the rather impressive endowment promised by the bulge in his pants. I knew little of his kind—not even what planet his people came from, much less the size, form, or uses of their genitalia. And I had no business wondering about that right now anyway, when he'd tried to steal from me.

"I have bills to pay," I added when he didn't reply. "That food you ate costs me money. So does the water, the coffee, and the air in here. All of which you consumed in significant amounts while sitting at that counter trying to figure out how to get away without paying for any of it." I came around the counter to face him, and to show him I wasn't afraid. "Hand it over. And don't forget the tip."

Something about what I'd just said made him grin, which only made me more furious. "I will knock that smirk right off your ugly face," I promised, my cheeks hot with anger. In truth, his face was far from ugly, but that seemed very much beside the point at this moment. I smacked the counter with my hand. "Money. *Now.*"

I expected him to curse or threaten, or to throw money at me and demand I unlock the door. Instead, he apparently chose a third option.

One moment he stood two meters away, his feet planted shoulder width apart, studying me like he couldn't decide whether to attack or just try to stare me down…

…and the next his hot body fitted against my side like he had turned to liquid or lava and shaped himself to me. But there was absolutely nothing soft about him.

Everything from his horns to his feet looked and felt hard as stone, and that included what I judged to be one of the biggest cocks I'd encountered—and I'd encountered quite a few. Through our clothes it pressed against my side, and I felt its heat and throbbing intensity.

Wait…it *throbbed?*

"A barter," he said, and his roar that only minutes ago had made the diner walls tremble and nearly knocked plates off the kitchen shelves had become a throaty growl that created a surprising amount of wetness between my legs. With any luck, he couldn't smell my reaction.

Stop it, I told myself sternly. *You aren't* that *hard up for attention. You can get it from Sakal over at the pilots' hostel anytime you want it. You don't need anything from this thief.*

"I barter food, water, and air for money," I said. My voice didn't shake, for which I was grateful. "That's how a restaurant works, if you're not familiar with the concept."

"Some things are beyond price." He leaned down and rubbed his nose in my hair, inhaling deeply as he moved along the nape of my neck, his breath hot against my bare skin. My sleeveless top offered him access to my upper back and shoulders, and he took advantage of that to inhale my scent.

Despite his proximity and the animalistic way he sniffed me, I didn't want to move away. I should, but I didn't. That made me instantly suspicious.

"What are you?" I demanded. "What are your people called?"

"I am Atolani." He inhaled very deliberately with his nose near my ear. The rush of air made me shiver. "Atolan is a desert world without much liquid. Very unlike your pussy, lovely lady of the diner. It gushes like a river for me."

I knew little about Atolani, but I did know they had no ability to influence the thoughts or actions of humans. If I felt reluctant to push him away, that was my own will, not his. If my pussy gushed for him, that was me.

"You're very mistaken, *thief*," I said, but that time my voice was anything but steady. "You've been in deep space so long you're hallucinating. The only thing I want from you is the money you owe me."

"I will make you a wager." His hot lips and nose continued their travels around my shoulders and along my upper back, and now I felt the harsh rasp of his tongue. "Lovely lady of the diner—"

"Ariel." It came out ragged, because now despite all my determination to get my money, I was thinking about how that tongue would feel on my most sensitive places. "My name is Ariel."

"*Ah-ree-ell.*" He sounded it out, each syllable oozing like plasma from a cut conduit. "I am Thalan."

I just couldn't help myself. "What's your wager, Thalan?" My fingers gripped his pants leg and clung to the tough, tear-resistant fabric.

"If I touch your pussy and you aren't sopping wet right now, I will pay you your money and go." Now his sharp teeth grazed the back of my neck and that element of danger sent another shiver straight to my core. "But if you are as wet for me as I believe you to be, I will earn my meal in work-in-trade, and I assure you I will earn it twice over."

"You owe me four thousand and ninety credits," I said. "Double that is eight thousand one hundred and eighty, *plus* a generous tip. That is quite a lot of work. More than I think you're capable of doing even if I gave you four hours."

"I will not need four hours." He said it with pride and certainty. "You accept the wager?"

I glanced at the locked airlock door. Outside in the corridor, the red light would tell potential customers I'd closed early and they needed to find their meals elsewhere on the station. So not only might I lose Thalan's four thousand credits if I said yes, but possibly far more than that in additional revenue. Orgasms, for all their benefits, did not pay any bills.

They did, however, relieve stress and loneliness, and I had that in heaps.

Oh, what the hells, I thought. Sakal hadn't done his best for me in ages. Plus, I'd never had an Atolani. I'd traveled to the frontier looking for adventure, hadn't I? Even if he didn't fuck me eight thousand credits' worth, an Atolani cock still might be considered an adventure. His pants seemed uncomfortably tight now. The size of the bulge made my mouth water. And no matter what Raxians claimed, size absolutely *did* matter.

"I accept," I said.

chapter four

thalan

I could have smelled Ariel's arousal from my ship. I knew I would win the wager. It was a sucker's bet and she had taken it. Now I would get to take *her*, and my cocks liked that idea very, very much. Their throb increased along with their hardness. They sensed her wetness and were ready to take and take and *take*.

Human women's pussies were so soft, so hot, so liquid and fire, but they hid them under clothes. That seemed blasphemous to me. Such pleasant softness should be a source of pride. Certainly not covered as if in shame.

I growled at her clothing. *In my way*. I unfastened the holster that held her firearm and tossed it aside. Then I ripped her pants apart and let them fall to the floor. She wore nothing underneath.

"Hey," she said, indignant.

I barely heard her. Her legs appeared even stronger and yet pleasantly soft without their covering, and now I clearly envisioned how they would look and feel wrapped around my waist. And between them, her lovely pink pussy captivated me, quivering and waiting to be touched.

"Look," I said, my voice a low purring sound. I trailed my finger tips over her thigh, toward the source of the wetness that ran down the inside of her leg. "Look at your pussy, so wet, so hungry."

She did not look down, though. She studied me, her brow furrowed, as if she thought I might be mocking her, and still clearly angry about her torn clothing.

So I turned her toward the shiny, mirror-like metal of the diner's wall and made her look at our reflection. We could not have been more opposite in appearance. I towered over her, though she was not short for her people. Her fair skin and shoulder-length brown hair stood out from the gray metal of our surroundings and my own red skin, black hair, and black clothing. I had yet to remove her shirt, but its hem hung to just below her navel and did not hide her pink folds at all.

"See," I said, my fingers gliding along her thigh to collect the slick moisture. "See it dripping. Why does your pussy drip?"

"I..." For the first time, she seemed unsure of herself. The woman who had threatened me with clenched fists had no words for me now.

"It drips for me," I stated. "That is my wager won. You agree?"

"Yes!" Now she was mad again, for reasons I did not understand. "You just have to rub it in, don't you?"

"Rub?" I frowned. "Why? Thrust, force, drive them in, as deeply as I can. You prefer I rub?"

She chuckled. Her reactions made as little sense as her obvious pride in that beast of a Bacorian coffee machine and the foul liquid it produced.

"It's an expression," she said. "I didn't mean literally—wait, what? What do you mean, *them?*"

I snarled. "No more talking." I wrapped my arms around her from behind and hooked one of her feet with mine to pull her legs apart. I held them in place with her feet off the floor and trapped behind my thick calves as I supported her weight. She squawked in surprise and tried to get away, but I held her still.

"Watch," I said, and pointed to the mirrored wall. "Tell me again: how much do I owe you for my meal?"

"Eight thousand one hundred and eighty credits, plus tip," she said automatically. "But—"

I interrupted her by squeezing her closer. "Keep track of my ledger," I commanded, and slipped my hand between her thighs, where she was softest and sopping and pink. Drops of wetness landed on my fingers. She moaned before I even touched her, her fingernails digging into my arm.

A promising start.

Carefully, I coaxed her delicate lips apart to delve into her wet folds. The guttural sound she made was quite gratifying, and I felt her relax against me, accepting that I could hold her up with no difficulty. My finger slid effortlessly through the wetness of her arousal as I explored, seeking the places that made her shake and whimper and curse in her own language.

Now satisfied that I had her full attention and cooperation, I slipped my finger into her slick tunnel for the first time. She arched against me and her eyes closed instead of watching us, as I had ordered her to do. I let her keep them closed for now. Seeing her bliss and hearing her moans was its own reward.

When she began riding my hand in earnest, I added another finger to give her more and begin the process of stretching her to accommodate my cocks. Even one at a time, they were considerably larger than a human male's. If she enjoyed pain with her pleasure, I could certainly provide both, but physical limitations were physical limitations.

One certain way to increase her pliability was attention to her most sensitive areas. I curled my fingers within her and began a slower, deliberate stroking, seeking a particular reaction I had learned to note from previous partners. She made a telltale sound low in her throat and shuddered in my arms. *There,* I thought with satisfaction.

I focused my attentions on that spot and she thrashed against me, her pleas turning to wordless cries. In the midst of the almost unintelligible sounds, I heard my name just before her tunnel clenched around my fingers and she wailed. Her nectar flowed over my hand.

I showed her no mercy. I did not pause, did not slow my strokes, and more spasms shook her body from her shoulders to her toes. Whether this was a second orgasm or simply a continuation of the first, I could not tell, but her head fell back against my chest, her mouth open and gasping for air as she mumbled words that tumbled over each other like poetry.

The scent of her and the sound of my name on her lips made my cocks strain the fabric of my pants. My level of arousal now bordered on pain.

"What does my ledger read now?" I asked as she panted.

When she did not reply, I slipped my fingers from her tunnel and up to the pearl hidden in the pink folds just above it. I began to circle this pearl and rub my fingertips over it. She made a ragged sound that was part protest, part demand.

"My ledger?" I asked again, my fingers slowing. "How much are you still owed?"

chapter five

ariel

MY ORGASM WENT ON AND ON. OH, GODS ABOVE, IT WAS SO FUCKING good.

Thalan's fingers, so hot and precise, somehow knew exactly where to find my g-spot, and he stroked it relentlessly. I lost sense of time and place or what if anything I said as I came, shuddering and gasping and crying out.

Only when he withdrew his dripping fingers and turned his attention to my swollen clit did I open my eyes. Of course, the first thing I saw was our reflection in the metal wall. I'd never been fingered to an orgasm in front of a mirror—in fact, I'd never been fucked in front of a mirror at all. I saw myself in the metal, flushed and trembling, my legs spread wide for his hand, which was so large it covered my pussy entirely. I felt self-conscious to be so boldly confronted with my reflection.

When he spoke, his voice seemed to come from a long way away, traveling though a thick haze of my pleasure. "My ledger?" His tone sounded like this wasn't the first time he'd asked. "How much are you still owed?"

How much…? I could barely understand his question, so I picked a

432

number I thought was less than the total he owed when he started. "Seven thousand five hundred."

His chest rumbled. I didn't know if his reaction was anger, laughter, or simply his own arousal. The enormous, rock-hard cock pressing into my lower back made it clear he was more than ready to fuck me.

When he reached for my shirt, I batted his hand away and pulled it over my head. I had to keep at least one or two pieces of clothing intact after this encounter. When I hesitated, somewhat inexplicably, to unfasten my bra, his fingers resumed their circular movement on my clit. I gasped and lowered my hands to grip his forearms.

"Remove it," he ordered, his fingers slowing again.

I did as I was told, but now with my eyes open I saw my nakedness reflected and tried to close my legs.

"No." He slapped my pussy, somehow making precise contact in a way that felt like more pleasure than pain. "Spread yourself open for me with your fingers. Show me your beautiful pussy."

No one had ever asked me to do that before, much less in front of a mirror. My face heated, and it had nothing to do with my orgasms. "I can't."

"Yes." He said it so forcefully that I almost obeyed reflexively. When I hesitated again, he pulled my hand to where he wanted it. "Spread yourself open," he repeated, but this time he accompanied the command with a slow drag of his tongue across my shoulder. "Show me how beautiful it is," he murmured, his lips against my skin. "I want to see."

My face burning, I rubbed my fingertips over my slick folds, then slid my index and middle finger between them to spread myself open as he'd demanded.

He cupped my freed right breast, his fingers large enough to do so and still strum and pinch my nipple into an even more painfully aroused nub. "Perfect." His murmur alone made me quiver now because it belonged to the same body as those talented fingers. "So beautiful," he said, laving my shoulder and the nape of my neck with his tongue until all I could think about was being fucked by its rough length. "You glow when you come, lady of the diner. Beautiful and powerful and strong, like a sun."

He met my gaze in the mirrored wall. His black eyes shone and glittered like space itself, with blue pupils that traveled slowly and very deliberately from my face down my chest and abdomen to where I'd opened myself for his admiring gaze. My whole body heated in a combination of desire still tinged with embarrassment.

"So very perfect," he repeated. "Don't move."

His fingers returned to my clit with a gentle circular motion that made my head fall back. He stopped immediately. "Eyes open," he ordered.

That dragged a groan of aggravation rather than pleasure from me. "This is *your* debt you're paying off," I said, breathless. I turned my head to glare at him. "You make a lot of demands for someone in my debt."

"And I am the one who won the wager," he countered, his expression suddenly grave. "Atolani take their wagers extremely seriously. It is a matter of life and death for us."

"Oh." That deflated my anger. Respect for the nuances of nonhuman cultures was important everywhere, but especially on the frontier, where disrespecting another culture could lead to war.

"So eyes open, Ariel," Thalan told me. "Eyes open, legs open, pussy open, all for me."

"What about my mouth?" I said it almost without thinking. My free hand slipped between us and found the hard outline of his cock. I could not wrap my hand around it fully. That made me wonder if I would even be able to take it, in my mouth or anywhere else.

"You will," Thalan stated.

I turned and blinked up at him. "What?" Then I realized what he meant, and I tried to free myself by digging my nails into the hot flesh of his wrists and pulling at his arm. "You bastard, are you reading my mind?"

He held me still with so little effort that my ego was irrevocably bruised. "Not in the least. It was not difficult to know what concerned you. *Now.*" His expression turned almost ferocious. "If you do not put your hand back where it belongs, you will never know for certain if you could accommodate what I have to give."

What a decision to have to make: continue to obey him, or spend the rest of my lonely days on this outpost wondering what an Atolani cock felt like.

Damn him for leaving me no choice.

I turned away resolutely and faced the mirrored wall. He made a satisfied sound and pulled my legs open a little wider, just to make a point, I thought. In the mirror, he met my gaze and then looked pointedly down.

I slipped my hand into my wet folds, shocked at how much liquid drenched my fingers. But instead of holding myself open and still, I rubbed myself the way I liked the most—the way I gave myself pleasure when I was alone in my quarters. He might take his wagers deadly seriously, but that didn't mean he got to make *all* the rules.

He watched me in the mirror, his free hand stroking my stomach and my hip as I touched myself for him, showing him precisely what I liked as his cock throbbed against my ass through his clothes. Soon he seemed to grow impatient and nudged my hand aside to take over. I held myself open for him without being asked again and was rewarded by a series of precise caresses that had me shuddering in his arms, despite already having come hard enough that I wasn't sure I could come again.

"Thalan," I moaned. "Yes, please. More."

I watched myself in the mirror grinding on his red fingers, my self-consciousness now all but forgotten. My wetness dripped from his hand. I'd never thought about watching myself come, but now I wanted to see how I looked in the throes of an orgasm.

A coil of heat and tension spread from my core. I saw myself reflected in the wall, flushed and wild, my mouth open wide as I gasped and moaned.

"Come for me now," Thalan commanded.

And I did, with a throaty cry, my body shuddering and writhing against his, fighting to get away because the intensity felt overwhelming. He continued to circle my clit as I wailed, and then dipped his fingers back into my pussy to feel me clench around him. He made a low thrumming sound that somehow made my pleasure even greater as he stroked inside me.

He met my gaze again in the mirror. "My ledger?" he asked.

I could not have cared less now about his debt, though I would when it came time to pay my bills for the month. But this was our game now and I would play along.

"Seven thousand," I panted. "If you want those numbers to drop faster, you need to be wearing less clothes, and I need to be back on my feet...or on my back. Or on my knees. Pick one."

His hand slid from me and I cried out to lose his touch. I wanted more of him, but I didn't want that talented hand going anywhere else.

He smiled at me in the mirror, revealing his sharp canines. "You are much too short to do anything for me while on your knees, Ariel."

"So we'll have to figure it out." I pulled on the arm that had been locked around my waist for...fuck if I knew how long. I'd lost all track of time. "Put me down."

Instead, he reached behind me, and I felt him unfastening something. Maybe his pants. *Finally!* My heart raced.

I wanted his cock so badly that I would have done anything right then to have it in my hands, my mouth, my pussy, wherever he wanted to put it.

The material of his pants slipped down between us, and suddenly something very, very large and very, very hot pushed between my parted thighs. What moved against my aching pussy did not feel like it could be a cock.

I looked at the mirror, at what Thalan had revealed by unfastening his pants. And I froze.

chapter six

thalan

Ariel stared at my cocks in the mirror, her mouth agape and eyes wide. Her astonishment more than made up for the orgasms I had provided.

She had offered her mouth, so that was what I would take first. And then I would take her pussy and her ass, first with one cock, and then the other. And then both, if she could take me fully.

There was indeed the matter of our different heights. She could not reach my cocks with her mouth if she kneeled, and standing she would have to bend over awkwardly. The best solution, I decided, was to pleasure each other at the same time.

But before that, she must see my cocks fully, and taste them.

I placed her on the floor facing me and released her. She stared openly at my cocks, at their red flesh with the black stripes that matched those than ran across my arms, legs, and sides.

I removed my boots, pants, coat, and shirt with the speed and efficiency of a trained soldier. She roused herself enough to unfasten and kick off her boots and I could finally see every square centimeter of her beautiful body.

I stacked all my weapons on the counter next to my empty plates.

Her gaze never left my cocks, and she licked her lips several times. *Hungry for me*, I thought. *I will fill you —do not worry.*

Now naked, I took my cocks in my hands and stroked them for her, one above the other, to show that while much larger than a human male's, their function and sources of pleasure were the same.

She raised her gaze to meet mine, a playful smile at the corner of her mouth again like when I had roared and demanded to be freed. "I must be dreaming," she said, and pinched her arm.

"What purpose does that serve?" I frowned. "Do you enjoy pain?"

"Sometimes." Her chuckle sounded a little strangled. "I have a feeling I'm going to find out how much I can take." She reached for my cocks with both hands, stroking hesitantly at first. Her hand, so much smaller than mine, could not come close to wrapping around one cock by itself.

Instead, she tilted her head, as if thinking, and then took my upper cock in both hands to stroke gently as she leaned down. With her tiny, soft, pink tongue, she licked around my cock head and then several times over its opening, where precum already dripped in earnest.

Gods. *Gods.* I let out a growl of pleasure.

She raised her head. "No? Not right?"

I took her head in my hand and urged her to bend again. "More."

"More *please*," she muttered, but she let me push her head back toward my upper cock.

Facing the mirror, I watched her from above and in the mirror's reflection as she explored my cocks with her hands and mouth. Since my upper cock was easier for her to reach, she took it in her mouth first, carefully, almost experimentally, likely to see how much would fit and how it might taste.

When her lips closed around my cock and she sucked, her tongue sliding against my cock head, I threw my head back and growled. She stunned me by immediately releasing me from her mouth. "Eyes open," she said sharply, and pointed to the mirror. "I watched you. Now you watch *me*."

I could not argue. Not with her hands on my cock and a thin rope of saliva running from her mouth to its swollen, sensitive head. Not when the sound of her commanding me made my cocks throb.

She stared at the cock in her hands. "It moves!"

"It does move." I undulated it, as well as my lower cock, and her mouth fell open again.

"This is the best bet I've ever lost," she said, and took my cock back into her mouth. I held her head with my hand on its crown, content to let her move as she chose, for now.

She could take less than a third of its length into her mouth at once, but she took more than I had expected by slipping its head into her throat. Then she pulled back, sliding her hands through her own saliva and spitting on my cock to provide lubrication for her steady, very pleasurable strokes.

Growling, I watched us in the mirrored wall and stroked my lower cock as she sucked me off. Her ass stuck out when she bent over, and I wanted to touch it, to lick it, to slip my fingers and then my cock inside her tight hole and bring her to climax that way as well. But first I had to taste her.

In one swift movement, I picked her up, spun her upside down, and held her so that her mouth could return to my upper cock while her pussy pressed to my lips. She would not be able to stay in this position for long, so I intended to make the most of what little time we had.

I slid my tongue into her wet folds and she screamed, "Oh, gods, Thalan!" It was part plea and part ecstasy. She trapped my head between her legs with her thighs on my shoulders and wrapped her arms around my waist to keep herself in place, though I held her weight without straining myself.

I parted her pink lips with my tongue, closed my mouth on her pearl, and sucked. Her scream this time was pure need, and a moment later she rewarded me with her mouth and hands again on my upper cock, stroking and sucking and drawing out growls from me that rolled from my feet to my lips and tongue. My growls vibrated against her pearl, making her squeeze my head between her legs and cry out. Her cries were muffled by my cock.

When she stroked my lower cock with one hand while still sucking and stroking my upper member, stars flew across my vision, and I roared into her pussy's wet heat.

Gods above, this woman, I thought. If I did not bury my cocks in her right now, I would lose my gods-damned mind.

With one last, long, lingering lick, I waited until her mouth had freed my cock before turning her upright. Her face was flushed and she gasped for air from sucking my cock and staying upside down for so long. As she caught her breath, I held her against my chest by her waist and thigh, her pussy poised just above my upper cock.

She grabbed me by my neck, pulled my head down to hers, and kissed me.

Atolani do not touch mouths as humans do, but I understood this was an intimacy, perhaps even more so than her mouth on my cock. I did not yet know what she meant by this kiss, or if it meant anything at all, but I chose to interpret it as her answer to my unspoken question.

I lowered her onto my slick upper cock and pushed its head inside.

ariel

GODS ABOVE.

Thalan's cock head pushed inside me, and I clenched around him immediately. *Too big, too big,* I thought desperately, freezing in place with my lips against his. If he drove himself into me right now, I'd find out how much pain I could really take.

Instead, he lifted me until his cock head pulled free. I cried out in protest against his mouth, and he immediately lowered me again so his cock could explore my pussy, sliding into me more carefully this time.

Oh, right. Because he could *move* his cocks.

And that had definite benefits, as I discovered a moment later when his cock head rubbed inside me, seeking and searching for the spot his fingers had found earlier—

And found it.

His hot mouth opened against mine to devour my cries as his enormous cock head rubbed against my g-spot in a way I had never felt before. I tasted myself on his mouth too—a musky sweetness I recognized, blended with his own smoky flavor and scent.

He'd held me with such strength and security while he'd tongued my clit and I'd sucked his cock that I'd felt small, but not afraid. I knew, though I couldn't have explained *how* I knew, that I was safe in his arms, even in that vulnerable position. I also knew he'd enjoyed what I'd done for him as much as I'd enjoyed what he'd done for me. I didn't trust easily and never had, but I'd never considered trying to make him put me down—and not just because he'd given me the best oral sex I'd ever experienced, albeit for only a minute or two.

Now I wrapped my legs tighter around his waist and hung onto his neck as his cock drove into me again and again, shuddering and pleading with him to *never fucking stop*, my words traveling from my mouth into his. In moments I came with a cry, shaking against him and writhing as his cock undulated inside me, driving deeper while still rubbing against my most sensitive place and drawing out my climax.

My orgasm made it easier to take him. He must have felt that too, because now he fucked me in earnest, holding me in place against his chest with his enormous hands under my thighs. His cock moved on its own to delve deeper inside me, one stroke at a time. His growls of what I'd learned was pleasure added to my own ecstasy because they traveled through his cock into me.

I hadn't intended to kiss him, but I couldn't help myself. I also couldn't stop crying out his name over and over into his own mouth as his cock went deeper and deeper and I stretched to accommodate him in a delicious combination of pleasure and pain.

"Ariel," he said, his mouth still against mine. "My ledger?"

How much was his debt? How much had I deducted? I didn't know and didn't care.

He slowed his movement then, his cock going still. "My ledger," he said again, and took his mouth away too. At my scowl, his smile turned decidedly wicked.

"Gods," I muttered, and tried to move on his cock, only to find I couldn't because he was a gods-damned behemoth with the strength of a Fortusian ox. "Five thousand credits."

When he grinned, I knew I'd given him the wrong number. "I mean six thousand," I said quickly. "Plus tip."

"No." His eyes glinted. "*Five* thousand. I have cut my debt by nearly half. I am pleased."

"You seem generally pleased with yourself," I shot back. "So that feeling shouldn't be too unique, Thalan the hotshot raider."

He stilled then, his expression going from amused to stoic in a heartbeat. "I am no raider," he said. I didn't like his voice now: harsh and flat. "I have left that life."

"Nobody just—" I started to say, and then closed my mouth.

No, nobody just left a raider squad. Only by death could a raider leave. Death, or a desperate and ultimately short-lived run.

Suddenly, everything I'd thought about Thalan changed. I didn't know why he'd deserted his squad, but there was a good chance he was running for his life. He'd likely come to my diner for a meal, hoping to find a moment's peace before taking off to some distant place where he'd have a chance to live in hiding.

I didn't feel sorry for him because I knew nothing about his life before this moment, but I understood what it meant to have to run— either away from something or toward some distant, unknown destination.

He watched my face, dark eyes searching my expression for what I thought of him. Did he expect a condemnation? Sympathy? Rejection? Well, I couldn't judge him. Not without judging myself too.

Only much later did it occur to me that he must have wondered if I would rat him out to the raiders the moment he left, hoping for a big reward. In this moment, the thought never crossed my mind. By telling me that he'd deserted his squad, this colossus of a man had bared his throat to me, both literally and metaphorically.

"Five thousand credits," I agreed, holding his gaze. I ran my nose over his lips before I kissed him again, this time less like I wanted to devour him and more in gentle reassurance. "Almost halfway to breaking even. Best get back to work, Thalan."

He moved so fast that I had no time to react. In the same kind of lightning-quick movement he'd used to approach me for the first time, he took me to the counter, set me down on its surface with my ass against its edge, and raised my legs so my ankles rested on his shoulders. From here I could see us reflected in the mirrored wall, and I felt a rush of heat that meant I'd gushed again for him.

My Atolani lover was magnificent, his body solid muscle, his red flesh with its black stripes now hot to my touch as if fucking me made him turn to lava inside. I could not count all of his scars, but I wanted to drag my tongue across them while he growled and writhed. And his thick cocks were as beautiful and imposing as the rest of him, with their bulbous heads and the ridges that ran from the tips down the length of the shafts.

Holding my legs raised and open, Thalan fucked me with his upper cock, pulling almost all the way out so that his cock head throbbed against my opening before plunging himself deep every time, never going so far that he would hit my cervix and cause me pain I didn't want. I cried out for him, helplessly spread, clinging to the sides of the counter to hold myself steady. His cock filled me up even more and its thick head and ridges rubbed against my g-spot nonstop. I screamed and screamed, calling his name.

When he pulled his upper cock out and pushed his lower cock into me, the angle changed and I climaxed almost instantly with a ragged cry. Apparently not satisfied with that, he circled my clit with his fingers as his upper cock rubbed against my folds.

I could die, I thought deliriously. *I could die getting fucked by this man, and I wouldn't even mind.*

It was a ridiculous thought. So was my next one.

I wanted him to stay here with me. Stay and help me run this diner. Fuck me senseless every night and every morning. It wouldn't be an adventure or dangerous or anything at all like his life as a raider, but it *would* be a life.

What a stupid thing to want, but I wanted it anyway.

When I reached for him, he picked me up again and kissed me as he settled my pussy back onto his upper cock. This time I wrapped my arms and legs around him and rode him more gently, almost tenderly, enjoying the way he growled and his cock throbbed inside me. I could get used to this.

Stop that right now, I chastised myself. *He's a dead man. It's only a matter of time.*

I sank my teeth into his massive shoulder and moaned.

Maybe no man fucked as good as one who thought he was about to die.

"Four thousand five hundred credits," I said without being prompted.

His grin made my stomach flutter, and not just with arousal. "My lady of the diner," he said. This time it didn't sound like he was being a smartass.

He carried me to one of the few booths in the diner. Most of my customers were singles. Occasionally pilots and copilots came in together. Once in a while, I'd get a whole ship's crew, and they'd crowd into the booths and line up at the counter, raucous and tiresome and drunk as they demanded food and directions to the brothel.

Thalan shoved a table out of the way and pushed two opposite benches together. I liked where this was going, but the makeshift bed wouldn't be big enough for him without his entire legs hanging over the end. Not comfortable at all for him, even for a wild fuck with a diner owner.

Instead, he put me on my knees on the benches with my ass facing him. Oh. The benches *were* a perfect height and size for that.

He stroked in and out of me slowly still, first with one cock and then the other. I'd learned how they each felt and the different angles and could tell which he used without looking. I leaned down on my forearms and he growled his appreciation for how deeply he could fuck me in this position.

This was a different kind of sex. Slower, deeper, more deliberate. I sensed a change in him, something less sarcastic or playful. Something more…primal. And I liked it.

While he fucked me slowly, I felt something new: the nudge of his other cock against my pussy too. I tensed.

He caressed my ass, then slid his hand around my hip and began to circle my clit in the way I liked. I arched against him with a moan, my hand joining his to drive me closer to a climax. I wanted to take both his cocks, but I didn't know if I could.

It seemed Thalan wasn't sure either. Instead, he slipped his upper cock out and slid the other in. I let out a breath and relaxed. He continued to rub my clit, however, and I felt another climax rising, softer this time.

As the warmth spread, his fingers dipped into my pussy along with his thrusts. I moaned and pushed back against his hand and cock, urging him to do that more. Maybe we could slowly work up to both cocks.

When I came with a groan and shudders, his fingers delved inside me, curled as if he was gathering the wetness of my release on his hand. The reason why became evident a moment later, when his wet fingers moved to my ass. I tensed again and stilled.

There was *no way*. No way at all I could take one of his cocks in my ass.

He withdrew his cock and kneeled behind me, pushing my legs farther apart as he spread my ass with his hands. Despite all we'd done, I felt another self-conscious flush creep over my flesh as he studied me, spread open for him again.

And then his tongue traveled from my pussy to my ass in one long, sinuous lick, and I forgot all about my embarrassment.

His tongue explored the contours of my asshole, seeking the sensitive areas and probing at the tiny opening. His fingers circled my clit as his tongue licked and stroked and prodded, until my asshole opened just enough for him to slide the tip of his tongue inside.

The raspy, wet heat of his tongue felt so good that I nearly collapsed, but he held me up and against him, stroking in and out first with his tongue and then with one wet fingertip, wonderfully hot and slick with my wetness and his saliva. And then he added another finger, still stroking and turning and curving slightly to make me shake and scratch my nails on the bench's worn seat.

A third finger joined the others and now I moved against him, fucking his fingers with my ass. I had done some ass play before with Sakal, but never with more than one or two fingers. And he'd never pushed me to go any further. I'd never been sure either of us wanted to. I was absolutely certain now that I wanted to go as far with Thalan as my body and his would allow.

I heard soft sounds and felt saliva dripping between my ass cheeks. More lubrication from Thalan's mouth. I wasn't sure it would be enough, though.

"Oil, in the kitchen," I told him, my voice hoarse.

He left me for only moments. When he returned, I heard the sound of a cap snapping off a bottle and then the soft sound of him stroking the oil on his cocks. Then he drizzled oil over my ass, where it dripped into my asshole and down my legs. I whimpered in need.

"One at a time, Ariel," he said, his mouth against my bare back. His fingers stroked my clit, circling, teasing, making me shake and arch against him, spreading myself even wider for him.

His lower cock slid into my pussy with a sensation that felt as comfortable as coming home. I loved that angle the most. *Not that I should pick a favorite cock,* I thought, and then almost laughed at the idea.

An hour or two ago, I would never have imagined such a thought would cross my mind. Not unless it was a single favorite cock attached to a single male.

A single cock might never be good enough again.

He stroked me gently, then more quickly, while his fingertips rubbed my clit just how I liked. Then the head of his upper cock pushed against my ass. The pressure was gentle, but unyielding. Without mercy. *Oh gods. Oh gods.* I might have been praying, which I'd never really done.

His cock head popped through my tight ring with a flash of blinding pain mixed with pleasure. I yowled, my body simultaneously trying to push him out and wanting more of him inside. My vision turned hazy and filled with stars.

"Easy," he said, holding me still with his hands on my hips. "Easy and slow. Just breathe."

I did. I breathed. I mumbled prayers mixed with Thalan's name and I breathed.

A little more oil flowed between my ass cheeks. And he moved again, still holding me in place. Then more, and more. I had never felt so very, very full.

When I moved back toward him, pushing more of him inside me of my own accord, he growled in pleasure for the first time since he'd breached my asshole. His rumble made me moan and try to find a handhold on the bench seat.

His cocks began to undulate inside me, throbbing with his need, and I sobbed as I came from a kind of pleasure I'd never felt before.

His cocks moved in my ass and my pussy, stroking in and out of me gently, and then not so gently. I held onto the bench as he fucked me and it felt so good—better than anything I'd ever known. Anything I'd ever dreamed possible.

His cocks throbbed faster and his growls rose in volume, becoming a keening, almost a song. I didn't need to speak his language to know what was happening.

Thalan was about to come.

He slowed and pulled me upright on my knees, his arm wrapped around my waist. The change in position was damn near too much for me to bear as his swollen cock heads rubbed inside me from entirely new angles. I made a sound somewhere between a groan and a mewl.

His fingers went to my clit, rubbing and circling, plying me. But there was no way I could come. I might never come again.

"You will," he rasped in my ear. He laved my shoulder with his tongue while his cocks plundered every available millimeter of my pussy and my ass.

I didn't know if he could read my mind or if I was just that easy to figure out. I wished I could figure *him* out. What he wanted. Where he intended to go. Why he'd left his raider squad and signed his own death warrant. Why he'd offered to fuck me rather than take the door code from me by force.

Maybe he'd seen something in me he liked. And maybe he was lonely too.

He stroked my clit more slowly, coaxing, always without mercy. I wanted him to make me come like this, with his cocks buried deep inside me and my name on his lips.

I'd go with him, if he asked. I'd run away from this diner without looking back. Kitbot could make meals without me. I wanted to go where I'd never have to worry about dealing with Raxians, or sex-starved freighter captains, or moody Pallasians demanding free food in return for hauling my scraps. Where Thalan could make me feel this good, whenever and wherever we wanted.

Was I stupid for wanting that? Maybe. I'd been stupid for running to this outpost. Maybe I still had it in me to do one more stupid thing.

I reached up to wrap my hand around the back of his neck and arched against him. His hands moved from my hip and my clit to cup my breasts, his thumbs playing with my sensitive nipples and sending sparks of pleasure through me. He hadn't used his tongue on them, or sucked them like I liked to have them sucked. Maybe next time.

While he pinched my nipples, I rubbed my clit and moved against him as his cocks throbbed and plunged in and out of my pussy and ass. It was a perfect moment of pure bliss.

A telltale warmth grew low in my abdomen. Thalan was right: I *could* come one more time.

He seemed to sense it too. His growl rose in volume as his thrusts turned more urgent. The throbbing of his cocks became a nonstop pulsation. I dug my nails into his thigh with one hand to brace both of us and rubbed my clit with the other.

When I clenched around him and cried out his name, he wrapped his arms around me, bellowed, and came—first with his lower cock in my pussy, and then with his upper cock in my ass.

The hot pulses of his release gushed from me and sent me right back over the edge in an orgasm so powerful that I'd never felt anything like it before. It rolled through my entire body like a tidal wave. I shuddered violently and went limp in his arms, sagging, somewhere between conscious and not.

Hazy minutes later—or maybe hours, I had no idea—I found myself nestled in Thalan's arms, wrapped in his long coat, my head against his chest. He was stroking my hair and smelling it, his nose traveling down its length until he twirled the end around his fingers and let it slip free.

As awareness returned, I immediately missed the sensation of his cocks inside me. I felt sore—not at all surprising, considering what I'd taken, and what I'd given. But I felt clean and warm and safe. More so than ever before.

Somehow, I knew he hadn't tried to get out and away while I was semi-conscious. That meant something, I thought.

"Don't run from me," I said drowsily. Fumbling, eyes half closed, I found his hand so I could lace my fingers through his. My hand looked hilariously small compared to his. In fact, all of me was small compared to him.

"What do you mean, my lady of the diner?" His voice was a low rumble.

"You're running, aren't you? You're about to run out of my diner and keep going until you find a place to hide."

His hand stilled, then continued stroking my hair. "I must go far from here. I cannot stay for long. I am…hunted."

"Yet you stopped for a quick meal."

"And a glorious fuck." He chuckled and tugged on my hair. "The meal was far less good than the sex."

I wanted to be mad, but he was not wrong about either the food or the sex. "Synthetic vegetables and meats and Kitbot's recipes can only do so much."

"You have done well. It is a good diner."

"I don't want it anymore." I said it without thinking, but it was probably the most truthful thing I'd ever said to anyone. "I want to go with you."

His whole body twitched. That was the first time I'd managed to startle him in any way. "It would not be a life for you," he said.

"*This* isn't a life for me." I gestured at the diner. "I'm just killing time here."

He'd straightened things up, except for our benches and the table that had once gone between them. I'd always thought these seats were terribly uncomfortable, but drunk crews didn't care. Not that I had the money to buy replacements anyway. But at the moment, I felt perfectly cozy. Thalan was very warm.

Finally, my mind cleared enough for me to ask important questions. "How did I get clean?" I asked. "And did I pass out from an orgasm? Not that I'm complaining."

"I cleaned us." He said it simply. "It was my pleasure."

"Well, it was all very much my pleasure too. And that final orgasm?"

"A…gift. A trait of my people."

"A mind-bending orgasm to finish off your partner. That is a pretty good gift." I squeezed his hand. "Tell me why you left your squad. I want to know."

"It is a long story, better suited for another day." His chin came to rest on top of my head, the pressure light despite his size. "I will say that I could no longer abide their ways, even if it meant my death. I chose the way of a coward and ran."

"A coward wouldn't have risked their wrath. A coward would have stayed and done what his squad demanded without questioning." I didn't push for more detail. I had nightmares of my own I did not want to share. "Take me with you, Thalan."

For a long time, he didn't speak. I didn't like the silence. I had learned to read silences. This one did not bode well.

But I did have one more card to play. "You owe me three thousand credits," I said sharply. "The law says you pay for your meals."

"I see no law here," he said.

I couldn't read his tone, and when I tried to crane my neck to see his face, he held me still.

"I'm the law in this diner." I pointed to the wall—not the mirrored wall, which I'd never be able to look at again without seeing us fucking in it. I indicated a metal plate bearing an official seal hanging crookedly to the right of the doorway to the kitchen. "See that? I'm deputized to protect my establishment."

"I find it difficult to believe that I did not pay my debt. You screamed a great deal. Came many times. Called my name again and again."

I shrugged. "You certainly made a valiant effort. I did warn you it would be nearly impossible to pay for double the cost of your meal in work-in-trade. You owe me three thousand credits. And that still doesn't include my tip."

His chest shook. I realized he was laughing.

"Why is that so funny to you?" I demanded. "You laughed last time too. You're lucky I didn't deck you for it."

"What is 'decking'?"

I huffed. "It's what I'm gonna do to you if you don't explain the joke."

"I gave you my tips," he said, very seriously. "Both of them. Quite large tips, as you discovered—and said so, many times."

I blinked at him, bemused. "That's the joke? A dick joke?"

"Indeed."

I drew him to me for a long kiss. When he raised his head, I skimmed my fingers along the ridge that ran down the side of his neck. "I want you to fuck me like that every morning and every night," I told him. "Until you pay off your debt, or we decide we don't like fucking each other anymore."

"Do you think we'll stop wanting to fuck each other?" His question seemed sincere.

"Honestly?" I shrugged. "I don't know. But if so, not for a long time. I like your cocks a hell of a lot."

"I like your mouth, your pussy, and your ass a hell of a lot." He said the last part awkwardly, as if he'd never used that expression before. And maybe he hadn't.

"Well, then it's settled." I rested my hand on his bare leg. "It'll take me ten minutes to pack and empty my savings. You start your ship's engine and I'll meet you at the airlock. We'll make a fast getaway."

I started to rise, but he held me still. "It will not be a pleasant journey," he warned. "You will be hunted with me. We may never find safety and peace."

"Or we might," I countered. "I've been searching for safety and peace all my life. I didn't find it here. Maybe I'll find it somewhere else with you."

chapter eight

thalan - two years later

FOR SOMEONE WHO ONCE OWNED A DINER, MY MATE WAS A TERRIBLE COOK.

She was, however, absolutely perfect in every other way—most especially early in the morning, when I woke to the suns-rise and the sensation of her mouth and hands on my cocks.

"Good morning, my lady of the diner," I said, my palm on the back of her head as she bobbed her mouth on my throbbing upper cock, her hand stroking its length. "I would not think you would have the energy for this. Not after last night."

Ariel sucked me hard as she withdrew her mouth and grazed my tender flesh with her teeth, eliciting a growl low in my chest. When she looked up at me, her eyes twinkled, and she licked my swollen cock head to catch a drop of precum on her tongue. "You know me better than that, Thalan."

I held out my arms. "Then bring that beautiful pussy to me, my love."

She gave each of my cocks one long last lick before obeying. I lifted her with my hands around her waist to settle her with her knees on each side of my face, so those slick pink folds were within reach of my tongue.

"Open yourself for me," I said.

Often she playfully argued when I demanded her cooperation as a reminder of our first encounter at her diner. But today she did as I asked, parting her folds with two fingers and showing me the sensitive pearl already swollen—or still swollen from last night's sex.

With my hands on her hips to guide her movements, I closed my lips on this sweet pearl, sucking and flicking it with my tongue. Her cries of ecstasy and the way she rode my face had become as familiar and welcome to me as my old ship had been. No, *more* familiar and welcome, because they signified how much she desired and loved me.

And for that, I would give her everything her heart desired, and everything that was in my power to give.

She came on my tongue with a wail, her hands clutching the metal bars of our new headboard. It was our fourth such piece of furniture since moving into our home on Pallasia, and much sturdier than previous versions. We were rough on our furniture and not just in our bedroom. My mate desired my attentions anytime we were together, wherever that might be.

A few minutes later, when she was astride my hips, her pussy and ass filled with my cocks, I watched her with her head thrown back, deep in the throes of pleasure. We had a mirror above our headboard as well, because now she loved to watch us make love, as she called it. It was an old-fashioned term from her home planet, she'd explained, but it made sense to me.

For a long time we had fucked: aboard my ship, on various space stations and planets, and finally here in the home we had built with our own hands. Somewhere during our journey, we began to make love, in the way her ancestors had called the joining of bodies for pleasure and comfort.

But we also still fucked, which was why we purchased new furniture at a rate that made the local shopkeepers quite curious.

I did not tell my Ariel to watch herself in the mirror this morning. For the moment, I was content to be the watcher while she braced herself on my chest with her hands and rode my cocks until my growls and her cries filled our home.

She came as many times as she pleased before I allowed myself to do the same. When she finally collapsed on my chest, dizzy and gasping and whimpering from our final shared release, I held her in my arms until her strength returned and her mind cleared.

At first, I had felt unhappy that the intensity of the orgasm caused by my ejaculations rendered her nearly unconscious each time we made love, but she had promised she did not mind. After hearing her gasping cries many times, and feeling her clenching in pleasure so powerfully that my cocks felt bruised, I finally believed her.

"My ledger?" I asked, my hand sliding down her side to grip her soft hip. Inside her pussy and her ass, her walls still twitched around my cocks. I was pleased by how sated she appeared. "How does my account look today?"

"Mmm." She gave me a drowsy look through her eyelashes. "Closer and closer to that five hundred credit mark, my love. It won't be long now before all you'll owe me is my *tip*."

I undulated my cocks so their swollen heads moved inside her. She rewarded me with a throaty moan, her fingernails digging into my chest in the way I liked.

"Your tip," I said, kissing her hair. She had grown it out long, in the way of the Atolani. "You may ask for more whenever you like, my lady of the diner."

"I can't take any more now." Ariel burrowed against my chest. "Last night, then this morning. Too much of a good thing." After a moment, she added reluctantly, "But I should make breakfast. We'll both need to leave for work soon."

I thought of the culinary abominations that came from our kitchen and had a far better idea. "Let us clean ourselves," I said, and moved my cocks just enough so she would raise her head and glare at me, because her glare made my blood rush and heart sing. "I do not hunger for breakfast—not when there are so many parts of you I would much rather have in my mouth."

"Gods above, Thalan." She sighed. "What part of *I can't take any more* did you not understand?"

"I understand none of those words." I slipped my cocks from her and gathered her in my arms. "I am a simple builder of homes now. But I insist that you can and *will* take more."

As I carried her to the adjoining room for bathing, she kissed me with her hands on either side of my face. "Stubborn man. What can I do with you?"

"Anything you want, Ariel," I promised. "And everything you can dream of."

Her smile turned mischievous. "In that case, I have an idea."

My cocks began to throb anew. "Tell me."

She did.

We did not go to our jobs that day. And the next morning, we had to purchase a new bathing tub. If the shopkeeper wondered why, he had the very good sense not to ask.

about lita grey

Lita Grey is the pen name of an urban fantasy author who wants to explore the endless possibilities of sci-fi, alien, and monster romance.

To learn more, visit www.lisaedmonds.com

one night with the blue billionaire

Megan Van Dyke

EVERYONE THIS SIDE OF THE GALAXY KNEW THAT THE BEST DESTINATION for a good time was the Golden Sphere, which was why Aivey and her two best friends didn't even consider another party station when planning their girls' week getaway during their last break before graduation.

The Sphere had not disappointed—not yet, anyway. After days of gaming, lounging in the manufactured sunlight of the dome crafted to mimic the pristine beaches of Traquila, dancing to hypnotic music, and tasting delicacies that left Aivey groaning in pleasure, there was only one way they could think of to cap off their vacation: a trip to the infamous and renowned sex club, Incandescence.

A shiver ran down the length of Aivey's spine as she stepped out of the cleansing enclosure. She should be used to it by now. After all, they had a similar one at the academy which all students were required to pass through when returning from off campus. But the woosh of air, sprinkle of tiny particles across her clothing and skin, and strangely mossy scent never failed to make her feel momentarily unsettled. Such things were necessary when citizens of various planets and systems mingled. Nobody wanted an accidental plague or anything.

"Woohoo!" Vesta raised her hands in the air as if making it through the cleansing was some big test. "Three for three!" The neon blue lights that illuminated the inner lobby of Incandescence—which was otherwise sleek and black like obsidian—caught on Vesta's pale hair which swayed from side to side as she gave a little celebratory dance.

"I can't believe we're almost in." Rima let out a little squeal and bounced in her spikey, golden heels.

A few other groups stood around, chatting excitedly. The distant thud of pounding music mingled with the hum of the nearby conversations.

The enthusiasm emanating from every pore of her friends—and seemingly everyone else—left Aivey even more unsettled than the cleansing chamber. The hard knot of anticipation sitting low in Aivey's stomach twisted tighter. Oh, she wanted to go to Incandescence. She'd perked right up the moment Rima suggested it. But now that they were actually here, about to walk into a club filled with people looking for their next fuck, she couldn't help but be nervous. Vesta and Rima seemed to have no such reservations, though, and Aivey wasn't about to be *that friend* and back out at the last minute.

It was just that sometimes a casual fling left her feeling... empty? Was that it? Unsettled? She could never quite pinpoint the exact feeling. All she knew is that sometimes, well, like *one* time, it was great, and most of the time it really wasn't. Though admitting that to her friends, close as they were, seemed impossible. Especially since that's what they were all about to do—go have a little fun without attachments.

No attachments, no chance of bumping into their hookup around the academy, and hopefully no regrets. Aivey glanced down at her pointer finger. Moments ago, she'd pressed it against a panel, had her blood sampled, been injected with a temporary fertility suppressant. Another club requirement, and one she was grateful for. After all, the club's slogan of "What happens at Incandescence stays at Incandescence" couldn't be true if there was the risk of getting knocked up. Thank goodness she didn't have to worry about any of that thanks to the club's strict safety protocols.

"I've been looking forward to this for ages!" Rima's exclamation drew Aivey's attention back to her friend. With the shimmering gold of her skin-tight dress against her bronzed skin and wavey pink hair, she'd stand out in any crowd, even as one as diverse as those in the

Golden Sphere. Which, Rima had proclaimed earlier that night, was just the point. "Seriously. Ever since I learned about this place, it's been top of my dream board."

Aivey sucked in a deep breath and shoved her worries to the back of her mind. "I know," she replied, attempting to sound way more relaxed and excited than she actually was. She wasn't about to dampen her friend's joy. "You've only told us about a million times."

Rima sauntered closer and booped Aivey on the nose. "Then one more won't hurt."

This was their last night of vacation. Rima and Vesta were determined to finish off the trip with the biggest indulgence of all: seeking to play out their inner fantasies with a stranger or two…preferably not of the Earthean variety. After all, their academy was mostly Earthean, so why not hook up with a different type of humanoid while they had the chance? This was a chance to break free, to indulge without judgment or consequence. After all, only the three of them would know about this little excursion and they'd already kept each other's secrets for years.

"Come on! I'm so ready to get in there already." Vesta looped her arms through Aivey and Rima's and marched them toward a sleek desk of shimmering black glass.

An exceedingly tall woman stood behind it. Two twisting white horns speared up through her violet hair that had been tied in little braids and fell down past her shoulders. Her attire, much like her skin tone, was nearly as black as the desk she stood behind—and just about everything else Aivey had spied in the club so far. They really took the dark tones and neon lights aesthetic and ran with it.

"Welcome to Incandescence," the woman behind the desk said as they approached. The silken tones of her voice made Aivey shiver with the way they slid over her senses and beckoned her closer. "Come forward and submit your cards to get your bands."

Before the cleansing chamber, they'd each filled out a card detailing their desired match, or matches, for the night. The questionnaire included their preferences on genders, species, number of partners, particular kinks they desired, and so forth. The list of choices was so exhaustive there was one gender and at least three species that Aivey didn't recognize, which was truly saying something since she had at least a cursory knowledge of the galaxy's primary intelligent races.

One by one, they inserted their cards in the illuminated slot and stuck their arm into the round opening. Aivey held her breath as the machine light up and then circled her wrist with a silver band almost an inch thick. Lights illuminated as words scrolled in galactic common across the smooth black panel screen in the center. The scrolling text confirmed Aivey's choices. Her band was silver for one desired partner. An orange light indicated she wished for a humanoid, and green represented the gender she wanted—in this case, male.

"Excellent. This is your whole party?"

Aivey glanced back at the woman, just as Rima answered her question. The hostess looked from one of them to the next, and it was impossible not to get caught up in the woman's dark eyes that sparkled with bits of violet. They certainly picked the right hostess for such a club.

"A quick reminder," the woman began. "If you wish to pair up with one or more individuals, you can tap your bracelet to theirs to see if you are a match. You'll both glow blue, if so. If not, your differences will be displayed on the band."

Rima and Vesta both nodded along silently, as if they were as entranced by the woman as Aivey.

"However, your bands are only your preferences," she continued. "You are free to choose outside of those if you wish and your selected counterpart agrees. The only exceptions are certain restricted kinks, but it doesn't look like any of you have chosen those." Her slow, knowing grin made Aivey's insides twist up, her pulse escalating and blood running hotter.

The woman clapped once and the feeling vanished. Aivey took a step back from the desk, standing a little straighter, her brows knotting.

"Any questions?" the woman asked, the hypnotic tone gone from her voice.

The three friends all looked between one another, blinking rapidly as if coming back to their senses.

"I am here if you do. If not, feel free to choose a starting room." The hostess gestured to three sets of double doors, each manned by an animatronic attendant. A few other groups stood around, possibly making their choice or just taking a breather before moving on to a new section of the club.

They all stepped away from the desk, making way for another group waiting to get their bands and likely listen to a similarly entrancing speech from the horned woman. There was something unique about her voice, perhaps a compulsion to make sure patrons paid attention.

"Are we ready?" Rima beamed as she turned toward Aivey and Vesta.

No. But Aivey never let the word leave her tongue. "As I'll ever be," she replied instead. That much was true. The first step was the hardest sometimes, and if she could just get inside, hopefully her worries would slip away. Until then, Aivey let her mind drift to her beloved Crathian mountains. With its soaring peaks dusted in pale purple snow, crisp air, verdant trees, and unique wildlife, there was no more peaceful and beautiful place in all of the galaxy. Which is why she'd made the mountains and their conservation the focus of her studies at the academy. Just the thought of it settled her.

"Which door do we want?" Vesta tossed her blond hair and drummed her black nails against one cheek. She'd gone simple and elegant with her look, sporting a sleeveless and short black dress in a similar style to Aivey's shimmering silver one that highlighted all of Vesta's generous curves.

"Actually..." Rima pulled her bottom lip between her teeth and wouldn't quite look at her two friends.

Rima uncomfortable? Aivey closed her mouth before she gaped too long at her friend. She was never shy, not from the moment they'd met at orientation day when she'd marched straight up to Aivey, wrapped her in a hug, and proclaimed that she just knew they were going to be the best of friends. She had been right, after all.

"Do either of you mind if I pick a different one from you all and go on my own?" Rima continued. "It's just, it's hard to explain, but in all my dreams I've come alone, and I feel like I need to do this, you know?

Live it out just like in my imaginings?" She continued to ramble, the words spilling out so fast Aivey nearly lost track.

"Rima…" Vesta whined, her shoulders drooping.

Splitting up, at least at the start, was not part of their plan. But now that Aivey looked closer, Rima had her hand tucked behind her back, her Incandescence bracelet out of sight. There was something about her selections she didn't want her friends to see, even with their promise to uphold the club slogan once they got back home.

"Yes, of course that's fine," Aivey said, interrupting Vesta's complaints. "We're good." She looped her arm through Vesta's and started to turn her away.

"But—" Vesta began.

Aivey cut her off and kept them moving. For once, Aivey wasn't the only one nervous, and from her extensive knowledge of the sensation, she knew there was nothing worse than other's pointing it out or lingering over it. Her friend wanted privacy and space to sort out her desires? She could give that to her. With a wave back at Rima, she said, "Have fun! We'll see you tomorrow!"

All trace of apprehension slipped away from Rima to be replaced by a blinding smile. "Tomorrow. Be back to the room by mid-morning or I'm going to worry. And we don't want to miss our check-out!" She bounced on her toes and waved before hurrying off toward the far door.

"Seriously, what was that about?" Vesta asked as soon as they passed through their door. A long hallway stretched out before them, colorful dancing lights and thumping music flooding in from the other end ahead.

Aivey shrugged and released her friend. "If she wants to do this on her own, let her. It's a safe environment. Besides, it's not like we're aiming to share."

"Speak for yourself." Vesta held up her bracelet with its golden band. "I'm hoping for at least a threesome. I mean, if we're gonna do this, let's go all-out, right?"

Aivey rolled her eyes. "You know what I mean. I don't think you want me in the room when you enjoy,"—she gestured around—"all that."

A wicked smile stretched across Vesta's face. "I plan to be so full of cock that I won't know or care who's there."

The beat of the music grew as they neared the end of the hallway, pulsing through Aivey's chest and easing some of her nerves. This was just a club. She'd been to dozens of those. No big deal. And if she found some male to enjoy the evening with, great. Aivey sucked in a deep breath of the strangely crisp air that, in a way, almost reminded her of the mountains. She could do this.

The hallway ended in a massive room with multi-hued lights illuminating a number of figures dancing just before them. That was normal enough, but it was the raised platforms jutting up amid the dancefloor that Aivey couldn't tear her gaze away from. People engaged in varied forms of public play for all to see. A blue-scaled Angrosian took an Earthean man from behind while he pleasured another with his hands. To the left, a female Taren rode both cocks of the massive figure lying on the platform below her. In the dancing lights, even more couples and groups played beyond them.

Nope. She was wrong. This was unlike any club she'd ever been to, and she'd only gotten her first glimpse of it.

Aivey's mouth gaped open as she caught sight of the ceiling, or lack thereof. Spanning the width of the room was a clear floor atop of which others played in a separate area a level above.

"Wow!" Vesta exclaimed above the music. "And I thought *I* was bold."

With effort, Aivey tore her gaze away from the spectacle and glanced at her friend. It wasn't shock or surprise glittering in Vesta's eyes, but something much closer to envy. *Stars.* Thank goodness Aivey hadn't mentioned being nervous, even though she had a right to be. Vesta probably would have laughed until her sides hurt.

"Well, should we grab a drink first?" Vesta suggested.

That was something familiar, something she could do. "Yes. A drink. Let's do that."

chapter two

WITH A LITTLE BOOZE IN HER SYSTEM AND THE NEWNESS WORN OFF, AIVEY finally didn't feel like rushing for the door at every moment. Two long and sweeping bars lined either side of the main room. Toward the back, hallways branched off, weaving around smaller rooms with lounges, slightly less public displays, and some locked private rooms. Aivey even enjoyed watching a couple entangled in a swinging contraption on the stage in one of the lounge rooms.

Not that she was ready to run off with anyone herself yet.

Hooking up was never exactly easy for her. Okay, it wasn't easy *at all*. There was always that fear that a stranger, or even an acquaintance, might leave her feeling less than satisfied or with morning-after regrets. In fact, she regarded hookups a lot like one of her favorite treats, Sweetened Duran Milk. On the surface it seemed incredibly enticing, promising something sinfully sweet that would tingle through her veins, flush her cheeks, and have her pressing her lips together with barely contained glee.

But only if it was made right.

Every so often the barista at the café forgot about her request to substitute the normal sweetener that she was allergic to for the Casae variety, which she wasn't, and her sweet treat turned into a painful nightmare full of regret.

That was how hookups were for her: laced with the worry her

partner would be full of the kind of sweetener that left her feeling awful long after. Seriously, some males were only interested in their own pleasure. Aivey dreaded the thought of picking another guy just to discover that he only wanted what he could get from her and not what they could find together.

Vesta, on the other hand, had no such fears.

Aivey half turned back toward where her friend sat on the lap of a green-skinned Garan, the top of his military uniform almost fully unbuttoned now to show his sculpted muscles. Another of similar dress and appearance sat beside him, rubbing Vesta's knee and grinning at her with his Earthean-like white teeth. Of all the species she could have gone for, Garans were quite similar to Eartheans, except for the green skin and the fact they were built slightly larger...everywhere. Vesta was in for quite a ride if she got her wish and took them both to a private room—though from the look on her friend's face, she wouldn't mind that outcome one bit.

She'd done her friend duty and waited to see if Vesta needed saving, but it was pretty clear that her friend had all but forgotten about her.

Great. Just fine. Aivey frowned down at her empty drink and set it aside on a small table containing a number of other consumed cast-offs. If she was going to survive in this place alone, she needed another and quick. The steep price tag would be a small price to pay to calm her nerves and make sure she didn't end up chickening out and leaving early.

Just as she was about to head back toward the main bar, two figures, Bhaargak males by the look of their pale purple skin and two tusks protruding up from their lower jaw, stepped in front of her.

"Hello there, pretty thing," one said with a thick accent. Saliva dripped from the corner of his mouth to splatter onto the floor at his feet.

Eww. Aivey barely stifled the urge to curl her lips back in disgust.

"Want to play?" He reached a beefy arm toward hers and tapped their bands together. A red light flared immediately, thank the fucking stars.

"Sorry." Aivey raised her voice to be heard above the music. "Doesn't look like we're a match."

"Ya can change your mind," the other said. "We'll show ya a good time."

"No thanks." She gave them her best *I'm-being-polite-but-please-fuck-off* smile. She bobbed on her toes, trying to look past their broad, bulky forms to catch sight of Vesta and hopefully snare her attention long enough to beg for help.

"Come on, give us a try." The first male grabbed her forearm, and Aivey instantly recoiled, trying to pull away. His skin was moist and clammy in a way that made her spine stiffen, and her drink burned back up the base of her throat.

She jerked her arm back, but the bastard held firm. "Let go!" When he didn't, she pulled back again, throwing the force of her body in the opposite direction, slipping in her heels, and—

Someone caught her from behind with a firm but gentle arm around her shoulders, tipping her back upright. A blue arm latched onto the Bhaargak's male's wrist and squeezed. "I believe she said no," the newcomer said, voice deep and powerful in a way that brooked no argument.

Finally, the Bhaargak yelped and let go before cradling his arm against his chest.

The male behind her steadied her on her feet and let go, half stepping between her and the two aggressive males.

"She might change her mind," the other Bhaargak insisted.

"I won't," Aivey snapped. "I already said no."

"There you go," the newcomer said. "She said no. Again. Or should I get one of the staff to remind you of the rules here and perhaps show you outside?"

At the threat, the two Bhaargak males grumbled and stomped off. Aivey let out a deep breath, her shoulders sagging as her adrenaline ebbed. With the males finally gone, she could see past them to where Vesta had risen from the lap of the Garan male and looked ready to rush over and save her. Aivey quickly shook her head and shot her friend a smile. She was safe now with this new male. Somehow, she knew that with a certainty.

Speaking of…

The male who'd saved her finally turned away from the retreating Bhaargaks. The snarl set on his features dropped away in an instant as his gaze met hers.

He was easily the most stunning creature she'd seen that night, with deep blue skin, silver hair that fell in long sheets past his shoulders, and a muscular humanoid body that filled out his black suit in the best of ways, accenting his broad shoulders and narrow hips. Two black horns speared through his hair just back from his forehead and sloped back past his pointed ears. He regarded her with ice-blue eyes set in a strong but balanced face.

"Are you all right?" he asked. He quickly slid his gaze up and down her body, not in the appreciative way several others had that night, but rather looking for injury or something else out of place.

"I am now." She exhaled. "Thank you for scaring off those goons."

"Of course." He nodded to her, his stance relaxing. "They should know better than to treat someone that way anywhere, but especially here."

"No kidding." Aivey hugged her arms around herself. "You'd think anyone who could shell out that entrance fee would have some decency about them."

His lips quirked up in the corners to reveal the hint of short fangs amid his otherwise Earthean-like teeth. "Some of us are decent."

She opened her mouth to say she hadn't been talking about him at all, but he winked and his smile broadened. "Perhaps I can buy you a drink? No pressure, though." He held his hands up in front of him. "Feel free to tell me to get lost if you like."

Aivey chuckled. As if she wouldn't want to spend a few more minutes with a gorgeous male who'd just saved her from an uncomfortable situation. "A drink sounds great. That's actually where I was headed."

"Excellent. Can I show you to the bar?"

"Please." She nodded.

No sooner had he turned toward the main room, Aivey a step behind, when her comms bracelet—a much smaller and more elegant version of the kind the club used—vibrated to alert her of a new message. She placed her thumb on the band, activating the message, as she followed in the wake of her savior through the crush of people milling about.

Message from Vesta: "Are you sure you're okay?"

With her thumb still on the bracelet she thought her reply for the communicator to transmit. *"Yeah, this one seems nice."* The implant that allowed such things was expensive but totally worth it in cases like this.

"Well, if I need to come kick his ass, let me know. I can bring some big green back-up, too."

Aivey laughed to herself. *"I'm fine. Go get laid."*

"Oh, I plan to." She could almost hear her friend's laugh. *"Hope you get to enjoy blue, shiny, and handsome!"*

Another huff of laughter caught in her throat. She'd share a drink with him for now and see how that went. After that? Well, who knew?

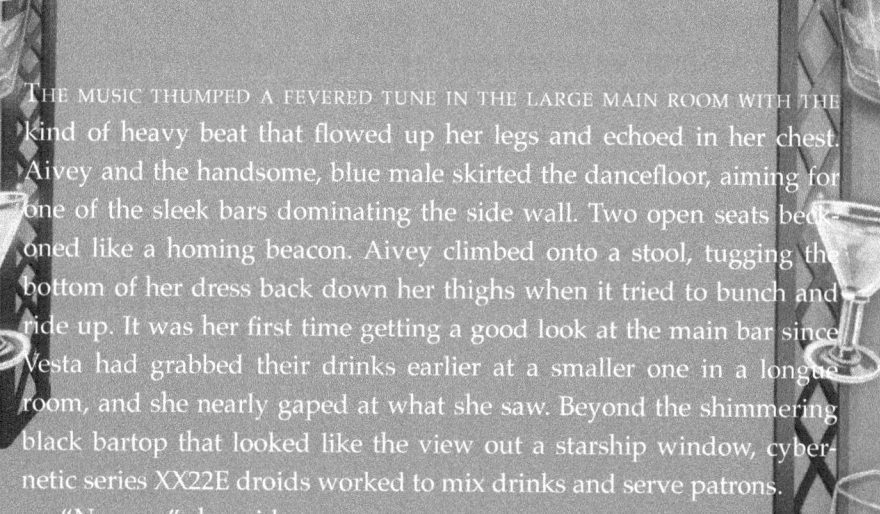

chapter three

THE MUSIC THUMPED A FEVERED TUNE IN THE LARGE MAIN ROOM WITH THE kind of heavy beat that flowed up her legs and echoed in her chest. Aivey and the handsome, blue male skirted the dancefloor, aiming for one of the sleek bars dominating the side wall. Two open seats beckoned like a homing beacon. Aivey climbed onto a stool, tugging the bottom of her dress back down her thighs when it tried to bunch and ride up. It was her first time getting a good look at the main bar since Vesta had grabbed their drinks earlier at a smaller one in a longue room, and she nearly gaped at what she saw. Beyond the shimmering black bartop that looked like the view out a starship window, cybernetic series XX22E droids worked to mix drinks and serve patrons.

"No way," she said.

The droids were famous for their skills, but not at bartending. Able to shift to multiple forms reminiscent of various humanoid species and genders, they were prized as the ultimate sex toy. And yet, here they were working the bar rather than pleasing customers in other ways.

"A shame, isn't it?" her companion mused, watching one of the droids zip past them. "I'm guessing this is your first time at Incandescence, given your reaction to the droids?"

She winced before sliding a little more firmly onto the seat. "Is it that obvious?"

A deep chuckle rumbled from his chest, barely audible over the music. "A little. You're not here alone, are you?"

"No, I came with two of my friends, but they're...occupied." Vesta certainly was, and if Rima was lucky, she was having a *very* good time off on her own as well. Aivey had briefly considered going to look for her, but just as quickly chucked that idea out her mental airlock when she remembered her friend's shyness about her band and request to go it alone. "And you?"

He shook his head. "I came with my brother. This is really more his scene than mine, but he was insistent." He shrugged. "He owns a private suite and comes often, and since I was visiting him, he dragged me along."

A private suite. Fucking stars. Renting a suite for the night was expensive. Owning a private one? The amount had to be astronomical. On first impression, it was clear that he dressed nicely and in clothes well-suited to his build, but now that little tidbit had her giving him another thorough once-over, noting things she hadn't before, like the nearly invisible seams and the little three moon logo barely on the far side of his chest. She knew that designer—heck, most people this side of the galaxy would. Knew it, but could never afford it.

"...I suppose you could say he's occupied as well."

Shit. He was still talking, and she'd totally zoned out while ogling him.

"So, I thought I'd grab a drink and relax for a little while. But then I saw that male grab you." He shook his head. "You looked terribly uncomfortable, so I thought I needed to step in."

"I'm so glad you did," Aivey replied. She wasn't above needing to be saved, especially by someone as gorgeous as him. Though more than that, he somehow made her feel comfortable. Safe. Almost like his presence was a balm to her nerves in and of itself. His looks were just a bonus.

He waved down one of the droids, who hovered over to their position. "A drink for the lady on my credits." He held out armband for it to scan. "Whatever she wants. And I'll take a Yenkoth Amber. No additives."

It was tempting to go for something high-end, but that would be rude. Though if she went with the bottom shelf crap they drank at the academy, and apparently was served here too since Vesta had purchased it, her sexy new companion might rethink his stay. Instead, she aimed for something just a little nicer than her usual. "Astrian blue, please. No ice."

He raised a silver brow. "Excellent choice."

The hint of a flush crept up her neck as the droid floated off to make their drinks. "I just realized that I never got your name," Aivey said.

His lips quirked up in one corner. "Baxian."

Baxian. She repeated to herself silently. It was an interesting name, one that felt right even as it rolled silently across her tongue.

"May I have yours?" he asked.

"I'm Aivey." She gave a nod of her head—the standard informal galactic greeting.

"Aivey. What a lovely name."

The compliment rolled through her like a gust of warm air, spreading out from her center.

"So, what brings a young Earthean female to Incandescence?"

The droid zipped back, drinks in tow, somehow managing not to spill any despite its speed. Both of them reached for the glasses at the same time and their bands nearly brushed one another. Blue light flared. Aivey froze, her head twisting toward Baxian. Not only was he handsome and considerate, they were a match. His blue eyes sparkled as he stared at her rather than the droid and their drinks. A rope of tension drew tight between them, nearly pulling Aivey right off her barstool and toward her alluring savior.

The droid beeped, severing the taut connection. Aivey relaxed back onto her stool and grabbed her drink, immediately bringing it to her lips and taking a small sip. She savored the light burn as it slid across her tongue and down her throat, only to be followed by a cool and refreshing aftertaste.

"Ah, sorry, about that. Where were we?" Baxian rolled his glass back and forth between his hands before setting it on the bar in front of him.

Aivey's lips twitched as she took him in. He almost looked as affected by the moment as her, but surely not. "I think you asked about why I came here tonight," she replied.

"Ah, that's right." His confidence returned as he sat a light straighter. "What *did* bring you to Incandescence?"

"Well." Aivey took another sip and crossed one leg over the other, trying to appear somewhat proper. "My friends and I are on break from Starborn Academy and are due back soon for our final term, so we thought this might be the perfect getaway to let loose during our time off."

Baxian gave her an appreciative look. "Quite a challenging academy to gain admittance to." It had been, damn it, though she was impressed he knew that. "What are you focusing on there?"

Should she tell him the truth or make up something to sound interesting? Most would probably find her research infinitely boring, but she opted to be honest with him anyway. "I'm finishing up my studies on the Crathian mountains on Elator and the impact recent mining practices have had on their sustainability and as well as the broader planetary environment."

He leaned back, shooting her an incredulous look. "I love the Crathian mountains. My family actually has a home along the southern range."

"You do!" She squeaked before plopping her drink down and leaning in. This male just kept getting better and better. The planet wasn't home to any native humanoid species, but it had become quite the vacation destination for wealthy galactic citizens—a fact that might have annoyed her had their own appreciation for the mountains not led many of them to donate substantial credits towards its preservation and study.

As they continued to talk, the bar, the music, and even other patrons around them faded into the background.

By the time her drink ran dry, Aivey had completely forgotten about where they were, her friends, and the public play happening just a few feet away on the raised platforms—and above their heads, for that matter. She and Baxian had been locked in conversation, and more than once had scooted their stools closer together to talk over the blaring music. Not that she noticed that much anymore either, the world outside of the two of them and it had stopped mattering the more they talked.

Baxian's long fingers flexed on the bare skin of her thigh where the bottom hem of her dress ended. His fresh, crisp scent enveloped her in its embrace, clouding out the scents of sex and booze that had filled her nostrils before she met him. Their legs rubbed against one another idly as they chatted, and Aivey discovered that this male knew almost as much about the Crathian mountains as she did, and even better, was a strong advocate for their preservation.

His skin was firmer than an Earthean, his body temperature just a bit warmer. He idly stroked her leg with this thumb, and though she tried hard just to focus on his words and his slightly hooded gaze, all she could think about was that touch. Back and forth. Firm and warm. *Stars.* Would the rest of him be so delightful? He would, wouldn't he?

There was a catching sensation in her chest as she stared at him. It pulsed in time with the thrumming through her veins, one that beat heavily in the juncture of her thighs. She couldn't remember being so interested in a male this fast, and not just for his looks, but his mind as well.

Finding someone she wanted to share the evening with had felt like a long shot when she first stepped into Incandescence, but now, after meeting Baxian, not spending the evening with him felt just as impossible. She yearned for him, plain and simple. The hesitation and uncertainty she often experienced with men, particularly potential hook-ups, was entirely absent.

All at once, the gentle stroking halted. "Aivey," he started, his features going stiff. "I wanted to ask—"

"There you are!"

Aivey startled, nearly falling backward. A new male threw an arm around Baxian's shoulders. The impact had his hand sliding up her thigh, but not in the way she'd longed for. He lunged forward with his other arm to steady her. Their little bubble of peace popped, and all the sound and scents of the club washed over her again.

An unfamiliar curse burst from Baxian as he snapped his head toward the male. "Phazian," he all but growled. Having steadied Aivey, he gave her leg one last squeeze and let go. She nearly whimpered at the loss of touch. He even slid his leg back from hers, leaving her suddenly cold and all too aware of her surroundings.

But that name slipped through the haze of lust and drink as quickly as a laser blast. Phazian. His brother? And now that she got a decent look at him, the resemblance was obvious. The same blue eyes and silver hair, though Phazian's was cut short and barely made it past his ears. They had a similar build, too, and while they dressed in equally fine clothes, Phazian's were even more elaborate and decorative with designs of shimmering silver and another pattern that had the hint of a rainbow hue.

Phazian smacked his brother across the back again, jolting him forward on the stool. "I've been looking for you, and you've ignored my comms. Are you ready to go?"

"Go?" Aivey squeaked before she could think better of it.

Phazian turned his head toward her as if noticing her for the first time. His pupils widened as he took her in from head to toe and then back again. "Well, aren't you a delicious little female." From the slur in his voice and slightly glazed look on his face, he'd had many more drinks than them already.

Baxian stood suddenly, placing himself between Aivey and his brother and giving the latter a little shove in the other direction. He looked back over his shoulder at her, his features pinched. "One moment."

While the two males were locked in conversation a few feet away, Aivey's stomach twisted itself in knots. She'd finally found what might be the only male in this bar she'd truly be interested in, and now his brother had to show up and ask him to leave. Could her luck be any worse? She should have just gotten to the point and asked him if he wanted to borrow a room with her. But, truly, she'd been enjoying their conversation and getting to know him first. It might be a little conventional for this unconventional club, but so what?

Baxian glanced over, catching and holding Aivey's gaze though his brother was still speaking and gesturing with his hands. Another couple walked between them, breaking up her line of sight. When they moved on, Baxian was looking at his brother again, saying something she couldn't begin to hear over the noise of the club and the surrounding patrons.

Her stomach dropped. Aivey grabbed her mostly empty glass and tipped it back, savoring the burn of the last few drops. She briefly considered ordering another, but what was the point? If he was going, she didn't plan to stick around and start at square one with someone else.

There was zero chance she'd find someone else like him anyway.

Baxian looked over at her again, and this time, Aivey willed all her hopes and desires into one look. *Please. Stay.*

Another agonizing few moments passed as Baxian addressed his brother once more. The two males clasped each other on the shoulders. Phazian headed wandered into the crowd as Baxian turned back toward her. Aivey sucked in a breath and sat a little straighter. Baxian still wore a serious expression. His lungs expanded on a deep breath that swelled his chest before he smoothed out his suit and strode toward her once more, his powerful body cutting through the space separating them with authority.

Aivey hopped off the stool as he advanced. This was it, where he said goodbye and walked out of her life forever.

Baxian stopped directly in front of her, their bodies nearly touching. "I'm sorry about that."

Aivey shifted from one foot to the other, unable to stand still. "You're leaving, too?" Her chest swelled in nervous anticipation.

His eyes hooded once more, a grin returning to his face. "No. Not unless you tell me you're done with me."

The breath she'd been holding whooshed out. "Thank the stars," she sighed.

"Although, I hoped you might want to get away from all of this"— he gestured around them— "and find somewhere a little quieter where we won't be disturbed again." The blue of his dark cheekbones deepened as he glanced away and then focused on her once more. "Since my brother is leaving, we can use his private suite. It hasn't been touched tonight and should be ready for us. If you'll join me, that is."

All her worry evaporated into nothingness, even her concern about potentially hooking up with a stranger who might leave her feeling less than satisfied or with morning-after regrets. Baxian wasn't that male. She knew it with a sudden certainty. He'd been nothing but respectful, and most of all, she felt comfortable with him. He was like Casac sugar: a sinful sweet that she could handle just fine. In fact, she ached for him body and mind, like even her senses knew that he would be good for her. How could that not be just what she was looking for?

He extended a hand to her, and she took it without hesitation. "I'd love to."

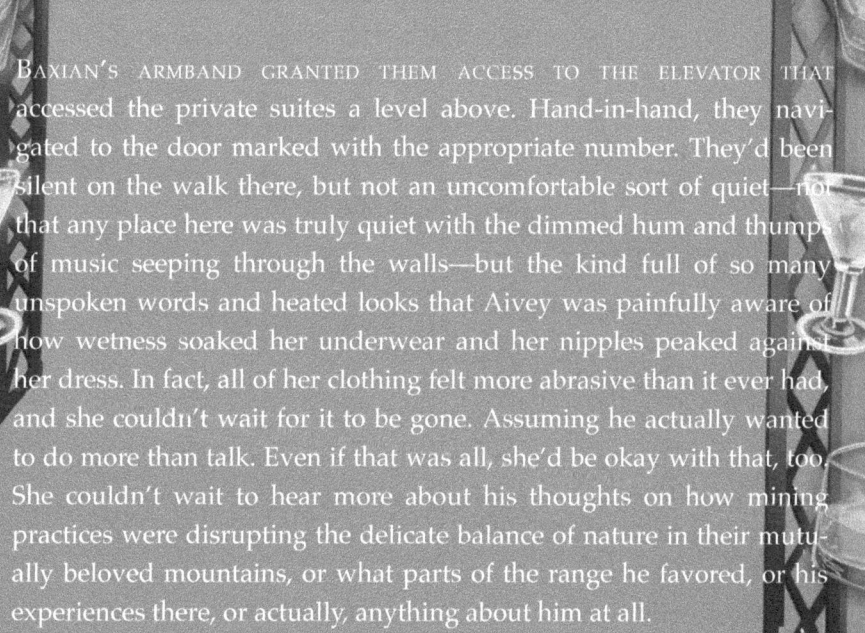

chapter four

Baxian's armband granted them access to the elevator that accessed the private suites a level above. Hand-in-hand, they navigated to the door marked with the appropriate number. They'd been silent on the walk there, but not an uncomfortable sort of quiet—not that any place here was truly quiet with the dimmed hum and thumps of music seeping through the walls—but the kind full of so many unspoken words and heated looks that Aivey was painfully aware of how wetness soaked her underwear and her nipples peaked against her dress. In fact, all of her clothing felt more abrasive than it ever had, and she couldn't wait for it to be gone. Assuming he actually wanted to do more than talk. Even if that was all, she'd be okay with that, too. She couldn't wait to hear more about his thoughts on how mining practices were disrupting the delicate balance of nature in their mutually beloved mountains, or what parts of the range he favored, or his experiences there, or actually, anything about him at all.

The door slid open with a soft whoosh as soon as Baxian held his band against the panel just to the left of it. Beyond lay a massive room that had Aivey stopping short the moment she stepped through the threshold and the door zipped closed behind them.

The space was large, as big as some of the lounges off the main floor. A multi-piece seating area lay directly in front of them with chairs and sleek sofas that could seat at least a dozen and an assortment of various-sized little tables. A chaise sat beyond that, pushed near the floor-to-ceiling tinted windows that looked out directly at the glass platform hovering above the main floor where the orgy was still in full swing.

To the left was a massive bed, perfectly made and flush with pillows in multiple sizes. A full bar hugged the wall with the entryway. Bottles of various beverages and crystal glasses glimmered atop it in strategic pools of light. The right side of the room was clearly designated for play. There were multiple sleek benches with straps and bindings. Another set hung from a wall. A swing occupied a corner. The far wall held a rack flush with toys—several of which she couldn't begin to know the use of.

All of the furnishings and accessories, from the chairs and tables to the bed and its pillows, were black with accents of silver. Even the carpet sucked up all the light, leaving the space dark despite the dimmed wall sconces and the dancing, colorful lights filtering in through the windows from the main bar.

"Wow," she breathed.

Baxian chuckled. While Aivey had been taking in the space, he'd watched her, seemingly documenting each reaction as she absorbed the various features of the room.

"Yes, it's quite over the top." He glanced toward the various toys and winced. "I forgot about some of that, actually. I've only been up here once, and that was for a party."

"It's fine." Actually, knowing that he wasn't a regular at using the room, but at least had enough familiarity to guide her, made her heart do a weird little flip-flop that it had no business doing given that they'd just met.

"If at any time you want to leave, just press the panel by the door. You have to have access to get in from outside, but it doesn't lock on this side. A little safety feature of the club."

Handy, that. And thoughtful of the management.

Aivey strode into the room, her heels making the softest thud against the floor. While they could hear the music in the hallways, in this room, it was barely audible at all.

"We can close the curtains if you like, if it's distracting. The glass is one way unless we choose to make it transparent."

The way he kept listing out the rooms features, filling the quiet with his voice, reminded her a lot of how Rima would ramble if something made her nervous. But Baxian couldn't be nervous, could he? She was usually the apprehensive one, always over thinking things and pondering worst-case scenarios.

"I thought this might be a more quiet and comfortable place for us to talk, free of interruptions. We don't even have to touch if you don't want to. There's plenty of seating."

Aivey ran one finger across the back of the smooth leather-like material of the black sofa before looking back over one shoulder at Baxian. He still hovered near the door, the dim light of the room casting shadows across his bold features and shining off his hair and the black of his horns. "I want you to touch me, Baxian."

He went absolutely still before loosing a heavy sigh. "Thank the fucking stars."

A giggle caught in her throat. "You're that surprised?"

"I wasn't sure." His powerful stride ate up the space between them before he stopped just in front of her and cupped her cheek, his long fingers threading through her hair. "I wanted. I hoped. But I was a little afraid you just wanted to hear more about my experiences in the Crathian mountains."

Aivey laughed. "Truthfully, I wouldn't mind that either, but there's so much more I'd like to experience with you." She leaned her head into his touch, his warmth, savoring the way that simple act had her whole body tingling. Without a second thought, she stretched up on her toes, wrapped her arms around his neck, and met him halfway in a kiss. His lips were softer than she expected given the firmness of the rest of him. Soft—but hungry, eager.

Baxian wrapped his arms around Aivey, pulling her close. She'd suspected he was strong, but now, her chest pressed against his, there was no doubt. Embracing him was like hugging one of the stone statues as the academy entrance. She'd done that once after a long night of drinking, but even then, those had never stirred anything beyond mild curiosity. Baxian lit her aflame from within as he conquered her mouth. His lips parted, and in the midst of their kiss, her tongue swiped against one elongated fang. It was her first time kissing a fanged male, but the oddity of it only enticed her further, beckoned her to discover what other unique features the male possessed.

The fingers toying with the back of her dress slipped lower to cup her ass. And then he was lifting her, hauling her up and further against him. Aivey wrapped her legs around his waist, holding tight and never breaking their kiss as Baxian backed her across the room.

Then they were tumbling backward, but never once was she afraid. Her back landed on the soft mattress, the feather-soft coverings tickling her arms as Baxian finally broke their kiss and stepped back. He rubbed his jaw as this gaze raked over her as if admiring a piece of artwork.

"Stars, you're beautiful," he said, his voice gone rough and low.

Aivey pushed up on her elbows. "You're not so bad yourself." Her attention dipped to the impressive bulge in his pants, her mouth going dry in anticipation.

Baxian noticed her stare and chuckled. The deep rumble in his chest made her thighs squeeze together to try and stifle the growing ache there. It wouldn't do if she came apart the moment he touched her.

Or maybe that would be the perfect compliment to such a glorious male.

"Have you been with a Vriks male before?" That intense blue gaze still roved over her, lingering briefly on her chest and the juncture between her thighs as if he could peel back her clothing with his sight alone and see what lay beneath. She didn't know a lot about his species but she didn't believe they could do that. He certainly seemed to be trying, though.

The flush in her cheeks burned hotter. Would he mind that she hadn't been with his kind? Aivey bit her bottom lip, and his gaze snapped right to that spot, his eyes flaring slightly wider. She shook her head slowly, watching him in return and waiting for his reaction.

The disappointment she feared didn't appear. Instead, the upturn of his lips hinted at pleasure or amusement. "Then there's something you should know before we go any further."

Aivey sat all the way up as Baxian claimed a spot on the end of the bed beside her, their sides touching. His large palm came to rest on her thigh, his fingers rubbing the hem of her short dress as he spoke. "Vriks males need to come twice to achieve full release. It's part of our mating ritual. The first time prepares our partner to receive our seed. The second release is the seed itself—not that we have to worry about any unintended consequences tonight." He lifted his braceleted wrist for emphasis.

Her brows pinched. "And that's a problem? Needing to have more sex?"

He shrugged. "I would hope not, but some only focus on their own pleasure, not their partner's."

Didn't she know it. Unfortunately, she'd been with a few partners like that, they were the ones that always left her with regrets.

"For a male to be left in between is not ideal," he continued. "My cock needs to be in the presence of my first spend to achieve the second. Otherwise, I'll be in some discomfort until my body resets."

How unique. She filed the data away in her brain for later. He worried it might be a turn-off, but the concept intrigued and excited her more than anything.

"Well…" Aivey turned, coming to straddle his lap. Her dress rode up, undoubtedly giving him a tease of her sodden underwear. She lowered herself onto his lap, her head spinning at the hard length of him pressing against her pussy. A small rock of her hips earned a deep groan from the male who had gone eerily still beneath her. "I'd like to think I'm not one of those people. I'm with you the whole way, Baxian. I don't plan to leave you wanting." Needing to fuck him multiple times was enticing. It meant even more chance of reaching her own release.

A deep rumbling, almost like a purr, vibrated his chest beneath her groping palms. Baxian grabbed her hips, pulling her tighter against his cock. He inhaled sharply. "Stars, Aivey." The way he said her name, so full and rich, nearly made her whimper. "I can smell your desire."

One large hand slid inward, his thumb finding the seam of her underwear and slipping beneath. "So wet for me. Fuck. No, you won't leave me wanting, will you, little beauty?"

All sensation narrowed down to his digit stroking the sensitive skin at the edge of her pussy. "Never," she promised.

His finger inched further, slipping across her clit, and she jolted against him.

His eyes widened. "Sensitive there?"

A breathy chuckle slipped from her lips. "I take it you haven't been with many Earthean females?"

"None," he admitted. "And I'm eager to discover what you look like beneath this dress." Baxian's finger retreated from between her legs to shove at the hem of her dress.

And she was eager to show him. Aivey rocked herself against him one more time before slipping off him. She kicked off her heels and then reached under her armpit to the little panel sewn into the dress. It registered her fingerprints, and the material shifted, expanding so that the dress loosened and fell to the floor in a puddle of silver. With the tech woven into the dress, she hadn't needed a bra. Only her underwear remained, a scrap of translucent silk that teased more than it covered.

A sharp inhale signaled Baxian's reaction before she glanced over at him with a shy grin. He gripped the bed coverings, bunching them up tight in his fists.

"Well?" She tossed her hair over her shoulder as she turned to face him fully.

He blinked. Once. Twice. "Stunning. Absolutely stunning."

The honesty ringing in his praise gave her the courage to slip her fingers through the hem of her underwear and draw it down her legs.

"Fuck, Aivey." He rubbed at his jaw and leaned forward. "I can see your pussy glistening."

She drew her bottom lip between her teeth. "Do I get to see you?"

Baxian was on his feet in a heartbeat, reaching inside his jacket. A moment later, his clothing loosened like hers had and slid down his body like a loose sheet of obsidian. Not one scrap remained on him. She knew his clothes were fancy, but she had no idea they could *that*. All pieces at once? How new.

But the wonder of his attire paled in comparison to the form he revealed—all navy blue, lean sculpted muscle. Defined abs. Narrow hips. Powerful thighs. And between them... Aivey's knees went weak. Saliva flooded her mouth. His proud erection jutted forward, long, thick, and a shade darker than the rest of him toward the bulbous tip. The smooth skin nearly glistened like a polished stone.

She licked her lips and closed the short distance between them. "May I touch you?" Aivey looked up at him under her lashes.

"As long as I can touch you." Baxian's fingers traced the curve of her ear, slid through her hair.

She grinned up at him before dropping her attention to his impressive cock. The shape was similar to that of Earthian men, but his girth and length would put them to shame. Little horizontal ridges ran along the top of his length, and she reached out a tentative finger to touch them. Like much of his skin, he was harder there than an Earthian would be, each ridge a little bump under her finger as she stroked the tip down his length. Stars, he would feel amazing inside her, if he could fit. She wrapped her hand around his length, her forefinger and thumb not even close to meeting.

Baxian let out a soft moan and rocked his hips, thrusting his shaft through her hold. "Your hands are so soft." He trailed the back of his down her neck, along one shoulder. "All of you. Soft, delicate, and so delightfully scented, like sweet berries."

Up and down, she caressed his length, her other hand running idly across the hard planes of his stomach, which tensed under her ministrations. Baxian covered her hand with his own and used the other to tip her chin up. "Too much of that, and you'll have me spilling early."

"We don't want that," she replied, dropping her hands. Especially if that meant he might not be able to find full release this night.

Baxian turned them until Aivey's back was to the bed again, and gently lay her back across the plush, cool coverings. But as she made to slide further back and draw him with her, he grabbed her hips and tugged her body to the edge of the mattress.

"Wha—"

And then he dropped to his knees before her, spreading her legs as he went. Cool air swept in, a sharp contrast to her wet heat.

He leaned in and placed a kiss at the crook of her knee. "I need to make sure you're ready for me." His breath teased her sensitive skin.

"You don't think I'm ready for you?" Her body practically wept for want of his cock. He scented it, he saw it—she knew he did.

"You're smaller than me, little beauty." His thumbs rubbed circles on the insides of her thighs as he held her legs apart. "I don't want to hurt you when you take me inside you. Besides, I'd like to taste you, see if your flavor matches your scent."

"You—" But whatever she'd planned to say vanished into nothingness as his tongue swept up her seam. She gasped, her head falling back onto the mattress.

Another long swipe and he groaned against her. "Delicious."

Aivey could do no more than whimper in response as he settled in, the smooth planes of one cheek warm against her thigh. There was nothing tentative about his attentions. Rather, he devoured her like a man starved. Every sensation narrowed to the feel of that strong tongue lapping at her core. She reached for his head, sliding her fingers through the fall of his hair. The movement sent it tickling her thighs, but she barely noticed. Sweet pleasure sat heavily in her abdomen as she rocked her hips against him, eager for all that he had to give.

Tentatively, she reached for one horn, running her fingers down its ridged length. In so many ways it reminded her of another part of his anatomy, though much less forgiving and pointed at the end instead of round and bulbous. She circled her fingers around it and Baxian jolted back. Her hand dropped away in a flash.

"Did I— Did it hurt?" Her chest constricted at the thought.

The look in his eyes positively smoldered—the hottest blue flame. He shook his head, letting out a throaty huff of laughter. "Not at all. But to grab a male's horns is quite the show of claiming."

"Oh." A different type of flush stole to her cheeks. She tried to squeeze her thighs closed on instinct, but Baxian held her firm. "I didn't know. I'm sorry."

"Don't be." His thumbs rubbed circles against her skin. Tender, reassuring. "It surprised me, but I enjoyed it. It's..." He trailed off, searching for the right word. "I appreciate a female who knows what she wants and is eager to discover more. Besides," His gaze dropped back between her legs and a wicked grin stretched across his lips. "I have discovered things about you. Which reminds me..."

A shot of pure electricity raced through her as Baxian's tongue found her clit and flicked against it. She squealed and bucked her hips in pure reflex. The uncertainty that had momentarily plagued her vanished, obliterated by his eagerness. Any *faux pas* she'd made was swept away by a tide of desire. The way he sought her pleasure, hungered for it, made her skin tingle and the pressure building in her core knot tighter.

"This magical spot." He placed a kiss against it for emphasis before pulling back just slightly to stare up at her. "What a delight." His blue eyes almost glowed where he loomed between her legs.

That look alone would haunt her wickedest dreams for years to come.

They hooded further, glittering with mischief. "Perhaps if I…" He took her clit between his lips and sucked.

"Oh, God!" Aivey screamed.

He growled against her pussy. "There are no Gods here. Just me."

Then he shoved two fingers deep into her pussy and Aivey shattered. "*Baxian!*"

The sudden intrusion, the fullness of him inside her, combined with his lips against her clit sent her soaring into the stars. She gripped his horns, fingers tangled in his hair, holding on for dear life as her release rocketed through her in wave after wave. Baxian didn't let up and continued to stroke her with his tongue and fingers, drawing out the pleasure until her whole body was twitching with ecstasy. At some point, she must have closed her eyes because when she opened them again the room spun, and it had nothing to do with the drinks she'd consumed that evening.

From between her legs, Baxian looked up at her again, wetness glistening on his bluish lips as he grinned. The thrust of his fingers slowed, drawing her back to him in a smooth rhythm. "There's my little Earthean," he crooned.

His Earthean. Yes, she was. She wanted to be. Stars above, no one and nothing had ever made her feel quite like that, and she hadn't even had his cock inside her yet.

When he finally pulled his fingers free, she immediately mourned their loss. Not that she could do more than whimper, given the boneless, panting mess she'd become.

Baxian sat on the bed beside her and leaned over. With the back of his long fingers, he traced a path down her cheek, along her jaw, the column of her neck, and between her breasts. "You flush such a lovely shade, like the petals of the Lal'ae flower, and you're even softer."

The Lal'ae flower. Deep inside her chest, something unfurled, long tendrils spilling open like the petals of the flower itself. He didn't know, *couldn't* know, that it was her favorite. That during many of her research expeditions, she'd slipped away from her group at night just to wander through the valley in search of the elusive blooms that would close back up into tight buds when the sunlight touched them. They could not be pried open either, not with the tiny needle-like fibers along the back side of the petals. Those fibers could pierce many fabrics and cut skin as easily as a sharp blade. The flowers only bloomed on their terms when they felt the safest.

"Baxian," she whispered, awed.

Something soft and tender broke across his face. He cupped her cheek, rubbing his thumb across her skin. "Those flowers are beautiful, as are you. You know them?"

She gave the smallest nod. "Yes, from the Crathian mountains."

He mirrored her nod. "A secret bloom some call them, as many never wander out in the darkness to see them, but I'm glad I did." The way he looked at her, how his sapphire eyes seemed to reach into her soul, said he was no longer talking about the flower.

"Do you still want me, Aivey?" He caressed her cheek.

And she knew with a certainty that if she said no, he'd make no argument and would let her walk out the door. But she had no intention of that. He'd awakened something in her, a fearlessness and courage that she thought perhaps she simply lacked. Maybe it was because he made her feel safe and desired. She wasn't about to miss the chance to be with someone like that and soak in as much of that feeling as she could.

Aivey pushed herself up until their faces were a breath apart. His hand had fallen away as she moved, but she cupped his cheek now and smiled. "Yes. I want to know all of you, Baxian."

She closed the last of the distance between them and kissed him. Not hard and fast, not with the eagerness coursing through her veins, but softly, tenderly, like the gentle side of that delicate bloom that opened itself up to the cool night air.

The kiss transformed from sweet to searing as they scooted farther toward the center of the sumptuous bed, never breaking apart. If anything, they found a way to move as one, Aivey's nipples grazing the firm planes of Baxian's chest in a repeated tease that she could only assume was somehow deliberate. Their sensuous dance made it easy for Aivey to hook her legs around Baxian's hips, bringing her aching center against the muscles of his lower abdomen. Unlike most Earthean males, he had no body hair but was just smooth, hard flesh and muscle. She gasped against his lips as her backside met his hard length, which he thrust lightly against her.

Baxian eased her back onto the fluffy bedspread before covering her with his body, careful to keep much of his weight on his arms so as not to crush her into the mattress.

With one last kiss and a flick of his tongue against her lips, Baxian pulled back, rising on his knees between her spread legs. He took himself in hand, stroking from the base all the way to the tip where a bead of pearlescent moisture glistened.

Aivey watched in rapture as he positioned himself at her entrance. When the head of his cock pushed against her, she bit her lip, her body tensing in anticipation laced with uncertainty. He was massive compared to any male she'd had before. Could he fit? Would he?

It'd be a terrible turn to the evening if they were somehow incompatible and she couldn't give him the same pleasure he'd given her, at least not without leaving him partially unfulfilled given his biological needs.

"Eyes on me, little beauty."

Baxian smirked down at her, the portrait of a confident male who knew he'd enraptured her. The was no uncertainty there. No question. He believed they were compatible and that surety gave her body what it needed to relax as he pressed the tip inside her.

His pupils blew wide. She saw the breath catch in his throat as it did hers. He'd barely breached her, and yet her body stretched to the border between pleasure and pain. Despite the urge to watch as his cock sank into her, to marvel that it was possible, she didn't let her gaze wander from his. Nor did he. Baxian fisted the sheets as he slid ever so slowly deeper.

"Aivey?" Her name was nearly a growl. A question and a sign of the force with which he held himself back.

"More, Baxian." She wiggled her hips just slightly. "I can take it."

"Fuck!" He blew out a heavy breath and pushed forward.

Aivey whimpered at the feel of him inside her. Full, so full, but so incredible. It was like being consumed from within, taken over by the sheer magnitude of him. The ridges along his length rubbed against her inner walls, pressing into them and hitting her pleasure spot deep inside. A moan tore from her lips. She thrashed her head to the side as he quickened his glacial pace, each ridge sliding in one after another.

"Fuck, Aivey. You're so tight."

She might have responded. She wasn't sure, couldn't think over the feeling of him inside her as he finally bottomed out and held himself still, letting her body adjust to his size.

He leaned down, his forehead meeting hers and his pale hair falling around them like a curtain. "Still with me, little beauty?"

She stared straight into two pools of shimmering blue. Something about it, about his rapt attention on her, the rapid thump of his heart beating against his ribs so hard she felt it where their skin touched, about the careful way he was with her, cleared away the anxiety that kept trying to surface itself. It liked to taunt her at the worst times, to ask what if, as it had with his size, but he washed it all away.

Safe. Cherished.

That's what he made her feel. This male who she barely knew, had just met, accomplished what so many never did.

"Yes." She whispered. "Yes." *Always.*

Only then did he move again, a slow retreat and gentle glide forward. All the while, he watched her, his gaze flickering over her face as if searching for something, waiting for it.

Another thrust. Then another. The edge of pain retreated, leaving only pleasure. A deep moan tore from her lips as those hard ridges slid against her inner walls.

Baxian's look shifted then. The sharp edges of his face smoothed out. His shoulder drooped as he rested a little of his weight on her and let his face fall to the crook of her neck, where he licked at the column of her throat.

He'd been leashed before, restrained. But whatever he had seen, or didn't, let him loose. What had been slow and gentle turned more ravenous. He lapped at the pulse in her neck with the same fervor he'd devoured her pussy, all the while thrusting into her with increasing tempo that sent her whole body jolting and sliding up the bed.

"Baxian," she moaned and reached for his horn—for anything to hold amid the storm of his passion. Vaguely she recalled his comment about horns and claiming, but she *wanted* to claim him, to show just how much she desired him, too. He growled against her skin the moment she encircled it. He jerked his hips, driving hard enough to force a gasp from her throat.

Without thought, she wrapped her legs around his hips, adjusting the angle of his cock within her. She gripped his horn tighter, and his sharp teeth grazed her skin in response. Not enough to hurt, never that, but just enough for her to feel, for a thrill to race through her body at the contrast of sensation.

Baxian withdrew from her neck, and Aivey released her hold on him. He drew back until he was upright, sitting on his feet. His cock slid from her with a wet pop.

Aivey made to protest, but the determination on his face left no room for protest. He wasn't done with her, not nearly. Baxian pushed her knees toward her chest and planted his hands on the bed with his forearms lodged against her thighs. Like that, she could hardly move her hips or legs, all of her trapped by the force of him. While holding her still, he pushed back into her with a powerful thrust.

The sensation of suddenly being filled once more tore another moan from her lips. Aivey tried to move, to buck her hips and meet his movements with ones of her own, but he held her in place, fully at his mercy as he took control, driving into her over and over. With her movements restricted, every sensation was so much more acute. He owned her pussy. Filled it. Controlled it.

And she loved it. Craved it. Each rock of his hips had her coming more and more undone, every sensation narrowing down to his hard length inside her and those little ridges, one after another, rubbing against her inner walls.

One more deep thrust, and she screamed. There was little warning as her release barreled into her with the force of a ship going to light-speed. Her back arched, her pussy clenched around his cock, and the whole room blurred.

Baxian must have released her because she was rocking her hips again, spiraling through her pleasure as he leaned over her and claimed her mouth with his. The last of her satisfied cries were swallowed by him, as if he needed that too. His tongue flicked against hers, claiming and coaxing, and then his body went rigid. He tore his mouth away, arching his head back as he gave a bestial roar that might have terrified her if it had come from anyone else.

His thrusts turned shallow and he clenched the bedspread on either side of her in his fists. He jerked his hips a few more times before finally dropping his head to stare down at her.

"Aivey." He drew out her little name, giving it the fullness of a prayer whispered into the dark depths of space.

When he finally pulled out of her, a rush of liquid followed, dampening her thighs and the bed beneath them.

"I—" She started, blinking up at him.

But he wasn't surprised. It was his come, she realized. Much more than a human male. To him, it was natural, normal. And truthfully, she didn't mind. It was almost like a reward, a prize for a job well done.

"You're all right?" That look creased his features again, the one he'd worn when he first began to move within her. She knew it now. Concern. He'd worried about her being able to take him. He'd said as much earlier, but most males seemed to forget such things in the moment. Not this one.

"Better than," she promised him with a smile.

She expected soreness, or at least a twinge of pain or something given his size, but it didn't come. Maybe that was part of his release as well. It'd make sense given his species' need for multiple releases. That would be harder to accomplish if one party was sore from the first bout.

"Good." He placed a quick kiss on her lips before rolling to the side. One hand lay on his chest, which still rose and fell with each heavy breath.

Aivey started to sit, felt more wetness slide from her pussy, and promptly flopped back on the bed.

Shit.

"Aivey?" Baxian's brows pinched as he looked over at her.

She bit her lip and turned her head toward him. "I uh… I felt some of your come leak out when I tried to sit. I'm sorry. I didn't think about that. I hope it doesn't mess things up."

His nose twitched. Something sparkled in his eyes. Baxian's whole chest began to shake as he tried and failed to hold back a laugh.

Her lips thinned. If he'd lied about—

"My apologies," he said, reining in his humor. "I should have explained it better. Yes, you can sit up. As long as you don't submerge in water or clean too well, there will be plenty left for my body to react with."

A heavy sigh slipped from her lips. "Thank the stars."

"So worried about me?" he teased.

She swatted playfully at his chest. "Well, since you were so giving when it came to my pleasure, I wouldn't want to be selfish and deny you yours."

He reached over and slid a wayward piece of hair behind her ear, his fingers tracing along the shell of her ear and down her jaw before retreating. "You're a gift, Aivey. And you've already delivered more pleasure than I've had in quite some time."

A flush of pride raced to her cheeks. "Good, well, a little more never hurt," she said, suddenly embarrassed for reasons she couldn't name.

"Not at all," he grinned back at her. "It will take my body a few minutes to reset, as it were. Let me get you a towel to clean up the excess."

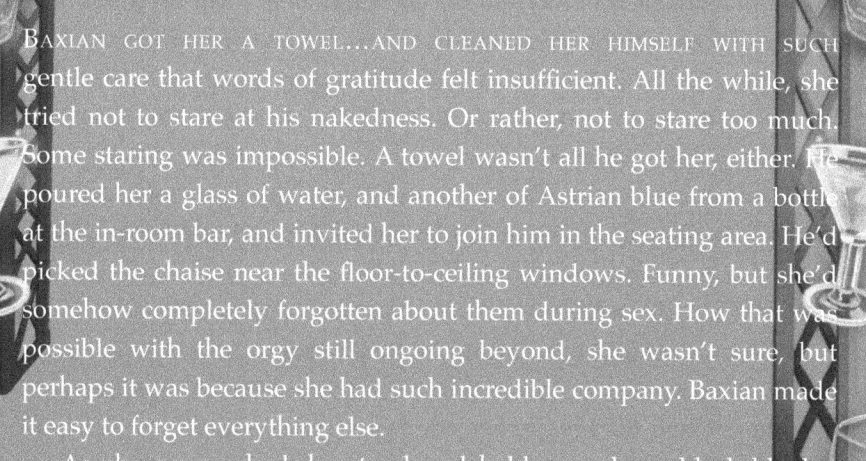

chapter six

Baxian got her a towel...and cleaned her himself with such gentle care that words of gratitude felt insufficient. All the while, she tried not to stare at his nakedness. Or rather, not to stare too much. Some staring was impossible. A towel wasn't all he got her, either. He poured her a glass of water, and another of Astrian blue from a bottle at the in-room bar, and invited her to join him in the seating area. He'd picked the chaise near the floor-to-ceiling windows. Funny, but she'd somehow completely forgotten about them during sex. How that was possible with the orgy still ongoing beyond, she wasn't sure, but perhaps it was because she had such incredible company. Baxian made it easy to forget everything else.

As she approached, he stood and held up a large black blanket which he wrapped around her. She nearly groaned at the soft texture against her still-sensitive skin. He didn't seem to mind his nakedness, but it was sweet that he thought she might prefer something to shield hers. Baxian drew Aivey down onto his lap, her back against his chest as they faced the scene beyond the tinted window.

"They really can't see us?" she asked.

"No." His breath teased her cheek. "Don't you think they might have been watching us if they could?"

At the suggestion, her thighs pressed tightly together to try and stifle her body's reaction. She'd never been one for exhibitionism, but being with him in any setting seemed to set her ablaze. "Perhaps."

His arm around her center pulled her closer, urging her to relax back against him. Beyond the windows, out on the raised platform, a female took two males at once, one at each end. Tears glistened on her cheeks in the neon lights shining from above, but from the eager way she stroked the base of the cock in her mouth and rocked back onto the cock behind her, she was enjoying herself quite well.

Baxian rubbed her leg through the layer of the blanket, soft slow strokes she knew were meant to put her at ease. "Would you prefer a different scene? The windows can change to project an image if you'd like."

"Oh?" she asked, genuinely intrigued. "What kinds of things?"

A soft chuckle echoed from his chest into hers. "Multitudes. I have an idea of something you may like." He tapped two fingers on the black panel of his arm band and a display screen flickered to life in the air above it. He moved quickly through the menus at first, but then paused. "Close your eyes."

Twisting her head toward him, she gave a side-eyed look but said, "Okay." Intrigued, she turned forward again and patiently waited. Light flickered beyond her closed eyelids.

"All right. Open them."

Aivey did, and gasped, breath lodging in her lungs.

"You recognize it?" Baxian asked, a hint of a tease in his voice.

She released the breath, her whole body relaxing against the male behind her. "Of course." He'd brought up a sweeping panoramic of her beloved mountains, the image taken from down in a valley, though from the angle she couldn't be sure which one. Towering trees with pointy needle-like leaves soared toward a blue sky dotted with lavender-tinged clouds. The shimmering pale purple of newly fallen snow coated the mountaintops and dusted some of the tops of the trees. If she closed her eyes, she could almost smell a hint of pine and the crisp iciness of the air. "This is beautiful."

He hummed in agreement. "The perfect place to spend some time together, don't you think?"

And spend time they did, sipping their drinks and talking while

Baxian held her. If he wasn't taking a sip of his drink, his hands were on her, holding her close, gently caressing her through the blanket. When she shifted and part of it fell away to reveal most of her leg, she didn't replace it. The room was the perfect temperature, and between the hard body of the male behind her and the desire coursing through her veins from his closeness, she was plenty warm enough, almost too hot, actually. His scent addled her senses. The frequent caress of his breath on her ear or face and the proof of his desire beneath her backside didn't help matters where her body temperature was concerned.

If his body reacted like an Earthean's, he was ready for another round. He had to want it, to achieve his release if nothing else, but he didn't ask for it, didn't redirect their conversation to that topic either. Rather, he asked about her life at the academy and shared about his role in his family's corporate empire of luxury travel retreats, which happened to be how he'd come to know and fall in love with the mountain range. He'd enjoyed it so much he'd purchased a home there himself—a fact that would have had Aivey tumbling onto the floor in shock at the thought of what it must have cost had he not been holding her. Even so, he didn't talk about it like the ridiculous luxury it was, which meant he was even more wealthy than she'd first thought.

Sitting with him, just sharing their lives, was a delight in itself, but she'd been lying to say she didn't ache to have him again. In fact, her pussy literally wept for want of him. The slow rub of his thumb across her skin didn't help matters, or the infuriatingly slow progress he made in inching his way down her leg toward the apex of her thigh, barely hidden by the edge of the blanket.

Aivey considered shifting her leg and letting the blanket fall away, or better yet, grabbing his hand and putting it right where she wanted it, but there was a delicious agony in the waiting, too. The catching sensation in her chest and the thrum in her veins was a high better than any drink could give. Though they talked casually, she was acutely aware of every bit of him beneath and behind her. Even one strand of his hair brushing across her exposed shoulder was enough to send a shiver down her spine. A burning urgency built in her abdomen, and she didn't just want him, she needed him.

He had to know how badly she wanted him again, *had to*. He'd scented her desire before, after all. But damn, the male was taking his time.

He paused his slow circling. "Aivey?"

"Hmm?" She twisted her head to the side and up to look at him, their breaths mingling in the narrow space between them.

The hooded, hungry look in his eyes dried her throat. "You haven't answered the last two questions I asked. In fact, I'd wager you didn't hear them at all."

"Oh, I…" She bit her bottom lip. "I was distracted. Sorry."

He chuckled, and his hand on her thigh slid lower until his fingertips brushed under the edge of the blanket and along the sensitive skin next to her pussy. "Thinking about?"

"You," she answered honestly. And then she did shift her leg, just enough to push the blanket away and give access to where she desperately needed him to wander.

He inhaled sharply, his pupils dilating.

As if he had read her mind, he reached between her legs and palmed her pussy. "Fuck, Aivey. You're drenched for me."

She was, damn it. Just the feel of his palm against her needy core had her rocking into it, desperate for friction, for him to touch her more.

"Said like you haven't been hard again for ages." She rubbed against him for emphasis, earning a little hiss.

He grabbed her breast with his other hand, eliciting a small gasp as he flicked her pearled nipple with the pad of his thumb. "So eager for me again?"

In response, she spread her legs further. Baxian sucked in a breath. He dipped his fingers between her lips then slid them up, right over her clit and back down again.

Her pulse thrummed at the apex of her thighs. "More. Please, Baxian."

The hand on her breast trailed down until his arm was a hard band around her. In one quick move, he lifted her up, removed his fingers from her core, and yanked the blanket away. With nothing between them as he settled her back on his lap, his warmth, the smooth firmness of his skin, and his throbbing erection were impossible to ignore.

Baxian pulled her ass tight against his abdomen, his cock sticking out between her spread legs in an erotic display.

Stars above.

A few small adjustments of their positions and he could be inside her again. Without even thinking, she angled her hips and rocked forward, spreading her wetness along his shaft.

"Aivey, fucking stars," Baxian ground out. He palmed her breasts with both hands, holding her secure as she leaned forward, letting more of their most intimate parts rub against one another with each roll of her hips. She'd never been much of one to take charge, had never had the courage, really, but with him it was so easy, so natural. He was a question her body knew the answer to.

She moved on him with abandon, seeking her pleasure, savoring his sounds of pleasure and the way he massaged the sensitive globes her breasts. Her breaths drew ragged, the coil of pleasure so tight within her—

Baxian banded an arm around her again and pulled her flush against his chest. His other hand knotted in her hair just above her nape, turning her head to meet his heated stare. "Turn around, Aivey." The sound of her name, all hoarse and desperate, sent a shiver across her skin. "I need to be inside you."

Her lips parted. "Oh." Some of the haze of her lust peeled back. Her cheeks flamed. She'd been so caught up in the feel of him she'd almost forgotten.

Baxian released her hair and she all but leaped to her feet, wobbling a bit as she did. In a heartbeat, she turned around and straddled him again. "Like this?"

A black tongue slid across his bottom lip as his gaze quickly devoured her from head to hips. "Good girl. You want to ride my cock?" He arched one silver brow.

Aivey bit her bottom lip and nodded.

He grabbed her hip, urging her up as he drew his cock between them and angled it toward her opening. "Then it's all yours. My first release should make it easier for you to take me again."

So there *was* something unique about his come after all. Handy, that.

Aivey hooked her arms around his neck and lowered herself until his tip brushed against her core. Warmth spiraled through her at the brief intimate touch, her body seeming to unfurl and reach for his.

With her eyes firmly locked on Baxian's, she lowered herself onto him.

"Oh, *fuck!*" she cried when he wasn't even halfway inside her.

Was taking him easier? Yes. Less exquisite? Not at all. If anything, now she was even more aware of his size and the firm ridges along his length, almost like her body had become attuned to his and awaited each bit with eager anticipation.

The fullness of him sent her thighs tingling as she slid the rest of the way onto him with a breathy whimper. Baxian groaned, his eyes falling shut and head tipping back. Stars above, he was a sight. Light from the projection caught on his skin and highlighted the sharp angles of his face. His pale hair almost seemed to glow where it cascaded over his shoulders. He was a work of art come to life, and right then he was hers, all hers.

He looked back down at her, his pupils wide, lips slightly parted, already panting hard. Aivey pulled in a deep shuddering breath as she adjusted once more to his size, and then finally began to ride him with slow, deliberate motions.

"You take me so well, Aivey." He ran his palms up her sides then in to tease her breasts. "Like you were made for me."

You too, felt insufficient. There were no words to describe his perfection. Instead, she leaned in until her breasts pressed against his chest and her breath ghosted across his lips. "Baxian," she whispered, then sealed her words with a kiss. Their tongues tangled, slow and deep as the strokes of his cock inside her. So close, entangled with one another, Aivey almost couldn't tell where she ended and he began.

Baxian palmed her ass with both hands, seizing control and dragging her up and down his cock. As the tempo increased, Aivey slipped from their kiss, a half moan, half whine filling the air between them.

"So wet, so fucking perfect," Baxian growled as he gnashed his teeth. Aivey leaned back just enough to see the desperate hunger in his gaze. Sweated dewed his brow. He surged up into her, his cock striking a new angle and threatening the tether on her sanity.

"I—I'm going to—" she gasped. There was no holding back, not like this, not with him working her body on his cock or the fullness of it.

"Let go," he commanded. "I've got you."

Aivey reached up and grabbed his horn, an anchor in the storm. He growled in response, bucking his hips.

She unraveled in a dizzying spiral.

Her inner walls clamped down around him in waves. Her whole body shook. All thought vanished, all feeling save for the endless bliss shuddering through her. She ground her hips down against him, trying to chase the sensation, to draw it out.

Baxian roared as he came, head tilting back in ecstasy. Jerking, shallow thrusts wrung out the last of her release as he found his, spilling inside her.

He abandoned his hold on her ass, drawing her body firmly against his chest and tucking her head into the crook of his neck. She came back to her senses there, feeling the rapid pound of his heart, the heavy rise and fall of his chest that mirrored hers, the firm planes of lithe muscle. Long fingers slid along her scalp and then down her sweat-dampened back in long, soothing waves.

They were still joined. And even though he'd softened like an Earthean male did after release, she was still full, so full of him. There was an odd comfort in it, and she had no desire to move. Not that her body would have let her if she tried, boneless as she was from her release.

Baxian continued to stroke her hair. Aivey closed her eyes and let herself go fully lax against him. She could fall asleep like that if he let her.

Not that he'd asked her to stay that long...

Cold reality smacked her in the face, and she tensed.

He'd met his second, complete release. Their agreement to each other was done.

His fingers stilled at the nape of her neck. "Aivey?"

"I just, um..." But she couldn't speak her worry, couldn't damn herself yet and make it real. Instead, she said, "I nearly fell asleep on you there."

"Oh." His features smoothed out into a soft smile. "Stay with me tonight?"

She blinked, dumbfounded. "Stay?"

His throat bobbed. "If you want to. The room is ours tonight."

"I..." It'd be better for her to leave. The thought of it struck like a laser beam through her stomach, but it'd be less painful than some awkward goodbye in the morning. The longer she spent with him, the harder it was going to be to let him go. It wouldn't be the first time she'd had that problem, wanting more, expecting it, when the guy she was with didn't want more than a quick fuck which hadn't even brought her to release. She bit her lip as she stared at him. He'd gone tense beneath her, and she wasn't entire sure if he breathed. "Okay," she said finally, her voice quiet.

Damn, she really was a glutton for punishment, but she couldn't let him go when he stared at her like that, like it might hurt him to let her go, too.

Just one night. They could have that. She could enjoy all of it, and that would be enough. It would. It would have to be.

He blew out a breath. "Good. I—" He closed his mouth, his brows scrunching before smoothing back out. "Good. I'm glad."

"Me too," she agreed, even if her heart already hurt at the inevitable future they faced come morning.

Aivey rose off him, and his cock slipped from her with a wet pop. His release slid down her thighs, some dripping to the floor with an embarrassing splat. Her cheeks flamed. *Fucking stars.* She should have thought of that after their first time together.

A nervous laugh bubbled from her. "I guess I should get cleaned up."

Baxian rose as well, his attention firmly fixed on her and not the mess. The full weight of his regard made her legs wobbly, or perhaps that was the after-effects of her release. Maybe both.

"Care to share a shower?" He arched a brow and extended a hand to her. "Or we could do that after we go again."

"Again?" For the second time in as many minutes, his questions left her almost speechless. "Twice more, you mean?" Damn. If he wanted to, she'd surely try, even if it left her exhausted and unable to walk the next day.

He chuckled. "After a reproductive release, it takes a few days for my body to reset itself fully. A Vriks male can continue to enjoy their partner until then without worrying about being left unfulfilled."

"Oh." A thrill raced through her blood. "Well, that's a nice perk." She took his hand, and his fingers closed around hers.

"It is indeed." He drew her hand to his mouth and licked at the back of it. A Vriks custom or claim? She had no idea, but it had her pulse thrumming between her legs again nonetheless. "Shall we?"

chapter seven

THEY SHARED ANOTHER TRYST IN THE SHOWER BEFORE CLIMBING INTO BED together. Baxian held her with his chest to her back, and though they likely didn't slumber long, Aivey couldn't remember waking quite so refreshed…or aroused given that she woke to Baxian stroking his fingers over her clit.

Not long after they both found release again, Aivey's comm bracelet vibrated with the reminder to meet her friends back at their hotel. Their time together really was at an end. Aivey excused herself, slipped out of bed, grabbed her discarded clothes from the night before, and hurried off to the bathroom. Cleaning herself and dawning her clothing was easy. Smoothing out her mussed hair was…fine. It would do. Wrangling in the tears that burned at the corners of her eyes? That was the hard part.

You just met him, for fuck's sake, she scolded herself. No one came to Incandescence looking for more than a little fun. That was all she had been looking for. But then, she never expected someone like Baxian. He was just too…everything. One in a million, and she'd certainly looked.

Walking out and never seeing him again was inevitable, but the thought pained her more than she ever expected. *Good job catching feels in the sex club, Aivey.*

She should have just turned and run right back out of the bar last night the first time her gut told her to. Hook-ups never ended well for her. Didn't she know that by now? How silly she'd been to think this time in this place would be different. Everything would have been easier if she'd just stayed at the hotel. She never would have met him.

But then... *She never would have met him.* And the thought of that, of erasing the moments they spent together and the knowledge there was a male out there like him, hurt worse than the thought of leaving.

So Aivey washed her face, pulled in a deep breath, let it out, and strode back out into the main room.

Baxian had donned his pants and sat on the edge of the bed, his head in his hands, that silvery hair spilling like a waterfall around him. The moment she entered, he lifted his head and whatever expression had been on his face shifted into something completely neutral.

"I..." Aivey's tongue was suddenly thick in her mouth. Her chest fucking ached and she hadn't even said goodbye yet. She sucked in another steadying breath. *Just get it out, Aivey.* "I have to go soon," she said so quickly it was almost one word. "My friends and I are leaving today," she continued a little more slowly, "and I'll be late to checkout and might miss our transport if I don't head back."

"I understand," he replied, expressionless.

She licked her lips, drinking in the sight of him one last time. "I enjoyed our time together."

Say something. Ask me to stay. Even if she couldn't, she wanted that, she needed...something.

"As did I."

Silence followed his words, hanging so heavy in the air it nearly drowned her.

Fuck, well, okay then. Aivey turned on her heel and headed for the door. She'd nearly reached it when a strong hand wrapped around her wrist and pulled her to a halt. She whirled and nearly smacked right into Baxian.

"Aivey." Her name was a broken rasp on his lips. His bare chest rose and fell. The hunger still lingering in his gaze nearly brought a whimper to her lips.

"I know you have to leave, but I want to give you this first." He dropped her wrist and pulled out a small silver card from his pocket. "It's my private comms card. It has my information across all the galactic channels, so you can reach me from wherever." He ran his other hand through his hair and looked away. "If you want to, that is."

Her mouth parted. Stars above, was he nervous? She blinked at him, her breath coming short and fast as her pulse hammered against her ribs. She could barely tear her gaze away from that little card. Reachable anywhere in the galaxy no matter the distance? That kind of comm required payment each use, and he offered it to her? A way to reach him literally any time anywhere?

Tears burned at the corner of her eyes again, but this time, it wasn't from sorrow.

"It's okay if you don't—" He started to drop the offered card, but Aivey snatched it up like lightning, blinking away her emotions before they overcame her.

"Yes, Baxian."

His gaze snapped back to hers, and she smiled at him.

"Thank you. I'd like to keep in touch, too." She held the card to the thin silver band of her comms bracelet to download the data. "I don't have a fancy card like you do, or cross-galactic comms…"

His lips turned up at the corners. "Just call my number, I'll cover any fees if we're not close. I'd like to see you again, Aivey. To talk, to spend time together, or more…" He glanced back toward the bed. "Whatever you're up for." The blue of his eyes positively sparkled.

The band around her wrist chimed, and Aivey held the card back out to him. Her arm nearly vibrated with barely contained joy. He wanted to see her again, and it didn't feel like a hollow, insincere offer.

The look he'd had when she'd come out of the bathroom had been sorrow, she knew it now, the echo of misery that she felt at parting from him. He'd offered a way to get in touch that few could. No one would do that on a whim, not without serious interest.

Baxian reached for the card, but instead of taking it, he wrapped Aivey's hand around it. "Keep it. Just in case the download failed or something."

It didn't. It wouldn't. He had to know that, but he wanted her to have it anyway as backup. Her chest swelled with emotion.

"I…" He rubbed the back of his neck, his gaze cutting away. "I know we just met, and I can't fully explain it, but I feel a connection between us. Some kind of pull that I can't ignore."

Aivey's heart skipped a beat. Her breath lodged in her throat.

Baxian muttered some curse she didn't understand. "Sorry. I should have kept my mouth shut."

"No!" She reached up and took his face between her palms. "Don't be." Aivey pulled in one desperate breath then another. "I feel it, too." Without another thought, she flung her arms around his neck and pulled him into a desperate kiss.

He tasted like passion, like dreams and hope. Baxian pulled her close, cupping her backside and tugging her up. She gave in to the invitation and wrapped her legs around his waist, locking them together. And then he was moving, pressing her back up against the wall as he all but consumed her. Aivey laughed amid the kiss, overcome, and she felt his lips stretch in a grin.

Whatever had sparked into being between them wasn't something she could put into words exactly, but the feeling was undeniable. And she wasn't alone in it, this crazy thought of so much more with a man she'd just met. Stars above, it wasn't just her.

She'd read about some species and their mating bonds. Tethers that connected two individuals and bound them in this life and beyond. But she was human. Humans could create deep connections, but not quite at the level of, or as quickly as, other species. Even so, she imagined it had to feel something like this.

All too soon, he pulled back. But Baxian didn't let go, just stared at her, their breaths mingling in the narrow space between their faces. His forehead leaned against hers. "You're something special, Aivey. I never…I never expected to meet someone like you here, but I'm so glad I did."

"Same. To think I nearly ran right back out the moment I stepped inside."

He laughed, his chest rumbling against hers. "I'm glad you didn't."

"Me too."

With one last peck on her lips, Baxian let her back down. "And now you really should go before I decide to keep you and piss off your friends before I ever get to meet them."

"Well…" She stroked her fingers down his bare chest. "We wouldn't want that."

"I'll talk to you soon, Aivey."

She stared at his hooded gaze, memorizing the shape of his face, the hue of his eyes, and the striking form of his body. "Soon. It's a promise."

Glowing within from the connection she'd forged and comfortable in the knowledge that their goodbye would only be temporary, Aivey left to return to her friends. They'd planned for the trip of a lifetime, for a finale they'd remember for years to come, but in all Aivey's imaginings she'd always thought it would be just one night. Somehow, she'd found so much more. Perhaps, she'd found forever.

about megan van dyke

Megan Van Dyke is a fantasy romance author with a love for all things that include magic and kissing. Many of her stories include themes of family (whether born into or found) and a sense of home and belonging, which are important aspects of her life as well. Megan also watched way too many Disney movies as a child, and adult, and has a deep love for fairytales and happily ever afters.

She began creating her own stories in elementary school, and has written on and off throughout her life. Despite this, she did not complete her first fiction novel until 2017. It was a trash fire, but it was that spark which grew into the flames of something magical and let Megan know she'd finally figured out what she was meant to do.

Megan is a former IT risk and security executive and current stay-at-home mom. When not writing, Megan loves to cook, play video games, explore the great outdoors, and spend time with her family. A southerner by birth and at heart, Megan currently lives with her family in Colorado.

She is the best-selling author of the Courts of Faerie, Reimagined Fairy Tales, and Stolen Empire series, all available now.

To learn more, visit www.authormeganvandyke.com

the twelfth ambassador

Mindi Briar

chapter one

day one

It's been ten years since I last set foot on Eiris. The thick humidity wraps around me like a welcoming hug as I stride down the ramp from Dad's private starship.

My father, Governor O'Rourke, lingers in the open airlock, like he's afraid to even touch the soil of the planet he rules as the Emperor's representative. "Remember, Sinead," he calls after me. "Six months to negotiate a treaty that favors our interests. Don't disappoint me."

I roll my eyes. He already spent the whole flight drilling that message home. *Don't bend to the aliens' threats, and don't get soft-hearted. You're on Eiris to get what we need and put the locals in their place.*

Turning back, I almost bump into my secretary, Cecily, floating my hover-trunks out of the baggage compartment. "Love you, too, Dad," I say pointedly.

He doesn't bother with the mushy stuff. Never has. And I, as always, have to pretend it doesn't sting.

Dad disappears inside the ship. The ramp retracts and the engines power up. Cecily and I back away. Wind ruffles my auburn pixie cut as the ship lifts off, leaving me alone on a planet I haven't visited since I was fourteen.

"Not to worry," Cecily says, falsely bright. "I messaged the embassy when we landed. Your new bodyguard will be here in a moment to escort us."

I sigh. My breath fogs the hard, clear, rounded breather mask that fits over my nose and mouth, connected to the air purification unit clipped to my collar.

Though Eiris's air won't be fatally toxic unless I breathe it for several days, it'll start making me light-headed and/or causing hallucinations within a few hours. The oxygen levels are passable, but the trees give off some chemical that, over long exposure, puts unaltered— or "Earth Classic"—humans into a comatose state.

But the view is worth the trouble. I've daydreamed of Eiris's natural beauty since Dad brought me here as a teenager to celebrate his new governorship. That was right after the Emperor had the old governor, Lady Crowe, executed. Back when Dad pretended to care about his only daughter.

I remember the first night in the resort, standing at our cabin window high in the trees. Dad pointed out a distant orange glow and said, "See that? They're burning Lady Crowe in effigy tonight. Good riddance to a bad leader, and welcome to a new one."

That might be the last time I remember being proud of him.

"Here he comes," Cecily announces, anchoring my thoughts in the present. I sweep my gaze down the path that leads to the resort but see no one.

Then a *whoosh* of wings catches my attention and I look up. My jaw drops.

When humans colonized this planet two thousand years ago, they didn't respond well physically to the lighter gravity and heady atmosphere. Rather than alter the planet to suit their needs, they altered themselves, splicing their DNA with one of the dominant local life forms.

And, for reasons unknown, they picked a fucking *butterfly*.

The man who floats from the sky to land in front of me is a dizzying blend of human traits with the colorful Eirisian insectoid. He's tall and wiry-thin, with skin the color of my favorite rose-pink lipstick. His elfin facial features and silky-straight brown hair tied back in a low ponytail make him look like a character in a fantasy holodrama, completely out of his element in a drab brown security uniform. He keeps his lower hands clasped politely behind his back, like he's used to working with Earth Classics who get freaked out when they see a man with four arms.

Then there's the *wings*. Folded, they create a brownish cape behind him, tapered back and stopping just short of brushing the ground. But in flight, the wings reach a massive span, at least twice his two-meter height, and they're vividly, eye-bleedingly rainbow-colored.

But the worst thing about the butterfly man is that *I recognize him*.

Ten years was almost enough time to forget the annoying boy who followed me around the resort as my "tour guide" when I was fourteen. Almost...but not quite.

"Jalus?" I exclaim.

I'm not entirely comfortable with the way my heart thuds as he walks toward me. When I last saw him, I'd just had a growth spurt and Jalus was shorter than me, a scrawny twig of a kid, with wings still shaggy from their first molt.

He's, uh, changed a lot.

Now he's a head taller, with devastating cheekbones and intense dark-purple eyes. His gaze feels like an x-ray scan. I cross my arms over my chest, even though I'm already sweating in my long-sleeved court robe.

He bows, keeping his eyes locked on mine. "Lady Sinead." Oh, stars, even his voice has changed. That husky rumble makes me forget how to breathe for a second.

"You're working as a bodyguard now?" I choke out.

"I was training as a protector before your last visit," he reminds me. "Since last longnight, I've successfully repelled twenty-nine swordbeak attacks on foraging parties." He sounds like he's used to reciting his résumé defensively.

Plenty of hybrids have jobs at the resort. I'm sure he's qualified. However, I'm surprised the embassy would entrust their governor's daughter's safety to a man who represents the opposing side of the dispute I've come here to resolve.

"I'm not worried about animals," I say. "What about people?"

Jalus blinks. "I'm not sure what you're implying, Lady Sinead. The people of Eiris are peaceful. Do you expect an attack from your own embassy?"

I lean in to whisper in Cecily's ear. "This isn't going to work. Get me someone else."

Cecily cups her hand over her mouth to hiss back, "There is no one else, my lady. He was the only applicant. So stop being mean to him before he changes his mind."

I paste on a smile. "Fine. Let's just go."

"This way, my lady."

This way, Nade! Come see this!

I blink away the memory of his childish smile, now nowhere to be seen. This isn't ten years ago. I'm not here to explore while Dad holds diplomatic meetings. We're both adults with jobs to do.

And my job is to bully his people into letting my father take what he wants from this planet.

The walkway from the spaceport to the resort is lined with little color-changing solar lights. The memory of how enchanted I felt walking this path for the first time brings a smile to my lips. The lighter gravity makes each step feel almost like floating.

Dad made me do a special lesson on Eiris before our last visit, so I know that the trees towering over me are called "Giant's Embrace." Eiris's landmass is one large megacontinent with vast lakes dotted across it, and there's hardly anywhere the trees haven't claimed. They're as tall as Hepburn City skyscrapers, draped with pinkish moss, and their trunks are thick enough that a starship could park inside a hollow log. The upward-curving branches give the illusion they're reaching toward Eiris's binary suns.

Tourism contributes a significant chunk of the planetary economy, since the hybrid communities live off the abundant natural resources and refuse to farm, manufacture, or mine anything. It's Dad's favorite rant: he can't tax people who don't use money. Which means the Emperor's "gift" of governorship is frustratingly hard for my father to use as a means to enrich himself. The resort at least draws a steady stream of tourists for the novelty of living suspended in trees.

But Dad never gave up trying other tactics.

Jalus frowns as he tilts his head back. I follow his gaze and spot the zipline above our heads, strung between two massive trees at least five stories up. The branches have been pruned back to make way for the zipline, allowing a rare patch of sunlight to fall on the path below.

"What?" I ask. Does the guy hate fun?

"The trees." Jalus doesn't take his eyes from them as he speaks. "They're injured."

I snort. "What, a little pruning? It's good for them."

"That may be true of the trees from other worlds," Jalus says. "The trees of Eiris mourn if they are cut." His eyes meet mine, deep and plummy.

I'm not used to people towering over me like he does. It's making me feel weird and unbalanced. I clear my throat and look away. "So I take it you're on the side of my father's opposition?"

"My loyalty lies with my Kin." There's no anger in his tone, but I shiver nonetheless. The hybrids call themselves Kin, but they consider all life forms on this planet their extended family.

"Then why volunteer to protect me, if you support my opponents?"

"The Kin aren't your enemies," Jalus says firmly. "We may protest a governor's bad decision, push for him to change his mind—but those aren't violent or dangerous actions. We're only trying to protect what can't speak for itself."

"The trees." We've reached the pulley platform that will raise us high into the branches. I step onto it and turn to face Jalus. "You talk about them like they're alive."

"Of course they're alive." He gives me a pitying look that strikes a spark of anger in my chest.

"I don't mean—" My skin prickles. I pull in a deep breath. *Do not go mega-glitch on him.* "I meant *sentient.* Like they understand what's happening."

"Do you think they don't?"

"They're trees," I say. "Trees can't think."

"You're still thinking of your domesticated, Earth-bred trees," Jalus says. There's a note of sorrow in his voice. "Again, they aren't the same."

I know they're not. That's why I'm here.

When Dad's scientists took samples of lumber from Giant's

Embrace for offworld testing, he was giddy to learn that the wood tested as uniquely sturdy, fire-resistant, and slow to decay. The chemicals the trees secrete, so dangerous when breathed in, harden into an amber-like sheen when the wood is cut and dried.

Dad wants to clear-cut a sample area and try to create a galactic market for this unique building material. It's a relatively cheap venture to start out, and if it takes off, we could basically print our own credits with the vast resources this planet has to offer.

But the second his lumberjack crew landed here, ready to begin the project, they met fierce resistance from the local communities. Both human hybrids and the Eirisian insectoids came out in force. They sabotaged machinery, kidnapped workers, and surrounded the embassy. Eleven different ambassadors quit because they couldn't handle the incessant protesting.

So Dad sent me. The twelfth. His heir.

"I don't trust anyone else to represent our family's interests in this dispute," Dad said when he broke the news. "You've been training since you were a child to bear the responsibility of governorship. This will be the first real test of your abilities. I don't think I need to say what's at stake here."

Oh, I know what's at stake all right: Dad's profit margins and bank accounts. But what he's holding over my head is worse: if I don't bulldoze over the protests and get him what he wants, he'll disinherit me.

I wish I could say I didn't care. That the comfortable Moon Palace apartment, the shallow political friendships I've forged with spoiled nobility, the invites to parties and balls, are all meaningless to me. But after a lifetime of living off Dad's money, it's all I know how to do.

Worse than that, the idea of disappointing Dad fills me with panic. Despite how distant he's been lately, I can't help bending over backward for his approval.

The platform raises us several stories into the treetops. I try not to look down as I step off onto a wide tree branch, where a handful of Earth Classic humans in breather masks are waiting. Cecily is ushered off with my trunks in tow, leaving Jalus and me to wobble along a rope bridge between trees as we make our way toward the embassy.

Well, *I* wobble. Jalus is infuriatingly surefooted.

The treetop resort stretches out between six or seven huge trees, connected by rope bridges and ziplines. Each upcurved branch cradles a one-bedroom treehouse made from enormous hollow seedpods. The roofs are thickly coated with the same pink moss that drips from every branch. It absorbs liquid like a sponge, keeping the houses dry and cozy even in torrential rain.

As a youth, I was enchanted with this place. It felt magical, like a fairy's home in a storybook. But Jalus is frowning again.

"What?" I challenge. "You think the trees don't like it when we build houses in them?"

"It isn't the burdens you place on their arms," Jalus murmurs. "It's what you have done to their bodies."

I follow his gaze to the bole of the tree on which we stand. A section of the trunk several meters high has been hollowed out to create a large room. The one we're passing is a dining hall. The other central rooms in the resort include a ballroom, a bathhouse, and, of course, the Imperial Embassy.

"It doesn't kill the trees," I argue. "These rooms were made a long time ago, and they're still thriving."

Jalus shakes his head. "Would you enjoy being hollowed out, even if your blood still runs?"

I have no easy response for that. Suspicion sprouts in the back of my mind: he didn't volunteer to protect me because he cared about our childhood friendship, or even his duty to the planetary governor. He's a spy, sent to convince me to support the hybrids' side.

Well, good luck. He'll have to go through my daddy issues first.

Inside the Embassy's hollow trunk, the room is partitioned into private offices. An intern ushers me to the one in the middle. "This used to be Ambassador Cora's," she says. "We cleaned out her stuff a couple of weeks after she disappeared."

"She…what?" I turn to stare at the girl. She's fresh-faced, probably a university student. Her short blond ponytail is losing its bounce, baby hairs straggling out at the neck and temples.

"Oh, um, I thought they would have told you," she says softly, darting a glance at her colleagues. They're all looking away, pretending not to hear. "There's been, um, a lot of disappearances in the past few months."

Jalus nods. "The previous eleven ambassadors have gone missing. That's why they hired me to guard you."

I gape. "No, they did *not* tell me." *Did Dad know? If he did, and sent me anyway...*

Blast me, that's cold, even for him. Enough to make a girl think her dear daddy wants to get rid of her. It already stung that he hinged my inheritance on the Herculean task of convincing a bunch of aliens that we're entitled to their planet's natural resources. Now he wants to throw me to kidnappers while he's at it.

"Has anyone investigated?" I ask. "The protesters—"

"Did *not* take them." Jalus folds all four of his arms across his torso.

"But have you checked?"

"I don't have to 'check.'" He glares at me, the most emotion I've seen from him so far. "The Kin are—"

"Peaceful, yeah, yeah. So maybe they didn't *kill* them. But what about holding them for ransom to try to blackmail my dad into stopping the clear-cutting?"

Jalus's reply is frigid. "If the Kin had taken your ambassadors, you'd know. You would've been given assurance that they were safe, and you would've already been presented with terms for their return."

"I see." Wrenching open the door to my office, I scan its bare amenities. The blank wallscreen, curved to fit against the bole. Uncushioned collapsible chairs. A desk folded up against the partition, able to flip down if I need a workspace. Nothing left of its former inhabitant or her possessions.

Nothing of the ten who preceded her, either.

I slide the door shut in Jalus's face and take a breath to collect myself. I've been dropped into the middle of a trap, set up for failure on all sides.

But I don't intend to disappear quietly.

chapter two

day two

Distant knocking is the first thing I register in the morning. "Lady Sinead. Are you awake?"

Jalus. Ugh. Go away.

Leaf-dappled sunlight streams through the treehouse window. I come to consciousness slowly, aware of a bone-deep fatigue. My muscles ache and my skin itches. I feel like I've been tossed out of a moving hovercar. What the blazes happened last night?

All I remember is retiring to my room, reading the Imperial news, drawing the window shade—the suns rarely both set at once on Eiris, meaning their "night" is still as bright as day--then lying down to sleep.

Nothing strenuous. Nothing that should have resulted in... scratches all over my arm?

I sit bolt upright, running my fingers across my freckle-dappled skin. Yes, there are thin welts all up and down my arms. I push back the covers and realize it's my legs, too.

Then I see the state of my nightrobe, and I scream.

My bedroom door slams open, and Jalus rushes in, a stiletto-sharp thorn weapon in each of his lower hands. "What is it, my lady?" Then he stops in his tracks. I watch as the pupils of his wine-dark eyes expand, his jaw hanging slack.

I struggle to gather enough scraps of my shredded, barely-there nightrobe to cover my breasts. "Get out!" I shriek.

He clears his throat. "My apologies." He whips around, wings ruffled just enough to show a peek of their rainbow undersides, and lets the door slide shut behind him.

Raking my fingers through my hair, I shuffle to the mirror over my washstand and examine the damage up close. The scratches are mostly confined to my limbs, but there are a few faint lines on my face. There's even one underneath my breather mask. How the blazes did that happen? The mask was firmly in place when I went to sleep, and it was there when I woke.

The cuts aren't serious; they'll heal up quickly. But I can't say the same for my nightrobe. It's in complete tatters. Barely qualifies as clothing anymore.

Jalus basically saw me naked.

Heat blooms in my cheeks as I remember the way his eyes darkened. Something about a man crashing into my chambers, weapons at the ready to defend me, was undeniably…compelling.

Although I'm fully dressed when I walk out of my cabin, Jalus can't quite meet my eyes. "Good morning, Lady Sinead. I apologize for intruding."

My face heats again. "It was nothing. I appreciate your speed in coming to my assistance."

"May I ask…" Jalus steps forward, his long-fingered hands reaching toward the cuts on my arms. He stops just shy of touching me, making my skin tingle with anticipation. "What happened? When I left, you were uninjured."

"I don't know," I admit. "Nothing that I can remember. You don't have rodents here, do you?"

"There are a few animals that roam the forest floor," says Jalus, "but they don't often climb to these heights, much less attack people in their sleep." He folds his lower arms, while using one of his upper hands to absentmindedly smooth his hair. "Lady Sinead, I think I should spend the night with you."

"Excuse me?"

"I'll stay in another room for your comfort," he adds hastily. "But I kept watch during your entire sleep cycle and saw no intruders. Whatever happened to you was cleverly orchestrated to avoid detection. I'm afraid it's connected to the disappearance of the other ambassadors. I won't allow that to happen again. Not to you."

My heart thumps. Is it me, or did he emphasize that last part with more warmth than is strictly appropriate? I might be suspicious of his motives, but he seems sincere in wanting to keep me safe.

Surely he can handle a couple of alien squirrels.

● ＼＼＼＼   ／／／／ ◦

"LADY SINEAD, if I may make a suggestion?"

I lift my head from where I'd let it fall onto my folded arms on the desk. My meeting with a Kin elder this morning was a disaster. He wouldn't budge, and I couldn't afford to concede. It's more embarrassing than I expected, having Jalus stand guard throughout the whole thing. Watching me fail.

Not quite able to meet his eyes, I mumble, "What?"

"Lady Crowe, the former governor, used to visit the Kin villages to hear our concerns."

I lift an eyebrow. "You think that might soften them up?"

"It wouldn't hurt," Jalus says cautiously.

I check the time on my keycuff. It's barely lunchtime, and the rest of today's meetings threaten to be equally unproductive.

"Cecily, can you take care of my appointments for today?"

My secretary glances up from her notes. "Of course, my lady."

Standing, I face Jalus with palms up. "You know your people best. Show me what to do."

Jalus steps closer. "The quickest way to the village is by flight. I can carry you, but…is physical contact acceptable? Your secretary warned me that you prefer not to be touched."

I flash an annoyed look at Cecily. She isn't wrong; I often flinch at casual contact and have to steel myself before handshakes with strangers.

But Jalus seems to be an exception. Because when we climb the ladder to the very top of the forest canopy and he hoists me into his arms, my heart starts to race, my insides turning gooey with desire. A faint sweet scent worms its way past my mask's filters, filling me with the sudden urge to rip my mask off and find out what his skin really smells like. I suppress a gasp when his lower hand settles on my waist. He's surprisingly warm for such an ethereal figure. With his four arms embracing me, I feel safe.

"Sorry if I'm heavy," I mutter. My cheeks burn.

"You're perfect." His voice rumbles through me, waking nerve endings in erogenous zones I didn't know I had. Then his eyes flit away, and a violet flush creeps across his cheeks. "I mean, you're not heavy. The foragers make me carry laden baskets all the time."

His heart is thumping under my hand on his chest. I try to catch his eyes, but he's resolutely focused on the horizon.

And then he extends his wings.

I can't hide my exclamation of awe as they shade the twin suns from my view. Light filters through the thin, fluff-covered membranes, creating a stained-glass effect.

Jalus's wings are *stunning*. Orange-red bleeds into violet-blue, natural stripes and swirls painting the colors into vivid shapes that make peacock feathers look drab.

"Hold on." His whisper in my ear turns me to jelly.

Then the wind catches us, and we're soaring.

The view from the starship couldn't compare to this. The warm breeze against my face, the hissing, chirping song of millions of insects, and the up-close texture of the trees' highest branches all combine to make it a stunning sensory experience.

But we're not alone in the sky.

As the flying shape swoops closer, I recognize the hooked, batlike wingspan and narrow, toothy jaw of a swordbeak. My Eiris geography lesson highlighted swordbeaks as the insectoids' main predator. I suck in a breath to scream, but Jalus already has his thorn weapons ready.

He waits until the swordbeak veers too close. Then, holding me secure against him with three of his arms, he executes a stomach-dropping loop and rakes the sharp weapon down the swordbeak's wing membrane. The creature shrieks and drops out of the sky.

My knuckles are white, fisted in his brown uniform. My breath fogs against my breather mask in little pants, my heart hammering so hard it feels like I might pass out.

The man's got *moves*. Blazingly sexy ones.

He angles his wings against the wind to slow us down, and faintly I hear his voice in my ear telling me to brace for landing. I squeeze my eyes shut as the canopy rushes up to meet us.

But the landing is painless. Just a jostle and a rustling noise as he folds his wings.

"Can you stand?" He gently sets me down. Despite his upper hand on my waist, I wobble and almost fall, grabbing a branch to steady myself. The rough bark skins my palm.

"What's one more scratch?" I joke, examining the new wound.

Jalus frowns. "You need medicine for that. This way." He guides me to a basket attached to a rope pulley. While he hauls on the rope to lower us, I catch myself watching his forearms flex.

Stars, what is wrong with me? I adjust my mask to make sure none of the hallucinogenic air is leaking through. Why can't I keep my eyes off this guy?

I drag my gaze away from him and focus on the Kin village instead.

Groups of winged children tumble through the branches, playing an airborne game of tag. Watching them reminds me of that summer I spent with Jalus and the few times he brought me here to visit.

I'm sorry, Nade. I forgot you can't play with us.

That's fine. Go ahead. You have fun.

No, I wanna stay here with you.

I chuckle to myself. Stars, I'd thought he was so annoying and clingy back then. Only now, ten years later, can I finally admit to myself that I was glad for his company. Visiting the Kin makes me feel…well, like an alien. And a familiar face, even if that face has antennae instead of eyebrows, goes a long way toward making me feel at home here.

We pass a large group working on food prep, boiling something vinegary over an ingeniously crafted hanging firepit.

"What are they cooking?" I ask. "Smells amazing."

Jalus says, "They're pickling foraged vegetables to store for later."

"Yum," I say without thinking. I love pickles, but the Moon Palace cookbots never served them.

"Would you like to try one?" Jalus offers.

I shake my head. "Oh, no, that's fine, I…"

"They are happy to share."

And that's how I end up being presented with a pickled alien fruit, served on a leaf to catch the dripping juices. It's shaped roughly like a banana pepper and smells mouthwateringly sweet-sour. I suck in a deep breath before lifting my mask and darting my tongue out to taste test. Jalus is watching me with an odd expression on his face. I probably look silly trying to hold my breath and eat at the same time.

The taste is pleasing, so I go in for a bite. It's still warm, invitingly soft with a firm crunch in the middle, and full of succulent flavor that reminds me of a tomato in balsamic vinegar.

"I could eat this forever," I tell the cooks fervently. "Delicious."

They dart glances at each other, giggling but looking pleased. They hand Jalus one, too, and to my shock his tongue flicks out and curls around the pickle, bringing it to his mouth like a frog catching a fly.

"Whoa." I stare. "Um. Your tongue…"

"It's retractable and prehensile." Jalus colors slightly. "I know eating in this way is considered rude by Earth Classic standards…"

"Eat whatever way you want," I tell him. "I think it's cool."

I'm carefully *not* thinking about other uses for that tongue.

"Come." Jalus beckons me to follow as he steps lightly across branches. This village doesn't have the safety nets that are everywhere at the resort. Trying not to look down, I follow his steps, wishing my stride was as long as his.

We arrive at a rope bridge connecting two trees together—only, unlike the ones back at the resort, this one is little more than a series of tightropes strung across a dizzying drop.

I back away queasily. "I can't go across that."

Jalus, already halfway across, turns with utterly perfect balance.

"Oh. I forgot." In two strides, he's back on the branch with me, scooping me up into his four arms.

My heart leaps into my throat. I thought I'd gotten used to his touch after that flight, but no. The sudden awareness of my own skin shocks me. I check my mask again. Still on. Still functioning. *What is happening to me?*

His steps are light and sure. I force myself not to look down.

Jalus sets me on my feet, businesslike, as if he hasn't just lit every nerve in my body on fire. I try not to hyperventilate.

"You're at a disadvantage here without wings," he observes. "Please, tell me if there are any more places you feel unsafe, and I'll carry you."

I mentally resolve not to ask for help, but that lasts all of two minutes before we hit another tightrope crossing. I'm drowning in a mix of embarrassment and confused arousal. Should I just fling myself off this tree and accept my fate?

But no. Jalus would probably dive to catch me.

Why do I *want* him to catch me?

We arrive at a storage area where a cluster of large plant-fiber cocoons hang close together from the branches under our feet. Jalus calls out to one of the Kin women and asks her for a healing salve, which she extracts from a pot sealed in one of the cocoons.

"Thank you," I say as she offers it to me on yet another leaf. I smear it across my palm and apply the extra to the cuts on my arms. Instantly, the stinging is gone, the redness fading.

"What is this?" I exclaim. "It works so well."

"A Kin secret," the woman tells me with a wink.

Jalus whispers another request, and she gives him a small gourd with a wax seal, sloshing with liquid. He stows it in his pocket, kissing his hand to her in thanks.

When he turns back to me, he seems almost shy. "This is my mother."

I look up in surprise and reevaluate the woman. I can see the resemblance. They have the same beautiful eyes, the same shiny brown hair. "Mother, this is Lady Sinead."

"The Governor's daughter." Jalus's mom gives me a once-over. "This planet has always turned easier when a woman rules us."

"*Mother…*"

"Are you talking about Governor Crowe?" I lift my eyebrows. "I thought she was unpopular. I saw the bonfires after her execution. Dad said they—you—were burning her in effigy because you hated her."

Jalus's mom raises her eyebrows right back at me. "Oh? Is *that* what he told you?"

"Burning is a sign of honor among us," Jalus tells me quietly. "We burned leaf dolls in the Lady Governor's memory because she had treated us kindly. Allowed us sovereignty over our own dealings. Often she visited the villages and spoke with us to learn our concerns. We mourned her passing greatly."

"*Oh.*" Governor Crowe must have done all that in secret, because she'd have been mocked out of the Ruling Council for such softhearted behavior. Maybe that was what got her removed and executed. "I'm sorry for your loss," is all I can think to say.

"As I said, a woman's rule has always brought this planet good fortune." Jalus's mother is staring at me with a calculating look on her face. "Especially a woman linked to our kind by—"

"It was good to see you, Mother," Jalus interrupts. "We have to go now. I'm taking Sinead to meet the Old Kin."

"Are you, now?" Jalus's mother gives a brief smile. "Good. Good." She reaches out to clasp my shoulder. "I will see you again," she says, sounding much more sure of it than I am.

Jalus leads me across a few more tightrope-bridges before he speaks again. "Mother is nearing the age of an elder, so she feels she's earned the right to speak her mind." He sounds apologetic.

"I like her," I say. "I didn't know about the former Governor. Thank you for telling me."

"I should have known the Governor wouldn't—" Jalus stops. "Forgive me. I don't mean to insult your father."

"He misinterpreted what he saw," I say, wishing I believed it. "Burning effigies means something else in Imperial culture. It would be beneath him to knowingly spread lies about his predecessor."

But that wouldn't stop him, whispers a voice in the back of my mind.

To distract myself, I ask, "Who are the Old Kin?"

"You'll see." Jalus flashes me a mischievous smile. It's the first one I've seen on his adult face, and it transforms him. He's handsome when he's solemn and cold, but smiling, he's so beautiful it's like staring directly into the suns.

He leads me to a separate section of the village, where I stop in my tracks. Nerves coil in my belly. This is where the non-hybrid, fully alien butterfly insectoids live.

They almost never show themselves to outsiders. I wasn't allowed to meet them when I was here as a teenager. As far as I know, Dad's never even seen one. Jalus does me a rare honor to bring me here.

Several of them take flight when they see us coming, and several more freeze in place, watching us warily.

I know I shouldn't stare, but I can't help it. I've only ever seen pictures of these creatures. They're smaller than Jalus, maybe half his wingspan. Their central bodies are segmented, pink-furred to resemble the moss that drips from the trees, with six long, thin legs ending in handlike appendages. They have huge, faceted eyes and tubelike mouths.

"Should we say hi?" I whisper.

"I already greeted them," Jalus tells me. "They speak in scents, not words."

"Does...does my scent say anything to them?"

Jalus chokes on what might be a suppressed laugh. "Don't worry. They can tell you're not able to alter your scent at will. They won't hold your fear against you."

"I'm not afraid."

"Of course."

Stars. What if he's been able to smell every thought I've had all day? What else does he know that I couldn't hide?

Maybe there's still time to jump off this tree branch.

He leads me straight to a large overhang of moss, where three of the butterflies are resting in the shade, slowly fanning their wings. I wait, silent, as he kneels and fans his own wings in response. Uncertainly, I kneel next to him.

"They want to tell you a story," Jalus says at last.

"All right…"

"This isn't for entertainment, you understand. Old Kin tell tales for education, to pass down knowledge."

I nod. "I'm listening."

He closes his eyes, inhaling deep. "Long ago, in the time before humans descended from the sky, there lived a youth named…um… Scent of Berries After Rain? I'll call him Berry. Right. So Berry was very fond of food, maybe too fond. He found a sort of delicious fungus that only grows on fallen trees, and he ate all of it without taking any back to the colony.

"He wanted to make more grow, but fallen trees are hard to find, and this fungus would not grow anywhere else. So he decided he would fell a tree purposely. He went deep into the forest where no one would see him. He took a sharp-toothed swordbeak skull and began to saw the wide trunk.

"It took him weeks to even cut halfway through. The whole time, he could sense the tree crying out, begging for him to stop. But every time his heart was moved with pity, he remembered those delicious fungi, and his gluttony urged him to keep working. At last, he weakened the base of the tree so much that he was able to topple it.

"It crashed into many others on the way down, damaging their branches. These trees felt the loss of their sibling and the pain of their own injuries. They cried out to Berry's colony, but Berry told them it would result in plenty of mouthwatering food for them all, so they chose not to punish him.

"The trees were angry that these people, whom they had fed and protected for millennia, would ignore their plea for help. So the next time Berry alighted on the ground to check his fallen tree, searching for the fungi he craved, the trees puffed out a poisonous scent that made Berry fall asleep. Then they sent out their roots to drag him into the depths of the earth. Berry was never seen again. But his colony apologized to the forest and promised they would never fell a living tree."

My jaw is hanging open by the end of the tale. "That's it? The trees killed him? Stars above, that's dark."

Jalus slowly rises from his crouch. "It happened a thousand generations ago. The Old Kin tell every child to remind them why we must respect the trees. Because if we don't, the trees will fight back."

"Do you think…" I put my hand to my mouth, the very thought sickening me. "Jalus, do you think that's what happened to the eleven ambassadors who disappeared?"

His eyes are solemn on mine. "I don't know. Nor do I know what happened to you last night." This time, he *does* touch me, the barest brush of his fingertips across the scratches down my arm. I shiver involuntarily. "But I'm certain that if your father continues to send offworlders to cut down trees, it's going to upset the delicate balance that makes it possible for us to coexist on this planet."

"Dad isn't the sort of person who just accepts 'no' as an answer." I gulp, imagining his face if I tried to explain all of this.

Both of us are quiet as Jalus guides me up into the canopy for our flight home. My thoughts spin in circles. If the Old Kin's warning is true, cutting down the trees will result in some kind of chemical reaction that will intensify the poison in the air. That's not good for anyone who lives on this planet. Yeah, maybe humans could get better protective equipment and still cut down as many trees as they like, but the resort's business would be ruined, and…

And every village like Jalus's would suffer. Maybe die.

I can't stand by and watch that happen. But nothing I say will stop my dad from doing what he wants. He'll just send more and more people, push harder and harder. It will take total devastation before he'll accept defeat.

Jalus eyes the sky. "There's a thunderstorm coming. I can't fly in the rain. We have to hurry." He lifts me into his arms and leaps into the air.

On the flight out, he kept low to the treetops; now he angles his wings to catch the air currents that will carry us higher. It's a bumpy ascent. I fight nausea and the urge to ask if walking back to the resort is still an option.

Dark clouds roll in fast. Jalus puts on a burst of speed. His labored breathing sounds harsh in my ears.

I've just caught sight of the resort in the distance when Jalus suddenly swerves and dives. I shriek, then seal my mouth shut in terrified silence as I catch a glimpse of what he's evading.

A swordbeak bursts up out of the canopy, circling us in tight spirals for an opening. Jalus is exhausted. What if he can't fight it off?

The avian swoops, its claw grazing my cheek. There's an agonizing snap. The bird's snagged my breather mask, breaking its cord. It falls useless around my neck, and I scream, my lungs filling with forbidden air.

My first unfiltered breath is humid, earthy with the smell of oncoming rain. Then Jalus's honey scent, unmuted, hits me like a shot of strong liquor. My brain goes fuzzy. *Blazes*, the man smells absolutely edible.

Jalus dodges and dips into the branches below. He lands hard on a wide limb and sets me down. I fall hard on my butt with my back against the trunk.

"What are you doing?" My voice is shrill with fear. "Don't leave me here."

His intoxicating dark eyes find mine. "Trust me," he murmurs.

Clinging to the tree's massive trunk, I squint through the treetops as he takes off again, lighter on the wing without me. He draws his thorn daggers from his belt. They're wicked-sharp, but half the length of a swordbeak maw. *What is he thinking?*

My breath comes in terrified gasps as Jalus grapples with the swordbeak. He's not just strong, he's *fast*, zipping in circles around the avian. When it catches him in its claws, he strikes, ducking under its sharp beak to stab the thorn through its neck. It releases him as it plummets, and he flits back up to land on the branch where I stand.

He's dripping blood from deep gashes on his shoulder and one of his lower arms. It's a shock to realize his blood isn't red, but a deep violet, nearly black. Surely his thin frame doesn't have enough of it to spare the amount he's losing.

I shrug off my outer robe, balling up the thin fabric to put pressure on the shoulder wound. He's breathing hard, dripping sweat that somehow smells honey-sweet, and gazing up at the sky in defeat.

A drop of rain hits my forehead. We're out of time. The storm is here.

"We'll have to walk now," he pants. "My apologies. Let's get down to the forest floor before I'm unable to carry you."

"Jalus…" My heart pounds as I look up into that unreasonably beautiful face. "Thank you. That was incredible."

He cups my cheek with one of his uninjured upper hands. "Your mask," he says hoarsely. He wipes a raindrop from my cheek with his thumb. I catch my breath at the intensity in his eyes. None of my previous bodyguards have ever looked at me like that after saving my life. If they had, I might have had them fired for inappropriate advances.

But I don't want him to stop.

"It's fine. The air won't be toxic for hours…" I trail off, my pulse pounding. The mask filters hid Jalus's scent from me before. Now that it's off, that sweet perfume goes straight to my groin, lighting up parts of me that have already been embarrassingly aroused all day.

Before I know what I'm doing, I'm kissing him.

The second my mouth meets his, Jalus groans. He presses me backward until the thin back of my dress meets the rough tree trunk. More scratches. I don't care. I hook my legs around his waist, my skirt riding up above my hips. I can't remember *ever* being this horny before.

Jalus pulls away first, with a deep guttural growl that doesn't sound like it should be able to come from a man who looks like a rainbow fucked a candy stick. He scoops me up in his arms and begins leaping from branch to branch, slowly lowering us to the ground level as raindrops fall faster.

"You need to take it easy," I protest. "You're losing a lot of blood."

He pauses on a branch festooned with pink moss. "Grab some of that for me."

I reach out, still held securely in his arms, and gather double handfuls of the stuff. It's soft to the touch, fragrant with an earthy petrichor scent, and drips moisture when I ball it up and push it against his shoulder.

Almost instantly, the flow of blood begins to slacken.

"Clots the blood," he explains, in response to my awed exclamation. "The Old Kin have used this to heal for many thousands of years. It's how they make the medicine you used earlier."

Dense underbrush envelops us as we reach the ground level. Jalus sets me down to wrap more moss around his injured arm. He's trying to put distance between us, but I can't resist moving closer. His scent draws me in like a bee to an open flower.

Shit. What am I doing? My relationships have been few and far between, and only a couple of them got further than kissing before Dad forced me to end them. "A governor's daughter can't afford to dally without any political benefit," he'd said, in a tone that brooked no argument. In other words, Vanessa the actress and Bowen the bartender weren't good enough for Lady Sinead the heiress.

Dad would be apoplectic at the idea of me fraternizing with an alien hybrid. Especially one who may or may not be attempting to torpedo Dad's latest fortune-building scheme.

I contemplate that for a moment, then decide I stopped giving a shit what Dad wanted when he sent me to Eiris to disappear like the other eleven ambassadors.

Jalus sinks onto a boulder, wings fanned behind him, and I close the distance between us, unable to stop myself. I plant myself in his lap, knees on either side of his hips, my nose buried in the crook of his neck. Dimly, I'm somewhat embarrassed at my own daring, but the attraction of his scent pulls me in like nothing I've ever experienced in my whole life.

"What—what is that perfume you're wearing?" I mumble into his neck. I want to lick it. Roll in it. Drown in it.

He tilts my chin back with his thumb and forefinger, and I close my eyes, ready to let him devour me.

Instead, he reaches for my mask and sets it over my nose and mouth, holding it there for my next two breaths.

My brain kicks back on, and I scramble backwards off his lap, mortified. "I am *so* sorry. Stars. The air—I must have—"

"Forgive me," Jalus says softly. His cheeks have a tinge of violet color, too. "I should not have taken advantage while you were in that state. I always wondered if you could sense…well, obviously you can."

I narrow my eyes. "Explain?"

Jalus clears his throat, shifting in his seat. "Among the Kin, scent is very important. You might say it's our first language, inherited from the Old Kin. Scent leads us to our intended mates. When we find someone with whom our scent mingles well, it can trigger…very strong instincts."

Both my hands press to the mask, my eyes widening. "You're telling me that smell is *mating pheromones?* When were you going to tell me you're in…what, like, butterfly heat?"

"It is not me alone," Jalus says, his eyes skittering away from mine. "Two scents must mingle to create the…pheromones, as you call it. My scent, mixed with others in the village, sparked no reaction. But when I'm close to you…Mother could sense it between us." He bows his head. "I didn't think you could tell. You gave no indication that you felt anything when we met years ago. I'm not even certain how it's physiologically possible for an Earth Classic…"

"When we met?" I stare at him. "You felt this way about me when we were *fourteen?*"

His miserable shrug says it all.

"Stars." I need to sit down, too. Somewhere other than his lap. "How the blazes did you resist? I can barely think straight when I…"

"How could I not?" Jalus says, hanging his head. "You don't care for me. You made that quite clear. No matter how strong the pull between two people, there is always a choice. A woman may choose to distance herself from a man she will not accept. There may be another mate for him someday. Her as well. A physiological reaction does not mandate a relationship." It's obvious he's thought about this a lot for the past ten years. "Your breather mask seems to mute the effects. Keep it on at all times, and you will not feel the urge to engage in anything unwelcome. I can…manage myself."

Fuck. This beautiful man promising to respect a "no" might actually be the sexiest thing anyone's ever said to me.

Jalus is still speaking. "I sincerely apologize if I made you uncomfortable. I can arrange for another guard, if you feel—"

"I don't want another guard," I say. And, very deliberately, I pull the mask from my face and drop it on the ground.

Jalus sucks in a breath and stands, his wings unfurling to their full glory. "Nade, please consider this carefully," he says in a low voice. His use of my childhood nickname sets wings fluttering in my belly. "The distance between our two worlds is great. It might be better if we don't entangle them."

He's not wrong. I've been raised in a world of privilege and excess, of getting what I want the second I want it. And all along, I was desperately lonely.

Returning to Eiris has made me realize that all the money and power in the world are no substitute for a place I feel at home. For arms I feel secure in.

My hand runs up his chest and his words get lost in a groan. I slide my fingers around to the back of his head, beneath the warm silken mass of his hair, and pull him down for a kiss.

If he wants me as badly as I want him, then I can imagine what it costs him to pull back. "Nade, don't tempt me unless—"

"Jalus," I whisper, in a voice I barely recognize. All my life, I have commanded. I have been groomed from childhood to take what is mine without a by-your-leave. But if he doesn't give me what I need right now, I'm prepared to beg. "Please."

The word has an instant effect on him, his pupils widening until there's almost no purple left in his dark gaze.

"You like it when I beg?" I look up at him through my lashes. "Then I'll get down on my knees."

A curse tears loose from his throat. In a single smooth motion, he scoops me into his arms again. My back hits the soft moss carpeting the ground as raindrops patter around us. His upper hands hold my wrists on either side of my head, the rainbow glory of his wings enveloping us like a tent and shielding us from the rain.

"If we are going to do this," he says, his voice roughened with desire, "I am not your bodyguard here. We are equals. Understand?"

"Yes, sir."

Oooh, he likes that. I roll my hips up into the bulge tightening the front of his brown jumpsuit. "Please fuck me, sir."

He chuckles. "Oh, no. I'm not going to fuck you."

I pout. "Do you not have the parts? That's fine, we can use—"

"Not until you're already screaming my name." He pushes up the hem of my dress and presses his nose into the moist center of my panties, inhaling deep.

My head falls back, my eyes closing as sensation takes over. He pulls my panties down just to the knee, keeping my legs trapped as his long tongue laps at my pussy, then wriggles deep inside. I'm moaning and gasping so loud I'm sure they can hear me back at the resort. And, just like he promised, his name rolls off my tongue, like…whatever the opposite of cursing is. Praising. Worshiping.

My back arches off the ground as he curves his tongue to hit the right spot inside me. "Yes, *please*, right there. Don't stop, Jalus, please—nooooo, *fuck*, you blasted tease," as he pulls back before I'm able to come. Desperately horny, I clutch at him, cursing and begging for him to come back, but he's peeling off his uniform and *oh, stars.*

That lean, lithe body packs some serious muscle, from his surprisingly meaty thighs to the ridges of his abs. His cock looks more or less human-shaped, long and thin and rigid against his belly. Corkscrew ridges spiral up the side, making me groan in anticipation. Before today, I would've claimed not to have a body preference. It's the person inside that matters, not the package they're wrapped in.

What a package, though!

I reach to pull my dress higher, but he says, "Leave the dress on," so commandingly I nearly melt into a puddle of arousal.

Slowly, he pulls down the neckline of my sundress to free my small breasts. His tongue snakes out to suckle on one, tickling the nipple with exquisite precision.

"Touch me, please," I beg. "Let me come."

He chuckles, then takes pity on me and thumbs my clit, sinking two of his long fingers deep into my pussy. It takes maybe thirty seconds before I shatter into the most intense orgasm I've had in…maybe my entire life.

And it only whets my appetite.

I want to demand his cock in me now, but I hold back the words. No, he likes me submissive. So I say, with fluttering eyelashes, "That was amazing, sir. Thank you. Will you allow me to suck your cock now?"

He groans and fists it. "Since you've been a good girl," he murmurs. "I want to see you kneel."

He plants his bare ass against that boulder again and spreads his legs for me. I slide between them, almost as eager for this as I am to feel him inside me.

The droplets at the tip of his cock taste salty-sweet when I lick them off. I take as much of him as I can into my mouth, then raise my eyes to meet his as I suck and stroke him, exploring the new and interesting ridges of him with my tongue. The dark lust in his eyes, the helpless pleasure in the O of his mouth, already have me excited again.

"Enough of that," he says harshly, gripping the base of his cock. "Get back up here. I want you in my lap."

I straddle him like before, squirming against his erection. He takes my mouth in a hungry kiss, and then murmurs in my ear, "You still want to be fucked?"

"Yes, please, sir."

"Then fuck yourself on me," he purrs. "Work my cock the way you want."

Stars, I could come just from the way he talks to me. I waste no time in raising my hips to sink down on him slowly. The ridges of him are heaven—I used to have a sex toy that was shaped just like this, but blast me if the real thing isn't twice as hot and a million times better.

His wings shiver as he strokes my nipples with his two upper hands. One lower hand plays with my clit as I fuck him, the other gripping my waist and then sliding around to palm my ass.

I'm starting to think every man ought to have four hands.

I kiss his neck and shoulder, nibbling just behind his pointed ear until he starts to moan. He's close, and I am too. If he keeps rubbing just like that, I'm going to—

"Fuck, Jalus," I groan as he brings me to climax again. I clench hard against him, and he bucks, swearing.

"Nade," he says, like a prayer, and then he's coming inside me, and oh, oh, the ridges *pulse* when he comes—

My head falls back in ecstasy, with his upper hands holding me up. The orgasm just keeps on going, waves of pleasure aftershocking into each other until I'm a boneless, satiated puddle.

He pulls me close to his chest and slides us to the soft mossy ground, our legs still entwined. I feel like I should say something, but I think he's fucked the words right out of me. For once in my long political career, I've got nothing to say.

Pillowing my head on his arm, I let sleep take me.

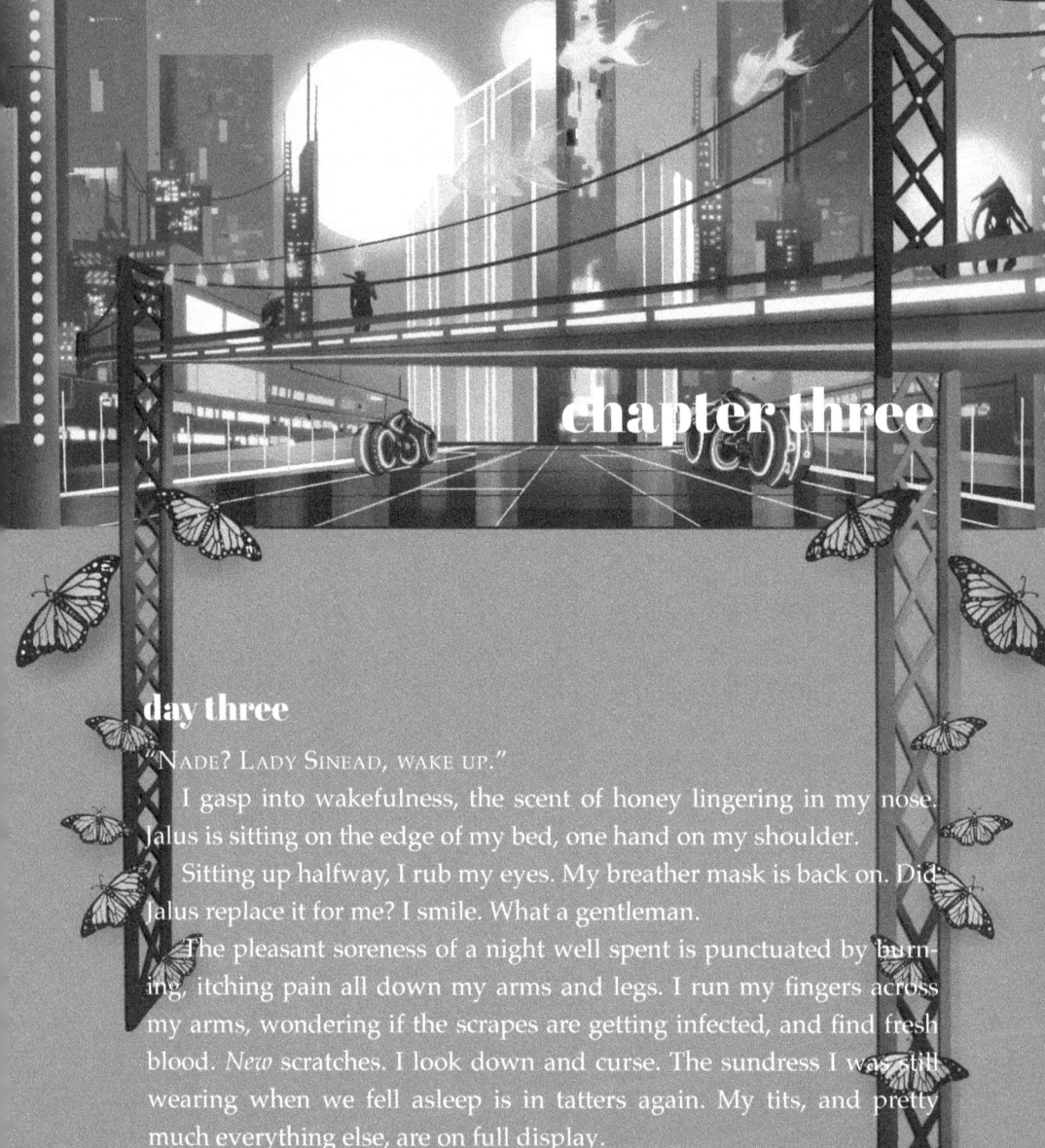

chapter three

day three

"NADE? LADY SINEAD, WAKE UP."

I gasp into wakefulness, the scent of honey lingering in my nose. Jalus is sitting on the edge of my bed, one hand on my shoulder.

Sitting up halfway, I rub my eyes. My breather mask is back on. Did Jalus replace it for me? I smile. What a gentleman.

The pleasant soreness of a night well spent is punctuated by burning, itching pain all down my arms and legs. I run my fingers across my arms, wondering if the scrapes are getting infected, and find fresh blood. *New* scratches. I look down and curse. The sundress I was still wearing when we fell asleep is in tatters again. My tits, and pretty much everything else, are on full display.

"What happened?" I mumble groggily. "Jalus? Did a squirrel get in?"

"I slept." He frowns. "I shouldn't have. Kin need very little sleep. I intended to stand guard while you slept, but...when I woke, I was alone. I scoured the forest, following your scent, and discovered you here."

I bolt upright. "Wait. *You* didn't bring me back here?"

Jalus shakes his head. "Do you remember anything?"

"No..." My hands start to tremble. The last thing I remember is falling asleep in his arms on the forest floor.

"You're still in danger, and I failed in my duty to protect you." Jalus bows his head. "I'm sorry, Nade."

"No...Jalus..."

At that moment, someone bangs on the cabin's front door. With a couple of choice swear words, I vault out of bed, bundle the ruined dress into the corner, and throw on another. My hair must be a riot, but I just run my fingers through it on my way to answer the knock.

It's Cecily, looking worried. "Lady Sinead? I canceled your first meeting of the day, but your next one is with your father. It's in ten minutes."

I check the time and groan. "Give me five to get cleaned up." Dad wouldn't appreciate me showing up to a meeting with sex hair.

Thankfully, Jalus seems ready to go. His hair is immaculate, wings folded, and that uniform fits his delectable frame with only a few wrinkles betraying that it spent the night crumpled up on the rain-soaked ground.

I don't want Dad asking questions about my injuries, so I cover my arms with a long-sleeved robe. I fairly sprint to the embassy, where the vid-call is already live on my wallscreen.

"Good morning, Dad," I say, proud of how cool and collected I manage to sound. "How are things back at the Palace?"

There's a long pause for the relay lag. When Dad replies, it's to wave my pleasantries away impatiently. "Tell me about the Eiris negotiations."

Typical. He gives me six months to get results, yet expects them within two days.

"They've just started," I tell him truthfully. "But I think I see a path forward."

I wait for Dad to receive my end of the message. When he does, he leans forward, stroking his chin. "You have a plan of attack?"

"I'm starting to formulate one, yes." Sweat trickles down my back.

"What's your estimated timeline?" Dad presses. "The contractors want a new landing date."

Shit. "I...don't know if I can give you one yet."

Long silence. Then, "Make an educated guess."

"Four weeks," I say. It's the first number that comes to mind. *Why didn't I say eight? Twelve?*

Dad sits back, looking pleased. "Well! If you're able to clear a path for the contractors by then, I'll be very impressed, Sinead. Keep me updated. Now, do you want to discuss details on your plan? I'm very curious what you've come up with."

A lead weight settles in my stomach. I can't tell him any obvious lies. If I say I'm planning to subdue the Kin with violence, he might show up with an army of mercenaries to help me. The only way forward is by twisting the truth just a bit...

I'm highly conscious of Jalus's presence in the corner behind me as I say, "I've made good progress connecting with the culture. I'm trying to build goodwill by listening to their folklore. Once they fully trust me, I'll use their own stories against them and convince them that the trees are harmful. That we'd be doing them a favor by cutting them down."

Another lag interval. Is the holo-capture picking up my nervous shaking?

"Not the approach I'd personally go with," Dad says, "but since our other attempts have failed, I'm willing to try a new angle. All right, Sinead. You've got four weeks. Don't disappoint me."

The call disconnects.

I sink into one of my office chairs, fanning myself. "Cecily, could you find me some coffee, please? Or tea? Or...honestly, I'll take anything liquid."

"Coming right up, my lady," my secretary says, and lets herself out of the office.

I meet Jalus's gaze reluctantly. "I'm sorry you had to hear that," I say.

His posture is stiff, his expression bland. "Why should you be? Nothing you say surprises me. I knew this was your intent from the start."

"No, Jalus..." I rub my eyes. "I mean, yes, I did come here intending to do whatever it took to get those trees cut down. But yesterday changed things for me. You have to believe I never would've…that I wouldn't lie about…" Stars, I don't even know what I'm saying. I'm losing him with every word.

Jalus shakes himself, his wings ruffling just enough to let the rainbow flash through before they settle. "I believe it would be best if I guard you from outside the room today," he says, his voice monotone.

He shuts the door behind him gently, but it echoes in my ears like a slam.

Jalus barely acknowledges me for the rest of the day, except to follow me at a respectful six paces behind when I go to the dining hall for lunch and dinner. When I retire to my cabin for a sleep cycle, he takes up his post outside the front door, making no motion to join me inside.

As I get ready for bed, I'm tempted to go outside and beg him. Not the sexy kind of begging, either. The pathetic, groveling kind.

But I don't know what there is to say if, after all that big talk about me trusting him, he still doesn't reciprocate that trust.

So I lie down in nothing but my panties, *because fuck you, alien squir-rels, I'm not ruining another nightgown,* and let sleep take over.

chapter four

jalus

As soon as Sinead lies down to sleep, I reach into my pocket for the stimulant I requested from my mother.

Breaking the wax seal, I wrestle the stopper out of the gourd and put it to my lips. The liquid inside is viscous, sticky, and sour-sweet. I swallow twice and wait for it to take effect.

When Sinead woke on the first day with scratches all over her body, I knew she was marked in the same way her eleven predecessors had been. Each of them complained of amnesia and strange wounds. And then, after three days, they disappeared.

I failed to protect her the first two days. With the stimulant to keep me alert, this is my last chance to save my lady.

Today's awkward silence gave me time to inspect my feelings, no longer carried away on updrafts of lust. It stung, hearing her words to Lord O'Rourke this morning. I had thought, after what we shared, she might finally stand up to him.

But I don't believe she meant those vile words.

The Nade I knew as a child held everyone at arm's length for fear of rejection. But there was a kind, openhearted soul hidden under that brittle shell, desperate for friendship and love. I keep seeing flashes of it, so much stronger and more beautiful now that she's grown into her power.

I'm confident I can coax that side of her into the light. But it *will* take time. I can't let her disappear before she's been given enough space to grow.

The substance works fast. Within minutes, my pulse begins to race. Adrenaline surges through my system, making it difficult to stand still.

It's been thirty minutes since Sinead went to lie down. She must be asleep by now.

Slowly, noiselessly, I push open her cabin door. It feels unseemly to be entering uninvited, but I remind myself that this is for her protection.

When I slip into her bedroom, there's a startled rustling sound. I open my mouth to apologize, thinking she's still awake.

But then, in the light filtering through the window shade, I make out the shape of her, sitting up in bed, breasts bare. Her eyes are closed, her head lolling to the side. She is asleep.

Her breather mask dangles next to her head, held in the prehensile grasp of a creeping vine tendril.

I suck in a breath and start forward, lower hands clenching on the handles of my thorn daggers. More vines shoot out from the floor, finding miniscule cracks in the seedpod to worm their way through. They wrap around my ankles and arms. Thorns prick my skin, a warning.

"Cousins," I murmur, releasing my weapons. Even when being attacked by the trees, I can't bring myself to disrespect them.

The vines encircling Sinead's arms and legs pull her horizontal, carrying her as if on an invisible stretcher, and begin to push her out the window.

They're taking her.

One of the vines puts out a bud, which blooms into a flower before my eyes. The scent is beguiling. Even with the energy from the stimulant coursing through me, I feel my eyelids droop, my breathing beginning to slow.

I let myself slump to the ground as the vines let me go. It takes all my self-control to lie still, silent, as the trees steal away the woman I'm sworn to protect.

When the rustling subsides and all is still, I leap to my feet and bolt for the front door. Following Sinead's scent is not hard; it calls to me, even at a distance. I spread my wings, floating down from branch to branch, thorn-daggers drawn in my lower hands.

They're taking her to the forest floor. My stomach turns, recalling the Old Kin tale. *They sent out their roots to drag him into the depths of the earth. He was never seen again.*

The trees buried that long-ago ancestor because he was beyond reason, unrepentant in the evil he was doing. I didn't know the eleven former ambassadors very well—they could've been just as hard-headed as Berry.

But I know Sinead. They're making a mistake to condemn her.

I just hope I'm in time to stop them.

sinead

IN MY DREAM, I'M BEING CARRIED THROUGH THE SKY. NOT BY JALUS. THE arms encircling me are cold, with fingernails that bite painfully into my skin. I struggle to wake, to roll over and comfort myself in his warm, strong embrace, but there is no waking. Only a cool breeze against my bare skin.

And there will be no Jalus in the morning, some distant part of my brain recalls. *I fucked that up, didn't I?*

It's only because it's a dream that a hot tear leaks out of the corner of my eye.

At last, the dream lays me down on a carpet of soft, wet leaves and moss. I inhale the earthy scent and realize that my mask is gone, allowing me to breathe in the dangerous perfume of Eiris.

Is this a dream? Or am I hallucinating? Surely it can't be real…

I sit up with a wince. Vines wrap around my limbs, their thorns digging into my skin. I watch in horror as they slide, snakelike, to more firmly encircle my upper arm. My instinct is to struggle, to rip them off, but when I try, they only bind me tighter.

Surrounding me are five enormous trees grown in a perfect circle. The clearing reminds me of one of the ancient stone rings I've read about from Old Earth's prehistory. Offerings scatter the ground and

549

hang from the trees' limbs: feathered ornaments, cloth woven from moss fiber, smooth pebbles with veins of crystal knotted into the drape of a necklace.

Vines writhe and tangle all around me. The trees lean in, their branches unfurling to reach for me. I catch my breath, but then force myself to reason through this weird figment of my brain's deepest fears. If the trees wanted to kill me, they could have sliced me to bits already.

They want me to do something. Dance? I don't speak tree language. How am I supposed to know? This feels like one of those nightmares where I show up to a royal ball, but everyone else knows some gossip I don't know, and they're all giggling behind my back.

Funny—I'm usually naked in those dreams, too.

The ground buckles under my feet and I stumble aside, staring as a root rises from underground. It's wrapped around something. What is—

Oh stars. My stomach lurches. *That's Ambassador Cora.*

More roots are worming their way up from the forest floor, carrying the rest of the missing diplomats. Eleven in total. None of them are decomposed, even though some of them have been missing for close to a year. They all appear to be asleep, limp in the grasp of the tree roots that hold them captive.

And now another root is pushing up underneath me, vines holding me in place as it wraps around my legs…

"NO!"

My head jerks up in time to see Jalus descending from the treetops above, wings spread in bright glory. Vines tangle toward him, but he slashes at them with his thorn weapons. His limbs move fluidly, a dancer's grace in a warrior's body. He lands at my side and takes hold of my arms, trying to wrestle me out of the trees' grasp.

"Thank the stars," I slur. "I was afraid this was a nightmare. Maybe now it can be a sexy dream."

Jalus curses under his breath, then seizes what looks like a flask from his pocket and takes a long pull from it. His lips crash onto mine.

I savor the kiss, drinking in his scent. His tongue parts my lips, making my pulse kick up a notch. Then he's passing a liquid into my mouth, something that feels like honey on my tongue but tastes more like kombucha. I swallow reflexively.

The world settles into sharper focus. The way the breeze caresses my bare skin, the sharp pain of thorns digging into my arms and legs…this isn't the hazy fog of a nightmare. This is real. I am awake.

I tug against the roots and vines holding me, but the trees hold me fast.

"They're trying to speak to you in scent-language," Jalus murmurs next to my ear, low and urgent. "They say that this is your last chance. If you won't save them from being cut and hollowed, they will bury you the way they buried all these others."

"Tell them…" My voice comes out high-pitched, words tripping over themselves to come out. I force myself to take a deep breath, to consider what I want to say. "Tell them I'm on their side."

Jalus's eyes meet mine. "I already have."

He believes me. Tears well, unbidden, in my eyes. "I'm sorry I didn't have time to prepare you before that vid-call today. I had to make something up to buy time for creating a real solution."

He leans close to the crook of my neck and breathes deep. Does sincerity have a scent?

I can't stop myself reaching for him. My fingers brush across the wound on his lower arm. It's been little more than a day since he was injured, but it's already nothing more than a raised pink-violet line across his skin. Imperial hospitals would pay dearly to get their hands on that kind of—

Wait.

"Jalus…I think I have an idea."

"Tell me," he murmurs hoarsely.

"The moss." I show him my palm, displaying the scrape from yesterday. It's so well healed, I can barely tell I was ever hurt. "Can it be harvested without harming the trees?"

"In moderation, yes. As I told you, the Old Kin have used it for millennia." Understanding lights his eyes. "You think your father would want…?"

A miracle medicine that millions will be eager to pay him for? *Uh, yeah, I think I can convince him.*

"I can draft a treaty with airtight protections for the Kin and all the Eiris wildlife." I'm thinking aloud, but Jalus's face is alight with hope. "I'll make Dad buy the moss at a fair price from the Kin. That'll cut the expense of bringing contractors and equipment to the planet. Kin harvesters can control where they take from so they don't disturb the ecosystem like outsiders would."

I glance around the clearing at the eleven unconscious ambassadors. "If I can guarantee the trees' protection, will they release the hostages?"

Jalus scents the air. "When a treaty is signed and these people no longer pose a threat, they will be released."

"Fair enough." I hesitate. "Of course, I'll probably have to stay here longer than six months, to make sure Dad's people keep their side of the treaty."

He tenses. "Is that...what you want?"

The Moon Palace already feels like a past life. Lonely, cold, sterile luxury compared with the bright, dangerous, sensual beauty of Eiris and the warm four-armed embrace of a man I think I'm already starting to fall for...

It's a no-brainer.

"Yes. I want to stay."

The man is beautiful when grumpy, but he's absolutely life-ruining when he smiles. The roots fall away from my legs as he lifts me into his arms.

When his mouth meets mine, I'm home.

about mindi briar

Mindi Briar's favorite book as a child was "Commander Toad in Space," an early sign that she was destined to become a gigantic nerd. She lives in the Seattle area with her husband and three cats, two of whom are named after punctuation marks. She will be your friend if you offer tea, or if you want to talk about Star Wars.

She is the author of the Halcyon Universe series, available now.

To learn more, visit www.mindibriar.com

red space

S.C. Grayson

chapter one

natalie

NEVER ANSWER A DISTRESS CALL.

Such a directive was stated in bold at the beginning of every intergalactic freight company's pilots' manual. If a cloud of debris or a psychogenic parasite managed to leave one ship stranded in the incalculable emptiness between galaxies, what would stop it from disabling whoever came to help?

The first step in helping somebody else is to not become a victim yourself, after all. It was a lesson taught to me early in the Space Force's basic training back on Earth.

So, when an orange light began blinking with startling urgency on the proximity monitors of the *Gokstad*, breaking the thick monotony of another day in the cockpit, my heart stuttered. For months, nothing had interrupted the Stygian gloom outside the viewports as I traversed the long quiet between star systems. Now the pinging light of a distress call cut through the stillness as thoroughly as the chiming of claxons on a Space Force Station.

I leaned forward to inspect the readouts, the worn synth-leather of the pilot's seat creaking in protest at my movements. My gaze swept over the control panel, checking how close the disabled ship would be to the *Gokstad*'s trajectory. My mechanical eye projected a series of calculations onto my vision, indicating the incoming signal originated not far from the edge of a passing galaxy, as if the source of the beacon had spun out of orbit and ended up in the nothingness of space by accident.

If a ship was not built for intergalactic travel, like my utilitarian but sturdy long-range freighter, its crew had little hope for survival.

My fingers drifted to the navigation panel but hovered over the controls. Common sense and manuals warned long-haul pilots away from distress signals for good reason. Pirates often used them as a lure for ships transporting rare commodities. Even if the signal was legitimate, I likely could do little to help.

After all, I was just one person: Natalie Jackson, former Colonel in the Earth Space Force turned lonesome freighter pilot.

I glanced over my shoulder toward the large cargo bay of my ship. The lights in the hold remained off, apart from the dim red running lights, leaving them to reflect eerily off the glass surfaces of row after row of empty stasis pods. I wasn't sure which was worse: the lifeless faces of hundreds of passengers kept in artificial sleep, looking almost like corpses as they careened through space, or the knowledge that there was no living soul besides myself for a megaparsec.

Except of course, in that moment, others nearby might be in need of aid. If the source of the distress call held any survivors, they would be the nearest lifeform I had encountered in months. The ache of loneliness throbbed in my chest at the thought of other beings so nearby, likely also lost and isolated in the icy vastness between planets. However, that ache was pushed to the background by the thought of what the ship's passengers might be going through, waiting to see if their distress signal would be answered—the panicked desperation that had clutched my own heart after an invading alien ship had disabled my Space Force fighter, costing me my eye and nearly my life. I wouldn't wish that fear on any being.

The vacant pods in my cargo bay stared at me, their emptiness standing in stark judgement, and my decision was made. I turned to the navigation panel and began making necessary preparations to drop out of hyper speed. Perhaps if I had held the lives of all my passengers in my hands, I would have made a different choice, not willing to risk the safety of those who had no say in the matter on something that might be a trap. But I was deadheading this transport back to Earth—a planet everybody wanted to leave, but nobody wanted to return to.

That's why this job paid so well. That was why I took it, resigning myself to the suffocating isolation of solo piloting. I would need those credits to start a new life, as far away from Earth as possible.

The floor shuddered beneath my feet as the roar of the fusion engines dulled to a pleasant hum. My ears rang with the newfound quiet, even as my stomach flipped at the sudden change in velocity.

I squeezed my eyes shut against the wave of nausea that rolled over me, acid sloshing in my empty stomach. I should have eaten something, but normal mealtimes had fallen by the wayside several weeks ago. The meaning of the cycling chronometer on the wall, and the ideas of normal social morays and even necessary life-sustaining practices like nutrition had disintegrated against the onslaught of isolation.

When the bile in my throat had eased its way back down to my gut, I opened my eyes, only to be left blinking at the sight in the viewport. The *Gokstad* approached the edge of a galaxy, a smattering of stars and planets in the distance scattered across the blackness like tossed confetti.

Much closer than the galactic rim, though, was a starship—or what was left of it. What had once been a sleek black hull was split down the middle, cracks running over the reflective surface out from the terrible rent that had cleaved it in two. I squinted, trying to get a gauge on what type of ship it was.

My mechanical eye automatically scanned the shape and design, comparing it to a reference database. Orange letters scrolled across the top of my vision as I stared at the seemingly lifeless vessel: *Escalon Class Entari Warship*

My eyebrows raised. I had never heard of the Entari before, but the ship, even decimated as it was, was clearly beautiful. If the pieces were joined back together, it would form a sleek, elongated disk, like the body of a stingray. It was much smaller than the reinforced bucket I currently flew, built for speed and maneuverability.

Unfortunately, it was clearly damaged beyond repair.

.C. Grayson

And even worse, such destruction would have left no survivors.

An unexpected pain pierced my heart, as hope I didn't realize I had harbored shattered as thoroughly as the ship before me. I'd hoped for an interruption to the long quiet nothingness of my current existence. I couldn't even hope to salvage the ship and sell the parts, hopefully making enough credits to cut a trip or two off my timeline before I could start a new life.

Now I'd just lengthened my journey for no reason. There were no survivors for me to rescue. Unlike when rescuers pulled me from my damaged Space Force fighter, down an eye but still clinging to life, I had arrived here too late.

I had failed.

Getting the *Gokstad* to fully accelerate the ship to hyper speed again would take hours. I swallowed around the lump of disappointment in my throat, turning back to the control panel and distracting myself by recalculating our flight path.

My finger hovered above the switch that would reengage the fusion engines when the shimmer of starlight reflecting off a piece of drifting debris caught my attention. I lifted my gaze to the viewport once again, and an unmistakable cylindrical shape floated away from the rest of the debris.

An escape pod.

I hurried to run a life-form scan, my heart in my throat as the radar pinged softly through its readout.

One lifeform. Type: unknown.

A survivor.

The *type: unknown* may have given me pause, but it wasn't uncommon on a ship equipped by humans. We knew shockingly little about life beyond Earth, despite the fact humans had fled their home planet for distant worlds by the thousands. *Unknown* was better than what we left behind, and it was better than leaving a survivor to die alone in the depths of space, clinging to the shred of hope that somebody would come.

After days on end of unhurried routine and not enough food, the adrenaline in my blood left me shaky, and my hands trembled as I hurried to engage the tractor beam. The beam locked onto the escape pod, artificial gravity reeling it toward the airlock. With bated breath, I watched the silver cylinder draw nearer until I was sure it approached unhindered by the surrounding debris.

My knees creaked and my back popped as I sprang from my seat, but I didn't care. Pushing the stiffness in my body from my mind, I strode purposefully toward the airlock. I shoved my faded purple hair from my face and tugged at my navy pilot's jumpsuit where it pulled tight around my generous hips and chest, trying to set myself in order as I walked. The pounding of my heart in my ears urged me to run, but my latent military training gripped my muscles and I measured my steps.

Several long years had passed since the adrenaline of battle had last coursed through me. The sizzle of energy and survival instinct had somehow kept me functional then as plasma bolts rocketed past my starfighter, allowing me to return fire against the forces invading Earth.

I wasn't in the midst of war now, though. The ship around me was quiet, not rocked by distant explosions or punctuated by blaring proximity alarms. Still, one overwhelming thought was the same as it had been during my time in the Space Force:

Somebody was in danger, and only I could help them.

I reached the ship's aft section and stopped at the end of the barren hallway. A painful groan of metal grinding indicated that the bay doors opened to allow the escape pod's entrance. I bounced impatiently on my toes as I waited for the titanium-composite door between me and the pod to slide open.

As soon as it did, I stepped forward without waiting for the jets of steam from the environmental regulators to dissipate. I had my gun on my belt, but my worry that whatever would come out of the pod would be dangerous was overshadowed by my need to lay eyes on the survivor—to assure them that they wouldn't perish in the vacuum of space, alone and unmissed.

Though the bay was spacious when empty, the cylindrical pod now dominated the area, giving me barely any room to maneuver. I hugged the wall as I inched around the space, inspecting the pod from all angles. A long minute passed, but no signs of life came from the craft.

Uneasiness worked up my spine, and my hand drifted to the plas-gun hanging on my belt.

The pod's inhabitant should be able to tell they'd arrived onboard a ship by now. The green blinking lights on the edges of the vessel indicated that the external sensors were intact, after all.

Slowly, I eased my gun from its holster, the biosensors on the handle recognizing my palm print and bringing the weapon to life. I gripped it with both hands, the tip pointed at the floor as I inched closer. It wasn't particularly wise to fire a plas-gun in an airlock, but the weight in my hands steadied me nonetheless.

Perhaps a squad of corsairs lay in wait within, waiting to jump out and hijack the ship the moment I let my guard down. Or maybe, whoever was inside was too injured or scared to come out.

I chewed my lips for a moment in indecision, before taking a deep breath. I had come this far.

"You are safely aboard the *Gokstad*, Intergalatic Federation License number RG1013," I said. My voice sounded hoarse from disuse. I cleared my throat and tried to sound professional and reassuring. "I intercepted your ship's distress signal. You should now be able to safely disembark from your escape pod."

The only response was the echoing of my own voice through the bay. I frowned. If I wanted to find out who was inside, it seemed my only way forward was to open the pod myself.

Keeping the gun in one hand, I stepped forward and ran my fingers over the panel of blinking lights on one side of the hull. Next to it, I could make out seams in the exterior that marked the presence of a hatch. The symbols on the buttons were in an alphabet I had never seen before, but a large button with a blinking green arrow seemed a pretty universal symbol for "Open." I pressed it, thinking that after an hour full of gambles, I wouldn't let fear of this last hurdle keep me from rescuing somebody in need. Not when they had been so improbably thrown into my path.

I was rewarded with a hiss and jets of mist that outlined the hatch as the pod depressurized. The sleek silver panel slid open but still no sound came from inside.

Perhaps the life-form scanner had been wrong. Maybe this escape pod had been jettisoned by mistake, and there really were no survivors.

I wouldn't know for sure unless I investigated for myself.

Awkwardly, I clambered inside using only one hand, refusing to holster my gun. As the dim running-lights flickered, casting long shadows over the cramped space, a dark shimmer on the floor caught my attention.

I squinted, only for my eyes to widen at the realization that the dappled pattern of shadows was the reflection of light off glossy black feathers. As my eyes adjusted, the pattern of feathers formed themselves into wings, spread across the entirety of the pod floor. My breath caught, startled by an unexpected sight.

Sprawled across the wings was a man.

Or not a man, for he clearly was not human. But my brain helpfully supplied that he was the most masculine creature I had ever encountered, despite his alienness.

Aside from the black feathered wings sprouting from his shoulder blades, the creature's form was mostly humanoid. What at first glance appeared to be dulled colors from dim light, turned out on second glance to be gray skin, pulled taut over a deliciously muscled torso. An impressive amount of that gray skin was on display, as the alien wore only a loose pair of black pants.

I tore my eyes away from the striking swell of his sculpted chest to look at his face. It, too, appeared mostly human, the features broad but handsome. The only difference was the glimmer of fangs, pressing lightly into a full bottom lip.

His eyes were closed, black lashes fanning over his cheekbones. In fact, he was completely black and gray, including the dark and wild hair that fanned out from his head. I saw only one single splash of color: the tips of his wings shimmered a dark crimson, the feathers there the red of blood spilled fresh from the vein.

I swallowed, wanting to say something, but my voice caught in my throat. Instead, I drifted forward one step, dropping to my knees beside the alien, careful not to tread on his wings. I hovered over him and my fingers trembled as I reached for him.

The pads of my fingers brushed across his cheekbone, but he did not stir. For a moment, my heart plummeted, like a starship shot out of the sky.

He was dead. I was too late.

Tears burned behind my eyes. This was not the first fallen soldier I had encountered, but the sight punched me in the gut, nonetheless. Maybe it was something about the alien's appearance, clearly speaking of strength and grace, that made his lifelessness so jarring.

Then, a tickle against my inner wrist made me freeze. Another second, and it happened again. A puff of air. *Breath,* brushing the hand that still gently traced his face.

He was alive, but he needed my help.

● ＼＼＼＼   ／／／／ ●

I CHEWED FIERCELY on my thumb nail, despite the fact that it was already bitten down to the quick. Under the harsh florescent lights of the med bay, my patient was even more magnificent, but seemingly no more alive. The mechanical aids in the bay had scurried to hook him up to tubes and contraptions, pumping him full of nutrients and hydration within minutes of me arriving with the alien on a hover-stretcher. They seemed unconcerned with him being of an unknown species, apparently finding his anatomy and physiology humanoid enough to proceed with standard protocols. But still the survivor didn't stir. If not for the strength and steadiness of his breathing, I might think my strange passenger had slipped away already.

Most strange of all, he bore no visible wounds on his body.

I tore my fingers from my mouth, berating myself for falling back on the nervous habit, and stepped closer. I turned my mechanical eye on him, taking in the swirling tattoos painted over his torso and upper arms, the black against the dark gray of his skin not offering enough contrast to be seen without the bright lights of the medical bay.

I zeroed my enhanced vision on the designs, and words began typing themselves across my vision in neat orange letters as my mechanical eye ran the patterns through the database.

Markings of the Entari Warriors. High complexity indicative of great skill or royal lineage.

My brows rose. I mentally focused on the words *Entari Warriors* with the odd sixth sense that I had gained since my cybernetic enhancement had been installed. At my will, more information began to appear, and I skimmed through it impatiently.

Perhaps the secret to this male's current state had something to do with his unique biology. While the medical pods of the ship were theoretically equipped to handle most humanoid species, it was mostly tailored to humans. Perhaps it had overlooked some unique needs of the Entari. After all, I had never even heard of the Entari before, and while there were certainly dozens of species common to the Intergalactic Federation that I had never encountered, I was relatively well-traveled.

I frowned at the information from the database flicking before my vision. Little was known about the Entari, as they were a relatively secretive species who tended to not venture far beyond their home planet without need. Given the few attempts to invade and colonize the Entari home planet had been quickly and violently rebuffed, the rest of the Intergalactic Federation decided it was in their best interest to leave them to their own devices.

The sections on culture and biology in the digital encyclopedia were woefully short too, including inconsistent reports of psychic powers that seemed to be unfounded, considering instances of its practice had been documented in a very small number of specific cases. However, my brain stuttered over something at the bottom of the entry:

Entari are known to be blood drinkers. Consumption of blood is thought to be the source of their incredible strength and potentially necessary for use of rumored psychic powers.

Blood. Water and other nutrients didn't seem to be reviving the male, but blood might be the key. It *would* explain the fangs, after all.

I hurried over to the cold storage at the back of the med bay, shuffling through the bags of fluids and medications until I found the few small packs of blood kept on board in case the need for infusion arose.

My fingers hovered over the bags, considering if it mattered which type I took. I didn't even know if human blood would work, after all. I shrugged and grabbed the O-negative. If it was the universal donor for humans, perhaps it would work for the Entari.

Hurrying back to the male's side, I spiked the bag with a length of IV tubing. I pursed my lips for a moment before dangling the free end over his lips. Carefully, I eased the clamp on the tubing partially open. A few drops fell from the rubberized end onto his lips.

I held my breath. He didn't move.

Disappointment fell over my shoulders like a weight, and I sat on the edge of the stretcher, careful to avoid his wings, which laid tucked behind him as neatly as I had been able to manage with his unconsciousness. His enormous body had proved challenging to lift and arrange on a hover stretcher.

Despairingly, I reached out a hand, using a rubber-gloved finger to wipe the crimson droplets of blood off the male's mouth.

As I pressed my thumb against his surprisingly plush bottom lip and dragged it out of the way, the length of a fang came into view, shining pearly white in the bluish fluorescence of the medical bay. I shivered but didn't draw my hand away.

The fangs would indicate the Entari had evolved to drink blood directly from the source. An image of those fangs dug deep into my neck, the male's body pinning me to the wall as he drank his fill, sprang unbidden to my mind. Maybe it was the lack of touch for months on end, but the vision awoke something inside me that wasn't fear.

Maybe the Entari needed fresh blood, and I was the only available donor.

My hands trembled slightly as I shucked off the protective gloves. Maybe I had really gone delirious with loneliness, but I had no reservations about what I was about to do. For some reason, it felt… right. Like a voiceless whisper in my ear reassured me that I was on the correct path.

With my hands bare, I grabbed a scalpel off a nearby cart. I lined it up at my wrist and paused for the barest moment. I looked away from my arm at the lifeless, handsome face before me and pressed down.

My breath hissed between my teeth at the sharp sensation, replaced in an instant by the warmth of blood gathering in the small cut.

Hurriedly, I lifted my arm to his face, a few droplets of blood falling on his exposed chest with the movement. They pooled in the valley between his pectorals, stark against the gray and black whorls of his tattoos.

I pressed the incision to his lips and held it there for a long, pregnant moment. Like most humans after the invasion and near destruction of Earth, I didn't believe in any higher power, but I found myself praying anyway.

His lips brushed my forearm. A hot, wet tongue licked at pooling blood, and heat coursed up my spine. I almost pulled away at the electric jolt that traveled from the top of my head toward my fingertips. Instead, I stayed frozen in place, staring at the Entari's face.

Then his eyes opened, fixing me in a glowing red stare.

chapter two

eacus

COLOR. I COULD *TASTE* COLOR.

I took a deep drag, trying to drown myself in the incandescent taste on my tongue. The blood was metallic and earthy, but at the same time floral, the bottled sunshine taste of summer wine—the kind made from my family's vineyards on the Entari homeworld. I wanted to get drunk on it.

The source of the taste twitched, and my hand shot up to hold it in place, my fingers wrapping around a slender wrist. An arm…

My eyes shot open, and there *she* was.

If her intoxicating blood flooding my mouth hadn't been enough to convince me that the creature I fed from was a perfect match in a mate, then my first look at her face would've been all I needed.

Waves of dark brown hair fading to a startling purple near the ends framed a pale, round face. Her pink mouth hung open in shock, her eyes also wide. Even as distracted as I was by the strength of her blood filling my veins, awakening my *xigia*, her eyes caught my attention. One was brown, the same as the roots of her hair, while one was solid silver, whirring in completely separate movements from the rest of her expression, which seemed to be frozen in shock. A scar bisected the socket with the silver eye, running from cheekbone to brow.

My *xigia* shuddered to life at the combined sight and taste of her, and a shuttered-out part of my mind opened. I took a mental step toward it as I latched my lips around her outstretched wrist and sucked. Her flavor exploded on my tongue once more, strengthening the warmth I felt growing in the newly discovered recesses of my psyche: the consciousness of my mate.

Suddenly her brows furrowed, and she wrenched her wrist out of my grasp.

A pained groan ripped its way from my lips at the loss, but it was drowned out by the fizzle of distress coursing through my mate's newly established presence in my mind.

I sat up so suddenly that the female lurched back and nearly tumbled to the floor. I caught her though, my tail wrapping around her leg as my hands came to cup her face. Her lovely eyes widened in wonder, but she didn't pull away. My wings flared out and came to wrap around us in a protective cocoon. I hadn't yet identified what had caused her distress, but already my instincts drove me to shield her from whatever would seek to harm her.

A shining red glow lit the dark enclosure of my wings. The female's eyes flickered to my chest, and she gasped. My markings glowed a deep crimson. While they had been black all my life, they would now glow every time I fed from my mate.

"You have awakened my *xigia*," I murmured in awe.

"Your…" she started, only to trail off with a frown. "I understand you, but you aren't speaking basic."

I nodded. "The *xigia* bonded us. Over time, we will not even need to speak to understand each other." I hoped she would still speak to me even then. Her voice was lovely: smooth and melodic, lacking the rough rasp of my own.

She shook her head, and her already pale skin took on a ghostly tone. I knew aliens came in all different colors, and some could even shift hues at will, but this pallor didn't seem natural to her. Perhaps I had taken too much of her blood, although the growing connection between us should strengthen her, helping replenish her supply.

Still, I flared my wings to let in more light and get a better look at her. The motion caused her to gasp, those perfect pink lips falling open. My gaze caught on them, but I refused to let myself be distracted from her wellbeing, studying her face carefully, discovering signs of distress in the furrows between her brows.

"Bonded?" she echoed.

I cocked my head. Perhaps her species were not blood drinkers—and perhaps she did not know the significance of such a feeding.

"When I drank your blood... that is how the Entari forge our mating bonds."

Her eyes went round, the silver one whirring in circles so fast I was afraid she might be dizzy. The bitterness of panic bloomed on my tongue, a taste of what my mate felt as our psychic bond blossomed.

"*Mating?* But—but the database said you needed it for nourishment. You were *hurt*, and I was just trying to help you—" Her words came more rapidly, as if in mounting distress, but I hummed gently, stroking her cheeks with my thumbs, and pushing reassurance into the edges of my mind where she had taken up residence. She stiffened against the foreignness of my psychic touch for a moment, but then softened.

"Hurt?" I echoed. I hadn't even taken a moment to think about how I had ended up here—wherever *here* was. From the moment consciousness returned to me, all I could think of was my mate.

"I found you in an escape pod," she explained, her words rushed for reasons I did not understand.

Images not from my memory passed through my mind—from her thoughts—a crashed ship, a stretcher carrying me to an empty medical bay. For now, they were just fragmented pictures.

"My ship encountered an unexpected asteroid field that knocked me off my trajectory while I was headed home from a diplomatic mission to the Intergalatic Federation," I thought out loud as memory returned. "I didn't have time to strap in safely before my escape pod launched. I must have hit my head." My gaze refocused on her still-bewildered expression. "You saved my life."

If the taste of her blood alone had not assured me that this female was meant for me, then her selfless actions would. Not many pilots answered distress calls these days. Most wouldn't have even considered doing so.

"And somehow bonded yourself to me? I don't even know your name!" Her words were breathless.

"I am Eacus, ambassador of the Entari. But you may call me whatever you wish."

"Natalie," she replied, all but panting the word, though seemingly comforted by the ritual of a simple introduction.

A smile toyed with the corners of my lips at the exchange of names, which nearly seemed superfluous given that we were beginning to share thoughts. Although with how little she reached into my mind at this point, I had to assume her kind had no psychic abilities. Perhaps she didn't even realize the connection.

She licked her lips, looking hesitant. "How do we undo the bond?"

I tried not to bristle, but my wings flared at the idea of severing our connection anyways. Once again, Natalie startled, jerking out of my hands that still cupped her face.

"It cannot be undone," I admitted, gently as possible. "Entari mate for life."

Her mouth fell open. "You drink somebody's blood once and it's permanent? How do you survive if you need blood for sustenance?"

"We don't need blood the same way we need food. We eat the same as most other creatures. But sharing blood is the source of our psychic powers. It helps us access our ability to forge mental connections. Thus, we only share blood with our immediate family…and our mates. Drinking from our mates awakens our bond with them, and for some —like it has for me—it awakens our *xigia*, the source of our abilities. A true psychic connection." I gestured to my chest, the whorls and swirls that decorated my body still glowing, but with slightly less intensity than they had when I first awoke. "You can tell by the markings."

Natalie's eyes fell to my chest. I didn't miss the way her gaze lingered on my pectorals and shoulders, and I puffed out my chest for her to admire.

"But I… I didn't mean to. I can't—*I have a life.*" Natalie deflated before my eyes. Her obvious worry and reluctance quickly doused my pride in my physique.

"Then I shall follow you wherever your life takes you." I grabbed one of her hands in both of mine. My fingers dwarfed hers, enclosing hers completely. "Whatever it is you are called to do, I shall do it with you."

The words were unplanned but rang true. While Entari largely preferred not to leave our homeworld, I had willingly taken on a role as ambassador that would take me into space often. The galaxy had called to me, as if I was searching for something that could not be found in my life among the Entari. Perhaps it was my mate who had called out to me, even from across the stars.

Her throat worked as she swallowed, but she did not immediately rebuff my offer. Carefully, I scooted closer to her on the narrow cot where we both sat. My tail, still wrapped around one of her legs, gently rubbed up and down, the tip tracing her upper thigh.

Her breath caught in a tiny gasp, and I smiled.

"Would having me as a mate be the worst thing in the world?" I asked.

She didn't answer right away, but the trail her mind traveled down was clear in my psyche. There was curiosity in her as she took in my muscles and my wings—and my fangs. I widened my smile, letting her get a better look at them, and didn't miss the responding shiver.

Under her curiosity was a hunger. I mentally pushed against that hunger and found that she ached, as if she had not been touched, even by herself, in far too long. And right beneath that ache was an endless well of loneliness. Her longtime solitude echoed so dark and bottomless that I nearly snarled at the isolation my mate had endured.

"No," she said, and I started, nearly forgetting I had asked her a question. "It wouldn't be the worst thing in the world."

Her response came directly to my mind, but I was glad she had said it out loud. The words on her lips made the glowing tattoos on my chest shine brighter for a moment, and Natalie's gaze traveled over them, admiring.

"Would you..." she hesitated, the curiosity in her clearly battling with the part of her that still seemed shocked that she had admitted I might make a good mate. "Would you have to drink more of my blood?"

"Have to?" I repeated. "No. But... feeding can be for more than just healing. It can strengthen the bond. And it can be... quite enjoyable. For both parties."

A tiny gasp caught in Natalie's throat as her gaze traveled back to my fangs. I itched to steal the rest of her breath by leaning forward and scraping my teeth along her collarbone, which had been left exposed by the slightly opened zipper at the top of her flight suit. I ached to let my tail inch even further up her leg, towards her hips. The flesh there was ample, and I was sure it would fill my hands as I pulled her towards me. In fact, she looked like she would be soft everywhere, and I would make a point to investigate everything about her, every secret place, leaving bitemarks to stake my claim.

The tiniest whimper escaped Natalie's lips, and I tensed. One part of the mating bond I hadn't mentioned was the wave of arousal that normally followed a new pairing, born of the psychic bond and amplified by the feedback loop of shared feelings. I myself had thought the claims to be exaggerated, tales told by new couples who just wanted an excuse to stay in bed together for a few days.

I was happy to be proved wrong.

Natalie leaned forward, her face drifting closer to mine. I clenched every muscle in my body, using every ounce of my warrior training to stay still and let her approach me. She had initiated this bond by accident, and as sure as I was that I accepted it, this was her chance to accept it too.

Her breath fanned over my face, and my mouth watered at her smell, already craving more.

An alarm blared, and Natalie reared back, nearly falling off the cot for a second time. I swallowed a snarl as she pushed free of my tail, stumbling to her feet.

"I need to check on the ship," she explained hurriedly. "You just—you stay there and rest. I'll be right back and then we can...um, talk."

Before I could say another word, she turned and left. My mate was gone as quickly as I had found her.

chapter three

natalie

MY FINGERS SHOOK AS I PUNCHED A FEW GLOWING BUTTONS ON THE control panel. Thankfully the alarm didn't require much brainpower to address, simply letting me know that it had been an hour since I had put the *Gokstad* on autopilot. I was honestly thankful for the interruption.

The weight of Eacus's glowing red gaze had been so heavy that it raised a layer of sweat on my skin. His pupilless red eyes should have been unnerving and alien, but instead, they held more feeling than I could have imagined—feelings that reminded me I hadn't been touched in a very long time. Even now, it made me want to strip out of my pilot's jumpsuit just to relieve the heat building in my flesh.

That was another thing. Eacus's touch had awoken something in me that had been dormant for months now. Even something as innocent as his palms cradling my cheeks made sparks dance over my skin. And when his tail—a lion-like appendage I somehow hadn't noticed until I transferred him to the med-bay—trailed up my thigh, I thought I would combust on the spot.

His insistence that we were mates didn't help the roiling inferno building within me either.

Even now, I could feel a foreign, though not unpleasant weight in the back of my mind. Even if I had wished his claims were untrue—which I wasn't sure I did—I could tell he wasn't lying.

The question was, what should I do about it?

Before the alarm had broken me out of my trance, I had been about to tilt my head back and ask him to feed from me again. To open my mind and body to this male I could somehow sense wouldn't betray me or leave me alone ever again.

Thanks to the *Gokstad's* interruption, I had a chance to think on the decision with a clear head. Or I would have, if my traitorous body wasn't begging me to go back and press my lips to his.

Maybe I just needed to give my body what it wanted, and then I could assess the situation with a clear head. After all, it had been months since I last sought release, my desire, like my appetite for food, shriveling up and dying inside me after weeks on end of listlessly drifting between galaxies.

Now that a male—a gentle, muscular, alien male—had banked the fire within me once more, I needed to satisfy it before I could decide anything.

Slowly, I pulled down the zipper at the front of my utilitarian khaki jumpsuit. As I did, my other hand drifted up to cup my breast, large enough to overflow my hand.

But it would fit perfectly in Eacus's large palm.

With that thought, I trailed my other fingers down my now bare stomach. They lingered at the elastic of my briefs, tracing back and forth for just a moment, before dipping underneath.

I had never been one to take my time with pleasure. Years in the military with minimal privacy made release something to be accomplished quickly and efficiently. Now, I didn't waste a second in reaching for my pleasure point for a different reason: desperation.

My core tightened instantly, somehow already wet from the short moments of contact with Eacus—his velvety black and red wings creating a cocoon around me, or his tongue darting out to lap at the blood on my wrist. The thoughts alone made me groan, and I used one hand to brace myself on the control panel while my other fingers quickened their pace.

Somehow, it still wasn't enough. The newfound presence in the back of my mind echoed my arousal back at me, amplifying it in the process.

Slowly, I worked a finger inside myself, and when I met little resistance, I added another. I found myself imagining it was Eacus's fingers instead. His cock.

It would surely be as big as the rest of him.

I hoped it was.

Another desperate sound tore from me as I thrust my fingers deeper. My breath was so ragged, nearly drowning out the subtle hum of the engines, that it took me a long moment to register the sound of footsteps behind me.

I whirled around, finding Eacus standing in the doorway to the cockpit, and froze. Slowly, his gaze trailed down my body, taking in my exposed, heaving chest and the hand I still had shoved into my underwear.

I swallowed thickly.

He took one step farther into the room, then stopped. He stayed there, although his tail flicked back and forth, the black tuft of hair at the end swishing across the durasteel floor. His wings flared slightly, showing off just how beautifully the glossy black feathers shifted to red at the tips.

Blood red.

"You think I couldn't feel you touching yourself, my beautiful mate? Thinking about my cock as you did so?" His words should have made me blush, but they didn't seem scolding. Instead he seemed curious, although the huskiness of arousal tinged his voice.

Carefully, I moved my fingers inside myself once more, and his muscles rippled as a wave of pleasure ran through me.

He *could* feel my actions.

"I..." I licked my dry lips and tried again. "I needed to be sure I didn't just want you because I was starved for pleasure."

The red glow of Eacus's eyes flared for a moment before settling back into their normal brightness.

"Then bring yourself pleasure," he said, his foreign voice practically a growl, although the meaning of his words was still clear in my mind. "Only you must touch yourself until you are sure... bring yourself to release as many times as you need to be certain you want me to feed from you again."

Slowly, he crouched down where he stood, resting his elbows lightly on his knees. The posture was relaxed, but somehow predatory, yet I didn't feel unsafe.

He intended to watch.

Slowly, I began moving my fingers again, pumping them gently in and out. I squirmed against them, but Eacus's eyes didn't leave my face. The heat within me grew, and I stroked faster.

It didn't take me long to work myself up to a fever pitch again, especially with the hunger growing in the back of my consciousness—Eacus's hunger, I realized. It was an all-consuming thing, but he didn't move a muscle. He just crouched there, watching me lose myself in the heat of his gaze with rapt attention.

I was so close, but I needed more. I shut off the control panel and used it as a seat so I could open my legs to give myself better access.

At this, the whirling tattoos on his chest—swirling black before they turned red when he drank from my wrist—pulsed with light.

My breath came from me in hard pants, each one punctuated by a breathless whine. Pleasure climbed up my spine, but I wobbled on the edge, not quite tipping over into my release.

I whimpered, and Eacus's façade broke infinitesimally as he smiled, showing off his glimmering fangs.

"Come for me, Natalie."

And I did.

I cried out and threw my head back as all my limbs shook, glad I had sat down on the control panel, for otherwise I surely would have fallen to the ground. Even as pleasure wracked my body, I felt a thrill of satisfaction that wasn't mine purring in my mind.

Eacus liked watching me come.

When I opened my eyes and came back to myself, I found Eacus standing now, although he hadn't moved any closer.

My ragged breath was the only sound in the room for a long moment.

"Well," he murmured, "was that enough to satisfy you, or are you still thinking about what it would be like to be my mate?"

I stared at him, and licked my lips, searching for my voice after such intense pleasure. A layer of tension had been stripped from my body with my orgasm, but the simmering heat of desire remained. It had only been bolstered by the feelings of his eyes on me as I touched myself.

Slowly, without breaking eye contact, I tilted my head to the side. Carefully, I drew my hair out of the way. The deep purple dip-dye I had attempted in a fit of boredom had faded terribly, but Eacus still watched my actions with feral attention.

He walked toward me, his long legs carrying him across the cramped cockpit in three slow, purposeful strides.

He stopped between my still-spread legs. Carefully, he placed his hands on my thighs, pulling me to the very edge of the control panel. His fingers dug into the ample softness there and I shivered. His tail wound around one of my calves, holding me in place—not that I wanted to move away. Still approaching at a painfully controlled pace, he leaned forward, his breath tickling the exposed column of my neck.

I nearly squeaked, and sparks danced up my spine as his tongue darted out to taste my pulse point. The sensation was followed by the gentle rake of his fangs, making my eyelids flutter, but he didn't break skin.

He pulled back a few inches to meet my eyes, and I felt his question in my mind, his thoughts already coming to me more clearly, despite the fact that he hadn't spoken.

"Yes, please. Bite me," I said, still feeling the need to speak out loud, as if it was imperative for him to know I chose this completely after falling into matehood accidentally.

He didn't have to be told twice, and I gasped as his teeth pierced my skin.

Instantly my eyes rolled back in my head and a foreign sort of plea-sure wracked through me as I choked on a broken moan. I could feel what Eacus felt when he fed from me—*taste* my essence on his tongue, how right it was, and how sure there could never be anybody else who felt like this.

A few long drags from my neck and I was lost in the ocean of his mind. What's more, I was welcomed there, drawn in by curling darkness and desire. I would be held and kept and cherished in this mind.

The vibration against my neck as Eacus groaned brought me back into my own body, although a tendril remained seated in his consciousness. My arousal blossomed anew, and I squirmed against him. I needed more than just his teeth inside me.

I needed *everything*.

Seemingly feeling my desperation, Eacus withdrew his fangs and pulled back from my throat with a moan that revealed how much effort that movement required. I rewarded his action by pulling my arms fully out of my jumpsuit to wiggle it the rest of the way off, removing my briefs with it.

The red glow of Eacus's eyes flared as the rest of my skin became bare to him. My curves were soft and generous these days, but the flare of lust in the back of my mind told me he appreciated every inch.

Eacus's hands trailed up from my thighs, his torso crowding me as he closed the small space he had given me to finish undressing. My skin burned in the wake of his hands, one coming up to cup my breast. It filled his palm perfectly, just as I had imagined.

The other hand traced over my collarbone, up to my neck. The heat of his touch mixed with the warmth of the blood slowly dribbling from his bite, and he dragged his fingers through the crimson liquid.

His gaze bored into me as he smudged his blood-coated fingers across my sternum, and a flare of satisfaction that was not my own rushed through me. I looked down to find that he had painted a symbol onto my skin in my own blood, stark against the pale skin of my heaving chest. The round swirls were reminiscent of the markings on his own skin.

"What is that?" I asked.

"My name."

His answer pulled a whimper from me. This mark was a claim, literally signed in blood. It was a claim I wanted more by the second.

My hands drifted to the ties of his pants, hovering there as I leaned forward to whisper in his ear.

"Make me yours."

eacus

AT MY MATE'S COMMAND, I REACHED BACK AND UNDID THE PANEL OF MY pants that held them in place over my tail. As they fell to a puddle at my ankles, my cock sprang free, so hard it slapped against my lower abdomen.

My mate's presence shuddered in my mind, the movement a mix of excitement and apprehension. I glanced up from my aching member to see Natalie's gaze raking up my length, eyes catching on each of the six silver piercings lining the underside.

I took myself in hand as she watched, stroking lazily up and down. I bit back a hiss at the sensation, as Natalie's fascination with the glide of my piercings under my palm became apparent.

I cocked my head at her, prodding her with a mental question.

"I've never…the piercings will be a first for me." Natalie's tone was a mix of arousal and nerves.

"I promise, it will feel good," I purred, continuing to stroke myself. "I got these for you, even though I didn't know it at the time. Entari warriors get them for their mates. I went along with the tradition, even though I had doubts I'd ever find a mate. I'm glad I did now."

Natalie's throat bobbed as she swallowed, the motion causing another drop of blood to drip down and pool in her clavicle, just above where my name adorned her chest. My mouth watered, despite the taste of her still coating my tongue.

"It's also…bigger than I'm accustomed to." Natalie licked her lips.

A satisfied snarl rumbled in my chest. "And it's going to fill you so well."

Natalie whimpered, and her hand drifted in between her legs again. At that, I leaned in close, fully invading her space once more. This time, her pleasure was mine to give. It was an opportunity I didn't intend to squander.

I let go of my cock in favor of touching her, as it was nearly painful to keep my hands off her for too long. I let my fingers trail up her sides before brushing my knuckles on the underside of her breasts. She arched her back with a shaky gasp at the touch, pushing her perfect chest toward me even further. I rewarded her by tweaking her nipples gently. Her mouth fell open and her head fell back against the star port with a dull *thunk*.

I wanted to keep teasing every last reaction from her, but the sight of her wet lips forming a perfect *O* as she moaned had my neglected member throbbing.

"Turn around, mate." I gave the command both with my voice, and with my mind. "It'll make it easier for you to take me."

A visible shudder ran up Natalie's spine, making her breasts quiver, in response to my instruction. I almost regretted her tight nipples being hidden from my sight as she hurried to comply, but that was quickly overshadowed by the pang of arousal at my new view.

With my right hand, I gripped the base of my shaft to keep myself from spending right there. Meanwhile, my left hand gripped one of Natalie's ass-cheeks as she bent over the control panel. Her flesh gave way under my fingers as I squeezed my generous handful, spreading her open to my perusal.

She was pink and glistening and *perfect*. I suspected the taste between her legs would be just as intoxicating as her blood, but confirming that would have to wait. Right now, her pretty hole clenched around nothing, and I ached to fill it.

My *xigia*'s power, already strong from drinking from my mate, surged within me, making my tattoos flash brightly and my tail swish insistently against the floor. It urged me to claim my mate and deepen the connection that had been forged by her blood on my lips.

I nudged forward, slipped the head of my cock between her folds, coating it in her wetness. She whimpered, falling forward onto her elbows, opening herself to me further.

Pulling back slightly, I slid my length into the cleft of her ass, rubbing it back and forth for a few strokes, letting the wetness I had gathered from her dripping cunt smooth the way.

"Please." Natalie's plea was echoed in my mind as she pushed back into me, grinding her hot sex onto my cock.

I wouldn't make her wait any longer. Not when she begged so beautifully.

With one hand braced on her hip, I reached forward and laced the fingers of my other through her hair, the dusty purple of the ends contrasting perfectly with the deep gray of my skin. A gentle tug pulled Natalie's head back, arching her back exquisitely. My tail wrapped around one ankle, nudging her legs even wider.

As the head of my cock notched at her entrance, I caught my mate's gaze in her reflection on the glass viewport ahead of us. I worked forward inch by inch, feeding my cock into Natalie. I pressed in slowly, letting her soft flesh give way to me even as I itched to bury myself to the hilt immediately.

A sharp smack echoed through the cockpit as Natalie slapped a hand to the star port to brace herself. She bit her lip and her eyelids fluttered, but she held my gaze until I was seated fully inside her wet heat. Her one human eye was half-lidded and glazed with pleasure, and even the silver cybernetic orb, which seemed to constantly flit about, stayed still as she stared at my reflection.

I shuddered, completely overwhelmed by the feeling of oneness. The clenching of my mate's cunt echoed in the back of my mind, enhanced by the feeling of fullness from Natalie. As she rippled around me, I felt the echoes of the pleasure caused by my piercings pressing against the sensitive points within her.

Then, I began to move. With short, slow thrusts, I somehow managed to work deeper, until Natalie was all I could see—feel—*taste*.

The edges between us blurred, until my mind was lost in a transcendent ball of ecstasy.

"*Eacus*." Natalie's voice was a whine for more, and I could deny her nothing. My grip in her hair tightened, arching her back into me even further. Her gaze held mine through our reflections in the viewport, her mouth hanging open and brows furrowed against the onslaught of sensations. I snapped my hips forward once more and snarled at the way her breasts swayed with the motion. I could just make out my name, smudged on her chest in her own blood, in the reflection. The sight spurred me on as my thrusts became relentless. Through her mind, I could feel the way her fingers dug into the unforgiving titanium of the control panel, and the building pleasure at the base of her spine.

My psyche fell into hers, wanting to be surrounded by Natalie in all ways. Her pleasure was mine, and my mouth watered with the craving for more. My hand at her hip snaked around to her core with the intent to stroke the bundle of nerves just above where we met, to stoke her pleasure higher.

Instead, my fingers drifted farther back to where I entered Natalie, tracing over the way her flesh stretched around me. The silver balls of my piercings popped in and out of her one by one. Each one sent a fission of pleasure up both our spines.

A growl ripped its way out of my throat. "I don't think I'm ever going to get enough of the way this tight little cunt strangles my cock."

Natalie's only response was a choked noise between a sob and a moan, but I understood it perfectly. I picked up the pace, pounding into her hard enough to drive her hips into the unforgiving edge of the control panel. She didn't seem to care, pushing back against me with equal force.

Finally, I dragged my fingers up to strum over her pleasure point. Earlier, she had touched herself with quick, vertical strokes and I mirrored them now, gritting my teeth against the thundering approach of my own release.

She shuddered around me, and I redoubled my efforts.

Supernovas exploded in my vision as Natalie's pleasure snapped with a breathless cry.

"Eacus."

The warm, salty taste of blood filled my mouth before I realized I had bitten down on the side of my mate's neck with the force of my release. I spent inside her with an almighty groan, my wings snapping fully open as our joined minds became nothing more than a burning ball of white-hot pleasure.

Mate.

She was my mate in every way now. Nothing in the charted galaxies and beyond would part us now. I would make it so.

The pressure and pain of the hard edge of the control panel against Natalie's hipbones seeped into my mind, gradually, as our brains continued to bleed into each other with little distinction. I gently pulled my teeth from her neck as I slid my softening cock from her, helping her shift away from the panel to ease her discomfort.

I relaxed my grip in her hair in favor of gently rubbing circles into her scalp. Another breathy moan escaped her lips, this one more a sigh of contentment than the cries of pleasure that had come before.

As I took a step back, the sight of my spend dripping down Natalie's thighs greeted me, almost more intoxicating than the blood trailing down her neck. Absently, I trailed my fingers through it before pushing it back inside my mate, her sex still pink and swollen with pleasure.

Natalie squirmed but didn't pull away.

"You took me at my word when I asked you to make me yours," she observed, teasing, but I sensed no regret. Only satisfaction.

"I do nothing by halves," I responded, pulling my fingers from her with a debauched squelch. The sound nudged my hunger again, but for now, the need awoken by the new mating was satisfied. There were other needs that overrode those desires.

The need to make sure my mate was cared for.

"What now?" I asked, stroking the length of her spine gently.

"Well, for now I think we need to clean up and find some clothes," Natalie sighed, finally standing up.

My arms came around her waist as I tucked her back to my front, unable to keep my distance for too long after all.

"I meant where are we headed?" I clarified, gesturing to the control panel before us as I rested my chin on the top of Natalie's head.

The sensation of heat in her face drifted through my consciousness as she realized how thoroughly we had defiled the ship she apparently piloted alone. I sensed no other life forms, and while my psychic powers had not been fully activated until I fed from my mate, they had always been accurate on such broad observations.

"Oh." Natalie let her head fall back onto my chest, looking up at me. "I was just bringing the ship back to the port after dropping off all the passengers at the new colonies."

"And this port is on your home planet?" I asked, sensing a strange sadness creeping into Natalie's psyche. My arms tightened around her, as if I could protect her from it, even though I did not know its source. "I will accompany you there," I assured, not wanting her to be afraid I would be unwilling to follow her to her home.

Natalie shook her head, the purple tendrils of her hair tickling my chest. "Earth isn't home. Not anymore at least. I'll never go back there again if I can help it."

Brief flashes of violence and war rattled through my brain: falling from the sky in a burning starfighter, losing her eye only to have to relearn how to see with a cybernetic one. I didn't mention these images, as I got the sense that Natalie didn't know she had shared these memories with me and had no desire to speak of them right now.

"Then where is your home?" I asked. I itched to know everything about my mate, and hear it from her own lips, even though we were already more intimately linked than I had ever been with another being.

"I don't have one. Yet," Natalie admitted, an aborted shrug an attempt at playing off her pain. "But these solo flights pay well, and soon I'll be able to settle somewhere far from Earth. Build myself a life there."

My heart panged in my chest, and my wings came around both of us in a protective shield once more, as if the black cocoon could protect my mate from the pain of her admission.

"I have a home with the Entari," I pointed out. "I'm not there much, because I've always felt like it was much too big for one person."

My mate shifted against me, and a bubble of hope grew between us, golden and bright and beautifully fragile. But I would protect it until it was solid and indestructible.

"It would feel more like a home with a mate there," I said, hoping she might like the idea. "And our homeworld is so far from Earth that we have never heard of your planet."

Natalie twisted in my arms, turning to face me. Her one organic eye was bright, light shining through like the lonely dark of space had been shattered to make way for a galaxy of stars within her. The heavy feeling in my mind, which I realized now had been my mate's oppressive loneliness, skittered away into darkened corners in the wake of the newfound light of hope.

"If I were at your home, would you be there too?" she asked, only slightly hesitant.

My fingers drifted over the punctures from my fangs in her neck, down to the now smeared tracing of my name on her chest. The sight made my *xigia* purr, the glow of my tattoos flashing to briefly illuminate the enclosed space made by the curtain of my wings. Such markings were a sign that her kind didn't appear to fully appreciate the significance of, but they were as binding of a promise as any I could make.

Perhaps I should be dismayed that it had happened so unplanned —although maybe it wasn't as unplanned as I thought. Maybe the uncharted asteroid that had knocked my ship off course, throwing me into the deep abyss of space on an otherwise uneventful trip, had been sent with a purpose—to put me into the path of this remarkable mate, a woman so unexpectedly wonderful I had never even managed to dream of anything like her.

"My mate, I will go wherever you go," I swore. "From here to the farthest star."

Natalie smiled, and joy bloomed in my heart, amplified exponentially, for it belonged to both of us.

My mate chuckled wryly. "I'm glad I responded to your distress signal."

I pressed my forehead to hers. "Perhaps you have saved us both."

about s. c. grayson

S.C. Grayson has been reading fantasy novels since she was a little girl, and that has developed into a love of writing and storytelling. She is currently focused on fantasy and paranormal romance. She has written several Gaslamp fairytale retellings, and looks forward to publishing additional epic fantasy, paranormal, and science fiction romances.

When she is not sitting in a local coffee shop writing and consuming an iced americano, Grayson is a nurse researcher, focusing her efforts on breast cancer genetics. She lives in Maryland with her loving husband and their two cats, who enjoy contributing to her work by walking across her keyboard at inopportune moments (the cats, not the husband).

S. C. Grayson is the author of the best-selling Talented Fairy Tales and Ballan Desert series, available now.

To learn more, visit www.scgrayson.com

thoroughly thrashed

S. L. Choi

chapter one

eau de orgy

NEITHER MOON HAD YET TO SET, AND I WAS ALREADY AWAKE. I SHUFFLED into the colony's communal dining hub, my jaw cracking on a wide yawn.

Suddenly, freezing-cold air pebbled my flesh, and my nipples to painful peaks. The blast of frigid air knocked me out of my trance-like state. Trembling, I looked down at my naked chest and the shirt I'd just peeled off my body dangling from my fingertips. Cursing beneath my breath, I quickly jerked the shirt back into place. As I did, its soft but stretchy material snagged on the messy bun piled atop my head, pulling it loose.

Fucking pheromones. I focused on breathing through my mouth while I tightened my drooping bun and glared at the alien responsible for the heavy cloud of *eau de orgy* hanging in the air.

Seated at one of the long tables in the otherwise empty room, Thrash shoveled a spoonful of highly sugared cereal into his mouth.

"Damn it, Thrash! Have you taken your compound today?" Without the suppressant made specifically for him, I put that alien's pleasure pheromones at threat level Alpha. Give me serrated spines, poison pinchers, or laser gun sharpshooters any day over five minutes with those unchecked pheromones. "Unless we're down for a colony-wide sex-pile before coffee—which I, personally, am *not*—you need to get that situation under control before anyone else wakes up."

The alien with way too much skin and scales on display than was appropriate for a communal dining hub looked up, a completely unrepentant grin splitting his too-handsome face. "Oops," he said, not bothering to look away while I adjusted my shirt.

Despite the fact I was on the verge of freezing to death—only a slight exaggeration—Thrash wore no shirt. Thick, glossy black hair draped over his obsidian shoulders. My traitorous gaze devoured the way the silky strands danced over his wide, sculpted chest.

He set his spoon in his bowl and leaned back, revealing the ridges of his hard abdomen. I couldn't see below the table, but my mind wandered. *Is he wearing pants?* The man was not ashamed of nudity. As a result, I'd seen—and begrudgingly admired—all of him.

"It's early," he said. "I didn't think anyone would be up yet."

My ice-cold fingers brushed against my ribs, shocking sense into me. My hands had gone in reverse, and I once again had my shirt halfway up my torso. I gritted my teeth. "Will you do something about that smell of yours?"

I crouched to grab the jacket I'd dropped before the pheromone-induced tit-flashing. Shrugging into the light-as-tissue, wool-like material, I went to the Meal Prep X9 and punched in the code for my usual.

"I know it's no big deal to you, but climate control is on the fritz again." I pointed out the obvious. "You and I are on colony habitat maintenance. Go take your compound before the humans among us freeze to death." At that moment, my teeth chattered as if to emphasize my point.

"You know I can control my body temperature. I have plenty of warmth to share with my future mate."

"Thrash..." I poured enough exasperation into his name to fill up the entire Belathar Asteroid Belt. For some reason, among all the women in this colony—in all the sun-scorched solar systems—he had zeroed in on me as his mate.

No matter how sexy I found those scales and horns, I would never be his mate. With my sights set on retirement from the stressful life in the terraform division of the Explore, Terraform, Populate department of UFIS—United Federal Interstellar Space—I'd been dodging romantic entanglements like they were colony raiders since I started this final job. Planet KR-732 was meant to be my last terraforming gig, and I planned to walk away with zero baggage.

Unfortunately, Thrash was a labyrinth of tangles waiting to trap me. He wasn't the first guy to try, but if anyone could tempt me away from my dream of settling down on an empyrean planet at the edge of some sleepy solar system, it would be Thrash. With or without the hormones, that guy did it for me on every level.

I enjoyed meaningless, for-the-sake-of-pleasure sex as much as the next deep-space terraformer. Existing on the edge of one lonely galaxy after the next meant there was little difference between meaningless and meaningful. With six days to go, I wasn't willing to trap myself—or my heart—in something I couldn't easily fly away from.

The X9 beeped and a basket slid out from beneath the machine. I grabbed the protein loaf, the heated plate warming my freezing hands as I made my way to the table and slid onto the bench seat opposite Thrash.

He watched me, a half-smile curving his lips. He took another bite.

My gaze dropped to the flex and feathering at the edge of his strong jaw. He had exaggerated features, which individually were strange to look at, but put together created a face almost as irresistible as his pheromones.

A scaled ridge that arrowed down from his hairline to end between his brows crested his forehead. Two sets of horns rose from just behind his hairline, accentuating the length of his oval face. His nose ran in a perfectly straight line from brow to tip without a bump or curve between. And then there were those lips. The bowed top lip and a lower lip with just enough padding to nibble. I'd had dreams about what those lips would feel like between my thighs. Moving against my clit, his tongue delving into my pussy.

"Victoria?" The snap of his tone and use of my full name rather than the abbreviated *Tori* implied this wasn't his first attempt at getting my attention.

Cold air blasted my shoulders. I looked down, to my shirt and jacket laying on the floor. My breath was all fluttery and damp, warmth gathered in my panties. Frustrated in every sense of the word, I shrieked and stomped my feet beneath the table. "Thrash, go take your compound."

He shoveled another spoonful of sugar disguised as cereal into his mouth. His species required a shocking amount of sugar. "Almost done."

"Damn it, Thrash, I am team lead of this base, and I'm ordering you to go. Now!" Five halls opened onto the common room. I jabbed my finger toward the branch which led to his living quarters, snatched my top from the floor and shook it in his face. "Before I use this shirt to strangle you."

He rose from his seat. Thankfully, he wore pants. "You win, my feisty little human."

"I'll show you feisty," I mumbled through the stretchy material as I jerked my shirt on, over my head. Maybe this time it would stay on.

Thrash spoke from the doorway. "I keep hoping."

I smoothed my shirt into place, opened my mouth to respond, and froze with one arm in my jacket. Instead of the hot retort sizzling on my tongue, only a strangled squeak came out.

He'd turned his broad back toward me and headed for his quarters. Thanks to his innate ability to regulate his body temperature and withstand a climate control system on the fritz, I got an eyeful of broad shoulders, rippling muscles, and a tapered torso as he disappeared down the hall. The *Earth Sunrise* setting of the overhead lights set his glossy black scales ablaze and lent his dark hair a blueish hue. Lights turned on as he passed beneath, while the lights behind turned off to save energy.

When the final light illuminating his impressive form went dark, my lungs deflated on a huge rush of relief. Ever since Thrash unexpectedly joined the team several months ago, I had been trying—unsuccessfully—to beat my hormones into submission. His frequent attempts to score a date and more didn't help. That guy had the smooth moves to back up his party-time pheromones. Worse, since this job was my swan song to terraforming, I hadn't jumped into another's bed or allowed anyone into mine since touching down on this planet.

To his credit, Thrash never used his intoxicating aroma to coerce.

Even when a wovvel—an indigenous, ferret-like rodent that continued to find a way inside the habitat—ate his supply of scent-blocking compound and it took a full three days for the colony's biochemist to engineer a new batch, Thrash had kept himself locked away in his quarters.

Unfortunately, by the end of the second day his pheromones had spread through the filtration system, resulting in the largest sex-party this side of the sixth moon.

Desperate to avoid an emotional landmine, I'd barely made it to my quarters on wobbly knees and locked myself inside. That night I'd rode my fingers so hard, I had to wear a wrist brace for a week.

Thrash had never asked how I'd hurt myself, but when he picked up extra shifts in my place until my brace came off, it was clear he knew, and he didn't feel good about what he'd inadvertently done.

Dangerous. That strong, sweet man was dangerous, to my sex drive and to my heart.

chapter two

forced proximity

BACK IN MY QUARTERS, I QUICKLY PLAITED MY PINK-TIPPED, PLATINUM-blonde hair before undressing. Instantly, the cold drilled into my joints, and an ache built in my temples. I rushed through the routine, applying an anti-atmosphere aerosol spray blended for the different levels, specific components, and toxins present on planet KR-732. The concoction countered any burning, blistering, itching, and eroding effects that might linger in the air. Chances were slim of running into a pocket of original atmosphere, but better safe than sorry.

Less than five minutes later I was thoroughly covered with the protective spray and clothed in my UFIS issued, spandex-like suit with its ridiculously impractical, decorative gold buttons. Despite the thin material, the uniform was designed to absorb and reflect body heat back into the skin as well as provide some protection from physical damage. A laser blast would burn a hole straight through, but claws, teeth, and regular blades would have a difficult time.

On my way out of the room, I reached for a cannister of company-issued repellent spray. After a brief pause, I also grabbed my weapon belt off the hook next to the door and settled it around my waist. The comfortable weight of the twin holsters for my precious plasma-edged daggers rested against my hips and outer thighs. The weapons were more than I would take on routine system check, but less than what I would bring into a raid. This outage didn't fit the typical raider attack pattern, but there was always a first time for everything. No reason to be reckless.

A rectangular panel mounted on the wall outside of my quarters remained dark until I pressed my palm against the opaque glass. Green light flared, outlining my hand. The locking mechanism *thunked*. As much as I liked my fellow crew, I didn't trust a bitch not to rifle through my shit. They'd steal my snack cakes, smuggled wine, and smut books that got me through these long, celibate months in a hot nanosecond.

I pressed a thumb to the center of the screen, and two more locks clicked into place, these on the top and bottom to prevent door removal. This wasn't my first terraforming rodeo. I knew all the tricks.

Geared up and dressed, I hurried to the dining hub. The closer I drew, my nerves came alive, turning my insides jiggly. The upcoming job and forced proximity with Thrash would be difficult. The Phase Four clean up team was due in less than a week. Until today, I thought I'd skate to the end of this job without the risk of temptation, but outside the habitat, there would be no escape from being near Thrash. Even with his pheromone blockers, I wanted to rip off his clothes. Any other day I could retreat to my quarters and get myself off on fantasies of holding onto those horns while I rode him. Or the one where—

Facing my direction, with his long, muscular legs stretched in front of him, Thrash looked up as I entered the room. Those delicious lips curled up at the corner, like he'd seen into my thoughts.

Oh shit, did he have that ability? My steps faltered. I covered the misstep by rearranging my holster belt. We locked eyes, and I shot him a scowl while I thought hard about shearing off the tip of his horns with my plasma dagger.

His expression remained the same. He didn't twitch.

My chest loosened and shoulders relaxed. I should have known. Telepaths were exceptionally rare. They wouldn't be wasted on a terraforming team. Though this was arguably the most vital part of the

ETP, it was also the most dangerous, with the highest casualty rate. Another reason it was time for me to clock out for good.

"Come on, we need to get the crawler loaded and get to the cave." I brushed past Thrash's legs and headed for the hangar.

chapter three

raiders in our midst

WHILE THRASH GUIDED THE CRAWLER TOWARD OUR DESTINATION, I focused on our surroundings. Miles of lavender sand and newly sprouted trees with blond trunks and teal leaves pulsing with biofluorescence dotted the landscape. Beyond those rose the lumps bumps of dark purple rocks that eventually led to a small mountain range and the cave which was our destination.

Everything appeared normal, but just because it seemed unlikely the climate control fault was due to raiders, that didn't mean it couldn't be. This sector of the planet was almost completely terraformed and habitable. The cleanup team was scheduled to arrive this week to initiate the transition to the final phase of the ETP. Guards would be placed around the equipment until the populate team arrived and permanent installments were erected.

Forty-five minutes into our trip, and I shifted uncomfortably in my seat for what had to be the hundredth time. After this morning's hefty dose of sexy-time pheromones this situation was less than ideal. Thrash was big in both height and breadth. My damn shoulder hummed from where it made constant contact with that man. Trapped in this cockpit designed for two average-sized people—which he was not—and I was ready to wriggle out of my own skin to escape the tiny crawler cabin.

Retirement was on the horizon, so close I could see the circled date on my calendar. Only six days, four shifts left, and after today, none of them would be with Thrash.

The vehicle slowed. I peeled my gaze from the view and glanced at Thrash. His hair was pulled back and tied off at his nape, revealing the stress lines on his face. "What's wrong?"

He jutted his chin in the direction we were headed. "We've got a problem."

Brows pinched, I squinted into the distance. All I saw was the beautiful terrain of KR-732, nothing alarming. Damn aliens and their enhanced senses.

I punched a button on the crawler's dash, and my side of the windshield zoomed in like binoculars. A joystick allowed me to pan around the area but with limited functionality.

As the magnified image on the screen slowly rotated to the right, something moved. I shot upright in my seat. Adrenaline twisted the muscles tight along my spine. Just a smudge of pixels, but there shouldn't be anything in the vicinity to cast a moving shadow.

I was afraid to blink, lest I miss whatever was out there. My eyes began to water. I sat stiff and still in my seat, staring hard at the screen, waiting for the image to pan fully to the right. Pixel by pixel, the screen focused.

Near the mouth of the cave that was our destination, several blurred shapes separated from the stony surface. "Son of a bitch," I muttered. The pixels continued to smooth and coalesce into something recognizable. Dread bubbled in the pit of my belly. The figures vanished off the edge of the area I'd focused on, but before they vanished, it was apparent they were humanoid.

"Raiders." I spat the single word like the curse they were.

Thrash made a growly grunt of agreement. The bioluminescent rings in his horns pulsed with the colors of a flame—a bright, rolling gradient of crimson to white gold. Briefly, the interior of the crawler glowed like an inferno.

My heartbeat pulsed in my throat. I swallowed and focused on my breath. Damn it to the nine suns and back, I'd only brought my daggers. They were good weapons, and I was lethal with them, but depending on the size of the crew, they weren't enough. I looked at Thrash. As usual, he carried no weapon. My nostrils flared with frustration. Was this man anything more than an aromatic aphrodisiac? How did he even end up on this team?

Since he joined, he'd been in dustups with raiders and survived, but I hadn't witnessed the skirmishes. I had no idea how capable he was in a fight. Sure, he was very large and visually formidable, but his continued existence could be because of his capable crewmates.

In the distance, at least three more blurry figures moved across the screen.

Why couldn't they come next week? I'd be gone, retired, and drinking too many starfruit daiquiris on the toasty beaches of the first empyrean planet I parked my space cruiser on. Some preferred Goldilocks planets, but I built these perfect worlds, and by the stars, I would live on one. Curse this entire situation to the black hole void.

Two more figures came and went while at least three entered the cave.

"Three raiders just entered the cave," I said. "I've counted at least seven—" A cluster of figures exited the entrance, carrying something enormous and huddled too close together to count their precise numbers. "Scratch that. We're at more than ten. If we don't play this right, we might not walk away."

There was a high probability we were about to follow in the footsteps of all the terraformers who had fallen before us, but if we could stop the raiders before they took all the life-sustaining machinery, we could at least save the colony and all the work we'd accomplished.

"I will handle this. Stay behind me." His tone was flat and authoritative, as if his words were law.

"The fuck I will." I swiveled in my seat and blasted a glare at the arrogant alphahole next to me, taking up too much space. My hand slipped from the console joystick and the front screen bounced back to regular viewing distance. "Maybe you don't know this about me, but there is a reason I'm team lead," I said, my words clipped. "Through all the jobs I've worked—and there have been a lot—I've fought off my fair share of raider parties."

We drove on, inching closer and closer to the raiders. Silence swelled inside the crawler's stuffy interior.

Thrash glanced in my direction and did a quick second glance, apparently realizing my lack of commentary and my death-glare meant I was waiting for some form of acknowledgment. "I reviewed all the team member's files before I joined."

Again, weird, since he was a nobody joining the most decorated terraforming team in the entire ETP, but whatever.

"Then you should know this planet's distance from anything habitable under jurisdiction of United Federal Interstellar Space has resulted in a higher than usual number of attacks."

He nodded. "That is the reason I was recruited. Allow me to handle the raiders."

A whooshing sound swept against my eardrums. My blood boiled through my veins while fire erupted in my chest. "Don't you worry your pretty little horns. I can take care of myself. Through all the raids we've endured on this mission, I hold the highest kill count." I sneered. "Perhaps *you* should stay behind *me*."

Beneath his forehead plate a deep *V* formed while iridescent light spiraled up Thrash's horns. Thin lines of fiery bioluminescence traced the edges of the flexible obsidian scales across his broad chest, arms, and shoulders. "I admire your bravery, but I will not allow you to be harmed."

"You will not *allow* me?" My voice went shrill, and I clenched my fists against my thighs. "I had no idea you were so damn sexist."

"You are my mate. I must protect you."

"Ugh! Not the mate thing again? If my response to your advances wasn't already a hard no, it would be now with this 'stay behind me, little woman' attitude."

As he steered us off the main path, he glanced in my direction, giving me a head-to-toe appraisal. His lips flattened, but he nodded. "You're right. I know you can handle yourself, but it's damn hard for me to disregard genetic instincts."

I softened, if only a little, at the apologetic tone and acknowledgment that I didn't need his protection.

The crawler rolled and bumped over the rocky terrain, shaking like an asteroid buster hard at work breaking up a belt. To avoid unintentionally piercing my tongue, I kept my jaw locked until we reached smoother terrain.

Finally, Thrash navigated the vehicle to a stop behind a rocky outcropping. "This appears to be a sizable group of raiders. Large enough they had the balls to power down the colony support while they worked, knowing it would draw attention."

Climate control was part of the colony support. The mammoth piece of machinery ran ultra hot. To stay cool, it siphoned icy runoff water from an underground iceberg deep below the cave. Hours were required to fully cool the equipment and drain the water.

I frowned. "Which means they probably have vibration detectors to know when we're coming."

"Precisely." He turned off the crawler and looked at me. "We need to go on foot. I will handle the crew outside."

I opened my mouth to argue, but he held up his hand.

"I will handle the crew outside because I am equipped to take on groups. Of the two of us, you know the machinery better and should get inside and get it back online as soon as possible."

Mollified, I closed my mouth and nodded. "Agreed."

It hadn't escaped my attention he'd pivoted his opinion, allowing me to put myself in harm's way. Confronting whatever was inside that cave was arguably more dangerous than what he would face outside. Warmth bloomed inside my chest.

Red alert! Red alert! Warning bells pealed in my head. I needed distance between me and this man before he ruined all my plans. As soon as we handled this situation and the machines were back online, I planned to lock myself in my quarters and avoid Thrash like the Sipphian Plague.

The crawler's doors retracted. I slipped on my helmet and climbed out. The helmet was no longer necessary for atmospheric reasons, but it provided an extra layer of combat protection. I hadn't expected to need it but was grateful for the last-minute equipment grab.

Thrash rounded the vehicle and stood next to me, far too close for comfort, a look of concern on his face. "Let me go first and draw their attention. I am not minimizing your abilities," he said before I could object. "We don't know how long climate control has been down. That endangers habitat stability and everything we have done here. You need space to handle the machinery. A distraction can give you that."

My hands clenched into fists at my sides. Damn him, he was right. If we had a full team here, we would be splitting up. I needed to get over this thing I had for Thrash that insisted on blocking out all logic. "Agreed. What's the signal for me to move in?"

He brushed a loose strand of hair peeking out from beneath my helmet behind my shoulder. I didn't shy away from the contact.

"You will know it when you see it." He dipped his head and gave me an intense look. "Stay alive, my mate."

Thrash sprinted into the predawn haze at an almost incomprehensible pace. The shadows quickly claimed his form.

Only after I'd lost sight of him, did it occur to me I hadn't objected to what he'd called me. *Mate.*

chapter four

sweet and spicy

HIDDEN BEHIND THE ROCKY OUTCROPPING, TOWARD THE MOUTH OF THE cave, I stared hard into the dusky, predawn darkness. Shadows from the mountain ridge lay in heavy layers across the path.

No raiders had emerged from or re-entered the cave. No movement came from the shadows. My gaze swiveled back toward the dark, silent space Thrash had disappeared.

I flexed my hands against my thighs, itching to unsheathe my daggers and run after him.

It wasn't that I didn't believe he could handle himself. Despite my earlier doubts, I knew he could. No matter what landed him on my team, he had arrived with official paperwork. Someone, or a group of someones, high up in UFIS had sent him our way, which meant he was more than capable of taking on raiders. I would trust any members of my team.

But I'm afraid for Thrash.

That could prove to be a deadly mistake. Space was a wide-open, wild frontier and UFIS had countless highly dangerous departments. The ETP, specifically, the terraforming division, was in the top five. As a terraformer, the quickest way to get dead was to grow soft emotions.

I cared for my team members, but it wouldn't hurt me if they fell. A stiff drink and good night's sleep and I could move on. Cold? Maybe. Necessary? Absolutely.

Staring into the silent distance, I knew it would break me if Thrash fell. Stars take me, but I'd known it within five minutes of meeting the guy. I could almost feel my dreams withering on the vine like the Elfusian sugar grapes he so loved.

A fierce burn ignited in my thighs from crouching so long. The discomfort pulled me from my melodramatic thoughts. Where was the signal? I shifted, settling into a comfortable position.

As I sank to one knee, a brilliant light erupted from the darkness, bathing the surrounding area in shades of red, orange, and yellow. The ground trembled from a concussive blast. Small stones hopped along the path from the force. Somewhere, men and women screamed.

A trio of raiders burst from the cave and sprinted toward the chaos.

Thrash's dark, impressive form stood out in stark relief at the center of an explosive light show. Even from this distance, the rings of bioluminescence flaring on his horns and between his scales were visible. Waves of light rolled away from him in a clearly directed path. More screams sliced through the murky dark.

At the last moment, he turned toward the trio closing in behind him. Another wave of light rolled away from him and collided with the raiders. I could just make out their crumpled bodies hitting the ground.

Holy oblivion! Equipped to handle groups, indeed. Another pulse, and this time I felt weight against my bones. I sucked in a breath. No wonder he didn't need weapons—that man *was* a weapon.

"That *has* to be the sign," I muttered. Tensing, I stood and cast a final look in Thrash's direction. Shrill screams continued, but Thrash had moved out of sight, probably herding the raiders toward their ship.

I turned my focus on the cave entrance, confirming no new raiders had joined the party. I had to hurry.

With quick, methodical movements, I rounded the corner and sprinted across the open space between the rocky outcropping and the shadowy entrance. No stragglers emerged as I approached, but that didn't mean the cave was empty.

Sliding to a stop on the silt and gravel, I pressed my back to the stone wall next to the entrance. After a few focused breaths to slow my erratic heartbeat, I eased forward to peek inside.

Empty. My lungs deflated and ballooned on a relieved breath. The smell of ozone, freshly churned soil, and barely-there evergreen notes rushed through my nostrils. I'd always loved the smell of a newly terraformed planet on the precipice of population phase.

Releasing the breath, I double checked the area behind me was still empty. No raiders, but also, no Thrash.

Damn it! This wasn't the time to lose focus. Thrash was a big boy— a very big boy. He could handle himself.

I pressed the heels of my palms into my tightly squeezed eyes until I saw stars behind my lids.

Refocused on the task at hand, I opened my eyes and slipped my daggers from their holsters, swiping my thumbs over the bio triggers to ignite the plasma blades. A glance inside confirmed the space was empty. I entered, daggers first.

Thrash's assault had indeed emptied this entire level. Either the raiders were overconfident or stupid. Or they were neither and there was a group waiting below who had been warned to expect company.

A single ramp led deep underground to the machinery. Nipping my bottom lip between my teeth, I looked from the cave entrance behind me, back to the dimly lit ramp, keenly aware I could be walking into a trap.

I approached the ramp, pausing to study the multiple sets of deep grooves carved into the hardpacked earthen and stone floor. The spitting plasma from my blades cast dancing light across the floor and on the walls.

If I were instructing my team, I would tell them to wait. While Thrash had taken on a larger number, he was in the open with plenty of places to take cover. The machinery room below was a small, enclosed space.

Cognizant that my only chance against an ambush lay in a silent approach, I carefully placed one foot in front of the other as I started down the ramp. My gaze swung between the gouges in the path and the dim length of tunnel in front of me. When the equipment had been installed, we'd rolled it in on platforms. Other than what was necessary to install the machinery, there had been no damage to the cave. This was all the raiders' doing.

Judging by the number of destructive trails leading up the ramp and out of the cave, my gut told me this place was empty. But there was a lot of equipment which meant there were no certainties.

One long, sloping turn after another crept by before pale pink light spilled onto the ramp from overhead. Those were the emergency lights. The fucking raiders had severed the power completely.

The lights flickered. With the total shutdown and so much equipment on the grid, the backup generators would have a hard time keeping up.

Still, no sound rose from below, so I continued my descent.

Despite the perilous situation, my stupid brain grabbed the reins and steered back to Thrash. He hadn't yet joined me. Was he hurt? Was he dying? *Was he dead?*

I was an idiot. He was fine. Or he wasn't.

Neither changed the fact that I had a job to do.

Pausing to center myself, I stared hard down the ramp while I drew in a deep breath and held it for a count of three. Nothing moved below. There were no sounds. I blew out for three seconds, and repeated.

Thoughts of Thrash, of empyrean planets and daiquiris scattered. I was close enough to the base of the ramp that soon the light and hiss from my daggers would alert anyone below of my approach. Naked daggers would have to do. I brushed my thumbs over the triggers and paused, allowing my eyes to adjust to the deeper dark of the tunnel. Tension ratcheted up my spine.

I rolled my shoulders, and holding my weapons in front of me, crept into the machinery room. Now when I entered, no noises echoed from anywhere. It was empty.

In the faint glow of the emergency lights and bioluminescent leaves of the subterranean trees similar to those on the surface, my gaze tracked from one dormant machine to the next, cataloguing the damage. Parts and tools were strewn across the room with several devices in various stages of dismantling. This setback would probably extend my time left on KR-732, but it wasn't catastrophic.

The raiders knew what they were doing, cracking open each machine and taking the most valuable guts—circuits and wires that could be sold on the black market or melted down for their rare precious metals.

I shifted my focus to the habitat regulator, a silent goliath against the far wall set between two stunted trees. Many people, including raiders, thought the planet stabilization equipment was the most important. They were wrong.

If the colony habitat failed, the mission failed. Habitat maintenance was of the utmost importance. The station was airtight. After five hours of downtime, all emergency power would be funneled to oxygen filtration, which had already happened judging by how cold it had been inside.

Enough heat still radiated from the colossal machine to prevent it from being taken apart. Pale teal light from the tree's bioluminescent leaves revealed the undamaged metal panels. Another hour, maybe two, and it would have been loaded and flying off planet. The length of time it took to power down and safely disassemble the habitat regulator was the reason raiders never messed with it. Not unless they were stupid or came prepared with a large team, like this group had.

Too bad they hadn't been prepared for Thrash. The corner of my mouth curled in admiration.

Heavy footsteps pounded on the ramp behind me. I spun to face whatever was coming. My thumbs brushed over the bio-triggers of my daggers. White-hot plasma flared along the blades. The momentary burst of light blurred out the enormous figure running toward the room. I crouched, ready to attack.

My muscles tightened but relaxed when I recognized the outline of Thrash's horns and broad shoulders before his strong features came into view. Unspent adrenaline ping-ponged through my body. I again brushed my fingers over the blades' triggers. The plasma along the edges went dark, and I holstered the weapons.

Thrash ran straight for me, invading my space. He laid his heavy hands on my shoulders. "You are safe?"

"I'm fine. No one was here." Instinct pushed me to rebel against his protective nature, but I didn't step away.

He lifted a hand to cup the back of my neck.

I swallowed. Maybe it was the surge of adrenaline with nowhere to go, but I was tired of fighting, tired of resisting his advances.

Suddenly, Thrash's head came up and he turned to the entrance, trying to push me behind him.

I heard it too. The rush of feet on the ramp, the rustle of clothes. I scowled and stepped around Thrash, standing at his side.

Raiders gathered on the ramp—five, seven. I lost count.

"This is bad." My focus shifted to the light already building beneath Thrash's skin. It flared around his scales in intricate tattoo patterns and illuminated his horns. Panic fluttered in my chest. "You can't use that down here. It'll bring the cave down on top of us."

"I am aware." He huffed a breath. "There must have been another ship. I was too concerned with your safety to do a thorough sweep of the area."

Sweet and spicy anger bubbled inside me. I was furious he hadn't done his job, hadn't trusted I could do mine, but weirdly touched my well-being meant that much to him.

Someone stepped forward from the group and tossed something in our direction. The object's distinct rattle and thump echoed off the ramp walls.

A small round metallic orb rolled toward us. Neon red flashed around its bulbous center.

My sluggish brain recognized the concussion grenade at the same moment Thrash projected a pulse of light towards the weapon.

They collided, and the cave imploded.

chapter five

pheromones gone wild

CONSCIOUSNESS CAME SLOWLY, AS IF SWIMMING THROUGH A LUGUWART slime swamp to reach the surface. My head throbbed with a dull ache. I groaned and snuggled deeper into the velvety heat surrounding me. My hand rested against a hard, hot surface that rose and fell beneath my touch.

The most delicious scent filtered into my nostrils; spicy and smooth, musky and sweet. *Sex*. It smelled like how mind-blowing sex should feel.

I knew that smell. My eyelids fluttered and snapped open.

"Pheromones," I croaked and licked my dry lips.

"Shh." Thrash gently brushed hair from my face, tucking it behind my ear. He drew his legs up, curling me against his chest. "It can't be helped, but I won't take advantage. We can take measures if it gets to be too much."

Too much? How did that alien make it through life, inciting orgies everywhere he went? Apparently, he couldn't go a full day before his blockers wore off. He hadn't arrived with any form of preventatives when he joined the team. What had he done before?

I pushed upright in his lap, away from his wonderfully naked chest but froze when the room tilted.

"Careful, Tori. Blowback from the explosion caught you on the temple." He shifted to sit behind me, bracketing my body with his legs and keeping his hands on my shoulders for support.

That explained the throbbing in my head and lack of helmet. Protocol indicated Thrash remove the gear and check for damage if I was unconscious. I leaned forward, away from his supporting form. Another wave of dizziness crashed over me, and I swayed.

His hands tightened, holding me steady. "Take it slow."

"Storage—"

"Was mostly wiped out by the raiders," Thrash answered my question before I could finish.

Blinking the grit from my eyes, I looked over the room. My gaze rose to the emergency lights mounted along the ceiling, still intact. The shock-proof casings on the lights had saved them, and the dim illumination allowed me to quickly assess our situation. The doors on two of the three large storage closets hung crooked on their hinges. They'd been completely cleared out. Even the awful never-goes-bad packed meals were missing. Dents and holes peppered nearly every piece of machinery. Debris and dust covered everything. The entrance to the ramp had completely caved in.

We were trapped.

I wouldn't panic. Not yet. It was only a matter of time before our continued absence would be noted back at the base. Since the climate control was out, the team would know where to look. The danger lay in the damage to the tunnel and the cave system as a whole.

If it was only the tunnel, we could be out by the end of the day, but if the integrity of the cave system was jeopardized, things would get tricky. It could be a month or more before they could safely dig their way inside.

Thanks to Thrash's body heat, the cave's frigid climate wasn't an issue. The underground ice would be difficult to reach but solved the question of hydration. My gaze slid toward the ravaged storage closets. Food was another issue. It had been a long time since I'd looked inside, but hopefully something remained in the untouched inventory.

Resigned, I sucked in a deep breath. Unprepared for the sultry scent that invaded my senses, a white-hot bolt of lust arrowed straight to my core, causing my pussy to clench.

Sweet, scorching solar systems! Slowly, my locked and straining muscles relaxed.

Thrash scooted forward, his groin behind my ass, broad chest against my back. The scent of him was *doing things* to me.

Squeezing my eyes shut, I bowed my head. My hair fell forward, hanging heavy and loose over my shoulders.

I laughed quietly to myself. On the bright side, it wouldn't be long before I wasn't concerned with food. Thrash's pheromones would soon be all-consuming, and I would be consuming him.

The touch of his fingers against my neck as he moved my hair behind my shoulder sent a cascade of shivers over my body. He drew his hand down my back to rest against my spine. "Are you okay?"

Not trusting myself to speak, I nodded.

"You won't like this suggestion, but I can bind you here and go to the other side of the room." Gently, he gripped my chin and turned my face so that I could see him over my shoulder, seated behind me. "It's the best I can do. I'm sorry."

Laughter grated against my raw throat. "How do you live like this?"

"I don't."

My brows drew together. "What are you talking about? If you aren't popping those pheromone blockers like candy, the base is a nonstop sex party." Not that anyone but me complained. "I thought Drakovian could control their pheromones."

Like a weapon.

"Of course we can," he said. Treating me as if I was woven of atohi yarn—fragile, delicate, and beautiful—he drew the back of his knuckle along my jaw. "But once we meet our mates, we lose control. It's a biological mechanism that ensures we attract our partner. This is how I know you are mine."

Something inside my chest cracked open. His touch and his words swept inside, while his scent continued to build, faster than I'd ever experienced. With each heavy beat of my pulse, my core tightened, and inner muscles clenched. I was a goner. "It could be anyone on the team."

And damn if that idea didn't turn my stomach. What was wrong with me?

"My pheromones did not slip the leash until I met you." His hands continued their gentle caresses, roaming along my throat, my shoulders, down my ribs and up my back. "And I met you last."

He was right. "I'd been on a remote job."

"A *solo* remote job." He clarified. "I was with the entire team for two days before you returned, and my pheromones flared." He smiled, and my gaze dipped to those kissable lips. "You, Tori, are my mate."

He inched back then, and I felt the loss of his touch like I'd stripped off my clothes. Bare, naked, and vulnerable.

"If you're near, I won't be able to keep my hands off you." His voice was deep and rough.

Exactly how I wanted him to fuck me.

Holy void! Where had that come from? Flustered, confused, and also never more sure of something in my life, I shook my head. I knew where that came from. I'd thought about having him inside of me from the moment I'd first laid eyes on this beautiful man.

I'd just returned from a remote mission and was greeted by my overly excited team who informed me that we had a new crew member. Annoyed at being assigned a new member without any notice, I went to learn who UFIS had the audacity to send and found Thrash exercising in the heavy gravity room, muscles flexing with exertion, and that glorious body glistening with sweat.

Immediately, I wanted to know him on every intimate level, and I knew I was in deep shit. I'd taken every opportunity to avoid him since.

And now we were trapped together in a cave. It was like the universe conspired to make this happen.

Thrash braced as if to stand. "If we are going to take precautions, we need to do it now."

I shook my head. "We don't have to do that."

Behind me, he went still. "What are you saying?"

For someone so sure of herself, I had a helluva time putting what I wanted—no, needed—into words. "Stay."

He didn't move. Fine tremors of restraint shook his body.

"I want you, so fucking bad, but it's the pheromones making you say this." His laugh was more of a growl. "I want your taste on my tongue, and my cock inside you, filling your tight, wet pussy, making you mine. I need it with the same violence of a newborn star, but not against your will. I will not coerce."

Weird thing for an alien from a race built for coercion to say, which was reason number five-hundred thirty-three he'd worn me down. I envisioned him doing everything he'd just declared and felt dizzy. My thin breath came out in quivering pants.

Time for full disclosure—for the raw truth. "It's not about the pheromones." Unable to meet his eyes, I tore my gaze away to look straight ahead, still keenly aware of his all-consuming heat at my back. "I want you. I've wanted you from the moment we met, but thought if I gave in, I might never walk away from this life. Maybe not even this planet. But right now, who knows if we'll walk away from this cave."

He went so still I'd believe I was alone if I wasn't trapped between his muscular legs. For a man who never missed a chance to come on to me, his brain crashed harder than a dimodian satellite when I gave him explicit permission.

"If that wasn't clear enough, I'm telling you I want you." Still, he didn't move. Had he fallen asleep? I twisted at the waist and angled my head to where I could see him seated behind me. Heat raced under and over my skin. I met his burning gaze and told him exactly what I wanted. "Fuck me so hard they'll hear me screaming your name from the base."

chapter six

foreplay for days

THRASH DIDN'T MOVE, BUT HIS INCREASED TENSION WAS OBVIOUS IN THE veins standing out on the slope of his shoulders and neck.

If someone told me this morning I would have to convince the al to have sex—

"Tori." His explosive breath heated the back of my neck. My v ne was so raw, it sounded like he was in pain.

His arms came around my middle, pulling me back until his groin pressed firmly against my ass. A wave of dizziness spun my head that had nothing to do with the hit I'd taken. The thick, hard length of him throbbed against my backside.

I laughed a little. "I didn't think you carried weapons." His size was considerable, and it had been so long.

Chuckling, he gripped my jaw and tilted my head to whisper in my ear, "I plan to destroy you." He bit down on my earlobe, skirting the edge of pain. "And you'll beg me to do it again."

His words short circuited my brain. My heart seemed to swell in my chest, crowding my lungs, turning my rapid breaths thready. Part of me wondered if this was really happening. I'd heard about head trauma and lucid dreams.

"Brave words." I rolled my hips, grinding against his cock. The pulsing heat pressed between my ass cheeks and the base of my spine nearly undid me. No, this was too real. I was awake and this was happening—*thank all my lucky stars*. "Prove it."

Thrash raised his arms from my waist to grip the neckline of my uniform. A rending sound hit my eardrums as he ripped my shirt from collar to waist. The dumb, superfluous gold buttons popped off and hit the ground, and I loved the sound of those little *plinks*. An official UFIS shirt meant to withstand blades and bullets, and he'd torn it in half, like tissue. The ruined shirt hung off my shoulders, its loose, frayed edges tickled my ribs.

Cold air buffeted my bare flesh, reminding me that without functioning machinery, this cave would quickly plummet to the same temperatures as the underground ice.

He released the halves of my torn top to skate his hands up my ribs. I shivered and moaned as he filled his large hands with my heavy breasts. Stroking upward, he took my aching nipples between his fingers and pinched.

Electricity zipped from his touch to my clenching core. My back bowed. I threw my head back against his shoulder, thrusting my breasts into his palms. "Again," I said.

"Mmm." His delight rumbled against my ear. "I knew you'd like a little pain," he whispered and squeezed my nipples.

Gasping, feet flexed inside my boots, my heels pressed against the hard-packed dirt and gravel floor. Damp heat flooded my undergarments. I panted, "Never been into it before."

"A first time then." He flattened a hand against my stomach and glided it downward to cup me through my pants. "Let's discover what else can make you scream."

"Sounds like a challenge," I said, and reached behind me. Wedging my hand between us, I curled my fingers around the outline of his cock—his astonishingly thick cock. *How was that going to fit?* His hips bucked, the friction from his movement doing my work for me. I smiled. "I bet I can make you scream first."

"Fuck. You're on." He wrapped one arm around me, caging me. His muscled bicep covered my entire middle while he worked magic with his other hand, rubbing his fingers toward my entrance and dragging them back until he pressed my clit through my pants.

The room seemed to tilt.

My hips jerked, but I quickly locked down the reaction. This was fun. He'd have to work for that scream. I let out a breathy little laugh. "My turn."

The squeeze between us was tight, but I guided my hand over his pants, down his length. The material gathered and smoothed beneath my palm until I could curl my fingers beneath the base of his shaft and cup his balls.

He grunted and jerked. His bicep flexed against my abdomen and his hand cupping my pussy spasmed.

I bit my lip to hold in the scream begging to escape and banged my head against his shoulder.

"Enough," he growled between ragged breaths.

My lips curled in a triumphant smile. "I knew—"

In one quick motion, Thrash let go of me and took hold of the front of my waistband. A soft snicking sound preceded the muffled thump of my dagger holster hitting the floor. Another tearing noise filled the room, and my pants sagged open. He pressed his fingers into my damp curls and parted my slick folds. "You are so fucking wet. Can you feel that?"

The sound of my pleasure came out as a hiss between my teeth. Something low in my belly pulled taut. I started to run my hand up his shaft, but he grabbed my arm and pulled it out from between us.

"No more games. Let me do this for you." Thrash released my arm to gently grasp my throat, holding me still while his free hand dipped between my legs. He pulled me against him, molding my back to his chest. Even through my shirt, his scales radiated enough heat to warm my chilled flesh.

I swallowed. My throat bobbed against his palm. This intimacy was something I'd resisted but thought about since I'd found him working out, sweaty and breathing hard. I'd gotten out of there as fast as I could, but I'd had a look. The man had been invading my dreams ever since. His impressive body covering mine. That thick dick I'd glimpsed when he traveled naked from the shower to his quarters, that I felt right now branding itself against my backside, filling me. Fucking me.

Holy constellations! This wasn't a dream. This was the real deal. My body quivered and tensed with anticipation.

"Relax, Tori." His pheromones flared, so powerful my muscles went loose and head fell back to rest against his shoulder.

The smell of him invaded deeper and deeper with each breath I drew, until his scent filled every cell of my being. I went boneless against him. My core felt hot and liquid—*ready*.

"Yes. Like that. Mmm." His hum of arousal was a level of sexy that defied description. He began tracing light circles around my entrance, not quite giving me what I wanted.

I gripped his thighs while my trembling legs fell open, inviting him inside.

"That's a good girl."

That did it. I whimpered and squirmed beneath his touch. My nipples tightened to the point I was pretty sure they could cut glass. They ached in the best way. "I swear, if there isn't some part of you inside of me in the next minute, I might combust."

He chuckled. With his large body curled around me, he leaned over my shoulder to press his cheek against mine. Our ragged breaths mingled. "Scream for me," he whispered and plunged his finger inside of me.

My hips bucked, and I gasped, nearly drowning beneath a wave of instant, intense pleasure. After so many fantasies about this moment, the feel of his long finger deep inside of me was almost unbearable.

Thrash dragged his finger back, nearly withdrawing, and reversed the action, pushing inside. Over and over, harder and faster. Each time he delved into me, his thumb circled my clit.

Harsh pants and the wet, sucking sound of his finger slipping in and out created a symphony of sex inside the cave. His heat surrounded me. His scent filled me.

My legs shook. I was close. So close. His hands were big and fingers strong, but this wasn't enough. "More," I demanded.

"If you insist." He pushed a second finger inside of me.

I tried to look down, to watch his pumping fingers, but the hold he had on my throat, the light grip of my jaw, prevented that.

A growl of frustration left me. "Still not enough," I said and wiggled my ass against his cock. "I thought you said you'd make me scream?"

The deep chuckle that vibrated against my back sent a cascade of shivers over my body, my nipples tightening once again. "Feisty little human. I've got what you need."

A third finger joined the party, stretching me. My core clenched, and I shuddered.

"Better, but not enough," I panted, completely undercutting my claim. It was enough. Everything was so damn good, but I wanted his dick inside of me, not his fingers.

I swallowed, once again feeling the pressure of his palm against my bobbing throat and tiny bursts of pleasure ignited everywhere we touched.

His lips brushed the shell of my ear as he leaned over my shoulder and whispered, "Tell me that after you come."

My eyes flew wide as his hand fell from my throat.

Freed of his hold, I tipped my head forward and watched his fingers working against me—inside of me.

He flicked my clit while his other hand continued to plunder my pussy. The pace grew frenzied, wet fingers filling me and withdrawing. His bicep flexed against me, and I felt him everywhere—behind me, inside of me, next to me as his ragged breath filled my ears. He moved his hips, griding his cock against my ass.

My body tensed and pants grew thready as I watched his fingers move toward my clit. He flicked and rubbed that ultra-sensitive bundle of nerves hidden between my folds.

Every nerve ending inside of me coiled. My legs shook as my core clenched and clit throbbed.

"I'll have that scream now." His words were a growl against my ear as I watched him push inside me, to the last knuckle, and felt his fingers curl.

Lungs seizing, my breath stalled in my throat.

At the same moment he stroked my clit, his other fingers hit that magic spot deep inside of me.

A scream tore out of me, so loud and long my throat burned. Every muscle pulled taut. My feet flexed. "Stars, yes!" I ground against his hand, felt my orgasm gushing over his fingers.

Waves of pleasure rolled in like a relentless tide, crashing against my senses over and over. White noise filled my ears. Bright lights flashed behind my eyelids like the lifespan of a planet, waking and dying and being reborn.

"Your pussy feels so good. So tight and hot. I bet you taste even better." With one wide hand splayed over my stomach, Thrash pulled his other hand free, fingers soaking wet with my arousal. "This is another way to know you are my mate." I heard the smile in his voice as he brought his fingers to his lips.

My eyes went wide.

"Your cum will be the best thing I've ever had on my tongue." He shoved his fingers in his mouth.

"Oh, fuck me," I groaned and twisted to watch.

"That's the plan," Thrash said and resumed licking and sucking his fingers like they were popsicles. "Amazing. You taste better than Elfusian sugar grapes."

The sight of his tongue tracing his fingers wet with my juices sent my insides spiraling into erotic chaos. I fisted my hands on his pants, balling the rough material against my palms.

"I…I want to taste you." I sounded so damn breathless. Probably because I was. My lungs felt as if they were filled with something lighter and fizzier than oxygen. Seated in the muscular *V* of Thrash's thighs, I twisted further at the waist, trying to look at the thick erection pressed against my back, still hidden inside his pants. That didn't seem fair.

A smile of pure, wicked delight bent one corner of his lips. "Better than butterscotch."

He knew butterscotch was my weakness. "Liar," I challenged.

His eyes narrowed and smile grew. Devious dimples pressed into his cheeks.

Uh oh. A moment of warning rattled in my brain. I tensed to move.

Suddenly, he had one hand under my butt and the other on the back of my neck. "I'll grant your wish, but I want to taste more of you."

"What—" I squealed as he pushed me forward and flipped me onto my back. The hard-packed dirt and gravel shifted beneath my weight. Tiny spikes of pressure pushed against what remained of my shirt and pants.

I'd never dreamed of allowing myself to be so utterly dominated, but I didn't fight this, and damn did it feel good. Thrash was different —special. Deep down I'd known that from the moment I laid eyes on all six-feet-four muscled-inches of him. That's why when capitulation came, it was easy to give in. I wanted to surrender, and I willingly handed over control. That alone told me I was already in too deep... *and I didn't care.*

As Thrash got to his feet, my gaze traveled up his body, locking onto the ridge behind his pants and the motion of his deft fingers unhooking the fasteners at his waist.

Shoving off his pants and undergarments, he stood over me gloriously naked. Every inch of him—*every inch of him*—was on mouth-watering display. His stiff cock jutted forward, veins standing out over the thick shaft. A dot of precum dampened the head, brilliant against his sleek, obsidian skin. He took hold of himself and pumped. The moment he gripped his cock, the same otherworldly shades of flame that rushed beneath his flesh and illuminated his horns before things exploded, flared in swirling tattoos of color around his shaft.

My eyes went wide. "I like danger as much as the next terraformer, but I'm not sure I'm on board with putting explosives in my vagina."

Thrash barked a laugh. "Don't worry, you'll enjoy this one. My *oreha* is my very essence, and it pulses with my emotions. Right now, it pulses for you."

nirvana

THRASH DREW HIS THUMB ACROSS THE HEAD OF HIS COCK AND GLIDED HIS hand down the shaft.

My gaze followed the path of his hand—down, up, down. I couldn't look away if I tried.

He quickened the pace, milking another glistening dot of precum to the surface.

Core tightening, I moved my legs restlessly, clenching my thighs together. He was so fucking thick. From about halfway down his shaft to the base, he couldn't completely circle his cock with his fingers... and Thrash had big hands.

My breath shook on my exhale as I sat up on my elbows. "You promised me a taste."

At my words, his *oreha*, that fiery essence burning inside of him flared from his horns to his cock beneath the surface of his skin. For a moment, his fingers tensed on his erection and the smooth glide of his hand faltered.

"It's only fair I do the same." From my reclined position, I reached for him, but he stepped out of reach. I laid back as he moved behind me. "Where are you goi..."

Words evaporated on my tongue as Thrash stepped over me, facing

625

my feet, and knelt over my face. With a knee on either side of my head, he bent forward. His balls hung low behind his shaft that jutted toward my lips. He pushed his hands under my butt, and gripped my cheeks, spreading me, forcing me to draw my legs up for stability as his pinkies teased the rim of my asshole and his index fingers found my tingling entrance.

I drew my knees up slightly, letting my legs fall open like a butterfly, exposing my most intimate parts to him.

"Your cunt is so beautiful." His breath brushed over my clit. Hot and wet, his tongue followed and pushed inside of me.

"Sweet solar orbits!" My back bowed. It was too much coming at me all at once.

He laughed against my pussy, the sensation sending a riot of carnal chaos coursing through me. His cock bobbed with his laughter. Its head met my lips, dampening them with droplets of precum.

Pheromones hit me harder than a freighter collision. The scent was richer, heavier, muskier. A spasm of pleasure short circuited my synapses and my grip on his thighs tightened, driving my short, blunt nails into his flesh.

Reflexively, my tongue darted out to capture his essence, and *I tasted him.* My eyelids fluttered, and I savored the indescribable flavor filling my mouth. Sweet and salty. Soft and velvety. I moaned as his taste seemed to sink into my very DNA.

Mate. Well, fuck me…

He was doing exactly that with his tongue. He spread me with his fingers while his tongue drove in and out. "You taste like nirvana, Tori." His lips and breath tickled that ultra-sensitive bundle of nerves as he spoke. "I knew you would."

"Nirvana," I repeated and drew my tongue over my cum-dampened lips. He was right. If paradise had a flavor, this was it. "Better than butterscotch."

It felt like he was everywhere all at once. He drove his tongue inside my drenched tunnel while ghosting a touch along my clit.

Panting, I tried to focus on his cock. The shaft grew thicker from head to base. Sex would work, but there was no way I'd fit the entire thing, or even half, in my mouth. I wrapped my fingers around the base while I drew the head between my lips and sucked.

His hips jerked in response and hands tightened where he held onto me, fingers pressing into my openings.

The sensation left me gasping, and I pulsed my grip on his shaft. "You're so big. So thick." I dragged my fingers up his cock while I sucked the head, taking as much into my mouth as I could.

"That's perfect." His voice was deep and ragged. "Just like that."

It wasn't enough for me. I sucked again as I glided my hand toward the head, but this time I released his shaft from my mouth and followed the path down his hard, hot erection with my tongue and teeth.

"Oh, yes," he groaned, his lips moving against my pussy.

I drew my hand and tongue back to the smooth, rounded head of his member, sucked, and repeated the action. Increasing the pace, I sucked, licked, and nipped. His flavor spilled onto my tongue each time I sucked.

His pheromones ballooned into the air around us, adding to the pleasure of his tongue and fingers delving into me. Time turned fluid, stretching and filling with the sounds of our pleasure.

This moment—the feel of him, the taste of him, his touch—was all I knew. All at once, everything seemed so vast, yet so small.

"I'm going to come," he growled.

"That's what I'm waiting for." I sucked harder, faster, and shifted my hand to cup his balls drawn tight with his need to climax and caressed his perineum.

"Tori!" His body tensed as he shouted my name. Hard ridges of muscles and veins stood out on his sweat-slick flesh while firelight pulsed beneath.

Drawing my tongue around his cock, I sucked on the head while I rubbed the sensitive flesh between his balls and his ass.

"Come with me," he growled. There was no time to object before he closed his lips over my clit and sucked.

All my senses narrowed to that pulling sensation. My toes slipped over the edge of the metaphorical cliff. "Please," I begged, and increased my ministrations to his shaft.

"You taste so fucking good." He sucked again, harder, and drove a finger inside me.

With the hyper-sensitivity and swelling pleasure centered directly where Thrash used his talented tongue, I didn't know how I focused on his cock, but I took as much of him as I could into my mouth. The sound of his pleasure pushed me closer to the edge.

I swirled my tongue around the head as I drew back. "So close," I panted, moving my hips, simultaneously trying to squirm away from and closer to his mouth.

Another wave of pheromones rose and ripped into me. From my clit to my core, the intensity stretched like a rubber band, ready to snap. I squeezed my eyes shut while I applied every sensual pleasure in my arsenal to his dick.

Thrash shoved a second finger deep inside of me and curled them into my g-spot as he sucked on my clit.

Everything I was drew inward, focused on that singular sensation. The universe paused. Time stilled. All at once I came apart, exploding on a scream.

"Tori!" He followed me over the edge. His hips jerked and he came. Cum sprayed onto my chest, throat, and into my mouth, hot, sticky, and delicious.

I swallowed. The flavor of ecstasy slid down my throat. I licked my lips, wanting more, and proceeded to lap at his erection until he groaned.

At the sound, another orgasm tore into me, or maybe it was the same one. Squeezing my eyes shut, I tilted my head back and rode the waves of undulating pleasure.

Lost in a haze of wanton delight, I barely noticed Thrash withdrawing his fingers from my pulsing core, but once removed, I was keenly aware of the absence of *him*.

Before I could form the words to object, I felt the molten, silky drag of his tongue over my center, lapping up my cum.

My chest shook as a breathy whimper left me. My bones were soft and liquid, my muscles hot and loose.

"Delicious," he murmured against me. "Your pussy is more beautiful than any nebula."

He rose, carefully stepping over me and away. Cold air swept over my bare skin thanks to all the torn clothing.

"Don't go," I mumbled the sleepy protest. The damp remnants of my arousal and Thrash's ministrations between my thighs exposed to the cold air caused me to shiver. My arms felt like sandbags attached to my shoulders, but I summoned enough energy to reach for him.

There was no telling when—if—the team would find us, but in this moment, I didn't care, so long as I was wrapped in Thrash's arms.

"Don't worry, I'm not done with you yet." He brought his big body down over me and nuzzled my neck, inhaling deeply. "I like the smell of me on you." His guttural voice sent another shiver through me for an entirely different reason. He worked his way up my throat, and then his lips were on mine.

The kiss was slow and teasing. A fizzy sensation tickled my chest. Lips parted, we shared breaths before his tongue pushed inside. The taste of our pleasure mingled on my tastebuds as our tongues stroked and swirled.

Slowly he pulled back. A few lingering pulls on my lower lip and he ended the dance.

A satiated smile curled my lips. My body felt heavy in the best way. I could sleep for days. Maybe I would hibernate in his arms until help arrived.

With my eyes closed, I drew lazy circles on his bare back. His scales were warm and smooth beneath the pads of my fingertips. A pleasing texture: hard but pliable, like a thin shell over thick leather. I drew my hands lower, where the scales transitioned to velvety flesh layered over slabs of hard muscles.

I could have been enjoying this all these long, lonely months. Why had I resisted? Because I was a stubborn idiot. Multiple orgasms didn't negate the fact that I was ready to be done with this life, but I was open to a conversation about the future—a future together.

Thrash found my neck again and delivered a soft kiss. "The floor is hard, and your clothes can't take much more." He rose and strode out of my line of sight, toward the single intact storage closet. Teal and pink light reflected on the glossy black scales layered over his shoulders and down his back, transitioning to flesh at the bottom of his ribcage. The moving light show of pink and teal was only interrupted by the swish of his dark hair.

"You ruined them first," I mumbled to his retreating back and forced my stiff body to bend as I sat up on my elbows. There was no way I would miss the opportunity to watch his gloriously bare backside. The muscled divots of his exceptionally firm ass flexed with each step he took. That man had a scrumptious derrière, and I had the ridiculous urge to take a bite.

"Hate to see you go, but I love to watch you leave." *And I can't wait for the return view.*

Completely out of character, I giggled and tried to pull the sides of my torn shirt together while I waited. Not because of embarrassment—I had great tits—but because without Thrash's body heat, the cold from the ice beneath the cave clawed under my skin. None of the machinery worked, so there was no ambient heat there, either.

At least we'd made it here before the raiders could do anything more than remove the ignition switch to the regulator. An easy fix if Thrash and I ever got out of here.

The reality of the situation sank in and the same concerns I'd toyed with earlier rose to the surface. By now the day team would be awake. They'd know Thrash and I had left to fix the problem, but when the habitat only grew colder, they'd realize something went wrong and eventually come looking. Who knew how much of the cave came down and how long we'd be trapped.

"Fucking raiders," I mumbled and flopped backward. "Son of an arnax hornet!" I winced and immediately sat up. Thrash wasn't wrong about the ground. My front might have been exposed, but he'd torn my clothes, not removed them, and my back had been protected. He'd been bare-legged, and his knees must be killing him.

I hugged my arms over my chest and tried to control my trembling limbs. *This sucks. All of this fucking sucks.*

Well, not all. Aside from the trapped-and-might-die part, I just had the most mind-blowing orgasms of my life, and his cock hadn't even been inside me yet. What would that feel like?

Could that thing fit inside of me?

It had been a long time since I'd been with anyone, and I would be tight. He'd used three fingers on me, but his girth would stretch me much more. Oh, well, what good came without a little pain? Besides, a whiff of those pheromones and I'd be sopping wet.

Thrash jogged into sight, several industrial blankets piled in his arms, dick swinging and slapping his muscular thighs.

One look and I was slick and ready.

i'm not sorry

THRASH'S HOODED GAZE LINGERED ON MY EXPOSED FLESH AND ROSE TO read my expression. Light spiraled up his horns and flared across his chest beneath the scales flexing with his movements. "For a human, you have remarkable stamina. I, on the other hand, need a moment to recuperate."

"Hey, don't flaunt it if you aren't about to use it." Holding the waistband of my pants together, I rose and relieved Thrash of several blankets, finding a pair of heavy-duty work pants folded on top. "Thank all the celestial bodies! I wasn't sure how I would walk out of here holding my clothes together." *Assuming we walk out of here.* "Don't suppose you found a shirt?"

"Right there." He jutted his chin toward a shapeless pile of rough canvas bunched on the ground as he finished fastening his pants.

I glanced at the indicated shirt and scowled. On two different occasions, contamination spills had forced me to change into the generic work clothes we kept stashed in the lockers, and they were not comfortable. "Scratchy but warm, I guess."

Thrash's beautiful lips curled into a smile as he came over and slipped my torn shirt from my shoulders. He used the material to gently wipe away what remained of his sticky cum on my face and chest.

"Thanks." My stomach fluttered at the thoughtful gesture.

He deposited a kiss to my forehead and set to work piling blankets on the ground. "You don't need to wear any clothes if you don't want to. I told you before, I can keep you warm." He winked. "It would be my pleasure."

I stood, removed my boots, dressed, and put my boots back on faster than I'd ever dressed before. No longer afraid I would freeze to death on the way to the restroom, I raced for the water closet in the corner. If there was one thing to be grateful for trapped in this cave, it was the natural running water fed from above to the subterranean flora on this level and the ice deposit below.

Feeling about ten pounds lighter and moderately cleaner, I jogged to the blanket pallet Thrash had created, toed off my boots—because I wasn't a heathen who wore shoes to bed—and climbed beneath the covers. I found the protein bar and tube of hydrating gel Thrash had placed next to my side of the blanket bed. *I guess it will be a slow starvation.* I chuckled at my gallows humor and quickly consumed the protein bar and gel tube before tunneling beneath the blankets.

The covers were warm, but Thrash was warmer, and I wiggled toward where he lay in the center of the makeshift bed. I drew in a deep breath, smelling him—just him. "Are your pheromones gone or am I just used to them?"

"Now that we are mated, they are under control." He smiled and gently brushed a tangle of hair from my face. "Do you know how happy I am?"

"I can guess. You know, we didn't technically *mate*." I returned his smile, but when I met his eyes, the intensity in his simmering orbs sent an unfamiliar feeling wiggling through me. Embarrassment? No. Living in close quarters with a large team very quickly cured everyone of any shred of self-consciousness. Worry for our situation? No. The possibility of death came with the job, and I'd made peace with that long ago. Hope? Hope for what? I was so close to retirement, to achieving all I'd wanted, but did I want more?

Question after unanswered question circled my brain. I frowned and rolled onto my side, facing away from Thrash.

"Our essences were exchanged. By my species definition, we are mated." He curled a heavy arm around my middle and pulled me against him as if I belonged there. He'd done it so often in such a short span of time, it was easy to believe I did. His heat radiated through the scratchy clothing, warming my back.

Instead of enjoying the smooth, silky feel of his flesh and scales, I had thermal-lined burlap rubbing on my ass. Damn it, what had I been thinking? "Not the sexiest description, but I get it." Whether we were mated or not was still debatable, but I understood his meaning.

A puff of air ruffled my hair as Thrash nuzzled my neck. "I would apologize for trapping us here with my *oreha* pulse, but I'm not sorry." He flexed his bicep, giving me a squeeze. "Look what I got out of it."

Smiling, I laughed. "Always good to experience sexual pleasure before you starve to death."

"You are more than my pleasure. You are my mate."

For once, I didn't argue his claim. I wasn't completely convinced, but I wasn't so stubborn not to recognize the signs. Whatever this was between us was more than a few good—*really fucking good*—orgasms. From the moment I gave in, I'd felt safe with him—happier, lighter.

In my thirty-two years of existence in the infinite universe, I'd been with plenty of partners. There had even been one relationship I'd almost walked away from terraforming for, but none had given me the starfruit daiquiris-on-the-beach feel I'd been chasing all my mostly lonely life.

Being tucked inside Thrash's arms felt even better.

Damn if I hadn't run headfirst—or pussy-first—right into that entanglement I'd spent the last couple years fervently avoiding.

I sighed and snuggled against my personal radiator. A renewed thread of worry flared in my chest. I'd been so distracted by, well, *distractions*, that I'd let myself forget we had bigger concerns. "The colony habitat can run on backup power for a month, but we can't. We should catalogue whatever rations are left down here."

"Mmm." Thrash mumbled sleepily into my hair.

My brow pinched. "Aren't you concerned about our situation?"

He chuckled. "I'm enjoying our situation."

"Sure, it was great and a long time coming, but have you considered what happens tomorrow? What about next week?"

Laughter vibrated his broad chest against my back. "No. I could not have put together a single coherent thought with my face buried in your luscious cunt and your hot mouth on my cock."

My thoughts came to a screeching halt. His declaration sent a tight, pulling sensation from my core to my clit. I squeezed my thighs together and tried to forget the soft appendage nestled against my backside. His groin was warmer than the rest of him, and despite the thickness of these uncomfortable pants, I felt his heat through our clothes.

"Okay, fair." My brain was still half-lost in the clouds, but I was team lead for a reason. "We need to make a plan. First, how many rations did you find?"

A groggy, mumbling chuckle ruffled my hair. "So full of questions."

"I am. I'd like to survive to be full of other things." I wiggled my ass against his dick, just in case he hadn't picked up on my not-so-subtle inuendo.

His fingers flexed on my hip. "We have the rations to survive. I do not have the stamina to survive your squirming."

"Sorry." I wasn't sorry.

"No, you're not. Get some rest." He slapped my butt, and with his face nuzzled against my neck, his deep voice vibrated in my ear. I heard the humor—and the challenge—beneath his words. "You're going to need it."

Chuckling, I shook my head. The blanket's rough material pulled at my hair. "Wake me when you're ready for round two."

He huffed a laugh and tightened his hold. It wasn't long before his breathing deepened, and he slept.

I lay silent, staring into the hazy, dimly lit darkness. I'd already outlived the average terraformer. Until today, I would have been fine with saying goodbye to what had been a good life. I'd lived it to the fullest, and not only made my mark, but carved out space in the infinite universe—perfectly engineered empyrean planets for others to live better lives.

But now there was Thrash. I wanted more years, more sex, more companionship, more everything with this man. I hoped we would survive to experience all of that, but in the meantime, I'd make the most of the situation.

chapter nine

pulsing for her pleasure

I WOKE TO A WARM PALM AGAINST MY LOWER BELLY, A FINGER STRUMMING my clit, and a thick cock against my ass. "Oh," I breathed.

"I am ready for round two." Thrash ground himself harder against my backside.

"So I feel." I simultaneously laughed and groaned.

He withdrew his hand, trailing fingers, damp from my arousal, over my belly.

"What are you doing? Are you trying to die today?" I was only half kidding. Don't wake me up by getting me all hot and bothered and stop mid-game.

Pushing me into a sitting position he said, "Take off your clothes."

"Just because you made my eyes roll back in my head does not give you the right to order…." My gaze dropped to his lap and throat tightened, turning my words into something that resembled the final breath of a deflating balloon.

The sheets had bunched at Thrash's hips. His pants were off, revealing a lot of obsidian flesh and the swollen head of his erection jutting past the blanket's edge.

"Good idea." I surged to my feet, but the covers had other ideas.

They tangled around my calves and thighs like a sardonian constrictor. I wobbled and tilted. "Shit!"

Thrash gripped my waist and saved me from a face-plant. "Careful. Don't bruise that beautiful body." He patted my ass.

"Thanks." I steadied myself and shimmied out of the heavy work clothes. They hit the ground with an audible whoomph.

Big mistake!

Immediately a spike of intense cold cleaved through my flesh to gnaw on my bones. The temperature in the cave had dropped several shocking degrees. Either that or Thrash eating my pussy while I sucked his cock had made me so hot, I hadn't noticed the cold. Probably the latter. Shivers wracked my body as I burrowed beneath the blankets and lay on my back, pulling the covers to my chin.

Thrash lay on his side facing me. He kissed my shoulder as he tunneled an arm beneath me and lay one over my middle, caging me in his hold as he pulled me against him. A lazy smile curled one corner of his mouth. He rocked his groin against my outer thigh. "Hi."

I choked on a response. How could he possibly expect me to be coherent with that beast pressed against me, flesh to naked flesh?

Heat from the steely length of him soaked into my skin, branding me, and shot liquid fire into my veins.

He moved his hips again and his cock slipped and slid against my leg.

A battalion of butterflies seemed to take flight in my stomach and flutter into my chest, turning me breathless.

Inside the circle of his arms, I rolled onto my side and faced him. His heavy erection fell against me, head nudging the seam of my thighs. Fuck, I was already wet. I took a deep breath to rein in my out-of-control hormones and smiled. "Hi."

He leaned in to kiss my neck. The hot swirl of his tongue and sharp nip of his teeth sent another jolt of molten heat from my core to my clit.

I placed my palms on his broad chest, letting my fingers explore the sleek feel of his scales. I drew my hands down his abdomen where scales gave way to ripples of muscle. Beneath my touch, his stomach trembled as I traced the ridges of his abdomen lower and lower. My knuckles grazed his jutting cock.

His hips jerked. A groan, deep and rough enough to be ripped straight from his soul, rumbled out of him.

The sound sank into every molecule of my being and caught fire. Dear gods but I needed more. More of him against me, filling me. My limbs felt jittery and restless. I threw a leg over his hip and pressed my heel into his thigh, urging him closer. His pheromones weren't doing this to me. The groan, while sexy as all hells wasn't the source either. The reason was Thrash—just him.

Mate. A word I never thought would be part of my vocabulary was harder and harder to deny.

He rolled me onto my back and rose over me looking like some god of pleasure I was ready and willing to worship. His molten gaze burned like undulating flames. "I need to be inside you."

Forearms braced on either side of me, he held most of his weight off me and moved his hips. His cock, heavy and hot, slid with delicious, silky friction along the seam of my thighs. The head nudged into my damp curls. "Already so wet. Do you like what you feel?" His heated gaze held mine as he moved again and this time his shaft pushed between my folds.

Fog clouded my brain. My tongue felt too thick and heavy to form words.

Withdrawing, he held his body still above me. "I asked if you like this."

"Thrash." I breathed past the lust-induced fog. "Yes. I like it very much."

"Do you want my cock in your mouth?"

This was torture. Could I die of pleasure? "Yes."

"Inside your beautiful, wet cunt?"

"Gods, yes."

"Which? Mouth or cunt?" His question was part groan part laugh. He still hadn't moved.

The light but persistent pressure of his dick against me fueled a very sudden and very feral need. "Fuck me already." I let my legs fall open and dug my nails into his ass.

Thrash hissed and his hips jerked. His cock pressed against my entrance. Despite the tight fit, I was so wet and slick, he easily pushed into me.

My body took him. One inch, more, growing thicker and thicker the deeper he sank. The movement stopped with a burst of burning pain that quickly melted into pleasure.

"Oh!" I let loose a trembling moan, and he froze. "Don't stop," I begged. "I want you inside of me. All of you. Fill me."

"I hurt you." He strained to hold himself steady. Veins bulged along his neck. He began to retreat.

"No." I bucked my hips.

Groaning, he slipped inside further. Sweat gathered along the edges of his scaled brow. His throat and chest glistened. Swirls of red, orange, and white-gold light spiraled up his horns and pulsed beneath his scales.

I felt a throbbing sensation inside my pussy. My muscles spasmed, going tense, and I almost came right then. "What…what was that?"

Another hot pulse.

Somehow, my core felt slicker, muscles looser.

He slid deeper.

I jerked, my knees came up, and my toes curled. Despite the tension in my body, my core relaxed further, allowing him to push deeper. I was fuller than I thought possible, and gods it felt good. "What is happening? Is that you?"

"Hmm," he rumbled. "I told you my *oreha* can also bring pleasure." A wicked smile curled his lips. Inside me, his cock pulsed, sending out a wave of heat and pleasure.

My clit thrummed and core tightened. *Scorching solar storms!* I was already so close to coming, and we had barely started. "This is going to kill me."

"It'll be worth it." Another pulse. He thrust hard and fast, stretching me with another snap of pain and pleasure as he pushed fully into me. "Tori!"

Our shouts mingled, echoing off the high dome of the cave.

He met my gaze and rocked his hips.

"Yes." I let my knees fall wide as he pulled back. When he thrust, he released another pulse. The vibration hit me everywhere. He moved again, slow at first, then faster and faster. Pull back, thrust, and pulse. I met him thrust for thrust, riding his cock.

He withdrew and shifted to kneel. Angling my hips, he hooked my knees over his shoulders and pumped into me, plunging deeper than I thought possible.

My eyes flew wide. I groaned at the new angle that hit in all the right ways.

With our gazes locked, he pulled back and thrust. His cock rubbed my g-spot with each pull and push. His *oreha* enhanced every sensation.

I looked down my body to where Thrash knelt between my legs, pounding into me over and over. The defined ridges of his abdomen flexed and constricted. His cock was wet with my juices. I glimpsed spirals of color before he thrust and released a pulse.

The slap of our flesh, the wet pull and push noises, and our heavy pants filled the air along with the musky scent of our sex.

"You're amazing," Thrash panted, his face and chest covered with sweat, his glossy skin shining in the faint glow of the lights. "You feel so good. Too good. I can't wait much longer."

"Please," I begged. "I want you to come."

"Tori. Fuck!" He jerked his hips forward, slamming his cock into me and withdrew, faster and faster, pulse after pulse. The heavy bedding bunched beneath my back as his pace increased. He pounded into me fast and hard, until I couldn't keep up.

Suddenly, the sweet and spicy, completely carnal scent of Thrash's pheromones ripped into me. Even though his hands were nowhere near my clit, I felt pressure there—a pinch. A pull where our bodies came together. My ragged pants matched the tightening inside of me.

"Come on, I can't… I have to…" His pheromones surged as he sank inside me on a roar. Iridescent light erupted in dazzling spirals and swirls across his glistening, obsidian flesh as another pulse hit me. He released my leg and collapsed over me, burying his face in my throat as he moved his hips in fast, hard jerks, creating friction against my clit.

I dug my nails into his back and held on for dear life as my climax tore through me. A scream of pure, carnal pleasure scorched a path from my lungs. I shattered into a thousand pieces that were now floating somewhere in space.

Eyes closed, my lips spread with a satisfied smile, and I wrapped my arms around his broad back, pressing my cheek against his shoulder, his scales hot and slick with sweat.

Still breathing heavily, Thrash rolled to his side. He held me tight and pulled me with him, so we remained connected. Chest to chest, our hearts raced against one another. Until exhaustion claimed us both.

chapter ten

dangerous dreams

ROSY-HUED WAVES LAPPED AT THE SANDY WHITE BEACH. AN OMBRE OF pink rippled toward the horizon, as far as the eye could see. In all my years of terraforming, I'd never seen anything as breathtaking as thi—

Except for Thrash.

He and I talked about sex in the sea, but turned out the pink hue was created by an intelligent amoeba that loved nothing more than to rub up against a warm body. Locals insisted they were harmless, and could, in fact, heighten anything you feel in the water—tangible or emotional.

While Thrash was more than willing to literally dive into that experience, I was still too freaked out to check that adventure off the sexual bucket list.

I leaned my forehead against the bedroom's glass wall. My shirt rose above my bare ass, and I tugged the hem. While I only wore a shirt, that was still one more layer than my hedonistic mate wore these days.

Every day I woke up to this view. It was everything I dreamed, but also a little less. I hadn't expected to miss the life we'd left behind, but I did. I missed the danger, but also the sense of accomplishment, the sense of purpose.

In the reflective glass, I watched Thrash enter the room behind me, dick out and a daiquiri in each hand. I was totally fine with his penchant for nudity, but it was probably a good thing we didn't have a neighbor for miles. I had saved a large enough nest egg to retire to the beach of my choice. Thrash had enough credits to buy that beach.

Turned out, while I had counted terraforming as one of the top five most dangerous jobs someone working directly for UFIS could hold, Thrash had worked for number one, and been paid accordingly.

Following the cave-in, we'd had two days to learn all about one another—our pasts, our dreams, our desires. Once the team safely dug their way to us, Thrash and I spent another seven months getting KR-732 back on track and then we'd gone planet-hopping, until we found *the one*.

Our gazes met in the reflection. Some days I wondered what would have happened if the raiders had never come. As it always did, my heart pinched at the thought of flying off into space without Thrash. He swore he would have followed me to the ends of the universe but thank the stars it hadn't come to that.

When he moved behind me, his cock, already semi-rigid, nudged my backside. He reached around me, holding a fancy glass filled to the brim with equal parts delicious frozen starfruit and sharp, tart, filda-cane rum.

After a deep drink that skated perilously close to brain freeze, I set my glass on the table and turned in Thrash's embrace. I wound my arms around his waist and nipped his earlobe.

His cock twitched against my hip.

"Put down your drink before you spill it," I told him, and he did.

Smiling, I pushed him backward, toward the bed. The back of his thighs made contact and he fell onto the mattress.

I hiked up my shirt and straddled his hips. While Thrash rarely wore clothes, I rarely wore underwear. No surprise, I was already wet, and I rubbed myself against his quickly thickening cock.

"How many more days do we have?" I reached beneath me and took hold of him.

His hips bucked and eyelids fluttered. "Tori, why the fuck do you ask me questions while you're holding my dick?"

I moved my hand to hold his shaft at the base. It wouldn't be long before he was fully erect, and I'd ride him like a champion racehorse. A lot—*a lot*—of practice taught me this was Thrash's favorite position. Might as well start the day off doing something nice for my man.

"If we are walking back into that life, we need to be at the top of our game," I teased.

I hadn't wanted to go back to terraforming, but I needed to do something. Thrash didn't want to be under UFIS' thumb, so we compromised and decided to enter the freelance game.

He groaned. "I promise to never be fucking you during a laser fight."

Working my hand up the velvety-soft flesh, I held his cock against me and rubbed the head in circles around my opening, already wet with my arousal. "I don't know, that could be hot."

Dick hardening enough to push inside me, his hands flexed on my hips. With a grunt, he impaled me on his rigid-enough length.

"Mate," he ground out the word.

I reached behind me to gently massage his balls. He hissed and his hips jerked in reaction to my touch.

Inside of me, he grew thick and strong. "You know how I like it," Thrash said, voice strained. His eyes, looking like twin flames with his rising *oreha*, were glued to where his dick pushed into my pussy.

"Faster?" I rose and sank down hard, gasping at the feel of him hitting me deep inside. I did that again, and again. "Like that?"

"Mmhmm." He rotated his hands to the front of my hips, pulling my folds apart with one hand so he could watch, and rub my clit with his other.

Electricity shot straight to my core. I gasped. My rhythm faltered.

"Fuck me, baby." Thrash's words were a growl.

This was so damn good. Was I an idiot for willingly walking away from this dream?

No, we had our own ship. Thrash never had to wear pants. I could suck his cock while he steered the ship. He could sit me on the console and eat my pussy while we streaked through space. We had a new dream together, and we'd always have this beach to come home to.

With this man, my mate, life would never be dull.

My motions grew shorter, but the pace increased. I rode Thrash's beautiful, perfect cock, bending backward slightly and grinding until he hit just right. He sent out a pulse and my core spasmed.

I came before he did, screaming and going rigid with the force of my orgasm.

He grabbed my waist, guiding me up and down as my core throbbed and milked his length. His pants grew heavier. Suddenly, he thrust his hips, slamming his dick into me and he roared his release.

My breathing was ragged as I collapsed over Thrash's chest.

We lay like that a long while, my cheek pressed to his shoulder, his hands beneath my shirt, trailing light touches over my back. "Promise me we come back to this beach at least once a year."

"Only if you promise we stay for at least a month," he said.

"Deal." The easiest promise I'd ever made. "When do we leave?"

"We depart for our first job next week."

I hadn't realized it was so soon. Lifting my head, I blinked up at him, but he stroked my hair and drew my face back down to his chest.

"Get some rest," he said. "We have a sexual bucket list to fill before we leave. Next up, we make love in the pink sea."

about s. l. choi

While Stacy's first loves are urban fantasy and paranormal romance, she is a multi-genre author who leans into humor, fast-paced action, and hit-you-in-the-heart feels. She grew up imagining goblins living in the rocks outside her bedroom window, while fairies flew through the flowers. Now she puts those stories to paper.

When she's not writing, she is either photographing the beautiful New England area, hiking, gaming with her equally nerdy husband, or attending to the small furry overlords who rule them both.

She is the award-winning author of the Blood Fae Druid series, available now.

To learn more, visit slchoi.com

you're it

Winter Elliott

chapter one

IF YOU CAN DRINK IT, YOU CAN DROWN IN IT.

That was the first thought to cross Vela's mind when she blinked onto the surface of Regnum Maris and was immediately assaulted by a humidity so dense it weighed on her limbs and made her pressure suit squelch.

Actually, humidity was the wrong word. Vela's home planet, Phaunos, was plenty humid—the air thick and sticky from an over-abundance of plants and bogs subjected to relentless, sweltering heat. This was more of a miasmic haze, chilled by unwavering night. The locals could breathe it just fine, thanks to a million-odd years of evolu-tion and strict adherence to a calendar that tracked the ebb and flow of density, like a tide chart. Vela had downloaded the data, but she didn't trust the underpaid planetographers at Central's intergalactic hub to account for shifts in current, and she definitely didn't trust her lungs to adapt swiftly enough to combat the condensation.

Suffice it to say, she'd be wearing her respirator a while longer.

The nearest city, Waldorf's Cradle, waited two kilometers off. Vela had plotted her coordinates for a wilderness arrival, worried her sudden appearance mid-metropolis would draw all the wrong atten-tion. The rare opportunity for a scenic hike had barely factored into the equation, though it certainly didn't detract from it.

With a few practiced taps on her wrist-console, her visor's optics attuned to her surroundings, and what had appeared to be solid darkness transformed into a jungle of living color. Like most sun-starved forests, this was more animal than floral. Tube worms sprouted from the silt, peeking from segmented calcium stalks to taste the air with glittering pink tendrils. Brine pools dotted gravel trails, clouds of bioluminescent krill tinging them milky teal. The fractal branches of coral trees tangled overhead, casting the faintest, ghost-pale gleam. When Vela ventured close to a trunk, hundreds of tiny polyps withdrew into coarse aragonite.

After several labored steps, she consulted her console a second time, adjusting her suit's propulsion and heat metrics to compensate for the atmosphere before continuing on. It still felt like wading through bog-water. Enough so that Vela's instincts pestered her to watch out for trilodiles.

Precisely fifteen minutes and forty-three seconds later, she came to a cliffside overlooking Waldorf's Cradle. Neon strips of every conceivable hue limned sleek commercial skyscrapers, reflected in triplicate on walls of gleaming chrome. Guide beacons encircled the external walkways of residential towers, while shuttle-lights and traffic signals turned the streets to artificial constellations. Banners advertising everything from cereal to strip clubs webbed between buildings, one pixelated image melting into the next with nauseating speed.

For all the light that blared below, a far more pleasant glow lured Vela's gaze skyward. Neither moons nor stars were visible from Regnum Maris, but sky eels writhed against the black, pockets of phosphorescence pulsing in tapered rows beneath their scales. She could practically see their loose-hinged jaws expanding to filter nutrients from algal clouds, their adipose lids flickering to clear three sets of sensitive eyes.

Ghosts of encyclopedias past and yellowing dreams swarmed around her skull. She swatted them away like fen flies. The local fauna made for an intriguing backdrop, but she'd blinked to this planet in pursuit of an entirely different class of sub-civilized creature.

Best not to keep the beasts waiting.

DETECTIVE PROGRAMS and mystery novels would have one believe criminals clung like mold to the dark corners of dive bars, their faces shrouded by tinted visors or oversized hoods. Even if that were true—and Vela knew from a decade of hunting it most certainly was *not*—the Silver Spire had no dark corners to speak of.

Located at the heart of a bustling tourist district, the drinkhouse was a climate-controlled menagerie of light, sound, and color. Tubes of blue and yellow neon wove across the ceiling, reflecting on a chrome floor so sleek it threatened the privacy of any who dared sport a skirt. A keening warble that vaguely passed for music rattled through the overhead speakers, not quite loud enough to cover the drone of the industrial humidifiers that made the place bearable to extraplanetary visitors.

Vela had stored most of her equipment in the locker lounge by the entrance, but she kept a bundle of tranq tags, a stun gun, and some gravitational cuffs in her belt-purse, as always. Her nylon jumper passed for understated fashion, wrinkle resistant and just fitted enough to flatter. The emerald hue complemented both her sage complexion and the hundreds of teal braids that swayed against her hips, and she'd undone nearly half of the buttons that stretched from collar to waist.

Several pairs (and trios, and octets) of eyes followed her with interest as she approached the bar. Vela could not return their admiration, but she carefully compared their faces to those she'd most recently committed to memory.

The crowd was among the most diverse she'd scoured in months. A cluster of leafy Floreans swarmed the nearest booth, chugging a foamy chartreuse beverage that reeked of mulch and phosphorus. A couple from Ceta sat to her right, tentacles twined beneath the table as they worked through a formidable heap of kelp chips. A Pherenese woman lounged alone in the far corner, shifting her fiber-optic hair through the spectrum in an attempt to lure company. Judging from the sheer number and variety of her limbs, she'd absorbed her fair share of hapless suitors already.

Not one of the so-called Seriville Six appeared to be present. But then, Vela had been in the game too long to trust appearances.

She claimed the last open barstool and rested an arm on the counter, tapping her fingers in feigned impatience as she eavesdropped on the closest conversations. Some of the chatter was a touch lewd for public, but none was damning in a legal sense.

The server was a native Marisian, tall and hearty of frame. Keeled scales glittered across her skin, and gills blossomed behind her ears with each breath. She assessed Vela with shrewd lilac eyes before pulling a dark bottle from the top shelf.

"Camdian Violet," she said, popping the cork free. "Strong stuff with a soft bite. Perfect for sleeping off blink-lag."

So, the server was familiar with Phaunids, the only people in the galaxies who could travel between planets sans spacecraft. Vela's kin adapted swiftly to extreme environs—not swiftly enough to blink long-distance without proper gear, but enough that their organs wouldn't burst en route. A convenient quality in a business where speed correlated directly to success.

"Well-drinks better suit my budget." Vela presented her wrist-console for the server to scan. She'd linked it to her civilian account to keep her cover, but Central would reimburse the expenses later. "On second thought, make it second-shelf. I'm in the mood to splurge."

The server scanned the device but ignored the request, filling a frosted tumbler to the brim. "How about we open a conditional tab?" she asked with the light, playful smile of someone always on the verge of laughing. "You only pay up if you collect your bounty."

Vela went rigid. Phaunids often stumbled into the hunting business, but it was rare for someone to suss her out so swiftly.

"Oh, don't look so shocked." The server nudged the tumbler toward her. "You're a decent actress—crossing your ankles in a show of class, contradicting it with an arm on the counter. You don't look like you're *trying* to look like anything." Her eyes sparked with approval. "I wouldn't have guessed your profession if it weren't for all those others, sniffing about. Most hounds aren't half so subtle."

Vela cursed under her breath. She'd been the last to view the file— the chief allocator had been bitter since she'd broken his capture record three orbits back—but only one crew was capable of beating her to a scene, even with a head start.

And they were the absolute worst.

"How long ago did those hounds pass through?" Vela wrestled her tone into something cordial, unwilling to let her frustration to spill over onto her first potential lead. "And who were they after, exactly?"

The server's smile tilted. That self-assured expression struck a familiar chord in Vela, though she couldn't recall where she'd seen it before.

"Tell you what..." She untied her tarpaulin apron, tossing it to a younger Marisian as he slipped behind the counter. "My shift just ended, and it's been a long one. Drink with me, and I'll answer whatever questions you'd like. Provided you answer a few of mine."

So, she was flirting. No wonder her smile set Vela on edge. This server must not have known much about Phaunids after all, or she wouldn't have bothered wasting her time.

Then again, Vela wasn't one to spurn an opportunity. Especially if it gave her an edge over Kalis and his pack.

She leaned forward, attempting a coy smirk of her own.

"Sounds like a plan."

chapter two

"STRONG STUFF WITH A SOFT BITE" WAS A FITTING DESCRIPTION FOR Camdian Violet. The burn was so subtle it barely prickled Vela's tongue, but the spirit's sweetness belied its potency. Judging from the boaty feeling in her skull, she needed to start pacing herself. This whole investigation would be pointless if she forgot her findings come morning.

The server, who'd introduced herself as Fyn, proved just as bold and bubbly off the clock as she'd been behind the counter. The moment they'd settled into a second-floor booth, she'd proposed a game: they'd trade off asking questions, as planned, but declining to answer meant taking a drink.

Fifteen minutes in, Fyn had yet to take a single sip.

Vela was on her second glass.

"You're making this too easy, Evie!" Vela's pseudonym rolled off Fyn's tongue, smooth as the pricey beverage. "I was aiming to get sloshed after a long night's work, but your questions are so hope-lessly...*professional*."

That was the point, yes. Vela had already plied the server for details enough to confirm that Kalis' crew had arrived on Regnum Maris four days prior, and that they treated strangers just as poorly as rivals. Fyn's queries, by contrast, had been entirely too personal: family, friends, exes, hobbies—all off-limits, where Vela was concerned.

"If your present is locked behind a firewall, let's try the distant past." Fyn ran a finger around the rim of her too-full tumbler, evoking a hollow whistle. The bar's upper level was calmer than the ground floor—quiet enough to hear such sounds but not so quiet they drew attention. "Here's a simple one: favorite childhood game."

Vela lifted her glass out of habit, only to set it back down. If she wanted to keep the conversation flowing, she needed to divulge a few details, and that one seemed innocuous enough. "Tag," she answered with a rigid shrug. "Cliché, I know. It's a game children on all planets somehow invent independently, like variants of 'the moss is magma' or 'pin the tail on the trilodile,' but blinking makes it different for Phaunids—less about following a path, more about predicting where it will end. I was my neighborhood's reigning champ until..." She shook the memories away before they could draw blood. "It's not that interesting. My turn?"

"Ask away." Fyn let the subject slide despite palpable curiosity. "Only try to ask about *me* this time. If I wanted to think about work all night, I'd have taken an extra shift."

Vela smothered a pang of guilt. Guarding one's secrets was a facet of the field, but being an ass was a personal choice. One she made a little too often.

"Why did you ask me to drink with you?" she asked, hoping for any answer but the obvious. Phaunids could not open up physically without first opening up emotionally, and few potential partners had the patience for that. Not that she was in the market.

Fyn answered with a chuckle so soft it was lost to the whir of the overhead humidifiers. "I wanted to get to know you, of course."

"Yes, but *why*?" Vela repeated. "I'm only passing through. What could you possibly hope to learn in a matter of hours?"

The server's smile tilted, and she took her first drink of the night.

A few seconds of uncomfortable silence oozed past before Fyn picked the conversation up where it had so clumsily dropped. "You're after the same group as the others, aren't you?" she asked. "The Semi-Evil Something or Others?"

"The Seriville Six." Vela practically growled the name. The syndicate had stolen from Seriville Senior Services, the most prestigious retirement care company in several galaxies. All criminals made Vela's trigger finger itch, but those who intentionally targeted the vulnerable?

If she found the Six before Kalis did, they'd arrive at Central in pieces.

"Let's pretend you're correct," she ventured. "Rumor has it their shuttle crashed on this planet seven days ago, not three kilometers off. I don't suppose you've heard anything about that?"

"I've heard what the programs report." Fyn cleared her throat before sweeping into a commendable newscaster impression. "Six individuals from vastly different fields funneled millions from their employer before stealing away in a company shuttle. The craft crashed in the Tenibris Quadrant days later, but no bodies were found at the scene. Suspects are still at large." She reverted to her previous, chipper tone. "Must've taken a lot of coordination, pulling off a heist like that."

"Perhaps." Vela wasn't convinced. She'd watched all thirty-two hours of video evidence several times, and the details still didn't sit right. "A clerk, an accountant, a custodian, a nurse, a community volunteer, and a dock operator. Together, they pulled off the heist of the century without ever working the same shift, let alone communicating on-site. Stranger still, only one member was seen boarding the shuttle they supposedly escaped in. Even if they doctored the tapes, the records reflect the same. It doesn't add up."

"Doesn't it?" A vocal uptick betrayed Fyn's interest. Perhaps she dreamt of becoming a bounty hound; Vela hadn't thought to ask. "Maybe someone on the outside coordinated the whole fiasco. I imagine it's hard to track a group of six, but it would be even harder if the members had never met."

Vela had already dissected that theory only to find it hollow. The footage had captured evidence enough. People seldom noticed the tics they picked up from their closest cohorts—common quips, facial expressions, even the occasional vocal lilt. In this case, all six thieves shared the same effortless, arrogant, lopsided…

Perhaps the drink had helped to untangle Vela's cluttered thoughts. Perhaps they'd sorted themselves as she spoke them aloud. Either way, the missing puzzle piece clicked into place.

Vela's breath hitched.

Fyn noticed. "Everything alright?"

"Just anticipating a hangover." Vela forced a laugh, swirling the remnants of her drink in one hand as she snuck the other into her purse. "If I'm going to suffer anyway, I might as well indulge. Care to top me off?"

When Fyn reached for the bottle, Vela surged forward and clasped a titanium cuff around her wrist. A gravitational anchor slammed to the table, and several expensive ounces of Camdian Violet spilled to the floor.

Fyn's too-familiar smile tilted further.

"You *are* a clever one, aren't you?" she asked, taking on a rich, masculine timbre.

Before Vela could react, the supposed-Marisian's arm began to pulse and shiver, stretching into the slick, purple tentacle of a Cetaloid. The captive slipped free and rushed away, waving freshly formed fingers before racing down the nearest staircase.

Vela gave chase, spitting swears. By the time she reached the first floor, the suspect had vanished. She spent another hour scouring the drinkhouse, knowing all the while her effort was pointless. Roughly two hundred bodies mingled in the crowd, and her target might have been wearing any of them.

LATER THAT NIGHT, as Vela crawled into yet another hard and lumpy boarding room bed, her wrist console chirped brightly. The image of an envelope appeared on the screen, both the sender and subject lines blank.

Upon opening the message against her better judgment, she was rewarded with a cryptic link and a simple, three-word taunt.

Tag, you're it.

chapter three

TWENTY-FIVE MILLION ZENNA.

It was more than the entire population of Phaunos made in a year, and it was sitting comfortably in Vela's bank account. The link that revealed as much vanished with a single click. She could find no receipt of transfer, no record of deposit, no evidence of a breach, but she knew exactly where the money had come from. If Central saw the numbers—and they *would*, next time they paid out a bounty—it would raise a lot of uncomfortable questions.

The last thing Vela needed was to be labeled an accomplice to the very crime she'd set out to avenge.

She logged out of the library database with a frustrated growl, having learned next to nothing in three days of research. The Wanderlings were...enigmatic, to say the least. No one knew which planet they hailed from, though they were sprinkled liberally throughout several galaxies. Their mutative qualities made them difficult to identify, let alone research. Most scholars posited they were an advanced variant of Vela's people, and that their shifting abilities had evolved from the Phaunids' own, less flamboyant adaptive traits.

"Advanced," as it happened, was a subjective term. No, Vela could not morph into other creatures. She could not grow gills to breathe miasma or sprout whiskers to sense electrical currents. But Wanderlings could not bend spacetime to leap between worlds on a whim. If one ever managed to blink, even after taking on a Phaunid's form, their final transformation would be into a puddle of putrid goo.

Disillusioned by the lack of hard data, Vela sulked toward the library entrance. It had been ages since someone had taken up so much space in her mind, and with so few factors to focus on. She'd nearly reached the locker lounge when she allowed the commotion beyond the picture windows to distract her. Marisians in hooded smocks scrambled in the glow of the streetlamps, holding mesh sacks open to catch falling flecks of green. Whenever a bag filled, they tossed it into a wheeled bin and ripped another from a tear-away roll.

Vela had read about the algal rains which accounted for much of the local diet. They only occurred when the tides were at their "lowest" —a term which had nothing to do with the depth of the miasma and everything to do with its density—leaving the air too thin to hold the clouds aloft.

Feeling inquisitive in the boldest way, Vela left her gear in the locker and marched through three sets of sliding doors to brave the dark of day.

The first breath was agony. It always was.

Miasma evaporated within her, coating her throat with condensation. Each droplet was a tiny, searing ember. She could feel them rolling down her bronchial tubes, pooling like magma in her lungs. For a frantic moment, her limbs leeched cold, and the world went white.

With a few desperate coughs, both the burn and chill subsided. Color returned to the city one garish billboard at a time. Pinpricks swarmed in her fingertips, trailed by comfortable warmth. She wiped miasmic dribble from her satisfied smile. Had she pulled the same stunt at high tide, she might have drowned before adjusting.

Giddy and thrill-drunk, she tipped her head back, hoping to catch the pastel pulse of a zephyr fish or the prismatic twinkle of a cloud jelly drifting through the sky. Unfortunately, the city's glow drowned the darkness, turning it to a charcoal haze sprinkled with drifting detritus.

Another time, perhaps.

Emboldened by how adaptive she could be, Vela pulled up the

city's business index on her console. If it was a game the Wanderling wanted, she would play by her own rules.

• ＼＼＼ ／／／ ๑

EVEN AFTER TRANSFERRING HALF the Seriville spoils to Vela's account, the Wanderling could have afforded an entire fleet of spacecrafts. Why, then, had they allowed a simple shuttle crash to strand them?

Vela could imagine only two possible answers: her target was unable to use the funds without alerting authorities, or they were saving them for a particular purpose. She needed to determine the details if she hoped to thwart her suspect's scheme.

Tag wasn't about following a trail, after all, but predicting where it would end.

She blinked to the entrance of Rager's Rocket Emporium, the only reputable spacecraft dealer in Waldorf's Cradle. There were plenty of *disreputable* options, granted, but she suspected the Wanderling was clever enough to avoid them. Honor was a rare commodity among thieves, and the common crooks who ran such enterprises would gain more from betraying their white-collar counterparts than working with them.

Vela steeled herself before stepping through the sliding doors and drinking in the dehumidified air. The sting, though intense, lasted mere seconds before her lungs remembered the atmosphere and adjusted accordingly. With more practice, she would hardly feel the change occurring, though she hoped to see her mission through long before that could happen.

She shook her braids, sprinkling the welcome mat with algae flakes before stepping onto the checked linoleum. Several customers wandered the salesfloor, eying sporty crafts they'd be paying off long after the engines died, but it took a while to find a staff member. The Marisian's smarmy grin was nearly a welcome sight. Though equally self-important, the Wanderling's smile had been bright and playful— genuine, even. This one was so slimy it threatened to drip right off the man's face. His nametag identified him as Rager, the owner.

"I'm interested in one of your window displays." Vela gestured in the craft's general direction. "Does the Magellanic Model 6 come in red, by chance?"

It absolutely did…for half-again the list price. Rager eagerly recited every customization the emporium offered as they marched toward the model in question. It was easy enough to steer the conversation toward payment plans, assessing each for how easy it would be to pay with stolen funds.

"The credit-lease option sounds fair, but I've been burned before." Vela tapped her cheekbone in mock contemplation. "I'd be more comfortable knowing it was a common choice. I don't suppose you've made any similar arrangements recently…"

Vela could practically hear a sales register chime inside Rager's skull. Unfortunately, when he opened his mouth to answer, it was another voice that found her ears.

"Still going with the 'hapless customer' routine, are we?"

Vela's jaw clenched tighter than her fists, but she managed a measured, "It's been a while, Kalis."

"Not long enough for you to come up with a new bit, apparently." Kalis stepped into her periphery, followed by his three loyal lackeys— Pryn, Zyl, and Tarah. "I swear, it's ploys like these that give bounty hounds a bad reputation."

"Pretty sure that's owed to the bribes and intimidation." Vela glared his way, nose wrinkling. He probably qualified as classically handsome, with sleek black hair, a razor-sharp jawline, and a marble-smooth maroon complexion, but the sight of him brought bile to her throat. "Granted, cheap tricks likely play their part. Or did you somehow find this place without scanning for gravitational waves?"

"If you didn't create them, I'd have nothing to track," Kalis replied with a haughty chuckle. "You lean into your advantages, and I'll make the most of mine. It's hardly my fault the two are linked." He turned liquid-amber eyes to the salesman. "I regret to say this 'customer' is only fishing for information, and you'll gain absolutely nothing from biting. Let me peek at your sales logs, however, and you'll find yourself fifty zenna richer. I sincerely hope that bait is enticing," he tipped his head toward Pryn, who rolled his sleeves up in a less-than-subtle threat, "because there's more than one way to skin a trout."

How Rager crammed so much greed and fear onto his face at once, Vela could only guess. She watched, fuming, as the Marisian ushered Kalis off to continue the conversation. The crew followed like the sycophants they were, though Tarah paused to stick a forked tongue out at Vela. A paragon of maturity, that one.

"Well, he's a massive prick, isn't he?"

The quip tugged Vela's attention to a Marisian mechanic peeking out from behind the hatch of a pre-owned shuttle. His plum eyes and spotted gills were unfamiliar, but there was no mistaking that syrupy voice and playful, lopsided smile.

Vela raced forward as the Wanderling ducked behind the spacecraft. By the time she rounded the shuttle, her target was gone.

chapter four

THERE ARE CERTAIN TRADITIONS WHICH, MUCH LIKE THE GAME OF TAG, ARE practiced by nearly every known population: annual rites like solstices, seasonal harvests, and—perhaps most unanimously—birthdays. Vela liked to think herself the exception to a good many rules, but she was not exempt from this one.

Every year, for as long as she was willing to remember, she'd celebrated alone with a slice of cake and a present. The dessert selection of Waldorf's Cradle left something to be desired, with words like "dulse" topping the ingredient lists, but the famed indoor swap market proved a trove of unique trinkets, any of which would mark the occasion well.

More importantly, the bustling crowd helped to distract Vela from the fact that Kalis had, once again, tried to use her as a springboard for vaulting ahead on a case. His new methods of exploitation were less invasive than hacking into her field logs while she slept, but only just.

Disgusted that she'd ever mistaken that prick's flattery for affection, Vela forced her focus to the vendor tables. They boasted everything from candles to coral sculptures, but nothing caught her eye until she wandered past a book seller near the middle of the marketplace. Every text ever translated to Galactic could be downloaded at the press of a button, but Vela had a soft spot for archaic prints, both leather-bound and paperback.

Xathar's Xenozoological Index Vol.3 (Planets Delthar-Geryon) serenaded her from atop a tower of precariously stacked tomes. She'd started amassing the volumes in her early teens, but at thirty-two, she'd secured only six of the thirteen. The vendor watched with palpable greed as she browsed the book, relishing the brittle texture and woodsy musk of each page. The first entry focused on the canopy lemurs of the Deltharian subtropics—a deceptively cute species with plush fur, massive eyes, and an alarming hunger for living flesh.

"Do they really glow during Delthar's rainy season?" someone asked.

The interruption would have startled Vela's heart from her chest, had she not, on some level, been expecting it. She glanced back to see the Wanderling hovering behind her, having donned the brawny body of a Lacertian man. That they'd snuck up on her was impressive. That scaly skin ought to have rasped like sandpaper.

"Seems counter-evolutionary," the target continued, slitted eyes roving the page with interest. Even on reptilian lips, their smile held its haughty tilt.

Vela turned to face them, forcing a genial grin. Either the Wanderling had overestimated their acting prowess, or they'd underestimated her powers of perception. Either way, playing along with the charade was her best shot at gaining the upper hand.

"Some adaptations are coincidental," she explained. "At the time this article was written, researchers believed the glow was a biological feature meant to attract mates. Dr. Xathar was the first to analyze the lemurs' diet. Turns out, the jungle's glow-worms hatch weeks before the rains begin, so—"

"When the lemurs eat them, their fur absorbs the oxyluciferin," the Wanderling finished, reading directly from the book. "Coincidence or not, doesn't it make them easy prey?"

"That's why they've developed such extraordinary defenses." Vela turned the page, revealing a detailed diagram of a lemur skeleton. Xathar was nothing if not thorough. "Those claws are actually elongated phalangeal spurs, and fossil evidence suggests they developed shortly after large predators migrated to the region. Never underestimate the power of adaptation. Small setbacks often result in massive leaps forward."

"A proven theory, at least in my own life." The Wanderling took the book and began thumbing through it. "I can only assume the same of you, given what I've seen these past few days. How else would you have developed such a brilliant glow alongside such wicked claws?"

Vela froze. Why would the Wanderling so blatantly reveal themselves when...

The reasoning mattered less than the opportunity it presented. In a single motion, she fished a tranq tag from her purse and pinned it to her target's shoulder. Their wince dissolved to a startled chuckle as their scales paled, parted, and peeled away. The tag clattered against the floor, trailing a sheet of shed skin, and the Wanderling darted off, unaffected.

Vela shouldered her way through the press, ducking beneath tables and veering around displays. She was gaining ground when a shriek cut through the crowd to her left. Several bystanders scrambled back as a Florean woman fainted, hands clasped over her heart.

Instinct took control, driving Vela to the woman's side as the Wanderling slipped away, a massive peripheral blur. She cursed her luck and checked for a pulse, but thick, leafy skin made assessment difficult. Vela pressed the heels of her palms to the woman's chest, prepared to pump.

"Wait!" The Florean lurched forward, dewdrop eyes flexing wide. "It's just a show! A prank, I was told. My troupe is known for them."

Vela's hands curled into fists around the woman's collar. "You're. An. *Actor*?"

"H-he paid me thirty zenna. Best money I've seen in months."

Vela's breath fled in an exasperated sigh. She released the woman to activate her wrist-console's recorder.

"Repeat the conversation, and don't skip a single word..."

● ⟍⟍⟍⟍   ⟋⟋⟋⟋ ◦

AFTER AN HOUR-LONG INTERVIEW that produced nothing of note, Vela returned to the boardinghouse, beleaguered, only to spot some curious new additions to her nightstand.

The slice of prepackaged cake—which she would definitely *not* be eating—was butterberry crunch, imported from Phaunos. The book beneath it had been acquired much more locally. Vela shook her head. She ought to have figured the Wanderling would note her birthdate upon accessing her account, and that they'd inevitably use the information to mock her.

Unsettling though the offering was, Vela mentally added a seventh volume to her Xathar collection as she plucked it from the nightstand. Before she could so much as flip the cover, her wrist-console chirped. She clenched her jaw and tapped the screen, fully expecting another childish taunt, only to find a set of coordinates and a blip of a message.

Let's take a time out.

chapter five

"TOLD YOU IT WAS CLOSED FOR THE NIGHT, MISS." THE SHUTTLE DRIVER tapped his tentacles against the steering wheel as he pulled up beside Waldorf's Bio Sanctum. "Why not try again tomorrow? Tours start at ten."

Vela ran a credit chip over the meter before exiting the cab. The driver lingered a moment more—probably concerned for her sanity—before leaving her to the midnight mists and a discordant din of unseen insects. She waited until his taillights vanished to adjust her visor and approach the fence.

Electric torches flickered along the perimeter, but the buildings beyond were blacker than brachiopod blood. Vela dropped into the sanctum to find a tangle of paved paths, pocked by garish tourist attractions. She kept an eye out for the hazy beam of a flashlight as she followed signs to the Visitor's Center, but not a single ray pierced the dark. The staff were probably deeper in, patrolling the coral forests, brine bogs, and kelp meadows. An enviable occupation, wages aside.

The Visitor's Center was more glass than chrome, with windows as numerous and tightly clustered as the compound eyes of a moon moth. A soft fluorescent glow spilled from the third of five stories. Vela readied her stun gun before slinking into the building. No matter how this conversation unfolded, she intended to leave the grounds with her target in tow.

669

Soon, she found herself in a sparsely-lit food court that reeked of braised kelp and chum. The Wanderling lounged in a hover chair roughly ten feet off, boots propped on a plastic table, arms folded casually behind their head. They still wore their Lacertian form—all bulk muscles and tawny scales. Vela centered a little red dot on their chest. Tranq tags were useless against reptilian races, but there was no sloughing off the effects of a shock ray.

"Would you believe that's not the rudest greeting I've ever received?" The Wanderling chuckled musically, leaning forward to plant their boots on the floor. "This isn't a trap, if that's what you're worried about."

Vela had discerned that much. If the Wanderling wanted to capture or kill her, they'd have already tried it. "What is it, then?"

"Why, an interview, of course!"

Vela didn't *intend* to lower her weapon, yet her trigger finger went lax and the gun drifted harmlessly to her side. "An...interview?"

"The last in a series, to be more accurate. The first, at the drinkhouse, gave me a chance to assess your intelligence. The next was a test of intuition. Going to the dealership would have been a brilliant move, had you been dealing with any ordinary reprobate."

"Let me guess," Vela sighed the words, "you're an *extra*ordinary reprobate."

They bowed from the shoulders, flourishing their arms. "The Camdian Violet of con artists."

Until that moment, Vela had never rolled her eyes at a target. "And what about the marketplace? Were you testing whether I'm naïve enough to play along with your little game, whatever it is?"

"Hardly!" They flashed their infuriating, lopsided smile. "All the cleverness and intuition in the world would be useless to me, were you not also *kind*. I needed to know you could cast your personal ambitions aside for the good of others. You passed the test with aplomb."

Vela plucked the broadest question from the storm in her skull. "Why would I work with you? Even if you weren't an intergalactic fugitive, you've done nothing but lie to me!"

"Only visually." The Wanderling shrugged. "You can't blame a man in my predicament for practicing caution."

"Oh? So you're name's really Fyn, is it?"

"Fyneas, technically, but a nickname hardly constitutes a lie."

Vele blinked, bewildered. She'd been certain they...er, *he* had given her an alias. Either he was supremely stupid, or he truly needed her help with something. Regardless, she could likely pry a few more details from those surprisingly loose lips of his.

"Well, *Fyn*, mind telling me what you're doing here? The whole Intergalactic Consortium knows you crash-landed on this planet, and I'm not the only hound on your trail. Why haven't you purchased a new craft and headed elsewhere?"

Fyn arched an eyebrow ridge. "What makes you think I have that kind of money just lying around?"

"*Fifty million* zenna isn't enough for your preferred spacecraft?"

"Oh, that?" He waved the notion away. "Those aren't my funds to spend."

Of all the perplexing answers he could have given. "What do you mean, they aren't—"

Rubber soles squealed against linoleum, shattering Vela's concentration and hopes alike. She'd been so cautious, forwent blinking in favor of a shuttle, and yet...

"How kind of you to keep our quarry occupied." Kalis's voice rang through the open space, turned brassy by chrome pillars and support beams. "You've played the role of decoy with grace, as always. Time to let the real hunters have a go, hm?"

Vela closed her eyes, exhaling slowly through her nose. He must have placed a trace on her credit account. If he'd given her cause to worry, she'd have switched services in the years since the breakup. Apparently, he'd been saving that particular blade for the moment her spine was most exposed.

"*This* is the creature who's been evading you?" Tarah said as the lackeys took up position, stun guns raised. "I know you're a shit aim, but who could possibly miss such a massive, metallic target?"

Vela smothered a laugh before it could burst free. Her rivals had been following her every move, yet they had no clue about their target's true identity. Amateurs, all.

"Capturing men has never been Vela's weakness." Kalis sauntered forward with all of his trademark arrogance, not a weapon on his person. "Keeping them is another matter. It's a pity my victories must always result in her failure, but to the brightest goes the battle."

"A lover's spat?" Fyn's face twisted, slitted eyes flicking to Vela. "You're a smart girl, but you have *horrendous* taste in partners."

Oh, didn't she know it.

"It's a foolish buck who mocks the hunter." Kalis wagged a finger, glancing back at his minions. "On my signal…"

He counted down from five. A split-second before he reached one, the Wanderling's body folded inward with a terse crackle of bone. Three sets of membranous wings sprouted from the small, gray body of an asteroid imp. It lifted into the air, leaving Fyn's clothing piled on the chair with the exception of a nylon jumpsuit that had shrunk with his figure. The transformation stunned the hounds, allowing him to flit down the nearest hall.

"What are you waiting for?" Kalis growled, shaking free of his stupor. "Split up and cut him off, dammit!"

The lackeys raced toward three different exits while their leader charged after Fyn. Vela spun on her heel and raced toward the staircase she'd just climbed. Bootsteps stormed through the building, delving far deeper than ground level. Vela surpassed three sets with ease, though the fourth maintained a steady lead. She allowed the railing to guide her as shadows bled across her vision, robbing the world of color and definition. Her helm tumbled free when she ducked beneath a landing, but she dared not retrieve it for fear of losing ground. The world was that much darker for its absence, but—thanks to her little low-tide experiment—the atmosphere no longer posed a threat.

She soon arrived at a storage facility cluttered with crates and empty cages, a single lamp dangling in one corner. Two figures squared off near the center of the space, both with stately frames, long black hair, and liquid amber eyes. In the gloom, even their outfits looked identical.

Vela leveled her weapon at the space between the doubles. The temptation to shoot them both was alarmingly strong.

"Get on with it!" barked the leftmost Kalis, waving toward his twin. "Shoot the blasted fraud!"

"Yes, please," quipped the Kalis on the right. "Anything to shut him up!"

"I-I'll split the bounty!" Leftmost offered, sounding nearly sincere. "You know it's me, my delicate swamp flower."

Vela cringed. She'd always hated that pet name. *All* pet names, really.

"And *I* know you'll make the right call," Rightmost countered, "my…fierce little… canopy lemur?"

Okay, that one was kind of cute.

"I heard voices! This way!" Zyl's shout rang from above, followed by racing bootsteps.

With the fuse running short, Vela pulled the trigger. The true Kalis gasped, eyes rolling back as he fell limp to the floor.

"I was counting on your good judgement," Fyn said with a tellingly nervous laugh.

As badly as Vela wanted to shoot him, there was no way she could drag him from the scene. Not before her rivals caught up.

"Shut up and follow me." She grabbed his arm and tugged him toward a metal door with a foreboding yellow triangle plastered on the front. Darkness waited beyond the threshold, too dense for even the strongest visor to filter.

Any other exit would have been preferable, but the encroaching bootsteps narrowed her options to one. She pulled the Wanderling into the shadows and jarred the door shut behind them. The deadbolt slid into place right as Kalis's crew burst into the basement.

chapter six

THE DEFAULT SETTING OF A CENTRAL-ISSUED STUN GUN COULD KNOCK A grown man out for an hour. Vela had adjusted hers to keep 'em down for three. After listening to Kalis's lackeys bicker beyond the door for several minutes, it became obvious they intended to linger until their leader shook off his stupor.

"Holding hands in the dark is romantic and all," Fyn's whisper tickled Vela's ear, "but we should probably search for another exit."

Vela released the Wanderling's arm, grateful the darkness hid her flushed face. The shiver of excitement she felt at the brush of his breath unnerved her. "Are you suggesting we feel our way to safety?"

"Only for a moment." Fyn placed a hand on her shoulder to guide her through the shadows, and she felt along the walls in an attempt to keep her bearings. Rough stone scraped beneath her glove, and the tangs of mildew and moss grew stronger with each step, sure signs they'd left the Visitor's Center behind.

After a few twists and turns, Fyn withdrew his hand. Light flooded Vela's vision, blindingly bright. She blinked the blear away to find that he'd shifted again, this time to a Pherenese man with pale lilac skin and fiber-optic hair. Males of the species were far smaller than their feminine counterparts, but Fyn still dwarfed Vela in both height and heft. He was not about to make himself easy to capture.

He tossed prismatic tresses over his shoulder. "In case you doubted my ability to brighten a room."

"Pity this isn't a room," Vela replied flatly, scanning their stony surroundings. The tunnel stretching out before them was too irregular to have been bored mechanically, though the lack of fresh claw marks and scat hinted at old age. "We're in an abandoned burrow, or at least the neglected wing of a warren. Probably the work of a rock gnawer or an anglerbeast."

"Good thing the architect's long gone. Neither option sounds particularly friendly."

They weren't herbivores, that was certain. "Don't let your guard down just yet." Vela scraped her boot on the ground, smearing a serpentine trail of soil. "Deserted dens often attract squatters of the toothy variety."

"So you're saying I should keep close?" Fyn looped an arm around her waist and pulled her flush against his chest—an act that, bizarrely, threw off the rhythm of her pulse.

She slipped away with a startled scowl. "I'm saying you should keep *quiet*."

"Shame." He pouted. "Here, I thought you'd have follow-up questions about the job."

The *nerves* on this one. "Why ask about a job I'm unwilling to take?"

"Curiosity."

He had her there. "I'll get the details from Central after the interrogation." She stepped aside to wave the Wanderling forward. "For now, I insist you walk ahead of me. For the obvious reasons."

It was hard to identify eyerolling in people without pupils, but Fyn somehow made it obvious. To his credit, he obeyed without much fuss. Vela followed as he wound through the tunnel, keeping well within the cast of his prismatic hair. They marched along in blessed silence for some time before he froze in place, arms splayed in an obnoxiously protective manner.

"There's something up there," he breathed.

Vela peered around him to see lights twinkling in the darkness—long strings of them, tangled together like noodles. Elated, she ducked beneath Fyn's arm. A heartbeat after she arrived at the edge of a hollow, his light spilled past her to fall on a nest of slumbering sky eels.

"Wait here," she whispered, tiptoeing forward.

"Wouldn't dream of following," came the bewildered reply.

Upon locating a juvenile eel, nearly two meters long, Vela crouched for a closer look. The creature was even more magnificent in reality than the illustrations—smog gray and sleek as an oil spill, with pockets of phosphorescence pulsing from gills to tail. A short, crimson dorsal ridge ran the length of its spine, and tiny pectoral fins of the same hue sprouted from its sides.

"Unlike most Marisian species, sky eels don't possess gas bladders," she explained. "They take flight when the miasma is at its densest, but during low tides, they're forced to settle down in whatever shelter they can find before they enter stasis." She removed a glove and stroked the creature's side. "The scales are smooth and hard as quartz flecks, just as Xathar described them."

A faint chuckle echoed off the cavern walls. Vela glanced up to see Fyn hovering beside her. His smile, though crooked as ever, was soft as silk. "It's a rare pleasure to observe someone truly in their element."

"Hunting is my element," Vela hissed, surprised by her own terse tone. Fyn's observation had warmed her, yet her response was frigid. She breathed deeply and tried again. "This is simply an interest. Some people are interested in baking. Some are interested in rock collecting. I'm interested in any resilient creature that thrives in seemingly unlivable circumstances."

"Feel a kinship, do you?"

Vela hadn't thought of it that way. Her interest in xenozoology far predated the events that nudged her toward a nomadic existence, though it had certainly piqued in the decades since.

But none of that was Fyn's business.

"Let's get going." Vela stood, dusting soil from her knees. "If the eels found this place, we can't be far from the surface."

They tiptoed carefully through the nest and into a tunnel on the opposite side, where the air smelled fresher and roots wove through the walls. A pit yawned open in Vela's stomach at the sight of so much loose soil, doubling in depth when a light appeared ahead of them, strong and bright as neon.

"We must be near a ranger's station!" Fyn exclaimed, breaking into a sprint.

Against her every instinct, Vela gave chase. She caught up with Fyn right as he slipped between the widespread jaws of an anglerbeast. A wet tongue squelched beneath his heel, startling him still. Vela grabbed him by the collar and pulled him to safety just before the creature's fangs crashed inward.

The anglerbeast bellowed, pelting them with spittle and spoiled-shrimp breath. Its bioluminescent lure bobbed wildly, reflected in its massive, milky eyes, as it struggled forward on limbs too squat to lift its belly from the ground. Vela and Fyn sprinted back toward the eel nest as it lurched along behind them with astounding speed. A fang snagged on Vela's jumpsuit, barely grazing her leg. The seam tore from ankle to knee when Fyn pulled her into a fissure, but she lost no skin to the bite.

A luminous lure dangled inches from Vela's nose as the anglerbeast clawed at the stoney crevice. Fyn tugged her deeper into darkness, dimming his radiant hair to dull mauve. Bedrock scraped their shoulders for several meters before the gap widened only to end in a wall of sheer limestone. At least there was space enough for two to settle side-by-side, which is exactly what they'd be doing until the creature lost interest.

"We're going to be here a while." Fyn didn't sound disappointed. "There's one sure way to pass the time."

Vela went rigid. The Wanderling's charms were undeniably appealing, but she would not allow him to manipulate her. "You'd better not be implying what I think you're implying…"

"I was only suggesting we pick our game up where we left it." He elbowed her side. "I believe it's my turn to ask something."

"You're serious?" She shook her head only to realize it was bursting with questions she desperately wanted answers to. "We've got nothing to drink, so you'd better be honest."

"Of the two of us, do you really think I'm the guarded one?"

"Is that your official question?"

"Far from it." Fyn's smile hiked up one cheek. "Mere interest or not, you looked far happier studying those sky eels than you have throughout this entire hunt, and don't get me started on the encyclopedia. Why in the galaxies would you waste time as a bounty hound when you have such a palpable passion for nature?"

Vela didn't have to answer. Her stun gun wasn't quite strong enough to faze a thousand-pound anglerbeast, but it would easily knock Fyn out for a while. Then again, she'd agreed to the terms, and playing along hurt nothing, and a foolish part of her *wanted* to tell him. Or someone, at any rate.

"I can't remember a time I didn't love animals—the stranger, the better." She fixed her gaze on the now-distant glow of one such creature. "My mom made a name for herself as a naturalist back on Phaunos. She was always more interested in fundraising than field work, but I devoured every textbook in her study. It was my greatest dream to explore the deserts of Haset. Most researchers flee the harsh conditions after a few weeks, but a Phaunid could weather the sandstorms with relative ease. Can you even imagine the undiscovered species skittering through those dunes?" A smile found her lips only to wither away. "Mom said it would be a waste of time. Apparently, donors care little for sand fleas and scavenger rats."

"Strange opinion for a scientist to hold. I don't suppose she ever took you into the field…"

"Her colleagues did." Vela warmed at the memory of Marcas helping her sift trilodile eggs from estuarine silt. "Mom had far too many hands to shake to bother holding mine, claimed it was her wit and winning smile that kept the cupboards stocked. That was probably the only truth she ever told me." She pulled her knees to her chest and wrapped her arms around them, feeling suddenly small. "Turns out, she tricked her way into the Naturalist's Society with a fake degree and some plagiarized papers. After securing twenty million in research grants, she vanished without a trace. No less than three species of river snail went extinct as a result."

"She left you behind?" The cocky smile fell right off Fyn's face. "Just like that?"

Vela shrugged half-heartedly. "It wasn't like she was really there before."

Fyn took a moment to gather his words, but they spilled out in a jumble. "That's awful, really, but I fail to see what it has to do with your career. Your mother faked an interest in xenozoology, but yours is obviously real. You shouldn't cast aside your passion for—"

"I didn't cast anything aside," Vela snapped. "I simply got a new passion: hunting down self-absorbed reprobates who see fit to take what doesn't belong to them."

"So, thanks to one woman's actions, you think all outlaws are slime mold?"

"Let me guess: you consider yourself an outlier." Vela laughed coldly, though she was beginning to suspect the same. "Since it's my turn, I might as well pluck the obvious fruit. You mentioned the stolen zenna wasn't yours to spend. Care to elaborate?"

Fyn grinned like he'd been anticipating that very question. Which was probably the case. "How much do you know about Seriville Senior Services?"

"The basics. They're responsible for housing over seventy million individuals. The brochures promise top-notch amenities and all-hours care staff, and there's not a single lawsuit or code violation to contest those claims."

"Strange, isn't it?" he asked. "It's hard to find a local diner without a flood of customer complaints, but a business that large is squeaky clean?"

"Maybe they're just meticulous."

"The best thieves are," Fyn replied with a bitter snort. "The CEOs of non-profits seldom make the broadcasts, so few know Hal Seriville lives in grander luxury than the princes of some planets. Three mansions, a villa in Avalonus, more household staff than a five-star hotel—none of which can be attributed to wages or grants."

"He's *not* misusing company funds?" Vela blinked. "Doesn't sound like a thief to me."

Fyn raised a finger, begging patience. "The Consortium keeps a close watch on anything they distribute. If Seriville misplaced a single government zenna, he'd find himself faced with at least a dozen audits. Bequeathals are another matter."

A decent theory, but not without weakness. "If the company was leeching assets from their residents, an estate lawyer would have caught on by now."

"Only if the company broke a law, which, technically, they haven't." A muscle in Fyn's jaw twitched. "Their contracts give them the right to cut off communication with any relatives they deem abusive or otherwise harmful to their residents' health. Records indicate they've played that card on no less than 10,000 occasions in the past three decades. Tell me, if Junior and Missy stop visiting out of the blue, abandoning Granny Dearest to the care of kindly strangers, who do you think will be cut from the will? More importantly, who will be added?"

Vela's stomach did a cartwheel. If Fyn's accusation was true, Seriville Services hadn't only stolen money from their residents, they'd stolen precious final moments from their loved ones. "That's a very big, very *convenient* claim. Do you really expect me to take your word for it?"

"Not at all." Fyn tapped Vela's wrist console. "Check your contacts, and you'll find a new entry for one Ms. Anyta Longsworth."

Vela pulled away. "Any chance you'll ever make a point without invading my privacy?"

"She was the first person I interviewed before taking this job," Fyn continued, unfazed. "I'm here to return some of the funds Seriville stole. It won't make up for the time she lost with her mother, but it'll pay the rent, perhaps put her kids through school. Hear her out, and if you're still not convinced, I'll let you cuff me. I might even let you turn me in."

Vela chose to ignore the bit about the cuffs. "It's a dangerous game, recruiting a bounty hound to your cause."

"If you haven't picked up on it, I'm fond of games." Fyn chuckled. "This job is too big for one person to pull off, and it's too important to abandon. I need someone clever, intuitive, and kind to help me see it through." He placed a hand on Vela's shoulder, which somehow made her light-headed. The Camdian Violet of con artists, indeed. "We haven't known each other long, but I'm positive we'd partner well."

"In business," Vela clarified, nervously shrugging his hand away.

"My mind was hovering far above the gutter, I assure you." Fyn winked. "I would hate to get between you and your amber-eyed oaf. At least, not while your stun-gun is pointed his direction."

To think, Vela's stomach had just settled. "Kalis was a mistake."

"A distant mistake you're ready and eager to move on from?"

"Why so curious?" Vela asked, though the answer didn't matter. Even if Fyn's tale was true, she needed to arrest him. Didn't she?

For some reason, the thought made her chest tighten.

"Never mind. I'm exhausted, and I'm not the only one." She nodded toward the anglerbeast, which was finally beginning to settle down. "If we're quiet, it might grow bored and leave."

For some time after, the only sound was the whisper of clothing against stone as Fyn and Vela both attempted to get comfortable. Eventually, most of him wound up pressed against her, probably by accident.

If she'd complained, he would have given her space.

So she didn't.

VELA SELDOM SLEPT SWADDLED IN LESS THAN FOUR BLANKETS, HER HEAD half-buried in a heap of overstuffed pillows. This is precisely the circumstance in which she assumed herself upon waking, warm and cozy, to the distant *plink* of water on stone.

After a smothered attempt at stretching, she realized it was not a blanket wrapped around her, but arms, and the silken pillow against her cheek was really a curtain of luminous hair. It hadn't been a dream, then. She'd dozed off in an anglerbeast burrow, her head tucked gently beneath a fugitive's chin, her body rising and falling with his every breath.

She wanted, so badly, to hate it.

Mustering urgency where resentment had failed, she shifted to peer down the fissure and was pleased to note their hungry host had vanished. The motion woke Fyn, who released her with a stream of mumbled apologies. If she wasn't mistaken, those glowing specks on his cheeks were the Pherenese equivalent of blushing. It would have been adorable on any of his faces.

"We should go." Vela felt the walls for a crack with which to pull herself upright. "Who knows when the anglerbeast will waddle this way again."

Fyn concurred—which mattered more than it should have—and they sidled back to the main tunnel. The low miasmic tide made their steps light and easy. Before long, they spotted another light pulsing in the tunnel ahead, this time shifting with shades of baby blue, petal pink, and buttercup yellow.

Fyn froze in place, having soundly learned his lesson. "Another charming local?"

"Several." Vela grinned, nudging him forward.

After walking a few more yards, they climbed out of a cave mouth into a silvergrass lea surrounded by coral trees. A ranger station overlooked the glade, tangled in course branches. Doubtless, a park map waited somewhere behind its darkened windows. Vela would retrieve it in time, but for now, her attention belonged to the zephyr fish.

An entire school bobbed throughout the glade, pastel light pulsing beneath their diaphanous skin. Their little fins fluttered wildly as they pecked invisible motes of detritus from the air. A brazen blue specimen flitted straight up to Fyn, who apparently couldn't resist reaching for it. At the slightest touch, the fish ballooned to three times its original size, then released its breath in a pigeon-like coo, looping around Fyn twice before flitting away.

Vela felt a prickle of envy. "I think it likes you."

"What's not to like?" Fyn flashed his crooked smile, and in that moment, Vela couldn't think of a single answer.

His expression soured as a familiar, spoiled-shrimp reek filled the air and sickly light swept across the silvergrass. The zephyr fish froze in place, eyes fixed on the cave mouth, before darting off in a colorful flurry. A surge of terror forced Vela's spine straight.

"Don't look back," Fyn mouthed, as though Vela was tempted. He tipped his head toward the ranger's station and counted silently backward. *"Three...two..."*

On the count of one, Vela sprinted toward the station ladder. She reached it a split-second before Fyn, who urged her upward with a frantic shove. Her palms barely grazed the rungs as she clambered toward a wooden hatch, which flung open with ease. She'd just pulled herself into the building when a startled cry rang out below. Fyn dangled from the ladder by one hand as several broken rungs fell to the grass. The anglerbeast pounced, its jaws snapping shut a twitch from the Wanderling's heel. Panic washed away the mistrust that had clouded Vela's thoughts. Fyn vexed, amused, and thoroughly fascinated her. She was not about to let his story end in the belly of a beast.

Gripping a table for support, she leaned forward with an arm outstretched. Fyn clasped her hand and hauled himself to safety, kicking the latch shut behind him. Momentum sent them both tumbling to the floorboards, tangled in an adrenaline-fueled outburst that forced them conveniently closer with each chuckle.

It felt so natural when he cupped her face, the last of his laughter gusting her lips. So perfectly, ironically, alarmingly *right*. There Vela was, nestled in the arms of the criminal she'd set out to capture, having only just escaped a grisly death for two, and she could not recall having ever felt so safe.

Before she could talk herself out of it, she kissed him.

It started as an innocent brush of lips, soft and halting, teasingly sweet. Then, those lips parted, and any remaining inhibitions melted away. Fyn tangled his fingers in Vela's braids and tugged, rousing a thrill in the nape of her neck, and another—far lower—that hadn't stirred in much too long. If the mass that stiffened against her thigh was any clue, she was not alone in her yearning.

Feeling suddenly smothered by her jumpsuit, Vela guided Fyn's hand to the topmost button. He took it for the permission it was, unfastening the garment from collar to waist and slipping his fingers beneath the fabric. He cupped her breast, his thumb skimming her nipple, as he trailed kisses down her neck, testing every inch until he found a spot that made her writhe.

Vela was on the cusp of losing herself when a prismatic tress fell over her cheek, and an inhibition clawed its way from the grave.

"Wait," she breathed, releasing her vice-grip on his waist.

"I'm so sorry!" He scrambled upright, cheeks alight. "I thought you wanted—"

"I do." She sat forward "Just...not like this."

"Oh." Fyn forced a grin, far more brittle than his usual. "I suppose everyone has a fantasy, and I'm nothing if not adaptable. Is it women you prefer? Tentacles? A brawnier build? Simply say the word and I'll..." He flinched, "Adjust accordingly."

The sorrow in his voice nearly broke Vela. She didn't need to know his history to tell he'd been used as a vending machine for all manner of kinks. It was enough to make her furious at every lover who'd come before her. And desperate to soothe the wounds they'd left behind.

"I want *you*." She rose to meet his gaze. "The real you, not a hair or freckle altered. Despite my best efforts, you've managed to see me more clearly than anyone has in years. I'm only asking for the same."

Fyn relaxed with a warm chuckle, and his form began to shift and shimmer. Lilac skin blanched to snowy silver, a shade paler than his frosty blue eyes. Ghost white waves spilled over slight shoulders, framing a delicate face that reminded Vela of the elves from Earthling Mythos. She could imagine no vessel more befitting the Wanderling's wit and poise, his trickery and tenderness. He looked very much like *himself*—a person whom Vela had, perhaps foolishly, grown to admire.

He must have read the awe on her face, because his confidence rushed back all at once. Those slender arms of his proved surprisingly adept at scooping her up and carrying her toward the bed in the corner. Giddy and impatient, she peeled his jumpsuit away en route. The second he set her down, her clothing joined his on the floor.

His pupils blossomed as they swept over her. "Here I thought the way you smiled while reading was the prettiest sight in the galaxies."

If Vela wasn't already smitten, that would have done it.

She pulled him onto the mattress and twisted atop him, stretching to give him a better view of the figure he'd been admiring. Somehow, his eyes grew wider. Though her body begged for his, she first treated herself to another kiss. The feral press of his lips was practically a plea, and the sweep of his tongue, a tender promise.

She lowered herself onto him slowly, savoring the sound of his groan and the pleasant ache of his entrance. With a few gentle thrusts, her body adapted to his, tightening to wring ecstasy from even the slightest movement. Judging from Fyn's reaction—something between a giggle and a gasp—the surprise was not unwelcome.

His every sigh and shudder emboldened Vela, and her pace reflected her fervor. Before she could push him over the brink, he grabbed her hip to temper her pace, sliding his other hand up her thigh to part her folds with his thumb. Bliss echoed his strokes, building steadily brighter and bolder until it crackled through her like lightning.

Vela fell into Fyn's embrace, a trembling rag doll. A moment later, he moaned her name, his entire body stuttering. Somehow, his release was even more satisfying than her own, and the way he melted against her, impossibly precious. He'd been stolen from as surely as those innocents he sought to help, and whatever small comfort she'd given him was a moment of healing for both of them.

"I wasn't expecting this," he whispered, nuzzling her cheek. "I'll admit I've fancied you since we first met, but I never dreamed—" His confession turned to a gasp when the mass that had just softened stirred anew.

"I-I should have warned you!" Vela blushed brightly, pulling herself off him while she could still muster the will. The aftershocks hadn't yet faded, and already, she ached for more. "My people don't really have casual encounters, so if it's been a while since we've last… connected, our body chemistry compensates."

"Are you saying you excrete an aphrodisiac?" Fyn's smile looked twice as devilish on his true lips. "Of your many impressive adaptations, that's probably my favorite."

He dragged Vela to the edge of the bed and flipped her, twining their fingers to pin her in place and dipping into her just far enough to tease. It took all of Vela's not-inconsiderable resolve not to whimper.

"Let's make a game of it, shall we?" he growled, pressing further only to pull back. It bordered on cruelty. "We test the limits of this little trait until one of us can't take it anymore. Winner is decided when the other cries mercy."

A dangerous proposition, given how stubborn they both were. But then, the past week had been rife with risks; what was one more?

"Challenge accepted." Vela arched downward, driving him deeper, and the game commenced.

* ⟍⟍⟍⟍ ⟋⟋⟋ °

"SURRRENDERRR QUIETTLY!"

The words sizzled through an amplifier, more static pops than voice. Vela woke to siren lights spilling through the windows, limning Fyn's silhouette in ruby with each pass. He sat slouched at the edge of the bed, fully clothed.

"You havvVe tennn MinNnuTes to Tturn yourssselF innN!"

The fog fled Vela's mind, and she furled upright to place a hand on Fyn's shoulder. He twisted to face her, a twitch of a smile tugging at one cheek.

"Kalis tracked us down," he said, voice threadbare from the night they'd shared. "He and the local authorities have us surrounded. They've probably set up patrols around the whole sanctum. I'm quite the prize, after all."

Vela grimaced at the ill-timed joke. "If we slip past them, we could return to the tunnels," she tried. "We'll hide until the fuss dies down, then—"

Fyn cut her off with a kiss deep enough to drown in. Even after it ended, she struggled to catch her breath. "This won't fall back on you." He touched his forehead to hers, sorrow glistening along his snowy lashes. "I'll tell them you were about to apprehend me when they interrupted, allowing me to turn the tides. It's an insult to your talent, I know, but it will keep your record clean." A tear broke free, and he blinked back the rest. "When you next check your contacts, you'll find information on fifty-seven families impacted by Seriville, along with the amounts I intended to return to them. You have enough zenna in your account to make it through half the list, and the rest will appear shortly. It's properly encrypted, so you won't raise any alarms if you're careful and clever. As though you could be anything less."

Vela had too many questions to voice and even more objections, so she summarized. "I can't do this without you."

"With that glow and those claws?" Fyn squeezed her hand. "You can do anything."

When he tore away, Vela scrambled to her feet, unwilling to let the conversation end there. Her vision dimmed and twisted, swaying like a spacecraft in an asteroid storm. Sore as she was, she'd dismissed the pang above her wrist as another in a sea of strained muscles.

She noticed the blink of a tranq tag right before the world went black.

epilogue

Three months, eleven days, and six hours after waking in Central's medical wing, the thought of returning to Regnum Maris still churned Vela's stomach.

Events had transpired exactly as Fyn predicted they would. He'd dressed and posed Vela before turning himself in, so no one questioned his testimony of her near-victory. The reward for his capture had gone to Kalis, of course, not that Vela minded. After fourteen years as a bounty hound, she was finally ready for a change. Or she would be, after finishing her final hunt.

Vela crossed another name off her list and steeled her nerves as best she could, then blinked to a parking garage on the outskirts of Waldorf's Cradle. She could tell from the pressure that the miasma was dense enough to choke her, but she removed her respirator anyway. For a moment, the tangible pain eclipsed the abstract. Too bad only one ache faded.

She shooed away the memories from her last visit as she searched the neighboring complex for apartment 115-A. Seconds after she rang the bell, a Marisian woman answered, gills flaring in surprise.

"I wasn't expecting a visitor." She smoothed her rumpled skirt. "Can I help you with something?"

"Other way around, assuming you're Ms. Anyta Longsworth," Vela said, adjusting the script she'd recited over fifty times before. "I'm here on behalf of my colleague, goes by Fyn."

"I…I can't believe you're really here," the woman replied, blinking wildly. "I was certain, when they arrested that poor man…"

After all Seriville Services had put Anyta's family through, she deserved an attentive ear, but the mere mention of the arrest sent Vela's mind to Tenibris Delta, where Fyn was being held. Vela could never visit the prison for fear of drawing unnecessary scrutiny. There would be no attending the trial, either, assuming Central granted one.

"Seems I've forgotten my manners." Anyta's bright chuckle jarred Vela back to Regnum Maris. "You must be exhausted after travelling so far. Please come in. I'll put a kettle on."

Having endured a version of this conversation on no less than twenty planets, Vela knew her protests would go unheard. So she allowed her host to lead her to the sitting room, where she'd wait patiently until the tea was brewed and the Marisian equivalent of cookies were arranged on a tray.

"I'll only be a moment," Anyta promised before rushing off.

Moments were a conveniently vague unit of measurement. It had been a moment since Vela last checked her wrist-console for messages, a moment since she added a new encyclopedia to her library, a moment since she fell asleep in Fyn's arms, lulled by the sound of his breathing. Another moment, or two, or twenty of waiting wouldn't kill her, though it would probably try its damndest.

The sitting room was cramped and cluttered. Handprints smudged the plaster walls, and a storm of toys littered the floor. A portrait of a woman, framed in gold, was the family's final vestige of wealth. It must have been a sentimental keepsake. Otherwise, they would have sold it to purchase more space. Hopefully, Fyn's funds would grant them at least that much.

Vela had been waiting only a few minutes when three young children raced into the room, playing tag, of all possible games. Blinking a pesky sting from her eyes, she looked past them to the screen in the corner. The animated antics of a pink Cetaloid and his pet anemone had nearly succeeded in distracting her when the program flashed over to breaking news.

"We've received word of a high-profile prison break." The reporter read directly from a print sheet. "A prisoner vanished from his cell in Tenibris Delta overnight, leaving authorities flummoxed. As of yet, details of the escape are vague, but Central has requested that anyone with information call…"

Vela was so lost in the newscast that she nearly missed the chirp of her wrist-console. The second an envelope appeared on the screen with neither sender's name nor subject line, she trapped a breath and clicked it open.

Having wanted to visit the desert planet of Haset for decades, she readily recognized the set of coordinates that greeted her. She scrolled right past them to find the simple, three-word message she'd dreamed of but hadn't dared hope for:

Tag, you're it.

about winter
elliott

Winter Elliot is a vaguely sapient collective of molecules drawn in from various galaxies. As such, they refuse to recognize most societal conventions, including species, gender, occupation, time, and location. They enjoy petting Earth floofs, eating fried things, and arranging letters in complex patterns to make humans hallucinate grand adventures. They do not wish to draw attention to their presence on this planet.

For your own sanity, inquire no further.

9 781963 525090